OXFORD ANTHOLOGY *of the* BRAZILIAN SHORT STORY

OXFORD ANTHOLOGY
of the
BRAZILIAN SHORT STORY

Edited by

K. DAVID JACKSON

OXFORD
UNIVERSITY PRESS
2006

OXFORD

UNIVERSITY PRESS

Oxford University Press, Inc., publishes works that further
Oxford University's objective of excellence
in research, scholarship, and education.

Oxford   New York
Auckland   Cape Town   Dar es Salaam   Hong Kong   Karachi
Kuala Lumpur   Madrid   Melbourne   Mexico City   Nairobi
New Delhi   Shanghai   Taipei   Toronto

With offices in
Argentina   Austria   Brazil   Chile   Czech Republic   France   Greece
Guatemala   Hungary   Italy   Japan   Poland   Portugal   Singapore
South Korea   Switzerland   Thailand   Turkey   Ukraine   Vietnam

Copyright © 2006 by Oxford University Press, Inc.

Published by Oxford University Press, Inc.
198 Madison Avenue, New York, New York 10016

www.oup.com

Oxford is a registered trademark of Oxford University Press

Library of Congress Cataloging-in-Publication Data
Oxford anthology of the Brazilian short story / edited by K. David Jackson.
p. cm.
ISBN-13 978-0-19-516759-7; 978-0-19-530964-5 (pbk.)
ISBN 0-19-516759-7; 0-19-530964-2 (pbk.)
1. Short stories, Brazilian. I. Jackson, K. David (Kenneth David)
PQ9676.O94 2006
869.3'0108981—dc22   2005028860

1 3 5 7 9 8 6 4 2

Printed in the United States of America
on acid-free paper

To my Brazilianists, Elizabeth, Sophia, Katharina, and Kenneth, and to all those who discover and come to love Brazilian literature

PREFACE

The invitation to compile an anthology of the Brazilian short story for Oxford University Press has led me to more than two years of unexpected and gratifying adventures. The labor of locating and selecting short stories in translation presented me initially with a complex literary puzzle, while the long process of contacting writers and their heirs, literary agents, and publishers added an unexpected human and legal dimension to the construction of this anthology. Even for someone familiar with the authors and their works, the few bibliographies of Brazilian short stories in English translation that exist are incomplete and fragmentary, thus my first task was to survey all of the published works in English that could be located. The sixteen floors of densely packed books in Yale's Sterling Memorial Library added a certain sense of mystery to my search, not to mention months of good exercise in hot, humid weather. Copying hundreds of stories and compiling new bibliographies occupied month after month. Were it not for Yale's immense library, where I spent a summer in the stacks, the task of locating rare published stories would have been much more difficult. One thing led to another, until I held in my hands, for example, the single issue of *Inter-American Magazine* from 1918 or the London journal *Life & Letters* from 1943. The interlibrary loan department was an essential resource, which was called upon to produce copies from even rarer titles, such as the anthology *Love Stories* published in São Paulo in English. I am grateful to librarian Cesar Rodríguez of the Latin American Collection, who gave valuable assistance in locating bibliographies of published stories in translation, and I would especially like to thank Lawrence Hallewell for a copy of his own compilation of Brazilian stories in English translation, which he sent to me from England. The number of Brazilian stories located was naturally much greater than could be included in a single anthology, and it was often difficult to choose.

In selecting stories for the anthology, my goal was always to include the classic stories that qualify to join the best of world literature. In doing so, the anthology seeks to familiarize its audience with the work of several dozen of Brazil's best short story writers, covering the period when its modern literature developed dynamically, with stories dating from 1882 to 1996. Too many of Brazil's major writers are underrepresented in English translation and therefore not widely known or appreciated, whether in university courses or on the shelves of readers. With the exception of several unpublished translations, the stories to be chosen for the anthology should have been previously translated and published, according to my charge from Oxford. Therefore, my objective needed to be, on the one hand, to avoid duplicating stories that had been frequently anthologized within the past fifteen years and, on the other, to include a large number of stories by the recognized masters of the short story, particularly Machado de Assis and Guimarães Rosa, that are no longer in print or difficult to obtain. Some well-known stories were irresistible because they deserve to be read by as wide an audience as possible.

Another high point of this adventure has been personal contact with many of Brazil's greatest writers, as I sought permission to include their work. It was especially exciting to contact authors whom I had read for many years but never met, as in an unexpected telephone call from Lygia Fagundes Telles, or letters and e-mails from Carlos Heitor Cony, Rubem Fonseca, Moacyr Scliar, and Dalton Trevisan. In other cases, I knew the writers well: Nélida Piñón and Edla Van Steen had given lectures for the Yale Portuguese program; Milton Hatoum was a visiting writer under a program from the Ministry of Culture; and Autran Dourado had been introduced to me many years ago by the writer and critic Silviano Santiago. I am grateful for their generous cooperation. I was privileged to contact relatives or representatives of writers in the anthology. During a visit to Salvador, Bahia, through the introduction of a close friend, I met Elizabeth Ramos, granddaughter of Graciliano Ramos, from whom I learned much about his personality and character. I am grateful to Luísa Ramos Amado, Graciliano's daughter, for her permission to print the stories. Telê Porto Ancona Lopez, my colleague from the Institute of Brazilian Studies at the University of São Paulo, once again generously provided contacts with the family of Mário de Andrade, and I would like to thank Carlos Augusto de Andrade Camargo for his cooperation. Heitor Martins helped me to contact the family of João Alphonsus, and I wish to thank Fernão Baeta Vianna de Guimaraens and Liliana Viana de Guimarães. In the same fashion, Ana Luiza Andrade introduced me to Lauro Oliveira, who handed my letter to the sisters of Osman Lins in Recife. I wish to thank Sílvia Rubião Resende for the story by Murilo Rubião and Renata del Giudice for the story by her late father, Victor Giudice.

I have likewise corresponded with many literary agents who represent Brazilian authors. Very special thanks go to Ray-Güde Mertin, literary agent for Brazilian literature in Germany, for making it possible to include stories by João Guimarães Rosa in the anthology, as well as for her delightful and generous correspondence. I am grateful to Agnes Guimarães Rosa do Amaral and to Vilma Guimarães Rosa for their cooperation. Bella Campillo provided advice about the works of Clarice Lispector and others. Literary agents in Brazil, among them Ana Luisa Chafir, Álvaro Gomes, Lucia Riff, and Patrícia Seibel, have been consistently generous and cooperative. Glória Bordini searched for original manuscripts by Érico Veríssimo in his archive and suggested that he wrote directly in English. From all of these sources, I have learned more about copyright law than I ever thought necessary, as well as the intricacies of markets and agents. I also wish to thank the many professional publishers and journals for their advice and permissions, which are listed in the acknowledgments of this book.

The Brazilian short story has attracted many talented translators over the years. Early journals, however, often did not even include their names, and therefore much good work remains anonymous. Where I have received rights directly from an author, I have also sought the translator's, and I would like to recognize the fine work and generous cooperation of Ana Luiza Andrade, Thomas Colchie, Fred Ellison, Earl Fitz, Adria Frizzi, Eloah F. Giacomelli, Elizabeth Jackson, Alexis Levitin, Elizabeth Lowe, Daphne Patai, Gregory Rabassa, Darlene Sadlier, David Treece, Nelson Vieira, Ellen Watson, and Richard Zenith.

At Oxford University Press in New York, my editors Elissa Morris, Eve Bachrach, Abby Russell, and Shannon McLachlan have been consistently encouraging, tempering enthusiasm with patience. Other debts are more long-standing, for the anthology could not have been conceived without the professors with whom I studied Brazilian literature and its masters of the short story, especially the notable author and critic Jorge de Sena at the University of Wisconsin, Madison. In Brazil, I learned much about the story from leading critics and professors, among whom are Antonio Candido, Walnice Nogueira Galvão, Luiz Costa Lima, Benedito Nunes, Fábio Lucas, and others who have written on the short story. I would like to thank my Yale colleague Claude Rawson of the Department of English for recommending and supporting this project and for his continuing interest in Brazilian literature. The introductory essays owe much to Elizabeth Jackson's careful proofreading and pertinent suggestions. Putting the anthology together has been a solitary labor, yet always full of enthusiasm, new discoveries, and fruitful personal contacts. I alone am responsible for it, yet all of the work has been done in pursuit of the goal of expanding knowledge of, interest in, and readership of Brazilian literature.

Contents

PART I
—◦❧ ❧◦—
Tropical Belle Époque (1880s–1921)

PART III

—◦❯ ❮◦—

Modernism at Mid-Century (1945–1980)

PART IV

—◦❧ ❦◦—

Contemporary Visions (after 1980)

Oxford Anthology *of the* Brazilian Short Story

INTRODUCTION

World World Vast World of the Brazilian Short Story

The World of the Brazilian Short Story

The short story, written in the Portuguese language and reflecting Brazil's cultural history, is one of the most prolific and popular literary forms in Brazilian literature. The sheer amount of writing, attested by Ítalo Moriconi's Brazilian anthology of the 100 best stories of the twentieth century (*Os Cem Melhores Contos Brasileiros do Século*, Rio de Janeiro, Objetiva, 2000), is complemented by the presence of four internationally respected masters of the short story: J. M. Machado de Assis (1839–1908), Graciliano Ramos (1892–1953), João Guimarães Rosa (1908–1967), and Clarice Lispector (1920–1977). Many of their stories have been widely translated and anthologized, and some of the best known—Machado's "Midnight Mass," Rosa's "The Third Bank of the River," Lispector's "Crime of the Mathematics Professor"—take their place among the best in world literature. Stories by other notable authors, such as Osman Lins, Nélida Piñón, Murilo Rubião, Moacyr Scliar, Lygia Fagundes Telles, and Dalton Trevisan, have reached an international audience in translations. Even writers who were primarily poets or novelists have published notable short stories, as did Brazil's most prolific poet of the twentieth century, Carlos Drummond de Andrade (1902–1987), whose often-quoted verse *Mundo mundo vasto mundo* / *World world vast world*, taken from a popular rhyme, is emblematic of the open horizons of the Brazilian story. The history of the modern Brazilian story covers approximately the past 150 years, and fully developed, artful stories have been penned by authors of every generation. Reflecting the nature and course of Brazilian civilization, as well as ties to Portugal and its empire, the modern story tradition is a confluence of widely diverse materials, brought together in expressive themes, images, and language. Being versatile, mobile, and appealing, the short story, like the oral tale before it, has proved to be an enduring repository of Brazil's cultural imagination.

What generally defines any short story is its concentrated, concise treatment of a unified theme, a feature that ties the form more closely to poetic or rhetorical techniques than to extended narratives. If there is a single characteristic that defines the story in Brazil, it is the capacity to receive and digest a broad international cultural heritage, to the extent that the imports often pass undetected before the eyes of readers, as if their own. Plasticity, adaptation, syncretism, and movement are general characterizations of the society that are transferable to the short story tradition. In late nineteenth-century Rio de Janeiro, for example, Machado de Assis, a supreme world master of the story and Brazil's greatest author, places the actions of his characters in the social context of the city, while at the same time forming parallels and suggesting references to works of classical and European literature, philosophy, and history. A century later, in Haroldo de Campos's poem *Finismundo* (1990), the epic hero Ulysses continues sailing west until he reaches the coast of Brazil, which thus finally absorbs classical mythology as its own. Through their stories, Brazilian authors could have been constructing a new literary continent to be discovered alongside the geographical one, in view of their assimilation of a wealth of sources, styles, and readings into their own language and lives, as personal references. Within this literary continent, in the words of literary historian Luciana Stegagno Picchio (*História da Literatura Brasileira*, Rio de Janeiro, Nova Fronteira, 1997), the story is the genre par excellence that most reveals the originality of new Brazilian literature. Machado de Assis once wrote in one of his ironically humorous notes that the story had a natural advantage over an extended novel, for if both were mediocre, the stories were at least short.

In view of Brazil's singular tradition, immediately apparent in the Brazilian Portuguese language, its short story in the context of Latin America also inhabits a world apart. In Rubem Fonseca's story "Large Intestine," an unnamed iconoclastic author is being interviewed. When asked, "Is there a Latin American literature?" he answers, "Don't make me laugh. There is not even a Brazilian literature, with a semblance of structure, style, characterization, or whatever. There are people writing in the same language, in Portuguese, which is already a lot and everything." Even discounting the provocation and insouciance, the author's reply is not uncharacteristic. If it seems surprising that Brazilians do not self-identify as Latin Americans and do not themselves describe Brazilian literature as Latin American, one should remember that Brazilian literature has traditionally been connected to Portugal and France, its major cultural referents, and its perspectives are Atlantic. Brazilians are aware that the description "Latin American" has come to refer almost exclusively to Spanish America in English-speaking countries, perhaps in view of a historical and geographical divide. Given Brazil's continental size, one notes the almost total lack of contact historically with Spanish America, which was at first a reflection of Portugal's long struggle to maintain its independence from Spain, accelerated over time on the American continent by geographical distance as well as political, linguistic, and cultural differences. Although Brazilian literature is sometimes categorized as an "exception" in the field of Latin American letters and is little studied in contrast to Spanish-language literatures, it is in fact the continent's largest and, indeed, features some of the greatest names in world literature.

Brazil is so large that Brazilians tend simply to divide the world into two parts: Brazil and all the rest. Brazil gives one the sense more of a continent than a country; indeed, it is the world's sixth-largest country in area, occupying half of South America, and is larger than the continental United States. Regionalism is a principal trend in a literature that confirms the individuality of the country's immense regions: the *gaúcho* Fandango in Érico Veríssimo's story of the southern plains lives and speaks a different language than the *caboclos* of Guimarães Rosa's interior *sertão*, the dry high plains of the interior coastal plateau. Within Brazil, a centripetal national force draws together a population formed over a 500-year period by miscegenation and immigration. The word *multicultural* is insufficient to describe the formation of the Brazilian population. Everyone is Brazilian because there are simply too many variations to be individually distinguished; yet precisely because of this grand amalgamation, the definition of a common national identity sought on nationalist grounds is always thrown into doubt. Literature provides the deepest investigation of national character, and the Brazilian story in particular possesses a special affinity with themes of language, culture, and history as they have come together in the last century and a half. They constitute central features of a composite national reality, which is constantly undergoing its own extended process of self-definition. Part of the story's appeal and force is its ability to epitomize a situation or encapsulate the essence of Brazilian culture in a single, concise narration.

In view of the hybrid nature of cultural constructs in Brazil, however, the story is shaped in its composition by inherent diversity and contrasts, if not by contradiction or paradox. Stories may take on the forms of chronicle, anecdote, tale, or case, for although its origins can be traced from a half millennium ago, the modern short story is a recent form. While the act of telling is timeless, the modern short story effectively dates from the development of a bourgeois, print-oriented society in the nineteenth century, following European models. It is tied to the press and to serial periodical publications, as literary critic Fábio Lucas reminds us (*O Livro do Seminário*, São Paulo, LR Editores, 1983), yet its history as a form encompasses and revalidates the oral tradition of ballads, fables, parables, exemplary tales, and other ancient forms of telling. Stories told by epic heroes to their immediate listeners had often been incorporated into such literary excursions as the *Thousand and One Nights*, *Decameron*, and *Canterbury Tales* or placed as episodes in the *Iliad* or *Odyssey*. In his narrative techniques, Machado de Assis exemplifies work with the oral, epic roots of the story, engaging his readers with a direct narrative voice and inviting them to participate through imagination in distant times, places, and events. The nineteenth-century Brazilian story, in many cases edited and printed in Europe, closely follows contemporaneous developments in European literatures, yet it draws on material from local realities and from the Brazilian oral tradition, almost without exception. To read the Brazilian story is to follow local situations that conform—if in bizarre and unexpected ways reminiscent of a curved mirror, or of Alice's looking glass—to the lessons, examples, and archetypes found in stories throughout the Western literary tradition. Above all, Machado's stories well illustrate how a Western literary form, placed in contact with diverse peoples, languages, and places over a long colonial period, can seem both uncannily familiar and strangely deceptive to a foreign reader of Brazilian literature. Even many of Machado's characters are no less deceived about the true nature of the situations and events in which they are involved as imitations of a distant original.

Brazil's Atlantic World

Ever since the Portuguese letter of discovery penned in April 1500 by shipboard scribe Pero Vaz de Caminha, Brazil and its civilization have been the source of a world of stories. Writing was an essential part of overseas expansion, and early historiography is rich in literary influences and reports of diverse cultures. The transcontinental voyages also conveyed the medieval oral tradition, whose themes of honor and chivalry were especially implanted in the folk literature of northeastern Brazil, now known generically as *literatura de cordel*. The Portuguese voyages spread ballads, canticles, proverbs, moral tales, chivalric prose, drama, and lives of saints. Once overseas, these were adapted for religious purposes in oral rhymes, plays, songs, and stories and repeated by contacted peoples who had almost no knowledge of Portuguese. As no printing was permitted in Brazil until the nineteenth century, unlike Spanish America, stories and oral literature of all kinds spread widely, as the only forms available to fulfill the role of national literature. Religious drama was the vehicle for José de Anchieta's polyglot plays in Tupi, *língua geral*, Portuguese, and other languages used for the conversion of Indians in São Paulo. Folk verses carried in ships along the Brazil and India routes became mainstays of local identity and culture. "Nau catarineta," a ballad spread throughout the Portuguese empire, is excerpted in a story by Rubem Fonseca, and Machado de Assis cites Fernão Mendes Pinto's infamous narrative *Peregrinação* (1614; *Travels of Mendes Pinto*, Chicago, U of Chicago P, 1985) in a story set in Siam, "The Siamese Academies."

Caminha's letter of discovery of Brazil has received intense analysis, being the prime foundational document that reveals the complex scope of the moment of encounter as a dialectic of here and there. At twenty-seven sheets, Caminha's letter of discovery could be considered Brazil's first short story. It is the first written description of the future nation as seen "inside" from "outside." Its events amount to decisive moments of the country under construction. For example, while Caminha describes the physique of the people as much healthier than that of the Portuguese, he reads in their beautiful robust bodies only the virtues of the land, diet, and climate. Another European, who never voyaged to Brazil, Michel de Montaigne (1533–1592) in his essay "On Cannibals" (*Essays*, New York, Penguin, 1958), would be the first to claim the superiority and value of their lives: "They are still governed by natural laws and very little corrupted by our own. They are in such a state of purity that it sometimes saddens me to think we did not learn of them earlier, at a time when there were men who were better able to appreciate them than we" (pp. 109–110). British poet Robert Southey recapitulates the utopian theme of discovery literature at the turn of the nineteenth century in his *History of Brazil* (London, Longman, Hurst, Rees, Orme, and Brown, 1817–1822): "If the territorial paradise exists anywhere upon this round world, they fancied that surely it could not be far from hence" (Part the First, p. 27). Indianism and utopian themes carry the chronicles into the modern story, alongside the exhausted cultural stereotypes of their times, which proved to be disastrous, implicated in the decimation of indigenous cultures they could not recognize and, more recently, ecological devastation resulting from another rush for land and riches.

The short story is constructed on the foundation of major forces that contributed to the chronological development of Brazilian civilization. These include remote origins reflecting tales, sagas, legends, epics, and exploits spread orally throughout the vast landscape since its discovery in 1500, bringing together Portuguese, indigenous, and African materials, although their collection and documentation began only in the late 1800s. Colonial travel literature embodied the sharp contrasts and emphasis on description that would shape early accounts of Brazil, from historical chronicles, on the one hand, to myths of riches and fecundity embedded in European cultural preconceptions, on the other. Expansionist themes of utopia and opulence fed an imagination as large as the landscape. The folk literature of the Northeast was seen to retain medieval European materials from the Carolingian cycle, hagiographies, chivalric prose, and exemplary tales. Oral literature from the Portuguese voyages and the Jewish diaspora from Iberia melded with indigenous Brazilian legends and languages, exemplified by well-known stories of the *jabuti* (tortoise), *onça* (jaguar), and *cobra* (great serpent). The relationship with nature, the landscape, and animals has continued to play a central role in the Brazilian story, apparent in the popular myths and legends collected in Luís da Câmara Cascudo's (1898–1986) dictionary of folklore (*Dicionário do Folclore Brasileiro*, Rio de Janeiro, Instituto Nacional do Livro, 1954). No comprehensive collection of indigenous lore was ever undertaken in Brazil, however, aside from materials collected by a handful of noted anthropologists, folklorists, or scientific explorers. The Brazilian people are known for the ethnic diversity of a highly mixed population: *mestiço*, mameluke, *caboclo*, and mulatto are only a few of the terms used to described the racial spectrum, which is popularly viewed in terms of gradation rather than defined categories. Afro-Brazilian culture, centered in Salvador, Bahia, which was named the colonial capital in 1549, flourished with the arrival of more than 5 million Africans as slaves, the largest number in the Americas. The lore, rhythms, and vocabulary of *candomblé* religious practice formed an enduring substratum of the national imagination, while Afro-Brazilian culture has played a significant role in literature, particularly through the works of the internationally known Bahian author Jorge Amado (1912–2001).

Modernists in the 1920s revisited historical chronicles from the sixteenth to the seventeenth centuries, exploiting them for their own devices. Oswald de Andrade ransacked Hans Staden's 1547 memoir of his captivity among the Tupinambás (*Warhaftige historia und beschreibung eyner landtschafft der wilden nacketen grimmigen menschfresser leuthen in der Newenwelt America gelegen*) for use in his cannibalist manifesto and magazine. He continued with excerpts clipped out of a chronological sequence of historical chronicles from which he constructed poems, selected for their effects of estrangement and humor when read in a contemporary urban context. The modernists had a deeper reason for rummaging in the historical descriptions of the colonial period, as by doing so they could turn back the clock, redefining Brazil by rewriting or repositioning the documents of discovery and description as modernist writings. Historical documents could be reread in new circumstances favorable to the Indian and black and sexually open. The short story provides a panorama of national types and experiences based on historical patterns. Stories kept arriving from different continents over the centuries, overwhelming indigenous cultures, and represent many epochs and genres, yet all have been assimilated as pieces of literature, as if they sprang naturally from Brazil's own realities or natural lore. Stories evoke by synthesis and comprise in number a vast aggregate of Brazil's regional diversity, colored by the historical, cultural, racial, and linguistic miscegenation responsible for creating the largest mixed culture in the Americas. To describe it succinctly requires a long string of hyphens: Euro-Luso-Afro-Asian-indigenous.

Brazil's long interface with the Portuguese world is not only unique in the South American context but remains a formative feature of its civilization. Portuguese poet Fernando Pessoa repeated the idea in his book of poetry *Mensagem* (1934) that the Iberian Peninsula is the head of Europe, as depicted on early Renaissance maps, and that Portugal is its face, looking out toward the Atlantic. One can imagine that this geographic face is looking toward Brazil, and Brazil is still very conscious of being seen, as well as visited, by a stream of Europeans. Some Europeans even attempted to take possession, as in the French settlement of what was called "Antarctic France" in the mid-1500s and the Dutch occupation of Recife for twenty-four years in the mid-seventeenth century. Returning transatlantic crossings carried elite Brazilians to centers of culture and to be educated. Indeed, Brazil faced more than its origins in Portugal, since it remained connected to half a world of Portuguese voyages over almost all of its existence. One of the most crucial distinctions in forming a sense of Brazil is its oceanic origin and history, as for centuries it was part of the world of Portuguese expansion that extended eastward to Africa, Goa, Malacca, Macao, and Japan. This wide geographical and oceanic sweep, although unseen today, underlies Brazil's contemporary international perspectives, reinforced historically by the country's demographic settlement in coastal cities interconnected by the sea. Well into the nineteenth century, Brazil's four largest cities were all coastal: Rio de Janeiro, Salvador, Recife, and São Luís.

Brazil's role in a world system was implicit in its discovery in April 1500 by Pedro Álvares Cabral, who continued on his voyage to southern India. Martim Afonso de Sousa, author of a diary of navigation to Brazil in 1530, returned to Portugal only to leave Lisbon soon after to become viceroy of Portugal's State of India in Goa, taking poet Luís de Camões along in his fleet. Duarte Coelho Pereira had fought under the great captains of the Portuguese in Southeast Asia and the Moluccas before obtaining a grant from D. João III to build a sugar plantation in northeastern Brazil. Citizens of the empire had long been emigrating to Brazil, as Portuguese ships often stopped at Salvador, Bahia, on the return voyage from India. The Chinese design and art of retables in the small baroque church Nossa Senhora do Ó in Sabará (Minas Gerais) is a well-known relic of Asian voyages. British historian Charles Boxer compared the town councils of Luanda, Goa, and Bahia, while Brazilian anthropologist Gilberto Freyre formed his theory of "Lusotropicalism" to unify the experience of what he called the Portuguese world in the tropics. In his controversial classic work *Casa Grande & Senzala* (1933; *The Masters & the Slaves*, trans. Samuel Putnam, New York, Knopf, 1946), Freyre developed the first comprehensive theory of Brazil in the context of a culture of "cordial" racial, social, and sexual relations. Effects of the Portuguese oceanic empire could still be felt in the 1950s, when poet Cecília Meireles and Freyre visited Goa, then part of

Portuguese India. Meireles composed a book of poetry there, and Freyre incorporated what he learned of Goan society into his theory of Lusotropicalism. Japanese emigration to Brazil began in 1908. Naturalist Aluísio de Azevedo had served in Japan in the late nineteenth century, as did modernist Raul Bopp in the 1930s. Many of Brazil's most distinguished writers in the twentieth century either were born overseas (Lispector), served in the diplomatic corps (Guimarães Rosa, João Cabral de Melo Neto, Murilo Mendes), or wrote about ethnic origins or immigrants (Alcântara Machado, Scliar, Piñón). Brazil's Atlantic world has now put on a global face for the twenty-first century.

Oceanic perspectives also can be applied broadly to Brazil's modern intellectual history, which looked so predominately toward the Atlantic for arrivals of Europeans in Brazil and Brazilians in Europe, particularly when the reciprocal visits concerned education, books, musical compositions, or art works. Brazilian statesman Joaquim Nabuco described the particular Brazilian preference for France: "what [Brazil] reads is what France produces. It is by intelligence and spirit a French citizen; it was born Parisian, in what place in Paris I do not know, it sees everything as a Parisian exiled from Paris would see it" (*Escriptos e Discursos Literários*, 1939, p. 44). In the 1830s, Brazilian romantics Gonçalves de Magalhães and Gonçalves Dias refined a national feeling of *saudade*, or melancholy longing, while studying in Europe. Modernists of the 1920s studied and lived in European capitals. For the Brazilian modernists, Paris was a passion, and they traveled there constantly during the 1920s. The celebrated Carioca composer Heitor Villa-Lobos took his music to France, where Arthur Rubenstein and others performed the Brazilian themes and rhythms written in the counterpoint of Western musical style. Villa-Lobos's enduring series of "Bachianas Brasileiras" attests to the genius of joining folkloric themes to baroque and modernist methods of composition. In Paris, aviators, owners of plantations, artists, musicians, and authors—Santos Dumont, Paulo Prado, Tarsila do Amaral, Heitor Villa-Lobos, Oswald de Andrade—formed their styles and concepts in contact with an international avant-garde.

Brazil too was fortified by waves of European intellectuals who arrived as professors, researchers, or in exile. Brazil's modern style in the arts and architecture is a direct descendant of Le Corbusier's (1887–1965) visit to Brazil in 1929, his futuristic sketches for the modernization of Rio de Janeiro, and his influence on architects Oscar Niemeyer and Lúcio Costa (see Philip Goodwin, *Brazil Builds: Architecture New and Old, 1652–1942*, photographs by G. E. Kidder Smith, New York, Museum of Modern Art, 1943). The most influential case of cross-acculturation between Europe and Brazil in the mid-twentieth century is arguably that of the French anthropologist Claude Lévi-Strauss, who arrived in São Paulo in 1935. Lévi-Strauss examined the city with the eyes of a Parisian, declaring such New World cities to be either new or decayed, but never capable of aging. His contact with three interior tribes was related in one of the classic books of twentieth-century anthropology, *Tristes Tropiques* (Paris, Plon, 1955). And between Brazil and Africa, beginning in the 1940s, the ethnographer and photographer Pierre "Fatumbi" Verger (1902–1996), whose work with Afro-Brazilian religions was commemorated in a film narrated by Gilberto Gil, Brazilian minister of culture, left a foundation in Salvador with an archive of more than 65,000 original photographs.

His legacy also includes an album of his photographs, a biography, and critical studies recently published in Brazil, where his presence is celebrated (Cida Nóbrega, *Verger: Um Retrato em Preto e Branco*, Salvador, Corrupio, 2002). In 1946, even after the isolation of the war years, the voice of writer and journalist Patrícia Galvão pronounced evocatively: "The Atlantic, our Atlantic life, so dependent on the Old World . . . European books, those precious rarities, have not yet begun to arrive" (8 February, *Vanguarda Socialista*). Brazil continued to look out onto something greater than itself: a post-imperial Atlantic whose vast world of stories is vitally connected to a heritage visible in the East, over the oceans.

A Brazil in Between

Perhaps it has been a tendency of American thought to wish to view Brazil either as a preposterous simulacrum of Europe, on the one hand, or as an original, multicultural entity, on the other. Historian Emília V. da Costa describes the problem as one that stems from defining historical processes from an assumed center of the capitalist world (*The Brazilian Empire*, 172), a point of view constituting both a narrative and a conceptual problem that continues to haunt postcolonial studies. Either one attempts to describe Brazil by searching for similarities with the center, or else one looks only to discover its specific points of difference. In either case, the analysis is dominated by the centrality of the observer, who usually has not participated in the actual local reality of Brazilian experience. What was called "Brazilian reality" by essayists in the 1920s–1940s (for example, Gilberto Freyre's *Casa Grande & Senzala*, 1933; Sérgio Buarque de Holanda's *Raízes do Brasil*, Rio de Janeiro, José Olympio, 1936) was often defined as the interplay between diverse intercontinental components and the country's vast interior reality.

In a theory proposed by author Silviano Santiago (*Latin American Literature: The Space in Between*, Buffalo, Council on International Studies, SUNY-Buffalo, 1973), Brazilian culture is neither a copy of Europe nor a separate autochthonous entity; rather, it occupies a sometimes eerie space between its arrivals from elsewhere and its luxuriant tropical nature. Its identity was forged through hybrid, multifaceted syntheses and, above all, oceanic crossings. Santiago speaks of the "in between" as a subtle and complex mixture of European and local elements, a kind of progressive infiltration put in motion by reference to indigenous cultural practices, since the road to decolonization would necessarily be the inverse of the one followed by the colonizers. The operation involves sabotage of the linguistic and religious codes or systems implanted by Western culture after discovery and occupation.

The theme of the assimilative nature of Brazilian civilization was captured in an original brainstorm by modernist intellectual Oswald de Andrade in his 1928 "Cannibalist Manifesto," according to which Brazilians, in the face of European arrivals, would take up the response of cannibal tribes and devour the Europeans in rites of ritual cannibalism. Their cultural goods would be transformed into local raw materials. Andrade's manifesto recapitulated the utopian ideal of Brazil before discovery, this time as a culture free from the conflicts and repressions associated with European civilizations. Yet the frightening metaphor of digestion is in itself a strategy, a mode of incorporating the alien with the indigenous, the cooked with the raw, while disguising resistance or converting aggression into play. The importance of Andrade's cannibal theory cannot be overstated as the scenario of a particularly Brazilian way of thinking, what is called a *jeito*, a creative synthesis and a turning of Western tables. The metaphor of cuisine expresses Brazil's traditional role of assimilation. The new Brazilian "cannibals," whom poet Haroldo de Campos ironically called "the new barbarians," occupy a cultural space in between, as they are not real cannibals, far from it, and even seem to depend on Europe for the source of literary protein upon which their manifesto depends. Nevertheless, the 1928 manifesto asserts the joyful originality of what they embraced as a simpler, more-direct way of life, an attitude useful at that time to supplant Lucien Lévy-Bruhl's studies of "primitive mentality" with savages of their own (*La mentalité primitive*, Paris, Librairie Félix Alcan, 1922). The modernists wished to create a difference with which they could provoke and challenge Europe.

Through centuries of voyages, Europeans and the inhabitants of their empires have arrived in a miscegenated, polyglot Brazilian space that assimilates traits of all, created by virtue of the alterations that Brazilian reality imposes on outside presence, and at the same time a space where European and Brazilian systems intermingle with others. Christmas under a tropical sun with palm trees, strange as it might seem, wrote Osman Lins, could perhaps be an enhanced version more authentic than the European original. Brazil's culture continues to embrace and encourage an identity conscious of its historical Atlantic, extracontinental position, neither totally here nor there, the intermingled space in between. In this literary space, European genres may be reproduced although strangely out of context, like a recording playing at the wrong speed, in which familiar content has been displaced through the transforming lens and crucible of a tropical reality. Such is the fundamentally disorienting scenario at the crux of João Guimarães Rosa's widely translated story "The Third Bank of the River."

Following the theory of a space in between, the Brazilian short story is an amalgam, a hybrid reflecting a multicultural place of encounter. The diverse threads all come together, however, either sweeping forward like a wave or flowing in reverse like the *pororoca*, the stormy ocean waves that surge up the rivers, reversing their flow. As if perpetuating this oscillating motion and rhythm, the stylistic, thematic, and linguistic qualities of the Brazilian story show consistency and coherence over time. Accounts of sailing or rubber tapping in the Amazon, for instance, may share similar literary qualities with contemporary stories of urban life, as part of a literature formed over the centuries by travel reports, descriptions, and memoirs written in the colonial period to be remitted to a distant central authority. Within this network, even the most remote corners of geography or of experience were conceived to be integral parts of a metropolitan Portuguese world, a unified geography where voyaging and writing were one: according to an old folk verse, the sea is ink and fish are scribes.

Brazilian Language

The Brazilian short story achieves its meaning and expressiveness through the singularity of its language. Brazilian Portuguese is one of the most assimilative and musical languages of modern times, particularly marked by words and expressions of Kimbundo, Yoruba, and Tupi origin. Portuguese is currently the official language of seven countries on three continents, including the world's newest nation, East Timor. Brazil is, however, the largest Portuguese-speaking country and the only South American country whose people speak Portuguese. Brazilians are in number more than half of the South American population, making Portuguese one of the ten most widely spoken languages in the world. The Portuguese language is one of the first early modern European national languages, developed from medieval Latin in the twelfth century and fully formed by the sixteenth. Because of Portugal's leadership in the age of sea explorations beginning in the fourteenth century, the Portuguese language loaned at least 1,000 words to contact languages extending from Africa to Japan, and even to languages in cultures never directly contacted. It served as a base for Creole and trade languages, while it also absorbed vocabulary from such diverse languages as Swahili, Tamil, and Japanese. Sebastião R. Dalgado's *Glossário Luso-Asiático* (Coimbra, Imprensa da Universidade, 1919–1921) documents the Portuguese language's sweep into Africa and Asia as the first global language of empire.

The differences between Brazilian and continental Portuguese are often compared to those of American and British English. Yet Brazilian Portuguese is even more flexible, assimilative, and idiomatic than American English, with a longer and more-diversified formative period. Brazilian Portuguese is particularly rich phonetically and in loan words from African languages of slavery and from Tupi and other major indigenous language families. Secondary American influences can be seen in imports from Nahuatl, Guarani, and Spanish. French has been the traditional second language for Brazilians, although in recent decades English has shown a pervasive influence.

Much more than a means of practical communication, spoken language gives one the sense of being an integral part of the essential qualities of Brazil itself. Brazilians are aware that their language has not been widely known or studied: in a sonnet dedicated to the Portuguese language, Olavo Bilac described it as a last occult and beautiful flower of Rome. In the modernist age, author Mário de Andrade described the language as one of the most rich and sonorous, possessing the "most admirable *ão*," by which he referred to a common nasal word ending, famous for challenging the phonetic prowess of all students of the language. Brazilian Portuguese, its vocabulary, expressions, melodies, and rhythms, its rebellion against grammar, is also an intimate part of daily life: in 1924, Mário described his Brazilian life as an aggregate of funny expressions, awkward sentimentality, and his knack for earning money, eating, and sleeping. In a 1924 manifesto, Oswald de Andrade praised the "millionaire contribution of all errors" in a "country without grammar." Language is what the short story is made of, and no translation, however competent, can replace or reproduce its expressive and linguistic features. Thus, the ultimate goal to which an anthology such as this can aspire is to motivate its readers to learn to read the stories in the original Portuguese.

Development of the Short Story:
Baroque to Modern

Two major formative aesthetic periods shaping Brazilian literature are the baroque, with its grand, expressive heterogeneity in the Portuguese overseas territories during the sixteenth and seventeenth centuries, and modernism, which was inaugurated at São Paulo's Modern Art Week in 1922. The story tradition took on the aesthetic contours of the maritime baroque, a monumental, decorative, and contrastive style found throughout the territories of Portuguese expansion. For more than two centuries, the Brazilian baroque age established and practiced a rhetorical, architectural, and theoretical paradigm for the developing civilization, characterized by sharp contrasts and elaborate dramatic expressions. Prime examples known today are the sculptures of Antônio Francisco Lisboa (1730–1814), known in Brazil as Aleijadinho, and the musical compositions of José Joaquim Emérico Lobo de Mesquita (c. 1740–1805). Its vital impact was propounded and defended in the twentieth century in studies by scholars Haroldo de Campos (*O Sequestro do Barroco na Literatura Brasileira*, Salvador, Casa Jorge Amado, 1989), Afrânio Coutinho (*Do Barroco: Ensaios*, Rio de Janeiro, UFRJ, Tempo Brasileiro, 1994), and Affonso Ávila (*O Lúdico e as Projeções do Mundo Barroco*, São Paulo, Perspectiva, 1971). It is frequently said that Brazil's literature was born already an adult, because of the elegant, ornate baroque style in vogue during its supposed infancy. Baroque features dominated the great cathedrals of Brazil, Goa, and Macao; peered out of animal faces elaborately carved in Indo-Portuguese furniture; and figured in the exchange of spices, fruits, and plants between India and Brazil. António do Rosário's curious treatise *Frutas do Brasil* (Lisbon, 1702) allegorized the role of thirty-six fruits in both governance and sacred scriptures, crowned by the pineapple. Linguistic versatility resulted not only from an increased amount of writing, but also from the diversity of languages in contact, particularly Portuguese and Tupi. Although the Brazilian baroque style became well known in the architecture of colonial churches, particularly those of the colonial towns in Minas Gerais, the literary baroque was supplanted after the country's independence in 1822 by the more-influential arcadist and romantic theories that came into vogue about the birth of national literature, emphasizing nature and the Indian. The centrality of the baroque in the formation of Brazilian literature is a scholarly reconstitution that has been reinforced by a recent surge of interest in its chief figures, both centered in Salvador, Bahia: poet Gregório de Mattos (1636–1696), known as "mouth of hell" for his satires, which got him exiled to Angola, and the foremost writer, intellectual, and religious figure of his age, the renowned Antônio Vieira, S.J. (1608–1697). In addition to its formal and conceptual sophistication, the baroque unites Brazil with the major architectonic style of Portuguese expansion in Africa and Asia in the sixteenth and seventeenth centuries. It is also a period that allowed for a full range of expressive writing, from the heights of religious poetry and philosophical essay to witty satirical poetry and scatological, erotic verse. The satirical tradition in the modern story has baroque antecedents, as does its preoccupation with linguistic innovation and the view of the world as a universe of forms, a prevalent theme in the masterful stories of Osman Lins and João Guimarães Rosa.

Just as Brazilian literature was said to have been born an adult because of the advanced conceptual and stylistic practices of the maritime baroque—and as if to prove the idea, in one of the major modernist novels, Mário de Andrade's *Macunaíma* (1928), the hero is born in the Amazon fully grown—the short story can likewise be said to have been born a modern adult. Beyond the parallel just drawn, one can consider several factors contributing to its majority when it first appears in print. The story comes of age in the period of the empire, thus descriptive narratives reflect a complex and historically charged international and colonial world view. In the atmosphere of the empire, the short story need no longer draw solely on its sources in tales, sagas, legends, and oral traditions firmly ingrained in the national consciousness, being distanced as well from the major national themes of romantic nationalism—Indianism, abolitionism, nature. Although its gestation attests to a kinship with all forms of story that arrived in Brazil, its appearance in written form corresponds with the publication of popular journals and newspapers. Many major novels were serialized, such as Manuel Antônio de Almeida's *Memórias de um Sargento de Milícias* (1855) and Machado's *Memórias Póstumas de Brás Cubas* (1880), and the *folhetins*, containing the first chronicles depicting daily life, connected the printed story to journalism, the novel, and local customs. Through Machado de Assis, the unquestioned master of the story, the workings of society— its psychology, politics, relations, and affections—were intimately those of Rio de Janeiro, although a hidden world of minor characters covered a full range of issues and social stratification. Given the atmosphere of post-Darwinism and positivism reigning in Brazil at the time, the short story would from its beginnings take up themes involved with the building of a modern, scientific nation, often subjecting them to the scathing satire and humor so adeptly ingrained in the story tradition. Authors of short stories were well acquainted with classical and modern European literature and philosophy, particularly Portuguese and French literature—although including Edgar Allan Poe in French translation—and their works reflected the characteristics of the successive chronological periods of major Western literatures. When rewritten in the Brazilian context, recognizable themes from the Western tradition were subjected to a kind of cannibalistic reacculturation, as theorized by Oswald de Andrade or practiced elegantly by Machado de Assis, a process through which original imported materials were absorbed into a vaster, more primal, and schematic Brazilian world.

Short-story writing from its beginnings in Brazil was influenced by sources as diverse as classical and European literatures, principally the French, journalistic chronicles of daily life, Portuguese imperial culture in Brazil, and the new sociopolitical circumstances of independence. In 1808, Rio de Janeiro became the capital city of the Portuguese imperial world, with the exile of Portuguese monarch D. João VI to his European capital in the tropics. Brazil's own empire under his descendants endured from 1822 to 1889. The bases for claiming a national literature were rooted in a romantic identification of the beauty and richness of nature with national independence. Indianism, with its idealized versions of the noble savage, dominated the literature of independence and romanticism. Ferdinand Denis first described Brazilian literature in French in 1826, in an epilogue to a discourse on Portuguese literature (*Résumé de l'histoire lettéraire du Portugal, suivi du résumé de l'histoire littéraire du Brésil*, Paris, Lecointe et Durey, 1826). More than a century later, critics in Brazil continued to debate the date when an autonomous Brazilian literature could be distinguished from Portuguese literature written in Brazil, in order to demarcate a formal birth certificate for the national literature. In influential histories of Brazilian literature in the mid-twentieth century, literary historian Antonio Candido located the first national characteristics in the arcadian nature of the mid-eighteenth century (*Formação da Literatura Brasileira: Momentos Decisivos*, São Paulo, Martins, 1959), while his counterpart Afrânio Coutinho claimed that any literature written in Brazil had always been Brazilian, ever since Caminha's first letter of description of the "Terra da Vera Cruz" (Land of the True Cross), later named Brazil (*A Tradição Afortunada*, Rio de Janeiro, José Olympio, 1968). The founding of the Brazilian Academy of Letters by Machado de Assis in 1897, with forty chairs based on the French academy established by Richelieu in 1635, was meant to provide an indispensable dictionary for Brazilian usage. It recognized the nation's most distinguished writers in a pantheon of glory equal to that of political fame, and many have served since as diplomats.

Brazil's overarching literary themes, consecrated by romantic nationalism, can be summarized as racial (the Indian, the black slave, the *caboclo*, etc.), economic (plantations), geographic (drought, the *sertão*), regional (Bahia, the Amazon, etc.), and metropolitan (empire). These broad themes remain valid as substrata of meaning upon which the modern story is constructed, although they were enriched by the naturalist approach to specific social and human problems so influential in the last quarter of the nineteenth century. Joaquim Norberto de Sousa e Silva (1820–1891) is credited with publishing the first short story, "As duas órfãs" (1841), followed by poet Álvares de Azevedo's (1831–1852) macabre tale "Noite na taverna," reminiscent of Poe and Maupassant. In the first history of Brazilian literature (1888; 6th ed., Rio de Janeiro, José Olympio, 1960), Sílvio Romero (1851–1914) defined and defended it as an expression of the scientific evolution of the land and people. The published story dates from this period, when printing was permitted in Brazil, although many books continued to be published in Portugal or France until the early twentieth century. At this time, folklorists and ethnographers such as Romero (*Cantos Populares do Brasil: Folclore Brasileiro*, Lisboa, Nova Livraria Internacional, 1883) were collecting traditional stories, as well as accounts of expeditions that included indigenous lore (Couto de Magalhães, *O Selvagem*, Rio de Janeiro, da Reforma, 1876). Themes of exploration and the natural environment were followed in the late nineteenth century by those of languages and cultures brought by waves of immigrants—from Lebanese to Italians to Japanese. All of this forms the complex texture of the modern story.

The Brazilian short story belongs to the country's long literary practice of collective self-definition through the depiction of human and geographic features and circumstances. In effect, this remains the function and purpose of the short story to the present day: to form contemporary visions in prose of etchings and drawings in order to characterize Brazilian natural, social, and human types. It is extremely rare to find a story set outside of Brazil, such as Érico Veríssimo's "The House of the Melancholy Angel," which is set in Germany, or Orígenes Lessa's "Marta: A Souvenir of New York." At the same time, the cosmopolitanism and internationalism of the Brazilian story is reinforced by the fact that Veríssimo wrote stories directly in English without a Portuguese original, just as statesman Joaquim Nabuco penned essays and lectures directly in English in 1908–1909 while serving as ambassador to the United States. Stories almost universally revive the Brazilian cultural world, as do historical paintings, such as the landscapes of the Northeast by Dutch painters Albert Eckhout (c. 1607–1655) and Frans Jansz Post (1612–1680) or the valued watercolors portraying a cross-section of the Brazilian population by Jean Baptiste Débret (1768–1848), who came to Rio de Janeiro with the French cultural mission in 1816 (*Voyage pittoresque et historique au Brésil* . . . , Paris, Firmin Didot Frères, 1834–1839). Such artists' work communicates the human and material culture of its time, and Débret's special interest is the world of labor, human types, and locales. The short story complements the visual depictions of Brazil through the depths of narrative imagination, specifying social, psychological, and existential meanings in its verbal canvases. In his 1916 history of Brazilian literature (5th ed., Rio de Janeiro, José Olympio, 1969), which is noted for its aesthetic emphasis, José Veríssimo (1857–1916) described the virtues of stories as communicating the characteristics of Brazilian life, expressing intimate feelings, and revealing idiosyncrasies, where readers could discover the Brazilian imagination, psychology, customs, national character, and reality. He thought of stories as mirrors of the Brazilian people, relating their outlooks, beliefs, relationships, experience, psychology, and humor. Veríssimo even categorized stories by kind and purpose: love stories, states of mind, customs, types, historical or true stories, cases of conscience, characterizations of people, and the habits of all classes.

Even during Veríssimo's time, the story was urbanizing, changing dramatically in focus, technique, and treatment but without either breaking its ties with the description of Brazil or losing its interest in recurrent themes of tradition, be they animals, regional traits, or a national ethos of perception and feeling. Contemporary critics Walnice Nogueira Galvão and Luiz Costa Lima divide the short story into two principal modes: the creation of atmosphere or theatricality, marked by colloquial scenes and language, and the story as concrete anecdote or plot (*O Livro do Seminário*, São Paulo, LR Editores, 1983). The former is more artistic or aesthetic, creating states of spirit or other nonrealistic experiences, while the latter develops practices of realistic or naturalistic description. Because of the story's ties to the journalistic chronicle and the scientific study of Brazil encouraged by naturalism, Galvão finds that the anecdotal story tends to dominate recent production, while the heritage of modernism encourages the experimental search for new aesthetic norms and forms of expression. An anthology of Brazilian short stories may not represent every category or tendency, but taken as a whole it inevitably amounts to a report and memoir depicting the vast world of Brazil. Read chronologically, it reconstitutes the waves that over time have so rhythmically advanced both how and what Brazilians wish to tell and their ways of telling. Its themes are commensurate with the portrait of a rapidly developing Western society over the past century: there are stories of love and death, internal migration and conflict, land, slavery, poverty, censorship and obscenity, sex, immigration, urbanization, crime and mutilation, rebellion, deception, tragedy and redemption, illusion and epiphany.

Stories constitute an important source and reinforcement of identity, invaluable expressions of continuity defining the national experience and character. As Roberto González Echevarría points out in his introduction to *The Oxford Book of Latin American Short Stories* (1997), which includes Brazilian texts, Brazilian and Spanish-American literary traditions are distinct, and Brazil, along with the United States, has the richest literature of the Americas. It should not be surprising that these two great literatures of the Americas, those of Brazil and the United States, share similar characteristics, although many of their common features are not widely known or studied. There is the issue of the enormous amount of writing, since state literatures in Brazil are equivalent to the national literatures of many Spanish-American republics, and one must consider the role of language and the creation of an assimilative, regional Brazilian Portuguese. Brazilian stories are likewise distinctly regional in theme, with characters depicting the speech, social worlds, and issues of their place and time. The vocabulary and speech of the Amazon and the Northeast, for example, have required authors to use footnotes and glossaries to identify indigenous flora and fauna and for regional vocabulary, all of which would not be familiar to readers in urban areas. Notable examples are the incorporation of Tabajara and Tapuia vocabulary from Ceará in José de Alencar's 1865 novel *Iracema*, first translated into English with notes by Isabella Burton (*Iraçéma, the Honey-lips: A Legend of Brazil*, London, Bickers, 1886). A glossary of northeastern terms for Brazilian readers was included in José Américo de Almeida's 1928 novel of sugarcane plantations, *A Bagaceira* (*Trash: A Novel*, trans. R. L. Scott-Buccleuch, London, Owen, 1978). In Érico Veríssimo's story about Rio Grande do Sul, "Fandango," the formal Portuguese taught at school is said to have very little to do with the language spoken by *gaúchos* on the ranch, where sayings and proverbs abound: "Sky with stony grain means wind or rain." The *sertão* of the interior dry lands beyond the coastal range lends its racial spectrum, folk language, and atavistic cultural practices of nomadic and messianic bands to the stories of Guimarães Rosa. More than a geographic region, the *sertão* in literature becomes a primordial, metaphysical setting for revealing and dramatizing the primitive roots of consciousness and social organization. It is a stage for the reenactment of medieval, allegorical drama. The immense Brazilian interior is above all a frontier, comparable to the American West in the *bandeirante* movement meant to conquer, tame, and populate it. Indianism is a common theme, which led scholar Renata Wasserman to compare the Indianist novels of James Fenimore Cooper with those of José de Alencar. There is the pervasive presence of slavery, which shaped northeastern plantation society much as it did the U.S. South and produced the consequent literature chronicling its abuses. The world of the plantation in northeastern Brazil in the fiction of José Lins do Rego has been compared to the plantation world of William Faulkner by Brazilian scholar Heloísa Toller Gomes (*O Poder Rural na Ficção*, São Paulo, Ática, 1981).

Immigration and urbanization, as in the United States, are the two major for-

mative forces in the twentieth-century story. Brazil received more than 80,000 immigrants from Italy alone in the period 1880–1900, and a Portuguese-Italian dialect
was common in the city of São Paulo and in the city press as late as 1950. In
Antônio de Alcântara Machado's bittersweet story "The Beauty Contest," reminiscent of pages of Mark Twain, a small-town girl from Corisco is selected to be the
state beauty queen by "one Brazilian, one Italian, one second-generation Italian,
and one Portuguese." Separated from her rural setting, Miss Corisco finds herself
at a loss in the competition in the national capital, where she must keep up a
cheerful appearance alongside Miss Brazil, who will represent the country in the
international competition in Galveston, Texas. Such links with actual events and
places help to characterize the modern story as a chronicle of daily life and events,
influenced by journalistic and camera-eye techniques. The rural-urban peasant migration is yet another link, whether evoked in Graciliano Ramos's novel of Northeast peasantry, *Barren Lives* (1938), one of the most widely translated works in
Brazilian literature, or in its American companion, John Steinbeck's *The Grapes of
Wrath* (1939). Rural emigration became a flood in the 1960s–1980s, transforming
São Paulo into the world's third-largest city and changing the nature of the national
landscape with the creation of dozens of cities with populations of more than 1
million people.

An even closer resemblance to U.S. literature is visible in modernism, a movement that swept over Brazil in 1922 and led many artists and writers to develop
their art while studying and living in Europe, particularly Paris, where Oswald de
Andrade mentions being in a studio with John Dos Passos. After 1945, a number
of Brazilian writers came to the United States, most to teach or lecture. Érico Veríssimo published a history of Brazilian literature in English and wrote "The Guerrilla," a parody set in Mexico, directly in English. Orígenes Lessa's story "Marta"
is his tribute to Hispanic immigrants in New York City. Modernism, whether focused internally on the cultural redefinition of Brazilian reality or internationally
on comparative techniques in France and the United States, has proved to be an
enduring legacy in the Brazilian story, continuing to shape contemporary writing
with its characteristics of youth, energy, populism, experimentation, and conscious
use of language. The most common elements linking Brazilian writing with that of
the United States are fruits of the modernism so well developed in Brazil's twentieth-
century architecture, music, and plastic arts: experimental style, an emphasis on
language and narration, use of native materials, and an open, individualistic sense
of creative imagination. Modernism in Brazil is said to have constituted the first
close look at national reality, replacing romantic myths with the authentic materials
of the day found in speech, song, labor, and the everyday lives of people. Forging
a national identity with new myths of its own, while developing in splendid isolation, modernism has had a more marked, centralizing effect in Brazil and dominates
the arts today in a more pervasive way than even would have been possible for its
counterpart in the United States. Where else but in Brazil would two concrete poets,
Haroldo and Augusto de Campos, be known on a first-name basis by almost any
high school graduate? Likewise, linguistic and formal innovation and experimentation are counted among the most constant features of the short story.

The modernist aesthetic that crystallized in the Modern Art Week in February

1922, with its documentation of the present moment and self-consciousness of the new, had a sharp and definitive effect on the writing of stories thereafter. After the Modern Art Week, Brazilian arts became more unified in developing a recognizable modern style, whether in music, architecture, plastic arts, or literature. The construction of Brasília (1959) is the most visible culmination of a long-existent dynamic, modernist, nationalist project, representing Brazil's commitment to and fascination with the forces of modernism. In the short story, the modernist contributions can be seen in urban themes and social critiques, Brazilianized language including regional and immigrant dialects, colloquial speech, fragmented discourse, cinematographic techniques, and humor applied to a culture marked by personal affection and sentiment. Mário de Andrade's stories dramatize the social, psychological, and economic problems of lower-middle-class immigrants in São Paulo, while introducing some technical innovations. In one of his stories, the main character is a number, while in another a character cites his story's author by name, using the interior monologue preferred by early modernism. In "The Christmas Turkey," Juca, the teenage narrator, subtly recounts the art of his strategic escape from suffocating paternalism to one of free indulgence and desire, neutralizing without offending the hovering ghost of his dead father at the family's meager yet ritualistic Christmas feast. Pleasure eclipses death only through a neobaroque sleight of hand, crafted in deceptively simple modernist language, and a pretense of madness that was his excuse to be different: "He's crazy, the poor kid." The dramatization of social issues and an artistic awareness of language are characteristics of the modernist story that again form a bridge with paintings of the period by Brazil's foremost artists, visible in the stylistic, formal landscapes of Tarsila do Amaral, the expressionistic mulatto women of E. Di Cavalcanti, and the stark, infinite landscapes of Cândido Portinari.

Stylistic and linguistic innovations based on modernist practices continued to lead the Brazilian story at mid-twentieth century, engendering some of the most radical yet enduring directions that have lasted to the present. Osman Lins writes in multiple perspectives of the events in his "Baroque Tale," whose sections are separated only by the word *or*, as if the different perspectives were angles of a geometric figure or plane. Dalton Trevisan introduces the inverted moral tale in his pathological monologues of sexually perverted narrators, as in "The Vampire of Curitiba." Trevisan continues to pare his stories, which demolish bourgeois desire, until arriving at the mini-story, or minimalist form. The stylistic innovation in Hilda Hilst's story "Agda" is produced by the vertigo of a continuous, free internal monologue, through which the aging woman attempts to capture the "ALL ALIVE" that lives outside and apart from her body. Clarice Lispector develops existentialist, occult, and primitivist themes in situations in which they might be least expected, wherein the dramas and anguishes of everyday life are unexpectedly confronted with human complexities. An often dark sense of comedy and satire, perfected perhaps in "The Smallest Woman in the World," a story that attracted Elizabeth Bishop's translation, demolishes some of the false and absurd cultural constructs that have come to dominate modern life. It is at the same time a hilarious satire of the anthropologist as hero, perhaps motivated by Lévi-Strauss's work in Brazil. In the world of language, Guimarães Rosa's formation and deformation of words, drawn from all periods of the Portuguese language and especially from usage in the interior *sertão*, constitute a kind of zenith of invention in the story, where narration becomes an amalgam of rhythm, form, and philosophy. Both Lispector and Rosa, although working from different directions, produce moments of epiphany that intensify one's admiration for their craftsmanship.

Poet Haroldo de Campos defined the postmodern in Brazil as post-utopian. One of the literary consequences of the dictatorship that governed Brazil from 1964 to 1985 is a form of despairing political satire, seen in Carlos Heitor Cony's "Order of the Day" or Moacyr Scliar's "The Last Poor Man." In these stories, the individual is sacrificed to the horde and mass psychology, enforced by ideological and militaristic posturing. In J. J. Veiga's "The Misplaced Machine," the population of a small town lives under the hypnotism of its messianic beliefs, its fear of power, and its ignorance of science when a strange, enormous machine suddenly appears on the town's square. In Victor Giudice's "The File Cabinet," an exemplary worker is given the absurd reward of having his salary continually reduced, until he is no more than an object. These are allegories of despair, just as Samuel Rawet's story of the arrival in Brazil of an old Jewish immigrant, "The Prophet," is one of disgust and alienation with urban commercial culture. The immigrant from the Old World cannot adapt to the secular ways of his relatives nor to the trivial, consumer culture that has occluded any awareness of suffering or history.

At the same time, stories of mythic imagination continue to recast the search for freedom and truth, however they may be conceived. Nélida Piñón's "Big-Bellied Cow" is a parable for the reverence, respect, and dedication that can exist between humans and animals on a plane much above that of ownership or service. Hilda Hilst's "Agda" is an interior narration on the fullness of sexual love, where energy and desire overcome age and death. In Lygia Fagundes Telles's story "Just a Saxophone," despair leads to apotheosis. When a woman's memory of a young lover who played the saxophone is equated with the lost love of youth, the narrator desperately demands to retain control over it: "If you really love me, then go out and kill yourself right away." A final trend that perhaps will show the way out of Brazil's postmodern dilemma is one that reconstructs a memory of lost culture. In Caio Fernando Abreu's "Dragons . . . ," an urban narrator searching for meaning and happiness compares his situation to that of medieval dragons. Perhaps he also is conflictive, ideological, and invisible? That crazy, ugly dragon stays with him, reminding him of his wait "for a happiness that never comes." The narrator learns from his imaginary dragon to abandon artificial paradises and illusions, even if the only certainty is that "none of this exists." In "The Truth Is a Seven-Headed Animal," Milton Hatoum produces in microcosm a critical review of Brazil's past worlds in all of their incongruity and difference. His suggestion that truth comes in different forms is a fitting conclusion to an anthology on Brazil. Hatoum returns us to the famous Manaus opera house, the subject of the film *Fitzcarraldo*, which is a replica of Milan's La Scala built during the rubber boom, where Caruso and other Italian stars of the day performed. In the story, an eighty-seven-year-old recluse who lives in the attic, a kind of phantom of the opera, still imagines that he hears and sees "the divine Milanese soprano" Angiolina Zanuchi in her performance of December 1910. What he actually sees is a homeless, destitute pregnant woman who takes refuge from a tropical deluge in the theater's front row. As Álvaro Celestino de Matos peers out of the stage curtain, he is led away by attendants from a mental hospital. Is he, perhaps, like Brazil, suffering from lunatic delusions, or is he caught in a memory of great intensity, frozen with the whole city in a timeless moment when art and fate cast a magical, eternal spell? Hatoum's story suggests that the truth of Álvaro's persistent paradisiacal memory will retain its power to transform a present of destitution and silence.

Major Themes

The unity and consistency of the Brazilian story becomes apparent through its overarching themes and issues, illustrated here by the selection of some of the principal lines of its chronological development and major concerns. These range from philosophical and ethical issues to humor and satire, altered realities and perceptions, abnormal psychological states, regionalism, primitivism, repression and sexual perversion, urban life, stylistic experimentation, oral tales, and myths.

Chief among them is the ethical, moral, and philosophical world of the story, a vision most fully developed in the works of Machado de Assis. Ethics is a form of philosophy in Machado's stories, where the author's ultimate interest is in the nature and meaning of the world and of experience. Machado subjects all of human behavior, its desires, motivations, and habits, to the eternal laws of fate, recounted in the twisted situations and contexts in which principles can be observed in play. One of the most devastating cases of moral choice is found in Machado's story "Father versus Mother," in which poverty and slavery lead to a fatal moment of crisis and choice in which survival and ethics are the opposing forces. The story is based on the duplicity of roles and questions whether grotesque and cruel acts can ever contribute to the building of a human social order. Because of the nature of slavery, slaves frequently run away, so Machado wryly observes—and large encampments have existed in the interior since the seventeenth century—and catching them was the profession of impoverished men, or those who thought they were enforcing a system of property rights. Candido Neves had been lucky at that occupation and made some money; yet when he married Clara and they had a child, profits dried up and there were no more slaves to catch. Impoverished, the couple was faced with abandoning their baby to an orphanage. Just as Candido is carrying the baby to its fate, in the street he spots a runaway slave woman, Arminda, pregnant with her unborn baby. When accosted and captured, she explains that her cruel master beats her severely; there is a struggle, and Arminda is dragged through the streets and returned to her master. As Candido receives his large reward, Arminda miscarries then and there in front of him. On hearing about it, Candido's aunt criticizes the slave woman severely for the miscarriage, yet Candido can only bless her for running away. The story closes with his motto: "Not all babies have the luck to be born!" Machado's narrative control of the story reaches well beyond the ironic or sardonic attitudes for which he is usually known and praised. Here, he has reached a point beyond words, for there is a profound level of truth in Candido's self-serving motto. To be born, as to live, is a struggle, as the science of the day proclaimed; yet that is hardly the whole story. Grotesque and cruel acts, implicit in a social order that proclaims itself humane, also intervene beyond ethics, and Candido invokes them with a blindness and self-interest protected by the social order and contentment in the sacrifice of the weakest.

In Machado's "Dona Paula," the main character's young niece Venancinha has gotten into marital troubles and calls on her aunt for assistance. Venancinha had quarreled with her husband, Conrad, to the point of separation, and she was desperate. He had seen her dance with a man twice and converse with him for a few minutes, and the next morning he accused her harshly. Dona Paula, entertaining some suspicion and curiosity, goes to visit Conrad at his law office to straighten out the matter. It seems there had been other incidents, and the two finally compromise that Venancinha will spend several weeks in temporary exile with her aunt in the Tijuca district. There, Dona Paula will lead her back to the habits of a perfect wife. When she first hears the name of the other gentleman, however, Dona Paula pales; it is not the former diplomat whom she once knew, but his worthless son. Once in Tijuca, Dona Paula begins her moral lessons, but when a tall stranger rides by on horseback, Venancinha confesses all and tells her aunt the story of her passion. In that story, Dona Paula unexpectedly relives her own past, for she never married after the passionate affair of her youth with the now-retired diplomat. Venancinha's catharsis leads her to beg her aunt for forgiveness, with the intention of forgetting the young man and returning to her husband. While listening rapturously to the niece's confession, Dona Paula is transported to her own past and revisits all of the raging emotions of yesteryear. She can only stare at the wind and rustling leaves, aware that her time has passed irrevocably and that she has just spoken to her niece of chastity, public opinion, and loving one's husband. The old servants in the kitchen, observing Dona Paula during her strange reminiscences, sense her distress and gossip that she is never going to get to bed that night. Are Dona Paula's actions hypocritical, Machado seems to ask the reader, or do they illustrate the delicious and sad human condition?

The creation of different realities and perceptions constitutes another major current in the Brazilian story. Guimarães Rosa's celebrated "The Third Bank of the River" proposes an ultimate difference that affects the very nature, psychology, and social organization of life. Rosa's tale is at once archetype and legend, parable and mystery, mixing biblical antecedents with the indigenous lore of the Brazilian *sertão*. A father, thought to be mad by his family, has a canoe built and bids them all goodbye. The mother considers it a betrayal, or madness, suicide, or crime. His oldest son asks to be taken in the canoe, but the father refuses. He paddles out into the middle of the river's current in the canoe that resembles a *jacaré*, a crocodile that is a master of metaphysics, where the father remains visible throughout the rest of time, to the family's surprise and horror. Their futile attempts to signal or call to the father constitute an allegory of the passing of the generations as a form of religious ritual and become examples, on another plane, of all human struggles for meaning, survival, and the eternal. The father performs a necessary but occult transmigration, when life must change its form, and he becomes the *jacaré*, the very current of the river, one of the prime symbols of life in the Platonic tradition. Yet by remaining visible, the father challenges the family he has left behind to come to an understanding of his strange anthropomorphic theology. The oldest son, who lives his life waiting on the bank of the river, becomes the guilt-ridden priest of the sacrificed father, thereby enacting a principal theme in Western religious belief.

Another very different story of the encounter of other realities is Clarice Lispector's "Beauty & the Beast," in which a wealthy, mature woman who has been at the beauty salon of the Copacabana Palace Hotel comes out onto the street and for the first time meets a beggar. Her disorientation crosses the boundaries of class and behavior, to the point of questioning the nature of personal communication and social organization. The woman wonders how much to give the beggar, then notices that she has only a 500 cruzeiro bill, a fortune at the time. Her strange question to the beggar, "Will this be enough?" is only a prelude to an intense, if limited, collapse of barriers on both sides, as she sits down on the sidewalk beside the beggar in her state of innocence and, perhaps, grace. Could she give the factory of her industrialist husband to the beggar? The limitless proportions of her gifts open the full wounds of economic and social inequality. They defy the normal common sense with which extreme wealth and misery are treated. Perhaps even the beggar will feel relieved when the chauffeur finally arrives to carry the wealthy woman back to her world of privilege and isolation. After Lispector's unlikely and magical story, however, can things ever be the same?

Yet another very different reality is invoked in Guimarães Rosa's "The Girl from Beyond." No one could ever understand Nhinhinha, that tiny bit of a girl with a big head and enormous eyes, who lived in the far backlands and whose few words were baffling, perhaps simpleminded. She was always only herself, and she spoke in short, inventive exclamations and told absurd little stories, like the bee that flew up to a cloud. Then, she began to work small miracles, asking for things that suddenly appeared, like a toad or guava jam, or curing her mother's illness with a hug. When she brought rain to end a drought, birds sang crazily, and she thought green-bird thoughts. Nhinhinha's sudden death was the blow from which all suffered, creating a time when there are no more miracles, no mysterious words, and no communion with the beyond. In the nature of a parable, Rosa's story tells of the unexpected and constant presence of grace, for acts of real living always take place far away, while Nhinhinha's mother now knows that her daughter was Saint Nhinhinha.

—◦❧ ❦◦—

Abnormal or unusual psychological states form the theme of numerous stories. In "The Thief," Graciliano Ramos, the master of modernist neorealism in the school of the northeastern novel, creates a tragic sense of life in carefully crafted language by accompanying the thoughts and actions of a most unusual thief. He is a novice who has not even completed his study of the layout of the house he plans to enter. Yet overcome with hunger and with cold, damp, and trembling hands, he faces what he inevitably must do. Each step in the house and every object encountered is a mystery and martyrdom. Having discovered some cash, he begins to leave, when he notices the girl with the green eyes, who has fascinated him before, asleep in bed with one breast exposed. Panic stricken, he hurls himself out of the room and onto the stairs, where he recovers. Yet in the silence, he begins to hallucinate and become disoriented, focusing only on his hunger. After searching for cheese in the kitchen, he is overcome by a mad idea, to return upstairs only to see the color of the eyes of the sleeping maiden. How could he do such a fatal thing, bending over to place a kiss on her lips, thinking himself beyond reality? The act that ruins his life is at once partly explained by his physical and psychological frailty, but it also has much to say about his need for other forms of affection and gratification, which society denies, available only in states of exception. The girl is a "Holy Mary" whom the thief encounters in the midst of his crime. Graciliano poses deep questions of social value and justice, as the reader follows the musings of a good thief, protected yet condemned by his naïve innocence, his psychological instability, and his inability to distinguish reality, just as he cannot quite make out objects in the dark house. In the story of a burglary one finds visionary questions about perdition and salvation, much beyond the conscious awareness of the good thief. Graciliano invents his own version of the absurd hero, solitary and frustrated, in revolt against forms of bourgeois reality and materiality, and capable of being misunderstood and condemned because of his inexplicable hypnotism by green eyes and a breast.

Sociopolitical satire and humor are vital currents in the Brazilian story, nowhere better illustrated than in Lima Barreto's "The Man Who Knew Javanese." An unemployed and impecunious student resolves to find his future niche and fortune by taking on a subject unchallenged by anyone else, the study of Javanese. The little he learns from an encyclopedia would not amount to two minutes of the first Berlitz class, yet he obtains a position as tutor to a baron, who wishes to learn Javanese in order to translate an obscure family document. Fortunately for our student, the baron "learns and unlearns" with equal rapidity, and by quickly perusing an English summary of the document, our student is able to build his reputation as an expert in Javanese. Through the baron's influence, he is ultimately named to the Foreign Office and assigned to an international conference in the Hague, but to a section having nothing to do with his "specialty." In the story's final twist, the hero wonders if there is still time to take on another career as an eminent bacteriologist. In microcosm, the story enlightens us about the entrenched systems of patronage and bureaucracy that, in the view of Emília V. da Costa, delayed the implantation of democracy and modernity in Brazil.

A much darker humor is employed in Monteiro Lobato's "The Funnyman Who Repented," which departs from strategies of the oral tale to weave the story of the illegitimate village comedian, Pontes, who gains a reputation for jokes and comedy so ingrained that citizens double up with laughter just at the sight of him. There is nothing he can do that is not taken to be funny or a practical joke. Now of a certain age, Pontes must decide his future, and he looks to a relative, Major Bentes of the Federal Internal Revenue Office, whom he hopes to replace in his sinecure in the city. After worming his way into the office and making himself indispensable, Pontes begins to plot the demise of the old major. After deepening his psychological fixation to the point of murdering the major at the height of a dinner anecdote, Pontes disappears for weeks in nervous agitation. He learns from a friend that during that interval the job has already been handed out to another; his delay has cost him his whole plan. When Pontes strangles himself with a leg of long underwear, it is taken by the villagers to be his last prank and the only task at which Pontes ever succeeded in his entire life. Lobato has created a setting for the themes of social immobility and stigma by creating a provincial comic hero, defined by his small-town existence and fatally marked by his illegitimate birth.

—◦❧ ❦◦—

Guimarães Rosa's "The Jaguar," one of the most masterful stories in all of Brazilian literature, embodies the theme of primitivism that was delineated theoretically in the 1928 "Cannibal Manifesto." Located far into the *sertão*, the story is narrated by an old *sertanejo* who has lived a full life as a hunter to clear the land of *onças* (jaguars). As he tells his life's tale, he is drinking *cachaça*, and thus his ability to speak in coherent Portuguese diminishes as the story progresses. The sole listener to his tale in a cabin deep in the interior is never identified, but the listener is addressed at times so as to indicate his position representing the law or learning. Perhaps he has come to bring the old *sertanejo* to justice, since the lengthy narration has the nature of a confession, a justification, and an autobiography. It is a psychological portrait of the values and demands of the *sertão* that have led the narrator to value and live exclusively with the animal world. He is full of the remorse and desires that have brought him close to madness, making strange the two main characteristics of his identity: a human being and a killer of jaguars. Now aged, he recognizes through telling his story that he is more like the very animals that he has hunted and killed by the hundreds. He declares his love and describes his courtship of the young female jaguars as if they were young maidens. His life and work have been nothing except an obsession to watch them and know them intimately, to the point that the violence of death is now transformed into the pursuit and fear of sexuality. When he tells of other jaguar suitors coming for his favorite, whom he names Maria-Maria, he becomes enraged and forgets how to speak Portuguese. Violence and sexual desire are the mainstays of his experience, which have brought him to the edge of an impossible transformation, surrender to the powerful female who dominates the interior lands and who could rip out his heart with a single blow. While his narrative asks for justification and exoneration in terms of society, it serves neither to expiate his crimes against the creatures he loves nor to bring about his physical transformation into the jaguar life. The narrator's language slowly fragments and alters, until in his last words he is speaking only jaguar language. Thus his final passion, inebriation, and exit from the human realm correspond with a final shift in language and in being. The narrator's episodic story of death and passion integrates the oral, frontier tale with the profound dramas that define the human realm, a structure Guimarães Rosa fully develops in his great novel, *Grande Sertão: Veredas* (1956).

Clarice Lispector's puzzling story "The Buffalo" captures something of the ineffable primitivism of the rites of spring and the awakening of fertility. A young woman is visiting the zoo, but at each instance of courtship or love among the species, she feels only a more desperate hatred. What she feels is just the urge for destruction, carnage among the beasts. Perhaps her rage comes about because of her petty life, as the day when all of the contents of her bag spilled out onto the road? Her repressed howl of agony is perhaps the outcry of a beast that has known only resignation, unhappiness, and love? If she could only learn to hate, then she would not die of the impossible love she feels as the spurned, shunned female, now without a partner in life. She looks at the white clouds without a shred of hope, and when she lowers her gaze, there is the black water buffalo, with its luminous, tranquil fury. With feelings of purity and veneration, she tries desperately to attract the attention of that black beast, and she feels that the dark liquids inside her have begun to flow, and some small happiness is coming into being. At the moment of epiphany, the buffalo turns around. Thinking of the man who has rejected her love, she says "I love you" to the buffalo, and "I hate you." The buffalo approaches slowly and deliberately, until their eyes meet, deeply fastened, without hope or escape. Lispector ends her story with this existential challenge in the meeting of apprentice and master in the quest for being.

Urban poverty and immigration affect the characters of stories set during the modernization of São Paulo in the 1920s by Mário de Andrade and Antônio de Alcântara Machado. Mário's story "It Can Hurt Plenty" recounts the young life of Paulino, who was a leftover in the dirty hut where he lives with his mother, Teresinha, and grandmother. Teresinha's husband is in prison, and she is a frustrated washerwoman, getting no pleasure out of life. Little Paulino feels hunger and hurt when his mother hits him. He sleeps on the cold floor and lives by the sounds and smells coming from the street. He plays with ants and eats them, an illusion of eating, and he eats cockroaches too. When Teresinha takes a boyfriend, the food improves, but the fights begin with her mother-in-law, who one day picks up Paulino and takes him away. Paulino thinks he will be torn to pieces. The mother-in-law has some money, and in her house Paulino adjusts to the first care he has ever known. At the same time, he still feels miserable because he cannot sense any real tenderness in her actions toward him. When he is caught eating dirt in the back garden, the punishments begin, and he begins to cough. As he sits on the ground afraid to move, Teresinha appears on the sidewalk. She is overcome with tenderness and squeezes Paulino until it hurts. But having become a full-time prostitute, she pretends that her son is being treated well and, after a last kiss, adjusts her clothes as she continues on her way. Mário's Paulino is the child of Italian immigrants in São Paulo, who moved to the city by the thousands in the period 1880–1920 and survived by sheer tenacity in the labor mills of the textile industry, where the working week was seven days, fourteen hours per day.

Alcântara Machado's "Gaetaninho" is the story of another immigrant child who lives with his mother and aunt on Orient Street in the factory neighborhood of Brás. Cars and horse-drawn carriages only appear for funerals or weddings. Gaetaninho's ideal dream is to be in a funeral procession taking his Aunt Filomena to the cemetery, with him sitting up on the box with the coachman in his sailor suit and white cap. He won't be satisfied until he can also hold the whip. Gaetaninho's dream is considered to be a very bad omen by the family. The local boys play soccer on the sidewalk, and when Gaetaninho runs into the street after a ball, he is hit and killed by a passing streetcar. In the next afternoon's funeral procession, Gaetaninho is closed in a coffin, and it is his friend Beppino on the coachman's box, proudly wearing a bright red suit.

—◦≫ ≪◦—

Sexual repression and perversion are treated with grotesque hyperbole in Dalton Trevisan's "The Vampire of Curitiba." Always in a state of exaggerated reality, the male narrator imagines the women he desires to be dangerous animals, "poisonous" virgins: "A virgin's kiss is the bite of a hairy caterpillar." The women of Curitiba should be locked up, as they only exist to excite the narrator with their vulgar sexual suggestiveness. Ornaments on young housewives at shopping malls must have been borrowed from the animal kingdom, and the narrator fantasizes about ripping them off to find evidence of a parallel animal nature underneath. He inflates himself by descriptions of his danger to women: not only is he a vampire, but any number of mythological and horrific creatures, violent and diabolical. At times, the façade crumbles into fears of insufficiency, however, as the lineup of fearsome beasts is reduced by the narrator to "a mangy dog tormented by fleas and turning around to bite his own tail." The ultimate ecstatic state desired by the hyped narrator is, however, to experience victimization, the poisonous bites of the feared yet desired females. He knows their power over him, which he extrapolates into the reason for their existence. Sexuality is implicit in the narrator's death fantasies, as he oscillates between lunatic and homicidal tendencies, sublimating the guilt he feels for his natural urges, which Curitiba's repressed culture would condemn as impure. Obsessions with the grotesque and with death are the narrator's perverted means of expressing the simple desire, but moral impossibility, to be close to a woman. Trevisan is a master of the intricacies of the repressed bourgeois middle classes under glass, which have, in some sense, replaced the severe moral strictures of Machado's aristocracy.

In Paulo Emílio Salles Gomes's story "Her Times Two," it is the ingenuous older male narrator who is deceived about the erotic machinations of Her in a context reminiscent of Vladimir Nabokov's *Lolita* (1955). "Her," the only name given the wife young enough to be his granddaughter, takes a scientific approach to the problem of consummating the marriage, even to the point of making an extended visit to a gynecologist. Her gentle nature and extreme cares and concern with the narrator's health and advancing age dominate his very generous, yet completely naïve, description of Her. The narrator's *carnet* splits into two parts, just as Her reveals to him the details of Her previous sexual involvements: "Mentally summarizing the skeletal plot of Her story, I saw a virgin crawling out intact from beneath the superior, inferior, and middle members of a first man to be twice deflowered by a second in order to marry a third." His deluge of laughter at the absurdity, followed by an unnatural calm, leads to an abyss of dualities and inversions. The narrator is not immediately aware that he has delivered a blow to the head, breaking teeth and bloodying Her. Her reaction in the language of a common street urchin gives him a glimpse of the only female he could love, the Her who now will never return to him. In a comic use of limited narration, Salles Gomes constructs a parody of urban mores while domesticating topics of sexual taboo with his touch of the absurd.

The heritage of the concise oral tale, employed by major authors Jorge Amado and Rachel de Queiroz, forms the core of such contemporary stories as Moacyr Scliar's "The Cow." After a shipwreck off the African coast, one sailor survives thanks to a cow named Carola, who swims him to a desert island and licks his face until he regains consciousness. In the form of a parable, the sailor relates how he makes use of the cow in every way for nourishment and survival: the foamy milk, the warm sleeping companion, the manure for fertilizer, and so on. The hyperbole of the tall tale enters at the point that the sailor begins to cut pieces of tender meat from Carola to satisfy his hunger. He uses her skin for clothes and shoes, and finally there is nothing of Carola that the sailor has not devoured. When the sailor is saved by a passing ship, he burns what is left of Carola and watches the black smoke rise from the horizon. Afterward his life is lonely and unhappy, and at middle age he travels to Europe by boat. At the moment he spots an islet on the horizon, he hears a voice say "hello." It belongs to a beautiful blonde named Carola.

The oral tale is applied to a darker and more devastating effect in the short masterpiece by Guimarães Rosa, "Those Lopes," an exemplary tale about the sufferings and repression of women. Flausina, now an old woman, narrates the story of her captivity by marriage to a series of men named Lopes, all of whom she calls members of a bad breed, arrogant seducers who seize everything, cruel and abusive lords over everyone. Her own nature is of a different paradigm: innocent, virginal, romantic, delicate. When she was a young girl, the worst of them, Zé Lopes, came by on horseback and saw her pretty white face, and her mother and father were helpless to defend her. Then, over the years, Flausina learned to survive by her own invention, to behave as expected, to deceive those watching her, and to learn completely in secret how to read and write from the newspapers used to wrap groceries. The Lopes men make money, but live like a nest of vipers. When her husband dies, the tough cousin and brother claim her. Flausina craftily sets them against each other in jealous rage, and both die in the duel. She weeps brokenhearted, according to custom. But there is one left, the oldest Lopes, and in this case Flausina has no solution but to outlast him, stuffing him with spicy foods and endless hours of pleasure. At last she is avenged, but only after arriving at the "bottom of my heart," after learning that all things are both good and bad for us. Her sons are all equally Lopes men, and her sacrifice has been long. Freedom and quality, however, have come with age. She will move miles away, where there are no more Lopes men, to live with a younger man she loves, where she can be happy in her day-to-day existence, talking out loud, governing her own life, but let no Lopes ever dare to approach her again. Guimarães Rosa expertly turns the oral tale into a memoir of the full sweep of life, making us aware of the existence of evil and of the difficulty and value of earning freedom, with the patience and invention of Flausina as an example.

—◦❧ ❦◦—

Brazilian short stories excel in examples of linguistic and formal innovation. Osman Lins's "Baroque Tale or Tripartite Unity," set in the baroque cities of Minas Gerais, fragments the narrative exposition eight times by presenting different possible accounts of the main incident, all separated by the sudden interruption "or" to introduce an alternate scenario. The planes of reality constructed by this device have a deeper thematic purpose within the story. They are neutral, disinterested images that protect the narrator from the pernicious intent of the human characters, and they place in question any possible objective narration of events, in favor of the indeterminacy of human observation, dreams, and memory. The narrator has been paid to assassinate José Gervásio, whom he has never met, but who has refused to meet his son, born to the black woman whom he would not marry. She is now reduced to prostitution, and the boy has died. The narrator will pay her for pointing out the victim, as she decides whether to take revenge. With each scenario, more of the ornate, florid eroticism of sexuality and assassination, loyalty and treachery, forgiveness and revenge is described in the bodies, objects, flora, and fauna of the setting: "arabesques, festoons, borders, conches, and scrollwork." The unity of events promised in the story's title is achieved only through the indeterminacy of memory, as one struggles as in a dream to reconstitute the skeletal objectivity of events. Does the narrator assassinate the boss who, drunk with anger, sent him on his murderous mission, or does he mistakenly assassinate the black woman, or does he kill Gervásio's father, who comes to offer himself in his son's place? Lins's labyrinth of events destabilizes chronological narration: as the narrator/murderer says, the victim, whoever it is, is not the one he came looking for.

In Clarice Lispector's "The Fifth Story," the narrator also destabilizes the story to be told, first by giving other possible titles and, second, by recapitulating the substance of the story in five separate new beginnings, each one called a separate story within the story. Each recapitulation advances the story to a new stage of events. "The Fifth Story" is based on Lispector's interest in Kierkegaard and, according to Barbara Slavinsky's thesis ("Clarice Lispector's Fiction: A Dialogic Study toward an Aesthetic and Ethical Exegesis," Stanford, 1993), demonstrates the fear and trembling necessary to maintain faith in life, even in daily surroundings. The structure, theme, and narrative exposition of Lispector's story is taken directly from Kierkegaard's *Frygt og bÆven: Dialektisk lyrik* (1843; *Fear and Trembling: Dialectical Lyric*), repeating the permutations of the story whose first four episodes treat Abraham's faith in the imperative to sacrifice his son, Isaac. The killing of cockroaches by the urban housewife opens the drama of the murder of innocents as an unquestioned role of our middle-class, sanitized existence. She conceives of her anxiety in the same terms as Kierkegaard's archetypal analysis of faith and murder, with four stories each of which increasingly torments her for her role of assassin. The first four of her stories always begin the same way: a female urban apartment dweller complains about cockroaches. She is given a mixture of sugar, flour, and gypsum to feed them, so as to dry up their innards. She does so and states dryly, "They died." The ever-expanding story gives details about their suffering and death, until their hard bodies cover the kitchen floor each morning, turned into stone like Pompeii, their dry antennas fluttering. The narrator becomes aware of the high, detached perspective of a human being, of her inability to love or coexist with cockroaches. She faces the terrible choice between the drying gypsum, the perverse pleasure of nightly deadly poisoning, and her role as assassin and the soul and vice of life in all of its pungent reality. Her heart carries the modern weight of an engraved sign: "This house has been sprayed with DDT." The fifth story within the story is indeterminate, never written. The narrator's description of its contents implies a new hope, however, far from urban fear and trembling, in its absurd title, "Leibnitz and the Transcendency of Love in Polynesia." Transcendent love is something far away, however, and the fifth story begins, as did all of the others, with an urban female complaining about cockroaches. Is transcendent love meant to be an answer for her fear and trembling? Using her experimental technique, Lispector has created another kind of labyrinth of stories, as in a hall of mirrors or a recurring dream full of the statues of death. Will Polynesia be a contrast, a lesson, a dream, or a solution? The reader has perhaps not even noticed that Lispector has written an absent or missing story, since the "fifth story" is incomplete, whether one refers to the story or to the story within the story. We are given only its first line, which is the same as all of the other stories, and we must try to imagine what will follow, and why. Our anxiety over the nature and contents of the story is elicited to make us aware of the two antecedents of fear and trembling that we encounter.

Nélida Piñón's "Brief Flower" is a story about the lessons and discoveries that carry an inconsistent and disoriented young woman through the hard rituals of living that put one in contact with life's allegorical and mythological truths. At first, the young woman must discover the immediate world and its mysteries, including the urge to stick her tongue inside a periwinkle, to discover the physical changes in becoming a woman. As a girl, she remained nameless, even after Pedro came to be her master, draining her of her will and nature. She would look intensely at the stars, wishing to be noble and free, and one day she leaves the house with her young son. She at first discovers the earth, raising chickens and massaging cows, but her inborn inconsistency drives her on. Seeking protection as a nun, she learns to fulfill her human duty, sharing belief, faith, and prayers. Yet her son must discover the world, and again they depart on an uncertain peregrination. After the son works for years at a mill, age overtakes his mother. She asks him to perform the ritual of throwing her gold coins into the stream, when she feels the illness and gravity of life amid the restlessness of approaching death. Brief flowers decorate her grave. Piñón's opaque parable of innocence and experience is a lesson in the strength of the human journey.

The mythical and allegorical strength of life "as it is" forms the substance of Clarice Lispector's story of communion, "The Breaking of the Bread." The guests come almost unwillingly, as if there were better ways to spend a Saturday, almost grieving their loss of a day. Yet the table with its white tablecloth is overfilled with fruits, vegetables, and wine, all fresh and clean, free from any human desires. That table is eternal and mythical: it exists as a mountain exists, free from the human sphere, an existence in purer form. And the hungry crowd consumes it all in the peace of a harvest gathering, cordially and directly eating with a material honesty of the moment, without hope or nostalgia. All desires and cares are lost, because they are unnecessary. There is the form and shape of existence placed before them, already existing like the mountain, without words, love, or desire. The act of eating in Lispector's story, reduced to an existential simplicity, is the bread of love capable of uniting humanity. The communion feast in her story has no symbolism or religious purpose; its transcendence lies in its simple, pure existence—only bread and hunger, equally strange and difficult concepts for a humanity that lives by symbols and passions.

The Anthology

This Oxford anthology assembles for the first time for readers of English a selection of the most notable short stories by the best-known authors in Brazilian literature, written since J. M. Machado de Assis (1839–1908) perfected the genre as its great master, authoring at least sixty stories considered to be masterpieces of world literature. With few exceptions, the stories in the Oxford anthology have all appeared in English translation, although spread over a long time period and often published in obscure journals not readily accessible to the general reading public. As a consequence, readers have not had the means to identify these authors and titles as belonging to a coherent tradition representing a singular, vibrant literature of the Americas. Containing stories by thirty-seven authors covering four stylistic and historical periods, the anthology encourages a comprehensive reading across the Brazilian tradition. Our goal is to allow readers to discover and experience the principal characteristics, qualities, and themes of Brazilian writing over the past century and a quarter.

PART I

Tropical Belle Époque
⟶⟶(1880s–1921)⟵⟵

The Second Reign (1840–1889) under Brazil's emperor D. Pedro II formed the historical context for the formal and informal institutions constituting national culture in the period of the belle époque, or the turn of the century. The period has been thoroughly studied by Brazilian literary critics Brito Broca (*A Vida Literária no Brasil: 1900*, 2d ed., Rio de Janeiro, José Olympio, 1960) and Roberto Ventura (*Estilo Tropical: História Cultural e Polêmicas Literárias no Brasil, 1870–1914*, São Paulo, Companhia das Letras, 1991), as well as by historians Jeffry Needell (*A Tropical Belle Epoque*, Cambridge, Cambridge UP, 1987) and Emília V. da Costa (*The Brazilian Empire: Myths & Histories*, Chapel Hill, U of North Carolina P, 2000). In this historical period, the very make-up of the capital city of Rio de Janeiro was understood to emphasize both an ideology and a set of cultural values in a stratified and polarized society. The extremes of social division were illustrated on one side by the urban redesign and reforms of 1903–1906, which created broad avenues and public spaces based on Parisian models, while on the other by crowded housing and public health emergencies, such as yellow fever epidemics. Brazil was still at this time a society of cities on a coastal strip, dominated by wealthy, powerful planters and merchants overseeing an underworld of slaves, freedmen and women, and their descendants. A thin urban class of liberal professionals, clerks, shopkeepers, and bureaucrats was forming, slavery was coming to an end, and urban commercial interests were becoming increasingly dissatisfied with the country's political organization. The institutions supporting the civilized life of the Rio elite included schools such as the Colégio D. Pedro II and the Collège de Sion, social clubs, the Casino Fluminense, the Jockey Club, the Opera Theater, and the salons, all contributing to a conscious re-Europeanization of the capital. This world, led by its wealth and the fantasy of being a copy of Europe, was conducted according to a rigid social code and inflexible unwritten rules. Marriage among elite families was fostered to concentrate wealth and power, reinforced by salons and social events frequented by bohemians and *littérateurs*. Elite women's lives were narrow, as they married young and were expected to fulfill certain social obligations that displayed grace and wealth, such as the abilities to read French, dance, play piano, and sing opera overtures, all in very restricted settings. Children were raised by black wet nurses, and child mortality was high. The lives of poor and middle-class women presented different patterns, noted by historian da Costa, with more freedom in the movements of vendors and the existence of a few exceptional outspoken women, such as Nísia Floresta, who defended progressive ideas as a teacher and abolitionist.

Elegant residential neighborhoods led the expansion of the city, and the consumption of imported European commodities epitomized the fetishistic imitation of a tropical European society. The web of patronage, according to da Costa, coexisted with capitalism and often superseded it, allowing for the absorption or incorporation of intellectuals and professionals through their ties to the elite, whereas these groups might otherwise have become agents of change. Patronage contributed to stability, at the cost of a bureaucracy of sinecures subject to the caprice of politics (da Costa, xxiii–xxiv).

The massive underworld is described in Aluísio de Azevedo's novel *O Cortiço* (1890; *The Slum*, trans. David H. Rosenthal, Oxford, Oxford UP, 2000), a tale of passion and greed in a tenement for the poorer classes behind João Romão's tavern, a beehive of love and death. Romão lives with his lover, Bertoleza, an escaped slave whom he appropriated from her absent owner to take on the endless drudgery of maid and cook, rising for work at four in the morning. Through the worlds of the characters who enter and leave the tenement, readers are presented with a panorama of a complex social world which, in spite of its poverty, is characterized by a wide range of behaviors and relationships, from noble to vile. In an influential essay first published in 1970, "Dialectics of Malandroism" (in *On Literature and Society*, trans. Howard S. Becker, Princeton, NJ, Princeton UP, 1995, 79–103), or "dialectics of the rogue," leading critic and scholar Antonio Candido called attention to the first novel of manners set in Rio de Janeiro, *Memoirs of a Militia Sergeant* (Rio de Janeiro, Tipografia Brasiliense, 2 vols., 1854–1855) by Manuel Antônio de Almeida, which mirrored the social hierarchy of the empire. Popular motifs were prominent in the music of the time, from the sentimental colonial *modinhas* sung with guitar to the salon tangos of such composers as Ernesto Nazaré (1863–1934) or the American Louis Moreau Gottschalk (1829–1869). In the same way, popular romantic sentiment entered the Carioca novel, as in Joaquim Manuel de Macedo's (1820–1882) *A Moreninha* (Rio de Janeiro, Livraria Garnier, 1844). In the Brazilian society of the capital, Candido perceives a system of human relationships capriciously balanced between order and disorder. Leonardo, the adventurous hero of the *Memoirs*, cuts across a flexible, movable social fabric and is motivated by an instinct of survival often evident in a picaresque hero, "a kind of irreverent common sense, which is pre-critical, but which . . . becomes in the end more demystifying" (100). Leonardo possesses a certain type of objectivity, marked by cynical reflections but without moral judgments; he optimistically and cheerfully accepts the given state of society. Disorder is the unruly expression of a vigorous young society, while order stands for its attempt to refine itself as an older colonial construct. The narrator/hero mediates between the dialectical categories, which give him a porous position in the social world, permitted by the hybrid composition of the social hierarchy. There is a rhythm in Leonardo's passage between institutions or types and the resulting irreverent social satire that, in its way, brings the two worlds together. Leonardo the rogue comes to represent the spontaneous enjoyment of all social life. In spite of the social mobility implied by the movement between classes, as historian da Costa states, racial democracy remained a myth, since the black population, like Bertoleza, was at the bottom of the social ladder without any personal means of economic improvement (234).

Multiple literary currents coexisted, but none was more typical of the age than the decadence and exoticism of aesthetes and bohemians such as Paulo Barreto, known as João do Rio, or Afrânio Peixoto, known for his exaggerated precious style. Parnassians Olavo Bilac and Coelho Neto were among the most popular writers of the age. In opposition were the naturalists and social critics, from Sílvio Romero to Euclídes da Cunha, whose great prose work *Os Sertões* (1902; *Rebellion in the Backlands*, trans. Samuel Putnam, Chicago, U of Chicago P, 1944) is a synthesis of the struggle to form modern Brazil, to Lima Barreto, satirist of the lower social world of Rio de Janeiro. Regionalists Monteiro Lobato of São Paulo and Simões Lopes Neto of Rio Grande do Sul employ dialects to create local types, such as Lobato's *caipira* Jeca Tatu, a common man of interior São Paulo. There were symbolist poets, led by the "black swan" João da Cruz e Souza (1861–1898), and Raul Pompéia's impressionistic novel of education, *O Ateneu* (Rio de Janeiro, 1888). Even old-school intellectuals, such as statesmen Rui Barbosa (1849–1923) and Joaquim Nabuco (1849–1910), the first ambassador to the United States, were promoting modern institutions in speeches, memoirs, and essays. "National regeneration" was the subtitle of a book on the Brazil of the future by Godofredo Barnsley, published as *São Paulo no Anno 2000* (*São Paulo in the Year 2000*, São Paulo, Typographia Brazi de Rothschild, 1909).

This fecund period of neocolonial transition to modernity was overshadowed in literature by the presence of Machado de Assis, whose extraordinary personal genius made him atypical, carrying him beyond the normal qualities and limitations of the age. He succeeded by literally defying his age, being a mulatto, the grandson of slaves, and self-educated, and he became the most learned figure of his generation and founder of the Brazilian Academy of Letters. After a long apprenticeship writing in all genres, Machado created a personal prose style, consistent from his first to last novels, characterized by a personal interactive relationship with technique and substance. His keen observation of the social world was matched by his literary *bricolage*, full of references to classical literatures and history employed to throw the reader off guard with unexpected descriptions and juxtapositions, full of ironic content. He invented literary modernity, sui generis. As if speaking for the belle époque, Machado's famous character Dom Casmurro confesses, "I knew the rules of writing, without suspecting those of loving. I had orgies with Latin and was a virgin with women" (*Dom Casmurro*, Cap. XIV "The Inscription," 1997, p. 28). Machado surprises in his writing, yet teaches the world. His short stories give us the capital of Rio de Janeiro in all of its human variety, a city that Machado left rarely and only for the mountain summer capital of Petrópolis.

Joaquim Maria Machado de Assis
—◦❧(1839–1908)❦◦—

Acclaimed as Brazil's greatest writer and founder of the Brazilian Academy of Letters, Machado de Assis (known simply as Machado in Brazil) is an incomparable figure and an exception for his time, whether for being the grandson of slaves, for being entirely self-educated, for never having traveled beyond the vicinity of Rio de Janeiro, or for his invention of an original moral, ethical, and philosophical world in his fiction. Machado's importance is that he changed the course of Brazilian and, by extension, other colonial literatures by making his characters, narrators, and readers self-consciously aware of their inauthenticity. His stylistic inventiveness and precocious modernity were effective in superimposing the idea that, in Brazil, old stories were being recycled in deceptively new forms. His persistent tone of irony, pessimism, and skepticism came in free doses, so as to allow his characters to meet their inexorable fates without any alteration in the eternal, measured pulse of his unorthodox and obtrusive narrative frames.

Machado published some 200 stories in the literary and social magazines of his day, many of which were reprinted in his seven books of short stories published from 1870 to 1906. The first two, *Contos Fluminenses* (1870) and *Histórias da Meia Noite* (1873), are usually grouped as early works along with his first four romantic novels, published every two years from 1872 to 1878 (*Resurreição, A Mão e a Luva, Helena,* and *Iaiá Garcia*). Beginning with *Papéis Avulsos* (1882) and followed by *Histórias Sem Data* (1884), *Várias Histórias* (1896), *Páginas Recolhidas* (1899), and *Relíquias de Casa Velha* (1906), Machado exhibits a polished, concise, and masterful style in sixty-three stories. A parallel style can be seen in his five major novels, which scholar Jorge de Sena called a "quintet" that includes two recognized masterpieces in world literature, the *Posthumous Memoirs of Brás Cubas* (1880) and *Dom Casmurro* (1899). Those novels are likewise composed in a series of short chapters resembling stories or parts of stories. Whether in the short stories or the novels, Machado is known for a subtlety and perfection of form, psychological suggestion, implication involving suspense and irony, narrative play and humor, and reflective analysis of behavior, social habits, motivations, desires, and illusions. The depth of futility of human endeavors falls within the perspective of a universal human comedy staged by forces that are beyond control or influence.

Fewer than two dozen of Machado's stories have ever been translated into English (*Brazilian Tales*, 1921; *The Psychiatrist and Other Stories*, 1963; *The Devil's Church and Other Stories*, 1977), whereas the critic Antonio Candido considers that at least sixty are masterpieces of world literature. Indeed, Machado is without equal in the whole of Latin American literature.

WEDDING SONG

—◦❧ ❦◦—

Just imagine that it is 1813. You are in the Carmo Church, listening in on one of those good old-fashioned celebrations that was one of the principal national pastimes and symbols of musical artistry. You know what a High Mass is, so you can imagine what a High Mass would have been like back then. I am not calling your attention to the priests and the sextons, nor to the sermon, nor to the young *carioca* women's eyes, which were already beautiful at that time, nor to the mantillas of the somber women, nor to the knee breeches, the wigs, the valances, the candles, or the incense. None of them. I am not even speaking of the orchestra, which happens to be superb. I am limiting myself to pointing out a grayish head to you. It is the head of that old man conducting the orchestra with such spirit and devotion.

His name is Romão Pires. He is probably sixty years old, no younger, and he was born in Valongo, or thereabouts. He is a good musician and a good man. All of the musicians like him. Maestro Romão is his known name, and to say known and public were the same thing in such matters at the time. "Leading the mass is Maestro Romão" was equivalent to another kind of announcement years later: "Appearing on stage is Actor João Caetano" or "Musical Artist Martinho is to sing one of his best arias!" There was a certain flavor to it, a delicate and popular attraction. Maestro Romão leads the celebration!

Who did not know Maestro Romão, with his cautious air, lowered eyes, sad smile, and slow-moving pace? All of that disappeared when he was in front of the orchestra; then a spark of life spread throughout the Maestro's entire body and all of his gestures. His gaze was brighter and his smile lit up. He was another person. Not that the mass was his. The one that he was leading in the Carmo, in particular, belonged to José Maurício. Nevertheless, he led it with the same love that he would have exhibited had it been his own.

The celebration ended. It was as though an intense light had gone out and left his face barely illuminated by ordinary light. There he was, coming down from the choir loft, supported by his cane. He went to the sacristy to kiss the hands of the priests and he took a place at the dinner table. He did it all indifferently and quietly.

He ate dinner, left, and walked along the Rua da Mãe dos Homens, where he resided with an old black man, *pai* José, who was like his own mother, and who, at that moment, was conversing with a neighbor.

"Here comes Maestro Romão, *pai* José," said the neighbor.

"Oh! Good-bye, *sinhá*!"

Pai José jumped up, went into the house, and waited for the Maestro, who, in a little while, entered in his usual manner. The house was neither luxurious nor cheerful. There was not even the slightest trace of a woman, old or young, no little birds that sang, no flowers, or lively or joyful colors. It was a gloomy, barren house. The most cheerful object was the harpsichord, which Maestro Romão would sometimes play while contemplating. On a nearby chair, there were some sheets of music. None was his.

Ah! If only Maestro Romão could, he would be a great composer. It seems as though there are two types of callings: those that have a voice and those that do not. The former are successful. The latter experience a constant and sterile struggle between inner impulses and the absence of a means of communication with others; Romão represented the latter. He possessed an innate calling for music. He carried within himself many operas and masses, a world of new and original harmonies that he did not manage to express or put down on paper. That was the real cause of Maestro Romão's sadness. Naturally, people did not fully understand that sadness. Some used to attribute it to one thing, while others attributed it to another: illness, a lack of money, or some old grief. However, the truth is this: the reason for Maestro Romão's unhappiness was his inability to compose, to express what he felt. It was not as though he had not scribbled a lot down on paper or probed his harpsichord for hours on end. But everything came out of him shapelessly, without either inspiration or harmony. He recently had come to feel ashamed of his lack of originality, and now he no longer tried.

And in the meantime, if he could, he would at least try to finish a certain work: a wedding song he had begun three days after his marriage in 1779. His wife, who was then twenty-one years of age, and who died at twenty-three, was not very pretty, not even somewhat. However, she was extremely kind and loved him as much as he loved her.

Three days after their marriage, Maestro Romão felt something like an inspiration come from within. He then envisioned the wedding song and wanted to compose it. However, the inspiration could not be expressed. Like a bird that had just been captured and tried to escape through the bars of the cage. Down, up, anxious, and frightened. It was in this way that the inspiration was thrashing about within our musician, locked inside of him, not able to come out, finding no door, nothing. Some notes flowed and he wrote them down, filling only one sheet of paper, nothing more. He persisted on the following day, ten days afterwards, and on twenty occasions during the time he was married. When his wife died, he reread those first conjugal notes and was again left sadder for not having been able to put down on paper that feeling of lifeless happiness.

"*Pai* José," he said as he came in, "I feel out of sorts today."

"*Sinhô* ate something that did not agree with you . . ."

"No, I have not been well since this morning. Go to the drug store . . ."

The druggist sent over something that Maestro Romão took that night. On the next day, Maestro Romão still did not feel any better. It is important to say that he suffered from heart disease—a serious and chronic illness. *Pai* José became frightened when he realized that neither medication nor rest alleviated the pain. He wanted to call the doctor.

"What for?" said the Maestro, "it will go away."

He did not get any worse that day, and he held up well throughout the night. Not so for the black man, who barely slept two hours. The neighborhood, which had just found out what was going on, spoke of nothing else. Those who had maintained a relationship with the Maestro went to visit him. They told him that there was nothing to worry about, that he was bothered by minor illnesses of the times. One added comically that it was a clever ploy on his part to avoid the beating that the druggist was giving him in backgammon. Another said it was love. Maestro Romão smiled, although he was telling himself that he was nearing the end.

"It is over," he thought.

One morning, five days after the celebration, the doctor found him really ill, and that was exactly what Maestro Romão read into the doctor's expression, behind the misleading words.

"It is nothing! It is better not to think of music."

Music! The doctor's very words gave the Maestro an idea. As soon as he was alone, with the slave, he opened the drawer where he had kept, since 1779, the wedding song that he had begun. He reread those difficultly formed and unfinished notes. Then he had an extraordinary idea. He would finish the work now, regardless of how it turned out. Whatever he could compose would be fine. At least he would leave a little of his soul on Earth.

"Who knows? If, in 1880, the work is performed, someone may say that a certain Maestro Romão . . ."

The beginning of the song ended with a certain *la*; this *la*, which fell nicely into place, was the last written note. Maestro Romão ordered his harpsichord brought to the back room, the one that looked out onto the garden. He needed fresh air. While standing by the window, he was able to see through the window at the back of another house. He saw newlyweds, who had been married for only eight days, leaning forward with their arms on each other's shoulders, hands clasped. Maestro Romão smiled sadly. "They are just starting out, whereas I am on my way out," he said. "I am going to compose this song, which perhaps they can play . . ."

He sat down at the harpsichord. He reproduced the notes and came to the *la*. . . .

La, la, la. . . .

Nothing. He did not get any farther. Nonetheless, he knew music as well as he did people.

La, do . . . la, mi . . . la, si, do, re . . . re . . . re . . .

Impossible! There was no inspiration. It was not that he wanted a profoundly original piece; but something, at least, that was not like any one else's, in order to complete what was already begun. He returned to the beginning again; he repeated the notes, hoping to recover a shred of the obscured sensation. He thought about his wife and the early years. In order to complete the illusion, he stared out of the window in the direction of the newlyweds. They were still there arm in arm, hands clasped. The only difference was that now they were looking into each other's eyes instead of looking down. Short of breath from his illness and impatience, Maestro Romão returned to the harpsichord; the sight of the newlyweds failed to provide him with the necessary inspiration. The succeeding notes did not come.

La . . . la . . . la . . .

In despair, he got up from the harpsichord. He grabbed the paper on which he had written; he proceeded to tear it up. At that very moment the young girl, enraptured by her husband's stare, spontaneously began to hum something never sung nor heard before. It had an unmistakable *la*, followed by a beautiful musical phrase. It was exactly the one that Maestro Romão had been pursuing, although not discovering, for so many years. The Maestro listened to it sadly, he shook his head, and that night he died.

The Siamese Academies

—◦❧ ❦◦—

Have you ever heard of the Siamese Academies? I know very well there were never any academies in Siam, but let's suppose there were, and that there were four of them. Listen to me:

I

Whenever the stars saw a host of milk-colored fireflies ascending through the night, they used to say they were the sighs of the king of Siam, who was amusing himself with his three hundred concubines. And winking at one another, they would ask: "Regal sighs, how is handsome Kalaphangko entertaining himself tonight?"

To which the fireflies would respond gravely: "We are the sublime thoughts of the four Siamese Academies; we bring with us all the wisdom of the universe."

One night there ascended such a quantity of fireflies that the stars, fearful, sought shelter in their alcoves and took charge of one part of space, where they settled forever and called themselves the Milky Way.

This enormous ascension of thoughts was caused by the four Siamese Academies' wish to solve this singular problem: why are there effeminate men and mannish women? And what had led them to consider this question was the temperament of their young king, for Kalaphangko was virtually a woman. Everything in him breathed the strangest femininity: he had gentle eyes, a silvery voice, a weak and obedient disposition, and a cordial horror of weapons. The Siamese warriors sighed, but the nation lived contentedly. All was dances, plays, and songs, in the manner of a king who cared for nothing else; hence the stars' assumption.

One day, however, one of the Academies suddenly found this solution to the problem: "Some souls are masculine, others feminine. The anomaly we observe is the result of his having the wrong body."

"No," thundered the other three, "the soul is neuter; it has nothing to do with external differences."

Nothing else was necessary in order for the alleys and waters of Bangkok to be stained with academic blood. First came controversy, then insults, and finally punches. The situation wasn't so serious at first; none of the rivals hurled an impropriety which wasn't scrupulously derived from Sanskrit, the academic language, the Latin of Siam. But later they lost all their sense of shame. The rivalry became disorderly, put its hands on its waist, stooped down to the mud, and resorted to stonings, blows with the fist, and vile gestures. Finally, the sexual Academy, in exasperation, resolved to put an end to the other three and devised a sinister plan. . . . Oh winds that pass by, if you would only carry away these sheets of paper so that I couldn't tell this tragic tale of Siam! How it grieves me (woe is me!) to write of such a singular case of revenge! The academics armed themselves in secret and went to confront their foes precisely when they were hunched over the famous problem, causing a cloud of fireflies to ascend to the heavens. Not even a preamble, not even pity. Foaming with rage, the aggressors descended upon their rivals, some of whom managed to flee hours later; others, pursued and attacked, died on the riverbank, on board launches, or in hidden alleyways. In all, thirty-eight cadavers. The victors cut an ear off their opponents' leaders and fashioned a necklace and bracelet out of them for their president, the sublime U-Tong. Drunken with victory, they celebrated with a huge revel in which they sang their magnificent hymn: "Glory to us, who are the rice of knowledge and lantern of the universe."

The city awoke in a state of shock, and terror took hold of the multitude. No one could absolve such a cruel and despicable act, and some couldn't believe what they saw. . . . Only one person approved of everything: fair Kinnara, flower of the royal concubines.

II

Lying meekly at fair Kinnara's feet, the young king asked her for a song.

"The only song I'll sing is this one: I believe in the sexual soul."

"You believe in the absurd, Kinnara."

"Then Your Majesty believes in the neuter soul?"

"Another absurdity, Kinnara. I don't believe in the neuter soul or the sexual one."

"Then what does Your Majesty believe in, if not in one or the other?"

"I believe in your eyes, Kinnara, which are the sun and light of the universe."

"But Your Majesty must choose: either believe in the neuter soul and punish the Academy that lives, or believe in the sexual soul and absolve it."

"How delicious your lips are, my sweet Kinnara! They are what I believe in: they are the fountain of wisdom."

Perturbed, Kinnara stood up. Just as the king was a feminine man, she was a masculine woman, a buffalo with swan's feathers. It was the buffalo which now paced around the room, but soon it was the swan which came to a halt and, curving its neck, asked for and obtained from the king, between two caresses, a decree in which the doctrine of the sexual soul was declared legitimate and orthodox and the other one absurd and perverse. That same day the decree was sent to the victorious Academy, the pagodas, the mandarins, the entire kingdom. The Academy hung out lanterns; public order was reestablished.

III

Meanwhile, fair Kinnara had an ingenious and secret plan. One night, as the king was examining some official papers, she asked him if taxes were paid punctually.

"*Ohimè!*" he exclaimed, repeating that word he had learned from an Italian missionary. "Few taxes have been paid. I don't wish to behead the delinquent tax-payers . . . No, never . . . Blood? Blood? No, I don't want any blood to flow . . ."

"And what if I give you a remedy for everything?"

"What?"

"Your Majesty decreed that souls were feminine and masculine," said Kinnara after a kiss. "Suppose each of use is living in the wrong body. It suffices to restore each soul to its rightful abode. Let's exchange our . . ."

Kalaphangko laughed heartily at the idea and asked her how they would go about making such an exchange. She replied that they could use the method of Mukunda, king of the Hindus, who placed his soul in a Brahmin's cadaver while a jester placed himself in Mukunda's body—an ancient legend passed on to the Turks, Persians, and Christians. Yes, but the formula for the invocation? Kinnara declared she possessed it; an old bonzo had found a copy of it in the ruins of a temple.

"What does Your Majesty think?"

"I don't believe in my own decree," he replied laughing, "but all right, if it's true, let's try it . . . but for six months, no more. After that we'll return to our former bodies."

They agreed the exchange would take place that same night. When all the city was asleep they called for the royal pirogue, got inside, and drifted aimlessly. None of the rowers saw them. When dawn began to appear, goading its resplendent cows, Kinnara uttered the mysterious invocation. Her soul detached itself and hovered, waiting for the king's body to be vacated. Hers had fallen on the carpet.

"Ready?" said Kalaphangko.

"Ready, here I am in the air, waiting. Please forgive the indignity of my person . . ."

But the king's soul didn't hear the rest. Cheerful and sparkling, it left its physical vessel and entered Kinnara's body, while hers took over the royal remains. Both bodies stood up and stared at each other, and one can imagine their astonishment. They were like Buoso and the snake, according to Dante's version of the tale; and here you will see how audacious I am. Dante tells Ovid and Lucan to be silent, believing his metamorphosis is more worthy than theirs. I'm telling all three to be silent. Buoso and the snake are no longer to be found, whereas my two heroes, once changed, continue to speak and live together—a situation which is clearly more Dantesque than any of the others, all modesty aside.

"Really," said Kalaphangko, "it's strange to be looking at myself and calling myself Majesty. Does Your Majesty feel the same?"

Both felt comfortable, like people who finally find the right house in which to live. Kalaphangko stretched out completely in Kinnara's feminine curves, and she stood up straight in Kalaphangko's firm torso. Siam finally had a king.

IV

Kalaphangko's first act (from now on we understand that Kalaphangko is the king's body with Kinnara's soul, and Kinnara the beautiful Siamese woman with Kalaphangko's soul) was nothing less than to bestow the highest honors on the sexual Academy. He didn't promote its members to the Mandarinate, since they were men of thought rather than action and administration, inclined toward philosophy and literature, but he decreed that all citizens prostrate themselves before them, as before the Mandarins. He also gave them great gifts, rarities or items of great worth: stuffed crocodiles, ivory chains, an emerald lunch service, diamonds, relics. The Academy, grateful for so many favors, also requested and was granted the official right to use the title of Light of the World.

This done, Kalaphangko attended to the public treasury, justice, religion, and ceremony. The nation began to feel the heavy burden of all this, for no fewer than eleven delinquent taxpayers were soon decapitated. The others, naturally preferring their heads to money, hastened to pay their taxes, and all was regularized. Many improvements were made in justice and legislation. New pagodas were constructed, and religious spirit even seemed to be revived as Kalaphangko, imitating the ancient Spanish arts, ordered the burning of a dozen poor Christian missionaries, an action which the bonzos of the land called the Pearl of the Kingdom.

A war was in order. With a more or less diplomatic pretext, Kalaphangko attacked another kingdom and carried out the briefest and most glorious campaign of the century. On his return to Bangkok he was greeted by huge and splendid celebrations in which three hundred ships, lined with scarlet and blue silk, went to receive him. Each one had a golden swan or dragon on its prow and was named by Bangkok's finest citizens; songs and acclamations thundered through the air.

That night, after the festivities had ended, his fair concubine whispered in his ear, "My young warrior, pay me for the longing I suffered in your absence: tell me the best of all celebrations is your gentle Kinnara." Kalaphangko responded with a kiss. "Your lips are as cold as death or disdain," she lamented.

It was true, the king was distracted and preoccupied, for he was brooding on a tragedy. The end of their time to live in each other's bodies was approaching, and he was considering breaking their agreement by murdering the beautiful Siamese woman. He hesitated, not knowing whether he would suffer at her death because her body was actually his, or whether he would have to succumb as well. These were Kalaphangko's doubts, and the thought of death cast a shadow over his face as he clutched to his breast a small flask filled with poison, in imitation of the Borgias.

Suddenly he thought of the learned Academy; he could consult it, not directly, but in a hypothetical manner. He summoned all the academics, who all came except for the president, the illustrious U-Tong, who was ill. There were thirteen of them, and they all prostrated themselves and said in the Siamese manner, "We, despicable pieces of straw, hasten to answer Kalaphangko's call."

"Rise," said the king benevolently.

"The place for dust is the ground," they insisted with their elbows and knees on the earth.

"Then I will be the wind which lifts the dust," replied Kalaphangko, and with a gesture full of grace and tolerance he held out his hands to them.

He immediately began to speak of diverse things so that the principal matter would emerge by itself; he spoke of the latest news from the West and the laws of Manu. Referring to U-Tong, he asked the academics if he really was a great man of wisdom, as he seemed to be; but seeing that they ruminated on their answer, he ordered that they tell him the whole truth. With exemplary unanimity they confessed that U-Tong was one of the greatest idiots in the kingdom, a vulgar spirit, worthless, who knew nothing and was capable of learning nothing. Kalaphangko was astonished. An idiot?

"It's difficult for us to say this, but he's that and nothing more: a vulgar and feeble spirit. But his heart is excellent, his character pure, noble . . ."

When Kalaphangko came to his senses after the shock, he sent the academics away without asking them what he had intended. An idiot? It was necessary to relieve U-Tong of his post without offending him. Three days later, U-Tong answered the king's call. Kalaphangko affectionately inquired after his health, then said he wished to send someone to Japan to study some documents, a matter which could be confided only to an enlightened person. Which one of his colleagues from the Academy seemed to him fit for such a task? One understands that the king's clever plan was to hear two or three names and conclude that above all of them he preferred the name of the president himself; but this is what U-Tong replied:

"Royal Highness, forgive the familiarity of my words: they are thirteen dunces, with the difference that dunces are modest and they are not; they compare themselves to the sun and the moon. But in truth, there were never thirteen more contemptible scoundrels under the sun than those thirteen . . . I understand Your Majesty's astonishment, but I would not be worthy of myself if I did not say this with loyalty, though confidentially . . ."

Kalaphangko was speechless. Thirteen dunces? Thirteen, thirteen. U-Tong spared only their hearts, which he declared to be excellent; no one was superior to them in character. Kalaphangko, with a refined gesture of complacency, bid farewell to the sublime U-Tong and grew pensive. Whatever his reflections may have been, no one ever came to know. It is known that he sent for the other academics, but this time one by one, so they would not see each other and would thus speak with greater frankness. The first one to arrive, who, by the way, was unaware of U-Tong's opinion, confirmed it entirely with the only correction that there were twelve dunces, or thirteen, counting U-Tong. The second did not differ in opinion, nor the third, nor any of the others. They differed only in style, some using the word "dunces," others employing circumlocutions or metaphors which had the same meaning, and yet there was no affront to anyone's moral character. Kalaphangko was dumbfounded.

But that was not the only shock to the king. Unable to consult the Academy, he attempted to deliberate by himself for two days, until fair Kinnara confided to him that she was going to be a mother. This news caused him to back away from the idea of the crime. How could he destroy the chosen vessel of the flower which was to emerge the following spring? He swore to the heavens and the earth that the child would live. At last the end of the six months arrived; the time to reexchange their bodies was at hand.

As they had done the first time, they entered the royal vessel at night and let themselves drift downriver, both reluctantly, feeling nostalgic about the bodies they were about to relinquish. When the glittering cows of daybreak began to tread languidly on the heavens, they pronounced the mysterious formula, and each soul returned to its former body. Kinnara, returning to hers, sensed her maternal instinct, just as she had felt paternal while she occupied Kalaphangko's body. It seemed to her that she was at once mother and father of the child.

"Mother and father?" repeated the king, restored to his previous form.

They were interrupted by strains of delightful music coming from afar. It was a junk or pirogue which was floating upriver, for the music was approaching rapidly. The sun had already inundated the waters and verdant shores with light, giving the scene a tone of life and rebirth which somehow made the two lovers forget the psychic restitution they had just undergone. And the music was nearing, becoming clearer, until at the river bend there appeared before their eyes a magnificent ship, adorned with feathers and streamers. Inside were the fourteen members of the Academy (including U-Tong), who in unison cast into the wind the ancient hymn: "Glory to us, who are the rice of knowledge and light of the world!"

The eyes of fair Kinnara (formerly Kalaphangko) were bulging out in astonishment. She could not understand how fourteen worthy men assembled together in the Academy were the light of the world, and separately a multitude of dunces. Nor could Kalaphangko, consulted by her, find an explanation. If someone discovers one, he or she can oblige one of the most charming ladies of the Orient by sending it to her in a sealed envelope, and for utmost security, addressed to our Consul in Shanghai, China.

THE FORTUNE-TELLER
—◦❯ ❮◦—

Hamlet observes to Horatio that there are more things in heaven and earth than are dreamt of in our philosophy. This was the selfsame explanation that was given by beautiful Rita to her lover, Camillo, on a certain Friday of November, 1869, when Camillo laughed at her for having gone, the previous evening, to consult a fortune-teller. The only difference is that she made her explanation in other words.

"Laugh, laugh. That's just like you men; you don't believe in anything. Well, let me tell you, I went there and she guessed the reason for my coming before I ever spoke a word. Scarcely had she begun to lay out the cards when she said to me: 'The lady likes a certain person . . . ' I confessed that it was so, and then she continued to re-arrange the cards in various combinations, finally telling me that I was afraid you would forget me, but that there were no grounds for my fear."

"She was wrong!" interrupted Camillo with a laugh.

"Don't say that, Camillo. If you only realized in what anguish I went there, all on account of you. You know. I've told you before. Don't laugh at me; don't poke fun at me . . ."

Camillo seized her hands and gazed into her eyes earnestly and long. He swore that he loved her ever so much, that her fears were childish; in any case, should she ever harbor a fear, the best fortune-teller to consult was he himself. Then he reproved her, saying that it was imprudent to visit such houses. Villela might learn of it, and then . . .

"Impossible! I was exceedingly careful when I entered the place."

"Where is the house?"

"Near here. On Guarda-Velha street. Nobody was passing by at the time. Rest easy. I'm not a fool."

Camillo laughed again.

"Do you really believe in such things?" he asked.

It was at this point that she translated Hamlet into every-day speech, assuring her lover that there was many a true, mysterious thing in this world. If he was skeptical, let him have patience. One thing, however, was certain: the card reader had guessed everything. What more could he desire? The best proof was that at this moment she was at ease and content.

He was about to speak, but he restrained himself. He did not wish to destroy her illusions. He, too, when a child, and even later, had been superstitious, filled with an arsenal of beliefs which his mother had instilled, and which had disappeared by the time he reached twenty. The day on which he rid himself of all this parasitic vegetation, leaving behind only the trunk of religion, he wrapped his superstition and his religion (which had both been inculcated by his mother) in the same doubt, and soon arrived at a single, total negation. Camillo believed in nothing. Why? He could not have answered; he had not a solitary reason; he was content simply to deny everything. But I express myself ill, for to deny is in a sense to affirm, and he did not formulate his unbelief. Before the great mystery he simply shrugged his shoulders and went on.

The lovers parted in good spirits, he more happy than she. Rita was sure that she was loved; but Camillo was not only sure that she loved him, but saw how she trembled for him and even took risks, running to fortune-tellers. However much he had reproved her for this, he could not help feeling flattered by it. Their secret meeting-place was in the old Barbonos street at the home of a woman who came from Rita's province. Rita went off through Mangueiras street, in the direction of Botafogo, where she resided; Camillo entered Guarda-Velha street, keeping his eye open, as he passed, for the home of the card reader.

Villela, Camillo and Rita: three names, one adventure and no explanation of how it all began. Let us proceed to explain. The first two were friends since earliest childhood. Villela had entered the magistracy. Camillo found employment with the government, against the will of his father, who desired him to embrace the medical profession. But his father had died, and Camillo preferred to be nothing at all, until his mother had procured him a departmental position. At the beginning of the year 1869 Villela returned from the interior, where he had married a silly beauty; he abandoned the magistracy and came hither to open a lawyer's office. Camillo had secured a house for him near Botafogo and had welcomed him home.

"Is this the gentleman?" exclaimed Rita, offering Camillo her hand. "You can't imagine how highly my husband thinks of you. He was always talking about you."

Camillo and Villela looked at each other tenderly. They were true friends. Afterwards, Camillo confessed to himself that Villela's wife did not at all belie the enthusiastic letters her husband had written to him. Really, she was most prepossessing, lively in her movements, her eyes burning, her mouth plastic and piquantly inquiring. Rita was a trifle older than both the men: she was thirty, Villela twenty-nine and Camillo twenty-six. The grave bearing of Villela gave him the appearance of being much older than his wife, while Camillo was but a child in moral and practical life. . . . He possessed neither experience nor intuition.

The three became closely bound. Propinquity bred intimacy. Shortly afterwards Camillo's mother died, and in this catastrophe, for such it was, the other two showed themselves to be genuine friends of his. Villela took charge of the interment, of the church services and the settlement of the affairs of the deceased; Rita dispensed consolation, and none could do it better.

Just how this intimacy between Camillo and Rita grew to love he never knew. The truth is that he enjoyed passing the hours at her side; she was his spiritual nurse, almost a sister,—but most of all she was a woman, and beautiful. The aroma of femininity: this is what he yearned for in her, and about her, seeking to incorporate it into himself. They read the same books, they went together to the theater or for walks. He taught her cards and chess, and they played of nights;—she badly,—he, to make himself agreeable, but little less badly. Thus much, as far as external things are concerned. And now came personal intimacies, the timorous eyes of Rita, that so often sought his own, consulting them before they questioned those of her own husband,—the touches of cold hands, and unwonted communion. On one of his birthdays he received from Villela a costly cane, and from Rita, a hastily penciled, ordinary note expressing good wishes. It was then that he learned to read within his own heart; he could not tear his eyes away from the missive. Commonplace words, it is true; but there are sublime commonplaces,—or at least, delightful ones. The old chaise in which for the first time you rode with your beloved, snuggled together, is as good as the chariot of Apollo. Such is man, and such are the circumstances that surround him.

Camillo sincerely wished to flee the situation, but it was already beyond his power. Rita, like a serpent, was charming him, winding her coils about him; she was crushing his bones, darting her venomous fangs into his lips. He was helpless, overcome. Vexation, fear, remorse, desire,—all this he felt, in a strange confusion. But the battle was short and the victory deliriously intoxicating. Farewell, all scruple! The shoe now fitted snugly enough upon the foot, and there they were both, launched upon the high road, arm in arm, joyfully treading the grass and the gravel, without suffering anything more than lonesomeness when they were away from each other. As to Villela, his confidence in his wife and his esteem for his friend continued the same as before.

One day, however, Camillo received an anonymous letter, which called him immoral and perfidious, and warned him that his adventure was known to all. Camillo took fright, and, in order to ward off suspicion, began to make his visits to Villela's house more rare. The latter asked him the reason for his prolonged absence. Camillo answered that the cause was a youthful flirtation. Simplicity evolved into cunning. Camillo's absences became longer and longer, and then his visits ceased entirely. Into this course there may have entered a little self-respect,— the idea of diminishing his obligations to the husband in order to make his own actions appear less treacherous.

It was at this juncture that Rita, uncertain and in fear, ran to the fortune-teller to consult her upon the real reason for Camillo's actions. As we have seen, the card reader restored the wife's confidence and the young man reproved her for having done what she did. A few weeks passed. Camillo received two or three more anonymous letters, written with such passionate anger that they could not have been prompted by mere regard for virtue; surely they came from some violent rival of his. In his opinion Rita concurred, formulating, in ill-composed words of her own, this thought: virtue is indolent and niggardly, wasting neither time nor paper; only self-interest is alert and prodigal.

But this did not help to ease Camillo; he now feared lest the anonymous writer should inform Villela, in which case the catastrophe would follow fast and implacably. Rita agreed that this was possible.

"Very well," she said. "Give me the envelopes in which the letters came, so that I may compare the handwriting with that of the mail which comes to him. If any arrives with writing resembling the anonymous script, I'll keep it and tear it up . . ."

But no such letter appeared. A short time after this, however, Villela commenced to grow grave, speaking very little, as if something weighed upon his mind. Rita hurried to communicate the change to her lover, and they discussed the matter earnestly. Her opinion was that Camillo should renew his visits to their home, and sound her husband; it might be that Villela would confide to him some business worry. With this Camillo disagreed; to appear after so many months was to confirm the suspicions and denunciations of the anonymous letters. It was better to be very careful, to give each other up for several weeks. They arranged means for communicating with each other in case of necessity and separated, in tears.

On the following day Camillo received at his department this letter from Villela: "Come immediately to our house; I must talk to you without delay." It was past noon. Camillo left at once; as he reached the street it occurred to him that it would have been much more natural for Villela to have called him to his office; why to his house? All this betokened a very urgent matter; moreover, whether it was reality or illusion, it seemed to Camillo that the letter was written in a trembling hand. He sought to establish a connection between all these things and the news Rita had brought him the night before.

"Come immediately to our house; I must talk to you without delay," he repeated, his eyes staring at the note.

In his mind's eye he beheld the climax of a drama,—Rita cowed, weeping; Villela indignant, seizing his pen and dashing off the letter, certain that he, Camillo, would answer in person, and waiting to kill him as he entered. Camillo shuddered with terror; then he smiled weakly; in any event the idea of drawing back was repugnant to him. So he continued on his way. As he walked it occurred to him to step into his rooms; he might find there a message from Rita explaining everything. But he found nothing, nobody. He returned to the street, and the thought that they had been discovered grew every moment more convincing; yes, the author of the previous anonymous communications must have denounced him to the husband; perhaps by now Villela knew all. The very suspension of his calls without any apparent reason, with the flimsiest of pretexts, would confirm everything else.

Camillo walked hastily along, agitated, nervous. He did not read the letter again, but the words hovered persistently before his eyes; or else,—which was even worse—they seemed to be murmured into his ears by the voice of Villela himself. "Come immediately to our house; I must talk to you without delay." Spoken thus by the voice of the other they seemed pregnant with mystery and menace. Come immediately,—why? It was now nearly one o'clock. Camillo's agitation waxed greater with each passing moment. So clearly did he imagine what was about to take place that he began to believe it a reality, to see it before his very eyes. Yes, without a doubt, he was afraid. He even considered arming himself, thinking that if nothing should happen he would lose nothing by this useful precaution. But at once he rejected the idea, angry with himself, and hastened his step towards Carioca square, there to take a tilbury. He arrived, entered and ordered the driver to be off at full speed.

"The sooner the better," he thought. "I can't stand this uncertainty."

But the very sound of the horse's clattering hoofs increased his agitation. Time was flying, and he would be face to face with danger soon enough. When they had come almost to the end of Guarda-Velha street the tilbury had to come to a stop; the thoroughfare was blocked by a coach that had broken down. Camillo surveyed the obstruction and decided to wait. After five minutes had gone by, he noticed that there at his left, at the very foot of the tilbury, was the fortune-teller's house,—the very same as Rita had once consulted. Never, as at this moment, had he so desired to believe in card-reading. He looked closer, saw that the windows were closed, while all the others on the street were opened, filled with folks curious to see what was the matter. It looked for all the world like the dwelling of indifferent Fate.

Camillo leaned back in his seat so as to shut all this from view. His excitement was intense, extraordinary, and from the deep, hidden recesses of his mind there began to emerge specters of early childhood, old beliefs, banished superstitions. The coachman proposed another route; he shook his head and said that he would wait. He leaned forward to get a better look at the card-reader's house . . . Then he made a gesture of self-ridicule: it had entered his mind to consult the fortune-teller, who seemed to be hovering over him, far, far above, with vast, ash-colored wings; she disappeared, reappeared, and then her image was lost; then, in a few moments, the ash-colored wings stirred again, nearer, flying about him in narrowing circles . . . In the street men were shouting, dragging away the coach.

"There! Now! Push! That's it! Now!"

In a short while the obstruction was removed. Camillo closed his eyes, trying to think of other things; but the voice of Rita's husband whispered into his ears the words of the letter: "Come immediately . . ." And he could behold the anguish of the drama. He trembled. The house seemed to look right at him. His feet instinctively moved as if to leave the carriage and go in . . . Camillo found himself before a long, opaque veil . . . he thought rapidly of the inexplicability of so many things. The voice of his mother was repeating to him a host of extraordinary happenings; and the very sentence of the Prince of Denmark kept echoing within him:

> There are more things in heaven and earth, Horatio,
> Than are dreamt of in our philosophy.

What could he lose by it, if . . . ?

He jumped out to the pavement, just before the fortune-teller's door; he told the driver to wait for him, and hastened into the entry, ascending the stairs. There was little light, the stairs were worn away from the many feet that had sought them, the banister was smooth and sticky; but he saw and felt nothing. He stumbled up the stairs and knocked. Nobody appearing, he was about to go down; but it was too late now,—curiosity was whipping his blood and his heart beat with violent throbs; he turned back to the door, and knocked once, twice, three times. He beheld a woman; it was the card-reader. Camillo said that he had come to consult her, and she bade him enter. Thence they climbed to the attic by a staircase even worse than the first and buried in deeper gloom. At the top there was a garret, ill lighted by a small window. Old furniture, somber walls, and an air of poverty augmented, rather than destroyed, the prestige of the occupant.

The fortune-teller told him to be seated before the table, and she sat down on the opposite side with her back to the window, so that whatever little light came from without fell full upon Camillo's face. She opened a drawer and took out a pack of worn, filthy cards. While she rapidly shuffled them she peered at him closely, not so much with a direct gaze as from under her eyes. She was a woman of forty, Italian, thin and swarthy, with large, sharp, cunning eyes. She placed three cards upon the table, and said:

"Let us first see what has brought you here. The gentleman has just received a severe shock and is in great fear . . ."

Camillo, astonished, nodded affirmatively.

"And he wishes to know," she continued, "whether anything will happen to him or not . . ."

"To me and to her," he explained, excitedly.

The fortune-teller did not smile; she simply told him to wait. She took the cards hastily once more and shuffled them with her long tapering fingers whose nails were so long and unclean from neglect; she shuffled them well, once, twice, thrice; then she began to lay them out. Camillo's eyes were riveted upon her in anxious curiosity.

"The cards tell me . . ."

Camillo leaned forward to drink in her words one by one. Then she told him to fear nothing. Nothing would happen to him or to the other. He, the third, was aware of naught. Nevertheless, great caution was indispensable; envy and rivalry were at work. She spoke to him of the love that bound them, of Rita's beauty . . . Camillo was bewildered. The fortune-teller stopped talking, gathered the cards and locked them in the drawer.

"The lady has restored peace to my spirit," he said, offering her his hand across the table and pressing that of the card-reader.

She arose, laughing.

"Go," she said. "Go, *ragazzo innamorato* . . ."[1]

And arising, she touched his head with her index finger. Camillo shuddered, as if it were the hand of one of the original sybils, and he, too, arose. The fortune-teller went to the bureau, upon which lay a plate of raisins, took a cluster of them and commenced to eat them, showing two rows of teeth that were as white as her nails were black. Even in this common action the woman possessed an air all her own. Camillo, anxious to leave, was at a loss how much to pay; he did not know her fee.

"Raisins cost money," he said, at length, taking out his pocket-book. "How many do you want to order?"

"Ask your heart," she replied.

Camillo took out a note for ten milreis and gave it to her. The eyes of the card-reader sparkled. Her usual fee was two milreis.

"I can see easily that the gentleman loves his lady very much . . . And well he may. For she loves the gentleman very deeply, too. Go, go in peace, with your mind at ease. And take care as you descend the staircase,—it's dark. Don't forget your hat . . ."

The fortune-teller had already placed the note in her pocket, and accompanied him down the stairs, chatting rather gaily. At the bottom of the first flight Camillo bid her good-bye and ran down the stairs that led to the street, while the card-reader, rejoicing in her large fee, turned back to the garret, humming a barcarolle. Camillo found the tilbury waiting for him; the street was now clear. He entered and the driver whipped his horse into a fast trot.

---

1. Italian for "love-sick boy," "young lover," etc.

To Camillo everything had now changed for the better and his affairs assumed a brighter aspect; the sky was clear and the faces of the people he passed were all so merry. He even began to laugh at his fears, which he now saw were puerile; he recalled the language of Villela's letter and perceived at once that it was most friendly and familiar. How in the world had he ever been able to read any threat of danger into those words! He suddenly realized that they were urgent, however, and that he had done ill to delay so long; it might be some very serious business affair.

"Faster, faster!" he cried to the driver.

And he began to think of a plausible explanation of his delay; he even contemplated taking advantage of this incident to re-establish his former intimacy in Villela's household . . . Together with his plans there kept echoing in his soul the words of the fortune-teller. In truth, she had guessed the object of his visit, his own state of mind, and the existence of a third; why, then, wasn't it reasonable to suppose that she had guessed the rest correctly, too? For, the unknown present is the same as the future. And thus, slowly and persistently the young man's childhood superstitions attained the upper hand and mystery clutched him in its iron claws. At times he was ready to burst into laughter, and with a certain vexation he did laugh at himself. But the woman, the cards, her dry, reassuring words, and her good-bye—"Go, go, *ragazzo innamorato*," and finally, that farewell barcarolle, so lively and gracious,—such were the new elements which, together with the old, formed within him a new and abiding faith.

The truth is that his heart was happy and impatient, recalling the happy hours of the past and anticipating those yet to come. As he passed through Gloria street Camillo gazed across the sea, far across where the waters and the heaven meet in endless embrace, and the sight gave him a sensation of the future,—long, long and infinite.

From here it was but a moment's drive to Villela's home. He stepped out, thrust the iron garden gate open and entered. The house was silent. He ran up the six stone steps and scarcely had he had time to knock when the door opened and Villela loomed before him.

"Pardon my delay. It was impossible to come sooner. What is the matter?"

Villela made no reply. His features were distorted; he beckoned Camillo to step within. As he entered, Camillo could not repress a cry of horror:—there upon the sofa lay Rita, dead in a pool of blood. Villela seized the lover by the throat and, with two bullets, stretched him dead upon the floor.

LIFE

—◦❦ ❦◦—

End of time. Ahasverus, seated upon a rock, gazes for a long
while upon the horizon, where two eagles fly, crossing each
other in their path. He meditates, then falls into a doze. The
day wanes.

AHASVERUS. I have come to the end of time; this is the threshold of eternity. The
earth is deserted; no other man breathes the air of life. I am the last; I can die.
Die! Precious thought! For centuries of centuries I have lived, wearied, mortified,
wandering ever, but now the centuries are coming to an end, and I shall die
with them. Ancient nature, farewell! Azure sky, clouds ever reborn, roses of a
day and of every day, perennial waters, hostile earth that never would devour
my bones, farewell! The eternal wanderer will wander no longer. God may
pardon me if He wishes, but death will console me. That mountain is as unyielding as my grief; those eagles that fly yonder must be as famished as my
despair. Shall you, too, die, divine eagles?

PROMETHEUS. Of a surety the race of man is perished; the earth is bare of them.

AHASVERUS. I hear a voice. . . . The voice of a human being? Implacable heavens,
am I not then the last? He approaches. . . . Who are you? There shines in your
large eyes something like the mysterious light of the archangels of Israel; you
are not a human being? . . .

PROMETHEUS. No.

AHASVERUS. Of a race divine, then?

PROMETHEUS. You have said it.

AHASVERUS. I do not know you; but what matters it that I do not? You are not a
human being; then I may die; for I am the last and I close the gate of life.

PROMETHEUS. Life, like ancient Thebes, has a hundred gates. You close one, and
others will open. You are the last of your species? Then another better species
will come, made not of clay, but of the light itself. Yes, last of men, all the
common spirits will perish forever; the flower of them it is which will return to
earth and rule. The ages will be rectified. Evil will end; the winds will thenceforth
scatter neither the germs of death nor the clamor of the oppressed, but only the
song of love everlasting and the benediction of universal justice. . . .

AHASVERUS. What can all this posthumous joy matter to the species that dies with
me? Believe me, you who are immortal, to the bones that rot in the earth the
purples of Sidonia are worthless. What you tell me is even better than what
Campanella dreamed. In that man's ideal city there were delights and ills; yours
excludes all mortal and physical ailments. May the Lord hear you! But let me
go and die.

PROMETHEUS. Go, go. But why this haste to end your days?

AHASVERUS. The haste of a man who has lived for thousands of years. Yes,
thousands of years. Men who existed scarcely scores of them invented a feeling

of ennui, *tedium vitae*, which they could never know, at least in all its implacable and vast reality, because it is necessary to have journeyed through all the generations and all the cataclysms to feel that profound surfeit of existence.

PROMETHEUS. Thousands of years?

AHASVERUS. My name is Ahasverus; I dwelt in Jerusalem at the time they were about to crucify Christ. When he passed my door he weakened under the burden of the beam that he carried on his shoulders, and I thrust him onward, admonishing him not to stop, not to rest, to continue on his way to the hill where he was to be crucified. . . . Then there came a voice from heaven, telling me that I, too, should have to journey forever, continuously, until the end of time. Such was my crime; I felt no pity for him who was going to his death. I do not know myself how it came about. The Pharisees said that the son of Mary had come to destroy the law, and that he must be slain; I, ignorant wretch, wished to display my zeal and hence my action of that day. How many times have I seen the same thing since, traveling unceasingly through cities and ages! Whenever zealotry penetrated into a submissive soul, it became cruel or ridiculous. My crime was unpardonable.

PROMETHEUS. A grave crime, in truth, but the punishment was lenient. The other men read but a chapter of life; you have read the whole book. What does one chapter know of the other chapter? Nothing. But he who has read them all, connects them and concludes. Are there melancholy pages? There are merry and happy ones, too. Tragic convulsion precedes that of laughter; life burgeons from death; swans and swallows change climate, without ever abandoning it entirely; and thus all is harmonized and begun anew. You have beheld this, not ten times, not a thousand times, but ever; you have beheld the magnificence of the earth curing the affliction of the soul, and the joy of the soul compensating for the desolation of things; the alternating dance of Nature, who gives her left hand to Job and her right to Sardanapalus.

AHASVERUS. What do you know of my life? Nothing; you are ignorant of human existence.

PROMETHEUS. I, ignorant of human life? How laughable! Come perpetual man, explain yourself. Tell me everything; you left Jerusalem . . .

AHASVERUS. I left Jerusalem. I began my wandering through the ages. I journeyed everywhere, whatever the race, the creed, the tongue; suns and snows, barbarous and civilized peoples, islands, continents; wherever a man breathed, there breathed I. I never labored. Labor is a refuge, and that refuge was denied me. Every morning I found upon me the necessary money for the day . . . See; this is the last apportionment. Go, for I need you no longer. (*He draws forth the money and throws it away.*) I did not work; I just journeyed, ever and ever, one day after another, year after year unendingly, century after century. Eternal justice knew what it was doing: it added idleness to eternity. One generation bequeathed me to the other. The languages, as they died, preserved my name like a fossil. With the passing of time all was forgotten; the heroes faded into myths, into shadow, and history crumbled to fragments, only two or three vague, remote characteristics remaining to it. And I saw them in changing aspect. You spoke of a chapter? Happy are those who read only one chapter of life. Those who depart at the birth of empires bear with them the impression of their perpetuity; those who die at their fall, are buried in the hope of their restoration; but do you not realize what it is to see the same things unceasingly,—the same alternation of prosperity and desolation, desolation and prosperity, eternal obsequies and eternal halleluiahs, dawn upon dawn, sunset upon sunset?

PROMETHEUS. But you did not suffer, I believe. It is something not to suffer.

AHASVERUS. Yes, but I saw other men suffer, and in the end the spectacle of joy gave me the same sensations as the discourses of an idiot. Fatalities of flesh and blood, unending strife,—I saw all pass before my eyes, until night caused me to lose my taste for day, and now I cannot distinguish flowers from thistles. Everything is confused in my wearied retina.

PROMETHEUS. But nothing pained you personally; and what about me, from time immemorial suffering the wrath of the gods?

AHASVERUS. You?

PROMETHEUS. My name is Prometheus.

AHASVERUS. You! Prometheus!

PROMETHEUS. And what was my crime? Out of clay and water I made the first men, and afterwards, seized with compassion, I stole for them fire from the sky. Such was my crime. Jupiter, who then reigned over Olympus, condemned me to the most cruel of tortures. Come, climb this rock with me.

AHASVERUS. You are telling me a tale. I know that Hellenic myth.

PROMETHEUS. Incredulous old fellow! Come see the very chains that fettered me; it was an excessive penalty for no crime whatever; but divine pride is terrible . . . See; there they are . . .

AHASVERUS. And time, which gnaws all things, does not desire them, then?

PROMETHEUS. They were wrought by a divine hand. Vulcan forged them. Two emissaries from heaven came to secure me to the rock, and an eagle, like that which now is flying across the horizon, kept gnawing at my liver without ever consuming it. This lasted for time beyond my reckoning. No, no, you cannot imagine this torture . . .

AHASVERUS. Are you not deceiving me? You, Prometheus? Was that not, then, a figment of the ancient imagination?

PROMETHEUS. Look well at me; touch these hands. See whether I really exist.

AHASVERUS. Then Moses lied to me. You are Prometheus, creator of the first men.

PROMETHEUS. That was my crime.

AHASVERUS. Yes, it was your crime,—an artifice of hell; your crime was inexpiable. You should have remained forever, bound and devoured,—you, the origin of the ills that afflict me. I lacked compassion, it is true; but you, who gave me life, perverse divinity, were the cause of all.

PROMETHEUS. Approaching death confuses your reason.

AHASVERUS. Yes, it is you; you have the Olympic forehead, strong and beautiful Titan; it is you indeed . . . And these your chains? I see upon them no trace of your tears.

PROMETHEUS. I wept them for your humankind.

AHASVERUS. And humanity wept far more because of your crime.

PROMETHEUS. Hear me, last of men, last of ingrates!

AHASVERUS. What need have I of your words? I desire your groans, perverse divinity. Here are the chains. See how I raise them; listen to the clank of the iron . . . Who unbound you just now?

PROMETHEUS. Hercules.

AHASVERUS. Hercules . . . See whether he will repeat his service now that you are to be bound anew.

PROMETHEUS. You are raving.

AHASVERUS. The sky gave you your first punishment, now earth will give you the second and the last. Not even Hercules will ever be able to break these fetters. See how I brandish them in the air, like feathers! for I represent the power of millennial despairs. All humanity is concentrated within me. Before I sink into the abyss, I will write upon this stone the epitaph of a world. I will summon the eagle, and it will come; I will tell it that the last man, on departing from life, leaves him a god as a gift.

PROMETHEUS. Poor, ignorant wretch, who rejects a throne! No, you cannot reject it.

AHASVERUS. Now it is you who are raving. Kneel, and let me manacle your arms. So,'tis well you will resist no more. Bend this way; now your legs . . .

PROMETHEUS. Have done, have done. It is the passions of earth turning upon me; but I, who am not a human being, do not know ingratitude. You will not be spared a jot of your destiny; it will be fulfilled to the letter. You yourself will be the new Hercules. I, who announced the glory of the other, now proclaim yours; and you will be no less generous than he . . .

AHASVERUS. Are you mad?

PROMETHEUS. The truth unknown to man is the madness of him who proclaims it. Proceed, and have done.

AHASVERUS. Glory pays nothing, and dies.

PROMETHEUS. This glory will never die. Have done; have done; show the sharp beak of the eagle where it is to devour my entrails. But hear me . . . No, hear nothing; you cannot understand me.

AHASVERUS. Speak; speak.

PROMETHEUS. The ephemeral world cannot understand the world eternal; but you will be the link between the two.

AHASVERUS. Tell me everything.

PROMETHEUS. I speak nothing; fetter these wrists well, that I shall not flee,—so that I shall be here on your return. Tell you all? I have already told you that a new race shall people the earth, formed of the chosen spirits of the extinct humanity; the multitude of others will perish. A noble family, all-seeing and powerful, will be the perfect synthesis of the divine and the human. The times will be others, but between them and these a link is necessary, and you shall be that link.

AHASVERUS. I?

PROMETHEUS. You yourself; you, the chosen one; you the King. Yes, Ahasverus. You shall be King. The Wanderer will find rest. The despised of men shall rule over mankind.

AHASVERUS. Wily Titan, you are deceiving me . . . King,—I?

PROMETHEUS. You, King. Who else, then? The new world needs to be bound by a tradition, and none can speak of one to the other as you can. Thus there will be no gap between the two humanities. The perfect will proceed from the imperfect, and your lips will tell the new world its origin. You will relate to the new humanity all the ancient good and evil. And thus will you live anew like the tree whose dead branches are lopped off, only the flourishing ones being preserved; but here growth will be eternal.

AHASVERUS. Resplendent vision! I myself?

PROMETHEUS. Your very self.

AHASVERUS. These eyes ... these hands ... a new and better life ... Glorious vision! Titan, it is just. Just was the punishment; but equally just is the glorious remission of my sin. Shall I live? I myself? A new and better life? No, you are jesting with me.

PROMETHEUS. Very well, then; leave me. You will return some day, when this vast heaven will be open to let the spirits of the new life descend. You will find me here at peace. Go.

AHASVERUS. Shall I again greet the sun?

PROMETHEUS. The selfsame sun that is about to set. Friend sun, eye of time, nevermore shall your eyelids close. Gaze upon it, if you can.

AHASVERUS. I cannot.

PROMETHEUS. You will be able to, when the conditions of life shall have changed. Then your retina will gaze upon the sun without peril, for in the man of the future will be concentrated all that is best in nature, energizing or subtle, scintillating or pure.

AHASVERUS. Swear that you are not lying.

PROMETHEUS. You will see whether I lie.

AHASVERUS. Speak, speak on; tell me everything.

PROMETHEUS. The description of life is not worth the sensation of life; you shall experience it deeply. The bosom of Abraham in your old Scriptures is nothing but this final perfect world. There you will greet David and the prophets. There will you tell to the astounded listeners, not only the great events of the extinct world, but also the ills they will never know: sickness, old age, grief, egotism, hypocrisy, abhorrent vanity, imbecility, and the rest. The soul, like the earth, will possess an incorruptible tunic.

AHASVERUS. I shall gaze ever on the immense blue sky?

PROMETHEUS. Behold how beautiful it is.

AHASVERUS. As beautiful and serene as eternal justice. Magnificent heaven, more beautiful than the tents of Caesar. I shall behold you forever; you will receive my thoughts, as before; you will grant me clear days, and friendly nights ...

PROMETHEUS. Dawn upon dawn.

AHASVERUS. Ah, speak on, speak on. Tell me everything. Let me unbind these chains ...

PROMETHEUS. Loosen them, new Hercules, last man of the old world, who shall be the first of the new. Such is your destiny; neither you nor I,—nobody can alter it. You go farther than your Moses. From the top of mount Nebo, at the point of death, he beheld the land of Jericho; which was to belong to his descendants, and the Lord said unto him: "Thou hast seen with thine eyes, yet shalt not pass beyond." *You* shall pass beyond, Ahasverus; you shall dwell in Jericho.

AHASVERUS. Place your hand upon my head; look well at me; fill me with the reality of your prediction; let me breathe a little of the new, full life . . . King, did you say?

PROMETHEUS. The chosen king of a chosen people.

AHASVERUS. It is not too much in recompense for the deep ignominy in which I have dwelt. Where one life heaped mire, another life will place a halo. Speak, speak on . . . speak on . . . (*He continues to dream. The two eagles draw near.*)

FIRST EAGLE. Ay, ay, ay! Alas for this last man; he is dying, yet he dreams of life.

SECOND EAGLE. Not so much that he hated it as that he loved it so much.

THE NURSE

So you think that what happened to me in 1860 can be printed in a book? Do whatever you please, but with only one condition: do not divulge anything before my death. You will not have to wait long, perhaps a week, if not less; I am incurable.

Look, I could tell you about my entire life, during which time other interesting things took place; however, in order to do that, one needs time, spirit, and paper, and I have only paper. My spirit is weak and time resembles a night lamp at dawn. It will not be long before the sun rises on another day. It is the sun of demons, as impenetrable as life. Good-bye, my dear sir. Read this and wish me well; forgive me for whatever seems improper to you. Do not mistreat the rue if it does not smell like a rose. You asked me for a human document, and here it is. Do not ask me for the empire of the Great Mongol, nor for a photograph of the Maccabees; ask me, however, for my death shoes, and I will not give them to anyone else.

You already know that it happened in 1860. In the preceding year, during the month of August, I, being forty-two, became a theologian. What I mean to say is that I copied the theological studies of a priest from Niterói. He was a former schoolmate of mine who had graciously offered me room and board. In that same month of August, 1859, he received a letter from the vicar of a certain town in the Interior asking if he knew of an intelligent, discreet, and patient person who might be willing to go and serve as Colonel Felisberto's nurse for a good wage. The priest talked to me about it and I willingly accepted. I was already tired of copying Latin quotations and ecclesiastic formulas. I went to the Court to say good-bye to my brother, and then headed toward the town.

As soon as I arrived in town, I received negative reports about the Colonel. He was an unbearable, peculiar, demanding man whom no one could tolerate, not even his own friends. He used up more nurses than medication; he cracked the skulls of two of them. To this I answered that I did not fear healthy people, much less sickly ones. After conferring with the vicar, who confirmed the reports I had received and who advised gentleness and compassion on my part, I set out for the Colonel's residence.

I found him stretched out on a chair on the veranda; he was breathing rather heavily. The Colonel did not welcome me too poorly. Initially, he said nothing; he fixedly observed me with his two catlike eyes. Afterwards, a sort of malicious grin lit his harsh features. Finally, he told me that none of the other nurses that he had were any good. They slept a lot, they were rude, and they were always on the scent of the female slaves; two of them were even thieves!

"Are you a thief?"

"No, sir."

He immediately asked for my name, I told him and he appeared surprised. Colombo? No, sir, Procópio José Gomes Valongo. Valongo? He did not think it was a suitable name, so he proposed just calling me Procópio, to which I replied that it could be whatever he pleased. I am telling you this particular incident, not only because it seems to depict his mannerisms quite well, but also because my answer gave the Colonel the best impression of me. He said so to the vicar, adding that, when compared to the previous nurses, I was the most charming. The truth of the matter is that we had a "honeymoon" that lasted seven days.

On the eighth day, however, I began to experience the life of my predecessors. It was a dog's life; no sleep, no thought of anything but caring for the Colonel, being wronged, and, at times, laughing at the circumstances with an air of resignation and submission. I noticed that this was one way to court the Colonel. Impertinences caused by illness and temperament. He had a wide range of ailments: he suffered from an aneurysm, rheumatism, and three or four minor afflictions. He was nearly sixty and had been spoiled ever since the age of five. He always had his way. If he had only been grouchy, it would not have been so bad; but he was also mean. He reveled in the pain and humiliation of others. By the end of three months, I was tired of having to put up with him. I decided to leave as soon as I had the opportunity.

That opportunity was not far behind. One day, merely because I had not given him a massage on time, he took his cane and hit me two or three times with it. That was it! I resigned immediately and went to pack my bags. The Colonel followed me to my room and asked me to remain. He said it was not worth getting angry over the grouchy behavior of an old man. He insisted so much that I remained.

"I'm on the brink, Procópio," he told me that night. "I do not have long to live. I already have one foot in the grave. You must attend my funeral, Procópio. I will not excuse you for any reason. You must go and pray at the foot of my grave. If you do not go," he added with a laugh, "I will return at night and drag you around by your feet. Do you believe in spirits from another world, Procópio?"

"Of course not!"

"And why shouldn't you believe, you nitwit?" he quickly retorted, opening his eyes widely.

That was peace; you can imagine war. He abstained from the blows with the cane, but the insults were the same, if not worse. In time I grew callous and did not seem to mind anything. I was called a nitwit, a blockhead, a dope, an idiot, lazy, and so on. Unfortunately, there was no one else around who might have absorbed any of those names. He did not have any relatives. He did have a nephew, although he died of consumption in Minas, toward the end of May or the beginning of June. At times, the Colonel's friends came to praise and applaud him, and nothing more. The visits lasted no longer than five or ten minutes. I remained behind, the victim of an entire dictionary of name-calling. I decided to leave more than once, yet, because of the vicar's insistence, I remained.

Our relationship was strained and I was anxious to return to the Court. At forty-two years of age, it was not as though I had to become accustomed to constant isolation, especially at the foot of a rude, sickly man from the Interior. In order to be able to imagine the extent of my isolation, you need only know that I did not even read newspapers. Except for some important news that was brought to the Colonel, I knew nothing of the rest of the world. I intended, therefore, to return to the Court at the first opportunity, even if it meant that I had to quarrel with the vicar. I can say (since I am giving confession anyway) that, as long as I was saving my salary and was not spending anything, I was anxious to squander it back there.

It was very likely that an opportunity would arise. The Colonel was feeling worse and made out his last will and testament, upsetting the notary almost as much as he did me. His behavior was harsher; his brief periods of tranquillity and kindness were rarer. By this time, I had already lost the small amount of compassion that previously made me forget the Colonel's excesses. I was now carrying the seeds of hate and repugnance within me. At the beginning of August, I definitely made up my mind to leave; the vicar and the doctor accepted my reasons, but asked that I stay on a little while longer. I conceded them one more month, at the end of which I had decided to leave, regardless of the Colonel's condition. The vicar tried to find a substitute for me.

You will now see what happened. The Colonel had a fit of rage on the night of August twenty-fourth. He knocked me down and called me all sorts of crude names. He threatened to shoot me and ended up throwing a dish of mush at me just because he found it cold. The dish hit the wall and was smashed to bits.

"You will pay for that, thief," he bellowed.

He grumbled for some time after that. At eleven o'clock, he fell asleep. While he was sleeping, I took out a book. It was a translation of an old d'Arlincourt novel that I had found. I started to read it in the Colonel's room, a short distance from his bed. I had to awaken him at midnight in order to give him some medicine. Either because of my weariness, or the book itself, I, too, fell asleep before finishing the second page. I soon awoke to the shouts of the Colonel and jumped up, quite startled. The seemingly delirious Colonel continued his shouting and, before I knew it, he grabbed a jug and hurled it toward me. I did not have time to evade it. The jug hit the left side of my face and the pain was so great that I could think of nothing else. I attacked him. I put my hands around his neck; we fought and I strangled him.

When I realized that the patient was dying, I drew back frightened. I cried out, although no one heard me. I returned to the Colonel's bedside and shook him, hoping to revive him. It was too late; his aneurysm had burst. The Colonel had died. I then went into the adjoining room and did not dare return to his room for two hours. I cannot really tell you all that I felt during that time. I was in a daze, a vague and dull delirium. It seemed to me that the walls contained forms. I listened to muffled voices. The victim's cries, before and after the struggle, continued to echo within me. Wherever I turned, the air seemed interspersed with convulsions. Do not think that I am creating images or inventing a style. I tell you that I distinctly heard voices that shouted at me: "Assassin! Assassin!"

Everything else was quiet. The same slow, even, dull sound of the clock underscored the silence and the solitude. I glued my ear to the door of the room in the hope of hearing a groan, a word, an insult, or any sign of life that would restore peace to my conscience. I would have been prepared to take a beating at the hands of the Colonel ten, twenty, one hundred times. But I heard nothing, nothing. All was quiet. I began to wander aimlessly. I sat down in the drawing room and put my hands on my head. I regretted ever having come. "Damn the moment that caused me to accept such an assignment," I exclaimed. I then denounced the priest from Niterói, the doctor, the vicar, those who had arranged this position for me, and those who had asked me to stay longer. I was clinging to other men's complicity.

Because the silence frightened me, I opened one of the windows to listen to the sound of the wind, if, indeed, it were blowing. It was not. The night was tranquil; the stars glowed, with the indifference of those who take off their hats when a funeral procession passes by, only to continue speaking of something else thereafter. I leaned there for some time, staring into the night. Hoping to ease the feelings of grief, I allowed myself to think about my life. Only then did I clearly think of the possible consequences. I was responsible for a crime and I anticipated certain punishment. Fear complicated remorse. I felt my hairs stand on end. Minutes later, I saw three or four indistinct figures in the yard. They were spying, as though preparing to ambush; I moved back and the figures vanished into thin air. It was a hallucination.

I treated the contusion on my face before dawn. Only then did I dare return to the Colonel's room. I drew back twice, although, because I knew I had to, I entered; even then, I did not dare approach the bed. My legs shook; my heart throbbed. I thought about fleeing, but that would have been a confession of the crime, and, besides, I was determined to make all of the traces of the crime disappear. I went to the bedside; I saw the dead man, with his fixed eyes and open mouth, apparently allowing the utterance of those eternal words: "Cain, what hast thou done to thy brother?" On his neck, I saw the marks made by my nails. I buttoned his shirt all the way up and I raised the sheet up to his chin. I then called a slave and told him the Colonel had died in his sleep; I sent him with a message to the vicar and the doctor.

The first thought that came to mind was to go away immediately, under the pretext that my brother was ill. In truth, I had received a letter from him several days earlier, in which he stated that he was not feeling well; however, I realized that leaving so suddenly would cause suspicion, so I stayed on. I was the one who dressed the dead body, with the aid of an old, myopic black man. I did not leave the mortuary, for I was afraid they might discover something. If the others suspected something, I wanted to see it in their faces, although I did not dare to stare at anyone. Everything annoyed me: the steps of those entering the room, which were like those of a thief, the whispering, the ceremonies and the vicar's prayers. When the time came, I closed the coffin with trembling hands. They trembled so much that someone who noticed them said to someone else, in a compassionate tone: "Poor Procópio! Despite all that he has suffered, he is very mournful."

It seemed ironic to me. I was eager to see it all end. We went out into the street. The walk from the semi-obscurity of the house into the brightness of the outside shocked me; I feared that now it would be impossible to hide the crime. I stared at the ground and kept walking. When it was all over, I was able to breathe again. I was at peace with my fellow man; however, I was not at peace with my conscience.

The first nights were naturally filled with discomfort and affliction. It is not necessary to add that I then came to Rio de Janeiro, nor that I lived here in fear, even though I was far from the scene of the crime. I did not laugh, I spoke little, I ate poorly, and I had hallucinations and nightmares . . .

"Forget about the deceased," I was advised. "There is no reason for so much melancholy."

I capitalized on that illusion, often praising the dead man and calling him a good person. He was rude, yes, but he had a heart of gold. And by praising him, I also convinced myself, at least for several moments. Another interesting phenomenon, and perhaps one from which you might profit, is the fact that, even though I was not a religious person, I requested a mass in honor of the Colonel's eternal rest, in the Sacramento Church. I did not invite anyone and I did not tell anyone about it. I went alone and knelt the entire time, often crossing myself. I doubled the amount paid to the priest and distributed alms at the door, all for the deceased. I was not intending to deceive anyone. The proof is that I went alone. In order to clarify this point, I will add that I never alluded to the Colonel without saying: "May God rest his soul." And I told several amusing, spirited, and witty anecdotes about him.

Seven days after arriving in Rio de Janeiro, I received a letter from the vicar. It was the one that I showed you, telling me that the Colonel's will had been found and that I was his sole heir. Imagine my astonishment. I thought I had misread the letter. I went to my brother. I went to my friends. Everyone read it in the same way. It was written right there. I was the Colonel's sole heir. I began to think it might be a trap, although I realized that there were other ways of capturing me if my crime had been discovered. Besides, I knew of the vicar's honesty; he would not take part in such a scheme. I reread the letter five, ten, many times; the news was there.

"How much did he have?" asked my brother.

"I do not know, but he was rich."

"It proves he was your friend."

"He was . . . he was . . ."

That is how, by a quirk of fate, the Colonel's wealth came into my hands. I thought about refusing the inheritance. It seemed odious to me to receive even a cent; it would even be worse than my becoming a hired thug. I thought about it for three days; the possibility that my refusal might make people distrust me always entered my mind. At the end of the three days, I decided upon a compromise: I would accept the inheritance and then secretly give it all away, little by little. It was not only a matter of scruples; it was also a way of making amends for my crime through an act of virtue. It seemed to me that this was the way to settle accounts.

I got ready and departed for the town. On the way, as I was approaching, I recalled the unhappy event; the town's surroundings had a tragic air about them and the Colonel's shadow seemed to come at me from all sides. My imagination was reproducing the words, the gestures, and the entire horrendous night of the crime . . .

Was it a crime or a struggle? Actually, it was a struggle in which I was attacked, defended myself, and in that defense . . . It was a disastrous and fatal struggle. My mind was set on that idea. I weighed the wrongs; on one side I listed the blows, the insults . . . It was not the Colonel's fault. I knew that very well. It was the illness that made him grouchy, perhaps even evil . . . But I forgave everything, everything. The worst of it all was the death that occurred that night . . . I also considered the fact that the Colonel did not have long to live. Yes, he would not have had much longer; he himself felt it and said so. How much longer would he have lived anyway? Two weeks or one? It could have been even less. It was no longer a life; it was a thread of life, if the poor man's continuous suffering could even be called that. And who really knows if the struggle and the death were not merely coincidental? They could have been, and that was even the most probable explanation; it could not have been anything else. I was set on that idea as well.

Just as I was approaching town, my heart began to race and I wanted to turn back; however, I regained control of myself and continued on my way. They greeted me with congratulations. The vicar told me about the arrangements that were made in the will, as well as its pious bequests. He also praised my Christian gentleness and the zeal with which I had served the Colonel, who, despite being harsh and cruel, knew how to be grateful.

"Without a doubt," I said looking away.

I was stunned. Everyone applauded my dedication and patience. The business of the estate delayed me in town for a while. I retained a lawyer; things went smoothly. During my stay, many things were said about the Colonel. People came to tell me about him, but they lacked the priest's moderation. I defended the Colonel, I pointed out some virtues, and I noted that he was difficult . . .

"Difficult! He is dead; it is over; yet he was the devil."

And they told me about his violent acts and wicked deeds, some of which were extraordinary. Do you want me to tell you more? At first, I listened to everything, full of curiosity. Afterwards, a unique pleasure entered my heart and I sincerely wanted to expel it. I defended the Colonel and I explained him, while attributing some things to local rivalries. I confessed, yes, that he was somewhat violent . . . "Somewhat? He was like an enraged snake," interrupted the barber. Everyone, including the tax agent, the druggist, and the clerk, said the same things; and then there were the anecdotes. The Colonel's entire life was exposed. The older people remembered his cruelties, even as a child. An intimate pleasure, quiet and insidious, grew within me. It was like a moral tapeworm, which, although torn into many pieces, always regenerated itself and kept on going.

The commitments to the estate distracted me; on the other hand, the town's opinion was so against the Colonel that various places were losing the frightening character that they previously held for me. After receiving the inheritance, I converted it into bonds and cash. Many months had passed by then and the idea of distributing everything as alms and religious donations did not dominate me as it previously had. I even think it had been pretentious on my part. I scaled down the initial plan; I distributed some money to the poor and I gave some new vestments to the primary church in town. I gave alms to Santa Casa de Misericórdia, and so on: thirty-two *contos* in all. I also ordered an all-marble tomb to be built for the Colonel. It was the work of a Neapolitan who was here until 1866, at which time he left and then died, I believe, in Paraguay.

The years went by and my memories turned gray and faded. At times I think of the Colonel, although without the fears of those first days. All of the doctors to whom I described the Colonel's ailments agreed that death was a certainty. The only thing that surprised them was his ability to resist it for so long. It could be that I, involuntarily, might have exaggerated the descriptions that I gave them; but the truth is that the Colonel was going to die, even if not under those particular circumstances.

Good-bye, my dear sir. If you find these notes to be of any value to you, then reward me with a marble tomb as well. The epitaph that I am asking you to inscribe upon it will be this amendment to the divine Sermon on the Mount:

"Blessed be those who inherit, for they shall be comforted."

THE SECRET HEART

Garcia, who was standing, studied his finger nails, and snapped them from time to time. Fortunato, in the rocking chair, looked at the ceiling. Maria Luiza, by the window, was putting the final touches to a piece of needlework. Five minutes had now passed without their saying a word. They had spoken of the day, which had been fine, of Catumby, where Fortunato and his wife lived, and of a private hospital that will be explained later. As the three characters here presented are now dead and buried, it is time to tell their story without pretense.

They had also spoken of something else, something so grim and unpleasant that it took away all desire to talk of the day, the surroundings, and the hospital. Their conversation in respect to it had been constrained. Even now, Maria Luiza's hands still trembled, while Garcia's face had a severe look—something not usual with him. As a matter of fact, what happened was of such a nature that to make the situation clear it will be necessary to go back to its very beginning.

Garcia had obtained his M.D. the year before, 1861. In the year 1860, while he was still in medical school, he had seen Fortunato for the first time, at the entrance to the Santa Casa hospital. He was going in as the other was coming out. He had been struck by Fortunato's appearance, but even so would have forgotten him, if it had not been for a second encounter only a few days later. He lived on the Rua Dom Manuel. One of his rare diversions was to go to the Theater São Januário, which was close by, between that street and the bay. He was in the habit of going once or twice a month, and never found more than forty persons in the audience. Only the most intrepid were bold enough to extend their travels to that out-of-the-way corner of the city. One night as he was sitting in the orchestra, Fortunato came in and sat down beside him.

The play was a heavy melodrama, stabbed through and through with daggers, bristling with curses and remorse, but Fortunato heard it with singular interest. In the painful scenes his attention redoubled, his eyes kept going avidly from one character to another—so much so that the medical student began to suspect that the play stirred personal memories in the man. At the end of the drama, a farce came on, but Fortunato did not wait to see it, and left the theater. Garcia followed him. Fortunato went down the Beco do Cotovelo, along the Rua de São José to the Largo da Carioca. He walked slowly, with lowered head, stopping now and then to whack with his cane some dog that was lying asleep. The dog would howl and he would keep on going. In the Largo da Carioca he climbed into a tilbury and went off in the direction of the Praça da Constituição. Garcia went home without learning more than this.

Several weeks passed. One night, about nine o'clock, as he sat at home in his garret apartment, he heard the sound of voices on the stairway. He went down at once to the second floor, where an employee of the Army Arsenal lived: several men were helping him upstairs, and he was covered with blood. His black serving man came running to the door, the man groaned, there was a jumble of voices, the light was dim. When the wounded man had been set down on his bed, Garcia said they must send for a doctor.

"One's already on the way," someone replied.

Garcia glanced toward the speaker; it was the man he had seen at the hospital and in the theater. He supposed he was a relative or friend of the wounded man, but he dismissed the idea when he heard him ask if the fellow had a family or any close relative. The black man said he had not; then the stranger took full charge. He asked the others to leave, paid the porters, and gave the necessary orders for seeing to the wounded man. Learning that Garcia was a neighbor and a medical student, he asked him to remain and assist the doctor. Then he told what had happened.

"It was a gang of *capoeiras*.* I was coming from the Moura Barracks, where I had gone to visit a cousin, when I heard a lot of yelling and then a scuffle. It seems they wounded another fellow who was going by and he turned down one of those side streets, but all I saw was this gentleman, who was crossing the street, at the moment one of the ruffians brushed against him and stuck a dagger in him. He didn't fall immediately; he told me where he lived, and, since it was but a few steps away, I thought it best to bring him home."

"Did you know him before?" asked Garcia.

"No, I'd never laid eyes on him. Who is he?"

"He's a good man, an employee of the Army Arsenal. His name is Gouvêa."

"No, I don't know him."

The doctor and the police inspector soon arrived. The man's wound was dressed, and the information taken down. The stranger said his name was Fortunato Gomes da Silveira, that he was a bachelor, living on his income, a resident of Catumby. The wound was considered serious. While it was being dressed with the help of the medical student, Fortunato acted as servant, holding the basin, the candle, the cloths, without fuss, and looking coldly at the wounded man, who groaned a good deal. Afterwards he had a private conversation with the doctor, walked with him as far as the landing, and again assured the inspector that he was ready to assist the police with their investigation. After these two had left, he and the medical student remained in the bedroom. Garcia was dumbfounded. He glanced toward him, saw him calmly sit down, stretch out his legs, put his hands in his trousers pockets, and fix his eyes on the sick man. His eyes were a clear gray, the color of lead, they moved slowly and had a hard, cold, indifferent expression. His face was thin and pale, with a narrow band of sparse red beard clipped close and extending from beneath his chin to either temple. He was perhaps forty years old. From time to time he turned to the student and asked some question about the wounded man, but immediately returned his gaze to him while the young man answered. The feeling the student got was at once one of repulsion and of curiosity; he could not deny that he was witnessing an act of rare dedication, and, if he was disinterested,

---

* Members of gangs who menaced the streets of Rio de Janeiro during the greater part of the nineteenth century. They were finally wiped out by Ferraz, the first police chief of the republic, in 1890.

as he seemed, there was nothing else to do but accept the human heart as a well of mysteries.

It was almost one o'clock when Fortunato left. He returned on the succeeding days, but the cure progressed rapidly, and before it was completed he disappeared without telling the wounded man where he lived. It was the student who gave him the information as to name, street, and number.

"I'm going to thank him for the kindness he did me, as soon as I can go out," said the convalescent.

Six days afterward, he hurried to Catumby. Fortunato received him with a constrained air, listened impatiently to his words of thanks, replied in a bored manner, and ended by swinging the cord of his dressing gown against his knee. Gouvêa, sitting silent before him, smoothed his hat with his fingers, lifted his eyes from time to time without finding anything to say. At the end of ten minutes he asked permission to leave, and left.

"Watch out for *capoeiras!*" said his host with a laugh.

The poor devil left there mortified, humiliated, scarcely able to swallow his dislike, making an effort to forget it, to explain it away or excuse it, so that only the memory of the kind deed would remain in his heart, but the effort was vain. Resentment, a new and exclusive lodger moved in and kicked out the kind deed so that the poor thing had no recourse but to climb up into the brain and take refuge there as a mere idea. So it was that the benefactor himself forced upon this man the sentiment of ingratitude.

All this astonished Garcia. The young man possessed in germ the ability to decipher men, to unravel human character. He had a love of analysis, and felt a special pleasure, which he called exquisite, in penetrating layer after layer of spiritual strata until he touched the secret heart of an organism. Pricked on by curiosity, he thought of going to see the man of Catumby, but it occurred to him that he had not received a definite invitation to call on him. He needed an excuse, at least, and he could think of none.

Many months later, after he had obtained his degree and was living on the Rua de Matacavallos, near the Rua do Conde, he happened to meet Fortunato on an omnibus, and he ran into him a number of other times: these meetings brought acquaintance. One day Fortunato invited him to come visit him in near-by Catumby.

"Did you know I was married?"

"No."

"I got married four months ago—it seems like four days. Come have dinner with us Sunday."

"Sunday?"

"Don't go making up excuses. I won't take excuses. Come, Sunday."

Garcia went on Sunday. Fortunato gave him a good dinner, good cigars, and good conversation, in company with his wife, who was interesting. He had not changed in appearance. His eyes were the same steely disks, hard and cold; his other features were no more attractive than before. His courtesy, however, if it did not redeem his nature, at least offered considerable compensation. It was Maria Luiza who possessed charm both of person and of manners. She was slender and graceful, with gentle, submissive eyes. She was twenty-five, and looked nineteen. The second time Garcia went there he noticed a certain dissonance in their natures, that little or no spiritual affinity existed between them, and in the wife's manner toward her husband there was something that went beyond respect and bordered on subjection and fear. One day when the three were together, Garcia asked Maria Luiza if she knew the circumstances under which he had met her husband.

"No," she answered.

"You are going to hear of a handsome deed."

"It's not worth the telling," interrupted Fortunato.

"She shall decide whether it's worth telling or no," insisted the doctor.

He told the story of the Rua Dom Manuel. The girl listened in amazement. Little by little she stretched out her hand and clasped her husband's wrist; she was smiling and grateful, as if she had just discovered his heart. Fortunato shrugged his shoulders but he did not hear the tale with indifference. At the end of it, he himself told of the visit the wounded man had paid him, with all the details of his appearance, gestures, his hesitant words, tongue-tied silences—in short a clown. And he kept laughing as he told it. It was not the laughter of a two-faced man, which is evasive and sly. His laugh was frank and genial.

"A strange fellow!" thought Garcia.

Maria Luiza was upset by her husband's mockery, but Garcia restored her to her former contentment by again mentioning his dedication and rare qualities as a nurse—"such a good nurse," he concluded, "that if I ever start a private hospital, I'll ask him to be my partner."

"You mean it?"

"Mean what?"

"That we are going to start a hospital?"

"No, I was joking."

"We could do it. And for you, just beginning your practice, it might not be a bad idea. It so happens I have a house that is going to fall vacant; it will be the very thing."

Garcia refused to consider the proposal on that day, and on the next; but the idea had become fixed in the other's head, and he would not be put off. As a matter of fact, it would be a good beginning for a doctor, and might turn out to be a good business for both of them. Garcia definitely accepted a few days later. It was a disappointment to Maria Luiza. The high-strung, delicate girl suffered at the very thought of her husband living in contact with human illnesses, but she did not dare oppose him, and bowed her head. The plans were quickly drawn up and carried into effect. The truth is, Fortunato gave no thought to anything else, either then or later. After the hospital opened, it was he who served as administrator and head nurse: he inspected everything, supervised everything—purchases, broths, drugs, and accounts.

Garcia could see that the dedication to the wounded man on the Rua Don Manuel was not a matter of chance but suited with his nature. He saw him perform menial and obnoxious tasks: he did not shrink from anything, did not find any disease distressing or repulsive, and was ready for anything at any time of day or night. Everyone admired and applauded. Fortunato studied, and closely followed the operations. He, and he alone, handled the caustics. "I have great faith in caustics," he would say.

The sharing of a common interest tightened the bonds of friendship. Garcia became a familiar of the house. He dined there almost every day, and there he observed Maria Luiza and saw her life of spiritual loneliness. And somehow this loneliness of hers increased her loveliness. Garcia began to feel troubled when she came into the room, when she spoke, when she worked quietly by the window, or played sweet, sad music on the piano. Gently, imperceptibly, love entered his heart. When he found it there, he tried to thrust it out, that there might be no other bond but friendship between him and Fortunato. But he did not succeed. He succeeded only in locking it in. Maria Luiza understood—both his love and his silence—but she never let on.

In the beginning of October, something happened that opened the doctor's eyes still more to the young woman's plight. Fortunato had taken up the study of anatomy and physiology, and busied himself in his spare time with ripping open and poisoning cats and dogs. Since the animals' cries disturbed the patients, he moved his laboratory home, and his wife, with her nervous temperament, had to endure them. One day, when she could stand no more, she went to the doctor and asked him to get her husband—as if it was his own idea—to give up these experiments.

"But you yourself . . ."

Maria Luiza answered with a smile. "He probably considers me childish. What I would like is for you, as a doctor, to tell him that this is bad for me. And, believe me, it is."

Garcia promptly got Fortunato to put an end to these experiments. If he performed them somewhere else, no one knew of it, but it may be that he did. Maria Luiza thanked the physician not only for herself but also for the animals, which she could not see suffer. She coughed, as she spoke. Garcia asked her if she was ill. She answered, "No."

"Let me feel your pulse."

"There's nothing wrong with me."

She did not let him feel her pulse, and went out of the room. Garcia was worried. He thought, on the contrary, there might be something wrong with her, that it was necessary to observe her and warn her husband in time.

Two days later—it was the very day on which we first glimpsed them—Garcia came to dinner. In the hall he was told that Fortunato was in his study, and he started toward that room. As he arrived at the study door, Maria Luiza came out in a state of great distress.

"What's the matter?" he asked.

"The rat! the rat!" she cried in a choked voice and went on.

Garcia remembered hearing Fortunato complain the day before of a rat that had carried off an important paper, but he never expected to see what he did see. He saw Fortunato seated at the table, which was in the middle of the study, and on which was placed a plate with spirits of alcohol in it. The liquid was on fire. Between the thumb and index finger of his left hand Fortunato held a hook from the point of which the rat hung by its tail. In his right hand he had a pair of scissors. At the moment Garcia entered the room, he was cutting off one of the rat's paws.

Then he lowered the poor thing into the flame, rapidly in order not to kill it, and made ready to do the same to the third paw, for he had already cut off the first. Garcia stopped short in horror.

"Kill it at once!" he said.

"In a minute."

And with a strange smile, reflection of a soul replete with satisfaction, a smile that told of an inward savoring of the most exquisite sensation, Fortunato cut off the rat's third paw, and for the third time made the same movement into the flame. The wretched animal squealed and twisted its bloodied, singed body, and would not die. Garcia turned away his eyes, then looked again, and put out his hand as if to prevent the torture from continuing, but he did not complete the gesture, because the devil of a man compelled fear, with that radiant serenity of countenance.

It only remained to cut off the fourth paw. He cut it off very slowly, keeping his eyes on the scissors. The paw dropped and he remained looking at the rat, now half cadaver. He lowered it into the flame for the fourth time, still more rapidly, to save if he could some tatters of life.

Garcia, who stood on the other side of the table, mastered his repugnance and looked intently at Fortunato's face. Neither rage nor hate; only a vast pleasure, quiet and deep, such pleasure as another man might derive from hearing a beautiful sonata or from seeing a sublime statue—something resembling pure, aesthetic feeling. It appeared to Garcia, and it was actually the case, that Fortunato had entirely forgotten him. He could not have been putting it on, no, it was impossible. The flame was dying, it may have been that the rat still had a bit of life left, a shadow of a shadow: Fortunato took advantage of it to cut off the animal's little muzzle, and, for the last time, to bring its flesh to the flame. Finally he let the dead thing drop on the plate, and pushed from him all that mess of scorched flesh and blood.

As he stood up he came face to face with the physician and started. Then he displayed rage against the animal that had carried off his paper, but the anger was plainly counterfeit.

"Punishment without anger," thought the doctor, "the need for a sensation of pleasure that only another creature's pain can give—that is the secret heart of this man."

Fortunato expatiated upon the importance of the document . . . only loss of time, it was true, but time was precious to him right now. Garcia listened without a word, without belief. He recalled other actions of Fortunato's, serious and trifling things: he found the same explanation for all of them, a ringing of changes on the same set of sensations, a unique kind of dilettantism—a miniature Caligula.

When Maria Luiza returned to the study a few minutes later, her husband went up to her, laughingly took her hands, and said gently, "Coward!" And, turning toward the doctor, "Would you believe it? She almost fainted."

Maria Luiza timidly protested: she was nervous, and a woman. Then she went and sat by the window, with her colored wools and needles, and her fingers still trembling, just as we saw her at the beginning of this story. It will be recalled that after speaking of other matters, the three fell silent: the husband sat looking at the ceiling, the physician snapping his finger nails.

Not long after, they went in to dinner; but dinner was not cheerful. Maria Luiza's thoughts kept straying and she coughed frequently. The doctor asked himself if she might not be exposed to some vicious excess in the company of such a man. It was barely possible, but his love transformed the possibility into a certainty: he trembled for her and determined to keep a close watch over both of them.

Her cough grew worse, and it was not long before the disease put off its mask. It was tuberculosis, insatiate old hag that sucks the life and leaves a pulp of bones. Fortunato received the news as a blow. He really loved his wife, in his way, was used to her, it was hard to lose her. He spared nothing—doctors, medicines, change of air, all the remedies, all the palliatives. But it was in vain. The illness was mortal.

In the final days, in the presence of her last terrible torments, the husband's peculiar bent dominated whatever other feeling he may have had. He never left her for an instant, fastened a cold, dull eye on that slow, painful dissolution of life, drank in, one by one, the suffering moments of this beautiful woman, now thin and transparent, consumed by fever and sapped by death. His relentless egoism, ravening after sensations, refused to renounce a single minute of her agony, or repay her with a single tear, in public or in private. Only when she died—then he was stunned. When he came to his senses he saw that he was again alone.

In the night, a female relative of Maria Luiza's, who had been with her when she died, went to get some rest. Fortunato and Garcia stayed on in the parlor, watching with the corpse, both thoughtful. But the husband, too, was exhausted. The doctor told him to rest for a while.

"Go lie down and sleep for an hour or two. I'll do the same afterward."

Fortunato went into an adjoining sitting room, stretched out on the sofa, and fell asleep at once. Twenty minutes later he awoke, tried to go back to sleep, dozed a few minutes, then got up and returned to the parlor. He walked on tiptoe so as not to awaken the relative, who was asleep close by. As he reached the door, he stopped in astonishment.

Garcia had gone up to the corpse, had raised the face-covering and gazed for some seconds at the dead woman's features. Then, as if death spiritualized every-thing, he leaned down and kissed her forehead. It was at this moment that Fortun-ato reached the door. He stopped in astonishment. Impossible that it was the kiss of friendship, it must have been the epilogue to a book of adultery. He was not jealous, be it noted. Nature had so mixed the elements in him as not to give him either jealousy or envy, but she had given him vanity, which is no less subject to resentment. He stared in astonishment, biting his lips.

Meanwhile, Garcia again leaned down to kiss the dead woman; but this time he could not bear his grief. The kiss gave way to sobs, and his eyes could no longer hold their tears, which poured forth in a flood, tears of love that had been stilled—of love and of hopeless despair. Fortunato, from the doorway, where he had remained, quietly savored this outburst of spiritual pain, which was long, very long, deliciously long.

A Woman's Arms
—◦❧ ☙◦—

Ignacio quailed before the lawyer's yelling, took the plate he handed him, and began to eat under a thunderclap of names: loafer, blockhead, stupid, crazy . . .

"Where are your thoughts that you never hear what I say to you? I'm going to tell your father and let him shake the laziness out of you with a quince rod or a good big stick. You're not too old to get a whipping, and don't you ever think you are. Stupid, crazy! . . .

"And outside it's just what you see here at home," he went on, turning to Dona Severina, a lady who had lived with him, maritally that is, for a number of years. "He gets my papers all mixed up, goes to the wrong address, calls on one court stenographer instead of another, switches attorneys on me: it's the very devil! He goes around asleep all the time. Look at him in the morning—you have to break his bones to get him out of bed . . . Just wait! Tomorrow I'll wake him up with a broom handle!"

Dona Severina touched his foot as if begging him to stop. Borges spit out a few more abusive observations, and was at peace with God and men.

I do not say he was at peace with little boys, because our Ignacio was not, strictly speaking, a little boy. He was fifteen, a good, well-grown fifteen. A shaggy untaught head, but handsome, full of questions, a head that wanted to understand and never understood anything, set on a body that was not devoid of grace, though poorly dressed. The father was a barber in Cidade Nova and had placed him as helper, clerk, what-you-will, with the lawyer Borges, in the hope of seeing him practice at the bar because he had noticed that lawyers make lots of money.

The above scene took place on the Rua da Lapa in 1870.

For some minutes nothing was heard but the rattling of knives and forks and noise of chewing. Borges stuffed himself with lettuce and beef, only stopping, occasionally, to punctuate this gustatory eloquence with a dash of wine; soon he fell silent altogether.

Ignacio ate slowly, not daring to lift his eyes from his plate nor turn them to the place where they had been at the moment the terrible Borges lit into him. The truth is, it would now be very dangerous. His eyes never rested on Dona Severina's arms but what he forgot himself and everything else.

The fault was really Dona Severina's in leaving them naked like that all the time. She wore short-sleeved dresses around the house, the sleeves falling scarcely a finger's length below the shoulder; from there down her arms were bare. They really were handsome and plump, like their mistress, who was rather more solid than delicate. And they did not lose their rosy softness for all their exposure to the air. But, it is only fair to explain, she did not wear them thus out of coquetry; it was simply that she had worn out all her long-sleeved dresses. When she stood, Dona Severina was eye-filling; when she walked, she shook with delightful undulations. Ignacio, however, scarcely ever met her except at table, where, aside from her arms, he could not see much of her. She could not be called pretty; but neither was she

75

ugly. Not a single bit of finery. Even the way she combed her hair amounted to little: she smoothed it back, caught it up, twisted it, and anchored it on top of her head with a tortoise-shell comb her mother had given her. At her throat, a dark scarf; in her ears, nothing. All this and the bloom of twenty-seven good substantial years.

They finished eating. When the coffee appeared, Borges took four cigars out of his pocket, compared them, squeezed them between his fingers, chose one, and put the others back. After lighting the cigar, he propped his elbows on the table and talked to Dona Severina of thirty thousand things that held no interest at all for our Ignacio; but while he talked he was not yelling at him, and he could muse at pleasure.

Ignacio drew out his coffee as long as he could. Between sips he smoothed the table cloth, picked imaginary particles of skin off his fingers, or let his eyes travel over the pictures on the dining-room wall, which were two: one of St. Peter and one of St. John, prints brought from church on feast days and fitted with homemade frames. Let him pretend with St. John, whose youthful head gladdens Catholic imaginations, but with the austere Peter it was too much. The only excuse for young Ignacio is that he saw neither the one nor the other: his eyes passed over them as over nothing. He saw only Dona Severina's arms—either because he was stealthily looking at them from under his eyelids, or because their image was impressed on his memory.

"Man alive, aren't you ever going to finish?" suddenly bellowed the lawyer.

There was nothing for it. Ignacio drank the last drop, now cold, and withdrew as usual to his bedroom in the back part of the house. As he entered the room, he made a gesture of anger and despair, and then went to one of the two windows that looked on the sea. Five minutes later, the sight of the water close by and the mountains in the distance brought back the vague, restless feeling of confusion that both tortured and comforted him—something the plant must feel when it puts forth its first bud. He felt a desire to leave, and to stay. He had been there five weeks now, and his life was always the same thing: go out with Borges in the morning, haunt the courts, the record offices—running errands, taking documents to the notary, to process servers, to court stenographers, to justices. In the afternoon he came back to the house, had dinner, and retired to his room till suppertime, had supper, and went to bed. Borges did not permit him intimacy with his family, which consisted only of Dona Severina; Ignacio did not see her more than three times a day, at meals. Five weeks of solitude, of distasteful work, far from his mother and his sisters; five weeks of silence, for he only spoke, now and then, to somebody in the street—at home, never a word.

"Just wait! I'll run away from here and never come back."

But he stayed—caught, and held fast, by the arms of Dona Severina. He had never seen such pretty arms, with such a fresh bloom on them. His upbringing kept him from looking straight at them all at once. In the beginning, he even averted his eyes, ashamed and troubled. Little by little he came to look straight at them, seeing they had no other sleeves but his own eyes. Thus he made their acquaintance, looked long at them, began to love them. At the end of three weeks they were, spiritually speaking, his shelter tents. He bore all the drudgery out there in the world of men, all the loneliness of solitude and silence, all the coarse abuse from his employer: his only pay—a glimpse, three times daily, of that superb pair of arms.

On this day, as night came on and Ignacio lay stretched out in his hammock (he had no other bed), Dona Severina, in the living room at the front of the house, went over the episode at dinner point by point, and, for the first time, she suspected something. She as quickly rejected the idea—a child! But there are ideas of the same race as stubborn flies: no matter how we brush them away, they fly back and light in the same place. Child? He was fifteen, and she had noticed that between the young man's nose and mouth there was the beginning of a trace of fuzz. What wonder if he had fallen in love? And wasn't she pretty? This idea was not rejected, but, rather, fondled and kissed. She recalled his actions, his absent-mindedness, his fits of woolgathering, then one thing, then another; they were all signs . . . and she concluded "yes," he had.

"What's the matter with you?" asked the lawyer after several minutes of silence, as he sprawled on the sofa.

"Me? Nothing."

"Nothing? It looks to me as if you're all asleep around here! Just wait! I know of a good medicine to wake up sleepyheads . . ."

And he went on in the same angry tone, shooting off threats right and left, but actually incapable of carrying them out, because he was coarse and rough, but not really mean. Dona Severina interrupted him to say he was mistaken. She was not asleep, but thinking of her godchild's mother, Dona Fortunata. They had not paid her a visit since Christmas. Why not go over there one of these evenings? Borges retorted that he was too tired, that he worked like a slave and was not about to go making social calls and listen to a lot of silly chitchat. Then he lambasted the godchild's mother and the godchild's father and the godchild himself—not yet out of primary school, a great boy of ten! He, Borges, at ten years of age, could read and write and do sums, not very well perhaps but he could do them. Ten years old! A fine end he'd come to:—a lazy bum in a soldier suit! It would take a taste of army life to straighten him out.

Dona Severina tried to calm him by making excuses: the mother's poverty, the father's run of hard luck; and she gave him some timid caresses, half afraid they might irritate him still further.

Night had now come in earnest: she heard the *tlic* of the street lamp as the gas was lit and saw its great reflection flash in the windows of the house opposite. Borges, wearied from the day, for he really was a worker of the first order, began to close his eyes and fall asleep, leaving her alone in the room, in the darkness, alone with herself and the discovery she had made.

Everything seemed to tell the lady it was true. But this truth, once the first shock of amazement was past, brought her a moral complication that she recognized only by its effects, for she could not make out what it was. She no longer understood her own feelings, and could not see her way. She even thought of telling the lawyer everything, and let him order the brat out of the house. But what was everything? Here she pulled up short. Actually there was nothing more than surmise, coincidence, and perhaps illusion. No, no, it was not illusion. She began to piece together vague clues, looks and gestures, the boy's bashfulness, his fits of absent-mindedness;

and she rejected the idea of being mistaken. In a few minutes (O whimsical Nature!), reflecting that it would be wrong to accuse him without grounds, she admitted she might have deceived herself—admitted it for the sole purpose of having an excuse to observe him more closely and determine the actual state of affairs.

That very night, from under her eyelids, Dona Severina examined Ignacio's looks and gestures. She did not succeed in finding out anything, because tea time was short and the young man did not take his eyes off his cup. The next day her observation was more successful, and, on the following days, supremely so. She found that the answer was "yes": she was loved and idolized—an adolescent, virgin love, held back by social chains and by a feeling of inferiority that kept him from recognizing himself for what he was. Dona Severina saw at once she had no cause to fear any disrespect, and she concluded that the best thing was to say nothing to the lawyer: she would spare him an unpleasantness, and the poor child another. By now she had convinced herself he was a child, and she proposed to treat him as coolly as she had heretofore, perhaps with greater coolness. That is what she did. Ignacio could sense that her eyes avoided him, or that she spoke roughly to him, almost as roughly as Borges. Other times, it was true, her voice sounded gentle and even sweet, sweet and tender, like the expression of her eyes—though her eyes were generally turned from him and wandered so constantly elsewhere it was only for repose that they came to light upon his head, and that for a brief instant.

"I'll go away," he would say to himself out in the street, as he had the first few days.

He came back to the house, and he did not go away. Dona Severina's arms enclosed a parenthesis in the middle of the long, tedious sentence of the life he led. And this added clause contained a profound, original idea specially invented by God and the angels for him alone. He stayed on, and his life went on as before. Finally, however, he had to leave, never to return. Here is how and why.

For several days, Dona Severina had treated him with kindness. Her voice, it seemed, had lost its rough tone; it was more than gentle, it was full of tenderness and concern. One day she would warn him not to get in a draft, another not to drink cold water after hot coffee, bits of advice, reminders, attentions of a loving woman and a mother—that flung his soul into still greater disquiet and confusion. He grew so bold one day as to laugh at table, something he had never done. And the lawyer did not rebuke him on this occasion, for it was he who was telling a funny story and no one rebukes a person who is applauding one. For the first time, Dona Severina noticed that the boy's mouth, charming in repose, was no less so when he laughed.

The turmoil in Ignacio's heart kept growing. He tried to calm it, and could not; he did not understand himself. He was not at peace anywhere. He would wake up at night, thinking of Dona Severina. In the street, he would take the wrong turn, go to the wrong address—much oftener even than before. And he never saw a woman, near or far, who did not bring her to mind. When he crossed the threshold on coming home from work, he always felt a kind of wild joy, at times over-powering, when he looked up and saw her peering through the wooden grillwork of the gate at the top of the stairs, as if she had run to see who it was.

One Sunday—he never forgot that Sunday—he was alone in his room, at the window, looking toward the sea, which spoke to him in the same obscure tongue as Dona Severina. He amused himself by watching the sea gulls, as they made great circles in the air or soared above the water, or merely flapped their wings. The day was fair beyond description. It was not only a Christian sabbath, it was an immense sabbath of the universe.

Ignacio passed all his Sundays there, in his room, either at the window or re-reading one of the three little books he had brought home from the city, tales of olden days, bought for a copper or two under the bridge to the Largo do Paço. It was two o'clock in the afternoon. He was tired; he had slept badly the night before after all the running about of the day. He stretched out in his hammock, took up one of the little books, *Princess Magalona*, and began to read.

He could never understand why all the heroines of these old stories had the same face and figure as Dona Severina; but, the fact of the matter is, they did. At the end of half an hour he let the book drop and fixed his eyes on the wall, out of which, five minutes later, he saw the lady of his dreams emerge. The natural thing would have been to start in astonishment; but he was not astonished. Although his eyes were tight shut, he saw her tear herself loose from the wall, smile, and walk toward the hammock. It was she all right, and those were her very own arms.

And yet, it is certain that Dona Severina could not have come out of the wall, even if there had been a door in it, or a hole; she could not have, for the simple reason that she was at that very moment in the front room, listening to the lawyer's footsteps as he went down the stairs. When she heard him reach the bottom, she went to the window, to see him go out the front door, and she did not leave the window until he disappeared in the distance, down the Rua das Mangueiras. Then she went back and sat down on the sofa. She seemed strangely restless, almost crazy. She got up and went to the sideboard, where she picked up the water pitcher and set it down in the same place. Then she walked to the door, stopped, and came back, as it seemed, without design. She sat down again, for five or ten minutes. Suddenly it occurred to her that Ignacio had eaten little at breakfast and had seemed dejected, and she asked herself if he might not be ill, perhaps very ill.

She left the living room, went straight down the hall to the boy's bedroom; the door was wide open. Dona Severina stood still, looked in and saw him asleep in the hammock, one arm thrown over the side, and the little book fallen on the floor. His head was slightly turned toward the door so that she could see the closed eyes, the rebellious hair in disorder, and a great smiling look of happiness on his face.

Dona Severina felt her heart pound, and stepped back. She had dreamt of him during the night; perhaps he was dreaming of her. Since early dawn the boy's like-ness had been before her eyes like a temptation of the devil. She drew back another step, then returned, stared at him two, three, five or more minutes. Sleep seemed to accentuate Ignacio's adolescence with an expression that was almost feminine— the look of a little boy.

"A child!" she said to herself in that wordless language we all know. And this idea slowed her racing blood and partly cleared away the clouds from her under-standing.

"A child!"

She slowly looked her fill—at the head turned toward her, the arm fallen from the hammock. At the same time that she found him childlike, she also found him handsome, much more handsome than when awake, and one of these ideas corrected and modified the other. Suddenly she shivered and drew back in fear: she had heard a noise close by, in the ironing closet. She went to see. A cat had knocked a bowl on the floor. She stole back softly to look in at Ignacio again, and saw that he lay in a deep sleep. He slept like a log, the child! The noise that had so startled her had not even made him change his position. She stood there, and watched him sleep—sleep, perchance dream!

Oh, that we cannot see the dreams of one another! Dona Severina would have seen herself in the young man's imagination, standing beside the hammock, smiling and quite still. She would have seen herself lean down and take his two hands, raise them to her breast and enfold them in her arms—her marvelous arms. Ignacio, busily making love to them, still heard the words of his mistress, words that were beautiful, warm, and above all strange—at least they belonged to some language he did not recognize, though he understood it well enough. Two, three, and four times the figure vanished to return again, coming from the sea, or somewhere else, accompanied by sea gulls, or swinging through the hall with all the lusty grace that was hers. Each time, she leaned down and taking his hands again folded them to her breast. Then, finally, she leaned down further and further . . . until her eager mouth left a kiss on his.

Here dream coincided with reality. And the same mouths were joined in imagination and outside of it. The difference was that the vision did not leave him, but the real person had no sooner completed the gesture than she shrank back clear to the door, vexed and fearful. She passed quickly down the hall, stunned by what she had done, looking neither right nor left. In the living room, she strained her ears, went back into the hall to see if she could hear any sound that would tell her he was awake, and it was only after some time that her fear began to pass away. Really, the child slept like a log! Nothing made him open his eyes, neither crashing pottery nor real, true kisses.

But, if her fear was passing away, her vexation remained and increased. Dona Severina could not believe she had done this thing. She seemed to have swathed her desires in the idea that he was a beloved child who lay there unconscious and blameless; and, half mother, half lover she had leaned down and kissed him. Be that as it may, she was confused, disgusted, out of sorts, annoyed with herself and with him. The fear that he might be pretending to sleep began to peep forth in her mind, and made her shudder.

But the truth is, he slept on and on, and only woke up in time for dinner. He sat down to table in a gay mood. Although he found Dona Severina taciturn and severe, and the lawyer as coarse and rude as on other days, neither the rudeness of the one nor the severity of the other could dissipate the agreeable vision that was still with him, nor dull the sensation of the kiss. He did not notice that Dona Severina was wearing a shawl that covered her arms. He noticed it later, on Monday, and on Tuesday, and as late as Saturday, which was the day Borges sent word to his father that he could no longer remain with him. He did not do it in anger; he treated him comparatively well, and even said to him when he left, "If you should need me for anything, look me up."

"Yes, senhor. And Senhora Dona Severina . . ."

"She's there in her room with a bad headache. Come tomorrow or the day after to say goodbye to her."

Ignacio left without understanding at all. He did not understand the dismissal, or Dona Severina's complete change toward him, or the shawl, or anything. They had been on such good terms! She had treated him so kindly! How did it happen that suddenly . . . He thought about it for a long time and finally decided that some indiscreet glance on his part, some thoughtless act, had offended her. It must have been; and this was the reason for the frozen expression, the shawl over her lovely arms . . . No matter! He would take with him the fragrance of the dream.

And down the years, in other love adventures, more real and lasting, he never again found the thrill of that Sunday on the Rua da Lapa, when he was only fifteen. To this day he often exclaims, without knowing he is mistaken, "And it was a dream! Just a dream!"

DONA PAULA

—◦❧ ❦◦—

She couldn't possibly have arrived at a more opportune time. Dona Paula entered the parlor precisely as her niece was drying her tear-swollen eyes. She was surprised, as was her niece Venancinha, who knew that her aunt rarely descended from the Tijuca district, where she lived. It was May 1882, and Venancinha hadn't seen her aunt since Christmas. Dona Paula had come down the previous day to spend the night with her sister on Lavradio Street. Today, she had dressed and run off to visit her niece right after lunch. A slave who saw her wanted to announce her arrival, but Dona Paula told her not to—to avoid rustling her skirts, she tiptoed ever so slowly to the parlor door, opened it, and went in.

"What's this all about?" she exclaimed.

Flinging herself into Dona Paula's arms, Venancinha burst into tears. Her aunt kissed, embraced, and comforted her and insisted that she tell her what the matter was. Was she sick, or . . .

"I wish to God I were sick! Death would be better!" interrupted the girl.

"Don't talk nonsense! What happened? Come now, tell me."

Venancinha dried her eyes and tried to talk. After five or six words, the tears flowed again, in such abundance and with such force that Dona Paula thought she'd best wait until they subsided. Meanwhile, she took off her black lace mantelet and her gloves. She was a striking, elegant woman with large attractive eyes that must have been irresistible when she was younger. While her niece wept, she moved quietly to close the parlor door, then returned to the settee. After a few minutes, Venancinha stopped crying and told her aunt what had happened.

It was nothing less than a quarrel with her husband, so violent they had even spoken of separating. Jealousy had caused it. For some time her husband had been suspicious of a certain gentleman, but the evening before, after seeing his wife dance with the man twice and talk to him for a few minutes, he concluded they were in love. When they returned home he was sullen. The next morning after breakfast, he exploded and said cruel harsh things, which she answered in kind.

"Where's your husband now?" inquired her aunt.

"He's gone. I think he went to the office."

Dona Paula asked her if his office were still in the same building and told her not to worry; it wasn't a serious matter. Within two hours everything would be settled. She quickly put on her gloves.

"Are you going there, Auntie?"

"Going there? Of course I'm going! Your husband's a good man—it was just a lover's quarrel. Number 104? I'm on my way, and don't let the slaves see you looking like this!"

Dona Paula spoke with volubility, self-assurance, and kindness. She put on her gloves, and Venancinha, as she helped her aunt with her mantelet, swore she adored Conrad despite their quarrel. Conrad, her husband, had been practicing law since 1874. As Dona Paula left, her niece showered her with kisses of gratitude. In all truth, she couldn't possibly have arrived at a more opportune time. On her way to see Conrad, Dona Paula reflected upon the incident with curiosity, if not suspicion, a little uneasy as to what the whole truth of the matter might be. In any case, she was determined to restore domestic peace.

When she reached her nephew's office, he was not yet in, but shortly thereafter he arrived. After his initial surprise at seeing her there, he guessed the object of her visit. He confessed that he had overreacted with his wife and said he was not accusing her of loose morals or perverse intentions. But she was behaving like a scatterbrain: she was too friendly with other men and was given to coquettish glances and honeyed words in their presence. And indiscretion was one of the gate-ways to misconduct. Furthermore, he had no doubt that his wife and the man in question were in love with one another. Venancinha had only told her about the evening before—she had not mentioned four or five other incidents, one of which had occurred at the theater and had developed into a scandal of sorts. He wasn't about to accept the responsibility for his wife's reckless and indiscreet behavior. If she wanted to go around falling in love, she'd have to pay the price for it.

Dona Paula heard him out. Then it was her turn to speak. She agreed that her niece was flighty but attributed this to her youth. A pretty girl could not help attracting attention, and it was natural for Venancinha to be flattered by the ad-miring glances of other men. It was also understandable that her response to such flattery was interpreted as a sign of love, by other men as well as her husband—their infatuation and his jealousy were the cause of the quarrel. She, for her part, had just seen her niece crying in earnest. When she left, Venancinha was disconsolate and brokenhearted and had even talked of wanting to die because of what he had said to her. So if he really only attributed her actions to foolishness, why not pro-ceed with discretion and understanding? He should use counsel and common sense—he could help her avoid similar situations in the future and show her how even the appearance of friendship and good will toward other men could be mis-interpreted and harm her reputation.

The good lady spoke no less than twenty minutes, and she expressed herself so eloquently and diplomatically that her nephew felt his heart softening. He resisted, of course—two or three times, to avoid appearing overly lenient, he declared that everything between them was finished. In self-justification, he mentally evoked his arguments against a reconciliation. But Dona Paula looked down until his wave of indignation had passed and then looked up at him with her large, sagacious, im-ploring eyes.

Seeing that Conrad wasn't going to give in easily, Dona Paula proposed a com-promise: "Forgive her, and make your peace together, then I'll take her to Tijuca to spend a month or two with me. It will be a kind of temporary exile for her. Meanwhile, I'll take it upon myself to straighten her out. Agreed?"

Conrad accepted. As soon as Dona Paula had his word, she prepared to leave to tell her niece the encouraging news. Conrad accompanied her to the stairs, where they shook hands. Dona Paula didn't release his hand until she had repeated her recommendation that he proceed with tenderness and discretion. Then, as though it were an afterthought, she added: "And you're going to see that the man in ques-tion isn't worth even a minute of the time we've spent worrying over him."

"His name is Vasco Maria Portela."

Dona Paula turned pale. What Vasco Maria Portela? An elderly gentleman, a former diplomat who . . . no, he was retired, had been in Europe for a few years, and had just received the title of baron. It was his son, a worthless rascal who had returned to Rio from Europe a short time before. Dona Paula squeezed Conrad's hand and hurried downstairs. Confused and excited, she spent several minutes at the landing going through the motions of adjusting her mantelet. She stared at the floor, pondering the situation. Then she set out to meet her niece, carrying with her the proposal for a reconciliation with Conrad and the conditions under which it was to be achieved. Venancinha accepted everything.

Two days later, they went to Dona Paula's home in the Tijuca district. If Venancinha seemed to have lost some of her earlier enthusiasm for the trip, the loss was probably due to the idea of exile or to longing for what she had left behind. In any event, Vasco's name went up to Tijuca. If it wasn't in both heads, it was at least in Dona Paula's, where it was a kind of echo, a remote and pleasant sound, something that seemed to hark back to the time of the opera singer Stoltz and the Marquis of Paraná. Those distant echoes were just as fragile as youth itself, and where were those three eternities now? They were scattered among the distant ruins of the past thirty years. Dona Paula, having nothing else to look forward to, lived with those memories of the past.

The elder Vasco had also been young once and had loved. Unbeknown to their marriage partners, he and Dona Paula had filled their cups to the brim and for several years had slaked their thirst for one another. Since the passing winds are unable to record men's speeches, there is no way to reveal here what was said at the time about their adventure, which eventually came to an end. It had been a series of sweet and bitter hours mixed with pleasures and tears, ecstasy and anger, and various other intoxicants the lady had used when she filled her loving cup to overflowing. She drained the cup dry and never touched it again. Satiety was followed by abstinence, and public opinion was formed by this final phase. Her husband died and the years flowed by. Dona Paula was now an austere and pious lady, prestigious and respected by all.

Dona Paula's thought had been carried to the past by her niece. The two similar situations, mingled with the same name and blood, awakened some old memories. They were going to be living together in Tijuca for a few weeks, and Venancinha would be following her aunt's instructions. Dona Paula would attempt to challenge her own memory—to what extent could she reexperience those sensations from the past?

"Aren't we going to the city at all? Not even for a little visit?" asked Venancinha the next morning, laughing.

"Are you bored already?"

"No, I'd never be bored here, I was just asking if . . ."

Dona Paula, also laughing, shook her finger negatively. Then she asked her niece if she missed the city. Venancinha said no and gave more weight to her answer by allowing the corners of her mouth to droop, in order to reflect her disdain or indifference. It was as though she had written a letter saying more than she had intended to say. Avoiding the reckless abandon of someone rushing off to save his father from the hangman's noose, Dona Paula had the good habit of reading slowly. She fixed her attention on the spaces between the letters and the lines, took in everything, and found her niece's response excessive.

"They're in love with one another," she thought.

This discovery awakened her dormant memories of the past. Dona Paula struggled to shake off those persistent memories, but they returned like a group of chorus girls: some slowly and suggestively, others with quick and sprightly movements— they sang, laughed, and raised the very devil. Dona Paula's mind returned to the dances of yesteryear. She remembered the eternal waltzes that made everyone stare at her in wonder and boasted to her niece about the mazurkas, the most graceful dance in the world, the theater, card games, and, obliquely, the kisses. But everything—and this was the curious thing about her recollections—everything was described with the cold and faded ink of an old chronicle, an empty skeleton of history that lacked a living soul. Everything occurred in her head. Dona Paula tried synchronizing her heart and her head to see if she could feel something beyond a mere mental reproduction of her past, but despite all efforts to evoke the old feelings, none returned. Time had swallowed them.

If she could only peek into her niece's heart, she might be able to see her own image reflected there, and then . . . After Dona Paula was possessed by this idea, it became harder for her to concentrate on her niece's rehabilitation, even though she was sincerely preoccupied with her welfare and wanted to see her reunited with Conrad. In order to assure themselves of company in purgatory, habitual sinners may secretly desire to see others committing sins too, but sinning wasn't the issue here. Dona Paula stressed Conrad's virtues and superiority and also told her niece that uncontrolled passions could destroy her marriage and, even more tragic, cause her husband to disown her.

Conrad confirmed the validity of Dona Paula's warnings when he paid his first visit nine days later: he was cold when he entered and when he left. Venancinha was terrified. She had hoped that their nine-day separation would soften her husband, and, really, it had. But in order to avoid the appearance of an easy capitulation, he masked his true feelings and held back his emotions. And this had a greater effect than anything else. Venancinha's terrible fear of losing her husband was the principal factor in her rehabilitation. Exile alone could not have accomplished so much.

Just two days after Conrad's visit, when both ladies had approached the villa gate to set out on their daily stroll, they saw a gentleman on horseback coming in their direction. Venancinha fixed her eyes on him, let out a little cry, and ran to hide behind the wall. Dona Paula understood and waited. She wanted to see the man close up. After two or three minutes he approached. Seated upright in his saddle, he was a handsome, proud-looking, elegant youth with fine polished boots. He looked just like the other Vasco—the same large deep-set eyes, the same tilt of the head, the same broad shoulders.

After Dona Paula had pried the first word out of her niece, Venancinha told her everything that very night. They had first seen one another at the horse races, right after his return from Europe. Two weeks later, she was introduced to him at a dance. He seemed so interesting and Parisian that she spoke to her husband about him the next morning. Conrad frowned in displeasure, and this reaction gave her an idea she had never before entertained. She began to see him with pleasure, and then she longed to see him. He spoke to her respectfully and told her nice things: that she was the loveliest and most elegant young woman in Rio, that in Paris he had recently heard some ladies from the Alvarenga family praising her fine qualities. He was witty when he criticized other people and expressed himself more sensitively than anyone she had ever met. He didn't talk about love, but he pursued her with his eyes—no matter how hard she tried to look away from him, she couldn't help noticing. She began to think about him, frequently and with interest, and her heart fluttered whenever they met. It was probably easy for him to detect in her face the impression he made.

Leaning forward, Dona Paula listened to Venancinha's story with her whole past concentrated in her eyes. With mouth agape, she seemed anxious to drink in her niece's words, as if they were a cordial. And she asked for more, telling Venancinha to omit nothing whatsoever. Dona Paula looked so youthful and her request was so gentle and full of potential forgiveness that she seemed like a confidante and friend, despite a few harsh words interspersed among the pleasant remarks through a sort of unconscious hypocrisy. It wasn't intentional, however: Dona Paula even deceived herself. She was like an invalid general who struggles to recover some of his old ardor by listening to the stories of another's campaigns.

"You can see your husband was right," she said. "You were foolish, very foolish."

Venancinha agreed with her aunt and swore it was completely finished.

"I'm afraid it isn't. Did you really come to love him?"

"Auntie . . ."

"You still love him!"

"I swear I don't love him any more, but I . . . yes, I confess I did. Forgive me, and please don't say anything to Conrad! I wish none of this had ever happened. Yes, I'll admit I was smitten at first . . . But what did you expect?"

"Did he reveal his feelings to you?"

"Yes, he did. It happened at the Lyric Theater one evening, as we were about to leave. He usually came by my theater box to accompany me to the carriage, and on our way out he uttered . . . three words."

Out of consideration, Dona Paula didn't ask for the gentleman's words, but she imagined the circumstances: the galleries, the couples leaving, the lights, the crowds, the sound of voices, and the scene she visualized allowed her to piece together some of the sensations her niece had experienced. With great interest and diplomacy, she asked her to describe her feelings in greater detail.

"I don't know exactly what I felt," replied Venancinha, her tongue gradually loosened by her growing emotion. "I don't remember the first five minutes. I think I maintained my dignity—in any event, I didn't answer him. I felt that everyone was staring at us, that they might have overheard him, and when people greeted me with a smile it seemed that they were mocking me. Somehow I managed to go down the stairs and without really knowing what I was doing, got into the carriage. I allowed my fingers to go limp when we shook hands good-bye. I can assure you that I wish I hadn't heard anything he said. When we were inside the carriage,

Conrad told me he was tired and leaned back against the far side of the seat. It was for the best, because I don't know what I would have said if we had talked on the way home. I leaned back too, but not for long—I wasn't able to sit still. I looked out the glass windows, and from time to time I could see only the glare of streetlamps, and then not even that. Instead I saw the theater galleries, the stairs, the crowds of people, and him next to me whispering those words, just three words, and I'm not able to say what I thought then—my ideas were jumbled and confused, and I felt a churning inside me."

"But after you were back home?"

"At home, as I undressed, I was at last able to reflect a little, but very little. I slept poorly and late. The next morning I was bewildered. I cannot say I was happy or sad. I remember I thought about him a lot, and to get him out of my mind, I promised myself I would reveal everything to Conrad, but the thoughts returned again. From time to time I shuddered, imagining I heard his voice. Then I remembered that when I gave him my hand my fingers were limp, and I felt—I don't know exactly how to say it—a kind of regret, a fear of having offended him. Then I wanted to see him again . . . Forgive me, Auntie, but you asked me to tell everything."

Dona Paula's answer was a tight squeeze of the hand and an understanding nod. Through these ingenuously narrated sensations, she had at last found something from her own past. Sometimes, in a dreamy trance of reminiscence, her eyelids were half-closed; at other times her eyes were sparkling with warmth and curiosity. She heard everything: day by day and encounter by encounter, including the details of the scene in the theater, which her niece had initially hidden from her. And the rest followed: the hours of anxiety, longing, fear, hope, depression, and dissimulation, all the deeply felt emotions of a young girl in this situation. To satisfy her insatiable curiosity, Dona Paula insisted on knowing every detail of her niece's story, which was neither a book nor even a chapter of adultery, but a prologue, interesting and violent.

Venancinha finished. Her aunt, in a state of rapture, said nothing. Then she came to, took her niece by the hand, and drew her closer. She didn't talk right away. First she stared intently at her niece's deep-set eyes, fresh mouth, and restless, palpitating youthfulness. She wasn't drawn entirely out of her trance until Venancinha once again begged her forgiveness. Dona Paula said everything with a mother's tenderness and austerity. She spoke so eloquently of chastity, public opinion, and loving one's husband that Venancinha wept, unable to contain herself.

Tea was served, but it wasn't really an appropriate time for tea. Venancinha retired immediately—as it was still quite light, she left the room with her eyes lowered so the servant wouldn't see her in such a state of emotion. Dona Paula remained seated at the table, in the presence of the servant. She spent about twenty minutes drinking her tea and munching on a biscuit. As soon as she was alone, she went to lean against the window which looked out from the back of the villa.

The wind blew gently and the leaves rustled with a whispering sound. Although they weren't the leaves of her youth, they nevertheless questioned her: "Paula, do you remember the leaves of yesteryear?" For that is the peculiar thing about leaves: the generations that pass on tell the newcomers what they saw, and that is why all leaves know and ask questions about everything. "Do you remember the leaves of yesteryear?"

She did remember, of course, but that sensation she had felt a short time before, which was scarcely a reverberation, had ceased. In vain she repeated her niece's words as she breathed in the pungent evening air, but instead of recapturing sensations from the past, she was only able to evoke the scattered lifeless reminiscences in her head. Her heart slowed down, and her blood ran at its normal speed again. When her niece was absent she felt nothing. Nonetheless, she stayed there, staring out at the night, which had nothing in common with the nights of Stoltz and the Marquis of Paraná. But she stared out anyway, and in the kitchen the slave women fought off their drowsiness by telling stories. Now and then they commented impatiently, "Seems like the old missus ain't never going to bed tonight!"

FATHER VERSUS MOTHER

—◦֍ ֍◦—

Slavery brought with it its own trades and tools, as happens no doubt with any social institution. If I mention certain tools, it is only because they are linked to a certain trade. One of them was the iron collar, another the leg iron. There was also the mask of tin plate.

The mask cured slaves of the vice of drunkenness by sealing up their mouths. It had three holes, two to see through, one for breathing, and it was fastened behind the head with a lock and chain. Along with the vice of drinking they lost the temptation to steal, because, usually, it was with pennies stolen from their master that they killed their thirst: here were two sins wiped out at once, and sobriety and honesty assured. It was grotesque, this mask! But a humane social order is not always achieved without the grotesque, and sometimes not without the cruel. The tinsmiths had them hung up for sale at the doors of their shops. But let us not concern ourselves with masks.

The iron collar was used for runaway slaves. Imagine a thick dog collar made of iron with a projecting iron shaft, on the right or left, clear to the top of the head. It too was locked on with a key. It was heavy probably, but it was less a punishment than an identification. A runaway slave wearing such a collar, no matter where he went, showed that he was a hardened offender, and was easily caught.

A half-century ago, slaves ran away frequently. There were many slaves, and not all of them liked slavery. It happened sometimes that they were beaten, and not all of them liked being beaten. A great part of them were only scolded: there would be someone in the household who acted as their sponsor, and the owner himself was not always mean; besides, the feeling of ownership moderated his actions, because money hurts too. Running away continued nevertheless. There were instances, though they may have been rare, in which the contraband slave, just bought at the smugglers' market in Vallongo, would take off at a run without even knowing the streets of the city. The cleverer ones followed along peaceably to the house, where they asked the master to set a price on their daily service, and went out and earned it peddling in the streets.

A man whose slave ran away would give a small sum to anyone bringing him back. He would put notices in the papers, with a description of the runaway, his name, clothes, physical defect, if he had one, the neighborhood where he had been, and the amount of the reward. When the amount was not given, a promise was: "will be generously rewarded," or "will receive a handsome reward." Many times, the notice had above it, or to one side, a vignette of a black figure, barefoot, running, with a pole over his shoulder and a bundle on the end of it. And it threatened to prosecute to the full measure of the law anyone who beat him.

Catching runaway slaves, you see, was one of the trades of the time. It may not have been a noble calling, but, as an instrument of the force by which law and property rights are maintained, it had that other nobility attaching to the vindication of private ownership. No one followed this trade out of a liking for it, or because he had been trained to it. Poverty, the need for a little extra cash, unfitness for other work, chance, and, occasionally, a natural taste for serving, though in a different way, supplied the incentive to a man who felt firm enough to reduce disorder and distress to a system.

Candido Neves—Candinho to his family—is the person involved in this story of a runaway. He yielded to poverty when he took up the trade of catching slaves. This man had a serious defect: he could not stick to a job or trade. He lacked stability; he called it "hard luck." He began by deciding to learn printing but he soon saw that it would take some time to become a good compositor, and, even so, most likely he would not earn enough. That is what he told himself. Commerce next attracted him, it was a fine career. With a little effort he got a job clerking in a haberdashery. The obligation, however, slavishly to wait on everyone and anyone offended his pride. At the end of five or six weeks he was, by his own volition, out of a job. Cashier in a registry office, messenger in a subdepartment of the Imperial Ministry, sales clerk, and other positions were left shortly after they had been obtained.

Then came the moment when he fell in love with Clara. He had nothing, except debts—though not so many of those either, because he lived with a cousin, a woodcarver by trade. After several attempts to obtain a job he decided to follow his cousin's trade, especially since the cousin had already given him a few lessons. It was a simple matter to obtain more. But, in his desire to learn quickly, he learned badly. He was not making delicate or complicated pieces, only clawed feet for sofas and simple raised decorations on chairs. He wanted something to work at when he married, and marriage was not far off, as it turned out.

He was thirty, Clara twenty-two. She was an orphan, lived with her Aunt Monica. The two women took in sewing for a living. Clara did not do so much sewing that she did not have time for a little flirting. But her admirers only wanted to kill time; they had no further thought. They would come by in the afternoons, ogle her and she them, till night made her go in to her sewing. She had noticed that none of them caused her any yearning or kindled any spark of passion in her. Perhaps she did not even know the name of many of them. Naturally she had marriage in mind. It was, as her aunt told her, fishing with a pole to see if the fish would bite. But the fish went by at some distance. If one stopped, it was only to circle the bait, eye it, smell it, leave it, and go on to other tempting hooks.

Love comes in an envelope with a name and address on it. When the young woman saw Candido Neves she felt that he could be her husband, her true, her only husband. The meeting occurred at a dance: it was—to recall the young man's former trade—the first page of that book, which was to leave the press badly printed and with a worse binding. The wedding took place eleven months later, and was the finest celebration the young couple's relatives had ever enjoyed. Some of Clara's friends, less out of friendship than from envy, tried to hold her back from the step she was taking. They did not deny the gentle manners of her betrothed, nor the love he bore her, nor even one or two virtues; they said he was too much given to fun and parties.

"All the better," answered the bride. "At least I'm not marrying a corpse."

"No, not a corpse! It's simply that . . ."

They did not say what. After the marriage, in the poor little house where the couple and the aunt had taken shelter, Aunt Monica did, one day, bring up the possibility of children. They wanted a child, just one, even if it should aggravate their poverty.

"If you two have a baby," the aunt said to her niece, "you'll die of hunger."

"Our Lady in heaven will feed us," retorted Clara.

Aunt Monica ought to have given the advice, or warning, when Candido came to ask for the girl's hand, but she too was fond of fun and parties, and the wedding was sure to be a big celebration—as it was!

All three of them were happy. The newlyweds laughed at everything. Even their names were the objects of puns: Clara (bright), Neves (snow), Candido (white). They did not produce food, but they produced laughter, and laughter is digested without effort. She sewed more now; he worked at odd jobs, at one thing and another, but had nothing certain.

Even so, they did not give up the hope of a child. But the child, not knowing of this specific wish, allowed itself to remain hidden in eternity. One day, however, it made itself known. Male or female, it was the blessed fruit that would bring the couple their longed-for fortune. Aunt Monica was dismayed. Candido and Clara laughed at her fears.

"God will help us, auntie," insisted the mother-to-be.

The word ran through the neighborhood. There was nothing more to do but wait for the dawn of the great day. The wife was now working with a will, and it was necessary to do so, seeing that besides sewing for others she had to make clothes for the baby, out of the scraps. Constantly thinking of it, she came to live with it, as she measured its diapers, its little shirts. The scraps, and the pay, were meager, the times between long. Aunt Monica helped, you may be certain, though not without grumbling.

"It's a sad life you'll have," she sighed.

"But aren't other children born?" asked Clara.

"They are, and they are always certain of something to eat, even if it is very little . . ."

"Certain of something . . ."

"Certain . . . a job, a trade, but what does the father of this unhappy child waste his time at?"

As soon as Candido Neves learned of the aunt's remark, he went straight to her. He was not rude to her, but still much less gentle than usual. He asked if there had ever been a day when she had not eaten.

"You have never fasted, senhora, except during Holy Week, and then it was because you did not choose to dine at my table. We have never gone without our codfish . . ."

"I know, but we are three."

"We shall be four."

"It's not the same thing."

"What would you have me do, more than I am doing?"

"Something more certain. Look at the carpenter on the corner, the fellow in the haberdashery, the printer who got married Saturday, all of them have a job that's certain . . . Don't be angry! I don't say you are a loafer, but the occupation you have chosen . . . it's not steady. You go for weeks without making a cent.

"Yes, but then there comes a night that makes up for everything, and more. God will not forsake me, and runaway slaves know I'm not to be trifled with. Almost none of them put up a fight, many give themselves up at once." He prided himself on this, and talked of hope as if it were actual capital in the bank. In a few minutes he was laughing, and he had the aunt laughing too. She was of a naturally happy disposition, and foresaw a party in the baptism.

Candido Neves had abandoned the trade of woodcarver, as he had given up many other vocations, better and worse. Catching runaway slaves held a novel charm for him. It did not oblige him to remain seated for long hours together. All it required was strength, a quick eye, patience, daring, and a piece of rope. He would read the notices, copy them out, put them in his pocket, and sally forth to the search. He had a good memory. With the physical appearance and the habits of a slave firmly in mind, he lost little time in finding him, seizing him, binding him, and taking him to his owner. Strength was the big thing, agility too. More than once, as he stood on a street corner, talking of other matters, he would see a slave go by, like other slaves, and would know at once that he was running away, who he was, his name, owner, the latter's address and the amount of the reward: he would interrupt his conversation and go after the criminal. He would not grab him immediately, but would wait for the right place and moment, then with one leap the reward was in his hands. He did not always come out of it without loss of blood, the slave's nails and teeth went into action, but generally he took them without a scratch.

And then, the profits began to fall off. Runaway slaves no longer came and thrust themselves into the hands of Candido Neves. There were new, skillful hands. As the business grew, more than one unemployed fellow upped and got himself a rope, went to the newspaper offices, copied down the advertisements, and joined the hunt. He had more than one competitor right in his own neighborhood. That is to say, Candido Neves's debts began to mount, and there were none of those prompt, or almost prompt, repayments as formerly. Life became hard and painful, food was scarce and poor, they did not eat regularly. The landlord sent for the back rent.

Clara scarcely had time to mend her husband's clothing, so great was the necessity to sew for money. Aunt Monica helped her niece of course. When Neves came home in the afternoon they would see by his face that he had not earned a penny. He would have dinner and go out again in search of some runaway. It even happened, though not often, that he made a mistake and grabbed a faithful slave who was going about his master's business: such was the blindness of necessity. On a certain occasion, he seized a Negro who was free; he melted into a thousand apologies, but did not escape a pommeling at the hands of the man's relatives.

"That's all you needed!" exclaimed Aunt Monica when she saw him come in the door. And after she had heard about his mistake and its consequences, she added, "Give it up, Candinho. Find some other way of earning a living, some other job."

As a matter of fact, Candido would have liked to have done something else. Not for the reason suggested by Aunt Monica, but for the simple pleasure of changing his trade. It would be a way of changing his skin, or his personality. The trouble was he did not know of a business he could learn fast.

Nature continued on her way, the fetus grew, became a burden to its mother before it was born. It was the eighth month, month of trouble and privation, less so, however, than the ninth; the narration of which I will also dispense with. It is better to tell only the outcome: it could not have been more bitter.

"No, Aunt Monica!" shouted Candinho, refusing a piece of advice, which it is painful for me to write—how much more painful for the father to hear! "Never! I will never do it!"

It was in the final week of that last, terrible month that Aunt Monica advised the couple to carry the child that was soon to be born to the Wheel of abandoned babies.* There could not have been a word harder for two young parents to hear, when they were waiting on tiptoe for their child, to kiss it, watch over it, see it laugh, grow, grow fat, skip about . . . Abandon? What did she mean abandon? Candinho stared at her, and ended by bringing his fist down on the dining table. The table, which was old, and weak in the joints, almost collapsed. Clara interposed.

"Auntie doesn't mean any harm, Candinho."

"Harm?" retorted Aunt Monica. "Harm or good, no matter what I mean, I say it's the best thing you can do. You owe everybody. The meat and beans are giving out. If some money isn't coming in, how can a family grow? And besides, there's time. Later, when you have a more secure livelihood, sir, the children that are born will be received with the same love as this one, or with greater love. This one will be well brought up, will not want for anything. After all, the Wheel isn't a barren coast, is it, or a refuse dump? No one gets killed there, no one dies there without good reason, while here it is certain to die, living on next to nothing. After all . . ."

Aunt Monica finished the sentence with a shrug of her shoulders, turned, and went into her bedroom. She had hinted at this solution before, but this was the first time she had done it with such frankness and spirit—such cruelty, if you like. Clara stretched out her hand to her husband, as if to brace his courage. Candinho made a wry face and, under his breath, called the aunt "crazy."

The tenderness of the young couple was interrupted by someone knocking at the street door.

"Who is it?" called the husband.

"It's I."

It was the landlord, who was a creditor for three months' rent. He had come in person to threaten his tenant. The latter asked him to come in.

"There's no need . . ."

"Please!"

The creditor came in but refused to sit down. He glanced around at the furniture to see what it would bring. He concluded, very little. He said he had come for the back rent, he did not expect more; but if it was not paid within five days he would put him out in the street. He had not worked hard just for the pleasure of keeping others in luxury. To look at him no one would say he was a property owner, but his words made up for what was lacking in his appearance, and poor Candido Neves preferred to keep still rather than make any reply. He inclined his head in a gesture at once of promise and of supplication. The landlord did not give an inch.

---

* Turn box in the wall of a foundling hospital in which an infant was placed.

"Five days, or out you go," he repeated, putting his hand on the latch, and he left.

Candinho left by another door. In such crises he never reached the point of despair. He counted on a loan. He did not know how he would get it, or from whom, but he counted on it. He also went and checked the notices of runaway slaves. There were a number of them, some old, ones he had already looked for without success. He spent several hours to no purpose, and went back home. At the end of four days, he still had not been able to lay his hands on the cash. He tried to get influential backing, he went to people on good terms with the landlord, but all he got was a notice to move.

The situation was acute. They could not find a house. They did not count on anyone lending them one, they would be out in the street. They did not count on their aunt. Aunt Monica had the cleverness to obtain lodgings for the three of them at the home of a rich old lady who was willing to lend them the use of some rooms under her house, in back of the stable, on an inner court. Aunt Monica had the even greater cleverness to say nothing about it to the young couple, so that Candido Neves, in desperation over the crisis, would begin by abandoning his baby and would end by getting some sure, regular way of earning a living—would mend his ways, in short. She listened to Clara's complaints, without joining in, it is true, but without consoling her either. On the day they had to move she would astonish them with the news of the old lady's kindness, and they would have a better place to sleep than they had hoped.

That is what happened. Put out of their house, they went straight to the lodgings that had been lent them, and two days afterward the baby was born. The father's joy was tremendous, his wretchedness too. Aunt Monica insisted they place the baby on the Wheel.

"If you don't want to take it yourself, let me do it. I'll go to the Rua dos Barbonos."

Candido Neves begged her not to go, to wait, he would take it himself.

Please note, it was a boy, and both parents had wanted that sex. They had just nursed it, but, as it happened to be raining that night, the father said he would take it to the Wheel the following night.

He spent the rest of the evening going over his notes on runaway slaves. The rewards for the most part were in the form of vague promises. A few mentioned the exact amount—niggardly sums. One, however, came to a hundred milreis. It was for a mulatto woman. There was a description of her looks and clothing. Candido Neves had hunted for her without success, and had given up; he imagined some lover was hiding her. Now, though, the sight of the amount and the need for it stimulated him to one last, great effort.

He went out the next morning to look and make inquiries all along the Rua da Carioca and its square, along the Rua do Parto and the Rua da Ajuda, where she had last been seen according to the notice. He did not find her. Only a pharmacist, on the Rua da Ajuda, remembered selling an ounce of a certain drug, three days before, to a person who fitted the description. Candido Neves spoke as if he were the owner of the slave and courteously thanked the man for the information. He had no better luck with other runaways for whom the reward was uncertain or cheap.

He went home to the wretched quarters that had been lent them. Aunt Monica herself had prepared a meal for the young mother, and had the baby ready to be carried to the Wheel. The father, in spite of the agreement, could scarcely hide his grief at the spectacle. He refused to eat what Aunt Monica had kept for him. He said he was not hungry, and it was the truth. He thought of a thousand ways to save his son from the Wheel. None of them were worth anything. He could not forget the cave they were living in. He spoke to his wife, who proved to be resigned. Aunt Monica had painted for her what the baby's life would be with them: it would mean greater poverty, most likely the child would be doomed to die. Candido Neves had to keep his promise. He asked his wife to give their son the last milk it would drink at its mother's breast. This done, the baby fell asleep, the father picked it up and went out in the direction of the Rua dos Barbonos.

That he thought more than once of turning back with it is certain. It is no less certain that he hugged it to him, that he kissed it, that he covered its face to keep off the night air. As he turned into the Rua da Guarda Velha, he began to slacken his step.

"I will give it to them as late as possible," he murmured.

But, since the street did not stretch to infinity, or even for a long distance, he was bound to come to the end of it. It was then it occurred to him to go by way of one of the alleys that link that street to the Rua da Ajuda. When he reached the end of the alley and was going to turn to the right in the direction of the Largo da Ajuda, he saw the shadowy figure of a woman just opposite. It was the runaway mulatto. I will not describe Candinho's commotion because I could not do it justice. Let one adjective suffice, let us just say it was tremendous. Since the woman was going down the street, he, too, went down the street. A few steps away was the pharmacy where he had obtained the information I mentioned above. He went in, found the druggist, asked him if he would be so kind as to watch the baby for a minute: he would be back without fail.

"But . . ."

Candido Neves did not give him time to say anything, he dashed out, crossed the street to reach a place where he could grab the woman without raising an alarm. At the end of the street, when she was about to turn into the Rua de São José, he came closer. It was she, it was the runaway mulatto woman.

"Arminda!" he called; that was the name given in the advertisement.

She turned around, never suspecting anything. It was only when he took the rope out of his pocket and grabbed her arms that the poor slave girl understood and tried to get away. By then, it was impossible. With his powerful hands Candido Neves tied her wrists. He told her to keep on walking. She was going to scream, and even uttered one rather loud cry, when she suddenly realized no one would come to set her free, but quite the contrary. She begged him then to let her go, for the love of God.

"I'm pregnant, dear master!" she cried. "If your honor has a child, I beg you, for love of him, to let me go. I will be your slave, I will serve you as long as you like. Le' me go dear young master! Le' me go!"

Keep going, Candido Neves repeated.

Le' me go!

"Don't keep me waiting! Get along!"

There was a struggle then, because the slave pulled back, moaning, dragging herself and her unborn child. Anyone passing by or standing in the door of a shop understood what it was and naturally did not come to the rescue. Arminda told Candinho that her master was very mean and probably would have her beaten with whips, and in her condition it would hurt much more. Yes, he would certainly order her to be whipped.

"You're the one to blame. Who told you to go having babies and then go running away?" he asked. He was in no joking mood, because of his baby that was back there in the pharmacy, waiting for him. It is certain too, he was not in the habit of making big speeches. He kept on pulling the slave woman down the Rua dos Ourives toward the Rua da Alfândega, where her master's house was. On the corner of that street, her struggling increased: she set her feet against the wall of a house and pulled back with great strength, but it was useless. All she gained was a few minutes' delay in reaching the house, already close at hand. Finally she reached it—dragged, desperate, gasping for breath. Even there she went down on her knees, but in vain. The master was at home and came running to the rescue at the noise and the shouting of his name.

"Here's your runaway," said Candido Neves.

"It's she all right."

"My dear master!"

"Come on, come in . . ."

Arminda fell in the entrance. Her master opened his billfold and took out the hundred-milreis reward. Candido Neves put away the two fifty-milreis notes while the master again told the slave to come in. There, on the ground where she had fallen, driven by fear and pain, and after some struggle, she miscarried. The fruit of some months came into this world without life, between the groans of its mother and the despairing gestures of its owner. Candido Neves saw the whole spectacle. He did not know what time it was. Whatever the hour, it was urgent that he run straight to the Rua da Ajuda, and that is what he did, without caring to know the outcome of the disaster.

When he reached the pharmacy he found the druggist alone and no sign of the baby. Candido Neves was ready to strangle him. Fortunately the man explained everything in time. The baby was inside with the druggist's family, and they both went back there. The father took his son with the same passionate fury with which he had grasped the runaway slave a short time before—a different kind of fury of course, a fury of love. He mumbled a few words of thanks and hastily left—not in the direction of the Wheel of abandoned babies, but in the direction of the borrowed lodgings—with his son, and the reward of a hundred milreis.

Aunt Monica forgave him for bringing back the child, after she heard the explanation, seeing that he brought a hundred milreis with him. It is true, she did have some hard things to say against the slave woman because of her miscarriage, as well as for running away.

Candido Neves showered his son with kisses and with tears, and blessed the slave for running away. He did not give a hang about the miscarriage.

"Not all babies have the luck to be born!" Those were the words his heart beat out to him.

WALLOW, SWINE!
—◦❧ ❦◦—

One evening, many years ago, I was strolling with a friend on the terrace of the Saint Peter of Alcantara Theater between the second and third acts of *The Sentence,* or *Trial by Jury.* I can no longer remember details of the play, only its title, but that's precisely what led us to a discussion of the jury system and a related event I've never been able to forget.

—◦❧ ❦◦—

I've always been opposed to trial by jury (said my friend). I'm not against the concept, which is liberal. My repugnance at the thought of condemning anybody is based on Scripture: "Do not judge, that you may not be judged." Nonetheless, I served on a jury on two occasions. At that time the district court was in the old Aljube district at the end of Goldsmith Street, near the Hill of the Immaculate Conception.

I had so many qualms that I voted to acquit all but two of the defendants. In fact, it never seemed to me that any of the crimes was proven beyond doubt, and a couple of the charges seemed particularly open to question. The first person I helped condemn was a clean-cut youth accused of forging a document for an insignificant sum. He didn't deny it, nor would it have been possible for him to do so. Although he admitted carrying out the deed, he said that another party, whose name he didn't mention, had suggested the possibility of forgery as a solution to his dire predicament. In a sad and subdued voice, he said that God, who could see into men's hearts, would give the real criminal his deserved punishment. His pale complexion and lifeless eyes inspired pity. The prosecuting attorney found a clear confession of guilt in the defendant's words and appearance. But the attorney for the defense showed that, quite the contrary, the accused's state of depression, distress, and paleness had been caused by the slandering of his innocent name.

I have seldom witnessed such a brilliant debate. Although the prosecutor's speech was short, it was eloquent, delivered in a tone that suggested indignation and hatred. The presentation of the defense revealed talent and was unusual in that it was the defending attorney's debut in court. The relatives, colleagues, and friends who had awaited the young man's first speech were not disappointed by his admirable defense, which would have saved his client if there had been any possibility of saving him. But the crime was as plain as the nose on your face. The lawyer died two years later, in 1865. What a loss for mankind! Believe me, I lament the death of a promising young man more than that of an older man . . . But let me get on with my story: the prosecutor gave his rebuttal and the defender rejoined. The presiding judge summarized the proceedings of the trial, which were then handed over to me, the foreman of the jury.

I won't reveal what took place in the jury room because it's secret. Besides, it's of no relevance to my story, which I confess would also be best left untold. I'll try to make it brief, as the third act is about to begin.

One of the jurors was a portly red-headed man who seemed more convinced of the defendant's guilt than the others. The proceedings were discussed and examined, and our decision was announced: eleven to one. Only the red-headed juror had been uneasy before the final decision was reached. After our vote had assured the accused's conviction, he was satisfied and said that an acquittal would have been a sign of weakness or worse. When the juror who had voted against conviction proffered a few words in defense of the youth, the redhead, whose name was Lopes, replied angrily: "What do you mean? It's a clear-cut case of guilt!"

"Let's not argue the point," I said, and the others agreed with me.

"I'm not arguing, I'm just defending my vote," continued Lopes. "The crime is more than proven. Like all defendants, he denies he's responsible, but the fact is, he committed a crime, and what a crime! And all for twenty dollars, a pittance. Let the swine grovel in his filth! Wallow, swine, wallow!"

"Wallow, swine!" I confess I was astonished. Not that I understood what he was getting at—quite the contrary, I neither understood him nor felt he was being fair, and that's why I was astonished. I finally went to the door of the jury room and knocked. When the door was opened for us, I approached the bench, handed our deliberations to the judge, and the accused was convicted. His lawyer appealed, but I don't know if the appeal was accepted or the conviction upheld. I lost sight of the matter.

When I left the courthouse, I walked along thinking about Lopes's statement and thought I grasped the meaning of it. "Wallow, swine!" was as though he had said the convicted man was the worst kind of thief—he was just a common thief. This interpretation occurred to me as I was coming down Goldsmith Street, just before I reached the corner of Saint Peter Street. I even retraced my steps for a distance to see if I could find Lopes and shake his hand, but there was no sign of him. The next day I came across our names while reading the newspaper, and his complete name was given. However, it didn't seem worth the trouble to look him up. "That's the book of life for you," my son used to say when he dabbled in verse. He also said that as the pages are turned, they are no sooner digested than neglected. Although I can't recall the verse form he used, that's how he rhymed it.

Some time thereafter, he told me in prose that I shouldn't refuse jury duty, to which I had just been summoned. I replied that I wouldn't serve and quoted Scripture to support my refusal. He insisted, saying it was a duty, a gratuitous service that no responsible citizen could deny his country. I went and sat in judgment three times.

The defendant in one of the trials was the teller at the Bank of Honest Labor, who'd been accused of embezzlement. I had heard of the case, which wasn't covered in much detail by the newspapers. I didn't actually care to read the news about crimes. When the accused appeared, he went to take his seat on the famous defendant's bench. He was a thin, red-haired man. I looked at him more carefully and shuddered, for he seemed to bear a striking resemblance to the juror who had served with me some years before. At that moment I was unable to positively identify him because he was so much thinner, but he looked like the same person, his hair and beard were the same color, and even his voice and name—Lopes—were the same.

"What is your name?" asked the presiding judge.

"Antônio do Carmo Ribeiro Lopes."

I had already forgotten the first three names, but the fourth was the same. Then other things began to confirm my suspicions, and it wasn't long before I recognized him as the very same Lopes who had been a juror several years before. As a matter of fact, I can now tell you that these circumstances prevented me from following the hearing attentively, and many things escaped me. When I came to my senses and was finally ready to listen carefully, the hearing was almost over. Lopes either firmly denied all the allegations or gave ambiguous answers that complicated the proceedings. He glanced about the courtroom without fear or anxiety, and I think I even detected a hint of a smile at the corners of his mouth.

Then the charges were read. He was accused of duplicity and the embezzlement of $110,000. I won't go into how the crime or the criminal was detected, because the orchestra is tuning up and we're running out of time. But I will say that I remember being most impressed by the inquiries, the documents, the teller's attempt to abscond, the testimony of the witnesses, and a lot of other incriminating evidence. While I was looking at Lopes, I heard people reading aloud or talking. He was listening too, but with his head held high, he looked at the court clerk, the judge, the ceiling, and the people—I among them—who were about to judge him. When he looked in my direction, he failed to recognize me. He stared at me and smiled, as he did with the others. His court manners were interpreted in different ways by the prosecution and the defense, just as the behavior of the defendant in the other trial had been interpreted years before. The prosecuting attorney saw a clear-cut case of duplicity in Lopes's manner, and the defending attorney tried to show that only innocence and the certainty of acquittal could explain his relaxed and confident demeanor.

While each lawyer presented his case, I began to consider the fateful turn of events which had placed Lopes in the same position as the young man he had once voted to convict, and I naturally repeated the scriptural precept: "Do not judge, that you may not be judged." I confess that on several occasions I felt a chill run down my spine. Not that I would have embezzled money, but what if I had killed somebody in a moment of rage or had been falsely accused of embezzlement? The same person who had once sat in judgment was now being judged by others.

As I thought about the scriptural precept, I was suddenly reminded of Lopes's "Wallow, swine!" You can't imagine how I was shaken by this thought. I recalled everything I just told you: the little speech Lopes gave in the jury room and those words, "Wallow, swine!" I saw he wasn't just a common thief—he really stole with class. It's the verb that defines the action so harshly: "Wallow, swine!" He meant that nobody should stoop so low unless the stakes are high. No one should wallow for a small sum.

Ideas and words were swimming through my head so fast that I was unable to catch the judge's summary of the proceedings. After he had finished and had read the charges, we retired to the jury room. I can tell you now that I was so certain of Lopes's embezzlement of the $110,000 that I voted for his conviction. Among the many documents was a letter written by him, which in my mind proved his guilt. But the other jurors didn't read with my eyes. Two jurors voted with me, nine denied Lopes's guilt, and he walked away a free man. The difference in the vote was so great that I began to have second thoughts. Perhaps I was mistaken. I still feel some pangs of conscience. Fortunately, if Lopes really didn't commit the crime, he wasn't convicted because of my vote. This thought offers some consolation, but the pangs still return. If you don't care to be judged by another, it's best to withhold your judgment. Wallow, swine! Let the swine roll, grovel, or wallow as they choose, but don't try to judge your fellow man. The music's stopped now. Let's return to our seats.

JOSÉ VERÍSSIMO
—∘❧(1857–1916)❦∘—

From Óbidos, Pará, the midway point of the Amazon River, José Veríssimo became the literary portraitist of his region, as well as a scholar of literature interested in its aesthetic and expressive qualities in contrast to the influential Social Darwinism of the day. He published native scenes (*Quadros paraenses*, 1878; *Viagem ao Sertão*, 1878) before his major collection of short stories, *Cenas da Vida Amazônica* (*Scenes of Amazonian Life*) was published in Lisbon in 1886. Veríssimo became a member of the Brazilian Academy of Letters in 1896 when he was director of the influential *Revista Brasileira*, third series, in Rio de Janeiro. His work as a literary critic is reflected in a series of studies of Brazilian literature (6 vols., 1901–1907), *Que é Literature* (1907), *Letras e Literatos* (1912–1914), and his classic history of Brazilian literature (1916), which showed sensitivity toward the works of Machado de Assis.

GOING AFTER RUBBER
—∘❧ ❦∘—

To go rubber gathering . . .
   A fatal phrase, which at certain seasons of the year runs from mouth to mouth in the wilderness.
   The man abandons the clearing, the wife abandons the hearth, the girl abandons her flowers.
   It is a fever.
   It is worse than the malaria.

—∘❧ ❦∘—

It is a country house.
   In the midst of a beautiful and leafy little grove.
   At its sides flowering orange trees, spreading in the atmosphere the agreeable fragrance of flowers like those used to crown brides, and fruit-bearing trees showing their delicious fruits.

In front, either on the ground or on a wooden platform, vases, baskets, pieces of meat-pots, remains of earthen pots are full of flowers.

Rose and camellia, pink and marigold, red and white columbines—beauty and perfume, sentiment and color.

A trellis of jasmine next to the bridal flowers.

Hummingbirds chirp in the trees; domestic fowls cackle on the ground.

Joy and life, health and abundance.

The light itauba boat is tied to the palm trunk bridge on the edge of the river.

Its japa bow is new, the sail has a light muruchy tint, and the boat is as flimsy as a fisherman's saraca.

On the rude bridge is piled the family's baggage.

Marupa trunks painted green, hampers of clothes, baskets of hammocks, willow baskets, the chief's uru, a little tin covered trunk, which is the girls' sewing chest.

Short swords, knives, axes, hooks, muskets, are the tools they carry.

Baskets of yellow manioc flour, jerked beef from Monte Alegre, good fish from the Lago Grande, fragrant tobacco from the Rio Presto, are the provisions.

They are going for rubber.

They are going for fortune.

The head of the family will be able to rebuild the house, the mother will be able to enjoy more leisure, the girls will have new clothes and ornaments, the children will have more playthings.

On returning they will go to enjoy the holidays in the city.

The father will have money to spend, the girls will be able to captivate the youths there by their graces and their rich adornments.

They are going for rubber.

They are going for fortune.

There are two men and three women.

Of the men one is the father, the other is his son.

The father, fifty years old, belongs to that amphibian class peculiar to Amazonia, he is husbandman and fisher.

He plants manioc as well as he fishes for the tucunare.

The son, a youth of twenty, robust and handsome, is the father's assistant and will be his successor, and like him amphibious.

Of the three women, one is the mother of the two girls and of the youth, and is the wife of the old man.

She is a woman of about forty, who still shows evidence of having been beautiful, Tapuya, fat.

The girls are two children.

Fourteen and fifteen years.

Flower buds who promise to be beautiful.

Lovable and clever.

Pure as the air they breathe when they put their beautiful brown faces out of the window in the morning.

And they are so gay!

If it were not for their flowers they would not look back.

The father promises them clothes and jewels when they return from the rubber gathering, and the father will not fail them.

They go for rubber.

They go for abundance and for riches.

—◦❧ ☙◦—

One day, the old man, dropping into his hammock on returning from fishing, was smoking his long pipe.

The wife, with her son, was preparing the manioc flour on the threshold.

The girls, seated in the hut, were making lace.

The burning July sun cast its rays over the earth.

All was silence and quiet.

Suddenly, the dogs, which were sleeping sluggishly on the ground, raised their heads and growled.

A canoe, an *igarité,* passed in the river in front of the house and put to shore.

The dogs continued to growl.

Someone cried from the bank:

"Hey there! . . ."

"With God's will, come in," answered the old man.

And the little girls, curious, dropped their lace and raised their heads to see who was coming.

—◦❧ ☙◦—

He was a young man.

White, blue eyes, whiskers.

He had one of those expressionless looks, one of those faces which express nothing, which neither attract nor repel.

Dangerous faces.

He wore pants of gray duck, a jacket of blue linen, a white shirt, without a tie, a Brago hat, and had a watch, with a gold chain, in the pocket of his pants.

He smoked a cigarette and played with a twig which he had in his hands.

He entered.

Whoever is accustomed to the Amazon valley would say immediately, as the old man said to himself:

"He is a trader."

A trader.

That is a thing, or a person, difficult to define.

He is a trader, and is not. He is something like a pirate. He travels by boat. At times he has a gentle voice; then his heart is evil. At other times, under the exterior of a dove, he hides the claws of sparrow-hawk. He is a nomad. Without having the courage of a Bedouin, he has the appearance of one.

The trader complimented the old man and his daughters.

His greetings returned, he seated himself in a hammock and began to talk to the old man.

They talked of many things.

The trader asked if he were going rubber gathering.

The old man answered that he was not.

"Why are you not going?" asked the trader.

The old man told his reasons.

He did not have provisions, it was time to harvest cocoa and to make flour, and other reasons which appeared good to him.

The trader facilitated everything.

He gave him provisions and money, big knives, goods, hatchets, everything.

And he proved to him that he was fool to let the rubber go for a miserable little cocoa harvest. Finally he deceived the old man.

"But I do not have any money to pay for your goods," said the old man, already persuaded, but still wishing to resist.

"You can have them on credit," promptly answered the trader. "This year rubber will be more plentiful than ever. You'll see, sir. Then you'll be grateful to me. And . . . I always have to be paid."

He uttered this last sentence in a low and harsh voice, looking at the two girls, who poor souls, blushed.

—◦❧ ❦◦—

And the trader left.

The man began preparing to go rubber gathering.

The trader had sold him goods for which he wanted payment in rubber.

He hastened the flour making, took care of the clothes himself, got ready the trunks, and washed the hammocks.

He spoke only of rubber, that is, of fortune.

The girls dreamed about clothes, the boy about another and better musket; all had already thought of what they needed, and of what they would buy on returning to the house.

Only smiles were seen on their lips; the preparation for departure was made with joy.

The day, so long desired, comes, everything is ready.

They are going out.

—◦❧ ❦◦—

Already the baggage is piled in the canoe. Already the food is cooked for the first day. Already the chickens which are to be taken along are put in the basket.

All is ready.

They embark.

What gay laughs from the girls!

What joy in the eyes of the youth!

What hope in the hearts of the parents!

The canoe is filled.

The mother is in the prow; the girls, seated in the first seat behind the prow, covering their heads with bright bordered white handkerchiefs, holding the ends in the corners of their mouths with their white teeth, ply two little oars, which are two toys.

The old man seats himself in the middle of the boat and lays hold of the oar with strong hands.

The son, leaning against the mast, awaits his father's order to raise the purple sail.

A little dog, at the extremity of the prow, raises his well-shapened head, looking longingly at the house they are going to leave.

That is to say that, among them, the dog alone is sad.

—◦❧ ❦◦—

"Let it go!" shouted the father.

At this command the sail was spread and opened to the wind.

The powerful arm of the old man put the oar in the water and drove the boat, which went like the arrow that this same arm was wont to send to seek the *jaraqui* in the bottom of the lake.

The wind was favorable.

The sail swelled, the oars struck the water with force, and the boat glided as lightly over the waters of the river as the wild duck which the alligator pursues.

The old man, smoking his long cigarette, smiled contentedly.

And no one looked at the house, which remained closed and silent, where in another day the petals of the flowers on the platform would wilt away from lacking the drop of water they were accustomed to receive from the attentive hands of their mistresses.

On turning a point, the house disappeared.

The wind blew stronger on the sail and the boat moved faster.

Joy shone in the eyes of all.

And the canoe ran.

—◦❧ ❦◦—

A good wind takes them.

They are going for rubber.

Returning from Rubber Gathering

—◦❧ ❦◦—

The end of the month of . . . came.

The tree whose sap feeds the valley of the Amazon is exhausted.

It is like the mother who does not have milk for her grown son.

The rubber tree raises high its branches in the breeze and listens no more to the entreaties of those who live by its pain.

It is in vain that its bark is opened, that the hatchet cuts it, that the clay vessel waits patiently for the drops, which do not come, of that milk which is life for many.

And the rubber-gatherer desperately repeats cut after cut, opens the bark more, and waits.

But it is in vain. From the unfeeling tree not another drop of the precious blood escapes.

And the disconsolate, sad and vexed rubber-gatherer decides to abandon rubber-gathering.

Then begin the preparations for leaving.

—◦❧ ❦◦—

After these days during which the sap leaves the rubber tree in gushes, during which abundance and joy ruled in the hut, during which the sounds of the guitar accompanied the voices of the singers and the airy steps of the nimble dance, come the days of work for return.

The trunks are filled, fish and manioc four are prepared, everything is ready, the canoe is made ready, and they leave.

And how sad is this leaving!

The canoe no longer has the same happy appearance that we saw on going after rubber.

The old man, seated at the rudder, does not have hope in his face, or that same confident smile on the lips that press the long tauari forehead. The pallor on his low forehead makes one guess that the fevers prevalent in rubber-gathering have passed over it.

And he fixes his eyes on the mast, from which hangs a torn purplish sail, beneath which no longer stands his manly son, who remains in the rubber district to pay fictitious debts by his labor.

Those two girls, so young and tender hearted, so beautiful and pure, whom we saw grasping the little oars, their gentle little heads covered with white handkerchiefs with red borders with the ends gathered in the corners of their gracious mouths, where played frank smiles in the time that they did not know pain, those two little girls are not there now.

Only one, beneath the japa canopy, with a new-born son in her arms and her head hanging on her breast, looking at him with eyes full of the tears and griefs of a disgraced mother, remains in the company of her parents.

The other one, seduced and ruined like her sister, wanders—a camp follower of love—from hut to hut among the brutal jests of ignoble men.

The old mother, thin and pale, still shivering with chills, covered with a torn and thread-bare quilt, her head reposing on a hammock folded up like a pillow, observes with sad eyes her unhappy daughter and her thin little son who sleeps in her arms the tranquil sleep of careless innocence.

And from time to time two tears roll down her sunken cheeks, burning with fever, and moisten a corner of the old quilt, tucked under her chin.

What of those so happy days of the early times of rubber gathering?

Where are those nights passed in the delirium of dancing to the magic sound of the guitar, rich with melodies?

What of those nights in which the champagne and the healing draught—in crystal cups—passed from the lustful hands of the traders to the violet lips of gay little Indian girls?

Where are those nights in which, after the intoxication of wine, came the intoxication of love?

Nights in which, between smiles and tears, embraces and kisses, caresses and curses, promises of marriage and oaths of love, was made one maiden less and one courtisan more.

Where are these days of laughter? Where are these nights of love?

Oh! Curses on both of them!

One day the trader came.

He came joyfully, gayly, contentedly.

Well dressed, with his gold watch chain, full of ribbons, cashmere pants, linen jacket, blue tie, hat pulled down, a noisy laugh on his lips, a twisted mustache, a cigar in the corner of his mouth, a flower in the lapel of his jacket; clean, adorned, radiant . . .

He entered the hut.

He greeted the father pleasantly, spoke a trifle to the mother, pressed the hand of the boy, patted the girls lightly on the face and sat down.

"How goes our business?" he asked the old man.

"Badly. I came late. Rubber is hard to obtain."

Thus began the conservation.

In a little while the trader saw that his victim could not pay half of what he owed. But this did not cause the smile to disappear from his lips.

He said: "Then you have not made anything? Not even the worst grade of rubber?"

The old woman interrupted him: "E'carauara paresque," which translated means: "I believe that it is sorcery."

The trader scowled, but soon changed and smiled at the girls.

Then he placed his cigarette in his mouth and, holding it there, puffed several times without removing it—thinking. Finally he removed his cigarette and his hand, let a roll of smoke come out of his mouth and nostrils, and smiling to himself.

"Now, that's nothing. I lose with you, I gain with others. There is compensation. Look, to prove to you that I am not mad, I invite you to prayers tonight. Do you know where my hut is? You don't know? Well, I'll tell you. Look, it is near the Chico Purus. You understand, don't you? You know. Then that's where it is. Adeus, I'll see you soon. Bring the girls, don't forget."

And he said to the girls: "Come, don't change your mind. There'll be a big dance."

He said this and departed.

On leaving he cast at the two girls an endearing and almost sincere look.

The look of a cobra at a passer-by.

The "prayers" are a pretext for a ball and an orgy.

After the prayer—a supreme and most scandalous profanation—begins the dance, which always ends in an orgy.

That night, after the intoxication of the father and brother, and while the mother was talking to the other old women, the two girls were taken away by the trader and a companion.

The canoe which bore them sped rapidly over the waters of the river.

Days passed.

One night the two little wretches—ruined at fifteen, knocked at the door of their parents' hut.

The evil companions, after having dishonored the girls, had flung them in the mud, driving them away.

It was like the saliva on red hot iron.

And what could their parents do?

Lament with the girls over the dishonor of both.

And they wept.

The trader did not return, fearing that the brother's sharp knife might avenge the affront done to his sisters.

The father continued his always fruitless work.

The hands of the rubber gatherer are like the Danaides' jars:

Money passes through them, but doesn't stick, falling into the hands of the trader or rubber buyer for whom he works.

And so the months passed.

Nine months afterwards one of the girls has a son, and the other let herself be taken by whoever passed.

And when the exhausted tree did not produce any more, they departed for that place which they had abandoned a year before with as much lack of foresight as hope.

The canoe moved slowly, driven now by the single oar of the old man and by a feeble wind which hardly filled the sail.

Then they remembered the site where the abundance of cocoa had been lost, the terraces that the grass had invaded, that deserted house which the ants had ruined, and she—she remembered the flowers as beautiful and pure as she when she left them, and her sister, the beloved friend of her childhood, the companion of her innocent sports, who was now dancing in some hut to the sound of a guitar to see if the desire, not the love, of someone might be aroused.

And two tears danced on her eyelids, rolled down her cheeks and fell on the fair breast of her sleeping infant.

They arrived.

—◦❧ ❦◦—

Oh bitter grief!

The closed house was about to fall, pulverized by the heavy rains.

The cocoa grove was like a small enclosed forest, and there was scarcely any fruit on the orange trees, because worms had eaten the leaves.

All was desolation and silence, tough climing vines had clung to the walls of the house, opening cracks in it.

The flowers were dead on the platform, and it half fallen. In the flower-pots grew wild grasses.

Only a white rose extended its stems—as if still hoping for its beloved friends—and moved by the breeze it scattered around about its soft perfume.

The girl ran to it, raised it to her lips, kissed it.

The rose shattered.

No, they were not the same virginal lips which had kissed it at another hour.

—◦❧ ❦◦—

On another day, before there was peace in that abandoned house, in that ruined family, the trader came.

The old ones were frightened, because they could not imagine what this man came for, and what evil intent he had.

He came with that satisfied look that always accompanied his cynical smile.

The poor little girl, his, had in her tired eyes a ray of hope.

Who knows but that he came for her?

Who knows but that love throbbed in his breast?

And furthermore that child which she held in her arms was his, and he would not abandon his child.

Oh! No!

The miserable girl was deceived.

The trader came to settle his account. The honor of the two girls did not pay the miserable amount which their father owed him.

The old man did not know how to resist.

The girl came to him with the baby in her arms, and, with that courage that only mothers have, said to him between tears:

"He is your son . . ."

"You are not the first one who has told me that."

When he gave this cruel reply to the unhappy girl the little child extended his arms with a divine smile on his lips, but the scoundrel had no affection for it.

He turned to the father and said:

"All right, I'll take your boat. It doesn't pay all, it is true, but at least I don't lose so much. Adeus."

And he went.

The old man looked at him indifferently and saw him depart with the stupid resignation of a Tapuyo Indian.

Little by little the boat was taken away towed by the trader's craft.

They both disappeared.

In the hut remained only grief, wretchedness, and dishonor.

EMÍLIA MONCORVA BANDEIRA DE MELLO

(pseud. Carmen Dolores)

—◦❧(1852–1910)❦◦—

Writing in Rio de Janeiro at the turn of the century, Dolores wrote 270 short articles for *O País*, organized chronologically as commentaries on the preceding week, on subjects ranging from social activities and cultural life to the weather and crime. These were collected and published in 1910 (*Ao Esvoaçar da Idéia*) and republished in 1998 (*Crônicas, 1905–1910*, organized and introduced by Eliane Vasconcellos). Dolores wrote fervently about women's rights, arguing in favor of divorce and educational reform. She is certainly one of the forceful exceptions that historian Emília V. da Costa contrasts to the myth of the helpless woman in belle-époque society. Her first collection of short stories, *Gradações: Páginas Soltas* (1897/1989), treats women's dependence on men. She published several volumes of stories, including *Um Drama na Roça* (1907), *Lendas Brasileiras* (1908), and the posthumous *Almas Complexas* (1934), and the novel *A Luta* (1911/2001).

AUNT ZÉZÉ'S TEARS
—◦❧ ❦◦—

Pale and thin, for eighteen years she had lived with her youngest sister, who had married very early and now possessed five children: two young ladies of marriageable age, a third still in short dresses, and two little boys.

Maria-José, whose nickname was Zézé, had never been beautiful or winning. Upon her father's death it was thought best that she should go to live with her sister Engracigna's family. Here she led a monotonous existence, helping to bring up her nephews and nieces, who were born in that young and happy household with a regularity that brooked small intervals between the births.

A long, pointed nose disfigured her face, and her lips, extremely thin, looked like a pale crack. Her thoughtful gaze alone possessed a certain melancholy attractiveness. But even here, her eyes, protruding too far for the harmony of the lines upon her face, seemed always to be red, and her brows narrow and sparse.

Of late, an intricate network of wrinkles as fine as hairs had formed at the corner of her eyes. From her nose, likewise, two furrows ran along the transparent delicacy of her skin and reached either side of her mouth. When she smiled, these wrinkles would cover her countenance with a mask of premature age, and threatened soon to disfigure her entirely. And yet, from habit, and through passive obedience to routine, Maria-José continued to dress like a young girl of eighteen, in brightly colored gowns, thin waists and white hats that ill became her frail and oldish face.

She would remain for a long time in painful indecision when it was a matter of picking out some piece of goods that was of too bright a red or blue,—as if instinctively she understood the disharmony of these hues with her age, whose rapid oncoming they moreover placed in all the more noticeable contrast. And at such times Engracigna and her daughters would say to her with a vehemence whose effect they little guessed, "Why, Zézé! Buy something and be done with it! . . . How silly! Do you want to dress like a widow? What a notion!"

And at bottom they meant it.

None of them saw Maria-José as she really was. Living with her day by day had served to efface the actual appearance of the faded old maid. For, in the minds of the mother and her daughters, who were moreover of a frivolous and indifferent sort, Zézé had grown to be the type, very vague, to be sure, but the eternal type of young girl of marriageable years who always should be well dressed and smiling.

When she would be out walking with her nieces, of sixteen and seventeen years, who wore the same clothes as she herself did, but whose graceful and lively charm became their gay colors of youth so well, Zézé's intelligence saw only too plainly the contrast between her and them; she would hold aloof from the laughing set, morose, wounded, as if oppressed by an unspeakable shame.

Ah! Who can depict the secret chagrin of an old maid who sees pass by in useless monotony her dark, loveless, despairing days, without hope even of some event of personal interest, while about her moves the busy whirl of happier creatures whose life has but one goal, who feel emotions and tendernesses, and who look upon her simply as an obscure accessory in the household's affairs! They all loved her, of course, but not one of them suspected that she, too, could cherish those aspirations that are common to all human beings.

Her self-denial seemed to be a most natural thing; indeed, they hardly considered her in the light of a living person; she was no longer of any consequence.

This was an attitude that satisfied the general egotism of the family, and to which they all had grown accustomed, never suspecting the grievous aspect of her sacrifice which was hidden by a sentiment of proud dignity.

So, when they would go to the theater, and the box held only five—Engracigna, her husband, Fabio, and the three young ladies,—Maria-José knew beforehand that her sister, snugly wrapped in her opera cloak, would come to her and say gently, in that purring voice of hers: "You'll stay at home with the children tonight, won't you, Zézé? Little Paul isn't very well, and I wouldn't think of leaving him with anybody else . . ."

And she would remain behind, without betraying the revolt within her which, upon each occasion of these evidences of selfishness, would make the anemic blood in her veins tremble with agitation.

Alone in the dining room she would ply her needle mechanically, while her nephews would amuse themselves with the toys scattered upon the table—colored pictures and lead soldiers. Every other moment they would call her.

"Aunt Zézé, look at George pinching me!"

"I am not! Paul hit me first! . . ."

And the good aunt would quiet them. Then, after both had been put to sleep in their little twin beds, she would rest her elbows upon the window sill of her gloomy old-maid's room, and placing both hands beneath her sharp chin, her gaze directed towards heaven, she would lose herself in contemplation of the stars that shone in the limpid sky, less lonely, surely, than she upon earth. In vain did her eyes seek in the eyes of another that expression of sympathy and tenderness which alone would console her . . .

The truth is that Maria-José was suffering from the disappointment of unrequited passion. She had fallen in love with Monjardin, a poet and great friend of her brother-in-law, Fabio. Monjardin came to the house every Sunday.

Older than she, almost forty, but having preserved all the attractiveness of youth,—a black moustache, a vigorous, yet graceful figure, eyes still bright, charming and wide awake,—Monjardin, without knowing it, had conquered Zézé.

This had come about in a rather curious manner. Finding the conversation of Fabio's wife and daughters too commonplace, Monjardin, when he would recite some of his poems or tell some story connected with his literary life, preferred to address Maria-José, whom he saw to be of a serious and impressive nature.

"Let's have another poem, please, Mr. Monjardin!" she would ask in supplicating tone. "For instance, that one you call 'Regrets.' You know?"

And then he would describe in his verse the grief of a heart, disillusioned and broken by the cruelties of fate, that evoked in vain the remembrance of yesterday's lost loves, vanished in the mists of eternal despair.

He recited these bitter griefs in a strong, healthy man's voice, erect in the center of the parlor, looking mechanically, distractedly at Maria-José with his dreamy eyes; the concentrated effort of his memory brought to his face an involuntary immobility which Maria-José, most deliciously touched, drank in.

The poet had announced that he had written a poem which he would recite at Zézé's anniversary dinner. The date for this was but a few days distant, and ever since the poet's announcement the whole family had taken to teasing the old maid, christening her "the muse of inspiration," and asking her when the wedding would take place . . .

She smiled ingenuously; at such times her face would even take on an air of unusual happiness; her features grew animated, less wrinkled and more firm.

On the day of the celebration Maria-José came out of her room radiant with hope. At the belt of her white dress bloomed a rose; a little blood, set pulsing by her agitated heart, brought a feeble color to her marble cheeks, from which now protruded her long nose in a manner less displeasing than usual.

"See, mamma," remarked one of the nieces, "doesn't Zézé look like a young girl today?"

They dined amidst merry chatter. Seated directly across from Monjardin, Maria-José, hiding her glances behind the fruit bowls that covered the table, looked at him furtively without surfeit. Her poor heart beat as if it would burst, waiting in agonized suspense for the poem in which the poet, without doubt, was to declare his intimate feelings for her. Monjardin had already pointed to his pocket as a token that he had the verses with him, and Zézé had trembled with gratification as she bashfully lowered her long face.

Champagne sparkled in the glasses and toasts were given. Several guests of distinction spoke first, then followed the hosts and their children,—frolicsome little things. Finally Monjardin arose and unfolded a manuscript, asking permission to declaim the verses which he had composed in honor of Maria-José, the central figure of the occasion. The guests greeted his remarks with noisy and enthusiastic approbation.

"Hear! Hear!"

Engracigna and her daughters leaned over and cast malicious glances in the direction of Maria-José, but she was paying no attention to them. Her eyes were buzzing; it seemed that everything was turning round.

Monjardin, the center of all eyes, made pompous preparation; he pulled down his vest, arranged his sleeves and, in sonorous, cadenced voice, began to recite his alexandrines, scanning the lines impeccably.

His poem opened with a eulogy of the ineffable virtue, compounded of self-abnegation and chastity, that distinguished the angelic creature who, with her white tutelary wings, watched over the happiness of his dear friend's love nest. He then recalled that the date of this day commemorated the happy birth of a being of immaculate purity, Maria-José, a veritable saint who had renounced all her own aspirations so that she might consecrate herself entirely to the duties of her sister's family; gentle figure of the mother-guardian, who would soon be the beloved grandmother sharing with her sister the joys of younger households which would soon be formed, offsprings of that home which her devoted tenderness as aunt and sister at present cultivated. As he came to a close, the poet raised his cup of sparkling wine and, in exalted voice, drank to the health of Zézé amidst the loud huzzahs of all present.

"Long live Aunt Zézé! Hurrah for Aunt Zézé!" cried the children, glass in hand, while the nieces laughed loudly, blushing to the ears, for they had understood very well the poet's reference to future "younger households."

Fabio and his wife, their eyes somewhat brightened by the strong champagne, proposed in turn their toast to Zézé.

"Here's to Zézé and the eighteen happy years we've lived together! . . ."

Maria-José, as soon as she had seized the significance of Monjardin's verses, had grown deathly pale; stricken by sudden disillusionment, she felt a glacial chill overwhelm her body to the very marrow; she feared that she would faint straightaway and provide a spectacle for the guests, who were all drinking her health, their eyes focused upon her. A veil of tears spread before her sight . . . In vain she tried to repress them, to force a smile of thanks upon her face. The smile wrinkled into a dolorous grimace; she succeeded only in convulsing her contracted visage with the sobs that she sought to restrain. Overcome at last, humiliated, powerless, she broke into tears, and this unforeseen denouement put an end at once to all the pleasure of the dinner.

"Zézé! Zézé! What ails you? . . ."

Engracigna had rushed to her side in alarm; everyone rose, seeking the reason for the outburst; they surrounded the poor creature, whose head had sunk upon the table, in the midst of the rose petals, the fruits and the glasses which were strewn in charming confusion.

"What is the trouble? . . ."

A nervous attack, perhaps? . . . Confusion produced in her by the touching poem? . . .

Finally they raised Maria-José's head and bathed it in cool water; whereupon the face of the poor old maid stood revealed in all the ugliness that her spasms of convulsive weeping cast over it, with her large aquiline nose, her protruding eyes and her livid lips . . .

And now Monjardin drew near. Delicately raising the icy fingers of Maria-José he lifted them to the edge of his perfumed moustache and placed upon them a grateful kiss; then, turning to Engracigna's daughters he said, with a solemn, self-complacent tone, "Aunt Zézé's tears are the most beautiful homage that could be rendered to my poor verses."

PAULO BARRETO

(João Paulo Emílio Cristóvão dos Santos Coelho Barreto;
pseud. João do Rio)

—◦❧(1881–1921)❧◦—

Frequenting the boulevards and salons of belle-époque Rio de Janeiro, João do Rio, as he was called, played the witty decadent and social dandy of Brazil's capital city. From a background in journalism to which he added interests in philosophy, literature, culture, and etiquette, João do Rio's literary career included chronicles based on observations of city life and culture, literary essays, the short story, and theater. He translated Oscar Wilde's *Salomé* for the Rio stage in 1908. The chronicling of city life can be found in his portraits of "the enchanting soul of the streets" (*A Alma Encantadora das Ruas*, 1908) as well as in essays on literature and literary life (*O Momento Literário*, 1904; *Vida Vertiginosa*, 1910). Reflecting Paris, the bohemian and decadent life in Rio was lived in the elegant cafes and society salons, which João do Rio described using the aphoristic, paradoxical, and polished style of the period. His curiosity about all levels of society can be seen in his study of religions in Rio (*As Religiões do Rio de Janeiro*, 1905) and his fascination with technology in a collection of essays titled *Cinematographer* (*Cinematógrafo*, 1909). His volumes of short stories are *Dentro da Noite* (1910), *Rosário da Ilusão* (1912), and *A Mulher e os Espelhos* (1911/1918). Only two of his stories have ever been translated into English. The equivalent of a French or English late nineteenth-century decadent, the life of João do Rio is described more fully in Jeffry Needell's *A Tropical Belle Epoque: Elite Culture and Society in Turn-of-the-Century Rio de Janeiro* (1987).

THE BABY IN ROSE TARLATAN
—◦❧ ❧◦—

Oh! a story about masks! Who doesn't have one in his life? Carnival is interesting only because it gives us that sensation of anguished expectancy . . . Truthfully. Everyone has his carnival story, delicious or macabre, chilling or full of atrocious lecheries. A carnival without adventures is no carnival. I myself had an adventure this year . . .

And Heitor de Alencar stretched out lazily on the divan, enjoying our curiosity.

In the office were Baron Belfort, Anatólio de Azambuja, with whom women were so entangled, Maria da Flor, the eccentric bohemian, all burning to learn of Heitor's adventure. An expectant silence fell. Heitor, smoking an authentic *gianaclis,* seemed engrossed.

—Is it a happy adventure? —questioned Maria.

—That depends on one's temperament.

—Dirty?

—Frightening at least.

—Daytime?

—No. Early morning.

—But, my God, man, tell us! —supplicated Anatólio. —Notice that you're making Maria sick.

Heitor drew a long puff on his cigar.

—There's no one who doesn't go out during Carnival ready for excesses, apt for raptures of the flesh and the greatest extravagances. Desire, almost morbid, is all but inculcated, infiltrated by the surroundings. Everything breathes luxuriance, participates in the anxiety and spasms, and in those four paranoid days, of leaps, of shrieks, of unlimited licentiousness, everything is possible. No one is contented with just one female . . .

—Or one male—interrupted Anatólio.

—Smiles are passed around, eyes question, giggles spread like prickly shivers in the air. It's possible that many people can remain indifferent. I react to all of this. And going out at night, to the city's fleshpots, I depart as in Phoenicia navigators departed their spring procession, or the Alexandrians for a night with Aphrodite.

—A pretty speech! —murmured Maria da Flor.

—Of course this year I arranged a party with four or five actresses and four or five companions. I didn't have the courage to be alone like flotsam on the city's swell of sensuality and pleasure. The group was my lifesaver. On the first day, Saturday, we covered the balls by car, going indifferently to drink champagne at the gambling clubs that advertised dances and to the coarsest *maxixes*. It was great entertainment and by the fifth club we were all very excited. That was when I suggested a visit to the public ball at the Recreio: —"My God!" —said the top magazine starlet who accompanied us. That's horrible! Riffraff, sailors in civilian clothes, pretentious broads from the dingiest parts of São Jorge street, an atrocious odor, constant scuffles . . .

—What about it? Aren't we all going together?

—Yes of course. We were going together, the women in costume. There was nothing to fear, and we could realize our greatest dream: to debase ourselves, to roll in the muck. Naturally we went, and it was bleak, with thick-lipped toothless black women swirling stinking velveteen around the military band platform, the whole crowd of oilers from gloomy back alleys, and those strange figures like diabolic larvae, incubating in flasks of alcohol, like the prostitutes from certain streets have, mere girls, but with features pale and pasty, like blotters or rice paper. There was nothing new. Only, since our group had stopped in front of the dancers, I felt something plump and appetizing graze by me, a baby in rose tarlatan. I looked at her legs with short stockings. Pretty. I checked her arms, the slope of her shoulders, the curve of her breast. Very pleasant. As for her face, it was small and aggressive, with two perverse eyes and a fleshy mouth offering itself. Her nose was artificial, a nose so perfect, so correct, that only by looking closely could one tell it was false. I had no doubts. I felt her and gave her a pinch. The baby started a bit and sighed: —"Oh that hurts!" You can see I was immediately ready to leave the group. But I had five or six elegant ladies capable of debauching themselves but never of forgiving another's excesses, and it was improper to abandon them, in pursuit of a habitué of the Recreio ball. We returned to our cars and went to dine at the city's most chic and exclusive club.

—And the baby?

—The baby doll stayed. But on Sunday, in the middle of the avenue, riding alongside my chauffeur, in the colossal hubbub, I felt a pinch on my leg and a hoarse voice say: "To get even for yesterday's." I looked around. It was the rose baby, smiling, with her artificial nose, that perfect nose. I still had time to ask:

—Where are you going today?

—Everywhere! —she replied, losing herself in a tumultuous crowd.

—She was following you! —commented Maria da Flor.

—Perhaps it was a man . . . —genteel Anatólio whispered suspiciously.

—Don't interrupt Heitor! —commanded the Baron stretching out his hand.

Heitor lit another golden-tipped *gianaclis,* smiled, and continued:

—I didn't see the baby again that night, and I didn't see her Monday either. On Tuesday I broke away from the group and fell into the high seas of depravity, alone, with light clothes over my skin and all my bad instincts aroused. In fact the whole city was the same way. It's the moment when behind the masks young girls confess their passions to young men, it's the instant when the most secret liaisons come to light, when virginity is dubious to us and of no use, honor an annoyance, common sense a drudgery. At that moment everything is possible, the greatest absurdities, the greatest crimes; at that moment there is a laughter that galvanizes our feelings and kisses hold free rein.

—I was shaking, with an almost morbid urge to debase myself. None of your perfumed classy, too well-known broads, and nothing of family contacts, rather the anonymous debauchery, the ritual debauchery of finding, grabbing, finishing off, and going on your way. It was ignoble. Fortunately many people suffer from the same weakness at Carnival!

—You're telling me! —sighed Maria da Flor.

—But I was out of luck, with the *guigne,* with the bad luck of our dear departed Indians. No sooner did I come close, than I saw my intended captive flee. After one of those adventures through the streets and squares, I burst into the São Pedro, joined the dancing, rubbed against those rather unclean people, flirted here, there. No luck!

—That's when one feels most nervous!

—Precisely. I stayed on edge until the dance ended, I saw everyone leave, and I left even more desperate. It was three in the morning. Movement on the streets had slowed down. The other dances had already ended. The squares, lit up hours before by floodlights and multicolored roman candles, were plunged into shadows—

accomplices of the early urban hours. And as a measure of the madness, the city's excitement, one or another exhausted car carrying kissing masks or some costume jingling bells along the soft sidewalks of confetti. Oh! the enervating impression of those unreal figures in the semi-shadow of those dead hours, dragging along the pavement, tinkling here, there, the lost sound of bells! It's like something impalpable, vague, enormous, emerging from the darkness in pieces . . . And the dominos, the crumpled dancing girls, the motley collection of last-minute masks, dragged along exhausted! I turned to walk through the Rocio court, and was going alongside of the Secretariat of the Interior, when I saw, standing there, the baby in rose tarlatan.

There she was. I felt my heart palpitate. I stopped.

—Good friends always find each other —I said. The baby smiled without saying a word. —Are you waiting for someone? —She made a gesture with her head meaning no. I embraced her. —Come with me? —Wherever you want! I took her by the hands. They were damp but were well cared for. I tried to give her a kiss. She backed away. My lips just touched the cold tip of her nose. I went mad.

—I can't resist . . .

—Carnival couldn't give any more, especially as she said with a panting, lecherous voice:

—"Not here." I put my arm around her waist and we went on without saying a word. She leaned against me, but she was leading and her moistened eyes seemed to possess all the bestial desire that mine expressed. In these phases of love no one talks. We didn't exchange a sentence. I felt my heart's disordered rhythm and my desperate blood. What a woman! What vibrations! We had circled the garden. In front of the entrance that faces Leopoldina Street, she stopped, hesitated. Then she dragged me, crossed the square, we threw ourselves into a street, dark and with no lights. At the end, the silence of Belas Artes was desolate and lugubrious. I squeezed her more. She snuggled more. How my eyes shone! We crossed Luís de Camões Street and were well under the thick shadows of the Music Conservatory. The silence was enormous and the atmosphere had a vaguely faded color with the darkness pierced a little by light from the distant lamps. My plump, rose baby seemed like an oversight of perversity in that night's austerity. —Then, shall we go? —I asked. —Where? —To your house. —Ah! no, at home you can't . . . How about over there. —Enter, undress, leave. I don't go for that! What do you want, dear child? We can't stay here in the street. A few minutes from now the policeman comes by. —What about it? —No chance they'll think we're here for legitimate reasons, on Ash Wednesday morning. Then, at four you have to take off your mask. —What mask? —The nose. —Ah! yes! And without saying anything more, she pulled me to her. I embraced her. I kissed her arms, kissed her body, kissed her neck. Greedily her mouth offered itself. Around us the world was something opaque and uncertain. I absorbed her lips.

But my nose felt the touch of her false nose, a nose smelling like resin, a nose that was unhealthy. —Take off your nose! She whispered secretly, —No! no, it's so hard to put on! I tried not to touch the very cold nose on that burning flesh.

The piece of cardboard, however, stuck out, seemed to grow, and I felt a strange uneasiness, a state of odd inhibition. —What the devil! You're not going to go home with it! Later it won't hide anything. —Yes it will! —No! I felt for the string in her hair. There was none. But embracing me, kissing me, the baby in rose tarlatan seemed possessed and precipitous. Again her lips approached my mouth. I gave myself. Her nose brushed mine, the nose that wasn't hers, the costume nose. Then, unable to resist, I let my hand come close, closer, while my left held her tighter, and suddenly I grabbed the cardboard and ripped it. Captive in my lips, with two eyes fused by anger and fear, was a strange head, a head without a nose, with two bloody holes stuffed with cotton, a head that was in my hallucination a skull without flesh . . .

I released her, drew back with an immense nausea filling my insides. I was shaking all over with horror, with disgust. The baby in rose tarlatan melted on the ground with her skull turned toward me, in a cry that drew up her lip revealing her extraordinarily pearly teeth beneath her nasal cavity. —Forgive me! Forgive me! Don't beat me. It's not my fault! I can only enjoy myself during Carnival. So I take advantage, do you hear? You're the one who wanted to . . .

I shook her furiously, pulled her to her feet with a jerk that must have torn her apart. An urge to spit, to retch, convulsed my throat, and the urgent desire overtook me to smash that nose, to break those teeth, to kill that atrocious inversion of licentiousness . . . But a whistle trilled. The policeman was on the corner and looked at us, noticing that scene from the semi-darkness. Take the skull to the police station? Tell everyone that I had kissed it? I couldn't bear it. I withdrew, hurried my steps and coming to the square unconsciously began to run like a madman toward home, my jaws trembling, burning with fever.

When I stopped at the door to my house to take out the key, I then noticed that my right hand clutched an oily, bloody pulp. It was the nose of the baby in rose tarlatan . . .

Heitor de Alencar stopped, the cigar between his fingers extinguished. Maria da Flor's face displayed an expression of horror and kindly Anatólio looked sick. The narrator himself had to wipe drops of sweat from his forehead. There was an agonized silence. Finally Baron Belfort stood up, rang the bell for the servant to bring refreshments, and said finally:

—An adventure, my friends, a beautiful adventure. Who doesn't have his Carnival adventure? This one is at the very least gripping.

And he went to sit down at the piano.

AN EPISODE IN A HOTEL

—◦❧ ❦◦—

That hotel of the rua de Cattete was frequented by a heterogeneous society, but all well-to-do. The proprietor prided himself on harboring Senator Gomes, with his untidy frock coats; the ex-vice-president of the ex-mission to Mexico; the first ex-great actress of vaudeville, with her dog; Madame de Santarein, divorced for the fourth time, in different religions; the Baron de Somarino, of the Instituto Histórico; a tubercular merchant, just arrived from the Swiss altitudes, with his enormous bundle of a wife; the engineer Pereira with his wife, his seven children and his maid-servant; the notable tragedienne Zulemira Simões, back from a tour through the provinces, in the company of the elegant Raymundo de Souza; two widows, un-married or perfectly married; in short, an entire world, very varied, but each one paid well. The proprietor, as the ex-star of vaudeville assured me, was ready to reciprocate; that is, he served them delicately. There was electricity in all the rooms, a shower-bath on the roof, and a Chinese cook.

At the hour of lunch it was curious to see all these people in the dining room, on the first floor, ornamented with palms and common flowers, amid the polished metal of the tableware. The dining room had a low ceiling with illumination from a skylight. It looked like a submarine or an aquarium. At least so it seemed to me. The actresses assumed the grave airs of fishes evolving ceremoniously at the bottom of the water, as a compliment to the ladies who were not of the theater; the men were most reserved. All ate silently, each one at his own table, the noise of the covers hardly being heard. Only when there appeared a new guest did brief phrases fall on the air.

"Who is it?"

"The deputy Gomensoro."

"Oh!"

Always great names, important people, a heraldic conglomeration of celebrities of the bureaucracy and of bombastic titles. At night, in the vestibule at the en-trance—a vestibule of marble, which the manager had hung with ancient tapestry and adorned with unspeakable furniture, the styles of which oscillated between the Ottoman, the *belchoir* and the comfortable English—could be seen the represen-tatives of all the social classes, from diplomacy to the *outré*.

We had at the moment two new guests: the old minister of the supreme court, Melchoir, and his nephew, Raoul Pontes, an elegant youth, vivacious, spiritual, having to his credit twenty irresistible years. Everybody in the hotel respected Mel-choir and delighted in Raoul, and no one forgot his *verve* when the deputy Go-mensoro, after pressing Raoul's hand, noted the lack of his watch. What had be-come of his watch? In the streetcar? Robbed? Did Gomensoro go out with him? Dr. Raoul Pontes laughed with all his might. The watch had evaporated, certainly. It was the heat. Very opportune was this jest, all the more so, as the aged Melchoir, the representative of justice, showed irritation.

On the following day, as I was dressing for luncheon, I recalled that in my cream-colored necktie there had remained a pin of blue tourmaline, with diamonds from the Cape, a pretty trinket and a charming gift. I opened the drawer where I had left it the night before. It was not there. I opened other drawers, I moved the trunks and the furniture. The pin had disappeared. I thought of warning the manager, but I restrained myself. I might have dropped it in a corner. When one is looking for something, he sees it without seeing it. Besides, a complaint against a servant without proofs would gain his ill-will—less perhaps than a complaint with proofs, but always sufficient to cause one to be badly served; and I am prudent. Three or four days afterward, Senator Gomes, who had nothing but books and old clothes in his room, asked me suddenly:

"You have a pin of blue tourmaline, haven't you?"

Besides being prudent, I am intelligent. How the devil, in that distinguished hotel, would the senator be inquiring about a pin that had disappeared? Could it be a jest? It was little fitting in one of his high legislative position, but in me it would be a proof of sympathetic confidence. It had the effect on me of a blow in the stomach. I replied:

"Yes; I have. Why do you ask about it? Even today I had it when I went out."

Gomes had begun with the charming Zulemira Simões, the theatrical oracle of this and the other side of the seas, an elevated discussion regarding Calderón de la Barca, to whom both imputed several pieces of Lope de Vega's. In so exalted a sphere of Spanish drama Gomes did not reply to my question; and I, who that night did not leave the house, on retiring, before tea, found in the corridor only the ancient Melchoir, in a very low state; I locked the door on the inside, went to sleep and, on the following day, noted the absence of my silver purse. A sufficiently stupid thing after all.

The thief—because it was a thief, there was no doubt of it—the thief, or ill-timed jester, had left my pocketbook,—sparing even the nickels—in order to signify to me that this was his and that it was there because he would return. What should I do? Warn the proprietor? But I was in so distinguished a hotel! It was not very proper and it would upset the equilibrium of the general confidence! No! It would be better to wait.

On the following day, upon returning from hearing *Don César de Bazán*, with Zulemira Simões and de Souza, as the latter was coming up, the actress said to him:

"Ah! my friend, this hotel has curious things; do you know that I have been robbed?"

"Seriously?"

"Yes; the article has a relative value; it was a piece of jewelry that Raymundo gave me when we became acquainted. Do not tell him anything, as it will vex him. At all events, I am not the only one. Doctor Pontes was robbed of his purse."

"The same happened to me!"

"To the senhor also? Then we are in the cave of Ali Baba!"

Happily, some hours afterward, the scandal came to a head. In the morning Madame de Santarein complained that they had robbed her of her *face à main* of mother of pearl with gold incrustations, designed, she said, by a Hungarian painter. The manager discharged the servant Antonio, because he himself also missed napkin rings and napkins, two or three of which he had lost. Antonio left protesting, furious. He even threatened with a suit for injuries and damages. He was a cynical thief. During breakfast the conversation became general. No one had escaped. What had happened to me had occurred to de Souza, to the Baron de Somarino, to the tubercular merchant, to the ex-vice-president of the ex-Mexican mission, to the vaudeville star, to Doctor Melchoir. All had been robbed. Effusively they recalled particular circumstances. "Doctor Pontes, our dear Raoul," asked the genial Simões, "were you looking for the thief the day that I met you in the corridor?"

"No; I did not yet know anything. I had only a presentiment. I think they must have arrested the man."

"But if there are no proofs!" exclaimed Madame de Santarein. "They found nothing! He was very clever! The day that my *face à main* disappeared he had not left his room."

"Extraordinary thefts!"

"We are under the dominion of genial thieves. We need a great detective to discover the criminal."

"And to arrest the servant Antonio? For thieves of this kind our police is sufficient!"

Besides, this Antonio seemed to be a sick man rather than a thief. For the man never stole money, and the napkins of the hotel were insignificant in value. However, whether he was a genial thief or a sick man, Antonio went away, and confidence was again restored. We passed thus a week, and with great surprise to ourselves, Madame de Santarein and the actress Zulemira Simões, on the same day, at the same hour, found on their washstands, one, her *face à main*, and the other, her trinket.

"It is an adventure! It is a devil of a case," remarked the tubercular merchant.

The hotel was thrown into convulsions. Only Senator Gomes growled: "What a beast!"

That phrase, pronounced suddenly, took possession of me. Because, at bottom, the fellow, the illustrious gentleman, was right. The thief or *sportsman*[1] in theft was not Antonio, but another: he existed, announced his presence, he was there at our side. Audacity? Folly? Stupidity?

The following day the gold necklace with fine stones of the actress Simões was missed, as well as the bracelets of the wife of the tubercular man. Terror reigned. The guests barricaded their rooms, and when they went out they carried their articles of value in their pockets, even to lunch. The rooms were cleaned up in the presence of their respective occupants. No one spoke any longer. There was a thief among us, a thief! The ladies did not leave their rooms for fear. No one absented himself without urgent necessity, fearing he might be suspected, although but for an instant, like Antonio. We were all involved in these crimes; we must arrive at the tragedy. The manager, livid, carried on a fierce polemic; the servants served under a cloud, with a sorrowful humility, afraid of being suspected, and the ex-vice-president of the ex-mission to Mexico insisted on writing to the chief of police to have someone come to search all the rooms.

---

1. English in the original.

"For the love of God," groaned the proprietor.

"It is insanity," added Gomes. "All of us here are respectable."

"That is clear; you are right!" then rejoined Madame de Santarein, the fourth time divorced.

Yet in spite of vigilance, articles continued to disappear. It was impossible! Either one must leave there or complain to the police.

Once in the city I met Melchoir and Pontes, accompanying Madame de Santarein to a *confeitaria*.[2] It was two in the afternoon. I returned to the hotel. By a coincidence I lived on the same corridor with these three persons, near the room of Senator Gomes. I was about to undress when I heard stealthy steps. I opened the door slightly. It was the lively and always spiritual Pontes. He was going to his room, but no. He stopped in front of Madame de Santarein's door, drew a key from his pocket, opened the door and entered. Oh! The immorality of these respectable hotels! The fortunate fellow! Oh! these proper ladies! A little afterward I again heard a slight noise; again I played the spy. It was Pontes, who, with the most natural air, was closing the door, and he went away hastily. I was inclined to cry out, to say to him: "Stop, rascal!"—or any other kind of folly—because by nature I am a jester. However, I resolved to leave it for dinner. That night, Madame de Santarein, who had arrived some moments before, appeared in the dining room, agitated: she had been robbed of her brooch of rubies.

We were all prisoners to a feeling of madness when the charming lady cried: "They have just robbed me of my brooch of rubies. One more!"

My eyes fastened on Doctor Pontes, who had the same astonishment as the rest, the same air and look.

An idea crossed my mind. It was he—the thief! No doubt. But, could he be the lover? Because, after all, he was a man who must respect his name, his uncle!

The proofs were against him, absolutely against him.

No one even thought of leaving the hotel after these thefts. It was necessary to clear up the situation. I could hasten the scandal, say that I saw him enter Madame de Santarein's room, and explanations would come afterward.

I was going to speak, I was going to tell everything, when I felt upon me the gaze of Senator Gomes, who, shaking his head, moving his knife between his fingers, seemed by every means entreating me not to say anything. Gomes knew—from the day on which he spoke to me of my pin! I restrained myself. Also because at that moment Pepita entered with her dog, both distraught over the disappearance of a ring, an admirable marquise, as the star said.

The engineer Pereira rose.

"Manager! I cannot remain another day in your hotel! The situation is delicate for the first one who leaves this inferno, but I dare to do it. I have a family, I have a nervous wife, I have valuables. I am the engineer Salustrio Pereira. My bags will pass through your office in order that you may search them. Prepare my account."

The diplomat, who, by the way, owed the hotel for five weeks, made a gesture:

"I also am going."

---

2. A pastry cook's shop, where cakes, candies, ices, etc. are sold.

The others remained quiet; they were overcome; but, to my great wonder, Doctor Pontes spoke:

"We have lived for some time in a nightmare. There is here a thief, or a thief from the outside possesses a key."

"That is it—a key," I observed.

"But in spite of the mutual respect which we owe, distrust exists. Thus, I have already thought evil of my uncle. I propose therefore that as we leave here we visit all the hotel, examining each of the rooms. Are you agreed?"

I had just taken my coffee, and I admired Pontes: either he is, I said to myself, a splendid thief, or he is innocent. On the other hand, Senator Gomes looked at the door; he was very pale. What was going to happen?

"Does it suit you?" said Pontes.

"Certainly, yes," said Gomes.

"Let us all go out in a caravan, beginning at the entrance. It is a pleasant manner of ending a tragic obsession."

"Approved! This Pontes is always the same."

Gomes, however, amid the noise of the comments arose and went out. I followed him, overtaking him in the corridor. We were alone. "He is the thief," I murmured to him. "I saw him enter the room of Santarein."

"He is not."

"Who is then?"

"I do not know."

"It is impossible to deny any longer. Either you will tell me or I will reveal everything to the public. Only the great respect . . ."

Gomes took on the look of a person in hallucination, stopping near the stairway that led to the upper chambers.

"Let there be no useless words. Do you swear to keep a secret?"

"It is a crime."

"Do you swear?"

"I swear."

"Well then; let us save a poor woman, let us save a maniac, my friend, let us save her! Do not ask me why. I love her as a father, as a lover, whatever you will. It is she who steals, it is she. I have not the means of stopping it. I am going to put her out of here, and at the same time I fear to see her in prison. She is crazy. At this very moment we are at the mercy of chance and the folly of Pontes, whom I ought to hate. But we are going to save her. We must save her. All will be returned. I have already done it. Look out! Hide yourself! Hide yourself! There, under the stairway. Do not let them see you! Do not let them see you!"

Someone came running down the stairway. Hiding, my heart beating, while Gomes placed himself near the balustrade of the stairway, I heard his voice asking:

"All?"

"Yes; my fearful one, yes; I had it all together. Take it. Now, I also . . ."

A form passed toward the vestibule of the entrance. From the dining room came out the guests, impassioned over that police-like examination of the rooms. Tremulous, livid, Gomes forced a bundle into my hand, while he kept in the ample pockets of his frock coat and of his trousers, other small packages.

"Tomorrow," he said to me, "we shall restore everything by mail. Be good; save her!"

It was frightful, it was tragic, it was ridiculous, to see that illustrious man and honest, taking care of articles stolen by a satanic kleptomaniac, and it was stupid— what I was doing! Stupid, but irresistible! Whoever the intelligent thief might be she was of an audacity, a genius, a subtlety, an egotism diabolically splendid. I stretched my neck in eagerness of curiosity to see who it was, to see who could be, in a hotel so full of guests, the one of whom I was the accomplice, the one who, mysteriously and impalpably, throughout a month, should bring to the hotel an atmosphere of doubt, of crime, of infamy. Then, restraining a cry of horror, I saw Madame de Santarein enter the vestibule, smiling and tranquil.

AFFONSO HENRIQUES DE LIMA BARRETO
—◦❧(1881–1922)❦◦—

Lifelong resident of Rio de Janeiro, Lima Barreto severely criticized and satirized the city and its society in his novels and stories from the perspective of his poverty and struggles. His is an engaged, painful, and conscious critique with the tone of solitary protest of a mulatto writer in a class-conscious society. His Rio de Janeiro, in contrast to that of Machado de Assis, is one of the merchant and proletarian classes, and his life was marked by struggles with alcoholism and mental asylums. A reader of the great French and Russian novels, Lima Barreto had the political perspectives of a militant socialist and reformer. His literary fame rests principally on four novels (*Triste fim de Policarpo Quaresma*, 1911; *Recordações do Escrivão Isaías Caminha*, 1909; *Vida e Morte de J. J. Gonzada de Sá*, 1919; *Clara dos Anjos*, 1948). English translations of the last two were published in *Lima Barreto: Bibliography and Translations* (1979). His final work of caricature and lucid irony (*Os Bruzundangas*, 1923) is also the story of man's subjection to social forces. In his now-classic story "The Man Who Knew Javanese," those forces are parodied as the aristocracy, bureaucracy, rigid social stratification, isolation, and stultified education. The only hopeful future for the middle classes is to be found through deviation and subterfuge, a form of Brazilian *jeito*, a practical if often marginally honest way of accomplishing one's objectives. Lima Barreto's sole volume of published stories is *Histórias e Sonhos* (1920).

THE MAN WHO KNEW JAVANESE
—◦❧ ❦◦—

Once, in a sweet shop, I was telling my friend Castro of the pranks I had played on convictions and respectability in order to survive.

There was even one occasion, when I was in Manaus, when I was obliged to conceal my college degree in order to win the confidence of the customers who flocked to my sorcerer's and soothsayer's office. I was speaking of that.

My friend listened in silence, rapt, enjoying the picaresque tale of my life, until, during a pause in the conversation as we emptied our glasses he observed idly:

"You've had quite an amusing life, Castelo!"

"It's the only way to live . . . This business of a single occupation—leaving home at a certain time, returning at another—is boring, don't you think? I don't know how I've stood it there at the consulate!"

"It's tiring, but that's not what I find surprising. What surprises me is that you've had so many adventures here, in this imbecilic, bureaucratic Brazil."

"Nonsense! Right here, my dear Castro, one can find beautiful pages of life. Imagine—I once taught Javanese!"

"When? Here, after you came back from the consulate?"

"No, before. In fact, that's why I was named consul."

"Tell me about it. Another beer?"

"Yes."

We ordered another bottle and filled our glasses.

I had just recently arrived in Rio (I continued) and was living in literal poverty. I was spending most of my time away from the boardinghouse, not knowing where or how to earn some money, when I saw the following advertisement in the *Journal of Commerce*:

"Wanted: a teacher of Javanese. References, etc."

Now, I said to myself, there's a job without many competitors; if I knew half a dozen words I'd offer myself. I left the cafe and walked the streets, imagining myself as a teacher of Javanese, making money, riding on trolleys, and free of unpleasant encounters with creditors. Unconsciously I headed for the National Library. I didn't know for sure what book I would request; but I entered, handed my hat to the doorman, received the check, and went upstairs. On the stairs, it came to me to request the *Great Encyclopedia*, Volume J, in order to consult the article on Java and the Javanese language. No sooner said than done. After a few minutes I knew that Java was a large island in the Sunda archipelago, a Dutch colony, and that Javanese was an agglutinant language of the Malayo-Polynesian group, possessing a noteworthy literature and written in characters derived from the ancient Hindu alphabet.

The *Encyclopedia* indicated some works on the Malay language, and I was quick to consult one of them. I copied the alphabet, its phonetic pronunciation, and left. I walked the streets, wandering about and chewing on letters.

Hieroglyphs danced in my head; from time to time I consulted my notes. I went to the park and wrote the figures in the sand to store them in my memory and accustom my hand to writing them.

At night, when I was able to go home without being seen, thus avoiding indiscreet questions from the concierge, in my room I continued to ingest my Malayan ABC's, and such was my dedication to the task that by morning I knew them perfectly.

I convinced myself that this was the easiest language in the world and I set out; but not so early that I avoided running into the concierge: "Mr. Castelo, when do you plan to pay your bill?" I replied with the most enchanting hope: "Soon . . . Wait a bit . . . Be patient . . . I'm about to be made a teacher of Javanese, and—"

The man interrupted: "What the devil is that, Mr. Castelo?" I was pleased by the diversion and launched an attack on the man's patriotism: "It's a language spoken in the area of Timor. Do you know where that is?"

Oh, ingenuous soul! The man forgot about my debt and told me in that strong accent the Portuguese have: "I don't rightly know; but I heard tell they're some lands we have somewheres near Macao. You mean you know that stuff, Mr. Castelo?"

Encouraged by this happy outcome that Javanese had afforded me, I looked for the advertisement again. There it was. I cheerfully decided to offer myself to the professorate of the oceanic language. I drafted the proposal, stopped by the newspaper and left the letter. I immediately returned to the library and continued my study of Javanese. I didn't make much progress that day, whether from assuming the Javanese alphabet to be the only knowledge necessary for a teacher of the Malay language or from exerting myself more in the literary history and bibliography of the language I was going to teach.

After two days I received a letter bidding me to speak with Dr. Manuel Feliciano Soares Albernaz, Baron of Jacuecanga, on Conde Bonfim Street, I forget the number. You must remember that in the meantime I was continuing my study of Malay, that is, Javanese. Besides the alphabet, I learned the names of a few authors, and to ask and answer "How are you?" along with two or three rules of grammar— all of this knowledge ballasted by twenty words of vocabulary.

You have no idea of the difficulties I went through to arrange the money for the trip! It's easier—believe me—to learn Javanese . . . I went on foot. I was sweating profusely when I arrived. With maternal affection the venerable mango trees, aligned in a row in front of the nobleman's house, received me, welcomed me, and comforted me. In my entire life it was the only time I enjoyed the sympathy of nature.

It was a large house that appeared deserted; it was poorly maintained, but for some reason I had the impression that the lack of maintenance was due more to carelessness and weariness with life than to poverty itself. It must have been years since it was painted. The walls were peeling, and here and there the edges of the roof, made of those old-fashioned glazed tiles, were missing like poor or ill-treated dentures.

I looked for a time at the garden and saw the vengeful force with which the brambles and cockleburs had expelled the caladiums and begonias. The crotons, however, still survived with their foliage of lifeless colors. I knocked. They were a long time in answering. At last there appeared an elderly black African, whose cotton-white hair and beard gave his features an impression of age, sweetness, and suffering.

In the parlor there was a portrait gallery: arrogant bearded gentlemen in collars were lined up in immense gilded frames, and sweet profiles of ladies, their hair parted in the middle, holding large fans, seemingly wishing to ascend into the air, buoyed by their hoop skirts. But of all those old things, to which dust had added greater antiquity and respect, what I most enjoyed seeing was a beautiful porcelain pitcher from China or India, as they say. The purity of the china, its fragility, the ingenuity of design, and its opaque moonlike shine told me that this object had been made by the hands of a dreaming child for the delight of the weary eyes of disillusioned old men . . .

I waited an instant for the master of the house. He delayed a bit in coming. Somewhat unsteady, with a large red kerchief in his hand, venerably sniffing the snuff of olden times, his arrival filled me with respect. I felt like leaving. Even if he weren't the pupil, it would still be a crime to deceive this elderly man, whose age brought to the forefront of my thoughts something of the august, the sacred. I hesitated, but I stayed. "I am," I put forth, "the Javanese teacher that you said you needed."

"Have a seat," the old man replied. "Are you from Rio?"

"No, I'm from Canavieiras."

"What?" he said. "Speak a little louder; I'm deaf."

"I'm from Canavieiras, in Bahia," I insisted.

"Where did you study?"

"In São Salvador."

"And where did you learn Javanese?" he inquired, with that characteristic stubbornness of the old.

I hadn't counted on that question, but I immediately constructed a lie. I told him that my father was Javanese, a crew member on a merchant vessel who had come to Bahia and established himself near Canavieiras as a fisherman, gotten married and prospered, and it was with him that I had learned Javanese.

"And did he believe it? What about your looks?" asked my friend, who until then had listened in silence.

"I'm not all that different from a Javanese," I objected. "My hair, which is straight hair, stiff, and thick, and my *basanée* skin give me much the look of a Malayan of mixed blood . . . As you well know, we have a little of everything among us: Indians, Malayans, Tahitians, aborigines from the Canaries, Madagascans, even Goths. It's a throng of races and types that's the envy of the entire world."

"Well," my friend said, "go on."

The old man (I continued) listened to me attentively, carefully scrutinizing my features. It seemed he judged me the son of a Malayan and asked sweetly: "Are you willing to teach me Javanese?"

The answer came out by itself: "Of course."

"You must be surprised," the Baron of Jacuecanga offered, "that at my age I still want to learn something, but . . ."

"No call for surprise. There are many very fruitful examples."

"What I want, my dear Mr.—?"

"Castelo," I volunteered.

"What I want, my dear Mr. Castelo, is to honor a family vow. I don't know if you're aware that I'm the grandson of Counselor Albernaz, the one who accompanied Emperor Pedro I when he abdicated. When he returned from London he brought back a book in a strange language, which he greatly esteemed. It was a Hindu or Siamese who gave it to him, in London, in gratitude for some service or other that my grandfather had done. As my grandfather was dying, he called my father and told him, 'Son, I have this book, written in Javanese. The man who gave it to me said that it prevents misfortune and brings happiness to its owner. I know nothing for certain. In any case, keep it. But if you wish the fate that the eastern wise man conferred on me to be fulfilled, have your son understand it, so that our race may always be happy.' My father"—the old baron continued—"did not place much credence in the story; nevertheless, he kept the book. At death's door he gave it to me and told me of his promise to his father. At first I paid little attention to the story of the book. I stored it in a corner and went about building my life. I even came to forget it; but for some time now I have gone through such sorrows, so many misfortunes have befallen my old age, that I remembered the family talisman. I have to read it, understand it, unless I want my final days to herald the disaster of my posterity. And in order to understand it, of course I need to understand Javanese. There you are."

He fell silent, and I noticed that the old man's eyes had misted over. He discreetly dried his eyes and asked me if I wanted to see the book. I said I did. He called the retainer, gave him instructions, and explained to me that he had lost all his sons and nephews and nieces, with only a married daughter remaining. Her progeny, however, was reduced to one son, weak in body and of fragile and wavering health.

The book arrived. It was a thick, old-fashioned book, an ancient *in-quarto* bound in leather and printed in large type, on thick yellow paper. The title page was missing and I was therefore unable to read the publication date. There were also a few pages of preface, written in English, where I read that these were the stories of Prince Fulanga, a highly meritorious Javanese writer.

At once I informed the old baron of this. Not seeing that I had gotten there via English, he was quite impressed by my knowledge of Malay. I was still leafing through the large old tome, with the air of one who is the complete master of that variety of gibberish, until we finally settled on the conditions of salary and time, with my commitment to have him reading the old book within a year.

I soon gave my first lesson, but the old man wasn't as diligent as I. He couldn't manage to learn to distinguish and write even four letters. The first half of the alphabet took us a month, and even so the Baron of Jacuecanga was not really master of the subject matter: what he learned he soon forgot.

His daughter and son-in-law (I think that until then they knew nothing of the history of the book) heard about the old man's study; they were unperturbed. They found it amusing and thought it a good thing to distract him.

But what will astound you, my dear Castro, is the admiration the son-in-law had for the Javanese teacher. Truly unique! He never tired of repeating: "It's amazing! So young! If I knew that, ah, where I'd be!"

The husband of Dona Maria da Glória (which was the name of the baron's daughter) was an appeals court judge, a man with power and connections, but he unabashedly demonstrated to everyone his admiration for my Javanese. For his part, the baron was extremely satisfied. After two months he had given up the learning process and asked me to translate for him, every other day, a passage from the enchanted book. It was enough to understand it, he told me; nothing prevented someone else's translating it and his listening. That way he would avoid the fatigue of study and still fulfill his mission.

As you're well aware, to this day I know nothing about Javanese, but I composed some truly inane stories and palmed them off on the old man as being from the *chronicon*. He listened to that foolishness with such interest! . . . He was ecstatic, as if he were hearing words coming from an angel. And I grew in his eyes!

He had me come live in his house, showered me with gifts, raised my salary. In short, I began to live sumptuously.

What contributed greatly to all this was the fact of his receiving an inheritance from a forgotten relative living in Portugal. The kindly old man attributed it to my Javanese, and I almost believed it myself.

I lost all remorse; but in any case I was always afraid that someone might show up who knew that Malay patois. And my fear was at its height when the gentle baron sent me with a letter to the Viscount of Caruru so I could enter the diplomatic service. I offered every objection: my ugliness, my lack of elegance, my Malayan appearance. "Nonsense!" he retorted. "Go, my boy; you know Javanese!"

I went. The Viscount sent me to the Foreign Secretary with several recommendations. It was a success.

The director called the section chief: "Look at this: a man who knows Javanese—fantastic!"

The section chief took me to the officials and clerks, one of whom looked at me more with hatred than envy or admiration. And everyone said, "So you know Javanese! Is it difficult? Nobody here knows it!"

The aforementioned clerk, the one who looked at me hatefully, added: "That's true, but I know Kanaka. Do you?" I said I didn't and left to meet the minister.

The high authority stood up, placed his hands on his hips, arranged his pince-nez on his nose, and asked, "So, you know Javanese?" I answered that I did, and to his question of where I had learned it, related the story of my Javanese father. "Well," the minister said, "you shouldn't go into diplomacy; you don't have the right appearance for it . . . The best thing would be a consulate in Asia or Oceania. There's no opening at the moment, but I'm about to make some changes and then you'll begin. As of today, however, you're an attaché in my ministry and within a year I want you to leave for Bali, where you'll represent Brazil at the Linguistics Conference. Study, read Hovelacque, Max Muller, and others!"

Imagine: I knew nothing of Javanese but was hired to represent Brazil at a conference of scholars.

The aged baron died, leaving the book to his son-in-law so that he in turn might pass it on to his grandson when the latter came of age; he also made a bequest to me in his will.

I plunged avidly into the study of Malayo-Polynesian languages, but it was impossible!

Well fed, well dressed, and well rested, I lacked the necessary energy to get those weird things into my head. I bought books and took out subscriptions to magazines:

Revue Anthropologique et Linguistique, Proceedings of the English Oceanic Association, Archivio Glottologico Italiano, everything—to no avail! And my reputation kept on growing. In the street, people who knew of me pointed me out, telling others, "There goes the fellow who knows Javanese!" In bookstores grammarians consulted me about pronoun placement in that gobbledygook of the Sunda Islands. I received letters from scholars, newspapers made reference to my knowledge, and I turned down a group of students thirsting to learn Javanese. At the editor's request, I wrote a four-column article for the *Journal of Commerce* about Javanese literature, ancient and modern.

—◦❧ ❦◦—

"How, if you don't know anything?" the attentive Castro cut in.

"Very simple: I first described the island of Java, with the help of dictionaries and a bit of geography, then I quoted for all I was worth."

"And they never suspected?" my friend asked.

"Never. Or rather, once I came close to ruin. The police arrested a fellow, a sailor, a dark-skinned type who spoke only some strange language. They called in several interpreters but no one understood him. I was called in also, naturally with all respect due my wisdom. I stayed away as long as I could, but I finally went. The man had already been released, thanks to the intervention of the Dutch consul, to whom he'd made himself understood with his half dozen words of Dutch. And the sailor in question was Javanese—ouch!"

—◦❧ ❦◦—

The time of the Conference finally arrived, and off I went to Europe. It was delightful! I attended the opening ceremonies and several preliminary sessions. They put me in the Tupi-Guarani section and I took off for Paris like a shot. First, however, I had the *Bali Messenger* publish my photograph along with biographical and bibliographical notes. When I returned the director apologized for putting me in that section. He didn't know my works and had assumed that, being a Brazilian, I should be in the Tupi-Guarani section. I accepted the explanation and to this day have never managed to write my works on Javanese and send them to him as promised.

When the Conference was over, I had excerpts from the article in the *Bali Messenger* published in Berlin, Turin, and Paris, where the readers of my works gave a banquet in my honor presided over by Sen. Gorot. The whole affair, including the banquet in my honor, cost me close to ten thousand francs, almost my entire inheritance from the credulous and kindly Baron of Jacuecanga.

It wasn't a waste of either my time or my money. I became a national treasure, and upon disembarking in Rio, received an ovation from every social class, and some days later I was invited to lunch at the presidential palace.

Within six months I was off to Havana as consul, where I spent six years and to which I shall return to further my studies of the languages of Malaya, Melanesia, and Polynesia.

—◦❧ ❦◦—

"That's fantastic," Castro observed, picking up his glass of beer.

"Listen: if I weren't so happy with what I am, do you know what I'd be?"

"What?"

"An eminent bacteriologist. Shall we go?"

"Yes."

José Bento Monteiro Lobato
—◦❥(1882–1948)❦◦—

Publisher, writer, and owner of plantations in the interior of São Paulo (b. Taubaté, S.P.), José Bento Monteiro Lobato is best known for his children's stories with the unforgettable character of Emília, known to generations of Brazilians. He also invented the typical man of the interior, Jeca Tatu. Jeca symbolizes the *caipira*, or worker of the interior, as a primitive antihero, apathetic, ignorant, and obtuse. Lobato's book of short stories, *Urupês* (1918), was one of the most widely read of its day and the first to gain a mass audience in Brazil. During the Vargas dictatorship, Lobato lived in exile in Argentina. His stories tell of provincial life in the countryside of São Paulo, derived from oral history and sometimes violent. Monteiro Lobato lived as a publisher in São Paulo, following romantic causes but essentially didactic and moralistic in his literary judgments. He is remembered for a devastating negative review of the first art exposition in São Paulo by the young expressionist artist Anita Malfatti, titled "Paranoia or Hoax?" Lobato's short story collections include *Cidades Mortas* (1919) and *Negrinha* (1920). Translated into English in *Brazilian Short Stories* (1925) as "The Impertinent Wag," Lobato's story was retranslated in 1956 for the *Atlantic Monthly* as "The Funnyman Who Repented."

THE FUNNYMAN WHO REPENTED
—◦❥ ❦◦—

I

Francisco Teixera de Souza Pontes, illegitimate scion of a Souza Pontes who owned some large Barreiro plantations, began to think seriously on life only upon reaching his thirty-second year.

A natural clown, he had used his comic gifts until then to make his way and provide him with home, food, clothing, and the rest. The currency he used in payment consisted of funny faces, jokes, stories about the English, and everything calculated to produce an effect on the facial muscles of the laughing animal commonly called man, by summoning him to chortle or break into guffaws.

He knew by heart the *Encyclopedia of Laughter and Merriment* by Fuão Pechincha, the most insipid author God ever let into this world; but Pontes's art was so fine that the most pointless tales received, when recounted by him, a special tang, enough to make his listeners froth at the mouth with pure joy.

He was a genius at imitating people or animals. The entire gamut of canine noises, from the baying at the wild boar, to the howling at the moon, and the rest, all these were molded in his mouth with such perfection that he could fool the dogs themselves—and even the moon.

He could also grunt like a pig, cackle like a hen, croak like a toad, scold like an old woman, whimper like a crybaby, call for silence like a congressman in power, or harangue like a patriot on the balcony. Faced with a favorable audience, what cry of biped or quadruped could he not imitate to perfection?

On other occasions, he would hark back to prehistoric times. As he had received some education, when his listeners were not ignorant he would reconstruct for them the paleontological roar of extinct monsters—snarls of mastodons or the bellows made by colossal creatures at their first glimpse of hairy, apelike men lolling on tree ferns—a performance that would have greatly enhanced the lectures on fossils by our famous Barros Barreto.

On the street, if he ran across a group of friends standing on the corner, he would steal up behind and—bing!—he would deliver a slap with his wrist on the calf of the handiest leg. It was fun to witness the frightened leap and the startled exclamation of the unsuspecting victim, and, after that, the continuous laughter of the others, and of Pontes who guffawed in a manner all his own, a combination of the boisterous and musical as in Offenbach's operas. Pontes's laugh was a parody on the normal spontaneous laughter of a human being, presumably the only creature that could make that sound except a drunken fox; but he would suddenly stop, without being gradual about it, falling abruptly into a seriousness that was irresistibly funny.

In all his gestures and ways, in walking, reading, eating, in the most insignificant doings of life, this devilish fellow was different from all the others because he made them seem terribly ridiculous to one another. This reached such a point that merely to open his mouth or begin a gesture was sufficient to send all around him into spasms. Just his being present was enough. They hardly spied him before their faces were creased in smiles; if he made a move, ripples of laughter spread; if he opened his mouth, some roared, others loosened their belts, still others unbuttoned their vests. If he merely started to speak, Holy Mother! what outbursts, horse laughs, screams, chokings, snorts, and terrifying efforts to catch one's breath.

"That fellow Pontes is unbeatable!"

"Stop, man, you're killing me!"

The joker however wore an air of innocence on his idiotic face. "But I'm not doing anything. I didn't even open my lips."

"Ha! Ha! Ha!" the whole company shouted, tears streaming down their cheeks as they shook in spasms of uncontrollable laughter.

With the passing of time the mere mention of his name was enough to kindle boisterous merriment. If anybody uttered the word "Pontes," the round of snorting hilarity was set going, the noise by which man rises superior to the animals that don't laugh.

In this manner Pontes lived along into his early thirties in the midst of a smiling parabola, as it were, himself laughing and making others laugh, and never thinking of anything serious—the life of a sponger who exchanges funny grimaces for his meals and pays his small debts with a currency of excellent jokes.

A merchant to whom he owed some money said to him one day amidst sputters of laughter, "You at least are amusing—not like Major Sourpuss, who lets his bills go unpaid with a frown."

This left-handed compliment vexed our joker, more or less; but his debt amounted to fifteen milreis, and it seemed better to swallow the taunt. However, the memory of that prick stuck in his mind like a pin in the cushion of his self-respect. Later on he felt the pins stick into him more and more, some lightly, others right up to their heads.

In the end, he couldn't take it any longer. Fed up with the life he was leading, our playboy began to reflect on the pleasure of being taken seriously, of speaking and being heard without the exertion of facial muscles, of gesturing without breaking down the composure of friends, of walking along a street without hearing on his trail a chorus of "Here comes Pontes!" shouted in tones of people doubled up in bursts of merriment or all prepared to let out huge belly-laughs.

Reacting to this, Pontes tried to be serious.

Catastrophe.

Pontes, now harping on a sober string, naturally fell into the English style of humor. Whereas before he had figured as a diverting clown, now he was considered even more amusing as Gloomy Gus.

2

The resounding success of what everybody imagined to be a new facet of his comic gifts made more morose the soul of our repentant joker. Was it then fated that he would never be able to strike out afresh on a road different from the one he had followed and which he now hated? Laugh, clown, laugh, that is thy destiny.

But the life of an adult has its solemn requirements, calling for gravity and dignity not so essential in the immature years. The most modest position in an office, the job of simple town selectman, demands the facial steadiness of at least some idiot who doesn't laugh. One just can't imagine a boisterous city father. Rabelais's dictum has one exception: laughter is common to all the human species except to city aldermen.

With accumulating years, his judgment matured, his self-respect steadied, and parasitic meals began to taste sour. His currency of tricks seemed harder to coin;

he could no longer cast it with wonted freshness, for he was using it now for a livelihood and not for idle relaxation as formerly. In his mind he compared himself to a circus clown, old and ailing, whom poverty forces to make funny faces out of his rheumatic pains because the paying public enjoys them.

He began to avoid people, and spent several months studying the changes necessary in him for the attainment of an honest job. He thought of being a counter salesman, or working in some factory, or being foreman of a plantation, or possibly opening up a bar—for anything seemed preferable to the comic foolishness of his present life.

One day, his plans well advanced, he decided to change his way of living. He went to a business friend and earnestly explained his wish to mend his ways, ending by asking him for a job in his firm, even if only as sweeper. Hardly had he finished his statement when his Portuguese friend, and those who were watching them nearby waiting for the point of the joke, all broke out into loud guffaws as if someone were tickling them.

"That's a good one! It's the best he has pulled off! Ha! Ha! Ha! So that now . . . Ha! Ha! Ha! You're killing me, man! If you're thinking of what you owe me for tobacco, forget it, for I've got my money's worth. That Pontes is full of tricks."

And the clerks, the customers, the idlers at the counters and even the passers-by halted on the sidewalk in front to enjoy the joke, and made the air quiver with their roars like the beat of a rattle, till their diaphragms ached.

Perturbed and insistently solemn, Pontes tried to make them understand they were wrong.

"I'm speaking seriously and you don't have the right to laugh at me. For the love of God, don't make sport of a poor man who is begging you for a job and who doesn't want your laughs."

The merchant loosened the belt of his trousers. "He's speaking seriously, pff! Ha! Ha! Ha! Look, Pontes, you . . ."

Pontes walked out on him in the middle of his sentence and went off, his soul torn between despair and anger. This was too much. So society was rejecting him? Was he condemned to remain frozen forever in his comic mold?

He visited other firms, explained as best he could, implored. But his act was judged by unanimous agreement as one of the neatest tricks of an incorrigible joker. Many persons repeated the usual comment: "That devil of a fellow refuses to change his ways! And yet, he is no longer a child . . ."

Thwarted in his commercial quest, he turned toward agriculture. He sought out a ranch owner who had discharged his foreman and explained his situation to him.

After listening attentively to his statements, followed by the request to get the foreman's place, the Colonel exploded in a hilarious burst, "Pontes the foreman! Sh! Sh! Sh!"

"But . . ."

"Let me laugh, man, for I don't often get the chance here in the backwoods. Sh! Sh! Sh! That's a good one! I've always said that for making jokes, Pontes, old boy, there's no one your equal!"

And bellowing into the house, "Maricota, come out here and listen to this new one of Pontes. It's a scream! Sh! Sh! Sh!"

On that day our unhappy joker wept. He finally understood that one cannot destroy in a twinkling what it has taken years to build. His reputation as the unexcelled life of the party, and as a joker unequaled and monumental, was built of lime too good and cement too hard to be overthrown suddenly.

3

Yet he felt impelled to change his way of living. Pontes now turned his consideration toward a political job, for government is an accommodating employer, perhaps the only one approachable under the circumstances; it is impersonal, it has nothing to do with laughter and doesn't even know intimately the separate units that make it up. Such an employer alone would take him seriously—yes, the road to salvation led that way.

He examined the possibility of serving in the post office, or the Department of Justice, or with the tax collector, and all the rest. Weighing the pros and cons carefully, with all the trumps in the deck, he fixed his choice upon the Federal Internal Revenue Office, whose head, Major Bentes, would probably not last long because of his age and a heart ailment. There was talk about his aneurism or tumor in an artery that might burst any time.

Pontes's ace card was a relative in Rio, a wealthy fellow able to exert political pressure if certain changes in the government took place. Pontes followed him around and did so much to win him over to his idea that his relative finally dismissed him with a formal promise.

"Don't worry, for if I get the break I expect in the government and your collector's artery explodes opportunely, nobody is ever going to laugh at you again. Now get along, and tell me when your man dies, and don't wait for his corpse to get cold."

Pontes returned home radiant with hope and patiently awaited the movement of events, one eye on politics and the other on the tumor that was to provide his salvation.

The political crisis came first; ministers fell, others replaced them, and among the latter a party bigshot who was associated with Pontes's relative. The road now was half traveled. Just the second part remained.

Unfortunately, the Major's health seemed steady, affording no evident signs of an early decline. In the opinion of the doctors who killed patients allopathically, the tumor was a dangerous thing that might burst under the slightest strain. But the surly old tax collector, thus warned, was in no hurry to depart for a better world, leaving behind a life for which the fates had provided plenty of comfort and ease. He did his best therefore to double-cross his incurable malady by following a rigidly methodical regimen. If some violent effort was to kill him, they needn't worry, he just wouldn't make such an effort.

Naturally, Pontes, already mentally the occupant of that sinecure, became impatient with this unsettling stalemate to his project. How was he going to remove this obstacle from his path? He studied up in the Chernoviz medical volumes the chapters on tumors, in fact memorized them; he went about investigating all that was said or written on the subject; he began to know more about it than Dr. Iodope, the local physician, of whom it may be reported here confidentially that he never knew anything at all in his whole life.

Having thus bitten into this tempting apple of science, Pontes was gradually led to the notion that he might hurry the man's death by helping him to burst. Any exertion would kill him? Very well then, Souza Pontes would bring him to make that exertion.

"A burst of laughter is an exertion," he reflected satanically to himself. "A sudden guffaw could kill. Well, I'm an expert at making people laugh . . ."

Pontes passed many days in seclusion, holding a mental dialogue with the serpent of his temptation.

"Is it a crime? No! According to what code is it criminal to cause laughter? If a man should die of it, the blame should fall on his weak aorta."

The mind of our evildoer became a battlefield where his plan fought a duel against all the objections sent against it by his conscience. His embittered ambition served as judge and God knows how many times said judge prevaricated, influenced by scandalous partiality for one of the contending parties.

As was to be expected, the serpent won and Pontes emerged once more into society a bit more lean, with hollows under his eyes, yet with a queer light of victorious resolution shining in them. Also noticeable to those who looked at him with penetration was the nervousness of his manner—but penetration was not an abundant virtue among his fellow citizens, and moreover the state of mind of a Pontes was a matter of no significance.

The future officeholder now began to forge careful plans for his campaign. First it was necessary to make contact with Major Bentes, a man who lived a retired life and was very little given to idle conversation; then to insinuate himself into his intimacy; study his whims and hobbies until he found in what part of his anatomy was located his heel of Achilles.

He began to frequent regularly the collector's office under various pretexts, now for stamps on documents, again for information concerning taxes, anything that served as an opportunity for a bit of clever skillful conversation intended to undermine the old man's hostility.

He even went there on the business of other people, to pay excise taxes, obtain permits, and errands of the sort; he made himself very useful to friends who had dealings with the Treasury.

The Major was astonished at the frequency of his visits and told him so but Pontes parried this remark by inventing masterful pretexts and persisted in his well-calculated plan of letting time take its course in wearing down the sharp angles of his acquaintance of the weak heart.

By the end of two months Bentes had become accustomed to that lively "chipmunk," as he nicknamed Pontes, who after all seemed to him a kind-hearted fellow, eager to be of service and quite inoffensive. It was only a step from that point to the time when he asked Pontes to help him out on a day when the work had piled up, and again after that, and even once more. This development finally made Pontes a sort of unofficial associate in his department. For certain services, there was no one like him. What industry! What subtlety! What tact! On scolding one of his clerks once, the Major held up Pontes's diplomacy as an example and a reprimand. "You big idiot! Learn from Pontes who is skillful in everything and who is witty into the bargain."

On that same day he invited him to dinner. Great was the exultation in the heart of Pontes! The fortress was opening its doors to him.

That meal marked the beginning of a series of movements in which the "chipmunk," now an indispensable factotum, had a free field for his tactics.

Yet Major Bentes appeared invulnerable. He never laughed, but limited his manifestations of hilarity to ironic smiles. A jest that forced other table companions to get up from their chairs and stuff their napkins in their mouths, hardly did more than bring a curl to the Major's lips. And if the humor was not of extraordinary keenness, he used to humble the narrator without pity. "That's an old joke, Pontes. You'll find it in the Laemmer almanac for 1850; I remember reading it."

Pontes smiled meekly, but within himself he took comfort with the reflection that if he hadn't caught him that time, he would catch him some other time.

4

All his sagacity was focused now on the single goal of sounding out the weakness of the Major. Every man has some preference for a certain type of humor or satire. One is fond of licentious tales about fat friars. Another dotes on good-humored jests connected with German folk songs. Another would sell his life for a tale with Gallic spice. The Brazilian adores satire which exposes the boorish stupidity of the natives of Portugal or the Azores.

But the Major? Well, he didn't laugh at humor served English fashion, or German, or French, or even Brazilian. What was his type?

A systematic exploration, with the exclusion of humorous types proven ineffective, brought Pontes to the realization of the special weakness of his tough adversary; the Major licked his fingers for tales about Englishmen and friars. However, it was necessary for these to be worked in together. Separately, they misfired. Such are the peculiarities of an old man. Whenever in the same story, beef-eating, ruddy Englishmen, in checkered suits, with cork helmets, formidable boots, with a pipe in their mouths, figured together with chubby friars, addicted to pipes and to feminine flesh, there and then the Major would actually open his mouth and interrupt the process of chewing, like a child who is being enticed with coconut candy. And when the point of the joke was sprung, he would laugh with pleasure, frankly, although without any abandonment endangering his state of health.

With infinite patience, Pontes banked on this sole type of humor and never left it for any other. He increased his repertory, regulated the dosage of wit and malice, and systematically bombarded the Major's aorta with the products of a skillful combination.

When the story was lengthy because the narrator embellished it to delay and conceal the ending or heighten its effect, the old man showed his quickened interest and during the cleverly placed pauses he would ask for clarification or for the rest of the story. "Well, how about that rascal of a beefeater? What happened then? Did Mister John whistle?"

Although the fatal guffaw was slow in coming, the future tax collector did not despair, trusting in the fable about the pitcher that went to the water so often that it finally cracked. His plan was really not too bad. Psychology was working for him—and also Lent.

On a certain occasion toward the end of the Carnival, the Major gathered his friends around an enormous stuffed fish presented to him by one of his colleagues. The Carnival sports had enlivened the spirits of his table companions as well as those of their host, who on that day was contented with himself and the world, as if he had beheld some extraordinary marvel. The odors of cooking coming from the kitchen took the place of liquid appetizers and called forth upon all faces an expression of gastronomic anticipation.

When the fish was brought in the Major's eyes sparkled. He doted on excellent fish, all the more when cooked by his faithful Gertrude. And at that banquet Gertrude surpassed herself in the seasoning which excelled the limits of the culinary art and rose to lyrical heights. What a fish! Vatel would have signed it himself with the pen of his helplessness moistened in the ink of envy, one of the clerks remarked, an observation read in Brillat-Savarin and in other artists of the palate.

Amidst swallows of strong but inferior wine, the fish was gradually being inserted into stomachs with appreciative fervor. No one dared to break the silence of this alimentary blissfulness.

Pontes felt that this was the opportune moment for his final blow. He had prepared a story about an Englishman, his wife, and two Franciscan friars, an anecdote that he had elaborated by the effort of the best gray matter in his brain, perfecting it during long nights of insomnia. For a number of days he had his trap all set, always awaiting the right occasion when everything would cooperate to obtain for him the maximum result.

This was the final hope of our villain, his last cartridge. If it misfired, he was resolved to put two bullets into his own brain. He realized it was impossible to contrive a more ingenious explosive than this story. If the sick artery resisted this shock, then the so-called tumor was a fake, the aorta a figment of the imagination, the Chernoviz medical disquisition a stream of nonsense, medicine a failure, Dr. Iodope an ass, and he, Pontes, the most complete simpleton ever warmed by the sun—and therefore unfit to live.

Thus Pontes meditated, gazing appealingly with the eyes of psychology, on his intended victim, when the Major met him halfway; he blinked his left eye, a sign that he was all set to listen.

"Here goes now," thought our bandit; and with peerless naturalness, picking up as if by chance a bottle of sauce, he began to read the label. "Perrins: Lea and Perrins. I wonder if he can be a relative of that Lord Perrins who tricked two Franciscan friars?"

Intoxicated by the delicious fish, the Major's eyes sparkled with a lustful light of greediness for a spicy story. "Two friars and a lord! This story must be A-1. Tell it to us, chipmunk." And chewing unconsciously, he became absorbed in the fateful tale.

The anecdote ran along craftily, combining the usual threads of events until the denouement was near. It was related with a masterly art, clear and precise, in a strategic development full of genius. Halfway toward the end, the plot had the old man so spellbound that it held him in suspense, his mouth half-open, an olive stuck on his fork stopped in mid-air. A readiness to burst out laughing—now held in check but eager to explode—a roaring laugh about to erupt, illuminated his face.

Pontes hesitated. He foresaw the bursting of the artery. For an instant his conscience put a brake on his tongue, but Pontes kicked it aside and with a steady voice pulled the trigger.

Major Antonio Pereira da Silva Bentes let forth the first guffaw in his life, a loud resounding roar that could be heard to the end of the street, a bellow like that of Carlyle's Teufelsdröckh facing Jean Paul Richter. It was his first, to be sure, but also his last, for in the midst of it his astounded companions saw him slump face down over his plate, as a jet of blood reddened the tablecloth.

The assassin rose, hallucinated. Taking advantage of the confusion, he slipped out into the street like a second Cain. He hid himself in his house, bolting the door of his room; his teeth chattered all night long, his perspiration ran cold. The slightest noise filled him with terror. Could it be the police?

It took weeks for that agitation of his soul to begin to calm down. Everybody attributed his indisposition to his sorrow over the death of his friend. Nevertheless, his eyes constantly beheld the same vision: the collector slumped over his plate, his mouth spurting blood, while in the air there echoed that shriek of his last laughter.

While he was in this depressed frame of mind, he received a letter from his Rio relative. Among other things, this influential person wrote: "As you didn't notify me in time according to our understanding, it was only through the newspapers that I found out about the death of Bentes. I went to the Minister but it was too late, the name of a successor had already been selected. Your carelessness made you lose the best chance in your life. Keep in mind for your guidance this Latin dictum: 'tarde venientibus ossa, whoever arrives late finds only bones'—and be more alert in the future."

5

One month later Pontes was found hanging from a beam, stiff, his tongue out. He had strangled himself with the leg of a pair of drawers.

When the news spread in the city, everyone was amused by this detail. The Portuguese department-store owner passed this comment before his clerks: "What a funny fellow he was! Even at his death he thinks up a prank. To hang oneself on one's drawers! That's a trick that only Pontes could pull off."

And the group around him echoed in chorus a half-dozen "Ha! Ha!'s"—the sole epitaph granted by society to poor Pontes.

PART II

Modernism
—•⇒(1922–1945)⇐•—

Modernism in Brazil encompasses a broad movement in the arts that soon rose to the level of a new national definition for twentieth-century Brazil. Its most visible consequence in architecture and urban planning is Brasília, the futuristic capital city constructed on an inaccessible interior plateau and inaugurated in 1960. In music, Heitor Villa-Lobos left a legacy incorporating the rhythms, sounds, and instruments of Brazil's regions into the compositional techniques of European music, notable in his series of "Bachianas Brasileiras." The paintings of Tarsila do Amaral capture the naïve, geometrical, and tropicalized landscapes of early modernism, while in social theory, Oswald de Andrade's 1928 "Manifesto Antropófago" ("Cannibal Manifesto") has become the essential reference to postcolonial theory in Latin America. A thorough visual and documentary overview of this period, covering all fields, can be found in the illustrated catalog to a recent international exposition organized by Jorge Schwartz, *Brasil 1920–1950: Da Antropofagia a Brasília* (*Brazil 1920–1950: From the Cannibal Manifesto to Brasília*, São Paulo, Cosac & Naify, 2002).

The roots of modernization can be discerned in the impulse toward it seen in the scientific thinking of the late nineteenth century, promoted by patrician states-men, such as Joaquim Nabuco (1849–1910). It only became a definitive movement, however, with a generation of young plastic artists and writers who put themselves in contact with the European avant-gardes in the second and third decades of the new century, along with artists who immigrated to Brazil, such as the influential sculptor Vítor Brécheret in 1913. His monument to the *bandeirantes* still dominates Ibirapuera Park in São Paulo, and he won a prize for sculpture in the 1951 São Paulo biennial art exposition. This diffuse group gained the support of society through such figures as plantation owner Paulo Prado, diplomat Graça Aranha, and patroness Olívia Guedes Penteado. Their program was presented to the public in three evenings at the Teatro Municipal in São Paulo in February 1922, known as the Semana de Arte Moderna (Modern Art Week). The intellectual and theoretical force behind the movement was Mário de Andrade, musicologist, humanist, and one of the most prolific scholars and writers of his time. A tall mulatto, Mário carried on voluminous correspondence and wrote the book of poetry most closely associated with the modern city of São Paulo, *Paulicéia Desvariada* (*Hallucinated City*, trans. Jack Tomlins, Nashville, Vanderbilt UP, 1970), essays on aesthetics, and one of the most celebrated modern novels, *Macunaíma* (1928; trans. E. A. Good-land, New York, Random House, 1984). Mário was a folklorist and anthropologist, art historian, and later minister of culture, whose three volumes of short stories have been undervalued in his writings. Modernism was conceived as a movement of national poetics, as expressed in Oswald de Andrade's 1924 "Manifesto da Poesia Pau Brasil" ("Manifesto of Brazil Wood Poetry"), and its major figures count among the greatest poets of the century: Manuel Bandeira, Murilo Mendes, Cecília Meireles, and Carlos Drummond de Andrade. Their poetry still impresses for its fresh spirit of discovery, musicality, and colloquial linguistic inventiveness.

In the 1930s, the modernist impulse changed focus with the economic crisis of the decade, producing proletarian novels, such as Patrícia Galvão's *Parque Industrial* (1933; *Industrial Park*, trans. Elizabeth Jackson and K. David Jackson, Lincoln, U of Nebraska P, 1993), set in São Paulo's immigrant neighborhoods, and the social novels of the Northeast by four masters of the genre: Rachel de Queiroz, José Lins do Rego, Jorge Amado, and Graciliano Ramos. A prolific novelist, Amado's works were widely translated and produced as films and television *novelas*. Ramos, a writer's writer, was a self-educated perfectionist in whose works one see the lessons of Eça de Queiroz and Machado, although his subject matter was taken from the social themes of the northeastern landscape, drought, poverty, and emigration. The artist Portinari perhaps best portrayed the aesthetics of the period in his landscapes of penitents, emigrants, and the poor. Scenes of urban poverty in Rio de Janeiro are found in the stories and novels of Marques Rebelo and Aníbal Machado. During this period, the nationalist side of modernism began to be institutionalized by the dictatorship of Getúlio Vargas (1937–1945) into a conservative program of *verdeamarelistas* (the colors of the flag: green and yellow) and *integralistas*, a protofascist group. Nevertheless, Vargas gave positions of leadership in his government to many modernist intellectuals, and the image of the country became more associated with modernism (see Johnson, *Literature, Culture and Authoritarianism in Brazil, 1930–1945*, Washington, D.C., Latin American Program, the Wilson Center, 1989). The mid-1930s also saw the coming of age of a first school of modern sociological studies of Brazil, beyond Freyre's 1933 classic *The Masters & the Slaves*, including works by historian Sérgio Buarque de Hollanda (*Raízes do Brasil*, Rio de Janeiro, José Olympio, 1936), Caio Prado Júnior (*Formação do Brasil Contemporâneo*, São Paulo, Martins, 1942; *Colonial Background of Modern Brazil*, trans. Suzette Macedo, Berkeley, U of California P, 1967), and Nelson Werneck Sodré (*Formação da Sociedade Brasileira*, Rio de Janeiro, José Olympio, 1944), who is also the author of a socioeconomic history of literature (*História da Literatura Brasileira: Seus Fundamentos Econômicos*, 2d ed., Rio de Janeiro, José Olympio, 1940). With the opening of the University of São Paulo in 1936, more European intellectuals arrived, including scholar of Afro-Brazilian culture Roger Bastide and Italian poet Giuseppe Ungaretti.

In 1918, Monteiro Lobato had published a highly successful book of short stories, *Urupês*, based on folk characters and themes from the interior of São Paulo. In contrast, modernist stories of interior life, such as those of João Alphonsus in Minas Gerais, showed a taste for daily life and its unseen privations and psychological complexities, especially including stories about animals. Breno Accioly's story about the transcendent madness of the small-town character João Urso is a sensitive portrayal of society's treatment of difference and the abnormal. Érico Veríssimo's "Fandango" documents the speech, habits, dress, and environment of the *gaúcho*'s world on the southern plains. The rapid urbanization of the capital and its burgeoning Italian immigrant population gave rise to journalism and stories of the city's ethnic neighborhoods using dialect, a specialty of Antônio de Alcântara Machado, who wrote about life in the Italian areas Brás, Bexiga, and Barra Funda. Mário de Andrade's stories more directly concern the difficulties of the rising lower-middle class, including economic, social, and psychological problems, as his characters struggle to find more openness, freedom, and pleasure in their lives. His stories are characterized by empathy with all beings and a free narrative approach, in which a character once refers the reader to his author, Mário de Andrade.

With its intense psychological and social portraiture, colloquial language and characters, and changing narrative frame, the modernist story set new parameters for the story that would continue to the present. While modernism as a movement is said to have ended in 1945, with the Second World War, the end of the Vargas regime, and the death of Mário de Andrade, its effect continued and even intensified in the experimental groups and inventive works that followed at mid-century.

MÁRIO DE ANDRADE
—◦❖(1893–1945)❖◦—

Ethnographer, musicologist, poet, and theoretician who led the modernist movement in São Paulo from 1922 to 1945, Mário de Andrade was largely responsible
for the cultural and linguistic definition of modern Brazil through his humanistic
and multifaceted knowledge, research, and writings. His groundbreaking book of
poetry prepared for the Modern Art Week in São Paulo in 1922, *Paulicéia Des-
vairada* (*Hallucinated City*, 1970), marks the modernist as a man of his city, but
with unlimited imagination. A tall mulatto with an outgoing, didactic personality,
Mário was a professor of music at the Conservatory of São Paulo. In the 1930s he
became minister of culture, yet his major contributions come from his own research
and creative works. His extensive library, including works on music, dance, folklore,
anthropology, art history, the novel, the short story, criticism, and many volumes
of correspondence, today forms the core of the collection of the Instituto de Estudos
Brasileiros. Mário was the Renaissance man of the modernization of São Paulo,
sensitive to the population and life of the city at the same time as he was reading
all of the European vanguardists and theorists of his day. His short stories have
been undervalued in terms of his overall production. Not only do they show touching characters taken from the city's immigrant and lower-middle-class population,
but they also include innovative touches, such as the stevedore only known by his
number, and deeply humanistic themes. Mário famously defined the modern short
story as "anything I want to call a story." His short stories constitute three volumes
of his complete works, *Primeiro Andar* (1926), *Belazarte* (1934), and the posthumous *Contos Novos* (1947).

It Can Hurt Plenty

—◦❧ ❦◦—

You remember Teresinha whose husband went to jail for killing those two brothers, Aldo and Tino? In an indirect sort of way it was Teresinha who really killed them. And she suffered plenty, what with her two kids and no husband. But anyway, his sacrifice seemed to break the hex she put on people. Nobody committed any more crimes on account of her. Only, poor Alfredo was stuck in that retreat up the river, slowly chewing and swallowing the twenty years that his nemesis of a mate cooked up for him. Injustice, bitterness . . . things that are hard to digest. Result: Alfredo had such a stomach ache that he became one of the most unwelcome guests in the penitentiary. Nobody liked him and he was always in some kind of trouble. I'm wasting too much time on him.

Teresinha suffered, poor thing! She was still half-goodlooking, with a nice shape. She could brag that lots of guys wanted to sleep with her and were even willing to pay for it. She refused. At first because she was thinking of Alfredo the beloved; then later because she was thinking of Alfredo the murderer. She was sometimes on the point of giving in, but then she pictured Alfredo coming out of the penitentiary with a new knife in his hand to disembowel her. So she stayed virtuous in a cold sweat. She got no pleasure out of life. She was angry at the whole situation and she didn't have any outlet, so she'd come home and take it out on whoever was weaker than she was. She'd see her mother, prematurely old and practically dying on her feet, take five minutes to lift a suit of long underwear out of the washtub. Right away she'd throw some more dirty wash at her.

"If you don't look out, you'll fall asleep with that stuff in your hands."

She was home. But could you really call it a home? It looked like one of those road huts where the mule drivers rest. Just about as dirty. Two things that looked vaguely like chairs. One table. One bed. On the floor there was a mattress where the cockroaches lived. At night they came out and danced on the old lady's face. After all, where do all the insects of this world perform their tribal dances? On somebody's face, right?

There was another room, where nobody slept. Small and stuffy. A tiny stove was there, but sometimes for two days in a row nobody lit a match because that would have implied food to cook and coal to burn, of each of which there was often none. But the stove was there, so in Teresinha's and her mother's dictionary it had the grand name of kitchen.

They lived in this hut with Teresinha's whelp, who was a sort of leftover—in every sense of the term. How could Teresinha spare any feeling for him? Good heavens, living with all kinds of injustice, wanting a man and not having any, thinking all the time about what Alfredo might do to her, and with the death of the two brothers on her conscience . . . And all she had in her hands, dipped in the gentle water, was somebody's underwear and socks, hardened with seven days' sweat. Some of her customers owed her for two weeks, and she hated them. . . . So, you see, Teresinha was carrying quite a burden. And as if this wasn't enough to plug up the fountain of maternal love, she had to put up with her pest of a mother-in-law, a big mulatto woman, whom she despised but needed because of the ten milreis she left there every month. The *figlia dun cane* would strut up to the house, very superior because she had maybe thirty contos in the bank, and would find fault with everything.

How could Teresinha feel any love for the little guy? She was a grown woman who never had any real fun in her entire thirty years on earth. She had a warm, live body and a cold, dead soul. . . . Paulino was almost four, and not since the first eight months did he know what it was to feel the warmth of her breast with her arms hugging him and her mouth coming close to his face and saying *figlioulo mio* and then giving him a noisy little sucking kiss, a mother's kiss . . .

Paulino was just a leftover in that house. And he was all the more so because his smart older brother, when he saw that everything was going to pot, had his guardian angel put a typhoid microbe on his tongue. The microbe went down to his little belly and started having children of its own, millions every hour, and within two nights they had paraded around there so much that they wore out the pavement. And off went the unbaptized soul to the limbo of innocent pagans. Paulino was left over.

Being a logical little fellow he never thought he was a leftover, because in that house he never saw anything left over. Paulino grew up on hunger, hunger was his daily bread. Sometimes, in the small hours of the night, he would wake up terrified. His angel was standing there. His guardian angel? Hell, no. His wicked angel, waking him up so he wouldn't die. The miserable kid would open his eyes in the foul-smelling dark and would half understand that he was eating himself up inside. The first few times he wept.

"*Stá zito guaglion!*"

What do you mean, *stá zito!* Did you ever feel real hunger gnawing at your entrails? . . . Paulino would sometimes stand up on his bowlegs and, with a sort of rocking gait, go over to his mother's bed. Bed, did I say? She hurt her foot and didn't have any money for the doctor who fixed it up. She had a choice: she could either get into the bed with the doctor or sell it to pay him. She sold it. Then she cut the mattress in two and put one half on top of three big boxes. That was the bed.

Teresinha woke up out of a sound sleep with her son's little hand patting her face. In a rage she struck out blindly, hitting him in the eyes and then in the pit of the stomach, wham! Paulino rolled on the floor. He wanted to scream, but his body reminded him of once when he cried too loud and got hit in the mouth with the heel of his mother's wooden slipper, and so he lost his taste for screaming. He just whimpered, so softly that it sort of lulled Teresinha back to sleep. He was all curled up very small like a pill bug. His pain and anguish were so intense that he paid no attention to the pinching of hunger. Finally he fell asleep.

In the cold early dawn his body woke up, and Paulino was surprised to find himself sleeping on the floor, far away from his grandmother's mattress. He had an ache in his shoulder, another in his knee, another in the part of his forehead that had been against the floor. But he hardly noticed these aches because of the immense pain of the cold. He crawled apprehensively, for the beginning of day outside was throwing ghostly glimmers through the cracks in the wall. He scared away the cockroaches and curled in the illusory warmth of his grandmother's bones. He didn't fall asleep again.

Finally, about six o'clock, Paulino was brought back to a consciousness of life in the world by the sound of the first people in the street: milkmen, baker's men, and food vendors of all sorts. His body felt a vague warmth. The noises outside woke Teresinha. She stretched and sat up, vibrating with that matutinal sensuality that drives a person crazy with longing. She pressed her arms against her well-developed breasts and against her belly and all, and pressed her thighs together so hard it hurt around the kidneys. That restless, aimless hatred started up again. It came from a chastity preserved at great cost, a chastity which she herself knew must end sooner or later. She looked for her wooden slipper. Then she screamed at her mother: what was she doing in bed at this hour, why hadn't she put water in the tub, etcetera.

Before the women got up, Paulino had left the warmth of his place on the mattress and was prowling about the kitchen, for the grandest thing that ever happened to him was imminent: he was going to get something to eat, a piece of bread. It was a glorious holiday for him when a customer paid, or his rich grandmother came, or anything like that, because then, in addition to the bread, they had coffee with sugar! He always drank it too fast, that hot water flavored with a pinch of coffee, burning his tongue and his pale little lips. And then he went and ate his bread outside the house.

Not right in front of the house, for that's where the faucet, the tubs, and the bleaching stone were. The two women would be doing the washing there and fighting. Before long, they'd turn their wrath on him and, as a bonus, they'd give him a knuckle rap on the top of his head. Don't kid yourself, a knuckle rap can hurt; it can hurt plenty.

So he never ate there any more. He'd open the kitchen door—it never closed all the way—and go down the step. Then he'd run off, laughing for joy at his companion, the cold, and lose himself in the tall grass and the cocklebur thickets behind the house. This was his forest. Here Paulino nursed his sorrows without anyone seeing or scolding. He sat on the ground or stood with his heel on an ant heap, and began to eat. Then all of a sudden, ouch! He almost fell as he raised his little leg to kill the sauba ant that had its stingers embedded in his ankle. He picked up his bread, now buttered with dirt, and went on with his breakfast, enjoying the music of the grit as it crunched between his teeth. It sounded like a maraca.

But he didn't forget about the ant. When he had finished his bread, the boy warrior in him took over and he didn't even notice that he was still hungry. He looked for a piece of wood suitable for the hunting of ants in the great forest—a stunted forest, alas, penetrated by even the weakest sun.

With stick in hand he set out in search of ants. Not ordinary little ants; he couldn't be bothered with them. Only sauba ants. When he found one, he followed it patiently, breaking through the branches of the shrubs when necessary. Often his hand or leg burned because he had brushed against the stinging hairs of a butterfly larva. When he finally got the sauba ant into the open, he spent hours playing with the little wretch, until it died.

Then he felt hungry again. The sun was high, but Paulino knew that only after the factory whistles blew would there be beans and rice when things were going well or another piece of bread when they weren't. He tried to distract himself by hunting for another sauba ant, but it didn't work. His daily suffering from hunger induced a mood of meditative melancholy. He would sit down, turn his head, and rest his cheek on his hand. Then one day, in the lacy shade of a bush, he learned how to forget his hunger for a while by falling asleep. He never dreamed in his sleep. The flies came and buzzed around his open mouth, attracted by the vestige of sweetness. Paulino stirred a little, pressed his tormented lips together, spread his legs a bit, and urinated.

Paulino woke up long before the time for the factories to whistle. He passed his tongue over his lips and chewed. There was the grit with its rhythmic scrunch— and something more, something small and sweetish, in his mouth. He took it out with his fingers to see what it was. It was two flies. Yes, flies. Didn't you know they tasted sort of sweet? He put them on his tongue, sucked their flavor, and swallowed them.

This was the beginning of a sustained effort to hide his hunger from himself by eating everything in the forest that could possibly be swallowed. Instead of wasting time hunting for sauba ants, he treated himself to little picnics of damp earth. Then he found something better. With tongue in readiness he would place his cheek on the ground next to an anthill. When an ant appeared he would shoot out his tongue, which soon became skilled in this maneuver. He would retract his tongue with the ant stuck to it and would press the infinitesimally small, round thing against the roof of his mouth. He'd place it between his teeth, crush it, and swallow his saliva— an illusion of eating. And what a bonanza if he came upon a whole line of ants! He'd get on his knees, with his backside to the clouds, and lick the ground like an anteater. In twenty seconds he could liquidate a procession a yard long.

Once, in this effort to kill his hunger, Paulino descended from the high epicurean level that I've been describing: he caught a cockroach, put it in his mouth, and chewed it as he walked away. Totally unaware that he was doing something disgusting. Of course, you must bear in mind that these things he ate provided almost no nourishment. The factory would whistle, and the prospect of rice and beans found Paulino sated, his belly filled with illusions. He grew weaker and weaker. He looked as bleak as a day in midwinter.

Teresinha never noticed. Then rein of virtue was by then so spent that the mare would soon break free and run wild. As a warm-up, she clouted Paulino—blindly, at random, her blows landing on every part of his body.

Fernandez the carter generally walked her home these days. He was an erect young fellow, of decent family, no more than twenty-five years old, and somewhat slow in his mental processes but physically energetic. The rein broke. Teresinha let him carry her bundle of wash, he came into the house, and she offered him coffee and consent. The old lady dirtied her mouth with some filthy language that no one exactly understood, took her mattress and her utterly astounded grandson, and moved into the kitchen.

Anyway, the meals improved and the little belly learned the secret delights of baked macaroni. Only, he was afraid of the man. Fernandez had made a little fuss over him when he first came into the house. The next morning, when they were all having breakfast together, Paulino began to play with one of the man's long legs and got a shove that left him with his ears drooping.

Naturally, the mother-in-law learned what was going on and came over. Teresinha was embarrassed. She said good morning and got barked at in reply. But Teresinha didn't need the mulatto woman's money any more and so she came back at her like a wildcat. A terrifying scene! Paulino wanted to run away, but he stood there fascinated because the mother-in-law kept pointing to him and saying "my grandson" every other second. She said Teresinha would have to get along without her help now, because she wasn't going to pay for any hanky-panky of a cheap Italian girl with a Spaniard. Teresinha shouted that a Spaniard was a lot better than a Brazilian any day, you daughter of a Negro! Mother of a murderer! I don't need you, you understand? Mulatto! Mother of a murderer!

"You're the murderer, you pig! You made my son do it, you damned wop, you pig!"

"Get out of here, mother of a murderer! You never bothered with your grandson before, and now all of a sudden you're worried about him. Take him along with you if you want to."

"I'll take him all right! Poor innocent little thing, he doesn't know what kind of a mother he has. You pig! Pig!"

She picked up Paulino with one arm and, adjusting her Sunday shawl, walked quickly away. A few women of the neighborhood looked with curiosity at her and the boy, who was kicking furiously. To show these onlookers that she was in the right, she turned around and shouted:

"Listen! I'm not going to pay your rent any more. I protected you because you were the wife of my unfortunate son, but I'm not going to support a loose woman, understand?"

Teresinha, mad with hate, was already looking around for a piece of wood with which to beat her mother-in-law to death. The older woman thought it prudent to quit while she was ahead and stalked off in triumph, clump, clump.

Paulino, jostled rhythmically against all that warm flesh, wept with fear. He was bewildered: a street he had never seen before, lots of people, this strange-acting woman, and he without mother, without bread, without his forest, without grandma. . . . What was happening to him? Terror crept through his little bluish body, but he was afraid to cry very loudly because he noticed that the old lady was wearing shoes with big heels, bigger even than the heels on wooden slippers. If she ever hit him in the mouth with one of those heels, it would tear his lips to pieces. . . . And Paulino, horror-stricken, forced his hands into his mouth, thus inventing a kind of mute.

"My poor grandson!"

With her big, warm hand she took his little head and placed it against her rubbery neck. It was sort of nice being carried in those strong arms, with the shawl providing extra warmth. . . . And the old woman looking at him with eyes of compassion and comfort. . . . My heavens, what is all this, that makes a fellow feel so good? Don't you know, Paulino? It's affection, that's what it is. It's tenderness. It's love. The old lady hugged him against her breast, placed his cheek against hers, and then kissed him again and again. In short, she introduced the kid to the great mystery.

Paulino became calmer. For the first time in his life, his concept of the future extended all the way to the next day. He felt he was protected and that tomorrow he would certainly have coffee and sugar. For hadn't the old woman put her mouth to his face and given him those big, wonderfully noisy kisses? And so Paulino's thoughts extended to tomorrow, and he imagined a huge cup, as big as the old lady, filled to the brim with coffee and sugar. He smiled at the two tears running down her cheeks, but then he saw, in the middle of one of the tears, a shoe . . . growing, growing, until its heel was as big as the old lady. Paulino began to cry softly again, as he did back home in the early morning when his crying served Teresinha as a lullaby. Until she woke up and screamed at him:

"For Christ's sake, that's enough! Get up now. Come on!"

The heel grew longer, enormously longer, and became the chimney of a building on the other side of the street. Paulino, choked with fear, stopped sobbing. They had arrived.

This was a real house. You went in by the garden, with flowers, and you wanted to pick all the roses. You went up a few stairs and there was a parlor with two big pictures on the wall—a man and a woman. The woman was the old lady. Plenty of chairs, and one big one on which lots of people could sit at the same time. On a small table in the middle of the room, there was a vase with a pink flower that never withered. And those little white doilies on the chairs and on the table, they could keep you amused just counting the round tassels. The rest of the house was just as amazing.

Afterwards, two very pretty girls appeared, wearing the navy-blue skirts and white blouses of normal-school students. They stared unpleasantly at him. Those four dark eyes came down like hard knuckles on the skull of Paulino's soul. He stood glued to the floor, motionless, dizzy.

Then there was a terrible row. The old lady made some remark and one of the girls replied crossly. The old lady raised her voice and spoke of "my grandson." The other girl shouted at her, and there came a tempest of "my grandson" and "your grandson," with lightning striking all around Paulino's head. It got worse and worse. When the three voices could rise no higher, the old lady slapped the girl nearer her and aimed a spoon at the head of the other one, but she ducked and ran out of the room.

Paulino's imagination couldn't have conjured up a more terrifying situation. And the funny thing is that, for the first time, terror awakened his intelligence. His prior concept of the next day disappeared, and Paulino saw that there would be nothing but anger and abuse tomorrow and tomorrow and more than three million years of tomorrows.

"Go pick up that spoon!"

His bowlegs moved, God knows how. He picked up the spoon and gave it to the old lady. She put it away and left the dining room. Everything was settled, the room was empty. The shadows of late afternoon came in quickly and hid the unknown objects. Only the table stood out clearly, especially the red and white stripes of the tablecloth. Paulino leaned against one of the table legs. He was trembling.

A nice sizzling sound and a delicious smell came from inside, and a soothing tick-tock seemed to be trying to calm him.

Paulino sat on the floor. A great peace settled on his exhausted mind: he had nothing to fear from the old lady's heel. She wasn't like his mother. When she got angry she didn't throw a shoe, she just threw a light little spoon, all gleaming and silver. Paulino curled up, his cheek against the floor. He was so sleepy after all he had been through. There was no more danger of a rap in the teeth with the heel of a wooden slipper; the old mulatto woman would only throw a silver spoon at him. And Paulino didn't know whether a silver spoon could hurt. He fell asleep.

"Get up off the floor! How this child must have suffered, Margot! See how skinny he is."

"No wonder! With his mother enjoying herself in orgies day and night, what would you expect!"

"Margot . . . you know what 'whore' means, don't you? Well, I think Paulino is what the old writers used to call a whoreson."

They laughed.

"Margot!"

"Yes?"

"Send Paulino here so he can get something to eat."

"Go in there, boy."

The bandy legs rocked rapidly as Paulino went into the kitchen. He soon learned that in this room he must not move around or touch anything. The kind old lady pushed the door mat with her foot.

"Sit down there and eat everything, you hear?"

It was rice and beans. With longing eyes he watched the meat disappear through the door to the dining room. The old lady probably thought that a boy of four didn't need meat, especially in view of the financial burden of bringing up two daughters.

Paulino's life was still miserable, but the nature of the misery had changed. The food had improved and there was enough of it, yet Paulino was haunted by a longing for the things he used to eat in his little forest. The old mulatto woman never suffered any recurrence of tenderness. It must have been a sort of reflex associated with a sense of duty. Those kisses she gave him were sincere all right, but only within the framework of tragedy. When the tragedy, as she saw it, was ended, so was the tenderness. She left Paulino with a terrible yearning for kisses.

He wanted to be close to the two girls, but they were always annoyed with him and pinched him for no apparent reason. Nevertheless, the younger, Nininha, who had an immense curiosity and who never got grades as high as Margot's, took it upon herself to give Paulino his bath. When Saturday came, she put him in the tub. He was amazed. He was also scared that he'd get pinched again. But instead he felt the caress of a face, hot and pretty, rubbing against his little body. The bath always ended with her angry at him and putting the nightshirt on him very fast, almost brutally. "Stand up straight, you pest!" she'd say, and she'd give him a twisting sort of pinch. It hurt, it hurt.

Paulino went down the kitchen steps and walked listlessly along the alleyway at the side of the house leading to the front garden. With considerable effort he pulled open the gate, which was always slightly ajar. He went out, sat down, rested his cheek on his hand with his head turned sideways, and watched the world go by.

And so, between pinches and hard words, most of which he did not understand, he too went by, like the world: sad, bewildered, afraid, tied to the earth, and progressively failing. But what could he do? He would drink his coffee and they would tell him to eat his bread in the yard or—pig!—he'd mess up the whole house. He went to the yard. The earth was so moist, it was a terrible temptation. Not that he thought of it as a temptation, for no one threatened him with a knuckle rap on the head if he ate earth. *Treck-trrleck*, he chewed a little piece, swallowed it, chewed another little piece, swallowed it. And then, around ten o'clock, he had to sit down on that doormat, with its fibers always pricking him, and had to swallow beans and rice, which he found nauseating.

"Good heavens, this boy doesn't eat! Just see how he looks at his food! Why do you get earth all over your face like a pig, eh?"

Paulino was afraid he'd get a rap with a spoon, and so he swallowed some beans, dry. Then the old lady's mind suddenly clicked.

"Is it possible! . . . You've been eating earth, haven't you? Let me see."

She pulled Paulino to the door of the kitchen and, with those two enormous, hot hands:

"Open your mouth, boy!"

She drew back his lips. Earth between his teeth and on his gums.

"Open your mouth, I told you!"

And her fingers opened his little mouth wide. She looked at his tongue. It was the color of earth all the way back to the root. Paulino got hit so often he thought it would never end. First came a slap on the mouth, which was still open, making a funny sort of sound, pah! Then came an avalanche of slaps, wallops, twisting pinches, knuckle raps on the head. And nasty words, which for little kids are also slaps in the face, right?

Then began Paulino's greatest martyrdom. Nobody wanted him to be in the house, he practically had to live in the backyard. Along with his bread he always got a tongue lashing of threats that almost knocked him out, honest to God! Paulino went down the steps to the yard, munching his bread. He was dazed. He felt the whole world hitting him. And then? . . . The bread was gone, and the tasty earth was still there, calling to him, offering itself to him. But those three women, those pinchers, didn't want him to eat it. . . . Oh, what a temptation to our poor little Saint Anthony! He wanted to eat it but he couldn't. Well, he could, but then the old lady would come and stick her big fingers in his mouth. . . . To eat or not to eat? . . . He fled his temptation, climbed the steps, and sat down, looking at the wall of the house so that he could not see the good earth. But it was there, calling him, all his, just five small steps below . . .

Luckily, he suffered this temptation only three days, for then he started to cough. It got worse and worse. The old lady was fit to be tied. Paulino heard her say it was one of those rasping coughs that are so annoying. Maybe he caught it from the boys across the street; he was playing with them in front of the gate. Let's give him the syrup that Dona Emilia taught us how to make. But Dona Emilia's syrup didn't help, nor did the five milreis spent for a patent medicine at the cut-rate drugstore. He just had to wait and hope that the cough would lose its voice and slink away by itself.

Paulino didn't like the scratchy feeling in his throat. He swallowed a lot to see if he could make it stop. When he got a coughing attack he went over to a wall and leaned against it. His eyes were running, his nose was running, and he was dribbling from the mouth, which he kept open all the time. The little guy sat down wherever he was, because otherwise he would have fallen. The chair was spinning, the table was spinning, even the smell in the kitchen was spinning. Paulino felt nauseous and his whole body hurt.

"Poor thing! Look, go cough outside, you're getting the floor all dirty. Go on!"

Fear gave Paulino the necessary strength, and he went out. He had another attack. He lay down, his mouth pressed against the earth, but with no desire to eat. For a long time he was stretched out on the ground without moving. His body didn't hurt any more. His head didn't think any more. He just stayed there. The dampness of the ground would have made his cough worse and he might have died, but he finally got up. He wanted to go back into the house. But he might get it dirty and then they'd pinch him in the chest. And it wouldn't do any good anyway, because they'd just send him right out again. . . .

It was late afternoon. Streetcars were going by, carrying the workers home. Paulino sat down at the front gate and watched them with his moist eyes. Night would fall soon, bringing new life. A light, dusty April wind touched his cheek. The sun, clutching in vain at the horizon, stained the tired air of day with red and green. The groups of workers walking past looked almost black against the sky. Everything was mysterious in contrasted light and shadow.

At that moment Teresinha came walking down the street. Stunningly dressed. To start from the bottom: her shoes were a dull yellow, her stockings gave a pink glow to her pretty legs, which were revealed up to the knee, and her dress was of a light blue lovelier than the April sky. And mama's face, how beautiful it was, with some of that dark hair done up in a lustrous topknot and some of it drawn from the center across her forehead, giving a glow of Neapolitan blue to the swarthy skin, which was illuminated also by the colors of French cosmetics.

With a confusion of joyous instincts in his body, and not exactly aware of what he was doing, Paulino got up.

"Mama!"

Teresinha turned. It was her *figlioulo*. I don't know just what happened in her mind, but she ran to him and kneeled down on the sidewalk in her silk stockings. She hugged Paulino against her ample breasts. It hurt, but deliciously. And Teresinha cried, because after all she was very unhappy too. Fernandez had walked out on her and, after some indecision, she had become a full-time prostitute. Now, seeing Paulino so dirty and sick-looking, she suddenly had an impulse to give up the life she was living. She cried in remorse and self-pity.

Only then did she feel badly about her son, so horribly thin and more fragile than virtue. He must have been suffering there in the mulatto woman's house. . . . For a moment she considered taking Paulino with her. But she quickly hid the thought from herself, for he would obviously be in the way whenever . . . She looked at his clothes. They weren't of the very best material, but they were serviceable. She placated her conscience by pretending to think that her son was being treated well. She planted a kiss on the little mouth, moist with phlegm, and swallowed a tear. Then she hugged him and kissed him several times. She walked off, adjusting her clothes.

Paulino, not very firm on his feet, made no motion, no gesture. He watched the blue dress disappear in the distance. He turned away. A piece of greasy wrapping paper was rolling merrily on the ground. He would have to take three steps to catch it. . . . It wasn't worth it. He sat on the step again. The colors of the evening were gently blending into a common gray. Paulino rested his cheek on the palm of his hand. In an indifference born of exhaustion, he half heard, half saw the world about him. His mouth was open; phlegm and saliva ran out onto his hand. From there it dripped on his shirt, which was dark so that it wouldn't show the dirt.

THE CHRISTMAS TURKEY
—◦❧ ❦◦—

Our first family Christmas, after the death of my father five months earlier, had decisive consequences for the happiness of the family. We had always been so happy as a family, happy in that very abstract sense of the word: honest people (no crimes at all), a home without any domestic quarrels or serious financial problems. But, due primarily to the gray nature of my father—a being devoid of any lyricism whatsoever, of an insipid exemplarity, cushioned in the comfort of mediocrity—we had always lacked that joy of living, that love of material pleasures: a good wine, a trip to the mineral baths, getting a freezer, that sort of thing. My father had been a good man gone wrong—quite dramatically—a purebred killjoy.

My father died, we were terribly sorry, and all that. As we reached the Christmas season, I had come to the point where I could do no more to remove that choking memory of the dead man, which seemed to have inculcated for all time the obligation of a painful remembrance at every lunch, in the slightest move the family made. One time I suggested to Mom the idea of going to see a movie: the result was tears. Where did anyone go to the movies in full mourning! Grief was now being fostered by appearances, and I, who as a rule had hardly ever liked my father, and then more out of a son's instinct than the spontaneity of love, found myself on the verge of being sick of even what was good about the dead man.

It was surely from this that there sprang—oh yes, quite spontaneously—the idea of pulling one of my so-called "cute tricks." Besides, that had been, ever since I was very young, my splendid victory over the family circle. Since I was a boy, from my high school days, when I regularly managed some sort of failure every year; from a kiss stolen from a cousin when I was ten, discovered by Aunt Fogey, a horrible aunt; and particularly after the lessons I gave or received (I don't know which) from a maid of one of my relatives: I got, in the reformatory called home and among the vast group of my relatives, the conciliatory reputation of being "a nut." "He's crazy, the poor kid!" they used to say. My parents would speak with a certain condescending sadness, the rest of my relatives looking for an example for their children and probably with that special pleasure of those who have convinced themselves of some kind of superiority. They didn't have any nuts among their children. Well, that reputation is just exactly what saved me. I did everything that life offered me and that my inner being demanded in order to grow with integrity. And they let me do anything, because I was nutty, poor boy. From this came an existence without complexes, and I can't complain about it a bit.

Christmas dinner had always been a tradition in our family. A crummy dinner, you can imagine—along the lines of my father; chestnuts, figs, raisins, after Midnight Mass. Full of almonds and walnuts (how much we three kids argued over the nutcracker . . .), full of chestnuts and boredom, we embraced each other and went to bed. It was remembering that, that I came out with one of my "bright ideas":

"Okay, on Christmas I want to eat turkey."

Unspeakable shock followed. Then my aunt, a pious and unmarried woman who lived with us, reminded us we couldn't invite anyone over during the period of mourning.

"But who said anything about inviting anybody! The same old story. . . . When have we ever in our lives eaten turkey? Here at home turkey is for social occasions; all those darned relatives come."

"Don't you talk that way. . . ."

"Well I am and that's that!"

And I unloaded my complete indifference for our endless band of relatives: what if they did come from pioneers, big deal! It was just the right moment for me to elaborate my theory about being a nut, a poor kid—I didn't miss the chance. Moreover, I was struck with an immense love for Mom and for my dear aunt—my two mothers (three with my sister), the three mothers who made life wonderful for me. It was always the same: somebody's birthday would come and only then would turkey be prepared in that house. Turkey was for social occasions: a horde of relatives trained by past experience would invade the house to get their dirty hands on the turkey, the dainty meat tarts, and the candy. My three mothers for the past three days had known nothing of life but working, toiling to make candy and the finest beautifully prepared cold meats. The mob would devour everything and they would even carry little packages for those who hadn't been able to come. My three mothers were always so exhausted they could hardly go on. As for the turkey, only when its bones were buried the following day would Mom and my aunt even taste a morsel from a leg—elusive, obscure, lost in the snowy rice. And that's exactly the same thing Mom served, ferreting it all out for Papa and for her kids. Really no one in our house knew for sure what turkey was—only leftover turkey.

No, nobody would be invited; it was a turkey for us, five people. And it was to be with two *farofas*,* the fat one with the giblets, and the lean one, golden brown with plenty of butter. I wanted the crop stuffed only with the fat *farofa,* to which we were to add prunes, walnuts, and a glass of sherry, as I had learned at Rose's house, my best girl friend. Naturally I left out where I had learned the recipe, but everybody suspected. And so they stood in that ambrosial air, thinking that enjoying such a delicious recipe might be a temptation from the Demon. And well-chilled beer, I assured them, almost shouting. Of course with my "tastes," already quite refined away from home, I first thought of a good wine—completely French. But my love for Mom overcame the nut in me; Mom loved beer.

When I finished my plans, I noticed that everyone was very happy—with a wild desire to carry out all those crazy ideas I had let fly. Even though they knew it was really craziness, still everybody made himself think that I was the only one who wanted it a lot, and that was an easy way for them to pile on me the . . . blame for what they too wanted so deeply. They smiled while exchanging glances—timidly like lost doves—until my sister declared the collective opinion:

"You're just as crazy as you can be."

---

* *Farofa:* "a popular Brazilian dish made of manioc meal browned in a frying pan with grease or butter; sometimes mixed with bits of crisp fat, chopped eggs, etc. It is much used as a stuffing for roast turkey" (James L. Taylor, *A Portuguese-English Dictionary,* rev. ed., Rio de Janeiro, Distribuidora Record, 1973, p. 28).

The turkey was bought; the turkey was prepared, and so on. And after a rather bad service for Midnight Mass, we had our most wonderful Christmas ever. It was funny: as soon as I realized I was finally going to get Mom to eat turkey, I didn't do anything then but think of her—relishing my affection for her, loving my dear old mama. My sister and brother were also caught up in the same rushing wave of love, all overcome by the new happiness which the turkey was stirring inside us. So, still masking my feelings, I very calmly let Mom carve the whole turkey breast. A moment later she stopped, having cut one of the two sides of the breast into slices, giving into those laws of thrift which had always stupefied her into an almost senseless poverty.

"No, Mother, cut the whole thing! I'll eat all that myself!"

It was a lie. Family love was burning so brightly in me that I even could have eaten a little bit, just so the other four would eat a lot. And that was what everyone else was thinking. That turkey eaten in peace renewed in each one of us what the day-to-day routine had totally smothered: love—a mother's love, a child's love. God forgive me but I was thinking about Jesus. . . . In that house of rather modest members of the middle class, a miracle was taking place—a miracle worthy of the Birthday of a God. The breast of the turkey was now entirely reduced to large slices.

"I'll do the serving."

"You're as crazy as can be!" I said to myself. So why did I have to serve if Mom always did the serving in that house! Amid the laughter, the big dinner plates were passed to me and I began to dish out the food in grand style while I had my brother serve the beer. Then I took charge of a choice piece of the skin—nice and plump—and put it on the plate. And later some huge slices of white meat. Mom's reproachful voice cut short those agonizing moments when everybody was longing for his part of the turkey.

"Respect your brothers, Juca!"

How could she know, the poor woman! That was her plate—Mother's—my oppressed friend, who knew about Rose, who knew about my sins, to whom I alone confessed whom I had wronged! The plate was magnificent.

"Mom, this is yours! No! For pity's sake don't pass it!"

That was when she couldn't stand all the excitement any more, and she started crying. My aunt too, soon realizing that the magnificent new plate might be hers, joined the tearful refrain. And my sister, who never saw a teardrop without turning on the faucet herself, burst into tears. Then I started saying a lot of nonsense so I wouldn't cry too—not at nineteen. . . . "Darn this ridiculous family that sees turkey and cries!" That sort of thing. Everybody tried hard to smile, but by then it was too late to be happy. You see, by way of association, the crying had conjured up the unwelcome image of my dead father. My father, with his somber countenance, was coming to ruin our Christmas once and for all: I was furious.

So, we began to eat in silence, mournful, and the turkey was perfect. The tender, finely textured meat floated caressingly amid the flavors of the *farofas* and of the ham—bruised, disturbed, and annoyed from time to time by the more brusque intervention of a prune and the impertinent interference of little pieces of walnut. But Dad sitting there: gigantic, incomplete, a reprobation, a wound, a helpless hulk. And the turkey was so delicious that Mom finally realized that turkey was a delicacy worthy of the newborn King.

A silent struggle began between the turkey and Dad's presence. I thought that praising the turkey would strengthen him in the fight, and, it's obvious I decidedly took the turkey's side. But the dead have sly, highly hypocritical ways of winning: I hadn't even praised the turkey when Dad's image grew victorious, unbearably stifling.

"If only your father were here. . . ."

I neither ate nor could I any longer enjoy that perfect turkey: I was too interested in that struggle between the dead pair. I came to hate Dad. And I can't imagine what singular inspiration suddenly turned me into a hypocrite and a politician. At that moment which now seems decisive for our family, I seemingly took my father's side. Pretending, I said sadly:

"Yes, if only. . . . But Dad, who loved us so well, who died from working so hard for us, Dad up in heaven must be happy . . ." (I hesitated, but resolved not to mention the turkey again) happy to see us all together as a family.

And everyone very calmly started talking about Dad. His image was getting smaller and smaller, and it turned into a bright little star in the sky. Now everybody ate the turkey with relish, because Dad had been very good. He had been such a devoted family man—always putting us first even if he had to go without. He had been a saint: "You kids will never be able to repay what you owe your father." A saint. Dad had become a saint, a subject for pleasant contemplation, an immovable little star in the sky. He wouldn't hurt anybody again; he was an object only of peaceful contemplation. The only dead one there was the dominant, triumphant turkey.

My mother, my aunt, we all were flooded with happiness. I was going to write "full of happiness," but it wasn't only the food. It was a supreme happiness, a mutual love, a purge of other relations detracting from the great family love. And that first turkey consumed in the intimacy of the family was—I know it was, the beginning of a new, reborn love—more complete, richer and more creative, more congenial and more thoughtful. And so it was that a family happiness arose for us which (I must admit) some may consider no greater than theirs, but it's impossible for me to conceive of any more intense than ours.

Mom ate so much turkey that for a minute I thought it might be bad for her. But then I thought: "Oh, let her go ahead! Even if she dies, at least once in her life she will have really eaten turkey!"

Our unbounded love had roused me to such great selflessness. Afterwards came some sweet grapes and some candy which back home they call "happy couple." But not even this dangerous name brought to mind the memory of my father, which the turkey had already transformed into something noble, something right, a subject of pure and reverent contemplation.

We got up from the table. It was almost two in the morning, and we were all cheerful and relaxed by the two bottles of beer. Everyone was going of to bed, either to sleep contentedly or lie restlessly awake in glad insomnia. Everyone but me. You see, the trouble was that Rose, a dyed-in-the-wool Catholic, had promised to wait for me with a bottle of champagne. To get out of the house, I lied, I said I was going to a party given by a friend; I kissed Mom and winked at her—a way of telling her where I was going and making her worry a little (as she always did). The other two women I kissed without winking. And now for Rose! . . .

Aníbal Machado
—∘❧(1895–1964)❦∘—

A writer and scholar from Minas Gerais living in Rio de Janeiro, Aníbal Machado kept a kind of literary embassy and library for intellectuals in the capital. He wrote in a modernist style, influenced by surrealism, fragmentation, and cinematographic techniques in stories marked by intimate narration in polished syntax within a disoriented and tenuous frame. "The Death of the Standard Bearer" (1931) is drawn from Rio's carnival, in which two flag bearers in colonial dress head the procession of samba schools on the boulevards. His works remained unpublished until late in his career, when their style had already been exhausted, such that they appeared as remnants of modernism. The posthumously published novel in aphorisms *João Ternura* (1965) would have been a modernist classic had it been published in the 1920s. His stories were published under the title *Vida Feliz* (1944) and collected in *Histórias Reunidas* (1959).

THE DEATH OF THE STANDARD-BEARER
—∘❧ ❦∘—

What good is it for the black man to keep looking along the Mangue or toward the Central Station? The Madureira Samba School dancers and musicians are far away, and his girl will only enter the Square at the head of her group in the wee hours of the morning. What tortures him is the idea that her presence will turn many heads, just when the action of the night is at its climax. If the black man only knew what a sinister glow his eyes are giving off, like the first puffs of smoke between the cracks of a locked house where a fire has just started! . . . Everyone notices that he's nervous, that a passion is burning his insides. But only through his look can one read his soul, because otherwise he's strangely calm, boxed up inside his ebony skin. Why didn't he join his own group? And why isn't he dancing? Didn't a dark-skinned girl pass by a moment ago and touch his arm invitingly? It was his big chance, he should have gone with her . . . Ah, black man, don't let happiness get away. It's the image of the other girl he can't get out of his mind, that blinds him to everything else. After all, the other girl doesn't belong to him yet, but to her group; he shouldn't have forbidden her to go out. Hasn't she already shown he could trust her? Patience: that body will later be his, for sure. It's already promised to him. Him walking around the Square that way, everyone becomes suspicious. Especially now they're playing his samba . . . He's serious, restless, oblivious to the music, worried sick his beloved could be in the arms of someone else . . . The black has the wrong idea. The sailors are no stronger than he is, not even the stevedores . . . There's no one better built. And Rosinha likes him, is saving herself for him. Perhaps it's fear of the dress she's going to wear today, that marvelous dress that makes her a "queen from head to toe"? His agony comes from the certainty that no one could look at Rosinha without falling in love. And no way he'd admit that she would be unfaithful.

For the first time the black man feels sad.

And he's even feels threatened by the night, by the Praça Onze that's growing on a high tide of madness. The Square was overflowing. Of the throngs that flowed in, the greatest numbers were from north of the city or the hillsides. Low clouds absorbed the singing voices and the fused sound of hundreds of hand drums, of moaning *cuícas* and hammering tambourines. Indifferent to everyone else's joy, the black's heart was beating, expectantly. His carnival would begin only after Rosinha arrived. The trumpet blasts made his muscles quiver and produced a state of vague nostalgia; of heroism without a purpose. Oh, Praça Onze, ardent and shadowy, can there be places in Brazil where throughout this endless night there's more life exploding, more movement and human tumult, than in this resonant and multicolored aquarium where houses, bridges, trees, poles, seem to shake and dance along with the people, invited by an obscure God who brought them all together at the blast of that trumpet sounding the end of the world? . . . The whole square is singing, trembling. Rosinha's body would soon enough be floating there like a petal. The crowd gives way to the groups that open paths through the squeezing, shouting multitude.

"Watch what you do, Jerônimo! Careful with her, she's a virgin . . ."

New songs ring out. "Quintino's Fearless" and "Ramos' Devils" are on parade. The crowd scrambles to see them. Companions get separated, daughters get lost from their mothers, children stray off. Above the waves of humanity the standards flap like sails. It's thanks to the undulation of these pennants that those who can't come closer guess the movements of the standard-bearers.

No one sees their bodies, one sees only the rhythm of the dance steps that they transmit to the flags on high. But it's as if one could see their whole bodies, so faithful are the waving flags to their image.

"Oh! but how huge that one there is! . . . Too bad you can't see her: but she's a *mulata*, I'm sure of it . . ."

"Look how that girl over on the other side must be dancing! . . . Eighteen for sure . . . Terrific build . . . Clear out of her mind . . ."

"The one clutching the banner just coming our way must be out of this world. Black for sure . . . Just look how the banner's shaking, how the flag dances with her . . ."

"By the way they shake it you can tell who it is right away."

Dozens of standards seemed to be speaking, sending ardent messages, shaking, whirling, stopping, drooping, reclining for a kiss, running away . . .

—"Imagine how that one over there's breasts are bouncing; that she-devil must be bathed in sweat . . . Hey! this is the race of people for me"

—"Shut up, Jerônimo. Or I'll whack you . . ."

The carnivalesque groups cross, intermingling their songs. A crescendo of terrifying drum rolls. A terrific group's approaching. The love-sick black man interprets the semaphoric signals of the standard that's entering on the Praça da República side. The black, with his enormous body, plunges into the crowd, positions his enormous body up close. He listens hard to find out if the song is from hes group. The noise is tremendous. Some notes from the anthem . . . He feels a shiver. Will she be wearing that dress? The closer the mulatto woman approaches, in a wave of glory among the waves of people, the sadder he feels. Even if the black wanted to get out of there he can't any more, he feels nailed to the spot. The cavernous moan of a nearby *cuíca* reverberates to the bottom of his heart. "*Cuíca*, you're bad luck, go snort in hell . . . Can it be, her, my God! . . .

The black is trembling. But it can't be her. When Rosinha comes out, no one can resist, there'll be a commotion, total amazement . . . Don't you see that's happening . . . Even the air is different. And the standard pressing forward is blue velvet, with the image of St. Michael among stars and the insignias of the group. It's still not Madureira.

The black man was mistaken. It's a load off of him. It was better that way. He thinks about leaving, giving up. The next day, in the Engenho-de-Dentro factory, he'll feel light as air, hearing the pounding on the anvils and the flap of the pulley belts. Should his companions ask why he did't show up, he'll say he was sick, he went to some relative's funeral, an aunt's, for example. He's really ready to go back home. Let them think he's a wash-out, if they like . . . If Rosinha disobeys and comes to the square, that's all right. He's also ready not to care . . . He won't even ask if she was a success, if anyone else fell in love with her, if that sorry Geraldo kept making a play for her. Tomorrow, at work, he'll start life anew, he'll be free again. Let Rosinha come look for him later. He's the man and is he's strong. What's good's a man is his will. Besides that, one night is over in a hurry. He'll stick his head under the pillow and the shame will pass. He'll try to get some sleep. He already feels sleepy. Meanwhile, it's wouldn't be a bad idea if a storm came up. At least that way, Rosinha wouldn't be leading the group . . . Oh! how he wished, how he longed for a rainstorm that would ruin her dress! That kind that floods everything, overturns houses, stops streetcars, brings everything to a halt. Basically, he hates carnival. Not far away, they're playing a samba that would make even the lame want to dance. Everyone is moving. He's the only one not moving, under the weight of an enormous pain. The classy mulatto women pass close to him, smile, say things. Today he's not in the mood. He even feels ashamed to be so different. It never used to be that way. At soccer games, work, strikes, parties, he was always the most enthusiastic. For some time now a strange dark thing has begun to stir and grow in his breast, an evil force that seemed to come, how absurd! out of Rosinha's body, as if she were somehow to blame. Rosinha isn't to blame. How could she been to blame?—that's the truth. He's suffering. The lucky ones are having a good time. It would be better to be like the others, any one of the others she can still belong to, than to be someone like him, who might let her get away. A dish like Rosinha, the joy of having her, great as it may be, isn't as great as the fear of losing her. The black sighs and fells a blinding rage at Geraldo, the bastard. It was Geraldo, so he figured, who was the closest to stealing his bride. The other one was Armandinho, but he was the right sort, his friend, incapable of betraying him. He felt an unexplainable gratitude to Armandinho.

His legs are carrying him aimlessly. He doesn't think he's headed home, nor does he feel he's exactly in the Square. Some snatches of sambas come within his hearing and alight upon his soul:

> *Our love/Was a flame . . .*
> *Now it's ashes/Everything's over*
> *Nothing's left . . .*

Everything's finished, everything's sadness, caramba! . . . Mulatto women avoiding him, empty beds, unhappiness. He never saw such jealousy. He wasn't meant for this, he's no good at suffering. The sambas make him uneasy. Why isn't he dancing with the others? The black man hesitates. Time parades on and Madureira's group may not be coming at all. The English tourists contemplate the spectacle at a distance and combine fear with curiosity. The Englishwoman suggests from time to time: "Don't come too close, my dear, they'll come at you . . ." The blond girl then asks the Legation secretary if there's any danger—"But are they wild?"—"No, young lady, you can come as close as you like, the blacks are tame."—A Bahiana with *acarajés* was ofended and muttered oaths:—'We're the ones afraid of you, you miserable sons of I don't dare say what!: we're not animals, we're people! . . ."

A magnificent ebony torso passes right in front of the miss. She gets upset, excited, whispers in the secretary's ear, her voice trembling:—"I'd like to dance with one . . . may I?—"You're crazy, Amy! . . . exclaims the older woman, scandalized. But the tourists now are frightened. People are running here and there and panic grips the far side of the square. Whistles screech. Steel doors come down with a roar. The samba school songs get livelier, a symphony in the dusty space. The elderly Englishwoman, alarmed, pulls her family through a half-open door.

They killed a girl!

This news, that had come from the corner of Sant'Ana Street, then circulated around the Benjamin Constant School; it now spread everywhere, alarming mothers.

—"They killed a girl!—people commented in the bars.—Yes, they did, they killed a girl! . . ."

How terrible for them to kill a girl on such a joyous day! Can it be true? . . . But they killed her, yes ma'am, I'm certain they did! . . .

—"What was she like? Did you see?"

"They told me she's dark-skinned, about 19 years old, more or less . . ."

Dark-skinned? Nineteen! . . . Oh, my God! that could be my daughter! . . . Tell me more about her, right now . . .

Another woman expecting the worse came up to the informant:

—"The man with her was black, wasn't he? Was he wearing white?"

—"And didn't he have a scar? Oh! if he had one don't tell me anything else . . . don't tell me anything else! My God, they killed my daughter! . . . Nenucha! Nenucha! Where's Nenucha? . . ."

All the mothers get up and go to search for their daughters. The clamor of some arouses others. Each had a daughter that may have been assassinated. They plunge into the crowd, cut through the carnival groups, cry out for them. Their fiancés are horrible, their boyfriends always promise they're going to kill them.

The enthusiasm in the Square is pierced by the cries of the worried mothers. Nenucha's mother, however, the first to tear her hair in grief, has already returned to her place. She came back because she ran into a woman who was consuming herself with admonitions: "Laurinha, I told you not to come, that awful man swore he'd kill you. Holy Virgin, they killed my daughter . . . I know . . . I don't want to look." Nenucha's mother transferred her dispair to Laurinha's mother and calmed down. But a fat woman came by telling Laurinha's mother the dead girl was someone else, a small girl from Bangu, a factory worker. The beast had been arrested.

Distant from the deadly tumult, the other mothers who had already rescued their daughters held them firmly, safe from their threatening fiancés. They were the ones who had escaped death, who'd been saved. "Mariazinha, what a fright you gave your mother! Don't go there any more, do you hear? We'd best be on our way, your boyfriend is prowling around . . ."

Other mothers sensing the worst left still looking for their daughters.

One lady who was being courted by a Portuguese underneath the bandstand, on hearing the news broke away bellowing, still entangled in streamers, searching for her Odete. It was certainly Odete . . . She had not the slightest doubt . . . She was running up to people with her hand on her head. Everyone laughed thinking it was some drunken reveler. Odete by now must be expiring in a pool of blood. It was her boyfriend! He could never tear his eyes off her breasts, that monster . . . He always said she could only be his. And he had a mean face, that devil . . . Poor little Odete . . . Those breasts! . . . She really didn't want them to grow that much. Odete too, she was already fearful. Her mother was running around sobbing, asking everyone where she could find her dead daughter. It was Odete, yes, she was almost sure. She was walking like a sleepwalker. Talking to herself, shouting lamentations. Where could Odette have fallen? And she couldn't get it out of her mind that the tragedy was caused by the girl's breasts . . . Who couldn't see it? She herself, as a mother, knew that those breasts were attracting too much attention. She had the feeling that it would come to no good. Even streetcars stuffed with people turned around to savor them when Odete stopped on the sidewalk. At first Odete, poor thing, so inexperienced, felt they made her look cute . . . Later they grew more than she wanted and that scared her. They were already causing trouble . . . The Devil had control of that part of her daughter's body. Of late it had been hopeless. The poor little thing could hardly cross the street without being chased by men. And it wasn't just two or three who looked at her, no; from café doors, from inside dry goods shops, from balconies, from all sides, all of them wanted a look, and they'd keep staring, staring . . . She went by quickly, embarrassed . . . Because she had always been a serious girl, her Odete . . . What rude people . . . God save us from men. What good was her tight brassiere? . . . It was even worse. Oh my God, can any mother sleep in peace, seeing her daughter's breasts grow that way? . . . It wasn't just the size—her mother kept pondering obscurely—because her daughter's breasts were pretty, even her mother recognized that, but there were a lot just like them out there, she thought. What she couldn't explain was that in Odete the attractiveness of her breasts came mainly because they were hers, making up a set of secret relations with her body's proportions, her look, her humid lips, her neckline. And when she walked they gained a fullness of life and mystery. That was the danger, that is, Odete's, helplessly exposing herself to the public at a time like carnival when men are always excited and so bothersome. That's why everyone, when they think of Odete, thinks first about her breasts, because they always come first like the prow of ships . . .

The woman walked on sobbing. Ah! Odete isn't to blame. It was her breasts, it was . . . How she wanted to take her far away from these brutes. Now, there she is like a mad woman, looking for her daughter's body . . .

Walking along, she saw a red rose growing right on the left breast of her Odete. She cries out, falls senseless. Two blacks carry her into a bar. Now other mothers were returning bringing their respective daughters firmly in hand. They gave her ether to smell, fanned her. When she came to, she seemed to step out of a shower of resignation; she was calm as if she had accepted everything that happened. Then she begins to recite the story of her daughter with the criminal: they met at a costumed swimming party at Ramos beach: at first he looked distinguished; he had a job, gave her presents. Later . . . the malicious young man began to threaten the poor unfortunate girl, demand things of her. He didn't want her to go to dances, to wear a loose blouse. He said that she moved her hips too much when she walked. He forbid her from wearing a flower on her head, from talking with her best friends.

"But are you sure that it was your daughter?" a mask interrupted.

"Like I'm seeing her cadaver this very instant! . . . Oh, my God, how it hurts! No. No! What I want is to tell her story. That makes me feel better . . ."

She paused. Then she begain again, more pathetic:

"She wasn't even eighteen yet. A mere girl . . . You should've seen the way she did embroidery. Everyone liked her . . . She helped me a lot . . ."

A guy dressed like Hailé Selassié was moved by her story. Little by little the poor lady started to notice that she was surrounded by horses, helpful steers and pigs, besides a Mephistopheles and some Harlequins that had come to offer their services. That grotesque fauna seemed to her like apparitions from a land of nightmares. She stared at them goggle-eyed, gave a cry of horror. They understood, took off their masks. From inside the masks shapes full of compassion emerged who attentively tried to console her. Someone said that the victim was someone else, a mulatto woman from Madureira, the standard-bearer of a carnival group. The woman didn't believe it. It was no use deceiving her.

Outside a chorus of voices was still asking insistently about Maria Rosa:

Where is Maria Rosa
The perfect femme fatale?

And they announced that she could be recognized by

A scar
Two great big eyes
A mouth and a nose.

—◦❧ ☙◦—

The mulatto woman wore a rose in the crinkly hair on her head. A masked carnivalizer took off his companion's mantilla, folded it and made a pillow for the dead girl. But the policeman said not to touch her. Her eyes weren't totally closed. They asked for silence, as if it were possible to impose silence on that noisy square. The last of the stricken mothers arrives late, passes through the crowd, takes a good look at the cadaver, lets out a cry of joy:

—"Ah! I thought it was Raimunda! Thank God it wasn't my daughter!"

She departed happily. Some rogues holding ukeleles backed away, somewhat awkwardly. One of them spoke out:

—"I can't stand pain, you know . . . I'm opposed to suffering."

They tried again to get silence: A woman of the streets drying her tears commented:

—"If only you could have seen, Bentinha, the more the knife went in the more she smiled . . . I've never seen anyone die like that . . ."

The black man's crime opened a silent clearing in the midst of the crowd. They were all frightened to death to see Rosinha close her eyes. The black man, kneeling, silently drank in her last smile and tilted her head from one side to the other as if contemplating a child. A samba school was making its appearance. One could still hear the applause for the Mangueira group. When the singing came closer, the mulatto woman seemed like she was going to get up.

And she was smiling as if she were alive, as if she heard the words that her assassin was now whispering quietly in her ears. The black can't take his eyes off his victim. She seemed to be smiling; the curious onlookers felt like crying. At any moment she might get up and dance. No one ever saw such a live corpse. They waited for that miracle. People could hear a song that seemed to be saying to the criminal:

"Who broke my favorite guitar?/She did . . ."

Some mothers, late comers, still came by but kept their distance from the dead girl.

The dead woman had neither mother nor relatives; she only had the murderer himself to cry for her. He's the one who is caressing her hair, slowing confiding his thoughts to her, calling her by name:

—It's time, Rosinha . . . Get up, my dear . . . It's the "Love's Lyre!" that's coming . . . Rosinha, won't you do what I say! Now is no time to sleep . . . Hurry, we're missing . . . What happened? Did you fall down? How? Was it me? . . . No, not me, Rosinha.

He bends down to kiss her. Those who couldn't stand strong emotion were withdrawing. The murderer no longer knows where he is. He's being carried to a destiny he's indifferent to. The voice of the same song still speaks to his hopelessness:

"Who used my heart for her poor dwelling place?/She did . . ."

May no one bother him now. Turn loose his arms. Rosinha is sleeping . . . Don't wake Rosinha. It's not necessary to restrain him, because he's not drunk . . . The low sky opened up . . . A sudden storm like that is good because it'll keep Rosinha in. Patience, everybody . . . Leave Rosinha there, he wouldn't think of it, no . . . No! And those drums? Ooo! What a wind . . . It's war . . . He'll be spread far and wide . . . Why are they hammering inside his head? . . . The anvil at Engenho-de Dentro factory is like that . . . Stay back, because he'll fight for her . . . She's not here any more . . . Sliding through the ether . . . Make way for him . . . Everybody else stay put . . . Stay over there . . . He's going to take Rosinha from her bed . . . She's asleep, Rosinha is . . . To flee with her, into the country's interior . . . To put her down on top of the central high plain! . . . To hold her to him on top of the hill. . . .

The First Corpse
—◦❧ ❦◦—

We were climbing slowly. When we got to the top, would find out where we were going. Not find out—guess. But the men said nothing; they only grunted on the steeper slopes. I wasn't *that* heavy. On the contrary: after so many days in the open, I had been shrunk a good deal by the sun.

I knew these roads. Often in the past, when I was drunk or worn out, I used to fold up on the pebbly roadbed and lean against the saddlebag while my dog sniffed for fleas and my mule cropped the grass at the side of the road. I would only waken when it thundered farther up, afraid of being swept away by a flash flood, or when I heard one of the big trucks that had begun to invade these mountains since they opened the highway, which led over that slope.

The drizzle cleared away from the valley. I didn't know why the cocks were still crowing. We reached the top, where a coconut tree cast a short shadow toward the mine.

It must have been a little past noon. I hoped we would go in the opposite direction from the shadow. Not that sun or shadow made any difference to me, but I preferred this side, where the mule track must still be.

The men stopped. Then they made up their minds: we were going by the new highway! Just as I wanted us to. The day turned bright. I had never seen it like this. I was happy.

There was Josefina coming up, with her baby in her arms. I wanted to say hello to her, but I couldn't. If she knew who was going by! She passed without realizing.

On the temporary bridge one of the men stumbled, and my body rolled off. They went and fished it out. I had been afraid they would just leave it to wash downstream. I was beginning to be less indifferent to its fate.

In the distance—a bloodstain on the vegetation—a gasoline pump, the first in these isolated mountains. Then the inn. The landlord shouted, as his eye fell on my remains: "What's going on up there, the way they're sending dead people down? This is the second!"

The men did not answer. They were discouraged, I don't know why. They wanted to get rid of me then and there—leave me in a ditch, as they had found me. Before, I wouldn't have minded. But now I had been struck by a whim: to get there first, to win the race. They kept going, lugubriously.

How far ahead was the other one? A muleteer told us farther on: "I ran into him a couple of miles from the church. I lifted the covers. Know who it was? Antão the orchid-hunter. Stank, poor fellow."

And, recognizing the quality of the goods on the litter: "If you want to get there first, you'll have to hurry. It's going to be a great party. They're only waiting for the stuff. They seem to pay pretty well. I've never heard of such a thing—buying a corpse for a cemetery!" ended the muleteer, with a guffaw. Then, glancing at my wrapped-up body: "Look, his foot's sticking out!"

It was only now that I realized why I was being carried: the people in Arraial

Novo had set up their first cemetery, but had no deceased to inaugurate it. So they had asked around the neighborhood.

It was getting dark. The men were now faced with a flat waste populated by toads and glowworms.

"Swallow your rum and get going!" I said impatiently.

My voice made no sound, but it had an effect. The men hoisted the litter to their shoulders and I started off again, my face turned to the first star.

One of the men was bald, the other had a moustache. They crossed the marsh. If they hadn't known the way so well, the three of us would have been stuck in the mud. They hardly spoke.

"Get that bluebottle off your forehead," I shouted to Baldy. That is, I tried to shout. The man shook his head.

"If we don't get four hundred cruzeiros we take him back," said Moustache.

"I'd settle for three hundred," replied Baldy.

"But he doesn't even smell!"

This was my advantage over my competitor. From the conversation, and from our haste, I gathered that we had better catch up with the other one on the bend by the banana grove before sunrise. At this thought, they shifted me to the other shoulder and began to walk faster.

In the darkness a file of country women appeared. As I came up, they fell to their knees, crossing themselves. The youngest asked a question, to which Baldy replied, without stopping: "No, he wasn't shot; he just died."

"Hurry, hurry!" I shouted, without being able to shout.

The men were beginning to fear that other corpses, besides the one in front, were closing in on Arraial Novo. There's always someone dying in these isolated mountains. But what with the cold of the past few days, and the advent of the trucks, it would be easier than ever to find a dead man rotting by the roadside or in the forest.

The interest of the men carrying me was in arriving first and negotiating a profit quickly; mine was in winning the race against my colleague up ahead.

"He can't be far away now," said Moustache. "You can smell him."

In the distance the banana grove loomed up, its cold-parched leaves waving in the wind. I felt a certain contentment that I had never felt in life. Not exactly ordinary contentment, but a return of the feeling almost extinct in me when they picked me up in the ditch, that I was still wandering near my body and would do so for some time.

That carcass was more than forty years old. I floated out in front of it like the light cast by a lantern.

What a pleasant journey this was! It was so clear that I could see all that went on in the vicinity of my body.

And there went the muleteer Fagundes—that *was* my name, Fagundes, wasn't it?—being carried down on a litter to the cemetery of Arraial Novo.

Why all this haste to open it? Why not wait for some local dead people? Life was good there, I knew. There was plenty of water, there were cornfields and mills, fertile lands and strong men. No one would feel like dying there just to inaugurate a cemetery.

"Hey, Moustache! Hey, Baldy! Hurry up!"

By the Mulatto Girls' Creek we overtook the others. They were going to lose. Aside from everything else, their merchandise was spoiling so fast that it might be rejected even if it arrived first, while my body, lean and sun-cured, seemed intact.

My men passed by without a word. The others watched in a rage. My ectoplasm explored the area without finding anything. As if there was nothing left of that other fellow.

Catching a glimpse of the settlement among the trees in the distance, the two men breathed a sigh.

I was greeted by a band of children amidst a general barking of dogs. They laid me on a platform that was waiting for me in the middle of the little church. They ran to tell the schoolteacher, while in the doorway my two men discussed the price.

The curious were arriving. They uncovered my face. It was the first time they had ever seen a dead man. At the sight of my one tooth stuck in a pale gum, they burst out laughing. Most of them were boys.

"Now the cemetery will be a real cemetery," said one.

"There goes our soccer field," sighed another.

"I don't think we should have fallen back on a dead man from outside," argued a third.

"It's a disgrace for our region!"

A dog came in. His barks echoed in the little nave. Then an old woman entered and knelt beside me, silencing the boys and the dog. As the boys left, with handkerchiefs to noses, they met on the steps an ill-smelling bundle wrapped in newspapers and banana leaves. It was the other fellow. A good why behind, on a cart, came the third contestant. Three dead men altogether.

The boys got indignant. Arraial was being invaded by putrid people. Disgusting! They went to complain to the Founder: in their haste to open the cemetery the women were flooding the village with corpses! One—well, that would have been all right. But so many! Wasn't that dangerous, Founder?

That was what everyone called this robust old man, three times married, the leading citizen and almost the sole owner of this village that he had filled with children and grandchildren.

"Settle it with the women. They're the ones who invented this business of a cemetery. For my part, as I've already said, when my time comes I'm going up and die in the forest."

Suddenly one of the boys grew sad.

"Don't fret, boy," said the Founder, slapping him on the shoulder. "I'll see that you get another field."

"It's not the field I'm thinking about. It's the dead men."

"He's pretending, Founder," interrupted a companion. "He is too thinking about the field, and nothing else. Me too. Our club was challenged, you know that. We've been practicing every day. Now, after the burial, what's going to happen?" He added slyly: "Is just one dead man enough to make a proper cemetery? Not only that, but a fellow nobody knows, who isn't a citizen of Arraial."

"That's right, that's right," I whispered in the boy's ear. But he didn't hear me, he *couldn't* hear me.

"It's your fault," said the Founder. "I ordered a cemetery and you made it into a soccer field."

"But not on purpose, Founder, not on purpose!"

"Even the measurements are the same, so they tell me."

The first boy had been silent, his face troubled. Now, in a rush of feeling that overcame his timidity, he said to the old man: "Founder, we've never had anything like this here. No one ever talked about death. Everybody only thought about working and living. You can save our team. The game is scheduled for the end of the month. People will be coming from all around. Our club is new, but we're sure to win. It will be an honor for Arraial. If it's all right with you, we'll get rid of the body, the inauguration can be postponed, and in three weeks we'll make another cemetery. Perhaps even a better one than this."

"It's too late," replied the Founder.

It really was. The old women had already washed me and now they were changing my clothes.

I had never been so well dressed. They stripped off my rags and put me into some kind of black coat, partway between a suit jacket and a frock coat. I turned out to be a very passable corpse. Clean, anyway.

The teacher assumed a mournful air. Dressed in black also, her face doleful but tearless, she was in charge of the burial. Other women surrounded her. She was behaving as if she were my widow.

Perceiving in the Founder's behavior a certain indifference to the funeral preparations, the boys made up their minds not to show up, and even took to undermining the inauguration ceremony. They offered two arguments: one, that I was not a resident of the place; the other, that filling the village with corpses would bring on an epidemic. Just ask the doctors in the neighboring city.

The Founder made short shrift of the latter argument by ordering the roads blocked and the other dead men disposed of at once. To the former, the women replied that we never know when our own time will come, or what will be done with our remains.

The boys listened in confusion. Such a subject had never occurred to them.

"Yes, you don't think about it, because you're young," insisted the women. "You should know that in this world you don't only die of old age. Let's give a little thought to the future. Remember that death clings to our skin."

And as the bells were beginning to toll, announcing my burial for the next day, the boys retired in defeat. They went down to the little square, with bitterness in their hearts.

"That's that. We'll have to put off the game. What a thing to happen!"

In the talk around the fountain, terms hitherto unknown in Arraial were being bandied about—"bier," "coffin," "funeral," and others, introduced by the schoolteacher.

The girls did not seem downcast. They would have to do without the soccer game, true enough; on the other hand, they had the funeral to make up for it. The first public ceremony of its kind in Arraial. Many were home getting their clothes ready.

The sight of me dressed in black, surrounded by candles and by women praying or pretending to pray, had impressed the boys. They could still hear the old woman's gloomy warning, reinforced now by the tolling bell. They gave up their campaign against the burial. Sure enough, their field was going to become a cemetery.

I certainly was a convincing corpse. The children climbed onto the platform to sneak a look and recoiled, scared away by the spear of my single tooth.

Next day, the people got up early. It had been a strange kind of night, with everybody going to bed convinced I was beside him. The dogs howled unceasingly. No face showed at a window. An immense, omnipresent dead man presided over the Arraial night.

As a matter of fact, I didn't spend a single minute beside my corpse. That job was taken care of by the schoolteacher and one old woman.

I floated above the rooftops, I crept lightly into the houses. I was at people's side during their most intimate activities. How simple they all were behind closed doors! When they dozed off, I touched the backs of their necks lightly. Just barely, enough to feel them shiver. No one saw me. I was sorry I couldn't materialize, as in the days when people believed in ghosts. I couldn't even blow out the lamps lit because of me. Perhaps because my ectoplasm was losing its strength and it wouldn't be long before my body disintegrated.

I'm reduced to the minimum, I thought. But I'm perfectly well able to take a look at the cemetery where they're going to put me this afternoon.

The gate was in place, the walls freshly whitewashed. The grave was open. The goal posts had been taken away. Too bad—the place was really much more like a soccer field than like a cemetery. I wondered what the boys would do now.

The bell began to toll, the dogs to bark. The time was coming. I went back to my body, to attend the funeral. The same woman was there. (Why don't you let me go, teacher!)

Oh, if only I could speak out loud. What a funny way of looking at a dead body!

I was being lifted. The atmosphere was festive. Everyone but the Founder accompanied me. He had said he had to cut some stumps up the hill and had vanished, leaving Dona Maria, his wife, sick in bed with a baby coming. He didn't want anything to do with death. He said he didn't like the cemetery.

I didn't like it either. Mainly because of the circumstances of my burial—that horrible bell that sounded more like confused hammer blows. I had never heard the death knell so badly struck. The people were behaving with relative decorum. At least, they did their best. The boys came along, after all. Reluctantly.

The women's funereal aspect concealed enthusiasm. Some only just managed not to smile. I was close by, watching. From time to time they would remember and put on a show of distress. True distress reigned behind, however, near the band, where the boys were still lamenting the loss of their field. In compensation, they flirted with the girls.

"Not here," said one of the girls. "Look at the dead man!"

"Go ahead and let him," I whispered in her ear. "Don't worry about that fellow up front; he's just an abandoned corpse fixed up by old women with nothing to think about but death."

She seemed to have heard me.

The procession passed through the iron gate. My coffin was laid down near its final resting place. I was getting bored with my enforced role. To awaken so many sad notions in a village so carefree! I claimed no respect for my body. Was it going into the grave now? Just a moment. Let me fly over.

The priest was finishing his Latin phrases. Then he spoke of the meaning of the ceremony, presented to the future dead of Arraial Novo their true dwelling place, and exhorted the people "to think always of death." When he had finished, everyone looked down and pretended to be grieved.

Next came some fine words from the district alderman. He said that we were burying here one of the last muleteers of our beloved region, "a race that is being extinguished before the progressive advance of trucks," and that he had known me (where? how? he had never seen me, I had never voted!) and had an important statement to make: "He was not a stranger to this place, he was born right here." Cheap demagoguery—Arraial wasn't thirty years old! The boys smiled, and resolved under their breaths to expel from the club that sallow fellow who had stooped to the role of gravedigger.

The schoolteacher came forward and gave instructions. The girls surrounded me, and a wave of happiness washed over me. The aura of youth emanating from them! What to do with so much springtime going to waste? My ectoplasm brushed their necks. Only my ectoplasm. The invisible caress raised shivers on their skin, while the little band played a mournful tune under the trees.

It was time for me to go down. And who was that at the edge of the grave? My mule, with its packsaddle on! Oh, little mule, I'm glad you haven't forgotten your old master. Poor thing! You look a mess, like a discarded toy. And behind you, showing her white teeth in a smile, half hidden in shadow, who do I see? Izabela! Remember, Sweetheart, when we went swimming in the river? The only good moment of my life. Now I can't come, mule. I can't, Izabela. Don't you see I'm very busy inaugurating?

The skyrockets exploded and the old women rejoiced. They did everything but cry. In a frenzy they tossed a rain of flowers over my body. Then, lumps of earth, as if they were stoning me. They embraced and bade each other happy goodbyes. They had prepared a site for their remains.

The gate closed behind them. I remained inside, like a china egg. Waiting for the dead who were bound to come.

I remained, that is, in a manner of speaking; I was forever going out. At first my ectoplasm was lulled by the idea of my body's burial, and for days I lost my memory, took a deep dive into the void. But I came back. In a little while I even took an excursion to the town square. There was a shrub there where I liked to hang out. A girl passing by suddenly stopped, startled, and looked at me without seeing me. I lost no time in getting back to the cemetery. And a good thing, too, for a stray dog, the same one that had barked in the church and growled all through the funeral, was scratching furiously at my grave, in the direction of my bones. Thinking of his teeth, I felt an unpleasant sensation similar to what in life is called terror.

After all, I belong to my body; I can't get very far from it without running the risk of dissolving forever.

Frankly, what I disliked was being the only tenant of this place. As the boys said, one swallow doesn't make a summer, and one grave shouldn't make a cemetery. Lately they had been coming home late and tired. They smiled whenever they saw the old women. The women didn't catch on; they were satisfied with their cemetery.

The Founder had his suspicions, but he pretended to know nothing. To make sure, he resorted to a stratagem:

"Well, is the challenge still on?"

"We'll be playing all the same."

"Going to lose?"

"What else? We haven't any place to practice."

"Why don't you talk to the schoolteacher? She has the key to the gate."

"But she only opens it when she goes to pray there."

"For a dead man nobody knows," added another boy.

"That's it exactly," exclaimed the Founder. "They have invented death in Arraial Novo."

Indeed, the old women couldn't let the cemetery alone. They would come in the afternoons and kneel. They weren't praying for me, they were praying for the future dead, they were praying to death. A little while ago, the schoolteacher came. Bending over the grave, she murmured only: "José, my José. . . ."

Now, José wasn't my name. I had forgotten my name, to be sure, but I knew it wasn't José.

The Founder was right. The spirit of death had taken over Arraial. Only yesterday I noticed this when I was resting among the shrubs in the square. Everyone silent and sad, waiting for the church to open. The only ones I didn't see were the boys. It's the cemetery, I thought; it's my presence.

For several days now, while one part of the population occupied itself with routine tasks, the other had been busy questioning its soul.

The old women were saying that anyone who had any doubts should simply go out there at night. Strange sounds were heard, running feet. If it hadn't been for the noise of the mills, the whole village could have heard it. On learning this the population felt a certain pride: there were ghosts already at the cemetery of Arraial Novo!

One surplus dead man, one simple muleteer, had the power to change a flat piece of ground, an ordinary pasture, into a cemetery. Everybody must respect the cemetery now, and the souls that passed through it.

Almost always, there were twenty-two of these souls, besides another few who remained a little apart, watching. They would climb the wall and pull on their shorts hastily as soon as they were inside.

Washerwomen passing by and overhearing would run away. If they had had the courage to check up, they would have recognized familiar shapes in the moonlight.

I loved it there then. I would take part in the game, get into the play. I did everything but shout. I don't know why nobody noticed my presence. Sometimes the ball went over the wall into the next field. One of the players would wrap himself up in something dark and go after it. Then the game would resume. Suddenly, for no reason, it would break off.

"What was that? Who whistled?"

No one had whistled. It was me blowing the referee's whistle. I would often join in without anyone knowing, just to liven things up, just to show I was there, seeing, sharing. They would put in a new referee, but the scoring would still go crazy. No one suspected. Before sunrise, the field would be deserted. The "ghosts" would depart and I would remain. I would remain. It was too bad, having to miss the bull sessions.

I enjoyed waiting for other night games. Sometimes the boys would be late and I would get impatient. First they would toss in the ball; then I knew they were near, getting ready to climb over. The ball would roll to a stop near my grave. Waking up, I would quickly mount the wall and voicelessly call to them. Then another lively game would start.

I gave up the whistle episode, not only because it might scare off the players, depriving me of the spectacle, but because I feared the declining strength of my ectoplasm would become all too obvious.

The old women were becoming suspicious. Not all of them. And of course nobody would have if the schoolteacher hadn't come across my wooden cross lying on the ground. It was the boys' fault; they had forgotten to set it up again the last time, when morning surprised them and they had to make a dash for it.

"No ghost did this," she said suspiciously. "Who could it have been?"

The women went back to the Founder to complain.

"That's no business of mine. Talk to Dona Maria, but after the baby comes; she's in labor now."

"But they were playing soccer on the cross! It's a sacrilege!" exclaimed the schoolteacher.

"It was only some ghost," explained one of the boys.

"Or perhaps somebody kicked a ball over from outside," said another.

"They couldn't because of the wall," insisted one of the women.

"It had to be a curve, and no one here knows how to kick like that."

"Zequinha used to," recalled the gravedigger.

Now, everyone knew Zequinha ran away with the alderman's wife; he was such a good player that she eloped with him.

All that the boys could count on now was the mediation of Dona Maria, who hadn't been doing well since the baby came.

From then on there was no more soccer playing at the cemetery. A closer watch was kept and my "ghosts" did not appear.

I felt low. I wasn't strong enough any more to fly to the village. I wasn't strong enough for anything.

I could no longer see very clearly what was happening on the other side of the walls. The landscape was dissolving before my fading sight.

The song of a laundress beating clothes still seemed to ring in my ears. So far away.

But something was happening at the entrance. The gate was opening wide! People were coming!

Oh, is it you? Come in, make yourself at home. I couldn't be responsible for this whole cemetery all by myself. I'm fading. . . . Space closed in on me. My time was up.

I could only see opaque figures frozen in the act of kicking the ball. And that fixed thing, the last spot of distant light, that must be the sun.

Come in, Dona Maria, welcome to your cemetery.

ANTÔNIO DE ALCÂNTARA MACHADO
(1901–1935)

Alcântara Machado dedicated almost the totality of his work to Italian immigrants in the industrializing city of São Paulo in the modernist years of the 1920s. He wrote scenes in the Italian-Paulista dialect that was common in the city from 1900 through the 1920s and dramatized life in the urban neighborhoods (especially those of Brás, Bexiga, and Barra Funda) of lower-middle-class immigrants struggling to establish themselves. He wrote with a Kodak eye of the period, creating snapshot images, telling stories taken from real life, and painting with sympathetic caricature the new, mixed world full of themes of social integration into Brazilian life. Alcântara Machado joined the modernist group in São Paulo and served as editor (the term used was "butcher") of the *Revista de Antropofagia (Cannibal Magazine)* in 1928. He also wrote a historical work on the São Paulo *bandeirantes*, or historical incursions into the interior for conquest and settlement. His stories were published under the titles *Pathé Baby* (1926), *Brás, Bexiga e Barra Funda* (1927), *Laranja da China* (1928), and the posthumous publications *Mana Maria e Vários Contos* (1936), *Cavaquinho e Saxofone* (1940), and *Novelas Paulistanas* (4 vols., 1959).

THE BEAUTY CONTEST

I

Though certain nationalists in Corisco insisted on calling her Senhorita, her official title was "Miss Corisco." The town of Corisco was so tiny and poor that, when ten families bought an alms box for the church, there was no money left over to put into it. Hence there were not many rivals to eliminate: Bentinho's daughter was freckled; João's sister had something wrong with her hips. So right from the start Conceição was a favorite and was soon acclaimed Miss Corisco.

She started by giving an interview to reporters from the newspaper *O Cacho-*

eirense. They asked: "What was the greatest emotion of your life?" She answered: "There were three. My first Communion, a moving picture of Rudolf Valentino which I saw in the capital of my beloved state, and . . . the third I can't tell—it's a secret."

"We respect the secret," wrote the newspaper, "because of course it cloaks a sweet love story." Then they asked: "What is your dearest wish?" She answered: "To see Brazil always in the vanguard of every enterprise."

"An admirable answer," commented *O Cachoeirense,* "which reveals in Miss Corisco a patriot worthy to be compared with Clara Camarão, Anita Garibaldi, Doña Margarida de Barros, and other national heroines."

Finally they asked: "What do you think of love?" She said: "Love, in my humble opinion, is an incomprehensible thing which rules the world."

"Words," the newspaper pointed out, "which contain a profound philosophy, surprising in view of the youth and sex of the enchanting miss."

She was photographed in various poses: with a little dog in her lap; picking roses in her garden; with her chin resting on the back of her hands. She gave the journalists her autograph—on rose-colored gold-bordered paper, with faint pencil lines to make it come out even, with the letters balancing along them. Her married brother dictated the sentiments. The representatives of *O Cachoeirense* withdrew. Miss Corisco went off to sweep the kitchen, which was her duty every day including Sundays and holidays. But next morning, accompanied by her brother, she took the bus to the capital of her state, Paraíba do Sul, to appear before the beauty contest jury at the statewide level.

The Ciné Theater Esmeralda was full to bursting. On the stage behind the jury the C. Gomes—G. Puccini Music Society was playing two-steps. Every other minute the enthusiastic audience gave a cheer for Brazil and the Brazilian "race." The candidates filed out dressed in the most refined taste. There were five judges: one Brazilian, two Italian, one second-generation Italian, and one Portuguese. They were overwhelmed with patriotic feelings: they wanted to choose a really Brazilian type. Dr. Noé Cavalheiro outlined the ideal incisively as: small mouth and tender eyes. Miss Corisco, by a three-vote margin, was elected Miss Paraíba do Sul.

Then she heard the first speech, pronounced with such emotion that it choked the voice of Dr. Noé Cavalheiro, assistant district attorney, silk handkerchief and all. He recalled how the ancient Greeks dedicated themselves to a cult of physical beauty. He dwelt on the disadvantage of a *mens sana* unless embodied in a *corpore sano.* And though he granted that the beauty of woman had provoked wars and catastrophes, he cited various historical examples of how it had also more than once contributed to the general advancement of nations. He reminded his hearers that Brazil owed much to the love shown it by Emperor Dom Pedro I under the beneficent influence of his mistress the Marquesa de Santos. He then referred to the competence of the jury, its independence of spirit, and claimed that the only dissonant note was his own speech—which called forth the unanimous protestation of the audience.

In conclusion, he intoned an impassioned hymn to the transient pulchritude of Conceição. "Uniting the classic beauty of the Venus de Milo with the stupefying seductiveness of the legendary Queen of Nineveh, Miss Paraíba do Sul, greater than

Beatrice and happier than Natercia, has conquered the heart of an entire region! The Fatherland is not only, as certain spirits imbued with materialism seem to think, laws guaranteeing private property! The Fatherland is something more, something sublime and divine! It is the star which watches us from the sky and the woman who sanctifies our hearth! The Fatherland is you, Miss Paraíba do Sul, it is in your eyes that is mirrored all the virile strength of the nation! For us, honest patriots and eternal lovers of Beauty, Miss Paraíba do Sul is at this moment Brazil!" (Prolonged applause. Speaker enthusiastically complimented. Sincere shouts of "Encore! Encore!")

One by one the members of the jury kissed the delicate rosy little hands of Miss Paraíba do Sul, while the C. Gomes–G. Puccini Music Society vigorously attacked the immortal music of *O Guarani.*

Very flushed and with her velvety eyelids blinking ingenuously, Conceiçao granted her first interview as Miss Paraíba do Sul. She expressed her opinion on the coming presidential elections, the growing of oranges, the religious question in Mexico, the popular provincial priest Padre Cícero, monetary stabilization, Victor Hugo, Brazilian perfumes, the nineteenth-century writer Ceolho Neto, and the decision that cleared the famous madman Febrônio the Devil.

In the Great World Hotel, the pilgrimage to her shrine went on from morning till night. Miss Paraíba do Sul received everyone most amiably with a charming smile on her red lips. The room-waiter went so far as to declare to a reporter, "She is extraordinarily amiable about receiving people: whoever knocks on the door can go in." Her brother, without waiting to find out whether offense was intended, instantly assaulted the unfortunate man. They were all taken to police court, but there the prestige of Miss Paraíba do Sul settled the matter quickly, with charges dismissed.

Presents rained in every day, such as a typewriter and binoculars for the races. An automobile was put at her disposal. The promising young architect Barros Jandaia offered her his professional services gratis. The hairdresser would not hear of charging her, and even gave her twenty coupons for free shampoos with Pixavon. The Cosmopolitan Bookshop offered a deluxe edition of *Paradise Lost.* And so it went.

Miss Paraíba do Sul was received in special audience by the governor of the state: she answered His Excellency's questions most charmingly, and distributed Petit Londrino cigarettes (ovals) to the inmates of the state prison. She also visited the City Hall. There an alderman compared her to the delicate violet of our orchards, which not only attracts by its beauty and captivates by its perfume but also conquers by its exemplary modesty.

Fifteen full days. Really busy. Not one minute of rest. Miss Paraíba do Sul hinted delicately that glory was a burden almost too heavy for her fragile shoulders. And entrained in a private car for Rio de Janeiro, the national capital.

At all the stations along the route appeared the judge, the district attorney, the government delegate, the mayor, the federal tax collector, and the sacristan who was in charge of the customary fireworks. The train whistled. Cheers and applause. The train moved on. Miss Paraíba do Sul arrived in Rio with an unbearable headache.

2

Then began the days of wild hope and suspense. Parties and more parties to cover up the anxiety. And notes from anonymous admirers. And a ball on the Navy destroyer *Paraíba do Sul*. And tea parties with the rivals, spiced with delicious catty remarks. And interviews, interviews, interviews! And pictures of every description in the magazines. One photographer, more daring than most, invaded the privacy of her bedroom and made a very original shot. Next day, on opening their newspapers, the Cariocas were confronted with a shoe and the following caption:

"While Miss Paraíba do Sul was dining, we succeeded in penetrating into her apartment and committing the delicious offense of photographing a little perfumed shoe lying on the dressing table. We were indiscreet enough to ascertain the size . . . it was three and a half! For our readers' pleasure we show above the slipper of this young Maria Cinderella of Grace and Beauty."

Such things touch the heart. Miss Paraíba do Sul gave the little shoe to the photographer as a memento. It was practically useless anyway (as her brother pointed out), since its sole was already worn paper-thin. Enormous crowds were lucky enough to see it on exhibition at the newspaper office. There was not one discordant opinion: it was indeed an adorable little shoe.

Finally the great day of the competition arrived. Miss Paraíba do Sul paraded in her bathing suit for all the old men of the jury to appraise her figure, and submitted to anthropological measurement at the National Museum. Her record was discussed by scientific societies and provoked quarrels among people who had been friends since school days.

But it was all useless. It was not Miss Paraíba do Sul who was judged worthy to represent Brazil in the world contest at Galveston.

It is true that she cried. It cannot be denied. Yes, she cried. But only in the privacy of her hotel room. In public she behaved like a perfect lady. She was all smiles with Miss Brazil. Her admirers protested energetically. A group of students drew up a manifesto in her favor. She just smiled gratefully and said the most amiable sort of things about Miss Brazil. She was honored with further titles: Miss Pindorama (Lady of the Land of Palms); Miss Terra de Santa Cruz (after the original name of Brazil); and Miss Simpatia Verdeamarela (after the colors of the national flag). Everyone recognized that the moral victory was hers. This was a consolation.

Once back in the capital of her native state, however, she decided to change her attitude. She sharply criticized the jury's decision. "Miss Brazil? Certainly a beauty. But a dull beauty. And what good is that without active charm? And no taste at all. You should just see her clothes. All from the bargain counter. What's more, you can tell from her features that she had foreign blood. Brazil will be represented at Galveston; but *not* the Brazilian race." And on she went. Not even the contest's organizers came out unscathed. "Pleasant enough, but partial. One of them, a bald old fellow with a long beard, was always annoying the candidates with his idiotic gallantries. But he got what he deserved: one of the contestants asked him why he didn't cut off a piece of his beard and glue it on to his bald head to look like hair. Yes, that's what she said. Right to his face. Absolutely, And with people around. She actually did. He got as red as a beet."

Corisco received back its Venus with a mournful soul. Miss Paraíba do Sul's father shook his head and murmured: "What injustice! What injustice!"

She and her brother spoke in vain about the moral victory, the sympathy of the people, the protests in the public press. She told how once when she was coming out of the hotel some man had said to her that she was the winner in the heart of the Brazilian people! "What about *that*, Father?"

But the old man would not be convinced. It was all very fine. But the prize money, the eighty-four contos had gone to someone else. "That's the whole point. Someone else got the money. Injustice. Brazil is going from bad to worse."

But he soon had to swear he was wrong, that Brazil was getting on very well, that a moral victory was more than enough, that money never brings happiness—because Miss Corisco, Miss Paraíba do Sul, Miss Pindorama, Miss Terra de Santa Cruz, Miss Simpatia Verdeamarela was beginning to cry.

GAETANINHO

—◦❧ ❦◦—

"Gaetaninho,* what are you doing there!"

He was day-dreaming right in the middle of the street. He didn't see the Ford that almost hit him. He didn't hear the dirty word the driver shouted at him.

"Hey, Gaetaninho! Come into the house."

It was a real motherly scream: a deaf child could have heard it. He turned his face, homely with freckles. He saw his mother and saw the slipper in her hand.

"Hurry up!"

He started toward her slowly, slowly. Frowning a little. Studying the terrain. Just in front of his mother he stopped. He swayed a little. A trick of the soccer champions. He moved slightly to the right. Then he suddenly did a half turn and darted to the left through the door.

Boy, a perfect feint!

—◦❧ ❦◦—

When the people there on Orient Street rode at all, it was in a streetcar. Automobiles and coaches were only for a funeral. A funeral or a wedding. That is why Gaetaninho's dream had never come true. Just a dream.

Take Beppino, for example. That afternoon he got a ride across town to Araçá in a coach. But how? By being in his Aunt Permetta's funeral procession. That was about the only way. Patience.

—◦❧ ❦◦—

Gaetaninho buried his head under the pillow.

Boy, what a deal! In the front, four black horses with plumes were hauling Aunt Filomena to the cemetery. Then came the priest. Then came Savério, her fiancé, with his handkerchief to his eyes. Then came Gaetaninho. Up on the box, next to the coachman. In his sailor suit and white cap with the words *São Paulo Dreadnought* on it. No. The sailor suit was fine but instead of the cap he would wear the new straw hat his brother had brought him from the factory. And black garters on his stockings. What a deal, boy! Inside the coach his father, his two older brothers (one in a red necktie, the other in a green necktie), and his godfather Mr. Salomone. Lots of people on the sidewalks, in the doorways, and at the windows of the fine houses, watching the procession. Especially admiring Gaetaninho.

But Gaetaninho was not completely satisfied. He wanted to hold the whip. The coachman was mean and wouldn't let him. Not even for a few seconds.

Gaetaninho was going to holler but Aunt Filomena woke him up, singing *Oh Marie*, as she did every morning.

At first he was disappointed. Then he almost wept with hatred.

---

* Diminutive of the name Gaetano.

Aunt Filomena had an attack of nerves when she learned about Gaetaninho's dream. In fact, the whole family was alarmed at the bad omen. Gaetaninho felt remorse. To put their minds at rest, he decided to replace his aunt with someone else in a new version of the dream. He pondered, pondered, and finally chose the Gas Company's lamplighter, Mr. Rubino, who once had given Gaetaninho a rap on the head with his knuckles.

His brothers (wouldn't you know it) found some occult reason in the dream for picking a certain number to bet on in the numbers game. They lost and kicked themselves for not having seen that the actual winning number was the one that followed more logically from the dream.

The soccer game on the sidewalk seemed like a matter of life and death. Even though Gaetaninho wasn't paying attention.

"Did you know Afonso's father, Beppino?"

"My father once socked him in the face."

"Then they won't ask you to the funeral tomorrow. I'm going."

Said Vicente, indignant:

"I'm not going to play any more. Gaetaninho is goofing off."

Gaetaninho went back to his position as goalkeeper. So full of responsibilities.

Nino came toward him, dribbling the ball. He got very close. With his body arched, his knees bent, his arms extended, his hands open, Gaetaninho was all set for defense.

"Pass to Beppino!"

Beppino took two steps and kicked the ball. With all his might. It went over the freckled goalkeeper's head and rolled to the middle of the street.

"That's a hell of a kick!"

"Shut up, bigmouth!"

"Get the ball!"

Gaetaninho ran after it. Before he reached the ball a streetcar hit him. Hit him and killed him.

Gaetaninho's father was in the streetcar, coming home.

The kids were frightened. In the evening they spread the news.

"You know Gaetaninho?"

"What about him?"

"He got run over by a streetcar!"

The neighbors took out their Sunday clothes and cleaned them with benzene.

At four o'clock the next afternoon, the funeral procession started out from Orient Street and Gaetaninho was not on the coachman's box of any of the carriages in the train. He was up front in a closed coffin covered with inexpensive flowers. He had on his sailor suit and garters but not the straw hat.

There was a boy on the coachman's box of one of the carriages in the little procession. It was Beppino, wearing a proud, dazzlingly red suit.

João Alphonsus
—◦❧(1901–1944)❦◦—

Son of the great symbolist poet Alphonsus de Guimaraens, João Alphonsus advanced modernism in his state of Minas Gerais, contributing to the journal *Verde* published in the town of Cataguases. His stories concern specific cases or events, communicated with rapid strokes, impressions, and characterizations. He was particularly interested in stories about animals, further marked by a taste for daily life and an interest in the psychology of local society and behavoir. His collections of stories are *Galinha Cega* (1931), *Pesca da Baleia* (1942), and *Eis a Noite* (1943).

SARDANAPALO
—◦❧ ❦◦—

I'm a modest druggist from a poor neighborhood, but there was a time, sir, when I was much younger and dreamier, that I had a taste for the literary life and even enjoyed a certain renown as a student poet while studying pharmacy in Ouro Preto. My Ouro Preto of the bohemian republics, with its countless mansions filled with rooms, traditions and long-bearded, centuries-old bedbugs! An old city, Ouro Preto remains unchanged at a time when everything else has changed. But let's not talk about my timeless Ouro Preto, since my intention is to explain to you why I tremble with fear whenever a mere cat passes by the door of my pharmacy at this late hour. It has nothing to do with any superstition on my part. It's just that I don't like cats; or better, I was overly fond of cats during that time when I thought of myself as a poet and was openly leading the life of an intellectual. Baudelaire and cats! I had convinced myself that it was spiritual to have one of those animals—the friend of lunatics and poets—in my student quarters: an influence derived from the French bards, whose refinement *exquises* were often flea-ridden . . . I kept an enormous cat in my room, a well-fed, lazy and useless cat that I had baptized pompously, parnassianically, Sardanapalo. Imagine, sir, Sardanapalo. It's enough to make one burst out laughing . . . A grim subject for me, cats. The question isn't really whether I like or dislike them, it's just that they make me feel uneasy, somewhat guilty, all because of this Sardanapalo, who became a kind of dark spot in my life . . . As a poet's cat, my well-fed pet didn't lower himself by eating the rats that were passing through our republic. At times Sardanapalo would chase them for amusement or perhaps out of respect for family tradition. He was a black cat, as was fitting for a worshiper of good literature, who had already read Poe translated by Baudelaire. He was black and fat and lazy. So fat and so lazy that at a certain point I noticed he was losing altogether the most notable characteristic of his race, namely the mortal hatred of rats. He wasn't even chasing them any more! The rats of Ouro Preto are also dignified and solemn and—don't laugh—traditionalists . . . descendants of other rats who, in those very same mansions, witnessed important historical events. Imagine, sir, in the home of the chief magistrate, Tomás Antônio Gonzaga, a meeting of the conspiring dreamers with the forefathers of those rats, who scurried around the attic and even across the floorboards and between the legs of men caught up in the hopes of national independence! And later, the ancestors of those rats, which I saw just now gliding subtly into my room, may have climbed up the post of colonial infamy where the head of Tiradentes was put on display! And when his eyesockets were ignominiously rotted away, they might have even entered the recess of that cranium where the fever of nationalism, without literature and with the simplicity of heroism, truly burned . . . These are just some of the thoughts that came to me at that time, but they didn't excuse the lack of character in which Sardanapalo was wallowing, and to such a degree that the rats began trafficking freely on the very sofa where he would stretch himself out with total disinterest. I used to watch him half-open one of his eyes, look at them for a few seconds, and then go back to sleep. Meanwhile, my books, even my most cherished works by my beloved poets, had been gnawed! I began cutting down on his food, slowly but methodically. With this, Sardanapalo returned more or less to his role as cat by suddenly shaking off his customary apathy to chase any rat that dared pass by him too closely. I didn't starve him by any means, that wasn't part of the plan. Despite his being the literary animal to whom I had already dedicated an Alexandrine sonnet, or because of this, I only wanted him to fulfill his responsibility of policing my intellectual goods against the subversive actions of the rodents. Nevertheless, in spite of this reasoning, I found one of my notebooks containing my own verses partially destroyed. I stared at Sardanapalo contemptuously; the useless animal thought I was giving him a prolonged, affectionate look and came to thank me by rubbing himself between my legs! I ended up scratching his head and smiling at what seemed an impossible situation. Then I left for an evening that ended with one of those dinners responsible for my present dyspepsia . . . Later that night, as I was about to return home, I recalled the gnawed book of verses and decided not to take him, as I was in the habit of doing, the sausage left over from my dinner. At the last moment, however, giving in to my good nature, I collected a few scraps of bread that were scattered about the table. When I opened the door, Sardanapalo jumped off the sofa with gaiety and interest. I threw him the crumbs disdainfully and fell heavily into bed . . . I was awakened by a strange noise in the room; a chair toppled over, sounding like a bomb, a sound that echoed in the abandoned rooms of the floor below. The noise was accompanied by the frightened squeals of a rat. The pale Ouro Pretian dawn filtered through the skylight to reveal Sardanapalo sitting in the middle of the room, resting one of his paws on an enormous rat. I wondered, could it be a demonstration of his efficiency, a sign of his rehabilitating himself? At that moment he seemed so caught up in the joy of his capture that he didn't pay the slightest attention to my having noticed his triumph. He lifted his paw off the prisoner and lay down in front of him, lazily, as if he were about to go to sleep or at least to doze. Seconds passed and suddenly the rat took off, getting but a short distance, less than the length of a single floorboard. Just then, Sardanapalo jumped, caught the rat in his mouth, and brought him back to his original, humble, nullified position close to his nose, and with studied indifference, he stretched himself out next to the rat. He didn't actually bite the rat, which gives an impression of violence, rather he held him delicately between his teeth without hurting him, forcing him to return to the point of departure. This wasn't the first time that I had witnessed such a scene between a cat and a rat. But it was the first time I had ever seen Sardanapalo act like that; having just been awakened from my morning slumber, at a confused and uncertain hour of the morning, my body hadn't even left its reclining position nor the pleasant torpor of its half-awakened cells, and with my head still on the pillow, I followed the development of the events . . . In those few minutes only we three existed in the world, in the universe, in time and space: myself, the cat and the rat. Sardanapalo began stifling his prisoner's slightest attempt to move by dealing small blows with his front paws. After innumerable delicate, almost gentle taps that didn't harm the rat, Sardanapalo initiated his interpretation of a "struggle." The rat, being so insignificant, seemed to have diminished in size. Poor, miserable little rat, his desperate moves facilitated the cat's dramatized struggle. Without heeding the insistent delicacy with which the cat's paws ordered him to remain still, the rat tried to escape them with all his might. But Sardanapalo would pounce on him, toss him into the air and, quickly turning on his back, would catch the rat with all four paws and then roll with him into a ball. And they would roll together toward me, as if the rat were in fact struggling, and then they would roll back . . . There were scores of acrobatic moves, as when Sardanapalo caught the little animal in the air between his paws, once, twice, five times . . . Next he allowed the rat, appearing smaller in size by the minute, to run the length of the room while he jumped back and forth from head to tail above him, so that from one moment to the next his way was obstructed. Disoriented in despair, the rat first ran in one direction, then another, in a futile attempt to escape his captor. It indeed had all the appearances of a game, but we three knew that it wasn't. My cat was faithfully fulfilling the age-old call of race against race, or of species against species, by putting his physical superiority to work. The clarity of the early morning gave an added refinement to the natural development of those cruelties impregnated with elegance and gentility. I was no longer lying down, but sitting, without the least concern with the cold (it seems to me now that I must have been feverish); and my legs were dangling from the old, high bed. Not missing the smallest detail, I was deliriously absorbed in watching the cat's highly diversified movements—more than absorbed, I was overcome by some inexplicable cruelty, a bizarre sensation which made me proud to be Sardanapalo's master, an indirect yet willing participant in that endless torture! Sir, do you know perchance a story by Villiers de Lisle-Adam called *The Torture of Hope?* No? In a final attempt to test the salvation of a man's soul, a medieval inquisitor tortures one of his victims, tempting him with the hope of being able to escape prison. The man discovers that his cell door has been left unlocked; he pushes it open and walks through endless corridors; friars pass by him without seeing him hidden in a niche in the wall. One of the friars, who is discussing with another some theological problem, rests an absent-minded gaze upon the fugitive immobilized in a cold sweat in his hiding place; but both friars take their leave, repeating, among other pious words, the name of Christ. The fugitive now sees the door leading to the outside, beyond which is light and the air of freedom; he moves toward the door when suddenly he is embraced by the inquisitor who calls him son and tells him not to flee from there, not to flee from Christ . . . The incident in my room made me recall the story, which I had read during that period, and at that strange morning hour, I remembered the original system of torture revealed or imagined by the storyteller; and Sardanapalo—don't laugh—remembered to apply it, or better, I transmitted my thoughts to him . . . My cat laid down nonchalantly and allowed his prisoner to run as far as he could (the rat was already staggering and exhausted, although he was without a single scratch), even to the corner of the room where there was a mouse hole I had stuffed with newspapers. The creature approached the hole, discerning the somber opening, prematurely enjoying its darkness and the narrowness of the meandering corridors where no cat had ever entered or could enter, the freedom of the darkness . . . he was closing in on the hole, only a few centimeters from it! In two leaps, the torturer caught up with him and carried him back in his mouth once again to the point of departure. All this, from the very beginning, was the pure torture of hope, with all the variations imaginable, each variation repeated once, twice, five, ten times . . . And I was seated on the bed accompanying them, using nerves and muscles to repeat to a certain degree those diversions, a cat myself, yes, a cat myself, don't laugh! Possessed by a cruel enthusiasm, I was twisting just like today's boxing fans do . . . The rat was now a rag, martyrized with such skill that one didn't see even the slightest trace of blood. If it happened that he was thrown on his back by a blow from one of Sardanapalo's paws, he remained on his back, flailing his little paws in the air, seeking help from some divine source to return him to his normal position . . . We were now at the end. Yes, we were at the end. I and my cat against that little animal nearly devoid of life's breath, who no longer responded to the cat's renewed and final blows. Perhaps he could still move himself a little, but he didn't try, convinced of the utter futility of it all, nirvana-ized . . . And my interest in the incident, an interest devoid of pity, even contrary to it, was reaching its peak. Note that there was no vengeance intended on my part as a result of the gnawed verses, since such a feeling in a human being against an insignificant little rat would be an unpardonable monstrosity. It was pure cruelty, a strange and unique intoxication of the perverse, with my alerted nerves sending signals to my muscles; it was as if my muscles were all moving in accordance with those of Sardanapalo. I sat on the bed and bent over the persecutor and the persecuted, shaking my bare legs, waving my arms, without soul and without feeling the cold morning air. I was a man possessed! Yes, that's the word: possessed! Without the slightest aversion, even with a certain diabolical enjoyment, I saw the enormous cat, who filled the enormous room with his extraordinary importance, open his mouth, show his fauces, and close his mouth, with the little rat's head between his teeth, crushing and swallowing it slowly . . . The little tail followed even more slowly, like a little snake. Sardanapalo coughed, and was seized by a kind of choking fit as the fine, delicate point tickled his throat. Only then did he look at me. But what a look! Of a grateful and compassionate accomplice perhaps, who fulfilled the order to kill that my disdain had instilled within him earlier. But even more, it was the look of a very pleased acrobatic showman for my silent, patient applause. Perhaps it was none of this and merely an amiable look at me, his master, after having demonstrated how much he could do, and how able, agile, and powerful he was . . . What is clear is that I didn't fully understand his look, to which I responded with restraint, not because of the humiliation I felt for being an accomplice or because remorse had set in: but because I perceived, frightened and confused, that the cruelty awakened within me was not yet satisfied! Before returning to the sofa, Sardanapalo came alongside the bed and, gazing at me still, rubbed his furry, warm body up against my cold, bare feet. Once, twice, four times . . . I began to play nervously with him, pulling my feet back so that he would lose his balance when he leaned against them, and then gently rubbing his full stomach with the soles of my feet. Sardanapalo stretched out on the floor. Now he seemed very small, endearingly tiny. I placed one of my heels on top of his head, which he lowered reverently, gratefully, gently. And with a sudden, irrepressible urge, I jammed my heel down with all the force of my body and crushed his skull. He didn't die just then. He began pulling himself away, dragging his head, unable to lift it off the floor. With his spinal column broken, it was as if his head were stuck to the floor with glue. He didn't meow or moan but merely gave that kind of choking sound. I opened the window, picked him up by the tail, and threw him out into the clear morning air as far as I could. He fell over there to the bottom of the abandoned, overgrown orchard and rolled down a steep slope until some bushes broke his fall. He continued to move around a little bit down there. Then he disappeared among the leaves.

LAUS DEO

Breno Accioly
—◦❧(1922–1966)❧◦—

A northeastern writer from Pernambuco who was also a medical doctor, Breno Accioly's stories join modernist techniques, including a tendency toward surrealism, to an exposé of the psychological undercurrents of society. As in "João Urso," he created a hallucinatory climate of madness and brutality in which differing cultural perspectives and values clashed. The collection titled *João Urso* (1944) won the Graça Aranha Prize in 1945 and the Afonso Arinos Prize from the Brazilian Academy of Letters in 1946. His other collections are *Cogumelos* (1950), *Marina Pudim* (1955), and *Cataventos* (1962).

João Urso
—◦❧ ❧◦—

The hills are torn bundles. From the distance come echoes of loud voices; but the city is an enormous silence of heavy sleep, of sleep broken by the sounds of the hills. And it seems that the night in the hills is different from the night which wraps the city.

In the hills are the red colors of the lightning, the loud cries of the breaking thunder, the trees quickly changing color and quickly returning to the green of their leaves.

There are no stars shining above the hills. They are all burning dimly in the distance.

The winds, the raging clouds and the burning colors are far away. One could compare the city to a person at a play, sitting in the back row and having to use binoculars.

João Urso may never have seen binoculars. But he seems to be shielding his eyes, making of his two hands a screen against the fierce brightness.

Leaning from the window, João Urso sees the old hills fighting against the fury of the elements and even forgets the sadness which is always with him.

A machine has put out the lights. Only the white shapes of the cathedral tower stand out sharply, hanging cones, motionless, piercing the night.

The wall of the hospital and its wards are also visible but weaker blemishes;

and if the prison had not been painted red, it would have been another blemish to take note of, a gross smear, with its old roofing, sleeping with its punished passions.

João Urso lifts the collar of his pajamas and rubs his hands.

The fig trees, the *caraiberas,* all the trees of the city and of the banks of the river are quiet. There is no wind to shake their branches, or turn the small weather vane at the meteorological station.

Canoes wedged between punt-poles as if they are overloaded and unable to stir; like enormous abandoned wooden slippers; the streets without drunks, or prowlers, or howling dogs.

João Urso alone watches the spectacle in the hills. When the lightning, growing stronger, flashes through the window, his eyes ache; for a moment it lights up bits of the dining room: chairs reflected in an oval mirror; a foot of wall covered with a picture of the Sacred Heart of Jesus, a God with a blue and red robe, holding in his left hand a globe of the world, his right hand lying on his chest as if to relieve some deep pain; numbers of portraits of João Urso's ancestors are colored, bleeding in the flash of the lightning.

The old piano seems to be covered in blood.

When the lightning moves by the river, the glasses of the cupboard seem to be full of wine, left over from some strange party where nobody wished to drink.

João Urso sighs. He bows his head to the city, and lifts his eyes to see the towers and the stars shining. Yes! Those towers and those bells! He sighs again. So long ago. So many memories.

And he fixes his eyes as if he were actually seeing the bells inside the cones of the towers, the bells ringing, waking the city to proclaim: A Waterspout! Since he was small he had loved to think like this, terrifying things which would make shivers of fear run up his spine. How good it would be if a Waterspout fell and made a hole in the ground, so deep that a lantern was needed to explore it.

A Waterspout to tear up roofs, cut the statue of the Emperor in two, break the chains of the prison, the iron bars which cut the prisoners' faces as they look out onto the road; João Urso begins to laugh. To laugh as he had laughed throughout his childhood, a laugh which nobody understood, and which made many people call him mad.

Even he could not explain why. When he came to, his mother would be screaming in his ears, angry, worried, wanting to know the reason for these sporadic, inexplicable bouts of laughter. João Urso would begin to cry. For hours at a time, he would be in disgrace, perched on a high stool.

The hours would pass slowly, slowly. In disgrace João Urso's hands would hold a book of sonnets: how often had he memorized love poems, and stood before his mother to repeat his punishment!

Sometimes, before finishing a sonnet João Urso's voice would seem to run away: his mouth would open showing yellow teeth, his cheeks would become round and full, pressing against his eyes, transforming his face, while he laughed out that hidden and mysterious pleasure.

"Get back to the stool, you little fool. Three more, do you hear?" João Urso knew that three more meant three more sonnets to learn.

He would climb up once more and return to reality a long time after, his legs hanging from the high stool.

Suddenly the echoes of João Urso's laughter would cross the corridors, fill the room, disturb the monotony of the huge stone thick-walled house, with its enormous garden going down to the banks of the river. As he used to sleep in the next room, he would wake sometimes to hear a person cry. He recognized it as his mother.

He would press his ear against the wall, but the thick stone only allowed him to hear everything dimly.

But even without being sure, João Urso believed that his mother's sobbing at night was due to the bouts of laughter he loved so much. João Urso would be happy, would shiver with pleasure when he felt that coldness running up and down his spine before filling his body with repeated spasms.

On one occasion some people had called with their children. They had gone to play in the attic. Downstairs had been heard the happy cries of children at play; but suddenly a long bout of laughter had drowned all the noises, and shaken the children who had been jumping over boxes, playing at hiding behind wardrobes and mats, concealing themselves in doorways or in the dark, narrow steps of the staircase.

The children had begun to cry as if they were crying for help.

In the middle of the corridor was the figure of João Urso laughing nervously, possessed by uncontrollable laughter, filling the children with terror as they continued to cry, calling for their parents, begging somebody for help.

They were children crying as if they had heard voices from another world, the laughter of some terrible apparition.

He had thought he would be punished, and spend the whole afternoon perched on his stool, learning sonnets by heart, his mother slapping and shouting at him.

He had gone sadly downstairs, and had sadly looked out of the window onto the road, its paving of enormous stones burning, leading upwards as if it wished to reach the hills where the donkeys who came to steal water from the river were returning.

And João Urso had felt his heart burst, filling itself with hate and, at the same time, with cowardice.

And if, instead of being punished, he were to go to church; struggling for a lantern as it was carried slowly past the Stages of the Cross, and lighting them? It was impossible now. Even if he were to go to church, he would be unable to get hold of a lantern. The priest had forbidden him to do so. The pious old ladies had been full of loud condemnatory prayers before, and had crossed themselves repeating the word: Excommunicated!

When he had held the lantern, João Urso had laughed heartily, shaken in a convulsion of strange laughter: his hands had seemed to change the lantern into a glove, and had whirled the globe like a boy from a circus, a mighty-handed acrobat.

The procession had been interrupted. Everybody had stood back, the priest with his open book, his eyes heavy with surprise, his rosary abandoned on his right arm like a useless weapon.

The white dresses of the Daughters of Mary adorned bewildered virgins, terrified by the laughter of João Urso whirling the lantern, as the columns in the nave answered the screams with muffled echoes, echoes vanishing behind the altars, behind the pulpits, and creeping up towards the trap in the choir through the box of the staircase.

And amid João Urso's mysterious pleasure, they had sprinkled holy water, while the priest—from a distance, everybody at a distance—prayed in Latin. João Urso remembers that afternoon well; he remembers the holy water that dried out on the blue cuffs of his sailor suit, on the velveteen collar embroidered with anchors. Neither has he forgotten the priest, the pious ladies, the whole town.

Sant'Ana do Ipanema was a voice which told everything, unable to keep the deepest secret. The people in the neighborhood had heard the story. And in the market, in the butcher's shop, in the town hall, in the brothels of Rua do Sebo, they had talked about João Urso's illness. They had imitated his bouts of laughter, and had cut the silence of the night with their mockery of his laughter. It was fashionable to laugh as João Urso laughed.

João Urso had thought of the punishment, and had soon abandoned all thought of the procession. He had been sure, absolutely sure, that his mother would punish him, bind him to the high stool, fill his hands with sonnets—romantic sonnets to be recited without a single mistake.

He had been expecting punishment. And, as if he were a condemned man with a few moments of life before him, had stayed at the window, his eyes following the street upwards, and then down the opposite way, losing themselves among the ox wagons creaking along the roads. The flagstones had shone, and the river of still, seemingly stagnant water had changed into a swamp where canoes rotted.

João Urso had sensed his mother's footsteps. To try and protect his ears, he had twined his arms, lowered his head—and waited. He had waited so long that he looked up.

And with surprise he had seen his mother crying, stretching out her arms to him, wrapping him in a long maternal embrace, crying still, moistening his hair with tears, searching out his mouth, his eyes to cover them with kiss after kiss.

In the corner of the room, the stool had become a friendly shadow like the other furniture. The agony of the stool, and of memorizing sonnets was over.

But instead of crying to accompany his mother's tears, he had filled the whole house with peals of laughter, laughing nervously as he had laughed in church, as he had laughed terrifying the children in the attic, as if he were saying good-bye to a punishment, fleeing from a hated prison.

And at school, whenever anyone was caught laughing without good reason, without an explanation, the teachers would say:

"Could this be João Urso's disease?"

There was no school which would teach him.

Everything over there seems to be on fire. Flashes of lightning tearing the hills, covering the trees with blood, bending their streaks over the city, streaks with huge reflections which are splashes of blood on the towers of the Cathedral, on the few large houses, on the walls of the cemetery. They are like lanterns, strange lanterns that torture the city with their red eyes, off, on, quickly off again.

And the stunted chest, the small hands, the strange head, the João Urso that the window still cannot hide is a splash also.

The hills must have imprisoned the thunder. João Urso no longer hears mouths bursting as if they want to tear the sky and explode all the secrets of the hills.

He is only colored by the lightning now, disturbed by the wind, nursed by the song of the rain that begins to fall. And he hears the rain surge in the gutter, the song of a rivulet flowing between the flagstones, the strength of the wind sway hair and trees, uttering the wail of untidy and disheveled hair.

João Urso sighs again.

He lowers the window. And stays watching the rain washing the glass, running its quick drops down until they disappear in the window frames.

He can hardly hear the song of the rain, now. He can see only the lightning through the window pane, and hear the distant murmur of tossed trees; enormous drops of rain hammer on the roofs, flowing rapidly by the flagstones.

João Urso hears everything distantly, half hearing as if he has been wrapped by the silence of the house, his senses imprisoned in the big drawers in the dressing tables, in the dark wood cupboards; he runs his fingers through his hair, framing the deformed head of his frail body. Such a long time ago!

A stronger lightning crosses the window pane, reddening the portrait of João Urso's mother. And the portrait seemed to revive João Urso's mother in the March afternoons, in those quiet, restful afternoons, when they had gone up the hills, João Urso breathing slowly. The doctor had ordered him to breathe very lightly, and João Urso had done so. His mother had lain in the shade, her hands useless, her fingers resting on crochet needles. And when she had seen João Urso putting down his penknife, tired of writing his name on the tree trunks, she had dried her face, moistened the sleeve of her blouse and shaken her head.

This was after the punishments, after João Urso had memorized endless sonnets, and stayed long hours perched on the stool. She had thought João Urso's laugh was insubordination or disobedience. And only after the scandal in the church, after the children had cried from fright in the attic, after everybody in the city had made fun of João Urso, and the schools refused to admit him—only after this had she thought to call a doctor.

And the prescription was to breathe the fresh air of the hills, breathing slowly "as if he were asleep." The doctor had said: "as if he were asleep" and how often had João Urso seen his mother absent-mindedly talking to herself, muttering irreverently: "as if he were asleep . . . as if he were asleep."

How often had his mother in her morning prayers slipped in that phrase of the doctor's without noticing! And João Urso had breathed as if he were asleep, obedient, even to the extent of lying down on the leaves, pretending to be asleep. Since João Urso hadn't stopped his laughter, a horse ride at the end of a train journey had taken him away from the hills, from the gossip, and from his mother who had remained waving, full of tears, waving until the horses had disappeared.

The specialists had been alarmed and had held a joint consultation. They had never seen anything like it; no medical book had ever dealt with it. And João Urso had continued laughing, letting out enormous shouts, high-pitched screams which had run through the wards like the cries of a strange wounded bird.

They had forbidden João Urso to read his mother's letters. No emotion, nothing disturbing. The doctors had found him an unusual case.

They had written to Europe to consult with experts; cures had multiplied and a cupboard had been filled with bottles labeled: THE TREATMENT—JOÃO URSO. And they had been downcast, and completely thrown off balance, when after each new medicine João Urso had laughed as if he had been with his mother, climbing the hills to breathe the purer air.

One, two, five years João Urso had stayed in the sanatorium, five years of lost Christmases, separated from the eve of St. João, that he had anxiously awaited, counting the days. He had returned laughing worse, much worse than when he had gone galloping away, passing through the shrub country, traveling by the train from Quebrangulo. "Recife is over there." His father's arm made a curve, as if he had wanted to enclose the hillocks, the children of dromedaries on the green hills.

The gesture had seemed to say: "We are far away." They had whipped the horses, spurred on, and the horses had lengthened their pace, whinnied, their flanks damp with sweat as if they had just crossed a river. Afterwards the Recife train had passed through miles of sugar-cane plantations, glimpsing factories with tall chimneys: João Urso had been delighted. The heat and dust hadn't bothered him. His father had told him the names of the estates and stories about the factories. João Urso had lifted his deformed head and seen in his father's eyes the magic of adventure. When he had met his father, he already knew how to talk, all his teeth had already cut. And sometimes he had seen his mother leaning from the window, absent-mindedly looking from the veranda up the highroads, distantly searching for that shadow which she knew so well. And one day, when he woke up, he had seen his mother telling a tall broad-shouldered ruddy man:

"This is João Urso, your son!"

And he had felt that the hands of the stranger, the man who his mother said was his father, were hard as rock, bumpy with corns.

Afterwards his father had taken him to his room and opened leather cases and trunks stuffed with riches. And for the first time João Urso had heard of diamonds, and precious stones which his father said were worth a fortune.

He had gone away suddenly and without warning leaving in his mother's eye that frequent sadness, a sadness that by its frequency became normal.

Now João Urso had returned. He had seen his mother thirty years older and had heard that heart, which used to beat so strongly, almost silent.

He felt moved, an urgent wish to cry, to hold his mother and to sob. He had opened his arms, wrapped his mother's breast in a violent hug and had begun to laugh, to laugh as he had never laughed, a sick laugh, interspersed with deep cries and terrifying screams.

The doctor who had brought João Urso had felt ill, and for a moment petty and useless. But he had moved instantly forward and had tried to separate João Urso's arms, and release him from his mother's breast.

João Urso's arms had been like iron rods, immovable in their sudden strength. João Urso had torn his throat and forced open the cut of his mouth. And when João Urso had stopped laughing, the walls had returned his cries of laughter in distant echoes as if other João Ursos had been hidden and were answering him.

His mother had fainted. And in her unconsciousness, asleep under the effect of morphine, had shuddered, her legs shaking in convulsions, had waved her arms, and groaned distressingly.

And João Urso had never again seen those trunks full of riches, those leather trunks. Never again had he felt those calloused hands, never again had he heard talk of diamonds like his father's talks.

The town had remembered João Urso's father as it remembered the death of the powerful.

"He died sifting gold on the banks of the Rio Prata. He was the richest man there. He lit cigarettes with fifty-dollar notes. He had virtually an army of prospectors. And he was rich enough to be godfather to the Governor's son." Other stories had been repeated from mouth to mouth. Stories like fairytales, unbelievable at that time.

His woman, for a whole year afterwards, would go with no one. She needed to rest and to restore her powers.

Another story had been told of a woman who went around the world, visiting all the nightclubs, and living in Paris like a princess because João Urso's father had liked her and wanted her to enjoy herself.

The window pane doesn't stop João Urso from being covered with a splash of blood. The hills are red flashes that have brought rain, furious rain, hammering the roof tops, swelling the volume of the river. And the waters of the river become dark, each moment muddier.

João Urso's mind dwells on so many memories, so many broken recollections! So many fragments of his sad past João Urso lives again, so many, so many!

Not even the hands of the clock break the silence of the house. The clocks are like out-of-date maps showing the time of another age. Everything is far away.

And as if he is throwing a last glance over his life, João Urso sees himself orphaned of his mother, forgotten by his father from whom he has had no news for so long, dead perhaps, or dying amid the riches which the people spoke about.

He sees himself forsaken by the world, without even knowing whether his laughter was contagious (even at the sanatorium the doctors took precautions). He had lived like an animal that loves the dawn, the solitude of the sleeping streets. João Urso had felt happy when some passer-by in the night bid him good night or asked him for a match. He would watch the shadow move away with a look full of sadness. And João Urso too would go away, fearing to be recognized, terrified of seeing the passer-by take to his heels, fly away in fear at discovering that it was João Urso.

He had loved climbing up beside the cemetery to find the meteorological station and he had stood for hours watching the weather vane turn, marking the direction of the wind, with those four letters which looked to the four corners of the earth. And once João Urso had seen the instrument house open.

He had marveled at the thermometers, the tubes of mercury oscillating slowly and magically. He had touched the aluminum flasks with enchantment. His eyes had stared at everything, at that world enclosed by white boards, and striped by blinds. He had felt himself the lord of a world that only he visited at dawn. He had never tired of seeing the thermometers, the geography of the constellations, tracing the bright paths of the comets with shining tails, of distant stars.

João Urso had braved the rain, the cold, the heat of the stifling nights. And if on this night he didn't go out at dawn it was not for fear of the lightning or of the rain which failed to wash the blood from the hills. João Urso would have loved to be with his mercury tubes, walking beneath the rain. But he is a prisoner now.

They have turned the old house into a prison. Soldiers, shivering with cold, dig their hands into their coat pockets. They swear. They have received orders to let nobody in or out. Their guns are wet pieces of iron, as forgotten as the soldiers in the stormy night. The judge had spoken fiercely, in front of João Urso.

"You know what to do if this criminal tries to escape. Fire!"

And they had all thrown stones, breaking the glass of the veranda, shouting, with clenched fists raised with the anger of the crowd. The people had crowded together and had fought for a place in front of the house wanting to lynch João Urso. And from up there João Urso had heard his name slandered in the people's mouths. Fate? João Urso could not understand the reason for it all. Yes, it had been silly. He should have remembered that everybody was afraid of his laughter. He had always tried to hide himself. But the lights of the circus had seemed to call him: they pleaded with him. João Urso had hesitated.

The shadow of a woman balancing on a trapeze was a mark on the canvas, tracing complex movements.

From a distance João Urso had admired, following the shadow, balancing his eyes on those studied, dangerous movements. Another mark had outlined the shape of a sunshade on the canvas. It was the end of the Balance of Death. There had been a long silence. They had all seemed dead, because nobody had breathed. The dancer had prepared to leap for another trapeze. The canvas had traced the silhouette of an Outstanding Act. A voice had called for more silence. Everybody had been in suspense, mouths open, waiting. The drummer had held up his arm to strike when the Jump of Death was over. But he had never been able to do so. João Urso had approached, arriving at the entrance to the circus. And at the moment of jumping, when the dancer's feet had flown like two sequin wings, with trousers of red satin, and a firm brassiere, at this moment, João Urso had let out his sharp cry of strangled laughter, perhaps the greatest laugh of his life. And the dancer had been like a wounded bird, a falling flight.

Once more João Urso's eyes bleed in the lightning. The spectacle of the hills, the song of the rain hammering on the roof tops, running by the flagstones, tires him.

And he only feels the desire to sleep, as he waits to go on a long journey, a journey which not even he knows the end of.

He finds his bed, and closing his eyes, keeps inside them the uncommon geography of the constellations, the mathematics of the old thermometers, the beautiful uncertain flight of the dancer.

GRACILIANO RAMOS
—∘❦(1892–1953)❦∘—

A writer's writer, Graciliano Ramos was entirely self-educated in the small town of Palmeira dos Índios in the northeastern state of Alagoas. An admirer of Machado and Eça de Queiroz, Graciliano represented the social novel and story of the Northeast in its most synthetic, condensed, and aesthetic form, subject to its author's constant revisions and perfectionism. He is best known for his novel *Vidas Secas* (1938; *Barren Lives*, 1965), many of whose chapters were originally published as stories, including the unforgettable story of the dog "Whale." Ramos creates a dramatic allegory in the drought-stricken lands of the northeastern interior, where the *sertanejo* Fabiano and his nuclear family wander in search of survival. The author's prison memoirs, *Memórias do Cárcere*, document his arrest and imprisonment by the Vargas regime in 1935 and the months before his release in Rio de Janeiro. Graciliano Ramos is remarkable for his critical, carefully crafted language, his dark characters, their psychological, self-destructive mentalities, and his tragic sense of life and fate. Many of his stories deal with crime, psychological instability, or a hero in revolt. His narratives are dry, essentialized, and spare, whether telling of the marginality and frustration of *sertanejo* life, or searching though the skeptical underground of the self. Because of his intimate, omniscient style and his portraits of society—from painting to orality to sociology—Graciliano Ramos is considered to be a master of the genre. His stories are found in *Histórias de Alexandre* (1944), *Dois Dedos* (1945), *Histórias Incompletas* (1946), *Insônia* (1947), *7 Histórias Verdadeiras* (1951), *Histórias Agrestes* (1960), and *Alexandre e Outros Heróis* (1962).

The Thief

The good luck that favored him during the first month or two turned out to be a misfortune. It was strange indeed: with no training at all this fellow starts out, makes one mistake after another, breaks into houses without studying the neighborhoods, clumps around as if he were out in the street—and everything goes fine. Clumping around like that, it's a miracle. You have to know how to move quickly and noiselessly, like a cat: your body must become weightless, it must float, almost leave the ground, and your legs must have spring and elasticity. Otherwise your joints will crack, you'll take forever to move from room to room, and the job will become almost impossible. But no one can achieve this necessary skill without an apprenticeship, and you can't complete an apprenticeship if you get caught at it.

Perhaps there is a divinity that protects novices, however brashly inept. At the beginning no one suspects them. They seem just like other people. The police don't follow them. If they didn't bump into furniture and shine their flashlights in the eyes of people who are sleeping, they'd probably never get arrested and sent to jail, which is a sort of trade school for thieves. That's where they sharpen their ears and get used to gliding around. After they're out they won't have to wear rope-soled shoes on the job any more: they'll move like machines with well-oiled springs, rolling silently on rubber tires.

The individual to whom I specifically refer had not yet acquired this indispensable if prejudicial manner: indispensable inside a house at night; prejudicial in the street, for it reveals the thief. Doubtless there are other signs by which a cop can recognize a thief, but the primary characteristic is this furtive, slinky way of walking, as if he were barely touching the ground. As I said, this fellow didn't know how to walk that way, and so he could pass unperceived in the crowd. There was no immediate likelihood that he could adopt the necessary, telltale manner. Sponger, his friend, who started him in the profession, had told him frankly that he ought to seek some less hazardous occupation. But the fellow was hard-headed. Encouraged by two or three lucky experiences, there he was, prowling around the iron gate as if he knew what he was doing.

He had already gained admission to the house by posing as a stove repairman and had observed the disposition of the furniture on the ground floor. He was sorry he hadn't studied the layout in greater detail. He should have got himself hired as a servant in the house for a week or so. That had been Sponger's advice, and Sponger could speak from experience. But, in his folly, he hadn't listened to him. So now he didn't even know on which side of the dining room the door to the pantry was located.

He moved away from the gate, afraid that someone might notice him. He walked down the street, entered a café at the corner, looked at the clock, and felt like taking a drink. He had no money. Besides, it would be crazy to drink at such a time. He was trembling. His hands were cold and damp.

"I've got to do it."

He looked again at the clock. It was after midnight. Fortunately, the street could be entered only at this end; at the other it came up against a hill. Few people, except those who lived on the street, were likely to go there.

. . . It really wasn't important. . . . He worried for a moment about the possibility of running into someone who knew him. The trembling of his hands tormented him. He was almost certain the waiter had noticed how pale he was. He went outside and stood on the sidewalk, undecided, looking at the hill, wiping his damp fingers on his handkerchief, telling himself again that it wasn't important. He shook his head and tried to remember what wasn't important.

He felt like going home. But he smiled wryly and started up the street, staying always close to the walls of the houses. How could he go home? He lived in the streets. What wasn't important? Finally he remembered and he felt better. What wasn't important was whether the door to the pantry was on the left side or on the right side of the dining room. Should he go into the pantry and steal the silverware? Eh? No, it would increase the danger. But then he thought of the cheese he had seen on top of the refrigerator. His mouth watered.

As he approached the house, his legs felt weak. He was trembling like a child. Probably the pantry was on the right as you entered the dining room, near the stairway.

"I've got to do it."

He approached the house, circled the premises, and then stood with his back against the garden gate. If he stretched his neck to look down the street, the policeman (if there was one) on the corner might notice him. His heart beat desperately and his vision clouded. He could not even see the corner to determine whether a policeman was there.

He flattened his body still more closely against the gate. He looked at the window of the house on the opposite side of the street and imagined that someone was watching him from it, perhaps the owner of the dry-goods store who had stared ferociously at him through thick eyeglasses when he had approached the counter the day before. He tried to dismiss this troublesome thought. Why should he think that the same eyes which had immobilized him yesterday were looking at him now, especially at such an hour!

But suddenly panic seized him. He felt he was being observed from the front and the rear, so that he was impelled both to run away and to take refuge in the garden. The street was filled with ambushes. He began to tremble again. His thoughts became confused. It seemed to him, for a moment, that he had already finished the job. He leaned against the gate.

For several minutes he thought about his old school in the suburbs, and he saw himself as a sad, puny boy. The teacher seemed to ignore him. She rarely asked him questions. The evil-looking boy next to him used to stick him with a pin; when the boy grew up he became a soldier. The little girl with the braids was pretty; she had green eyes and whenever she spoke she shut them.

A shiver dispersed these memories. He wanted to smoke but was afraid to light a match. Raising his head, he was momentarily distracted by a trolley car far off at the end of the street.

. . . Yes, no, yes, no. . . . His thoughts turned to the man behind the window, now comfortably warm and calm, and to the girl with the braids, smiling tranquilly and shutting her green eyes. His teeth chattered softly like castanets and then loudly like an angry pig. This alarmed him: perhaps someone could hear the noise. He bit into the sleeve of his jacket, stifling the sound.

Yes, no, yes, no. There was a clock in the dining room. He was almost sure he could hear the strokes of the pendulum. His teeth stopped chattering and further damage to his jacket was averted.

He stirred a little and stretched. His fears were subsiding. Now he moved with confidence. He grasped the top rail of the fence and, with a burst of energy, vaulted over into the garden. He crossed some flower beds and walked along the path to the porch. There he sank down on the sofa. If they found him so, he would say that he had entered the premises before the locking of the gate and had fallen asleep. That's what he'd say, although it would hardly serve to exculpate him.

But why dwell on possible misfortunes? He rose, went over to the door, and put his penknife in the lock. His hands no longer trembled. The bolt slid noiselessly. He stopped in surprise. He had never before worked alone, and he therefore expected every lock to stick. He had planned to climb up on the sofa and to cut, with a diamond, a piece of the glass panel above the door. He would then push an opened newspaper under the door, roll a handkerchief around his hand, and dislodge the glass, which would fall noiselessly on the paper. He would grasp the empty frame, pull himself up and, through the panel space, enter the house head first, groping for the floor. He would probably remain hanging there some time, like a monkey, with his curved toes serving as hooks on the lower edge of the opening. Almost surely something would go wrong in this maneuver. He would fail, he was bound to fail.

He looked for the glass panel. In vain: there was none. Nor did he have a newspaper. What stupidity to think this way, to invent trouble.

He opened the door and went in. He advanced slowly, afraid that he might bump into things. As his eyes became accustomed to the darkness, he began to distinguish vaguely the shapes of long, low chairs that cluttered the little parlor. He slid toward one of them and fell into it, exhausted, breathing fast, his heart pounding. The springs squeaked. He rose quickly and flattened himself against the wall. He was afraid his knees would give way. All the joints of his body seemed to crack whenever he moved; the noise would probably wake everybody up and he'd be captured. He lit his flashlight and was immediately sorry. What a rash thing to do! He turned it off.

He went into the dining room. Stretching his eyes wide he could see objects pretty clearly. A gray shadow extended down the stairway; there must have been a light on upstairs.

Fine: he could see the door to the pantry. It was on the right, just as he had thought. Two days before, he had seen a cheese on the refrigerator. He went over to the stairway and leaned on the banister with his head turned toward the pantry. He really wasn't hungry. He felt a pang in his stomach, but his mouth was dry. He shrugged his shoulders. It would be stupid to risk so much for a piece of cheese.

He went up one step and stopped. He was breathing hard. He climbed farther and felt nauseous. The stairway was moving, the house was moving. The dryness in his mouth disappeared. He puffed out his cheeks to contain the saliva as he thought about the cheese. He climbed a few more steps and swallowed the saliva with repugnance.

"I've got to do it."

He repeated this to strengthen his will. Yet, although he was halfway up the stairs, he found it difficult to continue. Suppose someone was watching him in the dark. He remembered the fellow in the dry-goods store; maybe he lived in this house and right now was staring at him like a cat. He thought again of the little girl in elementary school, of her smile, of her eyelids with which she hid her green eyes, like those of a cat. He hated himself for vacillating, for wasting time on such nonsense.

He arrived at the top of the stairs, stopped to listen, and then started down a hallway onto which many rooms opened. He went quickly past the door of a room where a light was on, and headed for the master bedroom, hoping it would not be in use. His fear was counterbalanced by a childish feeling of pride. He had done well so far. This job was quite an exploit, yes sir, and he wanted to hear what Sponger would say about it. If nothing bad happened he would seek out Sponger the next day. If nothing bad happened. For a moment he almost panicked. He crossed himself. God would not permit anything bad to happen. It was foolish to think of such a possibility. He would tell his story the next day, omitting his fear, and Sponger would be proud of him.

He turned the knob very slowly. Fortunately, the door was not locked. He became terrified again, but suddenly he conceived the curious idea that the danger lay elsewhere, that he could find sanctuary in the master bedroom. He went in, shut the door behind him, made a gesture of fatigue, breathed deeply, and assured himself that he was safe. His slight dizziness must have been caused by hunger. Really, a dope like him shouldn't take on such a job. Did he have the skill, the competence, for it? No, of course not. His talent was limited to entering houses through windows that had been left open, stealing whatever lay nearby, and beating it. That's all he was good for. His childish pride withered. If they discovered him, he wouldn't know which way to run. What troubled him at this moment, however, was less the fear of capture than the conviction of his own inadequacy. He knew he was going to fail: his hands would tremble, his joints would crack, he would knock over furniture.

He clasped his hands together in a sudden resolve to finish the job quickly. He fixed his attention on the big bed, where an elderly couple was sleeping. In alarm he fell to a crouch: if one of them woke up, he must not be standing there like a statue. Still bent over, he moved forward and hid behind the head of the bed, where he remained in the same position so long that he felt cramps in his legs. The windows were open, and the room was bathed in light from the street.

Turning his head he saw himself in the wardrobe mirror. He looked ridiculous, squatting there with his head twisted. He turned away from this disagreeable vision and noticed an arm hanging over the side of the bed. It was the arm of a lady, the sickeningly fat arm of a rich old lady. The hand was short and flabby, with rings on its plump fingers. He thought of trying to remove the rings with a bent needle. Sponger had taught him this trick, and he had some needles in his pocket. But he preferred not to take the chance. Sponger had iron nerves. To steal rings from a person's fingers! What a man! Years of practice, several prison terms.

On hands and knees he crawled to the wardrobe cabinet, opened it, and began to examine the clothes. He discovered a wallet, put it in his pocket, and hurried out into the hallway. At the door of the room where a light was on, he examined the contents of the wallet and found several banknotes. He tried to discern their amounts, but the light was insufficient.

He thought of leaving, took a few steps, and stopped. Sponger would ridicule him mercilessly for quitting before he had gone through the entire house. His terror had disappeared. He was amazed that he had come through all the danger without mishap. Of course he hadn't yet finished, but somehow he felt safe.

He opened one of the doors with a crowbar, lit his flashlight, and saw an oratory. What splendor! He wanted to take the beautiful images, especially the heavy, gold staff of Saint Joseph. He withdrew quickly, afraid of the temptation. He would never commit such a sacrilege.

He went into some of the other rooms and took various small objects of little value. He felt impelled to enter the room in which a light was on. There he could count his money. Besides, he wanted to be able to tell Sponger that he had gone there.

He managed to slip the doorbolt, went in, and hid behind a wardrobe cabinet. There was a narrow bed in the room, but he didn't look to see what manner of person was in it. He drew the wallet from his pocket and, for a time, stared like an idiot at its contents. He began to count the money, became confused, started again, and finally gave up. His fingers were trembling, the numbers were all jumbled together. He stuffed the bills into his trouser pocket. He would count the money later when he was calm. He would take it and go and live in a suburb where nobody knew him. He would quit this profession, for which he had no talent anyway, no talent at all. He wouldn't tell Sponger; he would avoid all such compromising characters. He would straighten himself out, become a respectable person, and start a business of some sort, far away from Sponger. Yes sir. He felt the bulge of the mass of bills and buttoned the pocket. He would become a decent person, yes sir, and this was the stuff that could do it for him.

He looked at the bed. At first he thought its occupant was a child, but then he saw an exposed breast. He trembled, turned away, and started toward the door. Then he stopped, turned again, and observed the young lady in the bed. He saw in her traces of the girl with the green eyes. His heart beat so violently in his narrow chest that it seemed about to leap out through his mouth.

He straightened up and averted his face. It was a crazy idea. He tried to think of ordinary, everyday things. He took a deep breath. He counted to ten. The tattoo on Sponger's leg was a horrible thing, really indecent. By now the café at the corner must be closed. He counted to ten again and exhaled. A fit of coughing interrupted these endeavors.

He hurried out of the room, making an enormous effort to keep silent. He needed air, tears were streaming from his eyes, the veins of his neck stiffened like taut ropes. He hurled himself through the hall and down the stairs, his hand in his mouth. He sat down on the lowest step and remained there several minutes, shaken by the stifled coughs. He began to wheeze softly, trying to get rid of a persistent tickle in his throat. He wiped away a trickle of saliva.

Gradually he recovered. Surely the people upstairs had awakened. He turned his head and cupped his ear. For a moment he had the mad notion that he could hear moths gnawing at the clothes in the cabinets. He should have taken some of the clothes; Sponger's fence would buy them.

He heard the sound of a whistle in the street and broke out in a sweat. A rooster crowed. Then everything was quiet again, except for some indeterminate little sounds, perhaps the patter of cockroaches' feet.

He got up, no longer terrified, and tried to take stock of his situation. He was hungry. The tickle in his throat had disappeared. Nonsense to listen to the cockroaches on the wall or to worry about the policeman's whistle in the street. These things had nothing to do with him; he was out of danger. Yes, out of danger. If his cough came back he would stifle it by biting his sleeve. He cleared his throat softly. Calm. Calm and hungry. He turned in one direction and then the other, torn between the little parlor and the pantry. The tickle in his throat had completely disappeared. His mouth filled with saliva. He listened: no policeman blowing his whistle, no rooster crowing, no cockroaches moving about. He wanted so much to go into the pantry. Now that he had recovered from his suppressed coughing and suffocation, he felt a need for refreshments.

He pressed the button on his flashlight. The weak light shone on the glass cupboard, then climbed up the table, dividing it in half. He placed the flashlight on the tablecloth. He drew the crushed bills from his pocket, bent over, and tried again to count the money. After several failures he finally thought he had the right sum. He considered it sufficient for the establishment of a bar in the suburbs. He smoothed the bills, folded them, put them back, and buttoned his pocket again.

He had capital now. He felt cold and hungry. The policeman must be dozing down at the corner by the café. He turned up his jacket collar. He had capital; he would establish himself in the suburbs as the proprietor of a café, far from Sponger and these dangers. A small, modest café with a radio and with decent customers, drinking and talking about soccer. This was where his talent lay. He would listen interestedly to the conversations without taking sides, he would never offend anyone, and he would see that his employees did their jobs properly. A boss, yes sir; he would treat his workers firmly but humanely. And Sponger wouldn't even recognize him if he saw him—stout, serious, working the cash register. Sure. He felt the lump of money and grew in strength. Fine. But no political intrigue in his café. Sports, inoffensive subjects, perfectly okay; but whisperings, secret papers handed from one to another, absolutely not. Everything must be proper: no complications with the police.

He straightened up. A slight pain gnawed at his stomach. He took the flashlight and started for the pantry with the firmness and confidence appropriate to the proprietor of a tavern in the suburbs.

Suddenly he felt an overwhelming desire to laugh—softly, of course, lest he cough and gag again. He shook with this quiet laughter for several minutes, while his shadow danced on the floor. He had bungled everything from the start, he hadn't even known which doors were where, he had bounded noisily down the stairs—

and no one had awakened. These people must sleep like corpses. So why be so careful, why take such precautions? Sponger knew how to work right, he even took rings off the fingers of people while they were asleep. A man of genuine accomplishment. And yet he had been arrested twenty times, had served several sentences, and had had any number of narrow escapes. So Sponger's knowledge and skill were really of little value. When God wants people to stay asleep, they stay asleep.

Where could the cheese be? He had seen it two days earlier on top of the refrigerator, but now he searched for it in vain. He went into the kitchen, looked in the casseroles, and found some pieces of meat, which he ate almost without chewing. His fingers were greasy from the fat and he licked them. Then, very deliberately, he turned on the water in the sink, washed his hands, and wiped them on his jacket. Relieved and satisfied, he breathed deeply. His light-headedness had entirely disappeared.

He thought of the clumsiness and stupidity with which he had handled the job. Holy Mary, what a bungler! If he told Sponger the whole story, with complete frankness, he'd have to listen to a sermon. But he wouldn't tell him anything. He wanted to have nothing more to do with Sponger. He was going to open a café in the suburbs.

He returned to the dining room and turned off the flashlight. The people upstairs must have been in a coma all this time.

A mad idea occurred to him: he would go up and down the stairs again, just to prove to himself that he was not so awkward as he seemed to be. Then the girl with the green eyes surged into his memory with one breast uncovered. Absurd. It was the young lady sleeping upstairs whose breast was uncovered. He wondered what the color of her eyes was.

The clock struck two, filling the house with the sound. The ticktock began to torment him. A few moments before, there was silence, but now the ticktock hammered inside his skull.

He returned to the parlor, tempted to go back into the rooms upstairs and take some additional objects to sell to the fence. He thought that by beginning again and, this time, following the rules expounded by Sponger, he might vindicate himself. The mass of bills, acquired so easily, now gave him no gratification.

He stepped on the first stair and trembled. The reasons for going upstairs fled his mind. Only the uncovered breast remained.

He tried to make himself think about the bar in the suburbs but couldn't. He stopped for a moment at the head of the stairs. "I must be crazy!" He went to the door of the room where the light was on, pushed it open, saw that the woman was still asleep.

And from that moment on, until the dreadful outcome, he didn't know what he was doing. The following day he remembered having stood a long time next to the bed, but he found it hard to believe he had done the mad act that brought about his downfall. How did it happen? It began with a sort of dazzlement. The house was spinning, the room was spinning, and he himself was spinning around the woman. He was a fly, circling, approaching, flying away. He had to light somewhere, to stop this dizziness The image of Sponger came and quickly went; the eyeglasses of the man in the store and the panes of glass in the window of the house across the street, blended and faded away. The clock struck again, a whistle blew in the street, cocks crowed, and he heard all this; but it made no impression on him. And then came the disaster, the madness, the maddest of madnesses. He bent over and pressed a kiss on the young lady's lips.

The rest of the story is in the police records. Giddy, emotionally exhausted, he gives only fragmentary and contradictory information. In vain they question him, in vain they slap him around. All he knows is that he heard a scream of terror and then a noise in the other bedroom. He remembers having gone down the hall and having taken one step on the stairs. He must have fallen down the stairway and lost consciousness. While he was falling he had a quick dream: he saw dirty cubicles crawling with bedbugs, pallets on the damp floor, horrible faces, gangs of prisoners carrying heavy beams. People were insulting him, raining blows on his back. But the insults faded away, the blows ended. And there was a long silence.

When he came to, he found many hands grasping him. Blood was flowing from a wound in his forehead. It got into his eyes, coloring everything and everyone red. An old man, wrapped in a blanket and holding onto the banister of the stairway, seemed to be gesticulating at him. And a woman's scream came from above, probably a continuation of the scream that had ruined his life.

WHALE

Whale was dying. She had grown thin and her hair had fallen out in several places. Her ribs protruded from beneath pink skin where dark fly-covered patches oozed and bled. Mouth sores and swollen lips made eating and drinking difficult.

That's why Fabiano thought she was showing early signs of rabies and had tied a rosary of burnt corncobs around her neck. But Whale went from bad to worse. She rubbed against the corral posts or rushed pell-mell into the brush trying to shake off the mosquitoes by flapping her droopy ears, swishing her short hairless tail, thick at the base and coiled like a rattlesnake's.

So Fabiano decided to shoot her. He got his flintlock, filed it, cleaned it with a rod, and set out to load it carefully so that the dog wouldn't suffer too much.

Sinhá Vitória closed herself in the bedroom, dragging with her the frightened boys who sensed misfortune and kept repeating the same question:

Are you going to hurt Whale?

They had seen the lead shot pouch and the powder horn and Fabiano's movements upset them and led them to suspect that Whale was in danger.

She was like a member of the family. The three of them played together, one could say there was no difference between her and the boys. They rolled around together in the river sand and in the soft manure that accumulated, threatening to engulf the goat pen.

They tried to move the bar and open the door but Sinhá Vitória took them to the bed made of branches, pushed them down and tried to cover their ears. She held the elder one's head between her thighs and spread her palms over the ears of the second one. She became irritated when they resisted and struggled to hold them down, grumbling fiercely.

She also had a heavy heart but she had resigned herself. Of course, Fabiano's decision was necessary and just. Poor Whale!

She listened; she heard the sound of the shot as it poured down the gun barrel, the muffled thumps of the ramrod on the wadding. She sighed. Poor little Whale!

The boys began to yell and kick. And because Sinhá Vitória had relaxed her grip, she allowed the bigger one to escape. She swore:

Accursed demon.

In the struggle that ensued to regain hold of the rebel son, she became really angry. That dickens. She cracked him on the head that he had buried under the red blanket and her flowered skirt.

Little by little her anger subsided and Sinhá Vitória, cradling the children, began grumbling about the ailing dog, muttering contemptuous expressions and harsh names. That disgusting, slobbering animal. Such a nuisance to have a crazy animal loose in the house. But then she realized she was being too harsh. She thought it unlikely that Whale had gone mad and regretted that her husband had not waited one more day to see if the execution was really necessary.

At that moment Fabiano was walking through the shed snapping his fingers.

Sinhá Vitória hunched her neck and struggled to press her shoulders against her ears. As that was impossible, she raised her arms and, without releasing her son, managed to cover part of her head.

Fabiano crossed the lean-to, staring out at the brauna trees and the gates, setting an invisible dog on invisible animals.

Sic 'em! sic 'em!

He then entered the sitting room, walked down the hall, and came to the low kitchen window. He examined the yard, saw Whale scratching herself and rubbing the bare spots of her hide on the Jerusalem thorn, and raised the musket to his face. The dog eyed her owner with distrust. She coiled around the trunk and moved stealthily away until she reached the other side of the tree, where she crouched suspiciously, showing only her black pupils. Annoyed by this maneuver, Fabiano jumped through the window, stole along the length of the corral, stopped at the corner fencepost and again raised the gun to his face. As the animal was facing him and did not present a good target, he advanced a few more steps. On reaching the caatinga trees, he adjusted his aim and pulled the trigger. The charge hit Whale's hindquarters and crumpled one of her legs. She began to yelp desperately.

Hearing the shot and the yelps, Sinhá Vitória cried out to the Virgin Mary and the boys rolled on the bed, crying loudly. Fabiano withdrew.

And Whale quickly ran off, circled the clay pit, entered the garden from the left, passed right by the pinks and the pots of wormwood, slipped through a hole in the fence and reached the yard, running on three legs. She headed for the shed but fearing she'd find Fabiano, moved away toward the goat pen. She stopped there only a moment, somewhat disoriented, and set off hopping aimlessly.

In front of the oxcart her rear leg failed her, but bleeding heavily she continued like a human being, on two legs, dragging the posterior part of her body with difficulty. She tried to withdraw and hide under the cart but she was afraid of the wheel.

She headed for the jujube bushes. Beneath the root of one of them was a soft deep depression. She liked to wallow there: she would cover herself in dust, avoiding the flies and mosquitoes and when she arose there would be dried leaves and twigs stuck to her sores. She was different from other animals.

She fell before reaching this far-off retreat. She attempted to rise, lifted her head and stretched her front legs, but the rest of her body lay on its flank. In this twisted position, she could hardly move, as she scratched her paws digging her nails into the ground and grabbing at small pebbles. Finally she collapsed and lay quiet alongside the pile of stones where the boys threw dead snakes.

A horrible thirst burned her throat. She tried to look at her legs but couldn't quite make them out; a mist clouded her vision. She began to yelp and wished she could bite Fabiano. She wasn't really yelping: she was howling softly, and the howls diminished until they were barely perceptible.

Driven by the sun's glare, she was able to inch forward slightly to hide under a sliver of shade at the edge of the rock.

She looked at herself again, worried. What could be happening to her? The mist thickened and drew closer.

She detected the good smell of cavies descending the hill, but the smell was faint and mixed in were scents of other living creatures. The hill seemed to have moved much farther away. She turned up her nose, slowly breathing in the air, wishing to climb the hill to chase the cavies that jumped and ran about freely.

She began to pant with difficulty, feigning a bark. She ran her tongue over parched lips and felt nothing. Her sense of smell was growing weaker: surely the cavies had run off.

She forgot them and again felt a desire to bite Fabiano, who appeared before her half-glazed eyes with a strange object in his hand. She didn't recognize the object but began to tremble convinced that it held unpleasant surprises for her. She made an effort to avoid it and to pull in her tail. She closed her heavy eyelids and decided that her tail was hidden away. She couldn't bite Fabiano; she had been born near him, in a bedroom under a bed of branches and had spent her entire existence in submission to him, barking to round up the cattle whenever the herder clapped his hands.

The unknown object continued to threaten her. She held her breath, covered her teeth, and espied the enemy from beneath her sagging lashes. She remained this way for some time and then relaxed. Fabiano and the dangerous thing had vanished.

She struggled to open her eyes. Now there was a great darkness. The sun must have disappeared.

The goats' bells tinkled down by the riverside, the stench of the goat pen spread over the surrounding area.

Whale gave a start. What were those animals doing loose at night? It was her duty to get up and lead them to the water hole. She dilated her nostrils, trying to make out the boys' smell. She was surprised by their absence.

She couldn't remember Fabiano. Something horrible had occurred, but Whale did not attribute the impotent state in which she found herself to that disaster, nor did she realize that she was relieved of her responsibilities. Anguish gripped her little heart. She must keep watch over the goats: at that hour there would be a smell of jaguars along the riverbanks and circling the more remote stands of trees. Fortunately the boys were asleep on the straw mat, beneath the corner shelf where Vitória kept her pipe.

A cold, misty, winter night embraced the little creature. Complete silence, not a sign of life anywhere. The old rooster did not crow on his perch, nor did Fabiano snore in the bed of branches. These sounds did not affect Whale, but when the rooster flapped its wings and Fabiano turned over, familiar emanations disclosed their presence to her. Now it seemed that the ranch had been abandoned.

Whale was breathing fast with her mouth open, her jaw flapping and her tongue hanging, devoid of feeling. She didn't know what had happened. The blast, the blow she had taken in her haunch and the difficult journey from the clay pit to the rear of the yard faded from her mind.

She was probably in the kitchen, among the stones used for the cooking. Before going to bed, Sinhá Vitória raked away the coals and ashes, swept the burnt earthen floor with a small broom, leaving a fine place for a dog to rest. The heat chased away the fleas and the ground was soft. And, after nodding off, numerous cavies scampered and frolicked; a swarm of cavies invaded the kitchen.

The shaking increased and moved from Whale's belly to her chest. From her chest on back everything was numbness and amnesia. But the rest of her body shivered, mandacaru cactus thorns penetrated the flesh that had been half-eaten away by the disease.

Whale rested her tired little head on the stone. The stone was cold; Sinhá Vitória must have let the fire go out very early.

Whale wanted to sleep. She would wake up happy, in a world full of cavies. And she would lick the hands of Fabiano, an enormous Fabiano. The children would wallow with her, they would roll around with her in an enormous yard, in an enormous goat pen. The world would be full of enormous fat cavies.

JORGE AMADO
—◦❧(1912–2001)❦◦—

One of the most prolific writers of the twentieth century, Jorge Amado evolved from the early dramatic, expressionistic proletarian novels in his first phase before the 1950s to a celebratory exposition of historical and cultural episodes and personalities of Bahian life after the publication of *Gabriela, Clove and Cinnamon* (1958). His long narratives elevate cuisine, conflicts, and mulatto heroines as national actors. Many of his novels have been made into film, including the widely praised *Dona Flor and Her Two Husbands* and *Tent of Miracles*. Jorge Amado was important for popularizing the mulatto and the role of Afro-Brazilian religion in Brazilian life, at the same time that he satirized the dominant political culture. His memoirs constitute a valuable panorama of literary and political life in twentieth-century Brazil. While Amado never specialized in the story per se, his novels are full of stories, a genre in which he is an enchanting master. Amado is one of the most widely translated Brazilian authors of the twentieth century. His tall tale "How Porciúncula the Mulatto Got the Corpse off His Back" was originally published in an anthology edited by Adonias Filho, *Histórias da Bahia* (1963).

How Porciúncula the Mulatto Got the Corpse off His Back
—◦❧ ❦◦—

The gringo who dropped anchor here years ago was a tight-mouthed and fair-skinned guy. No one had ever seen anybody who liked to drink so much. To say he guzzled the booze isn't to the point, because we all do that, praise the Lord! He'd spend two days and two nights nursing the bottles and not turn a hair. He didn't start blabbing or picking a fight; he didn't begin on the old-time songs, and he didn't spill over with hard-luck stories from way back. Tight-mouthed he was and tight-mouthed he remained; only his blue eyes kept narrowing, a little at a time, one red-hot coal in every glance burning up the blue.

They told lots of stories about him, and some tricked out so neat it was a pleasure listening to them. But all hearsay, because from the gringo's own mouth you couldn't learn a thing—that sewn-up mouth that didn't even open on the big fiestas when your legs feel like lead with the booze accumulating in your feet. Not even Mercedes—with a weakness for the gringo that was no secret to any of us, and inquisitive as only she could be—could squeeze out one clear fact about that woman he killed in his country, or about that guy he kept hounding year in and year out, through one place after another, till he finally stuck a knife in his belly. When she asked about it on those long days as the booze drowned out all reserve, the gringo just kept looking at no one knew what, with those tight little eyes of his, those blue eyes now bloodshot and squinting shut, only to let out a sound like a grunt, not meaning much of anything. That story about the woman with the seventeen knife wounds in her nether parts, I never did get to find out how the thing ended up, it was so bogged down in details; or again, the story about that rich fellow he hounded from one port to another till the gringo stuck a knife into him, the same one he used to kill the woman with seventeen wounds all in her nether parts. I don't know because if he was carrying those corpses around with him he never wanted to get rid of the burden, even when drinking he closed his eyelids and those burning coals rolled onto the floor at everybody's feet. Listen, a corpse is a heavy load, and many's the brave man I've seen who let his load slip into a stranger's hands when booze loosened him up. Let alone two corpses, a man and a woman, with those wounds in the belly . . . The gringo never let his drop, which was why his ribs were bent, from the weight of it, no doubt. He asked for no one's help, but here and there they told about it in detail, and it turned into a pretty good story, with parts for laughing and parts for crying, the way a good story should be.

But what I must tell now has nothing to do with the gringo. Let that one wait for another time, just because it needs time. It's not over one damn little drink— no offense to anyone here now—that you can talk about the gringo and unwind his life's ball of yarn or undo the skein of his mystery. That'll have to wait till another day, God willing. And time or moonshine won't disappear. After all, what are the stills working night and day for?

The gringo only drops in here, as they say, in passing, but he came on that rainy night to remind us the Christmas season was at hand. And of the country he hailed from where Christmas was a real holiday, not like here. Nothing to compare with the feast days of São João, beginning with those of Santo Antônio and going through the days of São Pedro, or those days commemorating the waters of Oxalá, the fiesta of Bonfim, the holy days of obligation of Xangô, and—oh brother!—not to mention the feast of the Conceição da Praia, which was some holiday! Since there's no lack of holidays here, why go and borrow one from a stranger?

Now the gringo remembered Christmas just at the time when Porciúncula—that mulatto in the story about the blind beggar dog—changed places and sat down on the kerosene drum, covering his glass with the palm of his hand to keep the voracious flies out of his booze. A fly doesn't drink booze? Your honors will excuse me, but this will sound like nonsense because they don't know the flies in Alonso's place. The flies were really wicked. Crazy for a drop; they'd throw themselves way down into a glass, sample their tiny drop, then out they'd come, weaving and buzzing like May bugs. There was no possible way of convincing Alonso, that headstrong Spaniard, to put an end to such a disgrace. His story was—and he was right—that the flies came with the place he bought, and he wasn't about to get rid of them for being troublesome simply because they wanted a little snort. That wasn't reason enough, since all his customers liked it too and he wasn't going to throw them out, was he?

I don't know if the mulatto Porciúncula changed places to be nearer the kerosene lamp or if he already had the idea of telling the story about Teresa Batista and her bet. That night, as I explained, the lights went out all along that part of the waterfront, and Alonso lit the kerosene lamp grumblingly. He really wanted to kick us out, but he couldn't. It was raining, one of those crazy heavy rains that soaks you wetter than holy water straight through the flesh and to the bone. Alonso was a trained Spaniard who absorbed a lot of his training from being an errand boy in a hotel. That's why he lit the lamp and stood doing his accounts with a pencil stub. People were talking of this and that, swatting flies, skipping from subject to subject, killing time as they could. When Porciúncula changed places and the gringo grunted out his piece about Christmas, something about snow and lit-up trees, Porciúncula wasn't going to let the chance slip by. Driving the flies away and downing a slug of booze, he announced in a soft voice: "It was on a Christmas night when Teresa Batista won a bet and started living a new life."

"What bet?"

If Mercedes's question was meant to encourage Porciúncula she needn't have opened her mouth. Porciúncula didn't have to be prodded or coaxed. Alonso put down his pencil, refilled the glasses, with the flies buzzing around convinced they were May bugs, completely drunk! Porciúncula downed his drink, cleared his throat, and began his story. This Prociúncula, he was the best-talking mulatto I ever knew, and that's saying a lot. So literate, so smooth, you'd think, not knowing his background, that he'd worn out a schoolbench though old Ventura hadn't put him into any school but out on the streets and the waterfront. He was such a wizard at telling stories that if this one turns sour in my mouth it's not the fault of the story or of the mulatto Porciúncula.

Porciúncula waited a bit till Mercedes was comfortable on the floor, leaning against the gringo's legs to hear better. Then he explained that Teresa Batista only showed up on the waterfront after her sister was buried, a few weeks later—the time it took for the news to find them where they lived, it was so far away. She came so she could learn directly about what had happened, and she stayed on. She looked like her sister, but it was just a facial resemblance, a surface thing, nothing on the inside, because the spirit of Maria of the Veil no one else had and no one ever will. That was why Teresa all her life remained Teresa Batista, keeping the name she was born with, without anyone finding it necessary to change. On the other hand, who on any day of the week would have thought of calling Maria of the Veil, Maria Batista?

Nosy Mercedes wanted to know who in the world this Maria was and why "of the Veil."

She was Maria Batista, Teresa's sister, Porciúncula explained patiently. And he told how Maria had scarcely arrived in these parts when everyone began to call her

Maria of the Veil, and only that. Because of that mania of hers for not missing a wedding, with her eyes glued to the bride's gown. They talked a lot about this Maria of the Veil on the waterfront. She was a beauty, and Porciúncula, with his turn for phrases, said she was like an apparition risen from the sea at night when she wandered around the port. She was so much a part of the waterfront, it was almost as though she'd been born there, when actually she came from the interior, dressed in rags, and still remembering the beating she'd gotten. Because the old man Batista, her father, didn't fool around, and when he heard the story of how Colonel Barbosa's son had taken her virginity, which had been still as green as a persimmon, he grabbed her by the chin and beat the daylights out of her for giving it away. Then he kicked her out of the house. He wanted no fallen woman in his house. The place for a fallen woman is the back alley, the place for a lost woman is the red-light district. That's what the old man said, bringing the club down on his little girl, being so full of rage, and even more of pain, to see his fifteen-year-old daughter, pretty as a picture, no longer a virgin and useless except to be a whore. That's how Maria Batista became Maria of the Veil and ended up by coming to the capital because at home there at the end of the world there'd be no future for her as a prostitute. After she arrived she knocked around from pillar to post till she landed on the Hill of São Miguel, such a child still that Tibéria, madam of the brothel where she'd dragged her bundle, asked her if she thought it was a grade school.

Many of the story's details before and after this Porciúncula got from the mouth of Tibéria a highly respected citizen and Bahia's best whorehouse madam ever. It's not because she's my friend that I praise her conduct. She doesn't need that. Who doesn't know Tibéria and who doesn't respect her qualities? They're fine folk in there, women as good as their word, hearts of gold, helping half the world. At Tibéria's it's all one big family; it's not each one for himself and the devil take the hindmost—nothing of the sort. Everyone's in accord; it's a close-knit family. Porciúncula was very dear to Tibéria, a familiar of the house, always falling for one girl or another, always ready to fix a leaking pipe, change a burned-out light bulb, patch the gutters on the roof, and with a swift one to the backside he would kick anyone out who dared lose his self-respect and turn into an animal. And it was Tibéria who told him everything, item by item, so he could unravel her story from start to finish without stumbling over any part of it. He was so interested because as soon as he laid eyes on Maria he was madly in love with her, one of those hopeless lovers.

When Maria arrived she was the youngest in the house, not yet sixteen, badly spoiled by Tibéria and the other women, who treated her like a daughter, loading her with elegant dolls. They even gave her a doll to take the place of the Raggedy Ann she used for her engagement and wedding games. Maria of the Veil spent her time on the waterfront; she loved to look out to sea, as people from the interior like to do. She was there at the first hint of nightfall; in moonlight or fog, drizzle or storm, she walked along the sea bank soliciting. Tibéria would scold her, laughing. Why didn't Maria stay inside the brothel, be nice and cozy, dressed in her flowered gown, waiting for the rich men crazy for a fresh young thing like her? She would even arrange for a rich guardian, an old man who'd fall in love and give her a good life in the lap of luxury without her having to go to bed with every Tom,

Dick and Harry, at the rate of two or three a night. Right here in the brothel, not to go any further, there was the example of Lúcia, whom Judge Maia came to see once a week, and he gave her everything. Even got porter's jobs for the easygoing Barcelino, Luúcia's sweetheart. Tibéria also was flabbergasted that Maria didn't take to Porciúncula the mulatto, devoured with passion for the girl who slept with everyone but him. She strolled along by his side, hand in hand through Mont Serrat, looking at the sea, or better yet, swaying alongside as a lover would when couples went aboard at night for a moonlight fishing trip. Meanwhile telling the mulatto all about the weddings she'd been to, how beautiful the bride looked, how long her veil was. But when the time came to go to bed and do the right thing, that's when she'd say good night and leave Porciúncula drained, stupefied.

This was just how Porciúncula told it that rainy night when the gringo was reminiscing about Christmas. Why I like to hear the mulatto tell stories is, he doesn't twist anything around to make himself look good. He could easily have said he screwed her, many times even. That's what everybody thought, especially those who'd seen them together along the waterfront. He could have bragged, but instead he told it the way it really was, and for a lot of us that was no surprise. Maria slept with this one and that one; she got excited at the right time. It wasn't that she didn't like it. But when it was done, it was done; she didn't like talking about it. Any real emotion in itself, the sort of endless yearning that lovers suffer from not seeing one another, and so forth, well, she never felt that over anyone. Unless she felt it about the mulatto Porciúncula, but then why didn't she got to bed with him? She'd sit next to him on the sand, dipping her feet in the water, jumping with the waves, looking out to the edge of the sea that nobody can ever make out. Who's ever seen the end of the sea? Any of my honorable listeners? Excuse me, but I don't think so.

The one really in love was Porciúncula the mulatto. A night didn't go by when he wasn't watching for Maria on the waterfront, trailing her, wanting to shipwreck himself on her. That's how he told it, hiding nothing; and even then the pain of his love softened his voice. He was more lost than an ownerless dog, sniffing out anything that hinted of Maria of the Veil, while Tibéria went around whispering things in his ear. That's how he began to unravel the net, piecing together the scaffolding of Maria's story up until the event of the funeral.

When Colonel Barbosa's son, a well-heeled student on vacation, screwed Maria, she wasn't quite fifteen but she already had the breasts and body of a woman. A woman to look at but on the inside still a girl playing with her rag doll all day, the kind of doll you can buy for a dollar at the fair. She put together bits of cloth, sewed them into a dress for her rag doll, with a veil and a bridal crown. Any wedding day in church at her end of the world and Maria would be there watching, eyes stuck to the bride's gown. She was thinking only of how good it must be to wear such a gown, all white, with a trailing veil and flowers on her head. She made clothes for the doll, talking to it all the while, and every day contrived a wedding just to see it in a veil and crown. The doll was married to all the animals in the neighborhood, especially the old blind chicken, who made a terrific groom because he didn't run away, but squatted in his blindness, obedient. So when Colonel Barbosa's son told Maria, "Now you're ripe for marriage. Would you like to marry me?" she said yes, if he'd give her a pretty veil. Poor thing, she had no idea that the guy was talking fancy talk and that to get married was highfalutin for getting screwed on the riverbank. That's why Maria, all excited, accepted, and is still waiting to this day for the gown, the veil, and the bridal wreath. Instead she got a beating from old Batista, and, when the story got out, the name of Maria of the Veil. But she didn't lose her obsession. Thrown out of her house, there wasn't a wedding she missed, hiding in the church, because a prostitute isn't allowed to have anything to do with weddings. When that Barbosa fellow, the same one that did her the favor, married the daughter of Colonel Boaventura—a widely discussed wedding!—she was there to see the bride, a beautiful, well-heeled girl, in a dress the likes of which had never been seen, made in Rio, with a train half a mile long and a face veil embroidered all over, something really astonishing. It was after that Maria made her way to this port and tied up at Tibéria's whorehouse.

A good time for her didn't mean going to the movies, a cabaret, dancing, boozing in a bar, or taking some boat ride. It was just weddings and looking at the bride's gown. She cut pictures out of magazines, brides in veils, store advertisements of bridal outfits. She stuck them all up on the wall at the head of her bed. With new scraps of material she made a new bridal gown for her new doll, a present from Tibéria and the other women. A young girl, still so damn young she could tell Tibéria, "One of these days you'll see me in such a gown." They laughed at her, played tricks on her, jeered at her, but that didn't change her.

Around this time Porciúncula's patience gave out—sick of keeping his animal nature down, of going around with clenched fists, of hearing the talk on the waterfront. Every man has his pride, he saw it was hopeless; he had waited long enough, and he wasn't the type to die of love, the worst death of all. He turned to Carolina, the big husky mulatto who lived just to make love to him. He cured himself of Maria of the Veil with a few drinks and some of Carolina's belly laughs. He didn't want to discuss it any more.

At this point Porciúncula asked for more booze and was served. Alonso would give his eyeteeth for a good story, and this one was quickly coming to an end. The end was the flu a few years back that wiped out half of the world. Maria of the Veil fell into a fever; fragile, she lasted only four days. By the time Porciúncula got the news she was already dead. At the moment he was more or less out of circulation because of the hot water he'd gotten into over a guy named Gomes. Gomes, who owned a market stall in Água dos Meninos, had gotten hurt in a card game. Now to cut cards with Porciúncula was to throw your money away. He played because he liked to, and he couldn't take anyone who complained about it afterward.

Porciúncula was letting the storm die down when he got the message from Tibéria, begging him to come right away. Maria was calling for him urgently. She died the very hour he arrived. Tibéria explained the last request she'd made on her deathbed. She wanted to be buried in a bridal gown, with a veil and garland. The bridegroom, she said, must be the mulatto Porciúncula, who was waiting to marry her.

It was a very painful request, but coming from a dead person there was no refusing to honor it. Porciúncula asked how he was going to get a wedding gown, an expensive buy, with the stores closed for the night besides. He thought it was going to be hard but it wasn't. Because all those swarms of women from the brothel and the street, all the old whores tired of life, all suddenly found themselves becoming seamstresses, sewing a dress with a veil and a bridal wreath. They quickly put all their money together and bought flowers, arranged the cloth, got lace, God knows where from, found shoes, silk stockings, even white gloves. One sewed a piece, another put on some ribbon.

Porciúncula said he'd never seen a wedding gown to beat it, so pretty and elegant, and he knew what he was talking about because in the time he'd courted Maria he'd been everywhere looking at weddings and had worn himself out looking at those gowns.

After they dressed Maria, the train of her gown trailed off the bed and bunched up on the floor. Tibéria came with a bouquet and put it in Maria's hands. There never was a bride so serene and sweet, so happy at her wedding.

Standing near the bed, Porciúncula sat down. He was the bridegroom. He took Maria's hand. Clarice, a married woman whose husband had left her with three children to bring up, wept and pulled the wedding ring off her finger—the memory of happier times—and gave it to the mulatto. Porciúncula slowly put it on the dead woman's finger and looked into her face. Maria of the Veil was smiling. Before that moment I don't know, but at the moment she was smiling—that's how Porciúncula described it, and he hadn't been drinking that day, hadn't touched a drop. Tearing his eyes away from that beautiful face, he glanced at Tibéria. And he swore he saw, he truly saw, Tibéria changed into a priest, wearing those special garments for consecrating a wedding, with a tonsure and everything, a fat priest who looked a bit saintly. Alonso filled the glasses again and he drank up.

It was here the mulatto Porciúncula stopped, and there was no getting another word of the story out of him. He'd unloaded his corpse on us, he'd relieved himself of the burden. Mercedes still wanted to know if the coffin had been white-for-a-virgin or black-for-a-sinner. Porciúncula shrugged his shoulders and swatted flies. About Teresa Batista, the bet she'd won, and the new life she started, nothing was said. And nobody asked. I can't say a thing about it. I'm not someone who tells stories about things he doesn't know. What I can do is tell the gringo's story, because that one I do know, like everyone on the waterfront. But I know it's not the kind of story to tell over one drink like this, if you'll excuse my saying so. It's a full-length story to drink on over a long rainy night, or better yet a fishing trip in the moonlight. Still, if you'd like I could tell it. I don't see any reason why not.

Rachel de Queiroz
—◦❊(1910–2003)❊◦—

The author of classics of the northeastern social novel, beginning with *O Quinze* in 1930, Rachel de Queiroz would become the first woman to enter the Brazilian Academy of Letters (1977). She wrote in an expressive, modernist, yet plain neo-realistic style. Like the landscape, her style was simple and unadorned, although she included dialogue in the dialect of local *caboclos* and the lyrics of traditional northeastern folksongs. The problems of society in the *sertão* were also cast as the problems of women. Rachel de Queiroz continued to pen journalistic chronicles and novels into the 1990s. She was the first Brazilian woman writer of the twentieth century to gain national and international stature. While known principally for her novels, Rachel wrote hundreds of chronicles, prose pieces that fall between the short story and journalistic compositions. "Metonymy, or The Husband's Revenge," taken from the popular, oral tradition, is given literary garb and retold as an illustration of a poetic device. A collection of Rachel's chronicles was published as *Cem Crônicas Escolhidas* (1970), followed by *As Menininhas e Outras Crônicas* (1976). Her novels span more than sixty years: *João Miguel* (1932), *Caminho de Pedras* (1937), *As Três Marias* (1939), *Dora, Doralina* (1975), and *Memorial de Maria Moura* (1992).

METONYMY, OR THE HUSBAND'S REVENGE
(DRAMA IN THREE SCENES)
—◦❧ ❦◦—

Scene I

Metonymy. I learned the word in 1930 and shall never forget it. I had just published my first novel. A literary critic had scolded me because my hero went out into the night "chest unbuttoned."

"What deplorable nonsense!" wrote this eminently sensible gentleman. "Why does she not say what she means? Obviously, it was his shirt that was unbuttoned, not his chest."

I accepted his rebuke with humility, indeed with shame. But my illustrious Latin professor, Dr. Matos Peixoto, came to my rescue. He said that what I had written was perfectly correct; that I had used a respectable figure of speech known as metonymy; and that this figure consisted in the use of one word for another word associated with it—for example, a word representing a cause instead of the effect, or representing the container when the content is intended. The classic instance, he told me, is "the sparkling cup"; in reality, not the cup but the wine in it is sparkling.

The professor and I wrote a letter, which was published in the newspaper where the review had appeared. It put my unjust critic in his place. I hope he learned a lesson. I know I did. Ever since, I have been using metonymy—my only bond with classical rhetoric.

Moreover, I have devoted some thought to it, and I have concluded that metonymy may be more than a figure of speech. There is, I believe, such a thing as practical or applied metonymy. Let me give a crude example, drawn from my own experience. A certain lady of my acquaintance suddenly moved out of the boardinghouse where she had been living for years and became a mortal enemy of the woman who owned it. I asked her why. We both knew that the woman was a kindly soul; she had given my friend injections when she needed them, had often loaned her a hot water bottle, and had always waited on her when she had her little heart attacks. My friend replied:

"It's the telephone in the hall. I hate her for it. Half the time when I answered it, the call was a hoax or joke of some sort."

"But the owner of the boardinghouse didn't perpetrate these hoaxes. She wasn't responsible for them."

"No. But whose telephone was it?"

—◦❧ ❦◦—

I know another case of applied metonymy, a more disastrous one for it involved a crime. It happened in a city of the interior, which I shall not name for fear that someone may recognize the parties and revive the scandal. I shall narrate the crime but conceal the criminal.

Well, in this city of the interior there lived a man. He was not old but he was spent, which is worse than being old. In his youth he had suffered from beriberi. His legs were weak, his chest was tired and asthmatic, his skin was yellowish, and his eyes were rheumy. He was, however, a man of property; he owned the house in which he lived and the one next to it, in which he had set up a grocery store. Therefore, although so unattractive personally, he was able to find himself a wife. In all justice to him, he did not tempt fate by marrying a beauty. Instead, he married a poor, emaciated girl who worked in a men's clothing factory. By her face one would have thought that she had consumption. So our friend felt safe. He did not foresee the effects of good nutrition and a healthful life on a woman's appearance. The girl no longer spent eight hours a day at a sewing table. She was the mistress of her house. She ate well: fresh meat, cucumber salad, pork fat with beans and manioc mush, all kinds of sweets, and oranges, which her husband bought by the gross for his customers. The effects were like magic. Her body filled out, especially in the best places. She even seemed to grow taller. And her face—what a change! I may have forgotten to mention that her features, in themselves, were good to begin with. Moreover, money enabled her to embellish her natural advantages with art; she began to wear make-up, to wave her hair, and to dress well.

Lovely, attractive, she now found her sickly, prematurely old husband a burden and a bore. Each evening, as soon as the store was closed, he dined, mostly on milk (he could not stomach meat), took his newspaper, and rested on his chaise longue until time to go to bed. He did not care for movies or for soccer or for radio. He did not even show much interest in love. Just a sort of tepid, tasteless cohabitation.

And then Fate intervened: it produced a sergeant.

Scene II

Granted, it was unjust for a young wife, after being reconditioned at her husband's expense, to employ her charms against the aforesaid husband. Unjust; but, then, this world thrives on injustice, doesn't it? The sergeant—I shall not say whether he was in the Army, the Air Force, the Marines, or the Fusiliers, for I still mean to conceal the identities of the parties—the sergeant was muscular, young, ingratiating, with a manly, commanding voice and a healthy spring in his walk. He looked gloriously martial in his high-buttoned uniform.

One day, when the lady was in charge of the counter (while her husband lunched), the sergeant came in. Exactly what happened and what did not happen, is hard to say. It seems that the sergeant asked for a pack of cigarettes. Then he wanted a little vermouth. Finally he asked permission to listen to the sports broadcast on the radio next to the counter. Maybe it was just an excuse to remain there awhile. In any case, the girl said it would be all right. It is hard to refuse a favor to a sergeant, especially a sergeant like this one. It appears that the sergeant asked nothing more that day. At most, he and the girl exchanged expressive glances and a few agreeable words, murmured so softly that the customers, always alert for something to gossip about, could not hear them.

Three times more the husband lunched while his wife chatted with the sergeant in the store. The flirtation progressed. Then the husband fell ill with a grippe, and the two others went far beyond flirtation. How and where they met, no one was able to discover. The important thing is that they were lovers and that they loved with a forbidden love, like Tristan and Isolde or Paolo and Francesca.

Then Fate, which does not like illicit love and generally punishes those who engage in it, transferred the sergeant to another part of the country.

It is said that only those who love can really know the pain of separation. The girl cried so much that her eyes grew red and swollen. She lost her appetite. Beneath her rouge could be seen the consumptive complexion of earlier times. And these symptoms aroused her husband's suspicion, although, curiously, he had never suspected anything when the love affair was flourishing and everything was wine and roses.

He began to observe her carefully. He scrutinized her in her periods of silence. He listened to her sighs and to the things she murmured in her sleep. He snooped around and found a postcard and a book, both with a man's name in the same handwriting. He found the insignia of the sergeant's regiment and concluded that the object of his wife's murmurs, sighs, and silences was not only a man but a soldier. Finally he made the supreme discovery: that they had indeed betrayed him. For he discovered the love letters, bearing air-mail stamps, a distant postmark, and the sergeant's name. They left no reasonable doubt.

For five months the poor fellow twisted the poisoned dagger of jealousy inside his own thin, sickly chest. Like a boy who discovers a bird's nest and, hiding nearby, watches the eggs increasing in number every day, so the husband, using a duplicate key to the wood chest where his wife put her valuables, watched the increase in the number of letters concealed there. He had given her the chest during their honeymoon, saying, "Keep your secrets here." And the ungrateful girl had obeyed him.

Every day at the fateful hour of lunch, she replaced her husband at the counter. But he was not interested in eating. He ran to her room, pulled out a drawer in her bureau, removed the chest from under a lot of panties, slips, and such, took the little key out of his pocket, opened the chest, and anxiously read the new letter. If there was no new letter, he reread the one dated August 21st; it was so full of realism that it sounded like dialogue from a French movie. Then he put everything away and hurried to the kitchen, where he swallowed a few spoonfuls of broth and gnawed at a piece of bread. It was almost impossible to swallow with the passion of those two thieves sticking in his throat.

Until one day there was a greater provocation.

Scene III

When the poor man's heart had become utterly saturated with jealousy and hatred, he took a revolver and a box of bullets from the counter drawer; they had been left, years before, by a customer as security for a debt which had never been paid. He loaded the revolver.

One bright morning at exactly ten o'clock, when the store was full of customers, he excused himself and went through the doorway that connected the store with his home. In a few seconds the customers heard the noise of a row, a woman's scream, and three shots. On the sidewalk in front of the shopkeeper's house they saw his wife on her knees, still screaming, and him, with the revolver in his trembling hand, trying to raise her. The front door of the house was open. Through it, they saw a man's legs, wearing khaki trousers and boots. He was lying face down, with his head and torso in the parlor, not visible from the street.

The husband was the first to speak. Raising his eyes from his wife, he looked at the terror-stricken people and spotted among them his favorite customer. He took a few steps, stood in the doorway, and said:

"You may call the police."

—◦❦ ❦◦—

At the police station he explained that he was a deceived husband. The police chief remarked:

"Isn't this a little unusual? Ordinarily you kill your wives. They're weaker than their lovers."

The man was deeply offended.

"No," he protested. "I would be utterly incapable of killing my wife. She is all that I have in the world. She is refined, pretty, and hard-working. She helps me in the store, she understands bookkeeping, she writes the letters to the wholesalers. She is the only person who knows how to prepare my food. Why should I want to kill my wife?"

"I see," said the chief of police. "So you killed her lover."

The man shook his head.

"Wrong again. The sergeant—her lover—was transferred to a place far from here. I discovered the affair only after he had gone. By reading his letters. They tell the whole story. I know one of them by heart, the worst of them. . . ."

The police chief did not understand. He said nothing and waited for the husband to continue, which he presently did:

"Those letters! If they were alive, I would kill them, one by one. They were shameful to read—almost like a book. I thought of taking an airplane trip. I thought of killing some other sergeant here, so that they would all learn a lesson not to fool around with another man's wife. But I was afraid of the rest of the regiment; you know how these military men stick together. Still, I had to do something. Otherwise I would have gone crazy. I couldn't get those letters out of my head. Even on days when none arrived I felt terrible, worse than my wife. I had to put an end to it, didn't I? So today, at last, I did it. I waited till the regular time and, when I saw the wretch appear on the other side of the street, I went into the house, hid behind a door, and lay there waiting for him."

"The lover?" asked the police chief stupidly.

"No, of course not. I told you I didn't kill her lover. It was those letters. The sergeant sent them—but *he* delivered them. Almost every day, there he was at the door, smiling, with the vile envelope in his hand. I pointed the revolver and fired three times. He didn't say a word; he just fell. No, chief, it wasn't her lover. It was the mailman."

MARQUÊS REBELO

(pseud. of Eddy Dias da Cruz)

—◦❧(1907–1973)❦◦—

A chronicler of the city of Rio de Janeiro, Marquês Rebelo was also a lawyer, journalist, translator, and art critic. His works pictured the popular classes of his day, in the tradition of Lima Barreto, yet perhaps with more humor than criticism. He was elected to the Brazilian Academy of Letters in 1965. Having been raised on the classics of French and Portuguese literatures, Rebelo never lost his desire to write. Rebelo left medical school to become a journalist, publishing poems in the modernist journals of the day. His first short stories, including "Down Our Street," were published in 1931 under the title *Oscarina*. His novel *Marafa* (1935) won the prestigious Machado de Assis Prize in 1935, and his major success occurred in 1939 with the novel *A Estrela Sobe*, about a suburban youth who succeeds in radio. Along with the social novelists of the 1930s, Rebelo denounced poverty and spoke for the simple and humble population of Rio de Janeiro. After Manuel Antônio de Almeida, Machado de Assis, and Lima Barreto, Rebelo continued the tradition of chronicling life in Brazil's capital city, although in his day Rio de Janeiro enjoyed a cultural innocence and social tranquillity that would be the envy of today's citizens. Rebelo's three books of short stories were written in the early stages of his career, *Oscarina* (1931), *Três Caminhos* (1933), and *Stela me Abriu a Porta* (1942). His verbal paintings of popular life carried the story into the chronicle in "Cenas da vida familiar, crônica de viagem" (1943), "Cortina de ferro, crônica de viagem" (1956), and "Correio europeu, crônica de viagem" (1959).

DOWN OUR STREET
—◦❧ ❦◦—

As it was payday at the Treasury, he arrived home earlier than usual. The worm-eaten clock on the wall, whose slow, measured beats sounded like the clanking of old iron, had not yet struck two. The linnet was pecking at the little jar of birdseed. He placed his parcels on the bare table, scattering the flies, carefully folding the newspaper along its natural folds, and was engaged in brushing his badly worn, black felt hat, when Veva, becoming aware of his presence, called out from the kitchen:

"Did you get paid, Jerome?"

"Yes, my dear," he replied, hanging his hat on the Japanese bamboo hat stand which filled up the corner of the room under a roughly framed three-color print of the interior of a British submarine in action during the Great War.

"And did you bring everything?"

"All except the little shoes for Jujú, because I forgot the size."

"Size eight, and don't go and forget it again, you old scatterbrain! . . . She's already stayed away from school two days through being without shoes. The teacher even sent a school friend to ask if she was ill."

She just couldn't get the fork any brighter. The hen cackled in the little cemented yard. Veva was working hard with the bath-brick, and Fifina, the little wretch, kept meddling with the cutlery.

"Leave those knives alone, child, or you'll cut yourself!"

Jerome was coughing and admiring the linnet:

"What's wrong with you, you old rogue? So you won't sing, eh!"

Veva turned round:

"And the Venosina, did you find it?"

"They hadn't any at Gesteira's, so I just bought it at Pacheco's: three-and-six!"

Veva was dumbfounded. Three-and-sixpence!! She turned the tap full on to wash the saucepan. Jerome, at the far side of the alcove, was changing into his cord and canvas beach slippers embroidered with an anchor.

"You can put the coffee on."

Fifina tore round to the baker's for bread.

"You must pay Solomon without fail," continued Veva. "He came yesterday, as arranged, but I apologized and told him you hadn't been paid yet, because of the holiday, and fixed for him to come along today. I forgot to tell you. Did I do wrong?"

"No, Veva. How much is it?"

"I don't know, dear, offhand, only if I reckon it up. Wait a moment and I'll go and see."

She dried her coarsened hands on the very grubby teacloth, put the china away on the dresser, which was all decorated with green tissue paper cut out in fancy designs. Jerome placed his rusty pince-nez on the bridge of his flabby nose, and they seated themselves at the table, with the housekeeping book, just as Fifina returned, perspiring and out of breath, with the bread.

Mr. Azevedo, their elderly neighbor, and a kindly soul, a toothpick in his mouth, and wearing a striped pajama coat, came along with Lúcia and Ninita, the youngsters, to take a breath of fresh air—say what you will, there's nothing like the suburbs for good, fresh air—to talk politics with Jerome, gossip a bit with Veva, ask after the invalid, always in the same way. "And how's Auntie?" She was a little old paralytic aunt to whom Jerome had offered shelter and on whom he bestowed kindly consideration. But if he was good, he was also adamant as regards politicians. "They were all a bunch of gangsters."

"A calamity, my friend, that's what I say, a calamity. Everything lost. Yes, everything lost! Don't be surprised at the expression. What price dignity? What price honesty? Read the papers, ask yourself! There's no longer any honor, there's nothing any more! A pack of thieves! Just thieves! And the politicians? Oh! Oh! Oh! In a country like this we only want a President like our greatest gangster Lampião. Jerome, d'you hear? Just Lampião!"

He stopped, red-faced and short of breath. He came from the hill dotted with huts, their laundry hanging out to dry, a light breeze which carried the chirrup of a belated grasshopper hidden in the bright coloring of an Imperial acacia. Jerome was laughing—a sickly, short laugh, almost forced—well, anyway it was his kind of laugh. The grasshopper stopped. The breeze died down. Two pigeons settled on the roof. The girls' attention was on the young man who was passing backwards and forwards in front of the gate in the avenida, smoking and casting furtive glances around him.

"I think he's that blond with the face of a German who followed us up to here on Sunday afternoon, when we came out of the cinema," whispered Ninita to her sister.

"I wonder," replied the other, doubtingly. "No-o-o. Couldn't be. The other one had a dried-up looking face and a different walk."

"That's because you didn't notice what he was like."

"Shh! If Dad were to guess . . ."

"Silly!"

Their father was shamelessly declaiming at the Income Tax Office—Oh, didn't you know?—Jerome knew just a little of the Martin trouble, the chap that wrote poetry and embezzled two hundred and fifty pounds. "You don't know the half of it, my friend." I know, I know. He told in every detail the case of the theft, the names of the people involved, the intrigues of the various parties, the cynicism of the flatterers who denied everything, denied everything . . .

Veva came to the window. Her hair, gray and cut, was unkempt, and her lack of teeth emphasized her short chin. She was slightly anxious about Judith who had gone to town to deliver some needlework. Perhaps Madame Franco wasn't at home and she decided to wait . . .

Hands in trousers pockets, thin bony legs wide apart, Mr. Azevedo addressed her: "And we are the ones who suffer. We! . . ."

Veva was surprised. "We? Come, now!" And she would have added "Why?" But Mr. Azevedo went on.

"It's sad, very sad . . ." and poured forth abuse of the state of affairs which kept them small and kept them down—yes, under the heel, that's the expression—of the great, without hope, without opportunity, without a right to their own fate, just puppets in the clutching hands of the brazen and favored few.

"Good afternoon, neighbors." It was Pequetita, recently married, coming to sit on the porch with her workbox to get a little more of the waning sunlight while waiting for her husband.

They returned her greeting, and Mr. Azevedo summed up, with an air of indifference, and stroking his moustache:

"This world is a ball, Mistress Veva. This world is a circus . . ."

Veva, leaning her elbows on the windowsill, didn't hear properly—Mr. Azevedo's voice being a bit husky—and, shy to ask him to repeat, remained in ignorance as to whether the world was a ball or a circle. She therefore changed the subject, inquiring whether Mistress Maria was better of her rheumatism, with the Spiritualist's prescription. Mr. Azevedo had this weakness: he loved to talk about ailments. He started on his wife's rheumatism—"as yet no improvement at all, my friend. Well . . ."—and he went on and on.

"Do you know something?"—he opened his eyes so wide, raised his eyebrows to such an extent that Veva had to answer "No."

"Miranda, you know, that thin fellow who used always to travel with me on the bus; you remember?"

"Thin . . . ?"

"Yes, the one who never went without an overcoat, father of Tudinha, a shy little girl who used to come to play sometimes with Ninita."

"Oh!"

"That's the one. Well, he won't last long, poor chap—that's what I say. Note that! Also . . ." He shook his head sadly. "And Souza, d'you know him? Poor fellow . . . He can no longer walk. He doesn't breathe properly—he only makes grunts," and he imitated him. "It's heartbreaking to hear him. The arteriosclerosis is very advanced. The doctor himself told me, very privately, mind. I pretended to be surprised—oh yes, but I saw all right. The daughter isn't well, and he has only the one, as the mother died in the Spanish influenza epidemic, a fine girl, a regular peach of a girl! And does everything single-handed. She's so unselfish. You can't imagine how tenderly she treats her father. It's really touching."

The two boys from the last-but-one house, spotlessly clean and with hair nicely combed—people from Paraná—came out to play on the doorstep.

"Be careful, now, no rushing about," their mother called out to them.

Mr. Azevedo stepped to the side, unpuckering his lips.

". . . But to me he's a 'goner,' unfortunately. He's a splendid soul, old Souza! . . . And, mind you, he's very much younger than I. In '85 . . . In '85 . . . No, I'm wrong, wait a minute . . ." and he put his forefinger to his lips to invoke silence. "In '86, when I was living with Fagundes, Jose Carlos Fagundes, you remember him, Jerome?"

The little laugh emitted by Jerome was malicious.

"I should say I do, the scoundrel."

Veva was no longer listening. She was in pain. A want of air, a heaviness in the breast, like a weight which grew heavier and heavier, a lackadaisical feeling, an aching body when she got up in the morning, and her veins swelling from day to day.

Venosina was a luxury, a little bottle with thirty pills—three-and-six, take it or leave it—and what can you do if they are necessary? She only took them at dinner time, to make them last longer. This was in addition to the fervent promises she had made to Our Lady of Perpetual Succor, as she had five children to bring up. Sometimes she would start thinking about a lucky sweepstake and in the hopes of gaining a fortune buy tickets off Mr. Paschoal, who had already sold her many in the past, only to be left in deep depression on finding she had drawn a blank. Why did luck never come her way? she wondered, sighing, and beating her washing on the side of the tank, because Alfredo, with this football business, was always getting his trousers grubby. "What have I done that God should refuse to help me?" she thought. "Oh, if only I had won a lottery . . ." She wouldn't say a word to anyone . . . only to Jerome . . . she would put it all in the Savings Bank . . . to accumulate . . . not a penny for herself . . . but she would enjoy herself as much as if she had spent it all; her children's future would be guaranteed. They wouldn't miss her so much then if she were to die, as Jerome would have the wherewithal to educate them, putting them at a good boarding school. But nothing of the sort. She made less pretentious plans, however, when young Judith's boy came round, a nice natural young man, and priceless, especially when he talked about the office doings; he made his sweetheart fairly shriek with laughter. Veva at these times would offer up a prayer to God to help him in his job, to earn more money and so enable the young couple to get married soon. It wouldn't matter their being such children; he was very affectionate, hard-working and conscientious; she, Judith, had a good head on her shoulders—no fancy ideas, very domesticated.

"How late the child is!"

Veva felt jumpy. Had anything happened? She craned her neck in the hope of seeing her turn the corner into the gate. She had gone to take the red dress with bobbles. "Is that her?" . . . "Is that her?" . . . "Isn't she ever coming? I wonder if Madame Franco . . ."

Mr. Azevedo was still talking, facing Jerome, on the sufferings of Melo, the man with bladder trouble, a landowner in the district, who had consulted all the highest medical authorities—without finding any relief.

The "boa-noite" creeper which hung on the half fallen-down wall was opening its simple white flowers. The thin, expeditious lamp-lighter, looking like a prophet with his staff, had already passed, leaving a trail of sickly yellow, hissing gas lights, where the moths came to flutter and to die. Here and there in the grassy parts, which in the daytime were beaten by the anti-mosquito squads looking for breeding grounds, the intermittent bluish glow of fireflies was to be seen, and in the still air the strains from the piano on which Maria Heloiza the dentist's daughter was playing "The Pagan" for her fiancé's benefit. The moon came out.

—◦❧ ❦◦—

Indistinct and muffled voices filled the air, a dog barked savagely, shut in the shower-room; high up in the heaven a single star shines, and it's cold; it is only a little past five o'clock, yet the twilight deepens and it seems like night—so early in fact, that winter is on her way.

Grumbling, the coach driver, wearing a top hat, his overcoat covered with stains, touched his horses with the whip, and the funeral moved off, followed by two motorcars, amid the whisperings of the onlookers who crowded round the gate of the villa.

Veva was dry-eyed. "Great God, I can hardly believe it!" and she flung herself in the squeaking Austrian chair and remained as in a trance in the narrow, shuttered room filled with the smell of flowers and candle grease, thinking of her Jerome, who had gone forever, such a good man, such a friend in his last thoughts of her, his voice as he lay sinking, almost inaudible: "Veva, see to the benevolent fund." The benevolent fund he had paid into, five pounds, and the landlord would take the lot, and then there'd be something owing.

Who could help her now? Aninhas, her sister, married to Dr. Graça, who was so well off? Porcina who had been left a widow without children and owning a bakery which brought in a small fortune? They never even came to the funeral. Not even some simple flowers did they send for the brother-in-law who had done so much for them. "Oh, my own Jerome . . ." There he was, smiling, on the top of the what-not, between a little angel with a broken wing and a plate with faded postcards on it. There he was smiling, in the photo, next to her—How happy they were!—on their wedding day. He standing up, dressed in black, his moustache curled, his hand on her shoulder as she sat nursing a huge bouquet, her long white skirt modestly reaching her feet.

The tireless Mr. Azevedo who had made all the arrangements for the funeral— the little man from the Infirmary had been rather insolent—and had sent a wreath from the girls and his wife—she, poor thing, confined to her bed with the shock— came to console her, his voice even more hoarse with emotion:

"Life's like that, Veva, you know. The point is not to give in, be brave, and strong. And hasn't it always been the same? Ah! Mistress Veva, it's sad, very very sad. Veva, it's terrible. I feel it, you can be sure"—and he beat his substantial chest— "but one must be brave! Life doesn't end with the death of a soldier. Life no, but war. War, struggle, life . . ." Mr. Azevedo became confused.

The paralytic in her wheelchair, dumped in the middle of the kitchen—and she could be seen from the room—shaken with sobs till she looked like a limp rag, was thinking heroically of the sadness of the workhouse, a heap of children, whimpering perhaps without knowing why, clinging to her spotless black skirt which covered her poor useless legs.

That pest of a fly kept circling about the room, and Mr. Azevedo went on:

"He's gone, it's our fate, my dear, a Supreme Will which none of us can oppose, and as he was such a good man he's no doubt with God. But he hasn't left you alone, don't forget. There's the children. And . . ."

Veva turned her hollow and frightened eyes to Azevedo, who lapsed into silence, for when she thought of her five children, then she realized how alone she really was, and, throwing up her hands, she began to wail.

ÉRICO VERÍSSIMO

—◦❧(1905–1975)❧◦—

A popular writer from Porto Alegre in southern Brazil and associated with the publishing house Globo, Érico Veríssimo taught in the United States, where he published a short history of Brazilian literature in 1945. The three short stories in this anthology were probably composed directly in English. Veríssimo is best known for a trilogy of historical novels under the general title *O Tempo e o Vento*, depicting the saga of a family in Rio Grande do Sul from 1745 to 1945. He painted a historical and poetic panorama, drawn from English and German models. His interests included psychological and social analysis, conveyed with impressionistic descriptions in a clean prose of short sentences. His last novels opened a broader satirical phase, taking on themes of dictatorship (*O Senhor Embaixador*, 1965), the Vietnam War (*O Prisioneiro*, 1967), and political intolerance (*Incidente em Antares*, 1971). His memoirs (*Som de Clarineta*, 1973–1976) give a valuable overview of literary and social issues. *Fantoches* (1932) is his only collection of short stories. "The House of the Melancholy Angel" is an English version of the story "Sonata," considered to be one of the best stories in the literature, originally published clandestinely during the war in *As Mãos de meu Fillo* (Porto Alegre: Merediano, 1942) and probably translated directly by the author.

FANDANGO

—∘❧ ❦∘—

The Life and Death of a Gaúcho

I

I shall never forget that bleak winter morning when word came from my grandfather's cattle ranch that Fandango was dead. It's strange the way you sometimes react to good or bad news. I received the sad message not with my brain but with my heart, which started pounding faster and faster, before my mind had taken in the full meaning of the loss.

My father heard the news in silence, without so much as blinking, his dry eyes set on the overcast sky. I knew he was sorry, because he too loved the old man. His countenance, however, did not betray him. That's the way *gaúchos* are. The men of the green pampas are not supposed to cry. Crying is for women—young women, that is, because old ones like my grandmother had cried so much over their men, killed, wounded or mutilated in endless duels, revolutions, and wars, that they had run out of tears.

I forgot to say that the wind was blowing hard that day, wailing and moaning in a kind of despair. It too had heard the sad news.

I guess it's no use to go on with my story without saying a few words about the place I live in, of which most people have probably never heard. Oh, I don't mean Brazil. Of course practically everybody had heard of that big country one way or another. I mean my native Rio Grande do Sul, the southernmost state of Brazil, bordering on Uruguay and Argentina. It has been so to speak the battleground of the nation throughout its history. Almost all the foreign wars in which Brazil has been involved were fought on *gaúcho* territory.

At the beginning of the eighteenth century, Rio Grande do Sul was nothing but a vast green desert separating the last Portuguese settlement in southern Brazil from the Spanish possessions on the River Plate. Then Brazilians from other regions started going down to that no man's land, which for some odd reason was known as "The Continent." Those adventurers knew that the rich lands and the wild cattle in the South would belong to the first-comer. The pioneers followed the elusive trails of the cattle drovers. Many explored the rivers in search of gold and silver and precious stones. A few of them applied to the King for land grants but most just took over the lands they liked, and not infrequently stole them from other settlers. Eventually roving cattle thieves settled down and ranches were established; but for many years the Continent was infested with desperadoes. They were tough men who knew no law or allegiance. Who were their enemies? The Indians, wild beasts, snakes, fevers and the Regiment of Dragoons that the Portuguese Crown had recently sent to the Continent. And who were their friends? Their horses, their muskets, their pistols and their knives. To the beat of their horses' hoofs and the crackle of their rifles the Spaniards were thrust back. The frontier went marching with them. They *were* the frontier.

Settlements sprang up in the valleys and on the prairies, in the highlands and on the banks of many rivers. These were the seeds of the towns of today.

During the nineteenth century thousands of immigrants came from Europe, first from Germany and then from Italy. *Gringos*, we called them. That's why today one finds so many people with blond hair, blue eyes and foreign accents.

This last used to roil old Fandango. He had no patience with foreigners. He was suspicious of them. He thought immigration a bad thing, because "every man ought to stay put in his own country, minding his own business, with his relatives and friends."

2

When my grandfather was born, it's said that Fandango, in those days a cow-puncher of twenty, was sent from the ranch to the village, on the back of a burro, to fetch the priest to baptize the baby. He was well into his forties when my father was born. My father grew up in the shadow of Fandango, and a very broad and generous shadow it was. The *gaúcho* taught him—as he had previously done with my grandfather—all about horses, the winds, the weather, women and the routine of ranch life. Our ranch was called "Angico," which is the name of a tree. Now, for some mysterious reason Fandango always reminded me of a tree, something rooted in the soil of our ranch, something strong, friendly and beautiful.

It never occurred to me to ask Fandango who his parents were, because I had the feeling that he had not been born like other humans: he had just sprung up from the soil of Angico like a plant, the seeds of which had been brought by the wind from some faraway forest.

Of course his real name was not Fandango, but José Menezes. The nickname was due to his passion for dancing. (For the *gaúchos,* every party, every fiesta at which there is dancing is a *fandango.*)

When I was twelve, the old cowhand was already in his early eighties, but still strong of body and clear of mind. I used to spend my summer vacation at Angico, and that for me was the best time of the year.

"What do they teach you in school?" Fandango asked me one summer.

"Well," I answered, "reading, writing and arithmetic. Geography and history, too."

Fandango chuckled and shook his white-maned head.

"That's for girls, son," he said. "A man should learn other things. Come on, I'll start your *gaúcho* education today."

And that summer and in the summers that followed, I learned many practical things from the old man. The Portuguese that they taught me at school was a strange, elaborate tongue that had very little connection with the language spoken in the sheds and kitchen of the ranch. Fandango considered the knowledge of arithmetic unnecessary. He had a theory of his own about the four principal operations. "The hard-working man adds," he would say with a wink; "the rascal subtracts; the clever man multiplies; and only the fool divides." He had never gone to school, and yet he could make an accurate estimate of the cattle in a herd at a quick glance. Geography? Fandango had the whole geography of the province in his head. From boyhood he had earned his living journeying, driving carts or herds, and there was not a ravine or gap or hideout in Rio Grande that he didn't know as well as the palm of his hand. He knew where the water holes were, where the rivers could be forded, where the best grazing land or the best shelter was to be found. It seemed that there was not a cabin, ranch, village, town or city where he did not have an acquaintance. "Even the trees and the animals know me when I go by," he used to boast.

One day, after looking at the pictures in a French magazine to which my father subscribed, I asked my oracle: "Which way do you take to go to Paris?"

Fandango looked puzzled. "Where's that, son?"

"Somewhere in Europe."

"Oh, well . . ." He looked first to the right, then to the left, closed one eye, pointed an arm to the north and, with the air of one who had gone to Paris many times, said: "You go straight in that direction, by way of Dead Man's Creek."

I was very proud of my knowledge of history, and sometimes I would tell Fandango all I knew about the Punic Wars, Alexander the Great, or the French Revolution. The old cowhand listened to me in silence, but seemed unimpressed. He thought all those things—wars, generals, foreign lands and people—were nothing more than invention on the part of some wily city folk. I confess that I found it easier to believe in Fandango's tales than in my history books. For the old man knew the best yarns in the world: stories about ghosts, family feuds, wars, duels and all sorts of adventurers. At sixteen he had seen his first war, and that was why he used to say, "Ever since I have been big enough to hold a gun, I've been fighting with the Castilians." (A "Castilian" was any of our Spanish-speaking neighbors across the border.)

Fandango could tell signs of rain in the smell of the wind or the look of the clouds. There was one side of the sky—the west—which he called the "rain maker," because when the clouds darkened in that direction it was rain for sure. There was a saying Fandango used to repeat frequently in winter: "Frost on the mud, rain on the stud." One day I asked: "Why 'on the stud,' Fandango?"

"To make it rhyme, son."

It took me some time to realize that Fandango was an incorrigible joker. One day, when I asked him whether it was going to rain or not, the old gaúcho looked gravely at the sky, consulted the clouds and answered: "Sky with stony grain means wind or rain." He paused briefly, gave his little dry laugh, and added: ". . . or something else again."

One day as we were going across the country in the heat of the sun, after a rodeo, feeling very thirsty, we hunted eagerly for a water hole. Presently Fandango reined in his horse and began to sniff deeply, smelling the wind. After some time he said: "There's water nearby. Over that way." We turned in the direction indicated and found water.

"How do you know these things?" I wondered.

"Well, I have been around for a long time, son."

Fandango was a man of average height, his skin tanned to leather by the sun, his roguish little black eyes set deep in bony sockets, his moustache and beard snowy white, and his cheeks the color of a ripe guava. He had a voice like a splintered cane, very similar to a parrot's squawk. He used to sum up his dislikes in a sentence that had become widely known: "Three things there are in life that make it very hard: old women, dark nights and a dog pack in the yard."

He also liked to say that "a man's woman, his rifle and his mount are not to be lent on any account."

The cowboys were in the habit of drawing comparisons between horses and women. Fandango advised the ranch hands to marry girls they knew, if possible girls they had watched grow up. And he quoted a saying: "The filly for your eye is the one raised up nearby." He would also warn: "A freckled woman and a horse that shies—watch out, brother, if you are wise."

Many were the tales that Fandango told about himself. Once, when eighteen, he ended a dance with his knife. As the daughter of the house loudly refused to dance with him, he shouted: "You're not the first mare that ever shied away from me." A brother of the girl who was near him pulled his dagger. "The weather closed in," Fandango used to tell. "First thing I did was kick over the lamp. From that point on we fought in the dark."

One winter day after lunch Fandango sat enjoying the sun in the doorway of the ranch house. Someone approached him and said: "Basking in the sun like a lizard, eh, Fandango?"

"The sun's the poor man's poncho, partner," replied the *gaúcho*.

He had also mysterious sayings, the meaning of which I could never penetrate: "A big stone makes a shadow, but the shadow has no weight."

"What does that mean?" I asked.

"When you're older you'll understand without anybody explaining."

In his wandering life Fandango had known many people in many places. He had a prodigious memory: he never forgot names, faces, dates or places. One night in the lean-to at Angico, when the ranch hands and a stranger were talking, smoking and drinking *maté* around the fire, someone inquired: "Whatever happened to Joca Silva?"

Fandango promptly informed: "Killed by his brother-in-law a long time ago."

"And how about his uncle, Two-Gun Pedro?"

The old *gaúcho* thought a minute and then answered: "Got his throat cut in the last revolution."

"And that tall one-eyed drover who used to . . ."

"Manuel the Horsefly?"

"That's the one!"

"Killed by an accordion player at a dance . . . couple of years ago."

The stranger, a cattle drover from São Paulo, who had listened in silence, observed: "From all I hear nobody around here dies in bed."

Fandango spat in the fire and replied: "Right hard to do, young fellow. But some manage . . ."

It was with Fandango that I learned to swim, use the lariat, treat sores and round up cattle. But of all the bits of knowledge the old man passed on to me, the ones of which I was most proud in those days were those having to do with horses. I had absorbed them in practical lessons, on trips, during roundups and at horse-breakings in which I saw with my own eyes the tricks and habits of horses, the peculiarities of each breed, and each type of marking. When I questioned the old man about the qualities of a dark brown horse, he would close one eye, look at me for some time and say sententiously: "Dark brown? He'll die before he tires down."

"And a dapple, Fandango?"

"In water he's better than a canoe."

"If you meet a traveler on the road with his saddle gear on his back, you can ask right away, 'Where'd you leave the bay?' " And he would add: "Once, over yonder around São Sepé, I was left afoot by a bay."

Nobody ever found out whether the thing had really happened "yonder around São Sepé" or whether Fandango had chosen that settlement just for the rhyme.

That was old Fandango for you. I owed him many things, including my life. Yes, my life! Once I went to swim in the river and, becoming exhausted, I was carried away by the current. Realizing that I was going to be swept over the nearby waterfall, to death on the rocks below—more than one ranch hand had died that way—I started yelling at the top of my lungs. Fandango, who was riding on horseback somewhere in the neighborhood, heard my cries for help, galloped down to the bank of the stream, grabbed his lasso, whirled it in the air, and flung it out in my direction. When, a little later, bruised, panting, and scared, I was riding home behind him on the horse's crupper, he gave me a slap on the thigh and said: "I've lassoed many a bull and many a calf in my day, but this is the first time I ever lassoed a monkey!" And he began to laugh. His laugh rang out on the clear after-noon air, mingling with the song of the birds and the roar of the waterfall, and all alike faded away on the broad horizon of Angico.

3

Now Fandango was dead. I drove with my father to Angico, to attend the old *gaúcho*'s funeral.

My grandfather met us in front of the big ranch house. My father and I, fol-lowing the ancient custom of our land, kissed his long, parched hand. The old man told us that Fandango as usual was watching the sunrise that morning, leaning on the fence near the bunkhouse, and all of a sudden his head had dropped on his chest, his arms had gone limp and there he had stayed, propped up on the fence, as if he had fallen asleep.

"I was at his side," my grandfather went on, "watching the sunrise too. And I didn't have to touch him, feel his pulse or even look at his face to know he was dead. We old people are too well acquainted with death not to know it when it comes."

My father cleared his throat. He always did that when he was either annoyed or moved or both.

We walked in silence to the room where Fandango's body was laid out. Grandfather stopped at the door and whispered: "He didn't really die. It was just like a candle blown out by the wind."

The wind was still blowing hard. Under the gray sky the rolling fields of Angico were a depressingly dull green.

Fandango was lying in a rough coffin made by the ranch hands with lumber from our woods. You could have imagined he was just asleep. His face was serene and I think there was a faint suggestion of a smile on his pale lips. Yes, a mocking smile, as if he were making fun of all the sad-faced people who had gathered around him. It seemed I could hear his voice: "Come on, you folks! Why so serious? Everyone has to die sooner or later. Haven't I told you many times that I wanted my funeral to be gay like a party? Well, where are the musicians? Where are the dancers? Call them in! Where are the six pretty girls I told you I wanted to carry my coffin?"

But the silence persisted in that cold, somber room and all the faces were as pale and motionless as the dead man's. The flames of the four candles that burned at the corners of the coffin flickered agonizingly.

I gazed at Fandango's face, trying to cry to relieve the unbearable weight of grief I felt in my chest. But it was no use. My eyes remained dry.

My grandfather took my arm and whispered in my ear: "I know how you feel, boy." He squeezed my arm. "Fandango told me many times that he wanted to be buried by the crooked pine on top of the hill," he went on. "I'm going to give him his wish."

At five in the afternoon the funeral procession started. As the coffin had no handles, it was carried on a cart pulled by a horse. My grandfather, my father and I followed the cart on foot, heading the procession. From the neighboring villages, ranches and farms many people had come to say farewell to the old *gaúcho*—rich ranchers, cowboys, farmers, Negroes, tramps, even *gringos* from the Italian settlements. They all knew and loved Fandango.

Horsemen stood in a double line along the slope of the hill, and, when the coffin passed by, the *gaúchos* took off their hats. Up at the foot of the crooked pine a group of people—men, women and children—surrounded the open grave.

Contemplating the picture from the foot of the hill, I shuddered, as if suddenly pierced by the sad, grave beauty of that moment. It was like the funeral of an ancient warrior, in a silent country which knew no drums or fanfares. The only audible sounds were the moaning of the wind and the rustling of the trees.

It was too much for me. I covered my face with my hands and let the tears stream down. Fandango whispered in my mind: "A man never cries. Pull yourself together, son."

At my side, my father cleared his throat three times. My grandfather kept squeezing my arm, as if he were trying to speak to me without words. Finally we reached the top of the hill. Following an ancient tradition, the coffin was opened once again before burial.

I looked for the last time upon the dead man's face, and the serenity of its expression was such that a calm came upon me, and my weeping ceased.

I uttered no word; my lips did not move; but in my heart I addressed Fandango.

"Old friend, forgive my tears. I understand now. You are not going away from us: your body will be planted in the good earth of Angico, and from it perhaps will spring a tree in whose shade I shall come to rest. Old cattle drover, your soul is journeying down its last trail, and one day I shall come to join you on some rise in the prairies of Eternity. Then since you will already know everyone and everything there, you can be my teacher again, just as in times past. Everything is going to be all right now. Farewell!" I am sure no one understood why a smile came to my lips as the coffin was lowered into the grave.

My grandfather and my father took handfuls of earth and cast them upon the lid of the coffin. Others followed their example. Then a ranch hand took a spade and started to fill in the grave.

Little by little the crowd disbanded. Fandango was alone on the hill by the crooked pine.

THE GUERRILLA
— ◦❧ ❦◦ —

I had a prodigious uncle. His name was Nestor. He was thickset, ruddy, strong as a bull. When you met him, phlegmatic and placid, you would not imagine him capable of the agility and mobility he revealed in dozens of battles. For my uncle was first and foremost a guerrilla. Wherever there was a revolution, there was he— revolver at his belt, Winchester slung over his shoulder, yellow kerchief around his neck. On horseback, in his outfit, he resembled Wallace Beery playing Pancho Villa. Fighting was his favorite pastime. But he cherished other loves. He read cloak-and-dagger novels with passionate avidity and he had a Falstaffian thirst and appetite. A man temperate in gesture, soft of voice, incapable of bluster, he was nonetheless gifted with an irrational courage that he took as much for granted as the color of his hair, the shape of his nose, and even the disfigurement of his left eye, which was blind.

— ◦❧ ❦◦ —

One time, he was standing on the front line ready to shoot when his commanding officer, who was in the same position beside him, yelled:

"Things are getting bad, major. Let's lie down."

Bullets whistling past him, my uncle merely said:

"I'm no frog, to be stretched out on my belly on the ground."

And he remained where he was.

— ◦❧ ❦◦ —

On another occasion, the group he was commanding attacked a small city and rushed the town hall, where the last defenders of the square had taken refuge. He broke down the door with his shoulder and went in. In the vestibule an enemy was waiting, his shotgun at the ready and pointed toward the door. But Nestor shot first and cut him down. Later, when his companions, amazed at this feat, complimented him on the quickness of his draw and the accuracy of his marksmanship, he shrugged and explained:

"Well, I had a hell of an advantage over that boy. He first had to shut one eye to aim. But I'm like Camões, with one eye shut by nature, so all I had to do was pull the trigger."

— ◦❧ ❦◦ —

Once a price was put on his head by the government he was rebelling against. After the revolution was over, Nestor was sneaking back to his native town when he decided to stop at a roadside store for a drink. The yellow kerchief, symbol of his political party, still encircled his bull-like neck. As he entered, a man standing beside the counter recognized him at once and raised his hand to the butt of his revolver. Nestor knew who he was—in person, the chief of police of the district he was heading for. There was a moment of tension. The storekeeper paled. The other men there caught on to the situation, withdrew, and waited outside in expectation of the volley. Some seconds passed; the silence continued. Nestor approached the counter and asked for a bottle of rum and two glasses. Turning to the chief, he said:

"Let's drink. I want to see if this bottle holds friendship or enmity for us two."

The other accepted the invitation. They began to hoist glasses. By the third, they were conversing naturally, like old friends. By the fifth, they were exchanging embraces. By the sixth, they were lyrical, they were brothers, they were swearing to die for each other. Soon afterward, Nestor left, free and unseathed. And the police chief stayed on, shouting to the four winds that he had never met a finer fellow in all his life.

I remember the day I went to the movies with my uncle. It was a picture about the relations between parents and children. There were a dissipated father, a martyred mother, and an unhappy daughter, all against a background of sad, languid violins. Beside me, Nestor was squirming in his seat, sniffling, rubbing his eyes with his fingers. I noticed tears trickling down those cheeks turned to leather by the sun and wind of a hundred revolutions. Realizing that I was watching him, my uncle murmured:

"I get upset at the least little thing. I'm a cow."

THE HOUSE OF THE MELANCHOLY ANGEL

—◦❦ ❦◦—

The story that I am going to tell has no real beginning, middle, or end. Time is a river without a source, ceaselessly flowing into Eternity, but it may well be that in unexpected reaches of its course our boat may slip out of the main current, turning aside into the ancient, stagnant waters of some quiet inlet, and only God knows what may happen to us then. Nevertheless, to get on with the narrative, let us assume that it all began that April afternoon.

It was the first year of the War, and I was trying to avoid reading the newspapers or listening to those who talked of battles, bombardments, and troop movements.

"The Germans will easily break through the Maginot Line," I was assured one day by the stranger who had taken a seat beside me on a park bench. "In a few weeks they will be masters of Paris." I shook my head and replied, "Impossible. Paris is a city, not in space, but in time. It is a state of mind, and of heart, and as such is inaccessible to the *Panzerdivisionen*." The man eyed me askance, with a look of amazement and alarm. Well, I am used to being so regarded. A lunatic! That is what my fellow boarders say of me in the house where I have a rented room with the usual rights to a scanty table and a collective bath. It is only natural they should think so, I am a rather queer fellow, a timid, solitary soul, who sometimes spends hours on end in conversation aloud with himself. "He lives withdrawn in his shell," they say. Perhaps so, but this dim oyster has not even the consolation of having produced, in his solitude, a rare pearl, unless—But I must not get ahead of my story, nor is it for me to judge.

A man of modest needs, what I earn by giving piano lessons in my pupils' homes is sufficient for my support. Moreover, it permits me to buy phonograph records and, now and then, to go to a concert. Nearly every night, after wandering idly and alone through the streets, I retire to my room, start the victrola, and, stretched out on my bed, close my eyes and listen to the late quartets of Beethoven, trying to discover what the old man can have meant by this phrase or that. In my room I have a piano on which I play my own compositions, which I have never had the courage or the need to show to anyone. A poet has said that

> Between the idea
> And the reality
> Between the motion
> And the act
> Falls the Shadow.

Well, between that shadow and a scarcely glimpsed light of hope I lived, apparently, with no other ambition than that of holding to my peace and solitude.

In winter, spring, and summer I feel like an exile, finding my natural climate and habitat only in autumn, the season which envelops people and things in soft lilac. It is as if God had set and lighted the world as a stage for his favorite mysteries, so that at any minute a miracle might occur.

On that April day I wandered through the streets as if walking in my sleep, with the impression that autumn was an opal in which my city was set, with its people, houses, streets, parks, and monuments, very like those tiny ships, made of pieces of colored glass, that prisoners patiently construct, bit by bit, inside bottles. I had a sudden desire to compose a sonata to the afternoon. I began with a serenely melancholy *andantino* and toyed with it for two blocks, my attention divided between the music and the world. Suddenly the freckled hands of one of my pupils began to practice scales in my skull with an atrocious violence, and away went the *andantino*. I thought, vexed, of the lessons I had to give the next day. Ah, the monotony of the exercises, the obtuseness of most of my pupils, the incomprehension and the insolence of the parents! I must confess that I did not like my profession. If I did not abandon the work, it was because I knew no other way to make a living, for the idea of playing popular music in those public houses where one dances, dines, and drinks at night was repugnant to me.

When the *andantino* stole back into my mind, I followed its notes, amused, as one who watches children dancing around in a garden. Suddenly a frightful screech slashed through my reverie from top to bottom just as someone hauled me backward with violence. Now, I have no instinct of self-preservation. They say Shelley was the same. Perhaps it is absurdly pretentious for me to compare myself with the poet. But the truth is, I have none. It took a good couple of seconds for me to realize that I had nearly gone under the wheels of a bus, and that an unknown passer-by had saved my life. I stammered thanks to the man, who was still holding my arm, but what really impressed me, even in that moment, was the furious expression of the bus driver, who was yelling, "Can't you look where you're going, you idiot?" How was it possible that anyone could get angry and shout ugly things on an autumn afternoon? The bus went on its way. My savior became lost in the crowd.

I saw then that I was in front of the Public Library. The gray, severe building had such a protective, inviting air that, without knowing just why, I resolved to go in. I crossed the rose-marble lobby, entered the reading room, and approached the librarian in charge—the one I call Confucius nowadays for reasons soon to be clear. We were already old acquaintances, since it was my habit to go to the library quite frequently.

The man looked up and asked, "What can I do for you, my friend?" My indecision expressed itself in a smile. I could have asked for a book of poems or some essay on Mozart, but I surprised myself by saying:

"I want to see some old newspapers."

"Which one?"

I mentioned the name of the city's oldest morning paper.

"And the date?"

"Nineteen-twelve."

That was the year of my birth. The librarian went away returning shortly with two large bound volumes under his arm, and laid them on the table at which I had sat down.

I leafed absently through the papers, finding a nostalgic flavor in the movie and theater advertisements, in the social items, and principally in the faded reproductions of photographs in which men and women appeared in the clothes of the period. In the issue whose date corresponded exactly to that April day I found among the want ads one which caught my attention:

> PIANO TEACHER *wanted, well-bred, to teach young lady*
> *with four years' previous instruction. Apply 25 Willow*
> *Street (old house with angel in garden).*

I could not help smiling. The librarian came over.

"What have you discovered that seems so interesting?"

I showed him the advertisement. He mounted his spectacles on his nose, bent over the table, and read.

"Listen," I said in a low voice. "Twenty-eight years ago, in a house on Willow Street, a young lady waited for her piano teacher. I wonder whether he turned up. I wonder what ever happened to that young lady."

The librarian shrugged.

"Probably she got fat, grew old, became a grandmother—Or died."

"Don't be such a pessimist! Imagine something different: time has not passed and the girl is still there, waiting—"

"Oh, imagine I was born in China centuries ago and that my name is Confucius!"

"And why not?"

The librarian uttered a laugh, a muted laugh as befitted the place and time. I picked up my hat and left. The phrases of the advertisement sounded in my mind like the childish melody of a music box.

I discovered that Willow Street, which I reached just at dusk, now bore the name of a leader of three revolutions and ran through one of those districts laid waste by the latest city-planning project. The old dwellings had been torn down to make way for modern apartment houses. I could see no willow or anything else even faintly suggestive of the possibility that a house like the one in the advertisement might have survived. I walked on slowly to the rhythm of my thoughts, once more concentrated on the *andantino*. The thunder of traffic had faded to such a degree that it was now hardly more than a distant hum. Street lamps were still unlighted along the deserted sidewalks. I could no longer hear the sound of my own footsteps: it was as if I were treading on the fallen fibers of the kapok tree. The street was bathed in a milky fog of purplish iridescence which seemed to deform all images, and I had the impression of being at the bottom of the sea, like a forgetful diver who cannot imagine why he has descended to the depths.

When I again became aware of reality, I found myself standing before an old iron gate, on the upper part of which was a plate with the number 25. Spying through the grating, I saw, at the back of a garden, squeezed between two enormous apartment houses, a colonial home with a whitewashed façade and blue shutters. A few steps from its main door, under a flowering kapok tree, was the melancholy figure of a bronze angel, seated on a stone in the attitude of Rodin's *Penseur*. The angel! An indescribable content filled me then, a sort of pride in verifying that there was still someone in the world who prized the past and resisted the temptation of money, refusing to sell his property to the insatiable builders of skyscrapers.

I opened the gate, crossed the crepuscular garden, caressed the patinated head of the melancholy angel, went up to the door, and knocked. My heart was beating irregularly. Why was I doing this? What right had I? What was my purpose? What would I say if someone should come to the door?

Overwhelmed by a sudden fright, I was about to turn and flee when the door was opened, and in the shadows of the hall I made out the form of a woman.

A neutral voice reached my ear:

"What do you want, sir?"

The reply that occurred to me in the confusion of the moment seemed senseless to me then, but now I know that it was the right one, the most natural, the only one.

"Is this where a piano teacher is wanted?"

There was a brief hesitation on the woman's part.

"It is. Please come in, and I'll go tell the mistress."

She showed me into a drawing room illuminated by a lamp on whose globe of white, frosted glass was painted a yellow butterfly between two bunches of flowers. I looked around. It was one of those parlors much in vogue in the last decade of the past century, with its furniture of carved jacaranda and wine-colored upholstery, the sofa and chairs with rollers on their feet. In one corner stood the dark bulk of the piano, upon which bric-a-brac was aligned on crocheted doilies. On the walls were pictures, portraits of bygone people. The atmosphere was warmed by so inviting an intimacy, by such a suggestion of human comfort, that for the first time in all my life I felt completely at home in an environment. I was so absorbed in the pleasure of the place and the moment that I did not even notice the entrance of the mistress of the house.

"Good evening," she said. "You are a piano teacher, then?"

Her voice, like her countenance, was a curious combination of gentleness and determination. I took the hand she extended. She indicated a chair. I sat down and only then perceived that I had before me a graying lady dressed exactly like my mother in that portrait, taken early in 1913, which is in my family album: a white blouse with a high lace gorget and a very narrow waist, and a dark full skirt with its hem almost sweeping the floor. Her coiffure reminded me of the "Gibson girls" which used to appear in the magazine illustrations of my boyhood.

"What is your name?"

I told her.

"How old are you?"

"Twenty-eight."

"So young? I expected an older teacher—"

"If you prefer me to age," I said with a smile, "I can go away and return in twenty years."

Her laugh was sonorous, and I feared that its vibrations might break the spell.

Yes, because I felt that something marvelous was happening to me, I did not understand why or how. I knew only that I had found a home, a shelter. It may seem silly, but it was as if I had gone back, by some miracle, to my mother's womb.

The lady's face again became serious.

"I am going to be quite frank with you, as is my habit. I am a widow, I live alone in this old house with my daughter, and I thoroughly disapprove of certain liberties of modern life. Have you read of the foolish things those so-called suffragettes are doing?"

I nodded affirmatively.

"Well, in my opinion," she continued, "woman was made for the home and not to vote and go around dressed like men. My daughter is a young lady brought up in the old-fashioned way. That is why I am looking for a respectable and respectful teacher for her. Speaking of that, do you have some certificate or letter of recommendation?"

"Not here with me. But if you wish, I can bring it another day."

"Do so. Now let us go on to another matter. What is your fee?"

"Whatever you say—"

"We paid thirty a month to the last teacher. He came twice a week."

"Why, thirty is quite satisfactory."

"When can you begin?"

"Let's see," I murmured, taking out my fountain pen and notebook. "What day is tomorrow?"

"The twenty-ninth."

"Of April?"

"Of course."

I could feel my heart stop as I asked:

"What year?"

The lady frowned.

"My dear sir! Can it be that you don't know this is 1912?"

"Forgive me. I am a little absent-minded."

"I do not care much for absent-minded people. And if you will permit an observation of a personal nature, I do not like the extraordinary way you dress. The character of a man is revealed by his clothes."

For some instants her dark eyes appraised me with an intensity not devoid of liking.

"Very well. Your face inspires confidence. After all, it is not a question of marriage. If I find you unsuitable, I shall tell you so frankly. But let us see what days and hours you have free."

I examined my schedule, without, however, really taking in its indications, for the names, days and hours spoke of a world and a time that I did not like and which now were dead to me and nearly forgotten.

As my indecision was growing overlong, the mistress of the house helped me with a suggestion. Couldn't I give the lessons on Tuesdays and Thursdays, from five to six o'clock in the evening?

"Perfect!" I exclaimed automatically.

There was a short silence, and then she called, "Adriana!"

Adriana came in dressed all in white. She was at most, twenty, and resembled—I sensed it immediately!—the mysterious woman that visited my dreams, and whose face I had never succeeded in seeing clearly. The presence of that strange apparition used to make itself felt, at times incorporate in a white feminine silhouette, at times in the form of a melody which I vainly sought to capture. In more than one dream I had set out in pursuit of that phantom, across mountains, meadows, forests, and waters. Now there she stood before me, within reach of my hand. The lamplight struck full on Adriana's face. And when she looked at me with her eyes of humid seaweed green, the diver at last realized why he had descended to the depths of the sea. The joy of the discovery was transformed into music in my mind. It was a broad phrase, clear and impetuous as a bird's flight or as a silver arrow sped against the sun.

—◦❧ ❦◦—

That melody accompanied me as I left the house of the melancholy angel and crossed the garden murmuring to myself, "What has happened is impossible, yet I need give explanations to no one, not even to myself. It is enough that I believe. And I do believe—oh, how I believe!"

In a mild daze I set out along the street. Night had fallen completely. Streetcars rumbled past, automobiles with glaring headlights roared along the asphalt, shop windows spread their livid fluorescent light over the sidewalks thronged with passers-by, and I walked among those creatures, noises and lights carrying my dream with the tremulous, fearful care of one who bears in his hands a crystal rare and fragile, which the slightest touch may shiver into bits.

I quickened my step and took refuge in my room, the better to protect my memories against the brutality of the city night. Sitting down at the piano, I began to develop the theme suggested by Adriana's presence. I forgot the abyss, the shadow, time and the world. Day was just breaking when I finished putting on paper the first movement of a sonata. I threw myself on the bed so exhausted that I fell asleep instantly. When I awoke, the sun was at its zenith. The events of the day before came to my mind and I said to myself, "It was all a dream." But no! I found on my night table the ruled paper with the first movement of the sonata. I leaped from the bed, snatched up my notebook, opened it, and read: "Tuesdays and Thursdays, lessons for Adriana, 25 Willow Street, from five to six." Today is Tuesday! I discovered joyfully. I shaved in nervous haste, dressed and went out. On the stairs I met the landlady, who scolded me: "The other boarders are furious. You hammered on the piano all night long. You can't do that!"

"I can't do that," I repeated mechanically. When I reached the sidewalk, an anguishing doubt assailed me. Suppose I could never again find the house of the melancholy angel? My first impulse was to run to Willow Street. I restrained myself. It was better to wait for the hour of the first lesson.

That afternoon I gave scant attention to my teaching. Shortly before five, without the slightest explanation, I left a pupil in the middle of a Chopin *étude* and started out for Willow Street. When I caught sight of the two sky scrapers which flanked the garden at the house of the angel, I slowed my pace. The street was deserted, the street lamps not yet lighted. A golden haze filled the air, muffling all sounds, as if it were cotton. I opened the old gate, entered, crossed the garden, smiled at the angel and knocked at the door. Adriana was awaiting me, standing beside the piano. I saw that her eyes were bright with tears.

"Have you been crying?"

She bowed her head affirmatively, and, seating herself at the piano and tapping absently on one key and then another, she stammered:

"I have been reading the story of the shipwreck."

"What shipwreck?"

She fixed surprised eyes on me.

"Then you don't know? You haven't read? The wreck of the *Titanic*—"

"Ah!"

The *Titanic* disaster, which had taken place the year I was born, was to leave me profoundly moved when, ten years later, I saw it described in an illustrated magazine in all its dramatic details.

"Well—," I murmured. "Now play something, so that I can see how well you do."

Adriana began to play a Scarlatti sonatina with occasional hesitations but with much feeling. While she played, I could observe her features better. I do not think it possible to portray in words a woman's face. What matters is not its configuration, the color of the eyes, the shape of the mouth and nose, or the complexion of the skin. It is, rather, a certain inner quality that illumines the face, animating it and setting it apart from all others, and that quality rarely if ever, allows itself to be caught even by the camera. There are skillful artists, or perhaps merely lucky ones, who, as they paint a woman's face, now and then succeed in fixing on canvas that radiance, impossible to localize, which at first glance seems to come from the eyes, but which nevertheless continues to impart luster to the face even if the eyes are covered. It was just such a splendor which enveloped Adriana's whole person. Her presence was warm, simple, friendly.

"Very good," I said when she finished playing the sonatina. "I can see that you love music. You play with your soul."

"Do you really think so? How wonderful! I adore music. Mamma has even promised to buy me one of those phonographs that play disks—you know—not cylinders."

I told her I was a composer and was writing a sonata.

"Ah! Play it for me!"

"It is not ready yet. Only the first movement."

At that moment Adriana's mother appeared in the doorway. I assumed a grave, professional air and said:

"Well. Let us hear some scales now."

—◦⟫ ⟪◦—

My life underwent a complete change. I spent the hour waiting anxiously, eager for the time when I would be with Adriana in that twilit drawing room. Never did I breathe a word of my secret to anyone. The oyster was drawing still further into his shell, jealous of his pearl.

There were, however, moments in which I feared, not the world, but the sense of logic which dwells within each of us, and which at any minute might ask explanations about what was happening to me. And every time it threatened to raise the dreaded question, I put it off by saying, "I need to believe it; otherwise I shall be lost forever."

There were early morning hours when I walked the streets aimlessly and with an almost unbearable desire to go look at the house of the melancholy angel. A secret voice, however, advised: "Don't. If you go, you may discover that it is all an illusion." And I did not go.

But on lesson days, there I was, crossing the ancient garden rejoicing, patting the angel's head, knocking on the door, and entering Adriana's room, world, and time.

A sweet intimacy gradually arose between us, an understanding that did not depend on words or on points of reference in time or space.

When her mother was not in the room, Adriana would describe to me scenes and impressions of her childhood spent in that house. She told me about the night the new century had come in and she had gone, holding to her father's hand, to see the Great Exposition. Ah! Never had she forgotten the merry-go-round, the clowns, the games, the hall of mirrors, and above all the fireworks, which had burst precisely on the twelfth stroke of midnight, to the clangor of the bells of all the churches in the city!

Adriana wanted to know where I had been on that great night.

"On the sea," I responded without thinking. And she smiled, apparently satisfied with my answer.

At times it was I who talked most, surprised and charmed as I was to find someone interested in my person and my life. Thus I emptied my heart of many cares and secrets. Things that I carried locked tight in the recesses of my being came to the surface and were transformed into words.

As our conversations lengthened into suspicious murmurs, more than once Adriana's mother came to the door to ask why the teacher had interrupted the lesson. We then had to invent a stratagem which gave us much amusement: Adriana would play her exercises and we would talk through the curtain of music.

But how empty and sad were the hours I spent away from her! The only thing that could restore, almost literally, the presence of Adriana was the sonata, to the development of which I devoted myself passionately through all that month of May—during which I lost my pupils one by one, as a result of my unpunctuality and absent-mindedness.

The second movement, a *scherzo*, came easily to my imagination, and with the same spontaneity I set it down on paper. Then I plunged into the third, a *molto agitato*, which I composed on a day at the close of May when winter sent its first message on the wind. I feared the coming of the cold, for a mysterious premonition warned me that the July winds might impel my boat out of the backwater, restoring it to the main current of Time and tearing me forever from the creature I loved.

One afternoon, I had hardly entered the house of the angel when Adriana came to meet me smiling, with the day's paper in her hands.

"Look!" she exclaimed. "Yesterday a baby with your name was born."

She showed me the social column, and I felt a chill on reading there the news of my own birth.

"I wonder what that baby's destiny will be," I said.

"He may become President of the Republic."

"Or nothing more than a mere piano teacher."

Adriana gazed at me with so profound an expression of tenderness that I was disturbed, and to hide my embarrassment I babbled:

"Let us play that Bach saraband."

—◦❧ ❦◦—

It was on the last day of May that I took the completed sonata to the house of the angel. I played it for Adriana. The first movement translated my surprise and joy at finding her. However, it was an *allegro ma non troppo*, for in the background of that happiness could be glimpsed the fear I had of some day losing her. The *scherzo* painted in vivid colors not only the happy moments we had spent together in the drawing room but also scenes of Adriana's childhood. There was the little girl with long braids, now playing in her room with dolls, now running in the garden rolling a tricolored hoop. Next came Adriana laughing, startled, before those seven other Adrianas deformed in her eyes by the concave and convex mirrors in the hall of magic of the Great Exposition. This was followed by the *molto agitato* of short duration, describing the despair of a man wandering aimlessly through empty streets, seeking an impossible love, lost in Time. And the sonata ended with a prolonged *adagio*, steeped in the resigned misery of one who yields to the irremediable, without rancor toward life or toward other beings. It was a slow, nostalgic movement, suggestive of a river flowing to the sea, carrying with it a longing for things seen on its banks and the certainty that its waters will never again reflect those loved images.

When it came to an end, Adriana murmured:

"Beautiful, very beautiful!"

"It is yours."

I took out my fountain pen and, beneath the title, "Sonata in D Minor," wrote: *For Adriana. May, 1912.*

She looked at me sadly, her eyes filling with tears. I wanted then a confirmation that she loved me; I wanted her to put it into words. Perhaps I was not worthy of the miracle that had happened to me, for I longed to touch Adriana, to have her for myself, to take her into my world, my time. And if in my desire there was so troubled an urgency, it was because I had noticed signs of winter in the air outside: the angel's head was chill to my touch that afternoon when I came.

The knowledge that I did not belong to that place and hour—for I was not more than a phantom of the future—gave me a boldness of which I had never before been capable. I took Adriana's hand and exclaimed, "I love you, I love you!" She jumped up, snatched her hand away, and turned her face aside, whispering, "But it is impossible!" And with tremulous voice she informed me that she was engaged and would be married in July. She did not love her fiancé, no! But her mother was insisting on the marriage and she had no alternative but to obey.

I did something senseless then, for I should have known that no gesture, no word, no desire of mine could alter what had happened.

"But no woman can be forced to marry a man she does not love!" I cried.

At that instant Adriana's mother entered the room, and in a freezing tone said:

"Your behavior is disgraceful. You have betrayed my trust and have abused my daughter. Leave this house at once!"

Outside I found the first breath of winter and a leaden sky. The hours that followed were hours of despair. I retired to my room, but I found no consolation in either music or books. I sought, but in vain, to find palpable evidence that everything had been only a hallucination or a prolonged dream; I found nothing beyond my memories. I threw myself on the bed and wept as I had not for a long time.

The next day, when I went out to wander again through the streets, it was with the sensation of being lost in a strange and hostile city. My steps eventually took me to Willow Street, and I carried in my heart a cruel presentiment that I was not long in seeing confirmed. Square on the site where the house of the melancholy angel used to be, a twenty-story apartment building had now been erected. I crossed the street and entered a café. With an air of indifference I questioned the waiter who served me. Did he remember the old houses in that street?

"No, sir," he answered. "I'm new here. Ask the owner, he's one of the oldest residents in this district. Boss, this young man wants to ask you something—"

The café proprietor, a gray-haired man with an air of weary or disillusioned kindness, came over. I waved toward the street.

"What became of the white colonial house that used to be over there, with a bronze angel in the garden?"

The man gave me a curious glance.

"How old are you, sir?"

I told him my age, and he inquired:

"How can you remember that house if it was torn down more than twenty-five years ago?"

I shrugged. A strange calm was now dulling my spirit. All had ended as was to be expected. My boat was letting itself be swept along once more by the main current of the river, and I neither knew nor wanted to know what awaited me in the Great Ocean. Nothing mattered any more. I was now living out the *adagio* of the sonata.

The proprietor of the café, meanwhile, was still waiting for my reply.

"Do you believe in miracles?" I asked.

He shook his head:

"I don't. Do you?"

—◦❦ ❦◦—

My life again became what it had been before. The winter was long and gloomy. The memory of Adriana was my constant companion and it was with her in mind that I composed my pieces. I still refused to examine that singular episode of my life in the light of reason. As a child I had read in an anthology a poem about a Hindu, who dissected a dragonfly for analysis, with the result that he destroyed all its beauty. I had learned that lesson.

Nevertheless, it did not prevent my returning to the Public Library one September day to ask Confucius for some old newspapers of 1912 to 1920, and setting myself to leaf through them with a restless hope.

In the July 1912 file I found the news of Adriana's marriage. I glanced over several volumes, covering five years, without coming across the slightest reference to her or to her husband, whom the society editor had called "a pillar of society." But in a May 1917 issue I found the report of the birth of their daughter, who had been given her mother's name in baptism. And, on opening the 1919 volume, on the first page of the first issue for January, I saw an announcement of a funeral. There, between two black borders, under a cross, was the name of "my" Adriana. I read the address of the funeral home, which meant nothing to me now that she was no longer there, closed the volume amid confused feelings, waved a friendly hand at Confucius, went out of the library and got into a taxi. "To the cemetery," I ordered.

I pictured a simple grave for Adriana: a plain slab surrounded by grass, and on the slab, seated on a stone, the melancholy angel. On the contrary: from her husband's middle-class imagination had sprung a pretentious mausoleum of greenish marble, with a Greek portico and a Latin inscription on the base of the entrance. I rested my face on the glass of the door to the tomb and, after my eyes had adjusted themselves to the gloom inside, was able to make out, on top of a marble stand, a large portrait of Adriana. I shivered. While I was walking the streets on that unforgettable April afternoon, I reflected, Adriana was already dead and buried. And yet—

No. Best treasure those beloved memories and not try to learn the reason for anything.

I heard a voice.

"An acquaintance of yours?"

I turned and found myself face to face with a very young woman who was watching me curiously. She was dressed in green, her arms were full of jonquils and the wind was blowing her bronze hair.

"Someone I met a long time ago," I explained.

There was a brief silence during which I stood with downcast eyes staring at the stranger's shadow on the mosaic pavement.

"I ask," she went on, "because that is the tomb of my mother."

I felt not the slightest surprise. Before she spoke the words I had already anticipated them. I raised my eyes. The girl did resemble her mother. It was not the resemblance of a twin sister, a likeness of feature, but rather an identity of atmosphere, or aura, of—I do not know why I am always trying to define the indefinable. Of one thing, at any rate, I am certain: the eyes were the same in shape and color. They differed only in expression. In those of the dead Adriana there was peace; in those of the living Adriana, something that disturbed me.

"But how can you have known my mother? She died nearly twenty-two years ago. At that time you must have been a baby."

Once more I stared down at the shadow.

"I confess I lied when I said she was an old acquaintance of mine. What really happened was that I was passing and looked inside the tomb and—"

"That's all right. You don't have to explain. There's no harm in looking."

She opened the mausoleum door, then turned to me and asked whether I would like to come in. I said no. She entered, laid the flowers beneath the portrait, knelt at the foot of the altar and remained there in prayer. A voice whispered to me: "Fly, fly while there is time." And yet I stayed where I was, as if under a spell.

Adriana rose, came out of the vault, closed the door and, turning, said:

"You still there? I can take you downtown in my car. Come on!"

She spoke that "Come on!" with an authority that admitted no refusal. Side by side we walked through the cypress grove, and I watched our shadows on the mosaic sidewalks, bemused, uncertain what to think of it all.

The automobile was a beige convertible, shining with chromium. I got in, sat down beside Adriana, and, after the car started off, covertly examined my unexpected companion's profile.

I felt embarrassed, not knowing what to say. It was not, however, necessary for me to invent a topic, for Adriana never stopped talking, casting occasional quick, penetrating glances at me. What was my name? Where did I live? What did I do? Musician, eh? Interesting.

She told me she loved music, played the piano a little, and had a fabulous collection of records. She asked what I thought of Stravinsky and Béla Bartók. I replied that I preferred the early Italians. Ah! But don't you think the classics can no longer satisfy our overexcited sensibilities, living in chaos as we do?

"I am a little conservative—"

"That's plain, from your clothes," retorted Adriana with a laugh that increased my embarrassment and my sense of solitude. Nevertheless, I confess I did not want to be rid of the girl. Whatever else, she was a prolongation of the Other.

"Where do you want to get out?" she asked, as we approached the center of the city. "Ah! I know. You're going to my house. We'll have a drink and I'll introduce you to my father, who's an old darling. I want you to play one of your compositions for me. My friends will be green with envy if I discover a new musical genius—"

"Have no illusions. I'm only a piano teacher."

"I'll be the one to decide that!"

We got out in front of one of those modern houses which seem like white, cubical, smooth, cold sepulchers. We crossed a garden bristling with cactus, in the middle of which I caught sight of an old acquaintance: the melancholy angel.

"Looking at that old thing?" asked Adriana with a gesture toward the angel. "It has no connection with this functional residence. It was in the garden of the house where Papa courted Mamma. The old man, who's a great sentimentalist, had the monstrosity brought here."

The interior of the house was bright, airy, colorful, shiningly clean and utterly impersonal, betraying no signs of human habitation. In a corner of the vast living room stood a grand piano.

"Too bad the old man hasn't come in yet!" mourned Adriana. "But he won't be long."

She nodded toward the piano and said:

"Sit down and play something of your own."

I obeyed, and began playing the sonata I had composed for the other Adriana.

"Stop!" cried the daughter. "I know that piece. Wait a minute—"

She ran out of the room and returned shortly with a yellowed sheet of music which I recognized, deeply moved, as the "Sonata in D Minor." There was the dedication and the date in my own handwriting.

"This music was written in 1912 by an admirer of my mother's. How do you explain that, Mr. 'Composer'?"

I shrugged.

"Forgive me. I must have heard that melody a long time ago and forgotten it. Then it came back to my memory and I thought—Well, those things happen—"

"Of course they do."

She gave me a soothing pat on the shoulder and then offered me a cigarette. I told her I didn't smoke. She lit her own, blew out a puff of smoke, looked me in the eye, and said softly:

"Funny, when I saw you in the cemetery I had the feeling I already knew you. Only, I can't remember where it was—"

Adriana was tapping on a key in a way painfully reminiscent of the Other. Her voice lost its aggressiveness and became sweet and friendly as she asked:

"Do you believe in premonitions?"

"Certainly."

She gazed at me enigmatically, and then, resting a hand lightly on my arm as if she were an old friend, said:

"Go on playing that sonata while I find something for us to drink."

I began to play. I hoped the first phrase of the sonata might have the power to conjure up the presence of "my" Adriana. But what it brought to mind was the image of a woman in green with an armful of jonquils, the spring wind tossing her hair.

Then I sensed that I was in danger of losing my dream forever, and an all but blind terror of the future swept over me.

I rose, picked up my hat and tiptoed out of the house.

PART III

Modernism at Mid-Century
—◦❧(1945–1980)❧◦—

Brazilian literature at mid-century is dominated by neovanguard groups that launched new manifestos, aesthetic principles, and experimental techniques, often highly theoretical and bringing literary expression closer to plastic arts and architecture. After concretism (1956), there followed a burst of neovanguard tendencies (neoconcretism, *praxis, ptyx, poema-processo*), paralleled in the works of plastic artists Lygia Clark (1920–1988) and Hélio Oiticica (1937–1980). The "generation of 1945" had prepared a return to technical and aesthetic discipline, favoring rigorous artisanship in poetry over the freedoms allowed by early modernism. The poets of this generation, such as Ledo Ivo (b. 1924), read the masters of world poetry and were led theoretically by their interest in Pound, Eliot, North American poetry, and new criticism. Poet João Cabral de Melo Neto (1920–1999), who combined innovation and engineering in a poetics of self-conscious structures and materials, became the most important figure of the second half of the twentieth century.

Poesia Concreta, the concrete poetry movement led by Haroldo and Augusto de Campos, with Décio Pignatari, developed rapidly though early contacts with Ezra Pound and Eugene Gomringer in Europe. It launched visual poetry in its journals *Noigandres* and *Invenção* in the 1950s and 1960s, presented its works in the form of an art exhibition at São Paulo's Museu de Arte Moderna in 1956, and consolidated its principles in a 1964 book of theoretical essays (*Teoria da Poesia Concreta*, São Paulo, Duas Cidades, 1964). By forming avant-garde verbal, vocal, and visual relationships, concrete poetry produced different morphological and syntactical relationships, leading to new forms of reading and meaning. Although concretism was highly polemical and thought to be ephemeral and inconsequential by some critics, the movement left a rich legacy that has affected every genre of writing, as well as popular music and plastic arts, and its erudite critical essays were responsible for inculcating both a high level of scholarship and a consciousness of international literature and translation on a level not seen before in Brazil. The polemics it inspired became part of the fervor in experimental arts of the times. The concretists' program of critical invention and translation had an effect on all literary production in Brazil.

In tandem with the generation of 1945, major prose writers who would create highly individual, experimental styles in the short story and fiction came on the scene beginning in the 1940s. This neomodernist generation was led by João Guimarães Rosa, who published a volume of short stories, *Sagarana*, in 1945 (trans.

Harriet de Onís, New York, Knopf, 1966); Clarice Lispector, whose stories first appeared in book form in the 1952 *Alguns Contos* (in *Family Ties*, trans. Giovanni Pontiero, Austin, U of Texas P, 1972); and Osman Lins, a prolific story writer from 1953 to the classic 1966 *Nove, Novena* (*Nine, Novena*, trans. Adria Frizzi, Los Angeles, Sun & Moon, 1995). These three authors would advance both the spirit and technique of innovation rampant at mid-century, and all worked extensively with language. Rosa's formation and deformation of words were bases for his questioning of the nature of the world and its meaning in his stories of the interior world of the *sertão*. Reading Rosa is a challenge to any reader, in understanding both the linguistic constructs and the levels of meaning, approaching dense poetry, with which he has charged them. Perhaps because of the difficulties of translation, only one book of his stories, now long out of print, appeared in English after *Sagarana* (*The Third Bank of the River and Other Stories*, trans. Barbara Shelby, New York, Knopf, 1968). Likewise, Rosa's great novel *Grande Sertão: Veredas*, one of Latin America's major works of fiction, was so inadequately translated that Haroldo de Campos referred to the English version as a "spaghetti western" (*The Devil to Pay in the Backlands*, trans. James L. Taylor and Harriet de Onis, New York, Knopf, 1963). Clarice Lispector's interest in the occult produced stories of reality made strange, and her writings became more experimental in form, at times beginning with punctuation marks, or multiple titles, or they were supposed to be accompanied by the sound of a beating drum. After her discovery by French feminists in the 1970s, Lispector became an international star, and all of her works have been translated into French, English, and other major languages. Since she avoided publicity after her return to Brazil in 1959 and left no manuscripts, the mysterious appeal of her life and works has attracted both scholars and a dedicated international readership. Her international prominence was enhanced by the prize-winning film based on her novel *The Hour of the Star* (Rio de Janeiro, José Olympio, 1977). Her works have been the subject of academic essays and numerous scholarly conferences (see overviews by Diane Marting, *Clarice Lispector: A Bio-bibliography*; and Earl Fitz, *Clarice Lispector*). Northeastern author Osman Lins showed an interest in perspectivism and the hidden codes and patterns of reality by giving multiple versions of events in his stories and by structuring works on the bases of labyrinths, puzzles, or acronyms. Characters are sometimes identified by graphic symbols instead of names, and the order and content of events is put in doubt by his characters' perspectives and the role of memory. A further experimental current exists in the stories of Dalton Trevisan, which have grown increasingly shorter since his 1945 debut to the point of becoming mini-stories. His relentless satire of the ethics and sexual mores of the bourgeois class has led him to ape the grotesque pandering and perversion of popular culture, which began as an interest in satirizing classical titles of culture and thereby rewriting tradition in a degenerate context. His titles have grown more extravagant, as if they belonged to horror or X-rated films in entertainment arcades.

Modernism at mid-century was a time of aesthetic experimentation, internationalism in reading and tastes, a formal and constructivist poetics, interdisciplinary works among the arts, and an assumed role of avant-garde leadership in Brazil. The "pilot plan" for concrete poetry was consciously patterned after the pilot plan for the new city of Brasília, and a generally positive belief existed that the inventiveness and creativity of a new science and technology would bring attention and solutions to Brazil's endemic problems as a society. This is the period during which Rosa and Lispector left their masterpieces among the great stories of world literature.

CLARICE LISPECTOR
—◦❧(1920–1977)❦◦—

Internationally recognized and widely translated after her discovery by French feminists in the 1970s, Clarice Lispector's stories continue to pose a challenge to readers and critics alike. Her importance lies in her capacity to dramatize the existential anguish and doubt, especially in her female characters, that she finds in common, everyday situations and experiences. By exploring the poetic function of language, including occult, mystical, and hermetic allusions and experimental techniques, Lispector explodes the concept of realism. Her writing has been described using Barthes's concept of "degree zero," as she invents opaque, neutral spaces dominated by the strange immediacy of existentialist or phenomenological perspectives. Her main characters are women trapped in a cruel existence without motivation, or confined in a monotonous and irrational subjectivity. Her theme is their search for a desperate or different form of liberation, never social but rather redemptive and transcendental.

Of Ukrainian-Jewish origin, Clarice Lispector was educated in Recife and Rio de Janeiro, where she studied law. Beginning with an impressive first novel, *Perto do Coração Selvagem* (1944), Lispector built a career as a metaphysical, essentialist, experimental writer concerned with issues of women and of consciousness, and on another plane with questions of purpose, social justice, love, death, and salvation. Her writings convey an intentional simplicity and disarming directness, at the same time belonging to and at odds with her theme, while retaining a mysterious, undefined, and incessantly questioning character. Lispector is now recognized as one of the masters of the genre in world literature. Three volumes of her stories have been translated and published in English: *Family Ties* (1972), *The Foreign Legion: Stories and Chronicles* (1986), and *Soulstorm* (1989). Her original collections are *Alguns Contos* (1952), *Laços de Família* (1960), *A Legião Estrangeira* (1964), *Felicidade Clandestina* (1971), *A Via Crucis do Corpo* (1974), *Onde Estivestes de Noite* (1974), and the posthumously published *A Bela e a Fera* (1979).

THE BUFFALO

—◦❧ ❦◦—

But it was spring. Even the lion licked the smooth head of the lioness. Two golden animals. The woman looked away from the cage, where only the warm scent reminded her of the carnage she had come in search of in the zoological gardens. Then the lion passed, heavy-maned and tranquil, and the lioness, her head on her outstretched paws, slowly became a sphinx once more.

"But this is love, this is love again," the woman said in rebellion, trying to find her own hatred, but it was spring and the two lions were in love. With her hands in her coat pockets, she looked around to find herself surrounded by cages, and caged by locked cages. She walked on. Her eyes were so intent upon her search that at times her sight darkened in slumber, and then she felt refreshed as in the coolness of a cave.

But the giraffe was a virgin with newly shorn braids. With the simple-minded innocence of that which is large and light and without guilt. The woman in the brown coat looked away—sick, so sick. Unable—confronted with that lovely giraffe standing before her, that silent wingless bird—unable to find within herself the critical point of her illness, the sickest point, the point of hatred, she who had gone to the zoological gardens in order to be sick. But not in the presence of the giraffe, which was more landscape than being. Not in the presence of that flesh which had strayed in height and distance, that giraffe which was almost green. She sought out other animals and tried to learn from them how to hate. The hippopotamus, the humid hippopotamus. Its round mass of flesh, its round, mute flesh awaiting some other round, mute flesh. No. Then there was such a humble love in maintaining oneself only as flesh, there was such a sweet martyrdom in not knowing how to think.

But it was spring, and, clenching her fists in her coat pockets, she would have destroyed those monkeys leaping around inside the cages, monkeys as happy as larks, monkeys tamely leaping among themselves, one female monkey with the resigned look of love and another engaged in breast feeding. She would have destroyed them with fifteen sharp bullets: the woman's teeth clenched until her jawbone hurt. The nakedness of those monkeys. That world which saw no danger in being nude. She would have destroyed their nudity. An ape, too, looked at her holding onto the bars, its scrawny arms opened in the form of a crucifix, its hairy chest exposed without pride. But she would not aim for its chest, it was between the ape's eyes that she would aim, between those eyes which stared at her unblinking. Suddenly the woman averted her gaze: the ape's eyes had a white gelatinous veil covering the pupils and in their expression the sweetness of illness. It was an old ape—the woman turned her eyes away, clenching between her teeth a sentiment she had not come in search of: she hastened her steps, still looking back in terror at the ape with outspread arms. He continued to stare ahead of him.

"Oh no, not this," she thought and as she escaped, she pleaded, "God, teach me only to hate."

"I hate you," she said to a man whose only crime was not to love her. "I hate you," she gasped in haste. But she did not even know how to begin. How to dig in the earth until she would find the black water, how to open a passage in the hard soil and never find herself? She walked through the zoological gardens among mothers and their children. But the elephant supported its own weight. That whole elephant which had the power to crush at will simply with its foot. Yet which failed to crush anything. That power which meantime would meekly allow itself to be led to a circus, an elephant for children. And its eyes were as kind as those of an old man, fixed within its great inherited flesh. The oriental elephant. An oriental spring-time too, and everything coming to life, everything running through the stream.

The woman then tried the camel. The ragged humpbacked camel chewing on itself, absorbed in the process of recognizing its food. She felt weak and fatigued and for two days she had scarcely eaten. The camel's long dusty eyelashes shielded eyes that had dedicated themselves to the patience of its internal craft. Patience, patience, patience—this alone did she encounter in the spring breeze. Tears filled the woman's eyes, tears that did not flow, arrested within the patience of her in-herited flesh. Only the camel's dusty odor came in opposition to what she had come for—dry hatred, not tears. She approached the bars of the enclosure, she inhaled the dust of that old carpet where ashen blood circulated. She sought the impure warmth, and pleasure pervaded her shoulders to the point of uneasiness, but it was not yet that uneasiness which she craved. In her stomach the urge to destroy con-tracted itself in colic. But not the tow-colored camel.

"Oh God, who will be my partner in this world?"

Then she was alone in possessing her violence. In the small amusement park of the zoological gardens she waited pensively in the queue of lovers for her turn to take a seat in the car of the roller coaster.

And now she was in her seat, silent in her brown coat. The car still stationary, the machinery of the roller coaster still at a halt. Alone in her seat she seemed to be sitting in a church. Lowering her eyes she saw the ground between the tracks. The ground where simply for love—love, love, not love—where for pure love there sprang up among the tracks weeds of a green so soft and ridiculous that they forced her to avert her gaze, tortured by temptation. The breeze made the hair on the nape of her neck stand on end; she trembled, refusing, refusing the temptation—it was always so much easier—to love.

But suddenly there was that soaring of entrails, that arrested heartbeat taken unaware in midair, the terror, the triumphant fury with which the car precipitated her into emptiness and suddenly raised her like a doll with lifted skirts, the deep resentment with which she became mechanical, her body automatically buoyant— the shrieks of girls with their boyfriends!—her gaze pierced by her utter surprise, her humiliation, "they were doing what they liked with her," the terrible humilia-tion—the shrieks of girls with their boyfriends!—the utter bewilderment of this spasmodic game as they did what they liked with her and her innocence was sud-denly exposed. How many seconds? The seconds necessary for the prolonged whis-tle of a train taking a bend, and the joy of a new dive through the air insulting her with a kick from behind, as she danced out of step in the wind, danced frenziedly, whether she liked it or not, her body convulsed like that of someone laughing, the sensation of death in a fit of laughter, the death without warning of someone who did not have time to destroy the papers in his drawers beforehand, not the death of others, but her death, always hers. She, who could have taken advantage of the cries of the others to utter her howl of agony, forgot herself, and she only felt fear.

And now this silence which was also sudden. They were back on the ground, the machinery once more completely at a standstill. Pallid, thrown out of her church, she looked at the motionless ground which she had left behind and to which once more she had been delivered. She straightened her skirt cautiously without looking at anyone. Contrite, as on the day when in full view of a crowd everything had spilled from her handbag to the ground and everything which had retained some value while secret in her bag, once exposed in the dust of the road, had revealed the pettiness of an intimate life marked by precautions: face powder, a receipt, her fountain pen—gathering the props of her existence from the curbstone. She got out of the car feeling stunned as if she were shaking off a collision. Although no one appeared to notice her, she smoothed her skirt again, doing her utmost that the others should not observe that she felt weak and sullied, protecting her disrupted bones with pride. The sky went round and round in her empty stomach; the earth, moving up and down before her eyes, seemed remote at certain moments, the earth which is always so obscure. For an instant, the woman desired, in the exhaustion of silent weeping, to reach out with her hand to the obscure earth: her hand stretched itself out like that of a cripple begging alms. But, as if she had swallowed emptiness, her heart was taken by surprise. Only this? Only this? Of her violence, only this?

She started to move once more in the direction of the animals. The tumult of the roller coaster had left her subdued. She felt unable to walk much further and rested her head on the bars of a cage, exhausted, her breath becoming short and faint. From inside its cage, the coati watched her. She looked at him. No words were exchanged. She would never be able to hate that coati, which in the silence of its questioning form watched her. Perturbed, she turned her eyes away from the ingenuous coati. The inquisitive coati asked her a question like a child. While she looked away, concealing her mortal mission from him, her head was resting so close to the bars that for a second it seemed to her that she was the one who was caged while a liberated coati was examining her.

The cage was always on the side where she was: she gave a groan that seemed to come from the soles of her feet. Then yet another groan.

Rising from her womb, there came once more, imploring and in a slow wave, the urge to destroy. Her eyes moistened, grateful and black, in something near to happiness. It was not yet hatred; as yet it was only the tortured will to hate possessing her like some desire, the promise of a cruel flowering, a torment as of love, the craving for hatred promising itself sacred blood and triumph, and the spurned female had spiritualized herself in great expectancy. But where, where would she find the animal that might teach her to keep her own hatred? That hatred which belonged to her by right but which she could not attain in grief? Where would she learn to hate so as not to die of love? And with whom? The world of spring, the world of beasts that in the spring grew spiritual, with paws which scratch but do not wound. . . . Ah! no more of this world! No more of this perfume, nor this weary heaving, no more of this pardoning everything that will die one day as if it were in the act of surrendering. Pardon never—if that woman should ever pardon again, even if it were only once more, her life would be lost—she gave a harsh, broken sob that startled the coati. Caged, she looked around her, and as she was not the sort of person others might notice, she crouched like a solitary old murderess as a child ran past without seeing her.

She started walking again, now shrunken, brittle, her clenched hands once more mortified in her pockets, the unknown murderess. Everything was imprisoned in her breast—in that breast which only knew how to accept, to resign itself, which only knew how to ask pardon, knew how to pardon, which had only learned to possess the sweetness of unhappiness, and how to love, to love, to love. To imagine that perhaps she had never experienced the hatred of which her pardon had always been made, caused her heart to grieve without shame, and she began to walk so quickly that she appeared to have found a sudden destiny. Almost running, her shoes unbalanced her and gave her body an appearance of fragility that once more reduced her to a female in captivity. Her steps mechanically assumed the imploring desperation of the fragile, she who was nothing more than fragile. But if she could throw off her shoes, would she be able to avoid the happiness of going barefooted? How could one fail to love the ground one treads? Sobbing once more, she stopped in front of the bars of an enclosure and rested her feverish brow against the rusty coldness of the iron. Her eyes firmly closed, she tried to bury her face between the hardness of the bars, and her face searched for an impossible entrance between the narrow bars, just as she had previously seen the newborn monkey search in the blindness of its hunger for its mother's breast. A fleeting comfort came to her from the way in which the bars seemed to hate her, opposing her with the resistance of cold iron.

She slowly opened her eyes. Those eyes emerging from their own darkness saw nothing in the faint light of evening. She stood there breathing. Little by little she began once more to perceive, little by little, forms began to solidify, her weary body overpowered by the sweetness of her fatigue. Her searching gaze turned toward the trees with their sprouting buds and her eyes met the small white clouds. Without hope, she heard the gentle current of a brook. Lowering her head once more, she stood watching the buffalo in the distance. Dressed in a brown coat, breathing without interest, no one interested in her, she herself interested in no one.

A certain peace at last. The breeze was playing with the hair on her head like that of someone who had just died, their head still perspiring. She contemplated with detachment that wide dry expanse enclosed by high railings, the territory of the buffalo. The black buffalo stood still at the bottom of the enclosure. Then he sauntered with his narrow haunches, his compact haunches. His neck was thicker than his contracted flanks. Seen from the front, the buffalo's head, which was much larger than his body, like a severed head, prevented any view of the rest of his body. And on his head his horns. In the distance his great torso paraded slowly. He was a black buffalo. So black that from a distance his face had no features. Over the blackness rose the elevated whiteness of his horns.

The woman might have gone away but the silence soothed her as evening fell.

And in the silence of the enclosure, the slow steps of the buffalo, the dry dust under his dry hoofs. From afar, pacing tranquilly, the black buffalo looked at her for a moment. The next moment, the woman could barely distinguish the hard muscle of its body. Perhaps he had not seen her. She could not tell, because from the shadows of his head she could only distinguish the outlines. But once more he seemed to have seen her or felt her presence.

The woman straightened her head a little and retreated slightly in distrust. Keeping quite still, her head drawn back, she waited.

And once again the buffalo appeared to observe her. As if unable to bear what she had felt, she averted her gaze and contemplated a tree. Her heart no longer beat in her breast, but felt hollow in the pit of her stomach.

The buffalo broke into another slow canter. The dust rose. The woman clenched her teeth, her whole face smarting slightly.

The buffalo with his black back. In the luminous light of the approaching evening, his was a blackened shape of tranquil fury. The woman sighed softly. Something white had spread itself inside her, white as paper, fragile as paper, intense as whiteness. Death hummed in her ears. Another canter by the buffalo brought her back to her senses, and in another long sigh she came back to the surface. She did not know where she had been. She was on her feet and feeling extremely weak, having emerged from that white remote thing where she had been—from where she now looked at the buffalo. The buffalo now appeared to be larger. The black buffalo once more.

"Ah!" she exclaimed suddenly in pain. The buffalo with its back to her, motionless. The woman's pallid face did not know how to summon him.

"Ah!" she exclaimed, provoking him. Her face was transformed by a deathly pallor and with a sudden, emaciated look, assumed an expression of purity and veneration.

"Ah!" she incited him with clenched teeth. But with his back to her, the buffalo remained quite still. She picked up a pebble from the ground and threw it inside the enclosure. The immobility of the buffalo's torso, which seemed even blacker than before, remained impassive. The pebble rolled away—quite useless.

"Ah!" she cried, shaking the bars. That white thing spread itself inside her, viscous like saliva. The buffalo remained with his back to her.

"Ah!" she cried. But this time there flowed inside her at last the first trickle of black blood. The initial moment was one of pain. As if the world had shriveled up so that this blood might flow. She stood there, hearing that first bitter oil drip as in a grotto, the shunned female. Her strength was still imprisoned between the bars, but something incomprehensible and warm, something incomprehensible, was happening, something that tasted in the mouth like happiness. Then the buffalo turned around.

The buffalo turned around, stood rigid, and, from afar, looked at her.

"I love you," she said, out of hatred then for the man whose great and unpunishable crime was not loving her. "I hate you," she said, imploring love from the buffalo.

Provoked at last, the great buffalo approached without haste.

He approached and the dust rose. The woman waited, her arms drooping down alongside her coat. Slowly he approached. She did not retreat a single step until he reached the bars and halted. There stood the buffalo and the woman face to face. She looked neither at his face, nor his mouth, nor his horns. She looked at his eyes.

And the eyes of the buffalo—his eyes met her eyes. And a pallor so deep was exchanged that, drowsily, the woman grew numb. She was on her feet but in a trance. Small, crimson eyes watched her. The eyes of the buffalo. The woman staggered in amazement and slowly shook her head. The buffalo remained calm. The woman slowly shook her head, terrified by the hatred with which the buffalo, tranquil with hatred, watched her. Almost feigning innocence, she stood shaking her head in disbelief, her mouth ajar. Innocent, inquisitive, entering ever more into those eyes that fixed her without haste, ingenuous, wearily sighing, without wishing or being able to escape, she was caught in mutual assassination. Caught as if her hand had fastened forever to the dagger that she herself had thrust. Caught, as she slipped spellbound along the railings—overcome by such giddiness that, before her body toppled gently to the ground, the woman saw the entire sky and a buffalo.

THE CHICKEN

It was the chicken for Sunday's lunch. Still alive, because it was still only nine o'clock in the morning. She seemed placid enough. Since Saturday she had huddled in a corner of the kitchen. She looked at no one and no one paid any attention to her. Even when they had chosen the chicken, feeling the intimacy of her body with indifference, they could not tell if she were plump or thin. No one would ever have guessed that the chicken felt anxious.

It was a surprise, therefore, when they saw her spread open her stubby wings, puff out her breast, and in two or three attempts, fly to the backyard wall. She still hesitated for a second—sufficient time for the cook to cry out—and soon she was on their neighbor's terrace, from which, in another awkward flight, she reached the roof. There the chicken remained, like a displaced ornament, perched hesitantly now on one foot, now on the other. The family was hastily summoned and in consternation saw their lunch outlined against a chimney. The master of the house, reminding himself of the twofold necessity of sporadically engaging in sport and of getting the family some lunch, appeared resplendent in a pair of swimming trunks and resolved to follow the path traced by the chicken: in cautious leaps and bounds, he scaled the roof where the chicken, hesitant and tremulous, urgently decided on another route. The chase now intensified. From roof to roof, more than a block along the road was covered. Little accustomed to such a savage struggle for survival, the chicken had to decide for herself the paths she must follow without any assistance from her race. The man, however, was a natural hunter. And no matter how abject the prey, the cry of victory was in the air.

Alone in the world, without father or mother, the chicken was running and panting, dumb and intent. At times during her escape she hovered on some roof edge, gasping for breath and, while the man strenuously clambered up somewhere else, she had time to rest for a moment. And she seemed so free. Stupid, timid, and free. Not victorious as a cock would be in flight. What was it in the chicken's entrails that made her a *being*? The chicken is, in fact, a *being*. It is true that one would not be able to rely upon her for anything. Nor was she even self-reliant like the cock who believes in his crest. Her only advantage was that there were so many chickens that when one died, another automatically appeared, so similar in appearance that it might well be the same chicken.

Finally, on one of those occasions when she paused to enjoy her bid for freedom, the man reached her. Amid shrieks and feathers, she was caught. She was immediately carried off in triumph by one wing across the roof tiles and dumped somewhat violently on the kitchen floor. Still giddy, she shook herself a little with raucous and uncertain cackles.

It was then that it happened. Positively flustered, the chicken laid an egg. She was surprised and exhausted. Perhaps it was premature. But from the moment she was born, as if destined for motherhood, the chicken had shown all the signs of being instinctively maternal. She settled on the egg and there she remained, breathing as her eyes buttoned and unbuttoned. Her heart, which looked so tiny on a plate, raised and lowered her feathers, warming that egg which would never be anything else. Only the little girl of the house was on the scene, and she assisted at the event in utter dismay. No sooner had she disengaged herself from the event than she jumped up from the floor and ran out shouting.

"Mummy! Mummy! Don't kill the chicken, she's laid an egg! The chicken loves us!"

They all ran back into the kitchen and stood round the young mother in silence. Warming her offspring, she was neither gentle nor cross, neither happy nor sad; she was nothing, she was simply a chicken—a fact that did not suggest any particular feeling. The father, mother, and daughter had been standing there for some time now, without thinking about anything in particular. No one was known to have caressed a chicken on the head. Finally, the father decided, with a certain brusqueness, "If you have this chicken killed, I will never again eat a fowl as long as I live!"

"Nor me!" the little girl promised with passion.

The mother, feeling weary, shrugged her shoulders. Unconscious of the life that had been spared her, the chicken became part of the family. The little girl, upon returning from school, would toss her school bag down without disturbing the chicken's wanderings across the kitchen. The father, from time to time, still remembered. "And to think that I made her run in that state!"

The chicken became the queen of the household. Everybody, except her, knew it. She ran to and fro, from the kitchen to the terrace at the back of the house, exploiting her two sources of power: apathy and fear.

But when everyone was quiet in the house and seemed to have forgotten her, she puffed up with modest courage, the last traces of her great escape. She circled the tiled floor, her body advancing behind her head, as unhurried as if in an open field, although her small head betrayed her, darting back and forth in rapid vibrant movements, with the age-old fear of her species now ingrained. Once in a while, but ever more infrequently, she remembered how she had stood out against the sky on the roof edge ready to cry out. At such moments, she filled her lungs with the stuffy atmosphere of the kitchen and, had females been given the power to crow, she would not have crowed but would have felt much happier. Not even at those moments, however, did the expression on her empty head alter. In flight or in repose, when she gave birth or while pecking grain, hers was a chicken's head, identical to that drawn at the beginning of time. Until one day they killed her and ate her, and the years rolled on.

The Smallest Woman in the World

—◦❧ ❦◦—

In the depths of Equatorial Africa the French explorer, Marcel Pretre, hunter and man of the world, came across a tribe of surprisingly small pygmies. Therefore he was even more surprised when he was informed that a still smaller people existed, beyond forests and distances. So he plunged farther on.

In the Eastern Congo, near Lake Kivu, he really did discover the smallest pygmies in the world. And—like a box within a box within a box—obedient, perhaps, to the necessity nature sometimes feels of outdoing herself—among the smallest pygmies in the world there was the smallest of the smallest pygmies in the world.

Among mosquitoes and lukewarm trees, among leaves of the most rich and lazy green, Marcel Pretre found himself facing a woman seventeen and three-quarter inches high, full-grown, black, silent—"Black as a monkey," he informed the press—who lived in a treetop with her little spouse. In the tepid miasma of the jungle, that swells the fruits so early and gives them an almost intolerable sweetness, she was pregnant.

So there she stood, the smallest woman in the world. For an instant, in the buzzing heat, it seemed as if the Frenchman had unexpectedly reached his final destination. Probably only because he was not insane, his soul neither wavered nor broke its bounds. Feeling an immediate necessity for order and for giving names to what exists, he called her Little Flower. And in order to be able to classify her among the recognizable realities, he immediately began to collect facts about her.

Her race will soon be exterminated. Few examples are left of this species, which, if it were not for the sly dangers of Africa, might have multiplied. Besides disease, the deadly effluvium of the water, insufficient food, and ranging beasts, the great threat to the Likoualas are the savage Bahundes, a threat that surrounds them in the silent air, like the dawn of battle. The Bahundes hunt them with nets, like monkeys. And eat them. Like that: they catch them in nets and eat them. The tiny race, retreating, always retreating, has finished hiding away in the heart of Africa, where the lucky explorer discovered it. For strategic defense, they live in the highest trees. The women descend to grind and cook corn and to gather greens; the men, to hunt. When a child is born, it is left free almost immediately. It is true that, what with the beasts, the child frequently cannot enjoy this freedom for very long. But then it is true that it cannot be lamented that for such a short life there had been any long, hard work. And even the language that the child learns is short and simple, merely the essentials. The Likoualas use few names; they name things by gestures and animal noises. As for things of the spirit, they have a drum. While they dance to the sound of the drum, a little male stands guard against the Bahundes, who come from no one knows where.

That was the way, then, that the explorer discovered, standing at his very feet, the smallest existing human thing. His heart beat, because no emerald in the world is so rare. The teachings of the wise men of India are not so rare. The richest man in the world has never set eyes on such strange grace. Right there was a woman that the greed of the most exquisite dream could never have imagined. It was then that the explorer said timidly, and with a delicacy of feeling of which his wife would never have thought him capable: "You are Little Flower."

At that moment, Little Flower scratched herself where no one scratches. The explorer—as if he were receiving the highest prize for chastity to which an idealistic man dares aspire—the explorer, experienced as he was, looked the other way.

A photograph of Little Flower was published in the colored supplement of the Sunday papers, life-size. She was wrapped in a cloth, her belly already very big. The flat nose, the black face, the splay feet. She looked like a dog.

On that Sunday, in an apartment, a woman seeing the picture of Little Flower in the paper didn't want to look a second time because "It gives me the creeps."

In another apartment, a lady felt such perverse tenderness for the smallest of the African women that—an ounce of prevention being worth a pound of cure—Little Flower could never be left alone to the tenderness of that lady. Who knows to what murkiness of love tenderness can lead? The woman was upset all day, almost as if she were missing something. Besides, it was spring and there was a dangerous leniency in the air.

In another house, a little girl of five, seeing the picture and hearing the comments, was extremely surprised. In a houseful of adults, this little girl had been the smallest human being up until now. And, if this was the source of all caresses, it was also the source of the first fear of the tyranny of love. The existence of Little Flower made the little girl feel—with a deep uneasiness that only years and years later, and for very different reasons, would turn into thought—made her feel, in her first wisdom, that "sorrow is endless."

In another house, in the consecration of spring, a girl about to be married felt an ecstasy of pity: "Mama, look at her little picture, poor little thing! Just look how sad she is!"

"But," said the mother, hard and defeated and proud, "it's the sadness of an animal. It isn't human sadness."

"Oh, Mama!" said the girl, discouraged.

In another house, a clever little boy had a clever idea: "Mummy, if I could put this little woman from Africa in little Paul's bed when he's asleep? When he woke up wouldn't he be frightened? Wouldn't he howl? When he saw her sitting on his bed? And then we'd play with her! She would be our toy!"

His mother was setting her hair in front of the bathroom mirror at the moment, and she remembered what a cook had told her about life in an orphanage. The orphans had no dolls, and, with terrible maternity already throbbing in their hearts, the little girls had hidden the death of one of the children from the nun. They kept the body in a cupboard and when the nun went out they played with the dead child, giving her baths and things to eat, punishing her only to be able to kiss and console her. In the bathroom, the mother remembered this, and let fall her thoughtful hands, full of curlers. She considered the cruel necessity of loving. And she considered the malignity of our desire for happiness. She considered how ferociously we need to play. How many times we will kill for love. Then she looked at her clever child as if she were looking at a dangerous stranger. And she had a horror of her own soul that, more than her body, had engendered that being, adept at life and happiness. She looked at him attentively and with uncomfortable pride, that child who had already lost two front teeth, evolution evolving itself, teeth falling out to give place to those that could bite better. "I'm going to buy him a new suit," she decided, looking at him, absorbed. Obstinately, she adorned her gap-toothed son with fine clothes; obstinately, she wanted him very clean, as if his cleanliness could emphasize a soothing superficiality, obstinately perfecting the polite side of beauty. Obstinately drawing away from, and drawing him away from, something that ought to be "black as a monkey." Then, looking in the bathroom mirror, the mother gave a deliberately refined and social smile, placing a distance of insuperable millenniums between the abstract lines of her features and the crude face of Little Flower. But, with years of practice, she knew that this was going to be a Sunday on which she would have to hide from herself anxiety, dreams, and lost millenniums.

In another house, they gave themselves up to the enthralling task of measuring the seventeen and three-quarter inches of Little Flower against the wall. And, really, it was a delightful surprise: she was even smaller than the sharpest imagination could have pictured. In the heart of each member of the family was born, nostalgic, the desire to have that tiny and indomitable thing for itself, that thing spared having been eaten, that permanent source of charity. The avid family soul wanted to devote itself. To tell the truth, who hasn't wanted to own a human being just for himself? Which, it is true, wouldn't always be convenient; there are times when one doesn't want to have feelings.

"I bet if she lived here it would end in a fight," said the father, sitting in the armchair and definitely turning the page of the newspaper. "In this house everything ends in a fight."

"Oh, you, José—always a pessimist," said the mother.

"But, Mama, have you thought of the size her baby's going to be?" said the oldest little girl, aged thirteen, eagerly.

The father stirred uneasily behind his paper.

"It should be the smallest black baby in the world," the mother answered, melting with pleasure. "Imagine her serving our table, with her big little belly!"

"That's enough!" growled father.

"But you have to admit," said the mother, unexpectedly offended, "that it is something very rare. You're the insensitive one."

And the rare thing itself?

In the meanwhile, in Africa, the rare thing herself, in her heart—and who knows if the heart wasn't black, too, since once nature has erred she can no longer be trusted—the rare thing herself had something even rarer in her heart, like the secret of her own secret: a minimal child. Methodically, the explorer studied the little belly of the smallest mature human being. It was at this moment that the explorer, for the first time since he had known her, instead of feeling curiosity, or exaltation, or victory, or the scientific spirit, felt sick.

The smallest woman in the world was laughing.

She was laughing, warm, warm—Little Flower was enjoying life. The rare thing herself was experiencing the ineffable sensation of not having been eaten yet. Not having been eaten yet was something that at any other time would have given her the agile impulse to jump from branch to branch. But, in this moment of tranquillity, amid the thick leaves of the Eastern Congo, she was not putting this impulse into action—it was entirely concentrated in the smallness of the rare thing itself. So she was laughing. It was a laugh such as only one who does not speak laughs. It was a laugh that the explorer, constrained, couldn't classify. And she kept on enjoying her own soft laugh, she who wasn't being devoured. Not to be devoured is the most perfect feeling. Not to be devoured is the secret goal of a whole life. While she was not being eaten, her bestial laughter was as delicate as joy is delicate. The explorer was baffled.

In the second place, if the rare thing herself was laughing, it was because, within her smallness, a great darkness had begun to move.

The rare thing herself felt in her breast a warmth that might be called love. She loved that sallow explorer. If she could have talked and had told him that she loved him, he would have been puffed up with vanity. Vanity that would have collapsed when she added that she also loved the explorer's ring very much, and the explorer's boots. And when that collapse had taken place, Little Flower would not have understood why. Because her love for the explorer—one might even say "profound love," since, having no other resources, she was reduced to profundity—her profound love for the explorer would not have been at all diminished by the fact that she also loved his boots. There is an old misunderstanding about the word love, and, if many children are born from this misunderstanding, many others have lost the unique chance of being born, only because of a susceptibility that demands that it be me! me! that is loved, and not my money. But in the humidity of the forest these cruel refinements do not exist, and love is not to be eaten, love is to find a boot pretty, love is to like the strange color of a man who isn't black, love is to laugh for love of a shiny ring. Little Flower blinked with love, and laughed warmly, small, gravid, warm.

The explorer tried to smile back, without knowing exactly to what abyss his smile responded, and then he was embarrassed as only a very big man can be embarrassed. He pretended to adjust his explorer's hat better; he colored, prudishly. He turned a lovely color, a greenish-pink, like a lime at sunrise. He was undoubtedly sour.

Perhaps adjusting the symbolic helmet helped the explorer to get control of himself, severely recapture the discipline of his work, and go on with his note taking. He had learned how to understand some of the tribe's few articulate words, and to interpret their signs. By now, he could ask questions.

Little Flower answered "Yes." That it was very nice to have a tree of her own to live in. Because—she didn't say this but her eyes became so dark that they said it—because it is good to own, good to own, good to own. The explorer winked several times.

Marcel Pretre had some difficult moments with himself. But at least he kept busy taking notes. Those who didn't take notes had to manage as best they could:

"Well," suddenly declared one old lady, folding up the newspaper decisively, "well, as I always say: God knows what He's doing."

THE BREAKING OF THE BREAD
—◦❧ ❧◦—

It was Saturday and we had been invited to a duty dinner. But each of us loved Saturday too much to wish to spend it with someone we did not desire. Each of us had at one time or another been happy and had been left with the mark of desire. As for myself, I desired everything. And there we were, tied down, as if our train had been derailed, forcing us to spend the night among strangers. No one there wanted me, and I did not want any of them. As for my Saturday—which was swinging in the acacias and in the shadow beyond the window—rather than squander it, I'd enclose it in my implacable hand, where I would crumple it as if it were a handkerchief. While waiting for dinner, without any pleasure we drank to grievance: tomorrow would already be Sunday. "It's not you that I want," our eyes without any moisture would say, and slowly we would blow out the smoke of our parched cigarettes. The miserliness that prevented the partition of the Saturday was gradually gnawing and advancing like rust, until any joy would be an insult to the greater joy.

Only the lady of the house didn't seem to be saving the Saturday to spend it at one of night's smallholdings. And yet, how could she have forgotten—she whose heart had known other Saturdays—that we keep wanting more and more? She wasn't even impatient with the heterogeneous, dreamy, and resigned group that was in her house as if waiting for the departure of the first train, any train, rather than remain in that empty railroad station, rather than rein in the horse, which with a pounding heart wanted to run toward other, yet other horses.

We finally moved to the dining room for the meal that hunger had not blessed. It was then that to our surprise the table flashed into view. It couldn't have been for us. . . .

It was a table set for persons of good will. Who was that expected guest who had not shown up? And yet we were that guest. Did that woman then give her best no matter to whom? And joyfully she was washing the feet of the first stranger. Ill at ease, we watched.

The table had been covered with a solemn abundance. On the white tablecloth were piled ears of wheat. And red apples; and large, yellow carrots; round tomatoes with skins that almost crackled; chayotes of a delicate green; pineapples malignant in their savagery; placid, flame-colored oranges; gherkins bristling like porcupines, implacable cucumbers which walled in their own aqueous flesh; hollow, reddish peppers which stung the eyes—everything was intertwined with masses and masses of the moist beard of the ears of corn, a beard red like one surrounding a mouth. And the grapes—grapes so black that they looked purple, and which could hardly wait for the moment when they would be crushed. And it didn't matter to them by whom. The tomatoes were round for no one in particular—for the air, the round air. Saturday belonged to whoever showed up. And the orange would sweeten the tongue of whoever arrived first. Even without having chosen us, even without having loved us, the woman who washed the feet of strangers had placed beside the plate of each discontented guest an ear of wheat or a bunch of fiery radishes or a red slice of watermelon with its joyous seeds. Everything was sharpened by the Spanish acidity one sensed in the green limes. The milk was in the jugs, and it was as if it had crossed with the goats a desert of cliffs. The wine, almost black from so many bruises, vibrated in the clay vessels. Everything was displayed before us. Everything was cleansed of entangled human desires. Everything as it is, not as we would have liked it to be; everything merely existing in its totality, the way a field, or the mountain, exists. The way men and women exist—not like us, covetous creatures, but like a Saturday, merely existing. Existing.

In the name of nothing, it was time to eat. In the name of nothing, it was good, without any dreams. And little by little we became aware of the day, and little by little we grew anonymous while growing larger to reach a life made possible. Then, like magnanimous peasants we accepted the table.

There was no holocaust: all of that food wanted to be eaten as much as we ourselves wanted to eat all of it. Without saving anything for the following day, in that very place I made an offering of what I was feeling to the substance that was making me feel. It was enjoyment of life without my having paid beforehand with the sufferings of expectancy; it was hunger that is born only when the mouth is already close to the food. And because we were then hungry with that complete hunger which encompassed the totality and the crumbs, as we drank of the wine we watched over the milk with our eyes, as we slowly drank of the milk, we felt within ourselves the wine someone else was drinking. Outside, God was in the acacias, which existed. We ate like someone giving water to a horse. The carved meat was distributed. Cordiality was rustic and homely. Nobody spoke ill of anybody because nobody spoke well of anybody. It was a harvest gathering, and a truce was declared. We ate. Like a horde of living creatures, gradually we covered the earth, busy like someone who tills existence, someone who plants, and harvests, and kills, and lives, and dies, and eats. I ate with the honesty of someone who cannot deceive what she eats: I ate the food and not its name. Never had God been so deeply apprehended for what He is. The food—rustic, happy, austere—was saying: eat, eat and share. All of it belonged to me, and that table was my Father's. I ate without any tenderness, I ate without the passion of pity, and without offering myself to hope. I ate without feeling any nostalgia. And I was well worth that food because I cannot always be my brother's keeper, and I can no longer be my own keeper. Ah, I no longer desire myself. And I don't want to shape life because existence already exists. It exists like the soil on which all of us advance, without a word of love. Without a word. But your pleasure understands mine. We are strong and we eat. Bread is love among strangers.

THE FIFTH STORY

This story might have been called "The Statues." Another possible title might have been "The Killing." Or even "How to Kill Cockroaches." Therefore I'll tell at least three stories, all truthful because none of them belies the other. Although one single story, they might have been a thousand and one, had I been given a thousand and one nights.

The first one, "How to Kill Cockroaches," begins thus: I complained of cockroaches. A lady overheard my complaint. She gave me a recipe to kill them. I was to mix equal amounts of sugar, flour, and gypsum. The flour and the sugar would attract them, the gypsum would dry up their innards. I followed the instructions. They died.

The second story is like the first one, and it's called "The Killing." It begins thus: I complained of cockroaches. A lady overheard me. The recipe comes next. And then the killing. The truth is that only in abstract terms did I complain of cockroaches, which weren't even mine: they belonged to the ground floor, and by climbing up the pipe system of the building, they reached our home. Only at the moment of mixing the ingredients did they become mine too. Therefore, in our name, I began to measure and weigh the ingredients with a somewhat intensified concentration. A vague loathing and a feeling of outrage took hold of me. In the daytime the cockroaches were invisible and nobody would have guessed at the secret malignancy gnawing at such a peaceful home. And yet in the daytime while they slept like secret malignancies, I in turn was busy preparing for them the poison of the night. Meticulously and zealously I filled the prescription for the elixir of slow death. A frenzied fear and my own secret malignancy guided me, so that coldly I wanted but one thing: to kill every living cockroach. Cockroaches climb up the pipe system while we, tired, are dreaming. So lo and behold, the prescription was ready, and very white. As if dealing with cockroaches smart like myself, I spread the powder skillfully so that it blended with the environment. In my bed in the silent apartment I would imagine them climbing one after the other up to the utility room, where darkness was sleeping with only one watchful towel on the clothesline. I overslept and woke up startled. It was already dawn. I walked across the kitchen. There they were lying on the floor of the utility room—stiff, huge. I had killed them during the night. In our name, morning was rising. A rooster crowed in the hill.

The third story about to begin is "The Statues." It starts by saying that I had complained of cockroaches. Next comes that same lady. It proceeds up to the moment when I wake up at dawn and walk across the kitchen. The utility room with its perspective of tiles is even sleepier than I am. And in the dimness of dawn, its purplish color increasing the distance between things, I notice darkness and whiteness at my feet: scores of stiff statues lie scattered about—the cockroaches that had stiffened from inside out—some with their bellies upturned; others, in the middle of a gesture that would never be completed. In the mouths of a few, some of the white foodstuff. I'm the first witness of dawn in Pompeii. I know all about that last night, I know all about the orgy in the darkness. In some of them the gypsum had probably hardened slowly, like a vital process. As their movements became gradually more painful, they probably intensified the joys of the night in an attempt to escape from their own insides, until at last they were transformed into stones, and their eyes, with innocent astonishment, expressed a hurtful rebuke. Others had been suddenly assaulted by their own essence, and without even a forewarning from their internal molds, turned into stone; they were crystallized like a word cut off the mouth: I love . . . Those were the ones who called the name of love in vain and sang in the summer nights. Whereas that one over there, that one with the brown antenna besmeared with white, probably divined too late that it was being transformed into a mummy precisely because it knew how to use things with the gratuitous grace of the "in vain": "It's because I looked too often inward! It's because I looked too often inw . . ."—From my detached height of a human being, I look at the downfall of a world. Morning rises. Here and there, the dry antenna of a dead cockroach flutters in the breeze. The rooster is crowing about the previous story.

The fourth narrative inaugurates a new era at home. It begins as we already know: I complained of cockroaches. It proceeds up to the moment when I see the monuments of gypsum. Dead, all of them. Then I gaze at the pipe system, where a slow and living population in Indian file will be restored. Would I therefore restore the deadly sugar every night, like someone who won't sleep without the fervency of a ritual? And would each dawn, like a vice guiding me to the statues that my perspiring night has erected, lead me, sleepwalking, to the utility room? With a perverse pleasure I shuddered at the prospect of this double life of witchcraft. And I also shuddered at the warning of the gypsum with its drying-up properties: the vice of life would rend my internal mold. It's a difficult moment to choose between two paths which, so I thought, say farewell to each other, and for sure, either choice would contain the sacrifice—me, or my soul. I chose. And today I secretly display in my heart a plate of virtue: "This house has been sprayed with DDT."

The fifth story is called "Leibnitz and the Transcendency of Love in Polynesia." It begins thus: I complained of cockroaches.

Miss Algrave

She was vulnerable to criticism. Therefore she didn't tell anything to anyone. If she had spoken, they wouldn't have believed her, because they didn't believe in reality. But she, living in London, where ghosts dwell in dark alleys, knew for sure.

Her day on Friday was the same as any other. It only happened Saturday night. But on Friday she did everything as usual. Yet a terrible memory had tormented her: when she was little, about seven years old, she had played house with her cousin Jack; in grandpa's big bed they both had done everything they could to have little children, but without success. She had never seen Jack again, nor had she wanted to. If she was guilty, so was he.

Single, of course, a virgin, of course. She lived alone in a small penthouse in Soho. That day she had done her grocery shopping: vegetables and fruits. For she considered it a sin to eat meat.

When she passed through Picadilly Circus and saw the women waiting on street corners for men, she practically vomited. Even worse—for money! It was too much to take. And that statue of Eros, up there, so indecent.

After lunch she went to work: she was a perfect typist. Her boss never checked on her, and he treated her, fortunately, with respect, calling her "Miss Algrave." Her first name was Ruth. She was of Irish descent. A redhead, she wore her hair in a severe knot at the back of her neck. She had lots of freckles and skin so fair and delicate it seemed of white silk. Her eyelashes were also red. She was a pretty woman.

She was very proud of her figure: generously built and tall. But no one had ever touched her breasts.

She usually dined at an inexpensive restaurant there in Soho. She ate spaghetti with tomato sauce. And she had never entered a pub: the smell of alcohol nauseated her whenever she passed such a place. She felt offended by humanity.

She raised red geraniums which were a glory in springtime. Her father had been a Protestant minister, and her mother was still living in Dublin with a married son. Her brother was married to a real bitch named Tootsie.

Once in a while, Miss Algrave would write a letter of protest to *The Times*. And they would publish it. She would note her name with much pleasure: "Sincerely, Ruth Algrave."

She took a bath just once a week, on Saturday. In order not to see her body naked, she would leave on her panties and her bra.

The day it happened was a Saturday, so she didn't have to go to work. She got up very early and had some jasmine tea. Then she prayed. Then she went out for some fresh air.

Near the Hotel Savoy she was almost run over. If this had happened and she had died, it would have been awful, for nothing would have happened to her that night.

She went to a choir rehearsal. She had a melodious voice. Yes, she was a privileged person.

Afterward, she went to lunch and allowed herself to order shrimp: it was so good it even seemed a sin.

Then she took her way to Hyde Park and sat down on the grass. She had brought along a Bible to read. But—may God forgive her—the sun was so savage, so good, so hot, that she read nothing, but just remained seated on the ground without the courage to lie down. She tried not to look at the couples that were kissing and caressing one another without the least shame.

Then she went home, watered the begonias, and took a bath. Then she went to visit Mrs. Cabot, who was ninety-seven years old. She brought her a piece of raisin cake, and they drank tea. Miss Algrave felt very happy, and yet . . . And yet.

At seven o'clock she returned home. She had nothing to do. So she started knitting a sweater for winter. A splendid color: yellow like the sun.

Before going to sleep, she had some more jasmine tea with biscuits, brushed her teeth, changed her clothes, and tucked herself into bed. Her sheer white curtains, she had stitched and hung them herself.

It was May. The curtains wavered in the breeze of this singular night. Why singular? She didn't know.

She read a bit in the morning paper and then turned off the lamp at the head of her bed. Through the open window she saw the moonlight. It was the night of a full moon.

She sighed a great deal because it was difficult to live alone. Solitude was crushing her. It was terrible not to have a single person to talk to. She was the most lonely creature she knew. Even Mrs. Cabot had a cat. Ruth Algrave didn't have any pet at all: they were too bestial for her taste. She didn't have a television. For two reasons: she couldn't afford one, and she didn't wish to sit there watching the immoralities that appeared on TV. On Mrs. Cabot's television she had seen a man kissing a woman on the mouth. And this without any mention of the danger of transmitting germs. Oh, if she could, she would write a letter of protest to *The Times* every day. But it didn't do any good to protest, or so it seemed. Shamelessness was in the air. She had even seen a dog with a bitch. She had been much struck by it. But if God wished it so, then so be it. But no one would ever touch her, she thought. She went on enduring her solitude.

Even children were immoral. She avoided them. And she regretted greatly having been born of the incontinence of her father and mother. She was ashamed of their not having been ashamed.

Since she left grains of rice at her window, pigeons came to visit her. Sometimes they entered her room. They were sent by God. So innocent. Cooing. But it was rather immoral, their cooing, though less so than seeing an almost naked woman on television. Tomorrow, without fail, she was going to write a letter protesting against the evil ways of that accursed city, London. She had once seen a line of addicts outside a pharmacy, waiting their turn for a shot. How could the Queen permit it? A mystery. She would write another letter denouncing the Queen herself. She wrote well, without any grammatical errors, and typed the letters on the typewriter at the office when she had some free time. Mr. Clairson, her boss, praised her published letters highly. He even had said that she might some day become a writer. She had been very proud and grateful.

That's how she had been lying in bed with her solitude. However.

It was then that it happened.

She felt that something which wasn't a pigeon had come in through the window. She was afraid. She called out:

"Who is it?"

And the answer came in the form of wind:

"I am an I."

"Who are you?" she asked, trembling.

"I have come from Saturn to love you."

"But I can't see anybody!" she cried.

"What matters is that you can feel me."

And she really did feel him. She felt an electric shiver.

"What is your name?" she asked in fright.

"Not important."

"But I want to say your name!"

"Call me Ixtlan."

Theirs was an understanding in Sanskrit. His touch was cold, like that of a lizard, giving her goose pimples. Ixtlan had on his head a crown of interlaced snakes, made tame by the terror of dying. The cape which covered his body was of the most painful purple; it was cheap gold and coagulated amaranth.

He said:

"Get undressed."

She took off her nightgown. The moon was huge within the room. Ixtlan was white and small. He lay down beside her on the metal bed. And passed his hands over her breasts. Black roses.

She had never felt what she now felt. It was too good. She was afraid it might end. It was as if a cripple had thrown his cane into the air.

She began to sigh and said to Ixtlan:

"I love you, my darling! my love!"

And—yes, indeed. It happened. She didn't want it ever to end. How good it was, my God. She wanted more, more, more.

She thought: Take me! Or else: I offer myself to thee. It was the triumph of the "here and now."

She asked him: when will you come back?

Ixtlan answered:

"At the next full moon."

"But I can't wait that long!"

"That's how it is," he said almost coldly.

"Will I be expecting a baby?"

"No."

"But I'll die from missing you! What can I do?"

"Get used to it."

He got up, kissed her chastely on the forehead. And went out through the window.

She began to cry softly. She seemed a sad violin without a bow. The proof that all this had really happened was the blood-stained sheet. She kept it without washing it and would be able to show it to anyone who might not believe her.

She saw the new day dawn all in pink. In the fog, the first little birds began a sweet chirping, not yet feverish.

God lit up her body.

But, like a Baroness von Blich, nostalgically reclining on her satin bedspread, she pretended to ring the bell to call the butler who would bring her coffee, hot and strong, very strong.

She loved him and would ardently await the next full moon. She would avoid taking a bath so as not to wash away the taste of Ixtlan. With him it wasn't a sin, but a delight. She didn't want to write any more letters of protest: she protested no longer.

And she didn't go to church. She was a fulfilled woman. She had a husband.

So, on Sunday, at lunchtime, she ate filet mignon with mashed potatoes. The bloody meat was excellent. And she drank red Italian wine. She really was privileged. She had been chosen by a being from Saturn.

She had asked him why he had chosen her. He had said it was because she was a redhead and a virgin. She felt bestial. She no longer found animals repulsive. Let them make love—it was the best thing in the world. And she would wait for Ixtlan. He would return: I know it, I know it, I know it, she thought. She also no longer had any revulsion for the couples in Hyde Park. She knew how they felt.

How good it was to live. How good it was to eat bloody meat. How good to drink a tart Italian wine, contracting your tongue with its bitterness.

She was now not recommended for minors under eighteen. And she was delighted, she literally drooled over it.

Since it was Sunday, she went to her choral singing. She sang better than ever and wasn't surprised when they chose her as soloist. She sang her hallelujah. Like this: Hallelujah! Hallelujah! Hallelujah!

Later she went to Hyde Park and lay down on the warm grass, opening her legs a bit to let the sun enter. Being a woman was something superb. Only a woman could understand. But she wondered: could it be that I'll have to pay a high price for my happiness? She didn't worry. She would pay all that she had to pay. She had always paid and always been unhappy. And now unhappiness had ended. Ixtlan! Come quickly! I can't wait any longer! Come! Come! Come!

She wondered: could it be he liked me because I am a little cross-eyed? At the next full moon she would ask him. If it were true, she had no doubt: she would push it to the hilt, she would make herself completely cross-eyed. Ixtlan, anything you want me to do, I'll do. Only I'm dying of longing. Come back, my love.

Yes. But she did something that was a betrayal. Ixtlan would understand and forgive her. After all, you do what you've got to do, right?

This is how it went: unable to stand it any longer, she walked over to Picadilly Circus and approached a long-haired young man. She took him up to her room.

She told him he didn't have to pay. But he insisted and, before going off, left an entire one-pound note on the night table. In fact she needed the money. She became furious, however, when he refused to believe her story. She showed him, almost under his nose, the blood-stained sheet. He laughed at her.

On Monday morning she made up her mind: she wouldn't work any longer as a typist, she had other gifts. Mr. Clairson could go to hell. She was going to take to the streets and bring men up to her room. Since she was so good in bed, they would pay her very well. She would be able to drink Italian wine all the time. She wanted to buy a bright red dress with the money the long-haired fellow had left her. She had let her hair down so that it was a beauty of redness. She was like a wolf's howl.

She had learned that she was very valuable. If Mr. Clairson, that hypocrite, wanted her to go on working for him, it would have to be in quite a different way.

First she would buy herself that low-cut red dress and then go to the office, arriving, on purpose, for the first time in her life, very late. And this is how she would speak to her boss:

"Enough typing! And you, you fraud, don't give me your phony manners. Want to know something? Get in bed with me, you slob! And that's not all: pay me a good high salary, you skinflint!"

She was sure he would accept. He was married to a pale, insignificant woman, Joan, and had an anemic daughter, Lucy. He is going to enjoy himself with me, the son-of-a-bitch.

And when the full moon arrived—she would take a bath, purifying herself of all those men, in order to be ready to feast with Ixtlan.

THE BODY
—◦❧ ❧◦—

Xavier was a fierce, full-blooded man. Very strong, this guy. Loved the tango. Went to see "Last Tango in Paris" and got terribly excited. He didn't understand the film: he thought it was a sex movie. He didn't realize that it was the story of a desperate man.

The night that he saw "The Last Tango in Paris" the three of them went to bed together: Xavier, Carmen, and Beatrice. Everyone knew that Xavier was a bigamist, living with two women.

Every night it was one of them. Sometimes twice a night. The extra one would remain watching. Neither was jealous of the other.

Beatrice ate anything that wasn't moving: she was fat and greasy. Carmen was tall and thin.

The night of "The Last Tango in Paris" was memorable for the threesome. By the early morning hours they were exhausted. But Carmen got up in the morning, prepared a great breakfast—with heaping spoonfuls of thick evaporated milk—and brought it to Beatrice and Xavier. He was bewildered with sleep and had to take a cold shower to snap him back into shape.

That day—Sunday—they dined at three in the afternoon. Beatrice, the fat one, cooked. Xavier drank French wine. And ate a whole fried chicken alone. The two women ate the other chicken. The chickens were stuffed with a *farofa* made with raisins and prunes, nice and moist.

At six o'clock the three of them went to church. They seemed a bolero. Ravel's bolero.

That night they stayed home watching television and eating. Nothing happened that night: they all three were very tired.

And so it went, day after day.

Xavier worked hard to support the two women and himself, to provide big spreads. And once in a while he would deceive the two of them with a first-rate prostitute. But he didn't say anything about this at home because he wasn't a fool.

There passed days, months, years. Nobody died. Xavier was forty-seven. Carmen thirty-nine. And Beatrice was about to turn fifty.

Life was good to them. Sometimes Carmen and Beatrice would go out in order to buy sexy nightgowns. And to buy perfume. Carmen was the more elegant. Beatrice, with her overflowing flesh, would pick out a bikini with the smallest possible top to hold her enormous breasts.

One day Xavier came home very late at night: the two were desperate. If they had only known that he had been with his prostitute! The three were in truth four, like the three musketeers.

Xavier arrived with a bottomless hunger. And opened a bottle of champagne. He was at full strength. He spoke animatedly with the two of them, telling them that the pharmaceutical industry which he owned was doing well financially. And he proposed that they go, the three of them, to Montevideo, to stay in a luxury hotel.

In a great hurry-scurry, the three suitcases were packed.

Carmen took all of her complicated make-up. Beatrice went out and bought a miniskirt. They went by plane. They sat down in a row of three seats: he between the two women.

In Montevideo they bought anything they felt like. Even a sewing machine for Beatrice and a typewriter which Carmen wanted so as to be able to learn how to type. Actually she didn't need anything, poor nothing that she was. She kept a diary: she noted down on the pages of a thick, red-bound notebook the dates on which Xavier asked for her. She gave the diary to Beatrice to read.

In Montevideo they bought a book of recipes. Only it was in French and they understood nothing. The ingredients looked more like dirty words.

Then they bought a recipe book in Spanish. And they did the best they could with the sauces and the soups. They learned to make "roast-beef." Xavier gained seven pounds and his bull-like strength increased.

Sometimes the two women would stretch out on the bed. The day was long. And, although they were not homosexual, they excited each other and made love. Sad love.

One day they told Xavier about it.

Xavier trembled. And wanted the two of them to make love in front of him that night. But, commanded thus, it all ended in nothing. The two women cried and Xavier became furious.

For three days he didn't say a word to them.

But, during this period, and without any orders, the two women went to bed together and succeeded.

The three didn't go to the theater. They preferred television. Or eating out.

Xavier ate with bad manners: he would pick up food with his hands and make a lot of noise chewing, besides eating with his mouth open. Carmen, who was more genteel, would feel revolted and ashamed. But Beatrice herself was without shame, even walking about the house stark naked.

No one knows how it began. But it began.

One day Xavier came home from work with traces of lipstick on his shirt. He couldn't deny that he had been with his favorite prostitute. Carmen and Beatrice each grabbed a piece of wood and they chased Xavier all over the house. He ran like a madman, shouting "Forgive, forgive!"

The two women, also tired out, finally gave up chasing him.

At three in the morning Xavier wanted to have a woman. He called Beatrice because she was less vindictive. Beatrice, soft and tired, gave herself to the desires of the man who seemed a superman.

But the following day they told him that they wouldn't cook for him any more. That he'd better work it out with his third woman.

Both of them cried from time to time and Beatrice made a potato salad for the two of them.

That afternoon they went to the movies. They ate out and only came home at midnight. They found Xavier beaten, sad, and hungry. He tried to explain: "It's because sometimes I want to do it during the daytime!"

"Then," said Carmen, "why then don't you come home?"

He promised that that was what he would do. And he cried. When he cried, Carmen and Beatrice felt heartbroken. That night the two women made love in front of him and he ate out his heart with envy.

How did the desire for revenge begin? The two women drew closer all the time and began to despise him.

He did not keep his promise but sought out the prostitute. She really turned him on because she used a lot of dirty language. And called him a son-of-a-bitch. He took it all.

Until there came a day.

Or better, a night. Xavier was sleeping placidly, like the good citizen he was. The two women were sitting together at a table, pensive. Each one thought of her lost childhood. And of death. Carmen said:

"One day we three shall die."

Beatrice answered:

"And for what?"

They had to wait patiently for the day on which they would close their eyes forever. And Xavier? What should be done with Xavier? He looked like a sleeping child.

"Are we going to wait for him to die a natural death?" asked Beatrice.

Carmen thought, thought and said:

"I think we ought to figure something out, the two of us."

"What kind of thing?"

"I don't know yet."

"But we have to decide."

"You can leave it to me, I know what to do."

And nothing was done, nothing at all. In a little while it would be dawn and nothing had happened. Carmen made a good strong coffee for the two of them. And they ate chocolates until they were nauseated. And nothing, nothing at all.

They turned on the portable radio and listened to some excruciating Schubert. It was straight piano. Carmen said:

"It has to be today."

Carmen led and Beatrice obeyed. It was a special night: full of stars which looked at them sparkling and tranquil. What silence. But what silence! The two went up close to Xavier to see if he was breathing. Xavier snored. Carmen really felt inspired.

She said to Beatrice:

"There are two butcher knives in the kitchen."

"So what?"

"So we are two and we have two knives."

"So what?"

"So, you ass, we two have arms and can do what we have to do. God directs us."

"Wouldn't it be better not to talk of God at this moment?"

"Would you prefer if I spoke of the Devil? No, I speak of God who is the master of all. Of space and time."

Then they went to the kitchen. The two butcher knives were newly sharpened, of fine, polished steel. Would they have the strength?

They would, yes.

They were armed. The bedroom was dark. They struck blindly, missing, and stabbed the bedclothes. It was a cold night. Then they finally were able to make out the sleeping body of Xavier.

The rich blood of Xavier spread across the bed and dripped down onto the floor—a lavish waste. Carmen and Beatrice sat down next to the dining room table, under the yellow light of the naked bulb, exhausted. To kill requires strength. Human strength. Divine strength. The two were sweaty, silent, knocked out. If it had been possible, they wouldn't have killed their great love.

And now? Now they had to get rid of the body. The body was large. The body was heavy.

So the two women went into the garden and with the help of two shovels dug a grave in the ground.

And, in the dark of the night, they carried the corpse out into the garden. It was difficult because Xavier dead seemed to weigh more than when he was alive, since his spirit had left him. As they carried him, they groaned from exhaustion and grief. Beatrice cried.

They put the huge corpse in the grave, covered it with the humid and fragrant earth of the garden, earth good for planting. They went back into the house, made some more coffee, and pulled themselves together a bit.

Beatrice, great romantic that she was—having filled her life with comic book romances about crossed or lost love—Beatrice had the idea of planting roses in that fertile soil.

So they went out again to the garden, took a stem of red roses, and planted it on the sepulcher of the lamented Xavier. Day was dawning. The garden gathered dew. The dew was a blessing on the murder. Such were their thoughts, seated on the white bench they had out there.

The days passed. The two women bought black dresses. And scarcely ate. When night came sadness fell over them. They no longer felt like cooking. In a rage, Carmen, the hotheaded one, tore up the book of recipes in French. She kept the one in Spanish: you never know when you might need such a thing again.

Beatrice took over the cooking. They both ate and drank in silence. The stalk of red roses seemed to have taken hold. Good planter's hands, good prosperous earth. Everything was working out.

And so the story would have ended.

But it so happened that Xavier's secretary found his boss's long absence strange. There were important papers to be signed. As Xavier's house had no telephone, he went there himself. The house seemed bathed in "mala suerte." The two women told him that Xavier had gone on a trip, that he had gone to Montevideo. The secretary didn't much believe them, but behaved as if he swallowed the story.

The following week the secretary went to the police. With the police you don't play games. At first the police didn't want to believe his story. But, in the face of the secretary's insistence, they lazily decided to order the polygamist's house searched. All in vain: no trace of Xavier.

Then Carmen spoke:

"Xavier is in the garden."

"In the garden? Doing what?"

"Only God knows."

"But we didn't see anything or anybody."

They went out to the garden: Carmen, Beatrice, the secretary named Albert, two policemen, and two other men whose identities are unknown. Seven people. Then Beatrice, without a tear in her eyes, showed them the flowering grave. Three men opened the grave, ruining the stalk of roses which suffered this human brutality for no reason at all.

And they saw Xavier. He was horrible, deformed, already half eaten away by worms, with his eyes open.

"And now?" said one of the policemen.

"And now we arrest the two women."

"But," said Carmen, "let us be in the same cell."

"Look," said one of the policemen, right in front of the astonished secretary, "it's best to make believe that nothing at all happened, otherwise there will be a lot of trouble, a lot of paperwork, a lot of gossip."

"You two," said the other policeman, "pack your bags and go and live in Montevideo. And don't bother us any more."

The two women said: Thank you very much.

And Xavier didn't say anything. For, in fact, he had nothing to say.

PLAZA MAUÁ
—◦❧ ❧◦—

The cabaret on Plaza Mauá was called The Erotica. And Luisa's stage name was Carla.

Carla was a dancer at The Erotica. She was married to Joaquim, who was killing himself working as a carpenter. And Carla "worked" at two jobs: dancing half nude and cheating on her husband.

Carla was beautiful. She had little teeth and a tiny waist. She was delicate throughout. She had scarcely any breasts, but she had well-shaped hips. She took an hour to make herself up: afterward, she seemed a porcelain doll. She was thirty but looked much younger.

There were no children. Joaquim and she couldn't get together. He worked until ten at night. She began work at exactly ten. She slept all day long.

Carla was a lazy Luisa. Arriving at night, when the time came to present herself to the public, she would begin to yawn, wishing she were in her nightgown in bed. This was also due to shyness. Incredible as it might seem, Carla was a timid Luisa. She stripped, yes, but the first moments of the dance, of voluptuous motion, were moments of shame. She only "warmed up" a few minutes later. Then she unfolded, she undulated, she gave all of herself. She was best at the samba. But a nice, romantic blues also turned her on.

She was asked to drink with the clients. She received a commission per bottle. She always chose the most expensive drinks. And she pretended to drink: but hers wasn't alcohol. The idea was to get the clients drunk and make them spend. It was boring talking with them. They would caress her, passing their hands over her tiny breasts. And she in a scintillating bikini. Beautiful.

Once in a while she would sleep with a client. She would take the money, keep it well hidden in her bra, and the next day she would buy some new clothes. She had clothes without end. She bought blue jeans. And necklaces. A pile of necklaces. And bracelets, and rings.

Sometimes, just for variety's sake, she danced in blue jeans and without a bra, her breasts swinging among the flashing necklaces. She wore bangs and, using a black pencil, painted on a beauty mark close to her delicate lips. It was adorable. She wore long pendant earrings, sometimes pearl, sometimes imitation gold.

In moments of unhappiness, she turned to Celsinho, a man who wasn't a man. They understood each other well. She told him her troubles, complained about Joaquim, complained about inflation. Celsinho, a successful transvestite, listened to it all and gave her advice. They weren't rivals. They each worked their own turf.

Celsinho came from the nobility. He had given up everything to follow his vocation. He didn't dance. But he did wear lipstick and false eyelashes. The sailors of Plaza Mauá loved him. And he played hard to get. He only gave in at the very end. And he was paid in dollars. After changing the money on the black market, he invested it in the Banco Halles. He was very afraid of growing old, destitute and forsaken. Especially since an old transvestite is a sad thing. He took two envelopes of powdered proteins a day for energy. He had large hips and, from taking so many hormones, he had acquired a facsimile of breasts. Celsinho's stage name was Moleirão.

Moleirão and Carla brought good money to the owner of The Erotica. The smoke-filled atmosphere, the smell of alcohol. And the dance floor. It was tough being forced to dance with a drunken sailor. But what could you do. Everyone has his *métier*.

Celsinho had adopted a little girl of four. He was a real mother to her. He slept very little in order to look after the girl. And she lacked for nothing: she had only the best. Even a Portuguese nanny. On Sundays Celsinho took little Clareta to the zoo at the Quinta de Boa Vista. And they both ate popcorn. And they fed the monkeys. Little Clareta was afraid of the elephants. She asked: "Why do they have such big noses?"

Celsinho then told her a fantastic tale involving good fairies and bad fairies. Or else he would take her to the circus. And they would suck hard, clicking candies, the two of them. Celsinho wanted a brilliant future for little Clareta: marriage with a man of fortune, children, jewels.

Carla had a Siamese cat who looked at her with hard blue eyes. But Carla scarcely had time to take care of the creature: either she was sleeping, or dancing, or out shopping. The cat was named Leléu. And it drank milk with its delicate little red tongue.

Joaquim hardly saw Luisa. He refused to call her Carla. Joaquim was fat and short, of Italian descent. It had been a Portuguese woman neighbor who had given him the name Joaquim. His name was Joaquim Fioriti. Fioriti? There was nothing flowerlike about him.

The maid who worked for Joaquim and Luisa was a wily black woman who stole whatever she could. Luisa hardly ate, in order to keep her figure. Joaquim drowned himself in minestrone. The maid knew about everything, but kept her trap shut. It was her job to polish Carla's jewelry with Brasso and Silvo. When Joaquim was sleeping and Carla working, this maid, by the name of Silvinha, wore her mistress's jewelry. And she was kind of grayish-black in color.

This is how what happened happened.

Carla was confiding in Moleirão when she was asked to dance by a tall man with broad shoulders. Celsinho lusted after him. And he ate his heart out in envy. He was vindictive.

When the dance ended and Carla returned to sit down next to Moleirão, he could hardly hold in his rage. And Carla, innocent. It wasn't her fault she was attractive. And, in fact, the big man appealed to her. She said to Celsinho:

"I'd go to bed with that one for free."

Celsinho said nothing. It was almost three in the morning. The Erotica was full of men and women. Many mothers and housewives went there for the fun of it and to earn a bit of pocket money.

Then Carla said:

"It's so good to dance with a real man."

Celsinho sprang:

"But you're not a real woman!"

"Me? How come I'm not?" said the startled girl, who, dressed that night in black, in a long dress with long sleeves, looked like a nun. She did this on purpose to excite those men who desired a pure woman.

"You," screamed Celsinho, "are no woman at all! You don't even know how to fry an egg! And I do! I do! I do!"

Carla turned into Luisa. White, bewildered. She had been struck in her most intimate femininity. Confused, staring at Celsinho who had the face of a witch.

Carla didn't say a word. She stood up, crushed her cigarette in the ashtray, and, without turning to anyone, abandoning the party at its height, she left.

On foot, in black, on the Plaza Mauá at three in the morning. Like the lowest of whores. Alone. Without recourse. It was true: she didn't know how to fry an egg. And Celsinho was more of a woman than she.

The plaza was dark. And Luisa breathed deeply. She looked at the lamp posts. The plaza was empty.

And in the sky, the stars.

Beauty and the Beast, or, The Wound Too Great

—∘❧ ❦∘—

It begins:

Well, then she left the beauty salon by means of the Copacabana Palace hotel elevator. The chauffeur wasn't there. She looked at her watch; it was four o'clock in the afternoon. And suddenly she remembered; she'd told "her" José to come pick her up at five, not figuring that she wouldn't do her toe and fingernails, that she would just have a massage. What should she do? Take a taxi? But all she had with her was a five-hundred cruzeiro bill and the taxi driver wouldn't have change. She'd brought money along because her husband had told her that a person should never be out and about without money. It occurred to her that she could go back to the beauty salon and ask for her money in smaller notes. But . . . but it was a May afternoon and with its perfume the fresh air was an open flower. So she thought it was marvelous and strange to be walking the streets—with the wind ruffling her hair. She couldn't remember when she'd last been alone, with just herself. Maybe never. She was always with other people, and it was in these other people that she saw herself reflected at the same time that it was they who were reflected in her. Nothing was . . . was pure, she thought without understanding. When she saw herself in the mirror—her skin tanned by the sunbathing that made the golden flowers close to her face in her black hair stand out—she had to contain herself in order not to exclaim, "ah!" since she was fifty million units of beautiful people. There had never been—in the entire history of the world—anyone exactly like her. And even later, in three trillion, trillion years—there would still never be a woman exactly like her.

"I'm a living flame! And I light up darkness again and again!"

This moment was unique—and during her lifetime she would have thousands of unique moments. Until, because of all that had been given to her and by her avidly taken, a cold sweat broke out on her forehead.

"Beauty can lead to the kind of madness we call passion." She thought, "I'm married, I have three children, I'm secure."

She had a name to preserve; she was Carla de Sousa e Santos. The "de" and "e" were important; they marked her class and four hundred years of being a Carioca.* She lived among the herds of women and men who, yes, who were simply "able." Able to do what? Well, simply "able." And yet above all viscous, since their being "able" was well oiled from the machines that sped around without the clamor of rusting metal. She, who was a potency. A generation of electric energy. She, who in order to rest used the vineyards of her country estate. She possessed rotting traditions, but now she was on foot. And since there was no new criterion to sustain her vague and great hopes, those same heavy traditions still strengthened her. Traditions of what? Of nothing, if she were wanting to purify herself. She had in

---

* A native or long-time resident of Rio de Janeiro.

her favor perhaps only the fact that their inhabitants had a long lineage behind them, one that despite being a plebeian lineage was still sufficient to give them a certain appearance of dignity.

Then, completely entangled, she thought: "She being a woman, which seemed to her a funny thing to be or not be, she also knew that if she were a man she would naturally be a banker, this being the normal thing that happens with 'their kind' of people, that is, to people of their social class, to which her husband, however, had gained entry by dint of hard work and which therefore classified him as a 'self-made man' while she was not a 'self-made woman.' " At the conclusion of her long thought, it seemed to her that . . . that she hadn't thought about anything.

A one-legged man, dragging himself along on a crutch, stopped in front of her and said:

"Will you give me some money so I can eat?"

"Help!!!" she shrieked to herself when she saw the enormous wound on the man's leg. "God help me," she whispered.

She was exposed to that man. She was completely exposed. If she'd kept her appointment with "her" José at the Avenida Atlântica exit, the hotel where the hairdresser's shop was located would not have permitted someone "like that" to come around. But out on the Avenida Copacabana everything was possible; there were all kinds of people. At least different than hers. "Hers"? "What kind of people did she know that were 'hers'?"

She . . . the others. But, but death doesn't separate us, she thought, suddenly, and her face took on the beauty of a mask and not the beauty of a human being; for a moment her face hardened.

The beggar's thought: "that woman with the little golden stars painted on her forehead will only give a little if she gives me anything at all." Then, a little tired, it occurred to him, "She'll give me almost nothing."

She was terrified. Since she was almost never out on the street—she always went from place to place in a car—she came to wonder, is he going to kill me? She was confused and so she asked:

How much does one normally give?"

"Whatever you're able to give and wish to give," responded the beggar, utterly astonished.

She, who never herself paid at the beauty salon, the manager of the place sending a monthly bill to her husband's secretary. "Husband," she thought. What would he do about the beggar? She knew what—nothing. His kind don't do anything. And she . . . she was "his kind," too. Could everything be given to him? Could she give him her husband's bank, their apartment, their house in the country, their jewelry . . . ?

But something that was the touch of avarice everyone has then asked:

"Is five hundred cruzeiros enough? It's all I have."

The beggar looked at her, still astonished.

"Are you laughing at me, lady?"

"I?? No, I'm not. I've got the money right here in my purse . . ."

She opened it, took out the bill, and, almost seeking his forgiveness, humbly handed it to the man.

The bewildered man.

And after laughing and exposing his almost vacant gums, he said, "Look, either you're a really good person or you're not right in the head. I'll accept it, but don't go telling later on that I robbed you . . . no one's going to believe me. It would be better if you'd give me some change."

"I don't have any change, all I've got is this bill."

The man seemed startled. He said something that was almost incomprehensible because, having so few teeth, his diction was bad.

While all this was transpiring, his head was thinking: from her, *cachaça, cachaça, cachaça, cachaça* and more *cachaça*.

Her head was full of celebrations, celebrations, celebrations. Celebrating what? Celebrating the strange wound? One thing united them: they both had vocations involving money. The beggar spent everything he had, while Carla's husband, the banker, collected money. His daily bread came from the Stock Exchange, The Bank, and Swiss accounts. The beggar's daily bread came from his round, open wound. And more than anything else he must have feared being cured, she guessed, because if he got well he wouldn't have anything to eat, Carla knew that, and she thought, "after a certain age, if you don't have a good job . . ." If he were a boy, he could be a wall painter. Since he wasn't, he was investing in his big wound, in living and purulent flesh.

She leaned up against the wall and deliberately resolved to think. It was different because she wasn't in the habit of doing so and she didn't know that thought was vision and comprehension and that no one could simply order themselves to think, like this: think! OK. But it happens that to resolve something was an obstacle. She began, then, to look into herself and things really began to happen. She had only the silliest thoughts. Like this: that beggar, does he know English? Had that beggar ever eaten caviar while drinking champagne? They were silly thoughts because she knew clearly that the beggar didn't know English and that he'd experimented with neither caviar nor champagne. But she couldn't stop herself from seeing born in her one more absurd thought: did he do his winter sports in Switzerland?

Then she became desperate. She became so desperate that there came to her a thought made up of only two words: "Social Justice."

Death to all rich people! That would be the solution, she thought happily. But . . . who would give money to the poor?

Suddenly . . . suddenly everything stopped. The buses stopped, cars stopped, watches stopped, people in the streets were immobilized . . . only her heart was beating, and for what?

She saw that she didn't know how to run the world. She was an incompetent, with her black hair and long, red fingernails. That's how she was, like in an out-of-focus color photo. Everyday she made her lists of things that needed doing or that she wanted to do the next day . . . that was how she'd become so tied to idle time. She simply had nothing to do. Other people did everything for her. Even the two boys . . . for it had been her husband who'd determined they would have two children . . .

"You've got to make an effort if you want to win in life," her dead grandfather had told her. Would she, perhaps, be a "winner"? If to win meant to be down on the street in the middle of the afternoon, with one's face smeared with make-up and spangles . . . was that what winning was? What patience you had to have with yourself. What patience you had to have in order to save your own little life. Save it from what? From judgment? But who would judge? She felt her mouth go completely dry and her throat on fire—exactly like when she'd had to submit to her school exams. And there was no water! Do you know what that's like—not having water?

She tried to think of something else and forget the difficult present moment. Then she remembered some lines out of one of Eça de Queiroz's posthumous books that she had studied in school: "Lake Tiberíade glittered transparently, covered in silence, bluer than the sky, hemmed in by flower-filled meadows, by dense orchards, by porphyry rocks and by open stretches of earth between the palm trees and beneath the swooping of the turtle doves." She knew this line by heart because when she was an adolescent she'd been very sensitive to words and because she desired for herself the same glittering destiny as Lake Tiberíade.

Unexpectedly, she had a murderous impulse to kill all the beggars in the world! Just so that, after the killing, she could enjoy the usufruct of her extraordinary sense of well-being.

No. The world was not whispering.

The world was SHOUTING!!! through that man's distended mouth.

The young banker's wife thought she wasn't going to put up with the lack of softness that they'd given to her so well made-up face.

And the celebration? What would she say at the celebration when she was dancing, what would she say to her partner who would be holding her in his arms . . . ? The following: look, the beggar has sex, too, he said he had eleven children. He doesn't attend social engagements, he doesn't get into Ibrahim's columns or Zózimo's, he's hungry for bread, not for cake, he should, in fact, eat only gruel since he doesn't have any teeth to chew meat with. . . . "Meat?" She vaguely remembered that the cook had said that "filet mignon" had gone up in price. Yes. How could she dance? Only if it were a crazy and macabre beggar's dance.

No, she wasn't a woman given to swooning and fastidiousness and feeling faint or ill. Like some of her high society "colleagues." She smiled a little when she thought in terms of "colleagues." Colleagues in what? In dressing well? In giving dinners for thirty or forty people?

She herself, taking advantage of the garden in the summer that was extinguishing itself, had given a reception for how many guests? No, she didn't want to think about this, she remembered (why without the same pleasure?) the tables spread out over the lawn, candlelight . . . "candlelight"? she thought, am I crazy? Did I fall into some kind of game? A rich person's game?

"Before getting married, you were middle class, the secretary of a banker with whom you got married and now . . . now, candlelight. I'm just playing at life," she thought, "life really isn't like this."

"Beauty can be a great threat." Her extreme grace became confused with bewilderment and a deep melancholy. "Beauty frightens." "If I weren't so pretty, I would have had some other destiny," she thought, adjusting the golden flowers in her jet black hair.

Once she'd seen a friend become entirely undone, by a broken heart and driven crazy, crazy from a powerful passion. After that, she'd never wanted to experiment. She'd always been afraid of things that were too beautiful or too horrible . . . she just didn't know deep down how to respond to such things or, if she did respond, whether she'd become equally beautiful or equally ugly. She was frightened, like when she'd seen the Mona Lisa's smile right in front of her at the Louvre. Like when she'd become frightened at the man with the wound, or at the wound of the man.

She felt like shouting out to the world, "I'm not a terrible person! I'm a product of I don't even know what . . . how am I going to understand this misery I feel in my soul?"

To change how she was feeling—since she didn't want to endure those sentiments any more and, out of her desperation, since she felt like violently kicking the man's wound—to change how she was feeling, she thought: this is my second marriage, that is, the previous husband was alive.

Now she understood why she'd gotten married in the first place and why it was an auction: who'll raise the bid? Who'll raise the bid? Then, you're sold. Yes, she'd married herself off the first time to the man who had "raised the bid," she'd accepted it because he was rich and because he was also a little above her in terms of social class. She sold herself. And the second husband? Their marriage was coming to an end, he with his two lovers . . . and she putting up with it all because a divorce would be a scandal: their name was, after all, often cited in the social columns. And would she go back to using the name she'd had when she was single? Until she could become accustomed again to her single name, she was going to delay things a lot. Besides, she thought, laughing to herself, besides, she'd accepted the second one because he'd given her considerable prestige. Had she sold herself to the social columns? Yes. She realized that now. If there were a third marriage for her—she was, after all, rich and beautiful—if there were, with whom would she marry? She began to laugh a little hysterically because she thought: the third husband was the beggar.

Suddenly she asked the beggar, "Do you speak English?"

The man didn't even know what she'd asked him. But, obliged to respond since the woman had just bought him with so much money, he did so evasively.

"Yes, I do. Aren't I talking with you right now? Why? Are you deaf? Then I'll shout: I Do."

Frightened by the man's enormous shout, she broke out in a cold sweat. She was fully aware that until now she'd pretended that there really weren't people who were worse than hungry, who spoke no language, and who were anonymous multitudes begging just to survive. She had discovered this, yes, but she had also turned her head and covered her eyes. Everyone, yes, everyone . . . they know and they pretend they don't know. And even if they didn't pretend, they were still going to have a bad time. How couldn't they have? No, they wouldn't, not even this.

She was . . . after all was said and done who was she? Without commentary, especially because the question had lasted only an instant of a second: the question and its answer hadn't been thoughts of the head, they were of the body.

I'm the Devil, she thought, remembering what she'd learned as a child. And the beggar is Jesus. But . . . what he wants isn't money, it's love, that man got lost from the rest of humanity, just like I got lost.

She tried to force herself to understand the world and she succeeded only in remembering fragments of phrases said by her husband's friends: "Those plants will not be sufficient." My God, what plants? Minister Galhardo's? Would he have plants? "Electrical energy . . . hydroelectric"?

And the essential magic of life . . . where was it now? In what corner of the world? In the man sitting on the corner?

Is money the mainspring of the world? The question became her. But she tried to pretend it wasn't. She felt herself so, so rich that she became ill at ease.

The beggar's thought: "Either that woman's crazy or she stole her money, because a millionaire she can't be," millionaire for him being only a word and even if in that woman he'd wanted to see a millionaire incarnate: hey, man, where have you ever seen a millionaire get stopped on the street? Then he thought: is she one of those tramps who charge their clients dearly and who are always keeping some promise?

Later.

Later.

Silence.

But suddenly that shouted thought:

"How is that I've never realized that I'm a beggar, too? I've never begged for spare change but I've begged for love of my husband, who's got his two lovers, I beg for the love of God that people find me pretty, happy, and acceptable, and the clothes of my soul are ragged . . ."

"There are things that equalize us," she thought, searching desperately for another point of equality. Suddenly, the answer came: they were alike because they had been born and they would die. They were, therefore, sister and brother.

She felt like saying, look, man, I'm pathetic, too; the only difference is that I'm rich. I . . . she thought ferociously, I'm close to discrediting the money, threatening my husband's standing in the market. I'm about ready, any moment now, to sit down on that strand of sidewalk. My worst disgrace was to have been born. Having paid for that damned event, I feel like I've got a right to everything.

She was afraid. But suddenly she took the great step of her life; courageously, she sat down on the ground.

"You see, she's a communist!" thought the beggar, half-clearly. "And as a communist, she would have a right to her jewels, her apartment, her wealth, even her perfumes."

—◦❧ ❦◦—

She would never again be the same person. Not that she'd never seen a beggar. But she'd seen this one at the wrong time, as if she'd been shoved and gotten red wine spilled on her white lace dress. Suddenly she knew; that beggar was made of the same material she was. Simply that. The "why" of it was what was different. On the physical plane, they were equal. For her part, she had a median culture, and he didn't appear to know about anything, not even who the president of Brazil was. She, however, had a keen capacity for understanding. Was it possible that she'd lived up to now with a kind of built-in intelligence? But what if she'd done so only recently, since she'd come into contact with a wound that was asking for money to get something to eat . . . had she only now come to think about money? Money that had always been evident and visible to her. And the wound, she'd never seen it from so close up . . .

"Are you feeling ill?"

"I'm not ill . . . but I'm not well, either. I don't know . . ."

She thought: the body's a thing that when sick people carry around with them. The beggar carries himself.

"At the dance this evening madame will feel better and everything will have returned to normal," José said.

In truth, at the dance she would be regenerated by the things that were attractive to her and everything would return to normal.

She sat back in the seat of the refrigerated car casting, before departing, a final glance at that companion of an hour and a half. It seemed to her difficult to say good-bye to him, for he was now her alter ego "I," he would be a part of her life forever. Good-bye. She was feeling dreamy, distracted, her lips half-open as if there were some words about to come out of them. For a reason she didn't know how to explain . . . he was really her. And so, when the driver turned on the radio, she heard that the codfish produced nine million eggs per year. She didn't know how to deduce anything from that phrase, she who was in need of a destiny. She remembered that as an adolescent she'd sought a destiny and had selected singing. As part of her education, they had easily arranged a good teacher for her. But she sang poorly, she knew it herself and her father, a lover of operas, had pretended not to notice that she sang poorly. But there was one moment when she began to cry. The teacher, perplexed, had asked her what was wrong.

"It's that, it's that I'm afraid of, of, of, of singing well . . ."

"But you sing very poorly," the teacher had told her.

"I'm also afraid of singing even, even, even worse. Really, realllly badly!" She was crying and never had another singing lesson. That story about seeking understanding through art had happened to her only once; later, she dove into a kind of oblivion so profound that only now, at age thirty-five, because of that wound, and because she knew she had to sing either very badly or very well, only now was she disoriented. For a long time she hadn't listened to what they call classical music because to do so would awaken her from the automatic slumber in which she was living. I . . . I'm just playing at life. In the upcoming month she was going to New York, and she discovered that that trip was like a new lie, like a bewilderment. To have a wound in your leg—that's reality. And everything in her life, from the moment she'd been born, everything in her life had been soft and smooth, like the leap of a cat, like a charade.

—◦❧ ❧◦—

(riding in the car)

Suddenly she thought: I didn't even remember to ask his name.

João Guimarães Rosa
—◦❧(1908–1967)❧◦—

João Guimarães Rosa, originally from Cordisburgo, a small town in Minas Gerais, is considered to be one of the most difficult and challenging writers even for educated Brazilian readers to fathom. Rosa published seventy-nine stories characterized by his interest in language and its crucial role in creating awareness, consciousness, and even reality itself. Rosa forms and deforms words, using regionalisms, archaisms, Latinisms, borrowings from other languages, erudite constructions introduced ironically, and constant permutations of words and expressions. His stories are full of constant lexical surprises and linguistic inventions. Much of his material comes from his ethnographic research in the interior of Minas Gerais and Bahia, the *sertão* where he accompanied nomadic, messianic groups for several years as a folklorist, anthropologist, and incipient writer, after finishing his medical degree. His stories are thus close to the oral tradition, as found in the nomadic cultures of Brazil's interior, as well as to the exemplary and gnosiological tales found in those atavistic, chivalric, and messianic societies. Rosa became a career diplomat whose interests in language and philosophy led him to study the historical, morphological, and syntactical features of the Portuguese language over time, as well as classics of philosophical and esoteric themes. His stories tell of desperate searches for freedom and salvation, amid the allegorical trials of experience. Rosa synthesized his diverse interests in highly charged stories, always linguistically challenging, narrating regionalist Brazilian culture in terms of universal archetypes. International recognition of his work has been hampered by inadequate translations, made difficult by the complexity of his writing and work with the Portuguese language. His themes of transcendence, redemption, repentance, salvation, and love produced works of great beauty. Rosa's prose masterpiece, *Grande Sertão: Veredas* (1956), is widely considered to be one of the greatest novels of modern literature. His published collections of stories are *Sagarana* (1946), *Primeiras Estórias* (1962), *Tutaméia: Terceiras Estórias* (1967), and the posthumously published *Estas Estórias* (1969). Two translations have been published in English, *Sagarana* (1966) and *The Third Bank of the River and Other Stories* (1968).

The Girl from Beyond
—◦❧ ❦◦—

She lived behind the Sierra of Mim, in the middle of a swamp of clean, clear water, in a place called Fear-of-God. Her father, a small farmer, struggled along with a few cows and a patch of rice; her mother, a native of Urucúia, never put down her rosary, even when she was killing chickens or blessing out somebody. The little girl, named Maria—Nhinhinha, they called her—was always a little bit of a thing, but she had a big head and enormous eyes.

Not that she ever seemed to stare at things. She stayed quietly in her place, had no interest in rag dolls or other toys, but sat still, hardly moving, wherever she happened to be. "Nobody understands much of what she's talking about," said her bewildered father. It was not so much that she used strange words, although once in a while she would inquire, for instance: "**Did she surego?**"—but who or what she was talking about, no one was ever quite sure. Even more baffling was the oddness of her judgments about things, and the embellishments she might exclaim, with a burst of sudden laughter: "**Armadillos can't see the moon . . .**" she might say. Sometimes she told snatches of vague, absurd little stories: about a bee who flew up to a cloud; or a great many girls and boys sitting at a long, long table covered with cakes and candy, time without end; or the need to make a list of all the things people lost day after day.

Usually, though, Nhinhinha, who was not yet four years old, caused no one any trouble, and drew hardly any attention to herself except by her perfect calm, her immobility, and her silences. Nothing, no one, appeared to inspire her with any particular affection or distaste. When food was given to her, she sat with a leaf plate in her lap, eating first the meat, the egg, the cracklings, or whatever looked most appetizing and then consuming the rest—beans, cornmeal mush, rice, squash—with artistic slowness. Watching her perpetual imperturbability, one of us would suddenly exclaim in surprise: "Nhinhinha, what are you doing?" and she would reply in a long-drawn-out, mirthful, modulated voice: "**I'm . . . ju-ust . . . do-o-oing,**" with empty spaces between the words. Could it be that she was just a tiny bit simpleminded?

Nothing intimidated her. Hearing her father ask her mother to brew some strong coffee, she would remark smilingly to herself: "**Greedy boy . . . greedy boy . . .**" and she was in the habit of addressing her mother as "**Big girl . . . big girl . . .**" which vexed both father and mother. In vain. Nhinhinha would only murmur: "**Never mind . . . never mind,**" sensitive-soft, helpless as a flower. She would answer in the same way when summoned to see some new thing wonderful enough to excite adults and children alike. Events affected her not at all. She was subdued, but healthy and flourishing. No one had any real power over her; no one knew her likes and dislikes. How could she be punished? There was no way to chastise her. They would hardly have dared to strike her; there was no reason to do so, although the respect she felt toward mother and father seemed, rather, an odd sort of indulgence. And Nhinhinha was fond of me.

We talked together now and then. She loved the night in its heavy dark coat. "So full!" she would exclaim as she looked at the delible, superhuman stars, which she called "cheep-cheep stars." She repeated "Everything being born!"—her favorite exclamation—on many occasions, with the vouchsafing of a smile. And the air— she said that the air smelled of memories. "You can't see when the wind stops . . ." I remember her in the yard, in her little yellow dress. What she said was not always out of the ordinary; sometimes it was our ears that exaggerated what we heard. "Up so buzzard-high" was only "Up where the buzzard can't fly"—and her small finger would almost touch the sky. She would remark: "Jabuticaba fruit come-see-me!" and then sigh: "I want to go there." œere?" "I don't know." Then she said: "The baby bird's gone away from singing." The birds had been singing, and as time slid by I thought she was no longer listening; then the singing bird stopped. "There's no more birdie," I told her. After that, Nhinhinha called the *sabiá*—the thrush— "Mrs. Birdie No-More." Some of her answers were longer than others: "Me? I'm making me homesick." At other times, when dead relatives were mentioned, she would laugh and say: "I'm going to visit them." I scolded her, advised her, said she was moonstruck. She eyed me mockingly, with perspective eyes: "Did he surego you?" I never saw Nhinhinha again.

I do know, however, that she began to work miracles at about that time.

It was neither her mother nor her father who discovered the sudden marvel, but Auntantônia. It happened one morning when Nhinhinha was sitting by herself staring at nothing in front of her. "I wish the toad would come." If they heard her at all, they thought she was spinning fairy tales, talking nonsense as usual. Auntantônia, out of habit, shook her finger at the child. But at that very moment the little creature hopped into the room, straight to the feet of Nhinhinha—not a toad with a bloated throat, but a beautiful mischievous frog from the verdant marsh, a green, green frog. Such a visitor had never entered the house before. Nhinhinha laughed: "He's weaving a magic spell." The others were amazed, struck dumb with surprise.

Several days later, with the same easy calm, she murmured: "I wish I had a corn cake with guava jam in it." And not half an hour later a woman appeared, having come from a long way off, carrying the guava rolls wrapped in straw matting. Who could understand such a thing, or the new wonders that followed? Whatever she wanted was sure to happen at once. But she wanted very little, and always frivolous, careless things that made no difference one way or the other. When her mother was very sick, suffering pain for which there was no remedy, Nhinhinha could not be persuaded to tell them the cure. She only smiled, whispering her "Never mind . . . never mind," and refused to say any more. But she went slowly to her mother, hugged her, and kissed her warmly. The mother, staring at her little girl with astonished faith, was cured in a minute. And so they learned that Nhinhinha had more than one way of doing things.

The family decided to keep it a secret, so that malicious persons with ulterior motives, or the merely curious, would not stir up trouble, or the priests and the bishop try to take the child away to a solemn convent. No one would be told, not even the closest relatives. Auntantônia and Nhinhinha's parents themselves were not eager to talk about it. They felt an extraordinary fear of the thing. They hoped it was an illusion.

But what began to annoy the father, after a time, was that no sensible advantage was being taken of Nhinhinha's gift. A scorching drought had come; even the swamp threatened to dry up. They tried begging Nhinhinha to ask for rain. "**But I can't, ué,**" she said, shaking her head. They insisted: they told her that otherwise there would be nothing left: no milk, rice, meat, candy, fruit, or molasses. "**Never mind . . . never mind,**" she smiled gently, closing her eyes to their insistence and drifting into the sudden sleep of swallows.

Two days later she was willing to ask: she wanted a rainbow. It rained and soon the fairy arc appeared, shining in green and red, really a bright pink. Nhinhinha, no longer subdued, was overjoyed at the refreshing coolness that came at the end of the day. She did something they had never seen her do before: jumped and ran around the house and yard. "Did she see a little green bird?" her parents wondered aloud. As for the real birds, they sang like heralds from another kingdom. But that same day Auntantônia scolded the girl harshly, angrily, with such rudeness that her mother and father were angry and surprised. Nhinhinha sat docilely down again, inexplicably undisturbed, stiller than ever, thinking her green-bird thoughts. Her father and mother whispered together contentedly about how much help she was going to be to them when she grew up and got some sense into her head, as Providence of course willed that she should.

And then Nhinhinha fell sick and died. They say it was because of the bad water in those parts. All acts of real living take place too far away.

After that blow had fallen, suddenly every member of the household began to suffer from one illness or another. Mother, father, Auntantônia all realized that they might as well be dead as half dead. It was heartbreaking to see the mother fingering her rosary: instead of the Hail Marys, she could only moan fiercely: "**Big girl . . . big girl,**" over and over. And the father's hands stroked the little stool where Nhinhinha had so often sat, and which would have broken under the weight of his man's body.

Now they had to send word to the village to build a coffin and make preparations for the funeral, with virgins and angels in the procession. Then Auntantônia plucked up her courage: she had to tell them that on that day of the rainbow, the rain, and the little bird, Nhinhinha had spoken some wild foolishness, and that was why she had scolded her. It was this: she had said she wanted a little pink coffin trimmed in bright green . . . an evil omen! And now, should they order the coffin made the way she had wanted it?

Her father, in a shower of brusque tears, stormed "No!" If he consented to that, it would seem as if he were to blame; as if he were helping Nhinhinha to die.

But her mother did want it, and began to plead with the father. At the height of her sobs, however, her face grew serene and smiled a wide smile, a good smile, stopped short by a sudden thought. No, there was no need for them to order the coffin or to explain anything: it was bound to be exactly the way she had wanted it—rose-colored with green funeral trimmings—because it had to be! Because it would be another miracle, the last miracle of her little daughter in glory, Saint Nhinhinha.

MUCH ADO

—◦❧ ❦◦—

One morning when all the cats were nice and neat inside their fur, I was standing outside the gate (which was against the rules) waiting for the newsboy to come with the papers, although I was officially on duty. Along with two or three other more or less casual bystanders, I saw a certain gentleman walk by with a rapid, precise step. Very temporarily, we received the impression of a man unsullied and undefiled. And immediately myth was born again into the world, for portentous events unfolded, exploded, filling our urban day with hurly-burly, hustle-bustle, and hurry-skurry.

"Oh, senhor!" was the cry, unless maybe it was a war cry—"Ugh, Sioux!"— which it might just as well have been as far as I was concerned, since I was either absent-minded or concentrating at the time, mulling over my own personal quid pro quos, which are the stuff of life, to my mind. But: "Oooh . . ."—had that well-set-up gentleman stabbed some inoffensive passer-by? I had an inkling in a twinkling. No. All that had happened, as I half-perceived, was that a not very skillful pickpocket had clumsily allowed himself to be caught in the act of stealing someone's wallet. In a trice, with the erstwhile gentleman as the trigger, our banal interior vacuum was broken open to receive the imprint of the series of episodes which followed.

"But he looks respectable, and he's well dressed, too," said Dr. Bilôlo's chauffeur in surprise, crawling out of the car where he had been dozing. "It was a fountain pen he swiped off some guy's lapel," testified the newsboy, who had not appeared until the crucial moment. Finding himself pursued, the man ran so fast he left a streak in the air as he tore around the plaza with only the front part of his feet hitting the ground. "Catch him!" Well, rearing up almost in the middle of the plaza was one of those royal palms, maybe the biggest one of all, a really majestic-looking tree. Now the man in his decorous business suit, instead of running into it and without even stopping to get rid of his shoes, flung his arms around it and clambered up it with incredible alacrity, an absolutely sensational climb. Is a palm tree a palm tree or a palm tree or a palm tree?—a philosopher might inquire. Our man, not enlightened to that degree, had already scaled it to the thin, sharp tip. And he managed to stay there.

"Well, I'll be!" I shook myself and blinked twice, trying to get hold of myself again. Our man had gone straight to the top of the mast, as light as a woodpecker, without a single false move, and was perched on the very tip-top, in the empyrean vault, as sassy as a *sabiá*. His pursuers had halted, no less surprised than I was, and had come to a standstill here at ground level, before the infinite palm—the great Trojan wall. The sky was a flawless sapphire. On the ground you couldn't even count the people in the crowd, because its circumference was constantly being enlarged by people swarming maggotlike into the plaza. I certainly never would have believed that a crowd could be generated so spontaneously.

Our man was, shall we say, ostentatious at that unexpected height: simultaneously flower and fruit. Our man wasn't ours any longer. "**Well, I must say he's artistic about it**"—this pronouncement came not from the newsboy but from the Chaplain of our Institute, and was almost gleeful. The other observers sent up insults like kites, clamoring for the police and the devil, and some of them even calling for guns. Beyond their reach, very much master of the situation, he hallelujahed gaily in mellifluent imitation. It was a wonder he could be heard so well in spite of the distance. Was he giving a speech about fountain pens? He was a street vendor, then, and could spill a good spiel about fountain pens and ballpoints. He hadn't chosen his territory very well, though, I thought to myself. If it had not seemed unkind, I might have been insulted at the idea of anyone's coming to perform that kind of juggling act or acrobatic stunt right in front of our Institute. But I had to hand it to him, he certainly had a daring imagination. And I was only human: I went over to see the spieler.

I heard someone calling me in that small space of time and saw it was only Adalgiso, sobersided as usual, except that he was tugging at my arm. Pulling and being pulled, I ran across the plaza toward the cynosure, the center of the whirlpool. Because we were both wearing our white coats, the crowd opened a crooked kind of lane for us. "**How did he get away?**" asked the people, who cannot be fooled all of the time. Finally I was made to understand—poor, unlucky me. "**How are you going to get him down?**" Adalgiso and I were on duty that fantastico-inauspicious day.

That being the case, Adalgiso whispered a short, quick explanation: the man was not our patient. Alone and of his own free will, he had turned up at the Institute only a few minutes before. "**Nothing abnormal in his features or general appearance; even the form and content of his speech seem at first to denote a fairly firm mental foundation. . . .**" It was a serious case, very serious. Pressed forward by the mob, we were standing in the eye of the cyclone. "**He said that he was sane, but, seeing that the rest of humanity was mad and on the eve of becoming more so, he had decided to enter the asylum voluntarily; thus, when things went from infernal to worse, he would be in a safe place, with enough space, good treatment, and security, which the majority—those on the outside—would eventually lack. . . .**" And so Adalgiso did not even accuse himself of venial carelessness when he had gone to fill out his form.

"**Are you surprised?**" I avoided the question. Actually, the man had only slightly exaggerated a very old hypothesis: that of our own Professor D'Artagnan, who used to say that forty per cent of his students—us—were typical latent cases, and a good proportion of the rest as well, except that the diagnosis would have taken a little longer. . . . But Adalgiso went on in my astonished ear: "**Do you know who he is? He gave his name and occupation. Sandoval recognized him. He's the Secretary of Finance. . . .**" All this in a low, vapid voice.

Just then the crowd fell quiet as if on purpose; it gave our nerves a wrench. It was sad to look up, where the sky was so clearly a high, scornful blue. In any case the man was a little this side of it, in a kind of ivory tower among the green, hispid palm fronds, at the terminal point of his rocket-rapid ascent. He was fulfilled, sublimely absurd. I know I am subject to dizziness. Who wouldn't be, under and face to face with such a thing, such a down-and-uproar? It was enough to make the hair on a wig stand on end. But there was no denying this: it was a superhuman individual gesture, a hyperbolic commitment, a herculean act. **"Sandoval is going to call the Director, the Police, Government House . . ."** Adalgiso assured me.

Now a palm has no leafy foliage like a mango tree; nor, as it happens, does it offer the stability and comfort of a pepper tree. So how on earth or over it could he contrive to keep himself up there so long, statesman or not, sane or sick? He was not perilously balanced; on the contrary. Cozily settled on the apogee, the foxy scalawag, besides acting like a lunatic, was clearly in no hurry whatever. The only thing he was doing was casting a shadow. At that very moment he began to shout as if delirious, knowing exactly what he was up to and no end pleased with himself: **"I have never thought of myself as a human being!"**—looking down on us disdainfully. He paused, then repeated the phrase, adding: **"If you know me, it's a lie!"** Was he answering me? He laughed, I laughed, he laughed again, we both laughed. The crowd laughed.

Not Adalgiso. **"How could I guess? I don't know anything about politics,"** he inconcluded. **"Manic excitation, state of dementia . . . Acute, delirious mania . . . shouldn't the contrast have been enough for me to get the symptoms right?"** he argued with himself. But, psst! who was the V. I. So-and-So who was making his important presence known? The Director appeared, advancing in all his fullness. There were policemen pushing the crowd aside to make an imperial pathway for him and to prevent any trouble—cops, guards, detectives, a commissioner, and the Chief of Police. With the Director came the innocent young male nurses and stretcher bearers, along with Sandoval, the Chaplain, Dr. Aeneas, and Dr. Bilôlo. They were bringing a straitjacket with them. They stared up at our empalmed man. Then the Director said masterfully: **"This should offer no difficulty!"**

In diametrical refutation came Professor D'Artagnan from the opposing side: **"Hebephrenic paranoid psychosis,** dementia praecox, **I see it clearly!"** The two men cordially despised each other, not only in a theoretical-speculative-philosophical way, but also when it came to trifles. They were rivals, as a matter of fact, although one was bald and the other was not. And so, logically enough, the Director replied unscientifically, but striking an attitude of dogmatic authority: **"Do you know who that gentleman is?"** and named the title in a hushed voice which was nonetheless audible to some of the nearby more sagacious members of the crowd. Professor D'Artagnan amended his verdict: **". . . the disturbance is transitory, however, and will in no way affect his civil standing . . ."** and began expatiating on the question of auto-intoxication versus infection. Even a wise man can be mistaken in what he believes—and the rest of us think we're wiping spots off glasses that are already clean. And so every one of us is a prepalatine donkey, or rather, **apud** the vulgate: a jackass. And furthermore, there being both logic and illogic in the world, the stretcher bearers did not deposit the stretcher on the ground.

For our exalted man recried: **"Living is impossible!"**—a **slogan** of his; and every time he was about to speak, he achieved a multitudinal silence from the thousands of people there below. He did not even neglect the art of mime: he made gestures as if he were balancing with a parasol. Was he threatening, something or someone with his catastrophic creative impulses? **"Living is impossible!"** came the empirical, anhermeneutic statement out of the sheer egoism of logic. But he said the words not at all in the voice of a preposterous wag or a hallucinated humbug, but in a candid, generous tone. He was making a revelation which would benefit us all and instruct us in the truth, us substantial, sub-aerial beings, from whose milieu he had snatched himself. It was a fact: life itself seemed to be saying it was impossible. It looked that way to me. And in that case, it was necessary that a tremendous miracle take place unceasingly in every corner of the universe, which is what really is occurring, in actual fact. I could not resist a vague intellectual empathy toward the man who was now an abstraction—who had triumphantly nullified himself; who had attained the apex of an axiom.

Seven expert, official pairs of eyes studied him from inferior space. "**What is to be done?**" The Director summoned us to a council in a precarious clearing widened by the obliging Police after a preamble of **cassetêtes** and blasphemous appeals. To our confusion, however, our illustrious patient was proving difficult. He embodied the soul incarnate of all things: inaccessible. And therefore immedicable. We would have to induce him to come down, or find some suitable way of unhoisting him. He was not in a handy position to be picked off the tree and was not the kind to be lured down with coaxing and strawberries. "**What shall we do?**" we all said in unison, but it took us a while to hit on a solution. Then the Director declared, with the air of one who draws and lets fly: "**The firemen are coming!**" Period. The stretcher bearers laid the stretcher on the ground.

Boos were what was coming. Not directed at us, fortunately, but at the guardian of our public finances. He had been pinpointed. The identity of our hero had been broadcast swiftly through the jostling mass. From the midst of it, from one throat and then another, in buffoonish, scattered shouts, the ready rumor sped; and one vox-popular version, which was shouted formidably to the heavens, was: "**Demagogue! Demagogue! . . .**" and Echo answered: "**Magoog! . . .**" the beautiful and the good; good night; my stars. What a hue and cry it was, that ultravociferate hallooing drawn from the multitude—standing chockablock, pitiless, parboiled by the March-day heat. I have a feeling that some of the members of our group, including myself, were vociferating, too. Sandoval certainly was: it was the first time in his life he had even made a halfway start at rebelling. Professor D'Artagnan reproved us: "**Hasn't a politician the right to his mental disturbances?**" in pedantic vexation. It was certainly true that the Director vacillated wildly in his judgments as a psychiataster when someone with status was involved. As we observed him, we saw that our poor man was fighting a losing battle: he had not succeeded in hoisting his fame up with him to the pinnacle. A demagogue . . .

But he did finally succeed—with one fell swoop. Gently but abruptly he began to move about, to teeter-totter; and for good cause for he let fall . . . a shoe! Exactly, half of a pair of shoes—no more—with a lofty condescension. It was a real theatrical coup, designed not so much to intimidate as to pull off a hugely effective piece of burlesque. Of course, there were fluxes and refluxes among the stirring crowd when the banal object was cast down from its height and came spinning gravitationally in the air. That man—"**He's a genius!**" exclaimed Dr. Bilôlo. The people sensed it, too, and applauded him, and then redoubled their applause: "*Viva, viva! . . .*" they thrilled with enthusiasm and turned themselves inside out. "**A genius!**" They knew he was one; they praised him, gave him their oceanic applause.

By St. Simeon the Stylite! And no doubt he was a genius, a dramatic *persona*, and an opportunist as well, who had, as was soon to be confirmed, extraordinarily acute perceptions and a fine sense of timing. For after a short pause, down came the other shoe. This one described no parabola; it plummeted down as straight as a line drawn on a blackboard. The shoes were a yellowish color. Our man on the maypole—the high-flown author and target of the electrifying acclamation appropriate to his feat.

But the clapping was drowned out by sirens. The fire engine made its way with some difficulty through the crowd and emerged with a tintinnabulation of noise and fanfare. And there it was anchored, ruddy as a lobster sunrise. The cleared space was widened to give the firemen enough space to maneuver; they added to the scene a heady note of belligerence which garnered the leftover surplus of applause. By that time their Commandant had come to an understanding with the Police and then with us, of course. They had a second, longer truck which formed the base of the ladder: the walking apparatus needed for this undertaking, loftily deployable, essential, a lot of machine. Now they were going to act—and to a martial tempo, to cornet and whistle. They began. In the face of all this, what would our patient say—our exposed, conspicuous cynic?

He remarked: "**The nasty's turning thingy . . .**" Cleverly comprehending our plans and becoming even more intractable, he adopted a defensive mimicry, as ingenious as he was alienated. Our solution seemed not to suit him: "**I'll be taken in by no wooden horses!**"—evincing a vigorous Trojan humor, suspicious of Pallas Athena. And: "**Do you want to eat me while I'm still green?!**"—which, being a mere mimetic and symptomatic phrase (protective coloration, so to speak), neither clashed with nor reinforced his preceding words.

The ladder aside, the stout-hearted firemen were men enough to take the royal palm by assault; or maybe even a single one of them, as expert in the technique as any Antillian or Kanaka. And after all, they had ropes, hooks, spikes, blocks, and pitons. There ensued an even greater expectancy than before; conversation was spasmodic. Silence set its seal on the crowd.

Not on our hero, though, who protested: "**Stop!**" He made a gesture of further protest. "**You won't get me off, you won't get me down alive!**" and he was in earnest, oracular; his speech was skillful. Since he demurred, we had to hesitate, too. "**If you come, I'll go, I'll . . . I'll vomit myself from here,**" he declaimed. He took a long time to say it, sounding very free, almost euphoric, as he skylarked about among the luxuriant palm leaves, almost losing his balance over and over again, oscillating by a thread. He added in a croak: "**A barking dog isn't dumb.**" And now, if the skin of his teeth wore a little too thin, he would change from a warning into a subject for pity and terror. He seemed to be clinging with his knees to some narrowest knife edge: his palm, his soul. Ah . . . and almost, almo-o-ost . . . a-a-almost, almost . . . It made the roots of my hair tingle. Nix. "**He's from a circus,**" someone—maybe Dr. Aeneas or Sandoval—whispered to me. That man could do anything, but we were not sure. Maybe it was a fake? Could he do the rope trick, escape from himself and from the devil? In his sly, harebrained obstinacy, he hung over a little farther, utterly pertinacious. We felt death's soft touch alongside us, stroking its stylographic drum. A panic terror gripped us; I froze. Now the crowd was fiercely in favor of the man: "**No! No!**"—the mob-cry—"**No! No! No!**"—a thundering tumult. The plaza clamored out its demand. There would have to be a delay. Otherwise, a reflex suicide would be produced—and then the whole problem would collapse. The Director quoted Empedocles. The terrestrial chiefs were agreed on one point: the urgency of doing nothing. The first attempt at a rescue operation was interrupted. The man had stopped swinging on the horn of the dilemma. He depended on himself, he, himself, he. Or on the deus ex machina, which, indeed, immediately appeared.

From one-two. The Finance Secretary's Chief of Staff came up with the Chief of Police. Someone handed him a pair of binoculars and he applied them to his eyes, scanning the royal palm in front of and above him and letting his gaze rest on the titular head; only to deny him, out of humane respect: "**I am not quite sure I recognize him. . . .**" Making the choice that seemed most fitting, he opted for a pale-faced solicitude. The air took on the air of an antechamber: everything became increasingly grave. Had the family been informed? No, and it was better not: families only cause trouble and vexation. But some vertical steps must be taken, and those were left to our mismanagement. The demented man must be parleyed with, there was no other way. Talk to gain time: that was it. But how could a dialogue mesh on two such different levels?

Would a scaffold be needed? No sooner was the thought voiced than a conical tube was produced—the fireman's megaphone. The Director was going to bend his reasoning power to the cause: to penetrate into the labyrinth of a mind, and, applying sledge-hammer blows of his intellect, bring the fellow thudding to the ground with the weight of his doctority. Curt, repeated siren blasts generated an equivocal silence. The Director, master of the dancing bears, grasped the big black trumpet and brought it to his mouth. He pointed it up like a circus megaphone and boomed into it: "**Your Excellency . . .**" he began, subtly and persuasively; badly. "**Excellency! . . .**" with an inappropriate subservience. His bald head shone with a gleam of metalloid, or metal; the Director was fat and short. The crowd jeered unreasonably: "**Aren't you ashamed, old man!**" and "**Leave him alone, leave him alone!**" In this way the opinions of laymen only hinder the strategy of experts.

Losing his tone of command, the Director, all ready to abdicate, spat and was rinsed in sweat as he took the instrument from his mouth. But he did not pass the megaphone to Professor D'Artagnan, of course. Nor to eager Sandoval, nor to Adalgiso's ready lips. Nor to Dr. Bilôlo, who wanted it, nor to Dr. Aeneas, who lacked his customary voice. To whom, then? To me, me, me, if you please; but only as a last resort. I trembled as I obeyed, gathering all my wits. The Director was already dictating to me:

"**My friend, we are going to do you a favor; we cordially wish to help you. . . .**" I brought forth through the conduit; the words produced an echo. "**A favor? From low to high?**" came the sonorous reply. Well, he was as sharp as a needle, wasn't he? We would have to question him. And, at a new command from the Director, my voice called out authoritatively: "**Psst! Hey! Listen! Look!**" "**Am I going bankrupt?**" came his high shout. He was letting me go on, but he was obviously bored. After all, I was speaking of duty and affection! "**Love is sheer stupefaction,**" he replied. (**Applause.**) He did, at times, deign to let out a cavernous "**Wah, wa-wah!**" with his hand over his mouth. And he cried tauntingly: "**Can** patience keep on sitting on its monument?" "Eh? Who? Eh?" shouted the Director impatiently, seizing the loudspeaker from my hands. "You, I, and those who are neutral," retorted the man; his imagination showed no signs of flagging at that incongruous elevation. Our inefficacious cawing, crowing, and cockadoodle-dooing, all our lovely verbiage, was only stirring up his gray matter to a demonic peak. We left off, for better or worse, from what was the equivalent of trying to stir up a porcupine with our fists. From a long way up came the porcupine's final, perfidious question: "Were those your last hypotheses?"

No. There still remained the unexpected, the triumph of ipso facto. What was coming? Who? The very man! The real Secretary of Finance, alive and in his right mind—ipso. He seemed to be emerging slowly out of the earth. Oppressed. Opaque. He embraced each of us, and we fawned on him gratefully, like the Prodigal Son's father or Ulysses' dog. He tried to speak, but his voice was inharmonic; he mentioned motives; did he fear a double? He was lifted onto the fire truck, then stood upright and turned completely around as though on a stage, displaying himself to the audience. His public owed him something. "My fellow citizens!" on the tips of his toes. "I am here, as you behold, me. I am not that man! I suspect the exploitation, the calumny, the fraudulent tricks, of my enemies and adversaries. . . ." He was obliged to stop because of hoarseness, which may have been a good thing or a bad. The other man, now ex-pseudo, deposed, listened idly. From the perch he had won, he nodded yes, yes, yes, without stopping.

It was midday in marble. Curiously enough no one seemed to be hungry or thirsty, there were so many other things to think about. Suddenly: "I have seen the Chimera!" yelled the man impolitely, inopportunely; his ire had been aroused. But who and what was he? Now he was no one, a nullity, nobody, nothing, no-man, nil. He had left elementary morality as a relative concept below him; that was all too clear. He was annoyed. And yet he was still pretending, in a jocose way, to be a castle in the air. Or was he enacting an epidermic epic? He showed us what lay between his shirt and his skin.

For suddenly, without waiting for the Secretary to finish his peroration, he began to undress. The fact is, he brought himself to light, drop by drop. There floated down on us, one after the other, his jacket, shorts, trousers—unfurled banners. Finally his shirt wafted down—airy, ballooning, billowing, white. What an uproar there was then—it was bedlam sure enough. In the crowd were women, old maids, young girls, cries, fainting fits, skelter-helter and mell pell. The disrespectful public had only to raise its eyes, and it did—to behold him in puris naturalibus like a white, peeled cassava root in the green tuft and front of the palm tree, a genuine naked man. Knowing he could be seen, he felt of his corporeal limbs. "The syndrome," observed Adalgiso; we were thrown into confusion again. "Bleuler's exophrenic syndrome . . ." noted Adalgiso, pontifically. The man was simplifying himself into a scandal and an emblem, a sort of magnificent Franciscan, by contrast with everyone else. But he lolled benignly, his good humor restored, in a truly primitive state.

In the melting heat the authorities sweltered and lost their tempers at all the high jinks. Could nothing be done about this disorderly, subversive, reprehensible citizen? They would have to go back to the beginning, they decided, after a confabulation: the horns of the problem would have to be confronted. The wheels began to turn, the brief, bellicose command was thundered out again, with fanfare: let the firemen perform their daring feat! Our little arena and atrium had widened, roped off by policemen; and journalists were already milling about, a handful of reporters, photographers, and cameramen.

But the man was alert and persisted in his lofty intentions, in the guise of great activity. I could tell he was counting on perpetrating another hoax. He grew cautious. He was counterattacking. He hurled himself upward to still more horrible heights as soon as the rescuing began: he would not be rescued against his will! Until—yes, until. Ascending from the mobile palm fronds to the supreme vertex, he was about to attain the sharp point of the trunk itself and was in great peril of plunging headlong. He would have to fall—the thing was as self-evident as a waterfall. "Now!" was our ejaculation; what we felt was the opposite of lethargy. We held our breath. In the midst of all those separate silences, were the brave firemen advancing? Slyly the man shook himself on the topmost tip, swinging like a comic misanthropoid in expert balance on his own extraordinary axis. He blurted out: "Is my nature incapable of the leap from anthropoid to hominoid?"

Just as certainly, we were enjoying ourselves too. As though he still found it necessary to evince optimism, the man displayed an unexpected verve. He seemed almost to strut like a dandy. The pause was more complicated now, and worse. His impending fall and death hovered toweringly over us. But even if he fell and died, no one would understand a thing about him. The firemen were halted in their tracks. They fell back. And the tall ladder drooped, disjointedly, and was put back in its box. The diligent authorities, defeated once more, began to distribute tasks. I realized what was missing. Just then a loud, lively band struck up a military march. From the top of the palm tree, one solitary creature gazed down at us.

"Possessed by the devil," said the Chaplain, smiling.

Possessed were the students, certainly, whose name was legion and who rushed up excitedly from the south side of the plaza where they had been concentrated. All hell's devils broke loose and pushed their way through the crowd in a torrent. They had got it into their heads that the man was one of their own; right or wrong, they vowed they would liberate him. It was no easy task to contain the ardent band. They brought with them, besides their invisible banner, a hereditary fervor. They were pigheaded, too. Would squadrons of rampant horsemen come into action against the noble young people? Would they attack? Well, later. The confusion was greater than ever. Everything tended to evolve with the dizzying speed of revelation. Eventually reinforcements were requested, with a view to clearing the plaza; and it was none too soon. Unnational anthems were being chanted, spreading to the multimob. And where was peace?

From ace to joker to king, the Secretary of Law and Justice watched the hubbub from atop the fire truck. Stentorian and bulky, he wasted no time making jokes: "Young men! I know you like to hear me. I'll promise anything . . ." and it was true. They applauded him for it rebukingly, trusting his past record. Then there was a remission, and some measure of calm. In the confusion of yeses and noes, the Finance Secretary, worn out with a variety of emotions, escaped and made his way to private life.

Nothing else happened. The man could be glimpsed as he settled down among the palm leaves as though they were a cradle. What if he went to sleep or loosened his grip, grew torpid, and finally fell and was smashed to smithereens? Professor D'Artagnan undertook to explain to his circumstanding audience how the fellow was able to remain firmly in place for such an unconscionable length of time. He was taking advantage of our patience—a hebephrenic catatonic—a stereotyped attitude. **"Among the Paressi or Nhambiquara Indians, he would soon be felled by arrows,"** concluded Dr. Bilôlo, satisfied to find that civilization nurtures human solidarity. For even the Director and Professor D'Artagnan, both sincere and rational by this time, were being pleasant to each other.

Now a new invention was born of old necessity. Three times mad as the man was, would he not listen to the appeal of some nearby, discreet argument, and condescend? To make sure he would not become skittish, they consulted him and he agreed to listen. And the deed was plotted and grew wings: the exploratory ladder, like a kangaroo or a huge red praying mantis, expanded into a contraption that reached more than halfway to the top of the tree. It was ascended by our daring, dauntless Director, newly naturalized a hero. Up I went after him, like Dante descending behind Virgil. The firemen helped us up. We addressed the man in the gallery, disoriented in space ourselves. Many yards above us still, he listened to us waste our Latin. Why, then, did he suddenly shout brusquely for "Help!"?

There was more hubbub and commotion—and the lower world exploded. In fury, tumult, and frenzy, the crowd grew ever more unreasonable and irrational, responding to a thousand influences, a prey to delusions and ready for the madhouse. I prayed as hard as I could that they would not overturn fire engine and ladder. And all because of the above-said so-and-so; it was as if he had poisoned the city reservoirs.

The strange and human reappeared. The man, I see that he is visible; I have to notice him. And suddenly a terrible thing happened. He tried to speak, but his voice broke and died away. His reason was in equilibrium again: that is, he was lucid, naked, and hanging. Worse than lucid: elucidated, with his head screwed on tight again. He was awake! His access of madness, then, had worn off by itself and he had awakened from delirium to find that he had been walking in his sleep. He was delivered from the promptings of influences and intuitions; had merely, with a sick consciousness, detumesced his mind, retreating to what was real and autonomous, to the bad stretch of space and time, to never-ending moderation. The poor man's heart almost jumped out of his breast. And he felt fear and horror, at finding himself so newly human. He no doubt experienced a retrogessive fright at what he had so lately been able to do, dangerously and at high cost, when he was out of step, his intelligence becalmed. And now he might precipitate himself, from one moment to none. I trembled in sympathy. Would he fall over the edge? We shivered. It was an impasse. The fact is, he was himself again; and he was thinking. And suffering— from shame and acrophobia. Infinitely far below him the base mob ululated, a mad, infernal sea.

How was he to get out of his predicament, now that he had turned the staid town inside out? I understood him. He had neither the face nor the clothes—this buffoon, runaway, wretch—with which to present himself for the final judgment.

He hesitated, galvanized. Would he choose not to be saved, then? In the drama on the catafalque, the hero's cup was turned down. A man is, above all, irreversible. He saw himself dotting the misty sphere in some other, immeasurable distance, in the form of millions and trillions of palm trees. Did he find himself being propelled into space, poor man, and attempting to cling, in vain, to Absolute Reason? The raving mob—exalted, maddened—had sensed as much and turned against the man who had somehow deprived us of some marvelous sequel. And so they howled. Fiercely, ferociously. He was sane. The maniacs wanted to lynch him.

That man inspired a pity that was outside the human province. The necessity to live was defeating him. Now, like an opossum feigning death, he sought our aid. He was easy prey for the firemen, who hastened to make him reappear in an act of prestidigitation. They lowered him with the help of planks, ropes, and other apocatastatic means. At least he was safe. Just like that. For now. But would the crowd destroy him?

Still not concluding. Perched on the ladder as it was still descending, he looked more closely at the deogenesic, Diogenistic mob. As he gazed at it, something unexpected took place in his head. He offered us another color. Had the people maddened him again? He merely proclaimed: "**Long live the struggle! Long live Freedom!**"—a naked, adamic psychiatrist. He received a frantic ovation; tens of thousands were overcome with emotion. He waved and reached the ground unscathed. Picking up his soul from between his feet, he became another man. He stood erect, definitive, and nude.

The upshot was magnificent. They lifted him to their shoulders and bore him away in splendor. He smiled, and doubtless proffered a remark or two, or none. No one could have stopped anyone else in that commotion of the people for the people. Everything fell apart as it happened, sprawling into triviality. The day had been lived out. Only the royal palm remained, unchanged, unreal.

Concluding. After it was all over, the glow extinguished, we exchanged our white coats for jackets. Drastic steps to be taken in the future were discussed, with variations, by the ex-professo Professor D'Artagnan and the Director and Dr. Aeneas, alienists. "**I see that I still haven't really seen what I saw,**" observed Sandoval, full of historical skepticism. "**Life is a continuous progression into the unknown,**" explained Dr. Bilôlo—serious, I think, for the first time. He donned his hat elegantly, since he could be sure of nothing. Life was of the moment.

Only Adalgiso said nothing. Now, for no apparent reason, he made us uneasy. Sober, correct, all too circumspect; and terribly, unsatisfactorily, not himself. In our shared dream, he had remained insoluble. I felt a reminiscent, animal chill. He did not say anything. Or maybe he did, in line with everything else, and that was all. And he went to town for a plate of shrimp.

SORÔCO, HIS MOTHER, HIS DAUGHTER

—◦⧚ ⧛◦—

The railroad car had been on the siding since the night before. It had come with the express train from Rio, and now it was there on the inside track near the station platform. It was new and shiny—showier than an ordinary first-class passenger car. When you looked at it you could see how different it was. It was divided into two parts, and in one of the sections the windows were barred like the windows in a jailhouse. It had come to take two women far away, for good, on the train from the outback which always went by at twelve forty-five.

A crowd had begun to gather around the car, just waiting. Not wanting to make a sad occasion of it, they talked among themselves, each one trying to speak more reasonably than the others in order to show his wider practical knowledge of the way things were. More and more people arrived. There was a continuous stirring toward the end of the platform, next to the corral where cattle were loaded onto the train; just this side of the woodpiles was the switchman's lookout house. Sorôco was going to bring both women; he had agreed it had to be done. Sorôco's mother was old, at least seventy. As for the daughter, she was the only child he had. Sorôco was a widower. As far as anyone knew he had no other kin at all.

It was the time of day when the sun is hottest, and the people tried to stay in the shade of the cedar trees. The railroad car looked like a big canoe, a ship on dry land. When you looked at it, the heat shimmer in the air made it seem out of kilter, turned up at each end. Its roof, like a potbelly turned upside down, glittered blackly. The contraption looked as if it had been invented on some other planet by someone without human feelings; you couldn't possibly have imagined it, and you couldn't get used to seeing it; and it didn't belong to the world you knew. It was going to take the women to a town called Barbacena, a long way off. Places are farther away to a poor man.

The stationmaster came up in his yellow uniform, carrying a black-covered book and some little green and red flags under his arm. "**Go see if they've put fresh water in the car**," he ordered. Then the brakeman began to move the coupling hoses. Someone called out: "**Here they come!**" and pointed to the lower street where Sorôco lived. He was a burly man with a thick body, a large face, and a stringy, stained yellow beard, who usually wore only sandals on his feet. Children were afraid of Sorôco, especially of his voice, which, when he spoke at all, was at first very rough and then faded out. Here they came, with a whole retinue.

They stopped and stood still. The girl—the daughter—had started to sing, lifting her arms high. The song straggled uncertainly; it was off-key and the words were nonsense. The girl raised her eyes to heaven like a saint or a woman possessed. She was decked out in tomfooleries, a wonder to behold, with a cap made of varicolored pieces of cloth and paper on her scattered hair. Her figure bulged with its wild mixture of clothing, ribbons dangling, sashes tied on, and all sorts of gewgaws: pure craziness. The old woman, in a plain black dress with a black fichu, shook her head gently back and forth. So different, the two women were alike.

Sorôco gave an arm to each of them, one on each side, as if they were going into church for a wedding. It was a sad mockery, though, more like a funeral. The crowd stayed a little apart, not wanting to look too closely at those wild ways and absurdities for fear of laughing, and also because of Sorôco; it would have seemed like a lack of consideration. Today, in his boots, his overcoat, his big hat—all his raggedy best which he had put on—he seemed diminished from his usual self, bewildered, almost humble. Everyone paid his respectful condolences, and Sorôco said: "**God repay you for your trouble.**"

What the people said to one another was that Sorôco had been wonderfully patient and certainly wouldn't miss the poor disturbed things; it would be a mercy to have them gone. There was no cure for what was wrong with them, and they weren't coming back, ever again. Sorôco had gone through so much and borne so many misfortunes; living with the two of them had been a struggle for him. And then they had gotten worse as the years went by; he had not been able to manage any longer and had had to ask for help. The authorities had come to his aid and made all the arrangements, free of charge. The government was paying for everything and had sent the special railroad car. That was how it happened that the two women were going to be put away in the madhouse. That was what was coming.

Suddenly the old woman let go of Sorôco's arm and went and sat down on the steps of the car. "**She's harmless, Mr. Stationmaster**"—Sorôco's voice was very soft—"**but she doesn't come when you call her.**" Then the girl started to sing again, turning first to the crowd, then to the sky, her face in ecstatic repose. It was not that she wanted to make a show of herself; she was acting out grand, impossible scenes of long ago. But the townspeople saw the old woman look at her with an ancient, charmed foreboding—an extremity of love. And, starting out softly, her voice growing stronger, she began to sing too, following the other woman in the same song that no one could understand. Now they were singing together, on and on.

It was about time for the train to come, and they had to make an end to the preliminaries and get the two women into the car with its windows crisscrossed with bars. It was done in a twinkling, with no farewells—which the two women would not have been able to understand anyway. Into the coach went the people who were going along to do for them on the long journey; the bustling, cheerful Nenêgo and Blessed José, who was a very reliable person. Those two could be trusted to keep an eye on the women, whatever happened. Some young lads climbed into the car, carrying the bundles and suitcases, and the meat—there were plenty of eatables, they wouldn't lack for a thing—and wrapped-up loaves of bread. Last of all, Nenêgo appeared on the platform, gesturing to show that everything was all right. The two women were not going to make any trouble.

Now all that could be heard was the women's lively singing, that shrill, distracted chanting which symbolized the great vicissitudes of this life, which can hurt you for any reason at all, anywhere, early or late.

Sorôco.

If only it would end. The train was coming. The engine maneuvered to pick up the car on the siding. The train blew its whistle and glided loudly away and left, exactly as it always did.

Sorôco did not wait for it to disappear. He never looked at it, but stood with his hat in his hand and his square beard, deaf—that was what seemed so pitiful; the plain open sadness of the man, who seemed unable to say even a few words. He was suffering the way of things, in a hole with no way to climb out of it, bearing the weight uncomplainingly, setting a good example. They told him: "**That's the way the world is.**" All of them stared respectfully, their eyes moist. Suddenly everyone loved Sorôco.

He shook himself awkwardly, with a now-it's-over-with sort of shrug, as if he were worn out, not important any longer, and then turned to go. He started off for home as though on a journey that was too long to be measured.

But then he stopped. He hesitated in a peculiar way, as if he were no longer sure of his old self and had lost his identity. It was as if he were pure spirit, beyond reason. And then something happened that could not have been foreseen; who would ever have thought of it? All at once he burst out singing, high and strong, but only for himself—and it was the same meaningless song the two women had sung, over and over. He sang on and on.

The crowd stiffened and was nonplussed—but only for a second. A whole crowd . . . and then, with no agreement beforehand, without anyone's realizing what he was doing, all, with one voice, in their pity for Sorôco, began to accompany that nonsense song. And how loud their voices were! They all followed Sorôco, singing, singing, with those farthest behind almost running to catch up, but every one of them singing. It was a thing none of us will ever forget. There was never anything like it.

Now we were really taking Sorôco home. We were going with him, as far as that song could go.

THE THIRD BANK OF THE RIVER

My father was a dutiful, orderly, straightforward man. And according to several reliable people of whom I inquired, he had had these qualities since adolescence or even childhood. By my own recollection, he was neither jollier nor more melancholy than the other men we knew. Maybe a little quieter. It was mother, not father, who ruled the house. She scolded us daily—my sister, my brother, and me. But it happened one day that father ordered a boat.

He was very serious about it. It was to be made specially for him, of mimosa wood. It was to be sturdy enough to last twenty or thirty years and just large enough for one person. Mother carried on plenty about it. Was her husband going to become a fisherman all of a sudden? Or a hunter? Father said nothing. Our house was less than a mile from the river, which around there was deep, quiet, and so wide you couldn't see across it.

I can never forget the day the rowboat was delivered. Father showed no joy or other emotion. He just put on his hat as he always did and said goodbye to us. He took along no food or bundle of any sort. We expected mother to rant and rave, but she didn't. She looked very pale and bit her lip, but all she said was:

"If you go away, stay away. Don't ever come back!"

Father made no reply. He looked gently at me and motioned me to walk along with him. I feared mother's wrath, yet I eagerly obeyed. We headed toward the river together. I felt bold and exhilarated, so much so that I said:

"Father, will you take me with you in your boat?"

He just looked at me, gave me his blessing, and, by a gesture, told me to go back. I made as if to do so but, when his back was turned, I ducked behind some bushes to watch him. Father got into the boat and rowed away. Its shadow slid across the water like a crocodile, long and quiet.

Father did not come back. Nor did he go anywhere, really. He just rowed and floated across and around, out there in the river. Everyone was appalled. What had never happened, what could not possibly happen, was happening. Our relatives, neighbors, and friends came over to discuss the phenomenon.

Mother was ashamed. She said little and conducted herself with great composure. As a consequence, almost everyone thought (though no one said it) that father had gone insane. A few, however, suggested that father might be fulfilling a promise he had made to God or to a saint, or that he might have some horrible disease, maybe leprosy, and that he left for the sake of the family, at the same time wishing to remain fairly near them.

Travelers along the river and people living near the bank on one side or the other reported that father never put foot on land, by day or night. He just moved about on the river, solitary, aimless, like a derelict. Mother and our relatives agreed that the food which he had doubtless hidden in the boat would soon give out and that then he would either leave the river and travel off somewhere (which would be at least a little more respectable) or he would repent and come home.

How far from the truth they were! Father had a secret source of provisions: me. Every day I stole food and brought it to him. The first night after he left, we all lit fires on the shore and prayed and called to him. I was deeply distressed and felt a need to do something more. The following day I went down to the river with a loaf of corn bread, a bunch of bananas, and some bricks of raw brown sugar. I waited impatiently a long, long hour. Then I saw the boat, far off, alone, gliding almost imperceptibly on the smoothness of the river. Father was sitting in the bottom of the boat. He saw me but he did not row toward me or make any gesture. I showed him the food and then I placed it in a hollow rock on the river bank; it was safe there from animals, rain, and dew. I did this day after day, on and on and on. Later I learned, to my surprise, that mother knew what I was doing and left food around where I could easily steal it. She had a lot of feelings she didn't show.

Mother sent for her brother to come and help on the farm and in business matters. She had the schoolteacher come and tutor us children at home because of the time we had lost. One day, at her request, the priest put on his vestments, went down to the shore, and tried to exorcise the devils that had got into my father. He shouted that father had a duty to cease his unholy obstinacy. Another day she arranged to have two soldiers come and try to frighten him. All to no avail. My father went by in the distance, sometimes so far away he could barely be seen. He never replied to anyone and no one ever got close to him. When some newspapermen came in a launch to take his picture, father headed his boat to the other side of the river and into the marshes, which he knew like the palm of his hand but in which other people quickly got lost. There in his private maze, which extended for miles, with heavy foliage overhead and rushes on all sides, he was safe.

We had to get accustomed to the idea of father's being out on the river. We had to but we couldn't, we never could. I think I was the only one who understood to some degree what our father wanted and what he did not want. The thing I could not understand at all was how he stood the hardship. Day and night, in sun and rain, in heat and in the terrible midyear cold spells, with his old hat on his head and very little other clothing, week after week, month after month, year after year, unheedful of the waste and emptiness in which his life was slipping by. He never set foot on earth or grass, on isle or mainland shore. No doubt he sometimes tied up the boat at a secret place, perhaps at the tip of some island, to get a little sleep. He never lit a fire or even struck a match and he had no flashlight. He took only a small part of the food that I left in the hollow rock—not enough, it seemed to me, for survival. What could his state of health have been? How about the continual drain on his energy, pulling and pushing the oars to control the boat? And how did he survive the annual floods, when the river rose and swept along with it all sorts of dangerous objects—branches of trees, dead bodies of animals—that might suddenly crash against his little boat?

He never talked to a living soul. And we never talked about him. We just thought. No, we could never put our father out of mind. If for a short time we seemed to, it was just a lull from which we would be sharply awakened by the realization of his frightening situation.

My sister got married, but mother didn't want a wedding party. It would have been a sad affair, for we thought of him every time we ate some especially tasty food. Just as we thought of him in our cozy beds on a cold, stormy night—out there, alone and unprotected, trying to bail out the boat with only his hands and a gourd. Now and then someone would say that I was getting to look more and more like my father. But I knew that by then his hair and beard must have been shaggy and his nails long. I pictured him thin and sickly, black with hair and sunburn, and almost naked despite the articles of clothing I occasionally left for him.

He didn't seem to care about us at all. But I felt affection and respect for him, and, whenever they praised me because I had done something good, I said:

"My father taught me to act that way."

It wasn't exactly accurate but it was a truthful sort of lie. As I said, father didn't seem to care about us. But then why did he stay around there? Why didn't he go up the river or down the river, beyond the possibility of seeing us or being seen by us? He alone knew the answer.

My sister had a baby boy. She insisted on showing father his grandson. One beautiful day we all went down to the river bank, my sister in her white wedding dress, and she lifted the baby high. Her husband held a parasol above them. We shouted to father and waited. He did not appear. My sister cried; we all cried in each other's arms.

My sister and her husband moved far away. My brother went to live in a city. Times changed, with their usual imperceptible rapidity. Mother finally moved too; she was old and went to live with her daughter. I remained behind, a leftover. I could never think of marrying. I just stayed there with the impedimenta of my life. Father, wandering alone and forlorn on the river, needed me. I knew he needed me, although he never even told me why he was doing it. When I put the question to people bluntly and insistently, all they told me was that they heard that father had explained it to the man who made the boat. But now this man was dead and nobody knew or remembered anything. There was just some foolish talk, when the rains were especially severe and persistent, that my father was wise like Noah and had the boat built in anticipation of a new flood; I dimly remember people saying this. In any case, I would not condemn my father for what he was doing. My hair was beginning to turn gray.

I have only sad things to say. What bad had I done, what was my great guilt? My father always away and his absence always with me. And the river, always the river, perpetually renewing itself. The river, always. I was beginning to suffer from old age, in which life is just a sort of lingering. I had attacks of illness and of anxiety. I had a nagging rheumatism. And he? Why, why was he doing it? He must have been suffering terribly. He was so old. One day, in his failing strength, he might let the boat capsize; or he might let the current carry it downstream, on and on, until it plunged over the waterfall to the boiling turmoil below. It pressed upon my heart. He was out there and I was forever robbed of my peace. I am guilty of I know not what, and my pain is an open wound inside me. Perhaps I would know—if things were different. I began to guess what was wrong.

Out with it! Had I gone **crazy**? No, in our house that word was never spoken, never through all the years. No one called anybody crazy, for nobody is crazy. Or maybe everybody. All I did was go there and wave a handkerchief. So he would be more likely to see me. I was in complete command of myself. I waited. Finally he appeared in the distance, there, then over there, a vague shape sitting in the back of the boat. I called to him several times. And I said what I was so eager to say, to state formally and under oath. I said it as loud as I could:

"Father, you have been out there long enough. You are old. . . . Come back, you don't have to do it any more. . . . Come back and I'll go instead. Right now, if you want. Any time. I'll get into the boat. I'll take your place."

And when I had said this my heart beat more firmly.

He heard me. He stood up. He maneuvered with his oars and headed the boat toward me. He had accepted my offer. And suddenly I trembled, down deep. For he had raised his arm and waved—the first time in so many, so many years. And I couldn't . . . In terror, my hair on end, I ran, I fled madly. For he seemed to come from another world. And I'm begging forgiveness, begging, begging.

I experienced the dreadful sense of cold that comes from deadly fear, and I became ill. Nobody ever saw or heard about him again. Am I a man, after such a failure? I am what never should have been. I am what must be silent. I know it is too late. I must stay in the deserts and unmarked plains of my life, and I fear I shall shorten it. But when death comes I want them to take me and put me in a little boat in this perpetual water between the long shores; and I, down the river, lost in the river, inside the river . . . the river . . .

TREETOPS

—◦≫ ≪◦—

The Inverse Separation

It was once upon another time. And again the Boy was on his way to the place where many thousands of men were building the great city. But this time he was traveling along with his uncle, and the departure was arduous. He had stumbled bewilderedly into the plane, a lump of something like weariness rolling around in his stomach; he only pretended to smile when he was spoken to. He knew that his mother was ill. That was why they were sending him away, surely for a long time, surely because they had to. That was why they had wanted him to bring his toys. His aunt had handed him his favorite, lucky toy: a little monkey doll with brown trousers and a red hat with a tall feather, whose face was on the table in his bedroom. If it could have moved and lived like a person, it would have been more mischievous and full of tricks than anybody. The Boy became more afraid the more kindly the grownups treated him. If his uncle jokingly urged him to peer out the window or choose some magazines to look at, he knew that Uncle was not entirely sincere. And other things frightened him, too. If he thought only of his mother, he would cry. Mother and sorrow would not fit in the space of the same instant; one was the other turned inside out—it was horrible, impossible. He could not understand it himself; it was all mixed up in his little head. It was like this: something bigger than everything else in the world might happen, was going to happen.

It was not even worth looking at the far-drifting, superimposed clouds that were moving in different directions. And didn't all of them, even the pilot, seem sad, only pretending to be normally cheerful? Uncle was wiping his glasses on his green necktie. Surely he would not have put on such a pretty tie if Mother was in danger. The boy conceived a feeling of remorse at having the little monkey doll in his pocket, so funny and always the same, just a toy, with the tall feather in its little red hat. Should he throw it away? No; the monkey in the brown trousers was his little companion, and after all, did not deserve to be treated so badly. He only took off the little hat with the plume and threw it away; now it was no more. And the boy was deep inside of himself, in some little corner of his being. He was a long way back. The poor little boy sitting down.

How he did want to sleep. People ought to be able to stop being awake whenever they needed to and drop safely and soundly off to sleep. But it wouldn't work. He had to open his eyes again even wider, to look at the clouds experimenting with ephemeral sculptures. Uncle glanced at his watch. And what would happen when they got there? Everything, all-the-time, was more or less the same, things and other things like them. But people were not. Doesn't life ever stop so that people can live on an even keel and have time to straighten themselves out? Even the little hatless monkey would know, in the same way as he did, the size of those trees in the forest, beside the land on which the house had been built. Poor little monkey, so small, so lonely, so motherless; he held it inside his pocket, and the monkey seemed to be thanking him and crying down there in the dark.

But Mother was only a momentary happiness. If he had known that she was going to get sick one day, he would always have stayed near her, looking at her hard, and really conscious that he was with her and looking at her with all his might. He would never even have played with anything else but would have stayed close to her side, without being separated from her for even the space of a breath, not wanting anything to change. Just as he was now, in the heart of his thoughts. He felt that he was with her even more closely than if they had been together.

The airplane unceasingly crossed the enormous brightness, flying its seemingly motionless flight. But certainly black fish were passing them in the air beyond those clouds, hump-backed and clawed. The Boy suffered, was suppressed. What if the plane were hanging in one place as it flew?—and it flew backward, farther and farther, and he was with his mother, in a way that he had never imagined he could be.

The Bird Appears

In the unchanged house, which was just as it had always been with the trees around and behind it, everyone began to treat him with exaggerated care. They said it was a shame there were no other children there. If there had been, he would have given them his toys; he did not ever want to play again. While you were playing and not paying attention, bad things were laying traps for you, getting ready to happen; they lay in wait for you behind the doors.

He felt no desire to go out in the **jeep** with Uncle, either, just to see dust, earth, people. When he did go, he held on tight with his eyes shut; Uncle told him he shouldn't clutch so hard but let his body relax, joggling to and fro with the jouncing of the **jeep**. If he got sick, very sick, where would he be: farther from his mother, or nearer to her? He bit on his heart. He would not even talk to the little monkey doll. That whole day was good for only one thing: to spread his tiredness more thinly.

Even when night fell he could not get to sleep. The air in that place was very cold, but thin. When he lay down the Boy felt frightened; his heart thudded. Mother, that is . . . And he couldn't sleep just then, because of her. The stillness, the darkness, the house, the night—all of it walked slowly toward the next day. Even if you wanted it to, nothing would stop or go back to what you already knew and loved. He was all alone in the room. But the little monkey doll's place was no longer on the bedtable: it was the comrade on the pillow, lying belly up with its legs stretched out. Uncle's bedroom next door was separated from his own by a thin wooden wall. Uncle was snoring. So was the little monkey, almost, like a very old little boy. What if they were all stealing something from the night?

And when day broke, in the no-longer-sleeping and not-yet-waking, the Boy received a flash of insight—a sweet, free breath. It was as if he were watching someone else remembering the verities; almost a kind of film of thoughts previously unknown to him, as if he were able to copy the ideas of great men in his own mind. Ideas that faded into shreds.

But within that radiance, soul and mind both knew that you can never wholly apprehend the events that are beautiful and good. Sometimes they happened so swiftly and unexpectedly that you weren't prepared for them. Or you had looked forward to them, and then they didn't taste so sweet after all, but were only a rude approximation. Or there were awful things along with them, on both sides of them, nothing clean and clear anywhere. Or something was missing which had happened on other occasions and would have made this second event perfect. Or else you knew, even as they happened, that they were on the way to ending, gnawed by the hours, falling to pieces. . . . The Boy could stay in bed no longer. Already up and dressed, he picked up the monkey and put it in his pocket. He was hungry.

The porch formed a passageway between the little house lot and the jungle surrounding it, and the wide outside—that dark country under quick forays of fog, ice-cold, pearled with dew: stretching out of sight, to the rim of the eastern sky, on the far edge of the horizon. The sun had still not appeared. But there was a brightness touching the treetops with gold. The tall trees beyond the clearing were even greener than the grass the dew had washed. It was almost day—and from it all came a perfume and the chirping of birds. Someone brought coffee from the kitchen.

And—"Psst!"—someone pointed. A toucan had flown to one of the trees on noiseless horizontal wingbeats. He was so near! The high blue, the fronds, the shining bands of yellow and the tender shades of red on the bird, when it alighted. Such a sight: so big, in such gala dress, its beak like a parasitic flower. It leaped from branch to branch, feasting from the laden tree. All the light belonged to the bird and was sprinkled with its colors as it sprang into the middle of the air, preposterously free, splendidly suspended. *Tuk-tuk* in the treetop, among the berries . . . Then it cleaned its beak on a branch. And the wide-eyed Boy, unable to clasp the foreshortened moment to himself, could only count one-two-three in silence. No one spoke. Not even Uncle. Uncle was enjoying it too; he wiped his glasses. The toucan paused, hearing other birds—its babies, perhaps—from the direction of the woods. Its great beak turned skyward, it let out one or two of those rusty-sounding toucan cries: "Creeh!" . . . and the boy was on the verge of tears. Just then the cocks crowed. The Boy remembered, remembering nothing. His eyelashes were wet.

And then the toucan flew in straight, slow flight—it flew away, **shoo, shoo!**— mirable, grandly dressed, all hovering color; dream stuff. But before his eyes were cool, someone was already pointing to the other side of the world. There the sun was about to come up, in the region of the morning star. At the edge of the fields that were like a dark, low wall, there broke through at one point a golden rhombus with jagged edges. There swung upward softly, in light, unhurried steps, the half-sun, the smooth disk, the sun, the light complete. Now it was a golden ball hung by a thread on azure. Uncle glanced at his watch. All that time the Boy had not made a sound. His gaze seized on every syllable of the horizon.

But he was unable to reconcile that dizzying moment with the present memory of his mother—cured, oh no, not sick any more, just as happy as she would have to be if she were there. Nor with the momentary idea of taking his little comrade, the monkey doll, out of his pocket so that it too could see the toucan: the little red god clapping its hands, its beak upright. It was as if it hung motionless during each separate moment of its flight, but in that infinitesimal, impossible point, not in air— now, eternally, and forever.

The Bird's Task

And so the Boy, in the dejected middle of the day, struggled with what he rejected in himself. He could not bear to see things in their raw state, as they really are, as they always tend to become: heavier, thingier—when you let yourself look at them without taking precautions. He was afraid to ask for news; did he fear for his mother, lost in the evil mirage of illness? However reluctant he might be to go on, he could not think backward. If he wanted to imagine his mother as being ill, unwell, he could not fit his thoughts together; everything was erased from his head. Mother was just Mother; that was all.

He waited, though, for perfect beauty. There was the toucan—flawless—in flight and rest and flight. Anew each morning, returning always to that high-crowned tree, of the kind that is, in fact, called "toucan tree." Taking its golden pause at daybreak. Each dawn, at the same time, the punctual, noisy toucan . . . **comincom-incoming** . . . in easy flight, as if at rest, drawn softly on the air, like a little red boat lazily shaking its sails as if it were being pulled along like a toy; as horizontally as a duckling gliding forward over the light of golden water.

After that enchantment, he had to begin the common body of the day. The day that belonged to other people, not to him. The jouncings of the **jeep** shaped the next happening. His mother had always warned him to be careful of his nice clothes, but this place defeated all his efforts. Even the little monkey doll, though it was always kept in his pocket, got sweaty and dusty. The thousand, thousand men labored mightily, building the great city.

But the toucan infallibly came just as dawn was being painted, and all knew him. The coming had begun more than a month before. First there had appeared a band of about thirty of the loud-voiced birds, but in midmorning, between ten and eleven o'clock. Only that one had stayed on to return at first daylight each morning. With his heavy eyes dizzy with sleep, the little monkey doll in his pocket, the Boy rose hastily and went down to the porch, eager to love.

His uncle talked to him with excessive amiability and painful awkwardness. They went out—to see what was going on. The dust clouded everything. Someday the monkey doll ought to have another little hat with a tall feather; but this time a green one, the color of that remarkable tie that his uncle was not wearing now because he was in his shirtsleeves. At every given moment it was as though a part of the boy were being pushed forward, against his will. The jeep ran over roads which went nowhere and were always in the process of being built. But the Boy, in the strong core of his heart, swore only that his mother had to get well, that she had to be saved!

He waited for the toucan to alight on the tree on time, on the dot of six twenty each morning; it always perched on the main mast of the toucan tree and pecked at the fruit for just those ten minutes, gnawed away and consumed. Then it flew off, always in that other-direction, just before the dropped half-instant in which the red sphere of the sun rolled up from the plain; the sun rose at six thirty. Uncle timed it by his watch.

The bird never came back during the day. Where did it live? Where did it come from—the shadows of the forest, the impenetrable depths? No one seemed to know its habits or what timetable it kept to go to those other places, over the isolated spots where it ate and drank. But the Boy thought that was as it should be—that no one ought to know. It came from a place that was different, only that. The day: the bird.

Meanwhile his uncle, after receiving a telegram, could not help showing an apprehensive face—hope grown old. But whatever it was, the Boy, not wanting to speak of it even to himself, made stubborn by love, must needs repeat over and over silently to himself that his mother was well again, that Mother was safe!

Suddenly he overheard their plan to console him. They intended to catch the toucan: with a trap, a stone thrown at its beak, a shot in the wing. No, no!—he was angry and distraught. What he loved and wanted could never be that toucan made a prisoner. It was the thin first light of morning, and, within it, that perfect flight.

The hiatus, which in his heart he could now understand, lasted until the next day, when, as it had been each other time, the bird in its radiance was a toy, freely given. Just like the sun; from that little dark point on the horizon, soon fractured with dazzling fire and turned into an eggshell—at the end of the flattened, obscure immensity of the plain, over which one's eyes advanced like an extended arm.

His uncle stood in front of him without saying a word. The Boy refused to understand that there was any danger. Within what he was, he said and repeated: his mother had never been sick, she had always been borne safe and sound! The bird's flight filled his whole being. The monkey doll had almost fallen and been lost: its little pointed face and half of its body were hanging out of the pocket when it was caught! The Boy had not given it a scolding. The return of the bird was a passion that had been sent to him, an impression of the senses, an overflowing of the heart, until the afternoon. The Boy thought of nothing but the toucan in happy flight, in the resounding air. It would console him and ease his sadness so that he could escape the weight of those checkered days.

On the fourth day a telegram came. Uncle smiled, *fortissimo*. His mother was well, she was cured! Next day—after the last toucan sun—they would go back home.

The Moment out of Time

Some time later, the Boy was peering out of the window of the plane at the white fraying clouds, the swift emptiness. At the same time, he felt as if he were being left behind to feel homesick, loyal to what was back there in the clearing. To the toucan and the dawn—but to everything else, too, which was a part of those worst days: the house, its people, the forest, the **jeep**, the dust, the breathless nights—all of that was purified, now, into the almost-blue of his imagining. Life itself never stopped. His uncle, wearing another tie, not as pretty a one, looked at his watch, impatient to arrive. The boy was thinking with half his mind, already almost at the borders of sleep. A sudden gravity made his little face seem longer.

He almost jumped out of his seat with anguish: the little monkey doll wasn't in his pocket! He had gone and lost his little monkey comrade! How could he have done it? Ready tears sprang to his eyes.

But then the pilot's helper came and brought something to comfort him: "**Looky here, see what I found for you**"—and it was the little red hat with the tall feather, no longer wrinkled, that he had so thoroughly thrown away on the first flight!

The Boy could no longer torment himself by crying. But being in the plane with all the noise made him dizzy. He picked up the lonely little hat, smoothed it with his fingers, and put it in his pocket. No, his little monkey companion was not lost in the bottomless darkness of the world, nor ever would be. Surely it was just off having a good time, peradventure, perchance, in the other-place, where people and things were forever coming and going. The boy smiled at what had made him smile, as he suddenly felt like doing: out beyond primordial chaos, like a discreated nebula.

And then came the never-to-be-forgotten stroke of ecstasy by which he was transported, at perfect peace, at oneness. It lasted the barest second, not even that, and crumbled to dust like straw, for evanescence is its very nature and no man can contain it: the whole picture escapes the boundaries of its frame. It was as though he were with Mother, healthy, safe, and smiling, along with the others, and the little monkey with a pretty green necktie—on the porch of the yard full of tall trees ... and the good old jouncy **jeep** . . . and every place . . . all at the same time . . . the first stroke of day . . . where time after time they watched the sun's rebirth and— still more vivid, full of sound and living—in unending suspension—the flight of the toucan, as he came to eat berries in the golden treetop, in the high valleys of the dawn, there close to the house. Only that. Only everything.

"**Well, we're here at last!**" Uncle said.

"**Oh, no. Not yet . . .**" replied the Boy.

He smiled a secret smile: smiles and enigmas, all his own. And life was coming toward him.

Those Lopes

A bad breed, who make for bad peace: I want to stay far miles from them. Even from my sons, three in number. A free woman, I don't feel old or worn-out. Quality comes with age. I love a man, and my good ways make him marvel, his mouth water. My desire now is to be happy, in my day-to-day, whether suffering or celebrating. I want to talk out loud. Let no Lopes come near, or I'll chase him off with bared teeth. What's behind me, all I went through, repeated itself until it was forgotten. At last I found the bottom of my heart. The greatest gift in the world is to be a virgin.

But first it's others who write our story.

As a little girl I saw myself dressed in flowers. But what stands out earliest is poverty. What good were a mom and dad to a monetary orphan? I became a young woman without abandoning innocence: I sang children's tunes crossed with romantic melodies. I wanted to be called Maria Miss, never caring for the name I was named: Flausina.

God gave me this black beauty mark on the whiteness of my chin—I looked pretty even when I saw my face in the trough, in the pigs' swill. And he passed by, Lopes, big hat, brim turned down. They're all good for nothing, but this one, Zé Lopes, was the worst, an arrogant seducer. He looked at me: standing there in my helpless trembling, nailed by his gaze.

He passed on horseback, in front of the house, and my dad and mom greeted him, sullen like they weren't with others. Those Lopes were a breed apart, from another riverbank. They bought or seized everything, and if it weren't for God they'd be here to this day, lording it over us. People should be meek, mild, like flower blossoms. Mom and Dad didn't lift a finger to defend me.

Little by little it comes back to me . . .

With barely enough time to weep, I wanted at least a trousseau, like other girls, the illusion of an engagement. What did I get? No courtship and no church. With his hot hands and short arms the man grabbed me and took me to a house, to his bed. But I learned to be shrewd. Muffled my tears. Endured that body.

I did what he wanted: I talked dirty. That's exactly what the devil makes some men want from us: invention. Those Lopes! With them if there's no hay, there's no milk. When he gave me money, I acted nice, I said, "I used to be a two-bit virgin. Now I've got three bits." He liked that. Didn't know I was watching and waiting.

He put a scrawny black woman in the house to keep an eye on me. Miz'Ana. Whom I learned to deceive, finagling accounts, and whom I called godmother and friend. I managed to make life smooth on the outside. It was lying on my back that I felt the world's sordidness, the devil's nightshirts.

No one has no idea what it's like: all night scrunched up on a cot, with the dull weight of the other hemming you in, his stink, his snoring, any one of those things amounting to cruel and unusual abuse. I, a delicate girl, made into a captive, with him always there, smothering me, in the dark. Ruination, the man hatching his hidden thoughts, like one day devouring another—how do I know what perversities he snored? All of this tarnishes a bride's whiteness, infects like a disease, pierces the spirit. As sure as I'm here today in a way I never was before. I got squeezed smaller, and on the wall my fingernail scratched prayers, my hankering after other horizons.

I traced the alphabet. Needed to learn how to read and write. In secret. I began from the beginning, aided by the newspapers used to wrap groceries, and by the kids who went to school.

And the money rolled in.

As far as I could, I managed all he had to my own profit. I saved up. Had titles and instruments put in my name. He, oblivious, was making me rich. And once I gave birth to his son, his trust in me was total, almost. He got rid of Miz' Ana when I trumped up false charges: that she'd goaded me to make carnalities with another man, a likewise Lopes—who soon vanished from life, in nobody-knows-how fashion.

Like they say: he who hears only half understands double.

I became a nest of vipers. In his liquor I put seeds, just a few, from the black calabash tree; in his coffee, liana bark and belladonna. Merely to cool down his rabid desire—I confess to no crime. Liana bark makes a man gentler, more refined. He was already looking yellowish, like an egg just laid by an ostrich. In short order he died. My life was quite lethal. After the funeral I swept the house and tossed out the dust.

And do you think those Lopes left me in peace?

Two of them, tough types, demanded my hand—the cousin and brother of the lately departed. I maneuvered in vain to keep the brutes at bay. One of them, Nicão, set a due date: "Wait for me at the end of the requiem Mass." Which would be in thirty days' time. But the other one, Sertório, lord and master, with gold and dagger in hand, didn't even wait seven days before barging into my house to claim me. I suffered with composure. How did I lead my life? Year after year of submissive subjection, as tiresome as catching rain in a gourd or chopping kale real fine.

Both men raging, oozing with jealousy. And for good reason—I set it up. Nicão kept circling the house. Were the two sons I bore really Sertório's? The sum total, whatever was supposed to be his, I charged, quickly adding it to my account—honor included. I acquired new graces and enjoyed them in the garden of myself, all alone. I assumed a more maidenly air.

Smiling I leaned out the window, lips puckered: negotiable, impartial. Until my idea hardened into action. I knew he was a Lopes: unruly, fiery, water boiling out of the pan. I saw him leave the house, steaming with steam, clothed in fury, his pockets full of slanders. I'd sent the other one messages, coated with sugar. Lately I'd laughed for a definite reason. Good guy against good guy, my lightning bolts faced off amid shots and flashing metal. Nicão died without delay. Sertório lasted a few days. I wept brokenhearted, according to custom, pitied by all: unfortunate woman, two and a half or three times a widow. On the edge of my yard.

But there was still one left. Sorocabano Lopes: the oldest one, loaded with land. He saw me and got me into his head. I accepted with good grace; he was itching for consolation. I stipulated: "From now on only if thoroughly married!" So great was his fervor he agreed—which, for a man of his declining years, was like buttoning a button in the wrong hole. And this Lopes I treated very well and much better, fulfilling his desire.

I wracked half my brain: I gave him rich, spicy meals and endless hours of pleasure—the guy was sapped dry from so much love and cuddles. All good things are bad and good for us. The one who died, at any rate, was him. And I inherited all he had, without the slightest qualm.

So finally in the end at last I'm avenged. That vile breed is finished. As for my sons, all of them equally Lopes, I gave them money so they could travel their cattle far away from here. I'm done quarreling: I've found love. Those who don't approve can't sway me. I love, truly. I'm old enough to be his mother? Save your breath. I'm no respecter of calendars and dates.

I don't intend to give him free rein over my body. But I'd like, for my own sake, to have some children of another stripe, civilized and modern. I want the good portion I never had, I want sensitive people. What use are money and understanding to me, if I can't settle with my memories? I, one day, was a very little girl . . . Everybody lives to serve some purpose. Enough of those Lopes!—they turn my stomach.

THE JAGUAR

—◦⊱ ⊰◦—

—Uhnn? Eh eh . . . Yep. Yessir. Uh huh, you wanna come in, come on . . . Uhnn, uhnn. D'you know I live here? How d'you know? Uhnn, uhnn . . . Eh. No siree, *n't, n't* . . . This the only horse you got? Phaw! That horse's lame, knackered. Ain't no good t'you. Huh . . . 's right. Uhnn, uhnn. D'you spot this little fire of mine, from way off? Yep. Right then. In you come, you can stop here.

Uh huh. This ain't my home . . . Yep. Wish it were. Reckon so. I ain't no farmer, I's a tenant . . . Eh, I ain't really a tenant either. Me—all over. I jus' here for now, when I want, I move on. Yep. Here's where I sleep. Uhnn. Ehn? That's up to you. No siree . . . You comin' or goin'?

Uh huh, bring it all inside, go on. Whoopah! You unharness the horse, and I'll help you. Shackle the horse, and I'll help . . . Bring saddlebag inside, bring sack, your blankets. Uhnn, uhnn! Go ahead. You're *sipriwara,* visitor come to see me; ain't that so, ehn? Fine. Real fine. You can sit down, you can lie down on that pallet. Pallet ain't mine. Me—hammock. I sleep in the hammock. That's black fella's pallet. Now I'm gonna squat down. That's all right too. I'll blow on the fire. Ehn? Is that mine, ehn? Yep, hammock's mine. Uhnn. Uhnn, uhnn. Yep. No siree. Uhnn, uhnn . . . So, why don't you wanna open the bag, poke around at what's inside? Huh! You dog-in-the-manger . . . Huh! . . . Is any of it mine? What's it got to do with me? I won't take your things, I ain't gonna steal 'em. Oh ho, oh ho, yessir, I'll have some of that. That, I do like. You can pour some in the gourd. I sure do like it . . .

Good. Real nice. Uh huh! This rum of yours is real good. I could drink it by the liter . . . Aaww, hum-and-haw: just bletherin'. I'm just bletherin' on, hummin'-and-hawin'. Feeling just fine. Hup! You're a fine man, so rich an' all. Ehn? No sir. I do appreciate a drop now and then. Hardly ever. But I know how to make it: I make it from cashew fruit, from berries, maize. But no, it ain't much good. It don't have this handsome fiery taste to it. It's a lot of bother. I don't have none of it today. None at all. You wouldn't like it. It's filthy stuff, poor man's rum . . .

Uh huh, black fella won't be coming back. Black fella died. How should I know? He died, somewhere abouts, died of some disease. Disease clean took him. It's true. I'm telling the truth . . . Uhnn . . . Your partner's gonna be a while, he'll only get here late tomorrow. Some more? Yessir, I'll have some. Hup! Good rum. You only bring that one flagon? Eh, eh. Your partner be up here tomorrow with the transport? That right? You got a fever? Partner sure to bring medicine . . . Uhnn uhnn. No sir. I drink tea made of herbs. Roots of plants. I know where to find 'em, my ma taught me, and now I know 'em all. I never get sick. Just the odd scratch or ulcer on my leg, ailments like that, the itch. Somethin' real lousy, I lie low, lone wolf, me.

Uhnn, no point in lookin' any more . . . Them beasts far away by now. Partner shouldn't have let 'em go. Lousy partner, *n't, n't!* No siree. They bolted off, and there's an end to it. This big, big country: out there it's the wide, open ranges, all wild bush, *tapuitama,* injun country . . . Tomorrow, your partner come back, bring some more. Uhnn, uhnn, horse out in the bush. I know how to find 'em, I listen to 'em galloping. I listen, with my ear to the ground. Horse galloping, pa-ta-pa . . . I know how to follow their trail. Phaw . . . I can't now, no point, too many trails around here. They've gone way off. Wildcat be eatin' 'em . . . You sad? Ain't my fault; no way it's my fault, is it? Don't be sad. You's rich, got plenty of horses. But those ones, wildcat's eaten 'em by now, huh! Any horse gets close to the forest, be eaten up . . . The monkeys, they've done their screeching—so wildcat must be catching 'em . . .

Eh, some more, yessir. I likes it. First-rate rum. You got baccy too? Yep, baccy for chewing, for smoking. You got more, got plenty? Ah ha. It's good snout. Real nice baccy, strong baccy. Yessir, for sure. You wanna give it me, I'll have it. Real fond of it. Real fine smokes. This chico-silva baccy? Everythin's real fine today, don't ya think?

You want somethin' to eat? There's meat, cassava. Oh, yeah, meat and cassava mush. Plenty of pepper. Salt, I don't have any. Run out. It's meat, smells real good, tasty. That's anteater I caught. You not eatin'? Anteater's good. There's flour, muscovado. You can eat it all up. Tomorrow I'll catch some more, kill a deer. No, I won't kill no deer tomorrow: no need. Wildcat's caught your horse by now, bled him from his jugular . . . Big critter's dead as a doornail, but she don't let him go, she's right a-top of him . . . She's split open the horse's head, torn out his throat . . . Split it open? Damn right! . . . She's sucked out all his blood, eaten a hunk of meat. Later, she'll have dragged that dead horse away, pulled him to the edge of the forest, dragged him in her mouth. Covered him over with leaves. Now she's sleepin', in the thick of the forest . . . Spotted jaguar starts by eatin' the rump, then the haunches. *Suassurana* deer-cat starts with the thigh, then the breast. With the tapir, they both of them start with the belly: got a thick skin . . . Would you believe it? But *suassurana* don't kill tapir, she ain't able. *Pinima,* mean and deadly, she's a killer; *pinima*'s my kinsfolk! . . .

Ehn? Early tomorrow morning she'll be back, eat a bit more. Then she'll go and drink some water. I'll get there, along with the vultures . . . Stinking critters, them vultures, a whole bunch of them live over in Coffer's Crag . . . I'll get there, cut off a piece of meat for myself. Now I know what's what: wildcat does some hunting for me, when she can. Wildcat's my kinsfolk. They're my kinsfolk, my kinsfolk, hee, hee, hee . . . I ain't laughing at you. I'm just hummin'-and-hawin' to myself, s'all. Horse's flesh won't be rotten tomorrow. Horse meat's real good, first-rate. I don't eat rotten meat, huh! Wildcat don't either. When it's the *suassurana* who's done the killin', I don't like it so much: she covers it all over with sand, gets it dirty with earth, too . . .

There ain't any coffee. Uhnn, black fella drank coffee, he liked it. I don't wanna live no more with any black fella, not ever . . . Big ape. Black fella stinks . . . But black fella he say I stink too: different kind of stink, strong. Ehn? No, the shack ain't mine; shack don't have no owner. Didn't belong to the black fella either. Palm thatch got all old and rotten, but rain don't get in, just a little drip. Aww, when I move out of here, I'm gonna set the shack alight; so's no-one can live here any more. Ain't no-one gonna live on top of my smell . . .

You can eat, that mush ain't made with anteater meat. Mush made with good meat, armadillo. I killed that armadillo myself. Didn't take it from any wildcat. They don't save small critters like that: they eat them all up, every bit. Plenty of pepper, huh . . . Ehn? Uh huh, yep, it's dark. Moon ain't come out yet. Moon's bidin' her time, but she'll soon be up. Uhnn, there ain't none. There's no lamp, no light. I'll blow on the fire. Won't do no harm, shack won't catch fire, I'm looking out, look-a-looking. A little fire under your hammock, that's real nice, lights the place up, warms it up a bit. There's some twigs here, brush, good firewood. I don't need it for myself, I can manage in the dark. I can see in the forests. Eh, there's somethin' glowing out there in the bush: take a look, it's not an eye—it's the moonshine drippin', a drop of water, sap oozin' from the tree, a stick-insect, a big spider . . . You scared? You can't be a wildcat, then . . . You can't have any understandin' of a wildcat. Can you? Speak up! I can stand the heat, I can take the cold. Black fella, he moaned when it was cold. Black fella a worker, he worked plenty, he liked it. Went and fetched the firewood, cooked the meals. Grew cassava. When there's no more cassava, I'm out of here. Eh, this rum's real fine!

Ehn, ehn? I've caught plenty of wildcat. I'm a big hunter of wildcat. I came here to hunt wildcat, and for no other reason. Mas'r Johnny Guede brought me here. He paid me. I got the hides, got some money for every wildcat I killed. Money good: clink-clink . . . I's the only one knew how to hunt wildcat. That's why Mas'r Johnny Guede told me to stay here, to rid these parts of wildcat. Jus' me, s'all, no-one else . . . Aahn . . . I used to sell the hides, earned more money that way. I'd buy lead and powder. I'd buy salt, fuses. Eh, I'd go a long way to buy all that stuff. Muscovado too. Me—I'll go a long way. I know how to walk plenty, a real long way, walk light on my feet, I know how to step so as you don't get tired, settin' one foot straight in front of the other, I walk the whole night through. There was one time I went all the way to Boi do Urucúia . . . Yep. On foot. I don't want no horse, don't like 'em. I had a horse, it died, ain't around no more, got jinxed. Disease killed it. Honest truth. I'm telling the truth . . . I don't want a dog either. Dog makes a noise, wildcat kills it. Wildcat likes killing everything . . .

Aaww! Huh! Get away! You ain't to say that I've killed wildcat, no you ain't. Me, I can. Don't you say that, oh no. I don't kill wildcat no more, I don't. It's a wicked thing I did, killing 'em. Wildcat my kinsfolk. I killed heaps of 'em. Can you count? Count four times ten, that's it: now that big pile you add four times. That many? For every one I killed, I put a little pebble in the calabash. No more pebbles gonna fit in that calabash. Now I'm gonna throw that calabash full of pebbles in the river. I wish I hadn't killed no wildcat. If you say I killed wildcat, I'll get mad. Say I didn't, didn't kill none, okay? You said it? A' right, uh huh. Good, nice, real nice. You my friend!

Yessir, far as I's concerned, I'll keep on drinking. Good rum, special. You drink, too: rum's yours; that old rum's a medicine . . . You lookin' at somethin'. Why don't you give me that watch? Oh, you can't, or won't, that's all right . . . Okay, forget it! I don't want no watch. Forget it. I thought you wanted to be my friend . . . Uhnn. Uhnn uhnn. Yep. Uhnn. Aagh phaw! I don't want no pocket knife. Don't want no money. Uhnn. I'm goin' outside. You think wildcat ain't gonna come prowling round the shack, won't eat up that lame horse of yours? Oh, she'll come all right. She reaches out her huge great hand. Grass stirs all in a round, aswayin', nice and slow, nice and gentle: that's her. She creeps along through the middle. Wildcat hand—wildcat foot—wildcat tail . . . Creeps up all quiet, wanting to eat. You ought to be scared! Are you? If she roars, eh, my little stray critter hidin' in the bush, you'll be scared all right. She growls—she roars enough to swell up her throat and reach to the bottom of the deepest hollow . . . *Urrurraaugh-rrurraaugh* . . . Sounds like thunder, even. Everything shakes. A huge great mouth, big enough for a whole lot to fit in that mouth, big two-mouths! Hup! You scared? Right, I know, you ain't scared. You's buddy-buddy, fine and fancy, real brave fella. All right, so now you can give me the pocket knife and the money, a little bit of money. I don't want the watch, that's okay, I was just kidding. What do I want a watch for? I don't need one . . .

Hey, I ain't mean either. You want a wildcat hide? Uh huh, see there, uh huh. Ain't it a fine skin? They all hides I caught myself, long time ago. I stopped selling these. Didn't want to. Those ones there? Big-headed *cangussou,* he-cat, I killed that one down by the Sorongo. Killed him, speared him with just one shot, so as not to spoil the hide. Hey, spirit-raiser! Damn bo-hunk bruiser of a he-cat. He bit the head of the spear, bit it so hard he left his teeth marks sunk into the metal. That beast, that cat spun himself into a ball, twistin' round, nice and easy, then quick as lightning, awful like an anaconda, doublin' up his body in a raging fury under my spear. He was writhin' about, the devil, flailing those legs around, and roaring, growling something terrible, would have dragged me into the bush too, where it was all thick and thorny . . . Nearly had me done for!

That one there, spotted too, but blotchy, *pinima* jaguar, big cat with a heck of a roar. I shot her dead, she was sitting up in a tree. Sittin' on one of the branches. There she was, no neck to her. Like she was asleep. What she was doing was watching me . . . Almost a look of scorn on her face. I didn't even wait for her to prick up her ears: there, take that, bang!—blasted her . . . With a shot in the mouth, so as not to spoil the hide. Uh huh, she tried to grab hold of the branch below with her claws—where she find the breath in her body for that? She was left hanging there stretched right out, then she came crashing straight down, broke two branches . . . Down onto the ground, with a bump, wow, yeah!

Ehn? Black cat? There's plenty *pishuna* cats round here, plenty. I used to kill them too, just the same. Uhn, uhn, black cat breeds with spotted cat. Along they come, swimming one behind the other, their heads showing, their backbones showing. I climbed up in a tree on the riverbank, shot 'em dead. The she-cat up ahead, *pinima* jaguar, she came first. Does wildcat swim? Eh, there's a critter can swim! Crosses the big river, straight as a die, comes ashore wherever she likes . . . *Suassurana* can swim too, but she don't like crossing no river. That pair of them I's telling you about, that was downstream, on another river, without a name, dirty river . . . She-cat was a *pishuna,* but she weren't black like charcoal's black: she was coffee-colored black. I stalked those two dead 'uns in the shallows: I didn't miss those hides . . . Right, but you don't tell nobody that I killed a wildcat, ehn? You listen up and don't say a word. You're not to. Huh? Serious? Aaww! Hey, sure I like the red stuff! You know I do . . .

Right, I'll have a drop. Ooff, I can drink so it makes me sweat, until my tongue's burnt to cinders . . . Holy injun firewater! I need the drink, so's I can get happy. I need it to loosen my tongue. If I don't drink much, then I don't talk, just get all tired . . . Forget it, you can leave tomorrow. I'll be left on my own, hmmm. What do I care? Eh, that's a good hide, came from the little wildcat, the one with the big head. You want that one? Take it. You'll leave the rest of the rum for me? You got a fever. You should lie down on the pallet, slip the cloak around you, cover yourself up with a hide, get some sleep. You wanna? Get your clothes off, put the watch in the armadillo shell, put the revolver in there too, no-one'll mess with them. I ain't gonna mess with your things. I'll get the fire built up, keep an eye out, tend the fire, you can sleep. Armadillo shell's only got this bit of soap inside. Ain't mine, it was that black fella's. I don't like soap. Don't you want to sleep? All right, all right, I didn't say anything, I didn't . . .

You wanna know about wildcat? Eh, yeah, they in such a rage when they die, sayin' things we folks don't . . . In just one day I caught three. Yeah, that one was a *suassurana*, foxy-red, big wildcat same color all over. She was sleeping by day, hid in the tall grass. Yeah, *suassurana*'s real hard to catch: she runs fast, climbs up into the trees. Wanders about some, but she lives in the bush out on the high plains. *Pinima* won't let *suassurana* live close to the swamps, *pinima* chases *suassurana* off . . . I've eaten her meat. Good, tastier, more tender. I cooked it with a mush of bitter okra. Plenty of salt, hot pepper. From the *pinima* I'd only eat their hearts, *mishiri,* I've eaten them toasted, roasted over the fire, all kinds of ways. And I'd rub the fat all over my body. So I'd never be afraid!

Sir? Yessir. Years and years. Got rid of them wildcat in three places. Thataways is the river Sucuriú, it flows into the Sorongo. There the bush is all virgin forest. But on this side it's the Ururáu river, then twenty leagues on it's the Monk's Mouth, you could have a ranch there now, cattle. I killed all the wildcat . . . Yeah, ain't no-one can live here, no-one but me. Eh, ehn? Uh huh . . . Ain't no houses. There's houses behind the palm trees, six leagues away, in the middle of the swamp. Mister Rauremiro, farming man, he used to live there. Farming man died, his wife too, his daughters, little boy. All died of some disease. Honest truth. I'm speaking the truth! . . . No-one comes this way, it's too hard. Way too far for anyone to come. Just because it's so far, a week's journey, rich hunters come out here, jaguar hunters, they come every year in the month of August, to hunt wildcat, too.

They bring big dogs with them, wildcat hunting dogs. Each of 'em got a fine rifle, a shotgun, I'd like one of them . . . Uhnn, uhnn, wildcat's no fool, they run away from the dogs, climb up into the trees. Dog barks his head off, sets off on the trail again . . . If wildcat can find a way, it'll get into the thick of the forest, yeah, there a man can have trouble seeing whether there's any wildcat about. All barking, and chasing—the dogs after her: then she goes wild, *mopoama,* crashing through the bush, flying about this way and that, killing dogs left, right and center, oh, she can move every which way. Uh huh . . . Lying in wait, that's when she's at her most dangerous: she's gotta kill or be killed once and for all . . . Yeah, she grunts like a pig, the dogs won't go anywhere near her. Not one of them. Just one lash of her paw, that's enough! A hook, a swipe . . . She spins round and jumps aside, you can't see where she's coming from . . . Whoosh. Even as she's dying, she can still kill a dog, a big 'un too. She roars and growls. Tears the dog's head off. You afraid?

I'll teach you, eh; you keep watching over there, where there's no wind blowing—
then you stay on your guard, 'cause that's where wildcat could leap out at you
from, all of a sudden . . . She'll jump sideways, and turn in mid-air. Jump crosswise.
You should learn how. She jumps, but don't. She pricks up her ears, a rattling, a
crackling, like hailstones. She cuts along. You ever seen a snake? Well, then, Hup!
screechowl screeching, deadly *jucca* tree knockin' . . . Time to time a little sound,
dry leaves stirring as she steps over the twigs, eh, eh—little bird flies away. Capybara squeals, you hear it in the distance: *aooh!*—and jumps in the water, wildcat's
close by now. When *pinima's* ready to jump up and eat you, her tail curls round
with the end up in the air, then she pulls herself together, nice and steady. Taut as
a bow: her head out in front, up in the air, and when she opens up her mouth, the
spots stretch out, her eyes get pushed apart, her whole face pinned back. Hey: her
mouth—hey: her whiskers twitching . . . Her tongue all folded back on itself out
one side . . . She parts her front legs, wrigglin' now all ready to jump: she hangs
back on her hind—eh, eh—on her hind legs . . . Wildcat that's cornered gets the
devil in her, sits there on the ground breaking up, smashing up sticks of wood. She
gets up, stands up. You go anywhere near her now, you be torn apart. Yeah, gettin'
hit by a wildcat's fist is worse than a clubbing . . . You see her shadow? Then you
already dead . . . Hee, hee, hee . . . Ha ha-ha-ha . . . Don't be scared, I'm here.

Right then, I'll keep on drinking, if it's all the same to you. Now I'm feeling
more cheerful! I'm not one to be a skinflint neither, food and liquor's for using up
right away, while you fancy it . . . Nothing like a full belly. Rum real good, I was
missing that. Yeah, firewood lousy, your eyes watering with all that smoke . . . Eh?
Yep, if you say so. Ain't sad to me. Ain't pretty, either. Right, it's just the way it
is, like any place. Good hunting, ponds to go swimming in. Ain't no place pretty
or ugly, ain't meant to be. Places are for living in, I was paid to come here and kill
wildcat. I don't any more, not ever. I kill capybara, otter, and sell the skins. Yessir,
I like people, I do. There's times I'll walk a long, long way to see someone. I'm a
runner, like a field deer . . .

There was a married woman, at the foot of the highlands, head of the stream
called Winding Path of the Shounshoun. Trail goes by there, trail to a ranch. Real
fine woman, she was called Maria Quirinéia. Her husband was crazy, old Siruvéio,
spent the whole time shackled up with a heavy chain. Husband just talked nonsense,
on nights when the moon weren't clear he'd shout gibberish, calling out, talking
injun . . . They didn't die. Didn't neither of 'em get ill and die. My oh my . . .

Lovely drop of rum! I like to swill it around first, before I swallow it. Uhnn,
uhnn. Uhhhh . . . Here, whatever comes along, it's just me and the wildcat. The rest
is food for us. Wildcat, they know a lot, too. There's things she sees, that we don't,
and can't. Oof! so many things . . . I don't like to know too much, my head starts
hurtin'. I just know what wildcat knows. But about that, I know everything. I learnt
it. When I first came here, I's left on my own. Bein' on your own, that's real bad,
nothin' but torment. Mas'r Johnny Guede a real bad man, brought us here and left
us all alone. Huh! Missed my ma, she died, *sassyara*. Aaahn . . . Jus' me . . . —all
alone . . . Didn't have no help or protection . . .

Then I started learning. I know how to do everything just like a wildcat. Wildcat's power is that she's not in a hurry: that's a creature lies down on the ground,

she'll use the sound bottom of some hole or other, she'll use the grass, look for their hiding-places behind every tree, slide along the ground, softly-softly, in and out, ever so quiet, shee-shoo, shee-shoo, until she gets right up to the prey she wants to catch. She stops, and stares and stares, ain't nothing going to make her get weary of staring, yeah, she's sizing up the jump. Eeyah, eeyah . . . She lunges once, sometimes twice. If she misses, then she goes hungry, but worse 'n that is that she nearly dies of the shame . . . So then, she's about to jump: she stares so hard, does it to scare you, she ain't going to take pity on nobody . . . A shudder goes right down her body, she shuffles her feet into position, coils herself up like a spring, and takes one mighty leap!—it's beautiful to watch . . .

Aw, when she's on top of the deer, poor critter, going for the kill, there's every curve rippling and bulging on her body, and she and her spots look shinier, her legs are helping too, eh, her plump legs bent double like a frog's, and her tail tucked under; anything that might come her way, she looks set to rip it apart, her neck stretched out . . . Hup! She just goes on killing, eating, on and on . . . Deer flesh makes a cracking sound. Wildcat roars out loud, like a fanfare, with her tail upright and mean, then, claws out, hey, strong claws, she roars once more, and that's enough. An orgy of eating and drinking. If it's a rabbit, some small critter like that, she'll eat it right down to the joints; swallow everything, gobble it all up, so she hardly leaves even the bones. The guts and innards, she don't like to eat . . .

Wildcat's a beautiful thing! You ever seen one? When there's a little stirrin' in the bamboo thicket, just a tremblin' for no reason: then that's one, eh, that could be one . . . Have you seen then how—how along she comes, with her belly full? Uh huh! How she walks with her head down, slowly saunterin' along: keeps her back straight as a rod, like a mountain ridge, raises one shoulder, then the other, each of her thighs, each of her haunches nice and rounded . . . The handsomest she-cat is Maria-Maria . . . Hey, you want to hear about her? No, I ain't gonna tell you. I won't, no way . . . You want to know an awful lot of things!

They left me here all alone, jus' me. Left me to work at killing, hunting cats. They shouldn't have. Mas'r Johnny Guede shouldn't have. Didn't they know I was their kinsfolk? Oh oh! Oh oh! I'm bringin' down evil and misfortune, 'cause I killed so many wildcat, why did I do that? I can cuss, I can. I can cuss! *Sheess, n't, n't!* . . . When I've got a full belly I don't like to see folks, don't like rememberin' anyone: I get mad. It's like I got to talk to the memory of 'em. I won't. I keep good and quiet. To begin with, I used to like folks. Now I jus' like wildcat. Love the smell of their breath . . . Maria-Maria—pretty she-cat, *cangussou*, fine-and-pretty.

She's young. Look, look—she's just eaten, she coughs, twitches her whiskers, eh, tough, white whiskers hanging down, tickling my face, lovely the way she tickles you. She goes off for a drink of water. Ain't nothing finer than Maria-Maria she-cat sprawled on the ground, drinking water. When I call, she comes. You wanna see? You shaking, I know you are. Don't be afraid, she's not coming, she'll only come if I call. If I don't call, she won't come. She's afraid of me too, just like you . . .

Hey, these wide open ranges, goin' on and on, that's my country, hey, this here—all mine. My ma would've liked it here . . . I want 'em all to be scared of me. Not you, you're my friend . . . I ain't got no other friend. Do I? Uhnn. Uhnn, uhnn . . . Ehn? Hereabouts there were just three men, plainsmen, once, on the edge of the highlands. They were escaped criminals, fujees, came to hide out up here. Ehn? What were they called? Why you need to know that? Were they relatives of yours? Huh! Plainsmen, one of them was called Gugué, he was a bit fat; another one was called Antunias—he had some money stashed away! The other one was old Rio-poro, angry man, cruel man: I didn't like him a bit . . .

What did they used to do? Uh huh . . . Fujees fish, hunt, grow cassava; sell hides, buy powder, lead, fuses, all that gear . . . Eh, they keep to the highlands, the plains. Land there's no good. Further away, over in Black Dog, there's plenty of fujees—you can go take a look. Those ones milk the mangaba trees. Poor folks! Don't even have clothes to wear anymore . . . Eh, some go about with nothing on at all. Aaww . . . Me, I got clothes, my rags, my pan.

'Ehn? The three plainsmen? No, they didn't know about hunting wildcat, they were too afraid. Couldn't hunt wildcat with a spear, like I do. We used to trade baccy for salt, we'd chat with them, lend them a bit of muscovado. They died, all three, died, every one of 'em—so much for them tough fellas. They got sick and died, yeah, yeah. Honest truth. I'm talking the truth, don't make me mad!

With my spear? No, I don't kill wildcat no more. Didn't I say? Ah, but I know how. If I want to, I can kill all right! How do I do it? I wait. Wildcat comes. Yeeeah! She comes pad-padding gently along, you won't make her out with those eyes of yours. Eh, she growls but don't jump. She just comes stretching one leg out after the other, crawling close to the ground. No, she never jumps. Eh—she comes right up to me, and I raise the spear to her. Whoah! I raise the blade of the spear to her, point the tip right where her chest is. You touch her with anything, she'll lie down on the ground. Keeps trying to swipe or grab out, trying to clutch everything in a hug. Sometimes she'll get up on her haunches. Wildcat, she'll pull the tip of the spear towards her. Eh, then I stick it in . . . Right away she gasps. Red blood pours out, or more like black . . . Chriisst, poor wildcat, poor devil, that spear-stick going right into her . . . Poor darlin' . . . Be stabbed to death? Uhnn, uhnn, God forbid . . . Feel the iron pushing into your living flesh . . . Huh! You afraid? 'Cause I ain't. I don't feel pain . . .

Ha, ha, don't you go thinking it's nice and easy, quiet and gentle, oh no. Eh, yeeah . . . Wildcat's choked up with rage. She slithers, and writhes, and struggles under that spear. Wildcats are wildcats—like snakes . . . She twists about all over the place, you think there's a whole bunch of 'em, that she's turned into lots more. Eh, she'll lash out with her tail, too. She coils up, rolls into a ball, somersaults, eh, bends herself double, twists backwards, backs away . . . You not used to it, you don't even see, you can't, she slips away from you . . . You can't imagine the strength of her! She opens her mouth right up, makes an awful hawking sound, she's hoarse, she's hoarse. It's crazy how quick she is. She'll drag you down. Ah, ah, ah . . . Then sometimes she'll run off, escape, disappear into the bamboo, the devil. On her last legs now, and still she keeps on and on killing . . . She can kill quicker than anything. That dog drops his guard, wildcat hand grabs him from behind, tears open his coat . . . Hup! Fine, handsome. I'm a wildcat . . . Me—wildcat!

You reckon I look like a wildcat? But there's times when I look more like one. You ain't seen. You got one of them things—a mirror, is it? I'd like to see my face . . . *Sheess, n'y, n't* . . . I got a strong stare. Yeah, you got to know how to look at wildcat, straight in the eyes, look at her with courage in your eyes: huh, she respects that. If you look at her with fear in your eyes, she knows, then you're dead for sure. Can't be afraid at all. Wildcat knows who you are, knows what you're feeling. I'll teach you, you can learn. Uhnn. She hears everything, sees every movement. No, wildcat don't go after the scent. She don't have a good sense of smell, she ain't a dog. She hunts with her ears. A cow breathes in its sleep, or snaps a blade of grass: wildcat knows about it half a league away . . . No sir. Wildcat don't lie in wait at the top of a tree. Only *suassurana* walks from tree, to tree, catching monkeys. *Suassurana* jumps straight up into the tree; spotted cat climbs up, just like a house cat. You ever seen it? Yeah, yeah, I climb up in the trees and lie in wait. Sure do. It's better keeping watch from up there. No-one can see I'm watching . . . Slide along the ground, to get close up to the prey, I learned that best of all with the wildcat. So darn slow, you don't even realize you're moving yourself . . . You got to learn all the movements your prey makes. I know how you move your hand, whether you looking up or down, I know how long it takes for you to decide to jump, if I need to. I know which leg you raise first . . .

You want to go outside? Go ahead. Watch how the moon's come up: in that full light, they'll be hunting, on a moonlit night. When there's no moon, they don't hunt; only in the evening, at dusk, and round about dawn . . . In the daytime they all stay sleeping, in the bamboo groves, close to the swamp, or in the deep dark of the forest, in the caroa thickets, right in the bush . . . No sir, round this time wildcat don't do any yowling. They'll be hunting without making a sound. A whole lot of days can go by without you hearing a single yowl . . . What just made that noise then was a crested seriema. Uhnn, uhnn. Come on in. Sit down on the pallet. You want to lie in the hammock? Hammock's mine, but I'll let you. I'll roast some cassava for you. All rightee. I'll have another little drop then. You let me, and I'll drink it right down to the dregs. *N't, m'p,* aah . . .

Where I learn all this? I learned it a long way from these parts, there's other men over there, almost as fearless as me. They taught me to use a spear. Valenteen Maria and Joss Maria—two brothers. A spear just like this one, with a handle a yard and a half long, nice cross-piece, and a fine aim. There was Mas'r Inácio too, old Johnny Inácio: he was a black man, but a real fine black man, straight as an injun arrow. Mas'r Inácio was a master spearsman, the man would go out unarmed except for a spear, a really old spear, and play with the wildcat. His brother, King Inácio, he's got a blunderbuss . . .

Ehn? Uh huh. That's 'cause wildcat didn't tell each other, didn't know I came so as to get rid of them all. They didn't doubt me for a second, they got my scent, knew I was one of their kinsfolk . . . Yeah, wildcat's *jaguareteh,* my uncle, they all are. They wouldn't run away from me, so I killed 'em . . . They only realized later, when it came to it, and then they went crazy . . . Yeah, I swear: I didn't kill any more after that! I don't. I can't, it's wrong. I got punished: hoodooed, jinxed . . . I hate to think about those killings I did . . . My kinsfolk, how could I?! Aw, aw, aw, my kinsfolk . . . I gotta cry, otherwise they'll get mad.

Yessir, I been caught by some of them. They've taken a bite out of me, look here. It weren't here in the open ranges. It happened down at the river over yonder, somewhere else. My other partners missed their aim, got scared. Yeah, broad-spotted *pinima* ran into the middle of us all, rolled over and over with us on the ground. She went crazy. Ripped off the front of one guy's chest, tore out his lung, we could see his heart in there, still in him, beatin' away in the middle of all that mess of blood. She stripped the skin clean off the face of another man—Antonyo Fonseca. She scratched this cross on my forehead, tore open my leg, the claw went in real deep, ripped it to shreds, *mussuruca,* left a festering wound. Claw's poisonous, ain't a clean sharp edge, that's why it hurts you bad, makes a nasty mess. Teeth too. Ghrahh! Bah, bah, yeah, a swipe from a wildcat can knock the spear out of the spearsman's hand . . . They stabbed her more'n thirty or forty times! Uhnn, if you'd been there, you'd be dead by now . . . She killed near on five men. Took all the flesh off the spearsman's arm, down to the bone, with the big nerve and the vein sticking out . . . I was hiding behind the palm tree, with my knife in my hand. *Pinima* saw me, hugged me between her front legs, I ended up underneath her, all tangled up together. Uhnn, it's hard to get a grip on her hide, it's slippery like soap, okra slime, she writhes around from left to right, just like a snake, yeah, a snake . . . She would have ripped me to shreds, but she was tired by now, she'd shed a lot of blood. I grabbed hold of the critter's mouth, so she couldn't bite any more. She scratched my chest, I've no nipple left on this side. She went at me with three hands! Tore open my arm, my back, she died clinging to me, from the stabbings I'd given her, lost all her blood . . . *Manyuassah,* mean devil of a wildcat! She'd drooled all over my head, my hair ended up reeking of that stink for days and days.

Uhn, uhn. Yessir. They know I'm one of their own. The first of them I saw and didn't kill was Maria-Maria. I went to sleep in the bush, right near here, next to a little fire I'd made. In the early hours I was asleep, and she came to me. Woke me up, she was smelling me. I saw those pretty eyes of hers, yellow eyes with little black speckles afloat in that glowing light . . . Then I pretended I was dead, that's all I could do. She sniffed me, sniff-sniffing, paw in the air, I thought she was trying to find my neck. An urukwera cried out, a toad croak-croaked, the creatures in the forest, and me just listening, listening on and on . . . I didn't budge. It was a soft, pleasing sort of place, lying there in the rosemary. The fire had gone out, but the embers were still giving out some heat. She came and rubbed herself up against me, staring at me. Her eyes were bunched up together, and they were flashing—glint, glint: the look in those eyes was keen, sharp, like it wanted to pierce right into you, swallow you right up: and never leave you be. For a long time she didn't do anything either. Then she laid her great big hand on top of my chest, real dainty. I thought— now I'm a dead man: 'cause she could see that's where my heart was. But she was only treading lightly, with one foot, and feeling, fishing about with the other, trying to wake me up. Yeah, yeah, now I began to get it . . . That was some wildcat, and I knew it was me she liked . . . I opened my eyes and looked straight at her. I said softly:—"Hey, Maria-Maria . . . You ought to be smarter, Maria-Maria . . ." Yeah, she growled like she was pleased, and rubbed herself up against me again, miaow, yowl. Yeah, she started talking to me, jagajawing, jagajawjaw . . . Her tail was stiff now, wagging, *sasseh-sassemo,* wildcat's tail hardly ever keeps still: huh, huh. Then off she went, and crouched down to watch me from a little further off. I didn't move but stayed where I was, lying on my back, and kept on talking to her and staring at her face to face all the while, giving her nothing but the best advice. When

I stopped talking, she'd let out a chirruping mew—jagajawjaw . . . She had a full belly, she was licking her paws, licking her throat. Speckles on her forehead, dew like beads of moonshine around her nostrils . . . Then she lay down leaning up against me, her tail giving me friendly slaps on the face . . . She fell asleep right by me. Her eyes turn to slits when she's sleeping. Sleeping, then sleeping some more, with her face in her hand, her snout and nose tucked into a hand . . . I could see her milk was drying up, I could see her shriveled up teats. Her cubs must have died, who knows what from. But now, she ain't going to have any cubs ever again, oh no!—no she ain't . . .

Ehn? Afterwards? Afterwards, why, she slept. Snored with her faced turned to one side, showing that awful set of teeth, and her ears pinned back. That was on account of a *suassurana* that was heading this way. A light-brown, corn-colored *suassurana*. *Suassurana* stopped short. She's the worst, an evil, bloodthirsty critter. I saw those great green eyes of hers, gleaming too, so round they looked like they were about to pop out. Uhnn, uhnn, Maria-Maria snored, *suassurana* went, went on its way.

Hey, *catou*, fine 'n' handsome, *poran-poranga,* ain't none finer! Maria-Maria sat up all of a sudden, and pricked her ears forward. Yeah, off she slowly went, goin' about her business, to look at her you'd think she's lumbering along, but if she wants to she'll move quickly, nimbly, just as she needs to. She sways so sweet, a lovely, lazy lilting, fur flowing, paws padding . . . She stands up full-length at the peroba tree, digs in her claws, and scratches all the way down, sharpening them to a point, clawing that big peroba tree. Then she goes off to the white boxwood tree. Leaves a mark there, you can see where she's been doing it.

I could have killed her then, if I'd wanted to. But I didn't. Why'd I want to kill Maria-Maria? Anyways, in those days I was sad, real sad, here on my own, jus' me, and even sadder and jinxed 'cause I'd killed some wildcat, bewitched I was. From that day on I didn't kill any more, just the last one I killed was that *suassurana* I went after. But *suassurana* ain't no kinsfolk of mine, my kinsfolk is the black and the spotted wildcat . . . I killed that one as the sun came up. *Suassurana* had just eaten a red brocket fawn. I killed it but out of anger, on account of that place where I was sleeping bein' where she came and left her dirt, that's what I found in amongst the bamboo, nothin' but her mess. Yeah, they cover it up with earth, but the he-cat covers it up less, he-cat's more dirty that way . . .

Uh huh. Maria-Maria sure is pretty, you should see her! Prettier than any woman. She smells of garlic-wood blossom after the rain. She ain't so big. She's a *cangussou*, big-headed jaguar, apart from her spots she's a pale, pale yellow. During the drought they turn even paler. Shiny skin that's soft, real soft. The spots, well none of them is a really black shade of black: more dark crimson, like a purplish red. Aren't any like that? There's all kinds. You ever compared her spots and her rings? You count, and you'll see: they vary so much, you won't find two just the same . . . Maria-Maria's got a whole bunch of little spots. A tiny, pretty face all made up, all freckled, just like that. A little spot in each corner of her mouth, and others behind her little ears . . . Inside her ears it's snowy white, like cotton-wool. Belly too. Belly and underneath her throat, and in between her legs. I'm allowed to tickle her there for hours on end, she's real fond of that . . . She licks my hand, licks it in a lovin' sort of way, the way they do to clean the muck off their cubs; otherwise, no-one could stand the rasping of that rough, scratchy tongue, it's got a worse rasp than a *sambaíba* leaf; but then, how is it she goes on licking, and don't scratch her little cub with her tongue?

Ehnn? Her, Maria-Maria, have a he-cat? No, she don't have a mate. Phaw! Bah! Get away! If any he-cat comes her way, I'll kill him, I will, I'll kill him, whether he's my kinsfolk or whoever!

All rightee, but now you need to sleep. Me too. Hey: real late. *Sejussou* is high in the sky, look at his little stars . . . I ain't gonna sleep, it's almost time for me to take a wander out there, every day I get up early, long before daybreak. You sleep. Why don't you lie down?—you just gonna stay awake asking me things, then I answer, then you ask me something else again? What's the point of that? That way, yeah, I'll finish up all your rum. Uhnn, uhnn, I won't get drunk. I only get drunk when I drink a lot, I mean a lot, of blood . . . You can sleep tight, I'll look after things, I can keep an eye on everything. I can see you're sleepy. Hey, if I want I can scratch two circles on the floor—to be your eyes—then I'll step on them, and you'll go right off to sleep . . . Eh, but you're brave enough, too, to look a man straight in the face. You got a good strong stare. You could even hunt wildcat . . . Stay calm now. You my friend.

Ehn? No sir, I don't know nothin' about that. All I know about is wildcat. Not cattle. Cattle is for eatin'. Cows, bulls, steers. My pa did. My pa weren't no injun breed, my pa was a white man, white like you, my pa Chico Pedro, *mimbawamanyanassara*, a cowhand he was, mean and tough. Died in Tungo-Tungo, in the Goiás ranges, Wild Falls ranch. Got killed. Don't know any more'n that. Everyone's pa. The man was stupid.

Sir? Uh huh, yessir. She might be hereabouts, might be prowling around the shack. They're all around, each wildcat lives on its own, near on the whole year. You don't get pairs living together the whole time, just a month, a short while. *Jaguatirica*, big bush cat, they's the only ones who live in pairs. Ouff, there's plenty of them, a whole bunch of 'em. Yeah, around these parts I don't do any more killing: this is *jaguaretama*, wildcat country, crawling with 'em . . . I know 'em all, nothing I don't know about 'em. No more of 'em can come this way—them that live around here won't allow it, otherwise they'll finish up all the game. These days I don't do any more killing, now they've all got names. Did I name 'em? Huh! No, I didn't, not just like that, I knew those were their names. Huh . . . How are you gonna know if they weren't? Why you asking? You gonna buy a wildcat? You gonna have a talk with one of 'em? Poor critter . . . Huh . . . I know, you want to know, just so you can be even more scared of 'em, don't ya?

Huh, a' right. Here: in a hollow over that side, real close to here, there's wildcat Mopoca, *cangussou* she-cat. She's just given birth, got a new cub, *jaguaraín*. Mopoca, good wildcat mother, she was always movin' about with her young, carrying cubs in her mouth. Now she's settled down in a good place, over there. Never goes far, don't get enough to eat. Hardly ever comes out. She just comes out to drink some water. Since she gave birth she's skinny, always thirsty, the whole time. Her cub, *jaguaraín,* wildcat pup, kitten, there's two of them, little furry mites, they're like stick insects, can't hardly move properly. Mopoca's got plenty of milk, cubs suckling the whole time . . .

Sir? Eh, any others? Here: further on, in the same direction, 'bout five leagues, you find the worst wildcat of them all, Maramonyangara, she's the boss, fights with the others, stares 'em out. On the other side, at the edge of the swamp, there's Sledgehammer, broad-spotted, huge, you just have to see her massive great hands, her claws, flattened out hands . . . Further on there's Tatacica, black as black can be, *pishuna* jaguar; she's got long legs, she's real wild. That one catches a lot of fish . . . Ehn, another black one? Uinyua, she lives in a real fine lair, a hollowed out hole in the gully, under the roots of a banyan tree . . . There's Slasher, a crafty old broad-spotted *pinima:* she goes off and hunts up to twenty leagues away, she goes all over. Slasher lives in a cave—wildcat's real fond of caves, likes 'em a lot . . . Mpu, and Missy, they were chased off, a long way from here, the others chased them off, 'cause the food was running out . . . Yeah, they move their homes about a lot on account of that . . . I ain't heard any more about 'em, they're not around here no more. The real wild *cangussou* is Tibitaba—wildcat with eyebrows: you watch her, she stays over there, lies at the top of the gully, right at the edge, her hands kind of dangling, just like that . . . There used to be others, gone now: Coema-Piranga, deep red, she died choking on a bone, darn critter . . . Jinxy, an old, old wildcat, with sticking out ribs, she was always going hungry, dogged by hunger, in the forest . . . Ehn? Uhnn, uhnn, no I ain't gonna say where Maria-Maria lives. How I supposed to know you don't want to kill her?! Of course I ain't . . .

Uh huh. What about the he-cats? Plenty, ooff, heaps of them. Just take a look at Man-eater: broad-spotted bruiser of a tom-cat, you be scared just by the size of him . . . All those fangs on top like butcher's knives, stained yellow, eh, smoker's teeth! There's one, Pushuera, he's old too: his big back molars, for cutting hunks of meat, they're worn out, ground down. Suú-Suú is a *pishuna* jaguar, real black, he's got one hell of a scary roar, you hear that and you'll be shaking, shaking, shaking . . . He likes Mopoca she-cat. Apiponga ain't a *pishuna,* he's the handsomest spotted he-cat, you won't see another like him, with his big nose. And he's always well fed, he's the best of 'em all at hunting. There's a *cangussou* he-cat, Petessara, who's a mite crazy, wrong in the head, it's him who just wanders about by day, he's the one I reckon looks like a twisty-mouth croaker fish . . . There's Uitawera for one, and Uatawera for another, they're brothers, yeah, but it's me who knows that, not them . . .

A' right, that'll do for now. I'll stop nattering. Otherwise, sun'll be up, you won't have slept, your partner be coming with the horses, you won't be able to travel, be sick, be tired. You sleep now. You want to? You want me to go, so's you can sleep here on your own? I can go. You don't? Well I ain't natterin' no more. I'll keep quiet, quiet. This place is mine. Uhnn. Uhnn uhnn. Why you ask questions, ask questions instead of going to sleep? I dunno. *Suassurana* don't have a name. *Suassurana* not my kinsfolk, she's a yellowbelly. It's only the black-backed one is fierce. *Suassurana* laughs with her cubs. Yeah, she's red, but her cubs are spotted . . . Uhnn, I'll stop chatterin' now, stop nattering, stop fanning the flames. Leave be! You goin' to sleep, or what? Uhnn. Yeah. Uhnn uhnn. No sir. Uhnn . . . Uhnn uhnn . . . Uhnn . . .

Ehn? Partner gonna bring another flagon? You'll give it to me? Uh huh . . . Huuuh . . . Hup! You want to hear some more? I'll tell you. You real fine guy, you my friend. When do they mate? Phaw, is that mating? Disgustin' . . . You come here at the end of the cold season, when the boxwood tree's in bloom, and you'll see. They get all moonstruck. They rage, and roar and roar, yowling and growling the whole time, they hardly hunt any more for food, they get skinny, go off out into the forest, off their heads, they piss everywhere, at night it stinks to high heaven . . . She-cat on heat yowls more, makes a different, funny sounding yowl. Along she comes with the fur on her back up on end, rubbing herself up against the trees, she lies down on the ground, with her belly in the air, *aruey!* All you hear is *arraugh-arraugh . . . arrarraaughhh . . .* You don't hang about: if you do, you be eaten up in no time, for sure . . .

He-cat follows her, for league after league. There two after her? Three? Hey, you don't want to see 'em fighting . . . Fur starts flyin'. Then, later, one's left on his own with the she-cat. That's when things really get goin'. They shoot off after each other. Start howlin', they take to howlin' and yowlin' over and over, the whole night long, they roll around on the ground and start fighting. Grass gets trampled, bamboo torn down, bushes flattened on the ground, they tear out clumps of plants and break up branches. He-cat gets demented, his body goes stiff, he opens his throat up wide, aaww, bares his fangs. Hey: tail like a rod, beatin' hard on the ground. You better run, get away. You hear me? Me—I'll be off on their trail. One huge paw print after the other, no claw marks . . . I'm off. One day I'll be gone for good.

Oh no, he- and she-cat don't go hunting together. Each one for himself. But they keep each other company the whole day long, lying down, sleeping. Heads resting against each other. One turned one way, the other the other way . . . Here: I'm gonna bring Maria-Maria wildcat here, I ain't lettin' any he-cat be with her. If I call her she'll come. You wanna see? You won't shoot at her with that revolver of yours, will you? Hey, maybe that revolver of yours is jinxed, huh? Let me take a look. If it's jinxed, I'll fix it . . . Oh, don't you want me to? Won't you let me touch your revolver? That's three times you've closed your eyes, you've yawned too, you've yawned. If I keep on with these stories, I guess you're gonna fall asleep, eh?

Yeah, when they're raisin' their young I'll find the lair. Den's well hidden, even harder to find in the forest, a hollow in a cave. In the thickest jungle. Mom-cat gets the devil in her. When I first started killin' wildcat, I'd wait for six months, so as the cubs wouldn't be left to starve. I'd kill the mother, let the cub grow. Ehn? No, I weren't sorry for them, it was just so I wouldn't waste any of my earnings, or the money for the hide . . . Yeah, I can yowl just like a cub, she-cat comes running, she's desperate. There was a she-cat with her whole litter, a *pishuna* jaguar, real big, real pretty, real ugly. I yowled and yowled, jagameeow, jagameeoweeow . . . She came running, crazy she was, scoldin' the cub under her breath, she didn't know which way to turn. I yowled here from inside the shack, *pishuna* mom-cat came right up, callin' to me to go back to the den. She opened up her fist to me . . . I wouldn't kill her, though, didn't want to lose the cubs, to waste 'em. I stopped yowling, and fired the gun off in the air. *Pishuna* ran off again swift as lightning, moved her home, took her young half a league away, got herself another lair, in the forest where the swamps are. Her cubs weren't *pishunas*, they were spotted wildcat cubs, *pinima* . . . She grabs hold of each cub tight by the scruff of the neck and carries them along, jumping over gullies and bushes . . . Hey, dumb critter! But you can't say she's dumb, eh. Just me.

Yessir. I'm drinking your rum right up. Yeah, nice fiery taste, warms your body up too. I'm feelin' happy, yes I am . . . Ehn? I dunno, I like going about with no clothes on, just an old pair of pants with a belt around my waist. This here skin of mine's tough as leather. Uh huh, but I got some clothes put away, good clothes, a shirt, a fine hat. One day I'll put 'em on, I want to go to a party, lots of parties. I won't wear no boots, though: don't like 'em! Don't like anything on my feet, phaw, won't fall into that trap. Hah. No partyin' around here. Ehn? Church, no, no way! I do want to go to heaven. No priests or missionaries, I ain't fond of them, don't want anything to do with 'em. I got a little locket to hang around my neck, I like saints. Have I got one? Saint Benedict keeps the snakes away . . . But snakebite can't hurt me—I've got some deer's horn, I put it on and it heals up. No departed souls, *tagoaíba,* spooks, out here on the ranges there ain't any, I ain't seen any. There's the devil, but I ain't seen him either. Uhnn uhnn . . .

Ehn? Me? It's you who's askin'. But I know why you're askin'. Uhnn. Uh huh, on account of my hair bein' this way, eyes real small . . . Yep. Not my pa. He was white, weren't no Indian fella. Ah right, my ma she was, she real good. Not Craoh Indian. Pewa, my ma, Tacunapewa heathen, long way's away. Not Craoh: Craoh real scared, they was nearly all scared of wildcat. My ma was called Mar'Yara Maria, she's a breed. Afterwards it was I lived with Craoh, lived with 'em. Ma good, pretty, she fed me, fed me real good, plenty, heaps . . . I've been around a lot, I've traveled. Craoh use pike, only a Craoh knows how to kill wildcat with a pike. Whuh?! Joerkim Pereira Shapudo, his other name was Kim Crenye, that one weren't afraid of anythin'. My friend! Bow, arrow, arrow go far. Ehn? Oh, I got a whole bunch of names. Name my ma gave me: Bacuriquirepa, Bacuri, injun mauler. Breoh, Beroh, too. My pa took me away to the missionary. Baptized me, baptized me. With name of Tonico; fine name, don't you think? Short for Antonyo de Yesus . . . Later they called me Macuncozo, that was the name of a farmstead that used to belong to some other fella, yeah—a farmstead they call Macuncozo . . . Now I don't have no name, don't need one. Mas'r Johnny Guede used to call me Tonyo Tiger-catcher. Mas'r Johnny Guede brought me here, jus' me, all on my own. He didn't oughta! Now I ain't got a name any more . . .

Naah, ehn, that's not a wildcat making that noise. It's a tapir, teaching its young to swim. Lots of tapir around here. Real good meat. On a warm day, tapir stays in the water to do his thinking, he knows all that's going on. Ehn? Ah, no, *pinima* wildcat eats tapir, eats 'em all. Tapir won't fight, tapir runs off. Once wildcat's jumped on her, she can't run with that wildcat on her back, no way she can, she ain't able. When *pinima* springs on a tapir, she kills it there and then. Jaguar bleeds that tapir. A clear night like this 'un, right for wildcat to go hunting!

No siree. That's the humming of other creatures, pauraque, potoo screeching.

What called out then was a hungry otter. It went:—*eeha!* Otter swims upstream. Yeah, she can come out of the water anywhere and her coat's gonna be dry . . . Capybara? You'll hear their racket from way off, grazing, half in, half out of the water . . . If a wildcat roars, I'll tell you which one it is. Eh, no, no need. If she growls or yowls, you'll know straight away . . . It's a strangled yowlin', from deep down in her throat, yeah, her throat's huge . . . Heeyah . . . Hup! You scared? Ain't scared? Well you gonna be. The whole forest is scared. Wildcat's a butcher. T'morrow you gonna see, I'll show you her trail, her tracks . . . One day, new moon, you come here, come and see my trail, like wildcat trail, yeah, I's a wildcat! Uhnn, don't you believe me?

Hey, crazy man . . . Hey, crazy man . . . Me—wildcat! Huh? I ain't the devil. It's you who's the devil, you twisty-mouth. You's lousy, lousy, ugly. Devil? Maybe I could be . . . I live in a shack with no walls . . . I swim, all the time, whole time. I've had the black pox. Joerkim Craoh had a cap with hawk feathers, macaw, scarlet ibis feathers too. Bands of ostrich feathers around his knee, his legs, his waist. But I'm a wildcat. Jaguar my uncle, my mother's brother, *tutira* . . . My kinsfolk! My kinsfolk! . . . Hey, gimme your hand . . . Gimme your hand, let me touch it . . . Just for a second . . .

Hey, you got the revolver in your hand? Uhnn uhnn. No need to keep hold of that revolver . . . You scared wildcat gonna come here to the shack? Uh huh, Uinyua wildcat's crossed the marshes, I know she has, come to, hunt for spotted cavy, she's slinking her way along in the thick grass. She creeps along with her belly to the ground, sprawled out, with her ears pricked forward—she clicks her ears like that, ever so slightly . . . Uinyua wildcat's black, devilish black, gleaming in the moon-light. She keeps flattened against the ground. Tips of the grass tickle her nose and she don't like that: she snorts. She eats fish, waterfowl, heron, coot. You can hear the *wey-wey* of the snipe flying off, snipe flies this way and that . . . Little bird shivers and takes off without a sound. Uinyua didn't take much notice. But the cavy got startled, took a leap. You hear the splashin'? Uinyua wildcat must be real mad. Soakin' wet from the dewy grass, spattered with the white the mud from the riverbank. Along she comes . . . she's the chief, the boss. Along she comes . . . In a boilin' rage! Your horse there making such a racket, all scared. Hey, no need for all that, Uinyua's stopped short. She comin'? No, she ain't, it was some frog or other croakin', *tataca* . . . Don't be afraid, if she comes I'll chase her off, shoo her away. I keep still, real still; she don't see me. Let the horse whinny, he must be shakin', his ears are pricked up. Those shackles okay? Strong fetters? He won't escape. Anyways, that horse of yours ain't no good any more. Wait . . . You point your revolver the other way, whuh!

She's not comin' now. Today Uinyua wasn't brave enough. S'all right, let it go: she won't starve to death, that's for sure—she'll catch an agouti or somethin', a mouse, any critter she finds around. That one'll even eat a porcupine . . . First thing in the morning, you're gonna see the trail. Wildcat gives off her smell and we'll find her, if we get there early. First thing tomorrow, we'll take a bath. You want to? Ehn? Their smell's stronger where they had their litter and lived with their cubs, it sure does stink. I like it . . . Now you can just calm yourself down, stay nice and quiet, put that revolver back in your pocket. Uinyua wildcat ain't coming now. She ain't even from over this way. If she crossed the marshes, it was only because Maramonyangara went over there, where her patch is, and then Uinyua got sore at her, and moved away . . . Everything's got its place: place for drinking water—Tibitaba goes to the pond where the buriti palm's bent over; Man-eater drinks in the same place as Suú-Suú, at the head of the Little Swamp . . . In the middle of the broad swamp there's a flat rock: Man-eater swims over there, steps onto the rock, it looks like he's standing up in the water, it's a damn ugly sight. He shakes one leg, then shakes the other, shakes his body dry. He stares around at everything, stares up at the moon . . . Man-eater likes livin' on islands, islands of forest, oh yeah. Ehn? They don't eat people? Huh! Wildcat stuck his hand through a hole in a hut, grabbed a little kid from his bunk, ripped open his little belly . . .

It wasn't here, it was over at the Chapada Nova farmsteads, eh. Old wildcat, huge great tiger of a wildcat, a *pinima* jaguar everyone knew about, the people there had called her Whirlfoot. Little kid's pa was a smallholder, he grabbed his rifle and went after the wildcat, *sacakwera, sacakwera*. Whirlfoot wildcat had killed the little kid, and killed a mule. Wildcat that gets up close to people's houses ain't afraid of being chased away, old wildcat, boss cat, eats people, dangerous critter, ain't so different from a man who's wicked. Farmer went after her trail, *sacakwera, sacakwera*. *Pinima* walks plenty, she walks a long way the whole night through. But Whirlfoot had eaten, she'd sure eaten some, she'd drunk the mule's blood, drunk some water, she left a trail, went to sleep deep in the forest, in a clearing, all sprawled out. I found the trail, but didn't say anythin', didn't tell anyone. Didn't that farmer say it was his wildcat? Farmer went to get the dogs, a dog let out a yelp, they found the wildcat. Cornered her. Farmer came up, all in a rage and hollerin', but his rifle wouldn't go off. Whirlfoot tore the farmer apart, split open his head, pushed his hair into his brains. They buried the farmer with his little son, or what was left of him, I went along to take a look. They gave me some food, rum, good food; I wept with them too.

Yeah, then they offered money for anyone who would kill Whirlfoot. I was willing. They talked about tracking her. Uhnn uhnn . . . How could they track her, find her by her trail? She was a long way off . . . How they gonna do that? Uhnn uhnn. But I know how. I didn't look for her. I lay down on the spot, smelled her smell. Then I turn into wildcat. I mean, I really turn into a wildcat, huh. I start yowling . . . Then I got it. I headed for Little Mill, on the shallows in the marshes. And that was the place: in the early hours of that morning, Whirlfoot had come and eaten up a sow that belonged to one Lima Torquato, a rancher at Saó. Rancher promised more money, too, for me to kill Whirlfoot. I said I was willin'. I asked him to loan me another sow, and tied it to a gum-tree. As night was coming on, Whirlfoot didn't have any notion about me, so she came lookin' for the other sow. But she didn't make it. She only got there early the next morning, when it was gettin' light. She growled, opened her mouth close to where I was, I let her have it right down her throat, and shouted:—"Eat this, old matey! . . ." Then I got my money from everyone, and got given plenty of food for days and days. They lent me a horse and saddle. Then Mas'r Johnny Guede sent me out here, to clear the place of wildcat. Dirty swine! Lousy no-good! Still, I came.

I shouldn't have? Uh huh, I know, I should never have come here in the first place. Wildcat is my people, my kinsfolk. They didn't know a thing. Yeah, I'm crafty, real crafty. I ain't afraid. They didn't know I was one of theirs who'd gone bad, who could betray them. All I was afraid of was coming face-to-face one day with a big wildcat that walks with his feet back to front, comin' out of the virgin forest . . . I wonder if it exists, I wonder. Uhnn uhnn. It's never appeared, I ain't afraid any more. Don't exist. There was a wildcat called One-Paw, who stuck her hand into someone's house too, just like Whirlfoot. The people inside the house got scared. She got her hand caught, they could have gone out and killed her from the outside. But they got scared, and just cut her hand off with a scythe. Wildcat roared, they hacked it off at the wrist. It was a black wildcat. Not one I knew. They hacked off her hand, and so she was able to get away. But she took to scarin' the wits out of those folks, eating people, eating livestock, leaving three-legged prints, limping about. And no one could guess where she was, so as to catch her. They offered plenty of money; but nothin'. I never knew her. And that was One-Paw. After that, she disappeared off somewhere on this earth. To haunt us.

'Hey, you hear that? That's wildcat yowlin'. You take a listen. He yowled from a long way off. That's Apiponga he-cat, he's just caught a big critter, a wild boar. He's fillin' his belly. He did his killin' at the edge of that island of forest, in the gully, that's where he did his butcherin'. I'm going over there tomorrow. Yeah. You don't know Apiponga: he's the one who roars loudest, and evilest. Yeah—he sure can jump . . . Every night he's hunting, killing. And when he kills, he does a beautiful job! He eats, and leaves; then, later, he comes back. During the day he sleeps, gettin' warm in the sun, stretched out. A mosquito comes along, ah, he gets annoyed. Go and see for yourself . . . The place Apiponga likes to sleep during the day is at a wellspring in the forest, where there's a mass of forest, and a big quarry. It's right there that he ate a man . . . Eeh, phaw! Once, one day, he ate a man . . .

'Ehn? You want to know where Maria-Maria sleeps during the day? What do you wanna know that for? What for? Her place is in amongst the rosemary in a clearing in the forest, real close to here, so there! Where did that get you? You don't know where it is, hee-hee-hee . . . If you come across Maria-Maria, it won't count for anythin' that she's the prettiest wildcat—she's gonna scare you to death. Hey: open your eyes: along she comes, here she comes, with her mouth half open, her tongue lollin' . . . Panting ever so slightly, when it's hot, her tongue lolling this way and that, but it never leaves the roof of her mouth. She pats the ground oh so gently, then stretches right out, and shuts her eyes. Yeah, she puts her hands out in front of her, opens her fingers right out—sticks out her claws, each one bigger than your little finger. Then she looks at me, she looks at me . . . She likes me. If I gave you to her to eat, she would . . .

You take a look out here. Moon's big and round. I'm saying nothin'. Moon ain't my pal. That's just bull. You not drinkin', I get embarrassed, drinking alone, I'm finishin' up all your rum. Is moon Craoh Indian's pal? Craoh only ever talked bull. *Awah?* Craoh by name of Curiwan, he wanted to marry white woman. Brought her things, gave 'em to her; pretty mat, bunch of bananas, tame toucan with a yellow beak, a turtle shell, a white pebble with a blue one inside. Woman had a husband already. Uh huh, but this was the thing: white woman liked things Craoh Curiwan brought her. But she didn't want to marry him, that would be a sin. Craoh Curiwan started smiling, said he was sick, if only white woman would lie in the hammock with him he'd get cured. No need to get properly married, just enough to lie in the hammock once. He put up his hammock nearby, lay down in it, didn't eat. Woman's husband came along, woman told him all about it. White man got mad as hell. Pointed a shotgun at his chest, Craoh Curiwan started crying, white man killed Craoh Curiwan, he was in some helluva temper . . .

Uhnn, uhnn. Hey: I was there, but I never killed anyone. Or at Tiger-Heron, I didn't kill anyone there, either. I've never killed, couldn't, my ma told me never to kill anyone. I used to be afraid of soldiers. I can't be locked up: my ma said I can't be locked up, if I am I'll die—on account of me being born in the cold season, just when *sejussou* was right bang in the middle of the sky. You look, *sejussou*'s got four little stars, plus two. Okay: can you spot the other one that's missing? You can't? That other one—that's me . . . My ma told me. My ma a breed, good, real good to me, same as wildcat with her cubs, her *jaguaraín*. You ever seen wildcat with her little cubs? You ain't? Mom-cat licks and licks, talks to 'em, jagajawjaw, strokes 'em, looks after 'em. Momma wildcat, she'll die for them, won't let anyone get near 'em . . . It's only *suassurana* that screws up, runs off, abandons her young to whoever wants 'em . . .

Eh, my kinsfolk is the wildcat, jaguar, my people. That's what my ma used to say, ma knew, *wey-wey* . . . Jaguar's my uncle, my uncle. Uh huh. Ehn? But didn't I kill wildcat? So I did, okay, I killed some. But not any more, I don't! At Tiger-Heron, that Pedro Pampolino wanted me to, he wanted to hire me: to kill the other man, to settle a score. I wouldn't. Not me. And get caught by a soldier? There was Tiaguin, he would: he got the money that was meant for me, went and waited for the other man by the side of the road . . . Ehn, what happened? I dunno, can't remember. I didn't help him out, did I? Didn't want anything to do with it . . . Tiaguin and Missiano killed plenty of people. Later he did it for an old man. Old man in a rage, swearin' he'd drink the other one's blood, a young man, that's what I heard. Tiaguin and Missiano tied up the younger man, and the old man slit his throat with a machete, caught the blood in a basin . . . Then I left the job I was doing, went away, ended up stoppin' in Chapada Nova . . .

That Mas'r Johnny Guede, had the fat young missy for a daughter, worst man around: he put me here. He said:—"Kill all the wildcat!" He left me here all by myself, jus' me, so alone all I could do was listen to my own voice . . . By myself the whole time, parakeet flies past squawkin', cricket chirpin' and chirpin' the whole night long, just won't stop chirpin'. Rains come, and it rains and rains. Ain't got no pa or ma. Just used to kill wildcat. Didn't oughta. Wildcat so pretty, my kinsfolk. That Pedro Pampolino said I's no good. Tiaguin said I's a loafer, a lazy deadbeat. Killed heaps a' wildcat. Mas'r Johnny Guede brought me up here, didn't no one wanna let me work 'longside others . . . On account of I's no good. Just stay here on my own, whole time. Just weren't no good, didn't know how to work right, didn't like it. Only knew 'bout killin' wildcat. Oh, they didn't oughta! Didn't no one wanna see me, didn't like me, everyone cussin' me. Maria-Maria came along, she did. So was I going to kill Maria-Maria? How could I do that? I couldn't kill any wildcat, wildcat my kinsfolk, I got sad at havin' killed . . . I was scared about havin' killed. No one at all? Aagh, aagh, gaahh . . .

At night I kept tossing and turning, I dunno, tossing and turning 'cause that's all I could do, I couldn't sleep; somethin' starting, and no end to it, I couldn't tell what was goin' on. I got to feeling . . . A crazy feeling like I wanted to turn into a wildcat, me, me a big wildcat. Go off out into the half light of the early morning, like a wildcat . . . I was roaring, quietly to myself, deep inside . . . I had those claws . . . There was an abandoned den, used to belong to a *pinima* jaguar I'd killed; I went over there. Still a strong smell of her about. I lay down on the ground . . . Yeah, I get cold, real cold. Cold comin' out from the bush all around, from the fields . . . I'm shiverin' all over. Nothing like that cold, never known anything like it. Made me tremble like I'd fall to bits . . . Then I got cramps all over my body, got the shakes; had a fit.

When I'd got over it, I found myself on all fours, itchin' to walk. What a relief that was! There I was, master of it all, happy I was alone, just fine, everyone dependin' on me . . . I weren't afraid of anything! Just then, I knew what everyone was thinking. If you'd come along then, I'd know everything you were thinking . . .

I knew what wildcat was thinking, too. You know what wildcat thinks? You don't? Eh, take a lesson from me then: only one thing wildcat thinks—that everything's just fine, real nice, fine, on and on like that, without stopping. That's all she thinks, the whole time, for long stretches, always the same thing, and she keeps thinkin' that as she's walking about, eating, sleeping, doing what she does . . . When something bad happens, then she whines, growls, goes into a rage, not that she's thinkin' anything: just that second she stops thinkin'. After that, it's only when everything's settled down again that she goes back to thinkin' the same as before . . .

Yeah, now you know, don't you? Uh huh. Ehn? Uhnn, well I walked out of there on all fours, off I went. Got so mad, felt like killin' everything, tearin' everything apart, tooth and nail . . . I roared. Eh, I—growled! Next day, white horse of mine, one I brought with me, that they gave me, horse was torn to shreds, half eaten up, dead, I woke up all caked in dried blood . . . Ehn? No harm, don't like horses, me . . . Horse was lame in the leg, no good any more . . .

Then I wanted to see Maria-Maria. Ehn? No, I don't like women . . . Sometimes I do . . . I walk the way those wildcat do, through the thorn bushes, real slow, nice and slow, I don't make a sound. But I don't get pricked, hardly ever. When you get a thorn in your foot, and it goes bad, you get sick for days, can't go hunting, you go hungry . . . Right, but Maria-Maria, when she gets that way, I take her food to eat, huh, uh huh . . .

Uhnn, uhnn. No, that noise wasn't a wildcat. Urukwera cried out, and some little critter skedaddled out of there. Eh, how'd I know?! Might be a deer, boar, capybara. What's that? You got everythin' here—there's patches of bush, trees sproutin' in the clearings . . . Otherwise that'll be frogs, wood crickets. Birds too, chirpin' in their sleep . . . Hey: if I fall asleep first, will you go to sleep too? You can rest your head on that knapsack, knapsack don't belong to no one, knapsack belonged to black fella. Nothing any good inside there, just some worthless old clothes. There was a picture of black fella's wife, black fella was married. Black fella died, I got the photo, turned it away so I couldn't see it, took it a long way off, hid it in hollow of a trunk. Long way away; I don't like having photos around me . . .

Eh, there was a roar then and you didn't hear it. A whisper of a roar . . . You scared? You ain't scared? That's right, you ain't scared, I can see that. Uhnn uhnn. Eh, if you're close up to 'em, you'll know what being scared means! When wildcat roars, a man gonna shake all over . . . Spearsman ain't scared, not ever. Eh, it's hard to find a spearsman, there ain't many of them. Spearsman—those people are gutsy . . . All the rest are scared. Especially black fella . . .

Yeah, wildcat likes black fella's flesh. When there's a black fella on a hunting party, wildcat follows along, keeping up without being seen, along secret paths, followin' behind, all the way, all the way, stalking him, keepin' her eye on him. Black fella was praying for his life, held on to the rest of us, shakin' all over. It wasn't the one who lived in the shack; that one who lived here: black fella by name of Tiodoro. It was another black fella, by name of Bijibo, we were following the banks of the Urucuya river, then Dead Creek after that . . . Old man had a beard, white beard, boots, boots made of boa snakeskin. Old man with the boots had a blunderbuss. He and his kids and the drunk carpenter were heading for the other side, for the Bonita Range, they were cuttin' across that way . . . Black fella Bijibo weren't a brave man: he had to travel on his own, he was on his way back somewhere—I dunno where—a long way off . . . Black fella was afraid, he knew there was wildcat waiting in ambush for him: wildcat creeping along, *sacakwera,* every night I knew she was prowling around, making *wawaka,* near the campfire . . .

Then I talked to the black fella, told him I'd go with him to the Formoso place. He didn't need any weapon, I had a pistol, a rifle, I had a knife, a machete, my spear. I was tellin' lies: as a matter of fact I was coming back here, I'd been to do some tough talking with Mas'r Johnny Guede, to tell him I wasn't going to kill any wildcat from now on, and that was my last word. I was coming back here, I only went so far out of my way on account of the black fella. But black Bijibo didn't know that, he came along with me . . .

Hey: as far as I was concerned there wasn't anything wrong with him, I hadn't taken against him, I liked black Bijibo, I felt sorry for him, sure I did, I wanted to help, 'cause he had plenty of good food and supplies, and I was sorry for him having to travel on his own like that . . . Black Bijibo was a good fella, scared to crazy though, he wouldn't leave me alone for a minute . . . We walked for three days. Black fella talked and talked. I liked him. Black Bijibo had flour, cheese, salt, molasses, beans, dried meat, a hook for catching fish, salt pork . . . Hallelujah!— black fella carried all that stuff on his back, I didn't help, don't like to, I dunno how he managed it . . . I did the hunting: I killed deer, guan, tinamou . . . Black fella would eat it all. Huh! Huh, the way he used to eat and eat, nothing else he wanted to do, I never saw anythin' like it . . . Black Bijibo did the cooking. He'd give me some of what he'd cooked, and I ate until my belly was stuffed. But black Bijibo didn't stop eating. He'd eat and talk about food, too, so I'd just watch him eat and then eat some more myself, until I felt bloated, and when I'd had enough I'd belch.

We'd made camp under the branch of a tree, and lit a fire. I watched black Bijibo eat, sittin' there with that crazy look like he was so happy to be eating, the whole day, the whole day, stuffing his face, filling his belly. It made me mad, real mad, mad as hell . . . Huaugh, huh! Black Bijibo happily eating away, eatin' all this good food, like he was famished, and along came poor, hungry wildcat, wanting to eat black Bijibo . . . I got madder and madder. Don't it make you mad? I didn't say nothin'. Uh huh. Right, I just said to black Bijibo that that was the most perilous place, all around there were spotted-wildcat dens. Aw, black fella stopped eating straight away, black fella had trouble gettin' to sleep.

Yeah, then I weren't mad any more, I fancied having some fun with the black fella. I crept out, real, real quiet, so slow no one could have been slower. I took the food, every little bit, I took it and hid it in the branch of a tree, a long way off. Eh, then I came back, covered over my tracks, eh, I was fit to laugh I was so pleased with myself . . . I walked a long way, in one direction and then the other, came back and climbed up onto a high branch and stayed hidden . . . That devil of a she-cat, she just didn't come! First thing the next morning, it was a joy to see, when black Bijibo woke up and didn't find me . . .

The whole day he spent crying, lookin' and lookin', and not believing his eyes. Yeah, he was goggle-eyed. Eventually he started walking around in circles, like he'd flipped. He even looked for me inside an anthill . . . But he was scared of shouting out and conjuring up the wildcat, so he just spoke my name real quiet . . . Black Bijibo was shaking, I was listening and I could hear his teeth chattering. He was shaking: quiverin' like a piece of meat roastin' on a spit . . . After that he went into a trance, lay down on the ground, face down, and put his hands over his ears. He covered up his face . . . I waited the whole day, up in that tree, I was hungry and thirsty too, but now I wanted, I dunno, I just wanted to see the jaguar eatin' the black fella . . .

Ehn? No, black fella hadn't done me no harm. Black Bijibo real fine fella, peace-loving man. I wasn't mad at him any more. Ehn? It wasn't right? How'd you know? You weren't there. Uh huh, black fella weren't my kinsfolk, he shouldn't have got it into his head to come with me. I took the black fella to the wildcat. Whuh? If black fella came with me it was 'cause he wanted to. I just was doing what I was accustomed to . . . Uhnn, why you feeling about for your revolver? Uhnn uhnn . . . Hah, good weapon, is it? Uh huh, good revolver. Whoah! You let me take a hold of it, so I can see it properly . . . Won't ya, won't ya let me, eh? Don't you like me touching it? Don't be afraid. My hand won't put a jinx on a gun. I don't let anyone touch my gun either, but it's women, women I don't allow; not even to take a look, they ought'n to. They'll put a jinx on it, a hoodoo . . . Uhnn, uhnn. Yep. Yep. Uhnn, uhnn. Whatever you say . . .

Uhnn. Uhnn. Yep. Nope. Eh, *n't, n't* . . . Huh . . . Yep. Nossir, I dunno. Uhnn uhnn. Nossir, I ain't sore, it's your revolver, you's the owner. I was jus' asking to take a look, good, fine weapon, revolver . . . But it won't get jinxed from me touching it, boy no!—I ain't no woman. Na, I ain't hoodoo, I's—lucky man. You won't let me, you don't believe me. I ain't telling no lie . . . A' right, I'll have another swig. You drink some too! No, I ain't sore at you. Hup, real fine rum . . .

Hey: you like hearing stories, a' right, I'll tell you some. After what happened to black Bijibo? Why, I came back. I got here, found another black fella, already living right here inside the shack. First I set to thinking: this must be the other fella's brother, come to take revenge, whuh, whuh . . . It weren't. Black fella by name of Tiodoro: Mas'r Johnny Guede fixed it for him to take over, and kill all the wildcat, on account of me not wanting to kill any more wildcat. He said the shack was his,

Mas'r Johnny Guede had said so, he'd given the shack to black Tiodoro, for keeps. But I could live with him, I'd have to fetch firewood, fetch the water. Me? Uhnn, me—no, no way.

I made myself a tepee out of buriti palm, near Maria-Maria's den. Ah ha, black Tiodoro bound to come hunting thereabouts . . . A' right, a' right. Black Tiodoro didn't hunt wildcat—he'd lied to Mas'r Johnny Guede. Black Tiodoro a fine fella, he was scared, I mean scared, scared to hell. He had four big dogs—barking dogs. Apiponga killed two of them, one disappeared into the bush, Maramonyangara ate up the other one. Heh, heh, heh . . . Dogs . . . He didn't catch no wildcat. Besides, black Tiodoro only lived in the shack one turn of the moon: then he died, and that was that.

Black Tiodoro wanted to see some other folks, and take a walk. He brought me some food, called on me to take a walk with him. Yeah, I know: he was scared of goin' about on his own around those parts. He'd get to the edge of the clearing, and then get all scared of the boa. Me, yeah, I got my good old club, bound with a strong length of vine: I'd slip the vine around my neck, and carry the club hanging there like that: I weren't scared of a thing. Then, black fella . . . We went a good number of leagues, right into the marshland, good land for farming. Mister Rau-remiro, he's honest farming folk, decent man, but he used to whistle at ya, like you was a dog. Am I a dog, eh? Mister Rauremiro used to say:—"You ain't coming into our room, stay out there, you's a breed . . ." Mister Rauremiro used to talk to black Tiodoro, chat to him. He'd feed me, but he wouldn't talk to me. I left there mad, real mad at them all: Mister Rauremiro, his wife, his daughters, his little boy . . .

I called black Tiodoro: after we'd eaten, we were gonna be on our way. Black Tiodoro just wanted to pass by the head of the stream at Winding Path—lie down on the rug with the crazy man's wife, real good woman: Maria Quirinéia. We went to the place. Then, why, they asked me to leave the house for a long while, to keep watch out there in the bush, keep watch on the path, huh, to see if anyone was coming. Plenty of men accustomed to going there. Plenty of men: fujees, plainsmen, those three who died. Close by I saw some tracks. Round tracks, pawprints be-longing to Sledgehammer, from her hunting. It was drizzling down, just a fine mist. I hid under a tree. Black Tiodoro weren't comin' out from inside, with that woman in there, Maria Quirinéia. The crazy fella, her husband, weren't even hollerin', he must have been sleeping all chained up . . .

Why, then I spotted a plainsman coming along, that Mister Rioporo, lousiest fella around, always in a rage. Mister Rioporo was wearing a big cape made of buriti palm, so as not to get his clothes wet, the water was dripping off him and his feet were sticking deep in the mud. I came out from under the tree and went over to meet him, so as to keep him back, stop him coming closer, like black Tiodoro had told me.

—"What you doing around here, you low-down cat-hunter?!" was what he said, what he shouted, shouted at me, real loud.

—"I'm watching the tail-end of this rain . . ."—I said.

—"Well, you can just go watch the tail-end of your ma, you waster!"—he shouted back, even louder, real loud, he did. He had quite a temper, that one.

So, shout, would he? Oh boy! My ma, was it? So, that was it. Oh boy! Right then. Right then. So I told him Sledgehammer wildcat was hiding there deep down in the hollow of the gully.

—"Show me, show me this instant . . ."—he said. And—"Huh, you ain't lying, are you? You lying devil, you'd lie for the hell of it!"

But he went over, stopped at the edge of the gully, right at the edge, leaned over, peering down. And I pushed him over! I pushed him ever so gently, just nudged him: Mister plainsman Rioporo went flyin' through the air . . . Hup! Ehn, what'ya say? Kill him, did I kill him? No I didn't, so there. He was still alive when he landed down there, when wildcat Sledgehammer started eatin' him up . . . Fine, handsome! Heh, *p's,* heh *poran* my beauty! Take a bite of that, uncle . . .

I didn't say nothin' to the black fella: hey . . . Woman named Maria Quirinéia gave me some coffee, told me I was a handsome Indian. Then we left. Black Tiodoro kept quiet, he was mad at me. 'Cause I knew how to hunt wildcat, and he didn't. I was smart as a fox, knew the place like the back of my hand, I knew where to find the creatures, the trees, the plants in the forest, every one of 'em, and he didn't. I had all those hides, and I wasn't gonna sell them, ever. He was staring at them, greedy like a dog, I reckon he wanted all those hides for himself, to sell 'em and make a stack of money . . . Oh, black Tiodoro told lies about me to the other plainsmen.

That fujee Gugué, a decent man, but I mean decent, he never cussed at me. I'd want to take a walk, but he didn't like to: he just lay there, in his hammock, in the grass, the whole day long, the whole day. He'd even ask me to fetch some water in the calabash, for him to drink. Didn't do nothin'. He'd sleep, smoke, stretch himself out on his back, and chatter away. Me too. That Gugué could sure talk the hind leg off a donkey! Eh, didn't do nothin' else, didn't go hunting, wouldn't do a little digging to pull up some cassava roots, wouldn't go walking. So I decided I wasn't going to keep lookout for him no more. Eh, no, I weren't mad, just sick of it. Know what I mean? You seen anything like it? Idle, bone idle, that fella, malingerin' just for the hell of it, phaw, that was some jinx! I stopped caring in the end . . . I didn't want to get mad at him, didn't want to do anything, I didn't, no I didn't. A decent man. I said I was leaving.

—"Don't go . . ."—he said.—"Let's talk . . ." But he just slept and slept the whole day long. Then all of a sudden, eh, I turned wildcat . . . Right. Couldn't take it no more. I got some vine, fixed me a good, strong cord. I tied that Gugué to his hammock. Tied him quick, by his arms, by his legs. When he was about to start hollerin', uhnn, paah! I didn't let him, huh: I got some leaves, and then some more, and stuffed them all down his throat. There weren't no one around. I picked up old Gugué, all rolled up in his hammock. Heavy he was, yeah, weighed a ton. I took him to Maneater. Man-eater, chief of the wildcat, a big tom, he ate up fujee Gugué . . . Man-eater, huge great bruiser of a wildcat, he snarls and snarls while he's eating, you'd take him for a young cub . . . Afterwards, I got to feeling sad and sorry for old Gugué, such a decent fella, poor devil . . .

Then, it being dark by that time, I went to have a talk with the other plainsman that was still left, by the name of Antunias, why, he was a fujee. That was some mean skinflint! He never gave anything away, nah, he kept it all for himself, he'd lend you a lead pellet but only if you paid him two in return. Phaw! Paah . . . I went over to him, he was eating, so he hid his food under the wicker basket, I saw him do it. Then I asked if I could sleep inside the shack.—"All right then. But go and fetch some twigs for the fire . . ."—he said, just to annoy me.—"Hey, it's after nightfall, it's dark, first thing in the morning I'll gather some real nice firewood . . ."—was what I said. But then he ordered me to fix an old sandal of his. Said that early next morning he was going over to Maria Quirineia's place, and I couldn't stay in the shack on my own, in case I meddled with his stuff. So then I said:—"I reckon wildcat's got Gugué . . ."

"Hey, Tunia!"—that was how Gugué used to talk to him. He stared at me, asked how come I reckoned so. I said I'd heard Gugué shouting and the roar of a wildcat filling her belly. You know what he said? You ever heard the like of this? Huh! He said that wildcat had got Gugué, so everything that belonged to Gugué was his now. And soon he was leaving for the other range of mountains, and did I want to go along, and carry all his gear, his hammock an' all.—"Sure do . . ."—said I.

Oh, but I ain't gonna tell what happened next, no I ain't, no I ain't, no way! Why you wanna know? You a policeman? . . . Okay, okay, I'll tell you, you my friend. I raised the tip of my spear to him . . . Let me show you how, won't you? Oh, won't you, can't I? You scared of me pressin' the tip of my spear against your chest, eh, is that it, ehn? So why you askin', then?! Huh, you a weak fella . . . You afraid the whole time . . . Right then, he was obliged to keep walking, crying all the way, *sacemo,* in the dark, falling down, getting up again . . . —"You're not to shout out, you're not to shout out . . ."—I told him, nagging at him, prodding and pushing him with the tip of my spear. I took him off to Maria-Maria . . .

Early next morning, I felt like some coffee. I thought to myself: I could call in on someone for breakfast, ask that woman Maria Quirinéia. I headed over there, keeping an eye out: Chriis'! On every side, on the slopes of the plain, there were wildcat tracks . . . Hey, wildcat o' mine . . . But they all gotta know who I am, yeah, I'm their kinsfolk—yeah, otherwise I'll set the fields alight, and the forest too, the caves in the bush, their lairs, I'll set it all alight, as soon as the drought's over . . .

That Maria Quirinéia, she's a real good woman. Gave me some coffee, some food. Her crazy husband, mister Suruvéio, he was quiet, it weren't his time to be moonstruck, he was just laughin' away, he was, but not shoutin'. Yeah, but Maria Quirinéia started lookin' at me peculiar like, in a different sort of way: her eyes a-sparklin', smiling, nostrils flaring, and she took hold of my hand, stroked my hair. Said I was handsome, real handsome. Me—I liked that. But then she tried to pull me down onto the rug with her, hey, whoa, whoa . . . I got so darn mad, real mad, mad as hell, I wanted to kill Maria Quirinéia, feed her to wildcat Tatacica, feed her to all the wildcat!

Yeah, then I got up, and I was going to grab Maria Quirinéia by the throat. But then she said something:—"Hey: your ma must have been real pretty, a mighty fine woman, I guess, am I right?" That Maria Quirinéia sure was a good woman, and pretty too, I was real fond of her, I remember that. I said everyone had got killed, eaten up by wildcat, and she oughta take herself off and move home, right that minute, just go, just go, right now . . . Anywhere else, but she should leave.

Maria Quirinéia got mighty scared, scared as hell, said she couldn't leave, on account of her crazy husband. I said I'd help take him along. Take him as far as the Conceição Marshes, there were folk there she knew. Yeah, I went along with them. That crazy husband of hers hardly gave me any trouble. I'd say:—"Shall we take a walk, Mas'r Suruvéio, sir, just a bit further?" He'd answer:—"A' right, let's go, let's go, let's go . . ." It was high tide on the marshes, rainy season, that was what gave us the bother. But we got there, and Maria Quirinéia said her farewells:— "You's a decent man, brave man, handsome man. But you ain't fond of women . . ." Then I said:—"Dead right I ain't. I—I got big claws . . ." She laughed and laughed and laughed, and I went back on my own, skirting round all them marshes.

Why then, why, after that I took a wide berth, found a way round the back of them swamps: I didn't want to see farming man Mister Rauremiro. I was hungry, but I wouldn't take any food from him—too high and mighty, that one. I ate some custard apple and sweet beans, and took a rest next to a thicket. After an hour it turned real cold, I mean real cold, set me walking in a different direction . . . Eh, after that, I dunno: I woke up—and I was in the farming man's house, it was just before daybreak. I was lying in a thick mess of blood, my nails all red with blood. Farming man had been bitten to death, farming man's wife, daughters, little boy . . . Hey, deadly *jucca* tree knockin', huh, hugggh! Then I felt sorry, started feelin' sore. Uhnn, ehn? You say I killed 'em? I bit 'em but I didn't kill 'em . . . I don't want to be locked up . . . I had their blood in my mouth, on my face. Uhnn, I went outside, wandered by myself through the forest, out of my mind, must be what comes from climbing all them trees, yeah, forest's a real big place . . . I walked and walked, couldn't tell you for how long. But when I'd come to again, I was all naked, starvin' hungry. Covered in all kind of filth, earth, with a bitter taste in my mouth, aagh, bitter like peroba bark . . . I was stretched out on that very spot, amongst the rosemary. Maria-Maria came right up to me . . .

You listenin', ehn? You getting my drift . . . Didn't I tell you, I's a wildcat! Hughh. Didn't I say—I'm turning wildcat? Great big chief wildcat. Look at my claws: you look—dirty great claws, black claws . . . Come 'ere, smell me: don't I stink of wildcat? Black Tiodoro said I do, eh, eh . . . Every day I wash my body in the pond . . . But why don't you go to sleep, uhnn, uhnn, don't keep waiting on your partner. You's sick, you should lie down on the pallet. Wildcat won't come around here, you can put your revolver away . . .

Huuuh! You ever killed anyone with it? So you did, did you? Why didn't you say so right away? Uh huh, you really did kill someone. How many d'you kill? You kill plenty? Uh huh, you's a brave man, my friend . . . Yeah, let's drink some rum, enough to make our tongues sting like we been eatin' sand . . . I'm picturing somethin' real fine, real nice: why don't we go and kill your partner tomorrow? We'll kill your partner, bad, no-good partner, he let horse run off into the forest . . . Let's do some killin'?! Aaww, aaww, back off, stay where you are! You're real sleepy . . . Hey: you ain't seen Maria-Maria, that's right, you ain't. You oughta. Before long she'll be here, if I want she'll come, come and gobble you up . . .

Ehn? Ah right, okay . . . All that time I was lying in the rosemary with her, you should have seen us. Maria-Maria makes all sorts of faces, paws the ground, jumps sideways, light on her feet, the way wildcat do, real pretty, real nice. Her backbone bristles, she puffs up her tail, opens and shuts her mouth, gentle, like someone who's sleepy . . . Like you, eh, eh . . . She walks along, swayin' slow and easy, she ain't scared of a thing, raising her haunches one after the other, with her shiny coat, along she comes, thoughtful like, the prettiest wildcat of them all, real solemn . . . She was growlin' softly at me, she wanted to come along with me and catch black Tiodoro. That's when I felt that cold, cold chill, cramps all over . . . Yeah, I'm skinny, I can slip through the smallest crack, but the black fella was pretty fat . . . Along I crept, on all fours . . . Black Tiodoro's eyes were scared crazy, phaw, they were looking huge . . . Started roarin'! . . .

You enjoy that, huh? Black fella weren't no good, eh, eh, eh . . . Hey: you're okay, though, you my friend . . . Here: let me take a proper look at you, let me grab a hold of you for a second, just for a second, lay my hand there . . .

Hey, hey, what you doin'?

Turn that revolver away! Stop foolin' around, point the revolver the other way . . . I ain't movin', I'm keepin' still, real still . . . Hey: you wanna kill me, whuh? Chuck the revolver over there, go on! You's sick, you's delirious . . . You come here to arrest me? Hey: no, I ain't puttin' my hands on the ground for any reason, no particular reason . . . So damn cold . . . You crazy?! Huggh! Get outah here, this shack's mine, gerraway! Back off! You kill me, your partner come and have you arrested . . . Wildcat's gonna come, Maria-Maria, she's gonna eat you . . . Wildcat my kinsfolk . . . Eh, on account of the black fella? I didn't kill no black fella, I was just foolin' . . . Here comes wildcat! Whoa, whoa, you's a decent fella, don't do that to me, don't kill me . . . Me—Macuncozo . . . Don't, no, don't. . . . Ehh ehh ehhn . . . Heeyah! . . .

Heh . . . Aargh-aagh . . . Aaah . . . You grrraaazed me . . . Remuassi . . . Re-yucaanasseh . . . Aaawwh . . . Uuhn . . . Whoah . . . Whoa . . . Uh . . . uh . . . eeehh . . . eeh . . . eh . . . eh . . .

OSMAN LINS
—◦❧(1924–1978)❧◦—

The fiction of the northeastern writer Osman Lins is highly crafted, making use of experimental devices and techniques from shifting narrative voice and point of view to the use of graphic signs to identify characters instead of names. His highly self-conscious novels and stories, full of critical reflection, present moral and philosophical dilemmas, foregrounding social and existential problems, often involving race or politics. Two of his major novels have been translated into English (*Avolavara*, 1980; *The Queen of the Prisons of Greece*, 1996), as has the book of short stories *Nine, Novena* (1995).

BAROQUE TALE OR TRIPARTITE UNITY
—◦❧ ❧◦—

Her dress is old and sumptuous, velvet with a golden design on a crimson background, little rural and domestic scenes, a joyous, bustling, glimmering universe, wrapped around the black undulations of her body. The monkey, bound by a thin rusty chain which she holds in her hands, watches me attentively from under her left armpit, its leathery hands resting on the dancers who play tambourines and flutes and kick their feet in the air around a tree, and on the hunter shooting his crossbow at a pelican in flight.

—Do you know this man?

—What happens if I say I don't?

—I heard that you lived with him for some time. You even had a child.

—He never wanted to see the kid, that bastard. Not even once.

Coils of hair, eyes like almonds, round cheeks, flaring nostrils, arched lips, breasts like spiral shells. Behind her, on the wall, cages with birds, all in profile and silent, canaries, parakeets, scarlet with iridescent wings, white with blue tails, black with violet hues, green with white markings under their eyes, silver beaks, jasper breasts.

—How can I recognize him? He and his cousin are so much alike. And both are named José.

—His cousin's name is José Pascásio. His is José Gervásio. But now he's using another name.

—Why didn't he want to see the kid? Why didn't he marry you?

—Because I'm black. Good enough to lie with, but not to stand next to at the altar.

—Do you care if he dies?

—For me it would be a relief. I'd like to see him in a hole in the ground.

—Then you'll tell me where he lives.

Sharp and cunning the expression on her face. A small scar, parting her chin in the middle. I put the small roll of bills on the table. The monkey rushes over, grabs it, tries to bite into the money.

—Count it.

—I know how much it is. I have a good eye. I can count money from afar.

—Asking for more won't do you any good.

—Do you know how many men I have to go to bed with in this rotten town to make half that?

The monkey looking at me over her left shoulder; over the right one; over the table. The white hairs around its head, its mummy paws, its shiny and malicious little eyes. Its voice like sharp little bites. It leaps onto one of the cages and all the birds flutter around, frightened.

—Why don't you move?

—I want to live near you-know-who.

—He lives in town, then.

—No, but he comes every week. The place where he lives is worse than this.

—Where is it?

—I'll give you the information you want only if you tell me why you want to murder him.

—You mean execute him. I don't know why. I'm obeying orders.

—Take your money. He's coming tomorrow. If I make up my mind, I'll show you the prey.

—◦❯ ❮◦—

I have conquered the steep hill of Congonhas, full of Christs and immobile apostles, of restless rams, of indifferent goats. I am standing in the church plaza, in the purple light of the setting sun, amidst the prophets and the few animals—the tame lion, the diminutive whale—staring at those heavy leaves of sandstone with Latin sentences, those hands, unarmed and powerful, those vacant eyes. The woman, now wearing a white dress, half hidden behind Nahum's cloak, is waiting for José Gervásio, who will arrive at the church shortly. Next to Baruch's sandals, my arms crossed, I observe the steep street from which my victim will come. I cannot hear a thing. In the silence, treason is brewing, a net woven by the black woman's hand. She will point him out to me: "This is the man." I will give her the reward, she will be able to move.

Or:

The funeral in the streets of Ouro Preto. Covered with purple ribbons, fluttering in the cold afternoon wind, the somber silverplated coffin, with its fuses, niellos, fretwork and hooks on the cobblestone street, amidst the closed doors, balconies, old roofs. Two long lines lead the procession, the men on the right (I among them), the women on the other side, some with lilies, others with roses, dahlias, immortelles. Further back, the lines are entirely made up of women. Ahead of the coffin, a brotherhood, I do not know which one: red surplices and tall candles; accompanying it, two pairs of children, with bouquets and wreaths: carnations, lilies, banderoles. A bald priest with a wrinkled face is praying, flanked by three young altar boys with scarlet tunicles and white lace chasubles; one of them is swinging the censer. Among the group closing behind the procession the black woman and I walk side by side, she in a cotton dress with green and blue waves overlapping. She forcefully takes the arm of a man, they look into each other's eyes. My hunt, my search of months, is finally over, I will be able to return to Pernambuco. I fix in my memory these features so long sought for, and which, as a result, had acquired the artificial life born of portraits. I would not have been able to discover them by myself. Bells are tolling. Great black peacocks fly over the funeral.

Or:

I am in Tiradentes, in the parish church, in the City Hall, on the street, at the fountain, a hat on my head. The church is full of ladders and scaffoldings, men are working to uncover the acanthus, the leaves, the foliage, palm leaf decorations and garlands hidden beneath the whitewash. Workmen talk, standing several feet from each other, about a priest who hated the town, so much that he threw salt on the images to ruin them. Out on the street, under the green cypresses, children are throwing stones at the birds. The clerks glide through the silent rooms of the City Hall, where pensive lions adorn the decrepit walls. Even the soldiers open and close the doors with circumspection, disappearing in the concave shadows, without arrogance. The chief of police looks at me and assents. Furtive old men in felt shoes skirt along the corridors. The mayor deposits the tax collection in the clay money box, a fierce and hairy fish with a coiling tail. With most of the houses closed up, almost all the dogs starved to death or left. You cannot hear any barking or roosters crowing. Standing erect at the windows, girls with wavy hair wait for the passage of death with somnambulant pupils. A man leans against the wall; indifferent to him, a gray bird describes a sinuous curve and enters a hole a foot and a half from his head, where it must have made its nest; the man ignores the bird as well. Sitting on a bench next to the fountain, the black woman tells me that every Thursday, with business as an excuse, José Gervásio comes to see a woman at four, then goes back home on the eight o'clock train. But at times, when he can't come, he sends José Pascásio with some money. I ask her if lovers come to sit on these benches around the gargoyle on full moon nights. She answers that Tiradentes is a town where not even lovers exist. She seizes my arm and looks over my shoulder: "Here he comes. Don't forget his face." I pass her the money, caress the revolver in my pocket.

—◦❧ ❦◦—

She is lying on the bed naked, with her knees drawn up and her legs spread apart, her left arm resting next to her hip, her right hand on the curved railing of the bed. The chintz bedspread with poppies, interlaced palm leaves and great magnolias hides her sex and covers her up to the right shoulder. With her round belly button and sloping shoulders, she reminds me of an angel raising a chalice I saw somewhere. On the dresser, in a lamp with a shade the color of mud held firmly in the claws of a small dragon, the light tarnishes her body with verdigris. Next to the lamp, a bluish plastic fruit dish imitating glass, with bananas, oranges and two lemons almost white, translucent as eggs. Above the dresser, several butterflies with spread wings and colored beetles, pinned and framed. The house is big, walls with decals of garlands, dentils, pale violets and faded rose apples, tile floor, little furniture. Smell of mildew. The black woman keeps talking about José Gervásio, savoring every word. Mice scurry in the dark, cockroaches flutter around. The light projects on the worm-eaten ceiling a muddy star, full of holes. The house is so empty, the town so quiet, that it sounds as if there were another woman talking in another room, with the same voice, dark and crossed by flying roaches, skeletal mice. She says what she is planning to do with the money she received for her information: buy perfumes, a gold wedding ring, a collection of butterflies, sunglasses, an anklet, a silver knife, printed velvet clothes. "Nothing for the kid?" "No." "Why?" "Because." "Where is he?" "You don't know me, and yet you ask about the kid. His father never did. He didn't even want to see him. He showed up when my belly was out to there, spoiling for a fight, he wanted me to leave. He was getting married, didn't want me around. I hit him on the head with a stool, opened a slit bigger than my own. I left my mark." "He was right about not wanting to see his son." Without hearing me (did I really say that aloud?) she goes on. Or rather: she goes back to the beginning, the middle, to the tortuous turns of her story, cursing men, a man, this Gervásio who is at the same time himself and me, and others, talks about her son and men in a cavernous voice. Her sex, covered with green hair thick and shiny like steel, is exposed now. With my forefinger, I slowly draw a spiral on her belly: "I, too, have a son I'm never going to see." "What if you knew he was dying?" "Even so, I wouldn't." "You're just like him, then. He didn't come, when the boy died." Naked, sitting on the bed, she shows me the picture of the dead child and his clothes, diapers, wool shirts, booties, toys, ribbons, some faded roses. "When did he die?" "Last week, in this bed. Tomorrow I'm going to buy some hydrangeas, some lilies-of-the-valley, to take to the cemetery. That's another reason I don't want to leave this town." "So you had been here for some time, when you had the child." "I wanted to get even with his father. And now I have, I pointed him out with this hand. Why are you looking at me like that? Do you think I did wrong?" "I don't judge anyone. That's not my job. I simply bought something I was interested in, something you had to sell." "You can't be what you say you are. Tell me if I was wrong." She has put the dead child's mementos back in the big dresser drawer. She is standing next to the bed, greenish in the light carefully held by the small dragon.

Then:

Reaching for my shirt, I begin to get dressed. The sheet of glass between us shatters into fragments we cannot see; this lukewarm, rusty, smooth and excitable sketch becomes threatening, vomits all over me her flagellated intimacy, demands that I judge her. And I will not even be able to lie with her again on this bed reeking of lavender and putrescent roses.

—Why are you leaving?

—Because now you exist. Unfortunately.

—What did I do wrong?

—You began to be. I can't explain. But a whore, a victim, can't exist. If they do, they open a wound in the executioner. Do you understand?

—You can leave if you want. But don't give me that stuff.

—I'm leaving because I can't find any peace here any more.

Or:

Faced with my silence, she can only think of one response: open again the drawer where she thinks she has preserved a past reduced to dust and throw it at me, try to infect me with her disease, drag me into that business between her life and a dead child, annihilate me. Threatened by the invasion of these vestiges, which the woman intuitively knows capable of worming their way into a stranger with the same voracity and the same power of multiplication of roaches and mice, I turned the lamp off, and finding the supple resistance of her body in the darkness I let myself fall with her on the bed, where the child had died and where his clothes, wilted roses and useless toys were scattered. In the darkness, the presence of these things—all without master, without use—was prevailing, trying to gnaw at me as if I could see them. The black woman, sinking her nails in my back and moaning as if that pressure hurt her, was still asking if she was wrong, if she had done wrong in betraying that man whose negligence perhaps had caused the death of the bastard on whose remains we were wrestling. I was describing my own act between my clenched teeth, my eyes closed in the darkness, struggling to destroy the words uttered and their corrupting meaning at the same time.

Or:

I place the tip of my tongue between my teeth, look into her eyes with such intensity that I pass through them and cease to see them. I know she is intent on luring me into the trap with which human beings, like spiders, capture those outside the web. Butterflies, faded rose apples, poppies, magnolias, violets and garlands close in around me. The woman is trying to suck me into her guilt and nostalgia, her rotting love, maybe. I hear her calling me a murderer. She is wrong, though. I am, at most, an executioner, in any case nothing more than an exemplary employee. In order to do my job well, I do not discuss orders, do not judge them, avoid weighing them in my hand, as well as weighing or judging my fellow men, I just obey them. It behooves the executioner, with his reticent ethics, to become immune to the cunning and even pernicious intrusion of that which is human. I must hold onto some neuter image, a cube for example, until this woman has exhausted herself with her attempts to involve me and I can—with the same disinterestedness—leave her forever or lie with her again and possess her, beat her perhaps, but without any anger.

—◆◆◆—

Outside, among these old moonlit houses, through these winding streets, I remember my childhood. My sister, with her black braids and a glass compote dish full of red and yellow cashew fruits in her arms, is in the garden, hiding behind a black mouse. A white peacock with a golden and blood-red tail approaches and greedily devours the fruit as my sister watches, paralyzed, leaving only the empty compotier. The mouse turns around and swallows my sister up in the twinkling of an eye. He swears eternal love to the peacock, though, and leaves him alone. The capricious peacock spreads his tail, picks up a knife and bleeds the mouse, slitting his throat. My sister again, sitting on her little chair, her braids on her breast. A dog comes, takes her away and marries her. He makes a cake with dirt and decorates it with rubies and bones for my sister to eat. She refuses, my brother-in-law swallows up cake and dish. My sister returns to our house. We have breakfast together. I tear off a piece of bread and raise it to my mouth. My sister points to the loaf of bread in the middle of the table. *It's a little boy! Are you going to eat him?* I answer that it is not a boy, but a scorpion. Our dishes and cups are forever brimming with children, alligators, scorpions, buffaloes, horses, mothers and flowers, which we feast upon with a smile. Somewhere in a church a bell is pealing. I do not count the strokes and I do not have my watch with me. Empty streets. I do not know where the inn is, and there is nobody around to ask. The town, armillary sphere of silences, dissolving in the acid of the moon.

—◦❧ ☙◦—

"Are you the man who's looking for my son?" "No." "I'm his father." "That's what I figured." "I thought you'd be older." "Older than who?" "Than you." "No, I'm my age. Not a day older." "May I ask how old?" "Twenty-two. I'm neither looking for a son nor a father. I'm looking for a person, just him, and him alone, with no relation to anyone." "To kill him?" "That's none of your business." "What do you mean, none of my business? I heard you wanted to kill my son." "I've already told you I don't."

From the back the man looks normal, with his suppliant air, his hunched back, one shoulder higher than the other; from the front, if you do not pay much attention, there's nothing special about him either. If you observe him more closely, though, you can see that his dark glasses, too big for his face maybe, have a strange purpose: that of concealing the absence of his left eye, which does not exist, never did, he does not have an eye socket or an eyebrow, the tissue behind the dark glass is reminiscent of those pictures of naked women whose pubis was touched up in the negatives, a camouflage more glaring than the frank reproduction of the model. To compensate for this, below the right eye, in its proper place, another right eye observes me, coldly, through the lens. The two eyes take turns, they do not blink at the same time. On the worn carpet, where three gazelles among embroideries, sedges and digitate leaves, can still be discerned, the character's feet, in a pair of heavy yellow shoes, go back and forth, as if they were studying a way of attacking me.

—My son's name is José Gervásio. I'm sure you came here after him, but I beg you by all you hold dear, go back to where you came from. Say you couldn't find him, or that he was already dead.

—A promise is a promise. Get out.

For the first time the two eyes have closed. The old man holds his hands out to me at the height of my stomach, his palms up, trembling:

—I came to offer myself in the place of my son. I'm begging you.

—I don't have any choice in the matter.

His hands remain fixed in a gesture of entreaty, so effective and easy. His voice, on the contrary, resembles the one that implored me about as much as an aluminum structure before and after a violent explosion in its foundation. The two right eyes pierce me, throwing me off balance.

—Then, since you won't do as I ask, I'll go to the police.

—It's no use. I *am* the police.

Or:

He does not hold his hand out to me. He remains standing on the threshold, sullen. I close the door. Bowing slightly, he gives me his hat, his umbrella, sits down and remains silent, sucking his teeth. He has a frightened and submissive look. His black shoes are so old they look gray. He cleans his glasses with the tip of his tie, with somber boughs and sanguine honeysuckle.

—My real name isn't José Gervásio.

—I know. It's Artur. It wasn't easy to find you.

—And now that you have found me . . . I'm not like the others. I don't run from my persecutors. I hear you're looking for me? Well, then: here I am.

—This is the first time. Until today you've been an escape artist.

—What do you want from me?

—You'll see.

—You want to kill me? Is that it? Of course it is. That's what I've been, all my life: the sacrificial lamb. The immolated one.

He shows me the picture, in a delicate frame with stars and imbrications. He in swimming trunks, long hair, a beard, his feet and wrists tied with rope, on a cross. His mother on her knees, her hands clasped together in supplication, her eyes heavenward. Further back, an old man with dark glasses. Then what we heard was true, that this man traveled around the interior of Bahia, in the area of the São Francisco river, with his father and mother, carrying on the back of a mule the cross on which he had them crucify him. He put a leather bag at the foot of the cross, people came, gave alms, prayed. His parents exploited him, traveled by train or bus while he went on foot with the mule and the cross.

—I'm going to tell you something horrible, which hurts to this day. Have you ever heard of Santo Sé? It's not far from Juazeiro. I had been on that cross for over twenty-four hours, almost without eating anything. There were towns where what they gave me wasn't even enough to feed the mule. But in Santo Sé it was glorious. Like this . . . (He points to the walls of the room, where the painted border, now in a state of decay, once depicted pineapples, bows and pink mangoes.) A horn of plenty. There were even some big bills in the bag. Well, when night fell and the people went to sleep, my father and mother ran away with the money. I was crying from the cross, begging them for God's sake not to leave me. *Father, mother, why have you forsaken me?* They ran off on the mule without even looking back. No sacrifice surprises me.

—You seem to be grateful to your old folks.

—I'm not grateful. I've forgiven them, as I forgive everything. As everybody should. And, at the same time, I'm taking my revenge. I go everywhere in my carriage, while they walk. What do you want from me?

—You said it yourself, a while ago. I want to kill you.

He was cleaning his glasses again. He stops and looks at me puzzled, as if I had already shot him or pulled my knife. "I haven't done you any harm." "No, you haven't." "So?! What's my crime?""I don't know." "Why must I die?" "I don't know and I don't care."

—You don't know how . . . to forgive.

—Forgive? . . . I'm a loyal agent and I intend to kill you one of these nights, when you return from your daily visit to your mother.

—I can go to the police.

—You won't. You've been running from the Law for years.

Having said this, we remain silent for the indispensable interval between what has been said and the sentence he finally ventures, in the way of a threat, hesitating over each syllable:

—What if I kill you first?

—That would be one of the only two ways of surviving.

—What's the other?

I write on a piece of paper, in numbers big enough for him to read even without glasses, the amount, exactly the same, paid to the black woman the day before yesterday to point him out to me. He put all the money he had in his pockets on the table, along with a ring. I gave him the ring back, kept the rest.

—Tell the desk clerk to send up the bill. I'm leaving.

From the window, I see him getting into the carriage, a fragile spider, iron wheels, pulled by a melancholy sorrel with flop ears. He whips the horse and leaves, without looking up.

Or:

I was not expecting a visit from the black woman. I do not recall giving her any information as to where I would stay, I do not think I told her my name, either, yet I find it perfectly natural for her to be here, with new shoes, clothes and purse, exuding a perfume she must have poured over herself without parsimony, *Fleur de Rocaille* maybe, and which must not be very common in this musty room. The dress (sunflowers on an ultramarine blue background) goes well with the serge of the sofa, the color of corn, with a worn tapestry of garlands, scepters and fleurs-de-lis. I know from the very first moment that she regrets having come and is debating whether she should tell me what brought her here. While she is deliberating, she imitates with visible effort the conversation and behavior of a regular visitor, criticizing, for example, the separation of the sexes still in force in certain places of worship in Minas, or asking about countries where, according to what she was told, blacks are not considered human beings, compelling me to express my opinion, which I summarize thus: "Every country has its customs. It's not for us to judge them." She mentions with a smile the flowers she put on her son's grave and two pieces of printed silk she bought yesterday, one with birds, another with leaves. While she talks, she finally makes up her mind and confesses what I already suspected. She told José Gervásio about me, thus sinking deeper and deeper into an impossible game of betrayals and confessions of disloyalty, which are in turn new treacheries subsequently divulged. I listen to her without moving, remembering the glaucus undulations of her body, certain she will ask me if she did wrong, if what she did can be forgiven, as if these queries and the answers they elicit could alter the nature and the consequences of her actions.

—Nothing kept you from talking to José Gervásio. It was my mistake not to demand your silence in our agreement. Did he reward you in any way for the information?

—He said that he already knew and that it didn't matter. How could he know?

—I'm going to pay you the same amount I gave you before. Go back and tell him that I left today. That you managed to convince me. But now your loyalty is part of the deal. I'm only asking you to keep the secret for two days. Tomorrow, when he comes back from the visit to the woman he calls his mother, I'll execute him. Two days only. It's not much. I'll give you half the money now and the other half later.

Before the dream, or before the part I remembered clearly, there was a monotonous and rather long part in which my servile nature and my master's tyranny became evident. Starting from the moment he orders me to go to the village, to see someone or bring some message to an even more powerful lord, the incidents become connected to one another and gain strength. In a black carriage, pulled by two horses, I turned around in the courtyard paved with flagstone, scattering hens, pigs, ducks and turkeys. I was holding my hat in my hands and receiving the orders, my eyes lowered. I have barely given the signal of departure, with a loud whiplash, when I hear my master's voice, imperious, calling after me. The noise of the carriage and of the horses allows me to turn a deaf ear to him with no fear of punishment. So I crack the whip with assurance, swearing through my teeth, overcome by an anger that throws me into a paroxysm. The desperate voice calls me again. Letting the wind carry it away, I yell at the horses and, drunk with anger, race along the road which I know as well as my pockets. I can feel my master following close on my heels. I act as if I did not know he was pursuing me, I begin to sing, still shouting and whipping the horses hard: they go faster, stretching out their necks. Cats, dogs, rabbits and sheep get squashed between the wheels of the carriage, the wind has blown my hat away. The mouth of the tunnel through which we both will have to pass is opening ahead of us. I put the handle of the whip between my teeth and pull up on the reins deliberately, to slow the gallop and allow the master to catch up with me . . . In complete darkness, the two carriages continued at full speed, one next to the other, without giving ground. The horses' hooves were pounding, neither of us was saying a word, the smell of leather and sweat was suffocating me. In spite of the darkness, I could see the walls of the tunnel, painted red: oxen and panthers, falcons, serpents and jackasses, pelicans, peacocks, does, dragons, turtles, lions and elephants, all flying past me like bats. Suddenly, I thought: "Now!" and drove my carriage against the master's, pushing it against the blood-red animals of the tunnel, while I lashed about with my whip shouting like a madman: "Take this, and this, and this!" The master was cursing in a muffled voice. I grabbed him, felt the roughness of his neck between my fingers, his blood throbbing, his strangled cry. "Take this!" I pushed him from the carriage. As he was falling he gave off a smell of burnt hair. I welcomed with ferocious joy the cry of agony beneath the wheels and the flying hooves, made my whip whistle through the air. The horses were spurred on more by my laughter and a cloud of flies than by the whip. I enter the house I was sent to. Almost at the same instant, very pale, my master arrives and says to me: "Some servant we've got!" I ask him, humbly as usual: "What have I done?" The host, hearing me, intervenes: "Your master is just giving you a hard time. I can tell from your voice that you haven't done anything. Go on, sit there." I sat down, opened a book and eagerly began to discourse on the arabesques, festoons, borders, conches and scrollwork that illustrated it. I declared myself inferior to all enigmas and apologized for having the gift of penetrating them.

—◦❧ ❧◦—

Thick clouds covering the moon. I listen to the silence, which will soon be broken by my shots. I picture it: large glass bowl, nocturnal mold of the winding streets, of the hills, of the empty churches, of the houses with jutting eaves. Bodies safely tucked under blankets. The bedbugs arrive with circumspection, steal into the beds, vie with the mosquitoes for human blood; on the ceilings and in the window frames, under the furniture, spiders spit out their threads; termites drill holes in the wood, weevils hollow out grain in the warehouses, beetles dizzily drone hitting against walls, moths flutter around the lamps, scorpions, ants, centipedes, crickets and roaches are swarming all over the ground, grasshoppers are eating the leaves of the trees, ticks and flies sting the skin of horses, goats and cattle. I concentrate on the weight of the revolver on my ileum. Everything must be fast and neutral, so that the act to be performed does not lose its impersonal character. The execution must be like affixing a seal to a text to be signed. A little earlier than I expected (I did not hear the bells striking ten thirty) I hear, still far off, the hooves and the clatter of the wheels on the stones, disturbing the frogs and toads that leap across the street. Mentally, I measure the space between myself and the noise, finding a certain beauty in this convergence, in this man approaching his executioner with such precision and certainty. Bullet in the chamber, I calculate the distance: the shots must be fired without any possibility of error and, at the same time, the victim must not see me beforehand. He might lay the whip to the horse and dodge the bullets. The spider is in the street. Under the little canvas top, within my gun's sights, a figure holds the reins. It stops, strikes a match. I aim at its head, thinking my mission has been accomplished: the match goes out, the figure bends over, falls slowly, its legs get caught in the step of the carriage. The horse remains immobile, all the insects indifferent, not a door opens, not a window. I see that I have killed the black woman, always undecided in her choices, a victim of the lack of definition that was a fault in itself and led me into error as well.

Or:

Stars and moon illuminate the knife blade. In the silence I hear the joints of the town creaking and decay creeping over the two-hundred-year-old walls, over the beams and the girders, over the colors of the saints and their bodies, over the choirs, the carvings, gildings, altars and moldings, over the windows, the ceilings, the chairs, the beds, the drawers, the crosses, the oratories, decay with its fungi, its insects, its sharp claws, its corrosive tongue. Everything, suddenly, looks like a knife blade to me: the letter and the inkblot, the bird and the shot, intimacy and distance, building, destroying, being born, living, dying. I hide the blade in its sheath. Facing myself, less than six feet away, I ask: "Am I sure?" I answer: "Am I?" Before it occurs to us who is to make inquiries and who is to solve them, we hear the trot of a horse, the light wheels of a spider turning on the pavement, while the church bells strike once and we both move away, I on the right-hand side of the street, I on the left, I hesitant, I determined, waiting for the condemned. The black horse— which appears white in the moonlight—comes, pulling the spider with its master inside. Hiding in the shadows, I remain still, watching the animal, the carriage and the man; but I move forward, and before the whipped horse has a chance to gallop away, I jump into the spider and do my duty. From the street, the now useless weapon in my hand, I see the sad vehicle moving away, hear a stifled cry amidst the noise of the wheels and of the hooves, I see myself jump off, jump off and come back to me, while the spider races through the streets, with its wounded passenger.

Or:

I do not know why this hirsute dog, with huge paws, so similar to the lion curling at Daniel's feet, is following me. It was waiting for me on the way out and walked on ahead of me, I ahead of it, down the empty moonlit streets. Why do I think of my sister and her black braids on full moon nights? The Monkey was climbing a banana tree, with the heavy basket of jaboticaba and pitomba berries and sapodillas, which he was eating. My sister hit him with a stick. The Monkey ran away and still managed to eat a passion fruit, currants, a cherimoya, Brazil cherries, mangoes, inga fruits, sugarapples, guavas. The Ant came and ate the Monkey. The Hare came and ate the Monkey again. Then my sister and I went out arm in arm with him, we climbed up into a jackfruit tree, were surrounded by white dogs. Now I see dogs in the stars. Skeletons of dogs, dog ears, dog skin cut open, bitches and puppies, dog mandibles, winged dogs, with wavy manes, wagging tails, horns and crowns. They gallop on their big paws, like this dog's, they bark, and even the skins without dog, the bones without skin run high above, the entire town vibrates with the galloping. In the absolute silence, I hear the horse's unhurried steps, the iron wheels, the steps of the horse. The dog moves away, heads for the spider. It has stopped at the beginning of the street, someone has gotten off and is coming toward me. I take out the revolver, aim at the heart. *Do not allow any dialogue. Eliminate the victim quickly. Do not allow him, under any circumstances, to breach the distance that protects me from his wiles.* I lower the weapon: he is not the person I am looking for.

—I came in his place. Let me die in my son's place.

The dog, sitting, looks at me. The horse gets tired of waiting, comes pulling the spider along, stops next to us. The old man thinks that he will draw me into some troubled and difficult game, full of questions, of pressure, of deliberations, that he will introduce uncertainty, the vacuum and imbalance in my limpid rigor. Without answering, I fire my gun, blow his brains out. The horse bolts away, dragging the old carriage, the dog starts to bark. In the moonlight, I examine the old man lying on the sidewalk: he now seems to be looking at me with three eyes. The dog sniffs him.

EASTER SUNDAY

The long, sun-drenched floor boards smell of wax and cedar. From the bathroom comes a perfume as of pine forests. The sea breeze rustles the flowered curtains in slow undulant ripples that die out like the waves below, inaudibly, leaving a cool wetness on the narrow beach and the old people's feet. They walk by, almost always in pairs, their elbows slightly raised, or they sit on the beach, their legs outstretched, covering their joints with the black sand and the viscous ochery clay, which is constantly being replenished by the sea. Added together, their ages are alarming; as a group, they themselves become one monstrous ancient man, many millennia old, furtively observing with nostalgia, envy, and a strong urge to spit, my muscular chest, my inconceivable forty-four years. The fragrance of lotions, powders, and beauty creams mingles with the perfidious smell of the floor boards, alive with the whirr of wings and the scraping of scales: specters of birds and reptiles. Only one guest, her body lustrous with oil, is exposed to the sun in a reclining chair near the swimming pool. The rectangle, of an almost turbid green—the adult swimming pool—and the children's pool, farther away and also rectangular, the round and square table tops, the arrangement of the chairs, the harmonious nexus among so many geometric forms, tell me not to fear death or disaster today; that the next hours will maintain the essentials of this moment—the luminous sky, the companion on the floor above ours, the table with apples on it near the window, the sharp blade of the knife, the ribbons, the earrings, an almost girlish pair of slippers on the carpet—and only the chair of that guest there in the sun, placed at an absurd and perhaps even foreboding angle, threatens the order of things. The oil which protects her skin vaguely suggests machinery still intact.

[*The little girl is squatting in the bushes, skirts raised; urine palely trickles over an anthill. I don't know the time (afternoon, morning?), I don't know the month or the year but it is a hot day and we are surrounded by a dizzying sea of silence. I hold a beetle in my hand, its wings a metallic green, its legs restless. The girl has stopped urinating and I insert the beetle in her still dripping sex.*

Who was she? A neighbor? A cousin? Who? I have lost her face and her name.]

I turn off the light and sit down in the chair beside Narcelia's bed, where she reclines against fluffed pillows with their lacework pillowcases.

"I hate these hotel pillowcases. They are too hard and, besides, so many strangers have slept on them!"

The Holy Week moon, riding high above the ocean, lights up the fruit-laden table, part of the wooden floor, the embroidered bedspread, Narcelia's quiet feet, her lilac nightgown, which the moonlight turns into an evanescent mist. Clarity bathes her well-kept hands idly resting on her stomach. I follow the calm movement of her breathing and I can even see her breasts throbbing under the light material, their rhythmic pulsing, the blood pounding. But her face is in the shadow now, undiscernible: her hair almost hiding her shoulders, her eyes always moist and reflecting whatever shines, be it the remotest or the dullest of glimmers. In spite of the moon and the open window, it is difficult for us to breathe the heavy air.

"Many guests are arriving. There is a lot of commotion in the corridors and I even heard children crying."

"You're right. In the restaurant, there were three or four."

In front of a TV set, several women and a man watch a program about the conquest of space, others play cards at one of the tables in the bar, elevators move up and down, a Dodge stops at the main entrance and all the bellhops rush out of the brightly lighted lobby at once; on the TV screen the Hindenburg burns over Lakehurst after flying over Times Square with its inaugural escort of planes, ships saluting with flags and whistles the portentous arrival which (how could one know?) was really a farewell, then the huge shiny structure loses its equilibrium and falls, transformed in seconds into a smoldering cage.

"A crackling, shapeless skeleton."

Seen from above, the obstinately straight and arid main street, with its unattractive resort hotels, its shops as yet without customers, and its deserted restaurants with soiled, wind-blown tablecloths still awaiting the hoped-for Holy Week invaders, has something about it that suggests a completely obtuse form of life proudly advancing into nothingness.

Narcelia stirs, and the simple arm movement scatters her heavy perfume in the air, extends her hand to the bedside table, picks up her gold-plated cigarette case, opening it with a click.

"Light it."

I obey. By the light of the match, her small simian face emerges with its large crossed eyes.

As brilliant as precious stones, despite the wrinkles. "Do you want me to make you comfortable?" No, she's fine. At this same time day before yesterday, the light had not yet reached the bed.

"Next year, I want to spend Holy Week in Seville." An authoritarian voice—and when it expresses impossible desires—a yearning voice, and with a note of senility. However, in what she says, even in the most trivial things, there is a subtle hint of secret satiny fire indicating the wisdom that germinates like a fruit in her intimate, brooding, bristling, inner preserve.

"Will I be going too?"

"Too bad! You know you won't."

"Why?"

She raises the cigarette to her mouth, compresses her lips—rather like a biting dog—and her powerful, solemn, look shrivels me.

"The dead are not going to see Easter in Seville. They can rot anywhere." She laughs. A tense protracted sound, welling up in her throat. Happiness scrapped. The moonlight falls only upon her always immobile feet, and her toenails seem painted black.

—◦❦ ❦◦—

[I look up—I don't know if I am in a yard, on some deserted road, or in some open field—the sky appears to me as if I might punch its royal-blue shell with my still fragile fist and I think to myself: "Tomorrow I'll be seeing other stars." I feel restless and upset by my imminent trip.

But a trip where, by what means, with whom, for how long, and to do what?]

—◦❦ ❦◦—

The moon dips and the neon sign on top of the hotel rhythmically casting its green clarity upon the nearby buildings, is the only clear sign of life. The telephone rings at the main desk: someone is dying.

A secret plan is put into operation, similar to those that precede prison breaks and designed to make the dead man disappear, to transfer him outside the confines of the hotel, beyond this place where people come to flee all things evil. But why was the swimming pool chair, that particular one, allowed to be placed at such an unlucky angle? The elevator opens, the dead man emerges wrapped in a sheet, and with only his bald pate and a few white hairs visible, he seems to be almost gliding along, and his passage through the poorly lighted hallway is rapid: his widow follows hesitantly, purplish circles under her dry eyes, and she keeps turning around as if some piece of her husband might have dropped on the ground.

At the steps leading down to the beach, I set the wheelchair brakes, I take Narcelia in my arms, I extend her on the sand. She closes her eyes with a look of resignation and she opens them again only after I have settled her against the canvas back rest. In the blue sky where there are no clouds or birds, the sun is shining low on the horizon; our shadows and those of the old people, who are numerous at sunup, extend along the ground, in transit or motionless. Foundations rise above the level of the ocean and so near it that, at high tide, from the top floors one can spit on the waves. The crumbling walls of the building pulsate into the night, reflecting the hotel sign with its livid glow. I wonder if Narcelia has noticed that her still shapely legs are atrophying. I am supposed to rub this reddish-colored mud gently over them and without taking too much time.

Nothing that might suggest a caress. Next, I cover them with the slimy dark sand on which the invalids rely.

Invaded by them, the almost treeless and somewhat arid city, though bordering the ocean and with many new buildings, exudes negligence and penury.

"It reminds you of an asylum for indigent old people."

"Now, Canoas, you have fifteen minutes to yourself. But look in my direction now and then. I may need you."

My feet sink into the sand, which is strangely unstable beneath the water. I dive and swim, always mindful of Narcelia, alone and unprotected, the metal of her wheelchair glinting in the distance, at the top of the stairs. I get out and dry myself. Something for her? She doesn't answer. Isn't the sun too hot? Silence. She needs to be careful. "You can't afford to get sunburned."

"My feet are becoming uncovered. Put some sand on them. And stick to the essentials; mind what you're doing. You haven't brought a child to the beach. Right now, I need care, not baby-sitting. I'm forty-six, two years older than you."

I stroll up and down in the sun, a dog without its collar, insulting these declining bodies, redolent of rancid fat, faded dahlias, camphor—and still hopeful as they dig in the sand for strength. Suddenly, from the little group of oldsters a young black girl dashes out.

"She looks like the offspring of those old men and women, that they've produced in common."

They come and go, exchanging dull phrases like knife blades that have been ground a hundred times:

"Last night, did you get up to urinate?"—"It takes over two weeks for payment to arrive"—"It needs a railing, that high sidewalk along the beach. A person could fall and break his neck"—"Now that I think of it, I didn't take my medicine"— "The city is above sea level"—"If it were below, it would flood"—"Sorry about what? I was right to give him poison."

The black girl, who is missing a tooth and who is no more than ten or eleven, passes near me, pinning up her hair, her armpits not so dark and her eyes half hidden beneath eyelids puffy with desire. Her rump and smooth sex bite with a kind of passion into her faded old swimsuit, the waves lap her vibrant ankles, her knees, her thighs. She jumps backward into the first big wave, her legs apart, the white soles of her small feet turned toward the clouds. Ah, to put a beetle or a wasp in there!

[*I am traveling or about to travel. Anyhow, the place where I spent the night serves no meals and I enter the deserted cafe. The street is probably wide and it must be morning since the low sun can still shine in, reaching my table to the right on the far side of the dining room, and my back is to the entrance and against a brown wainscoted wall. On the marble tabletop, fresh rolls and a metal coffeepot.*

What city on earth can this be, why this trip, how old am I, and where am I going, where?]

With curtains closed, all lights burning as if it were night, I remove Narcelia's clothes and, likewise nude, I carry her in my arms to the shower. Sitting in her chair, under the jet of warm water that patters on her flowered plastic cap, she soaps herself from her hips up while I take care of her legs and feet, in silence: she forbids me to speak during her bath.

After placing her full length upon the bed, on a towel, I finish drying her, I rub her lightly with a fleetingly fragrant moisturizing cream, I sprinkle talcum powder on her ankles and knee joints and the area, always dry, where her legs join her torso, I help her to dress. I put on my own lounging robe, I open up the curtains to the morning, turn off the now unnecessary lights, and hold up the mirror while, with liner, powder, and rouge, she tries to bring her tiny waxen face to life. Her eyes (bottles of black ink hurled against a wall shatter: their stains); her wide eyes reflect the mirror's and the day's luminous surfaces: with her false lashes and make-up, they gain in size. Suddenly, they stare into space, voices rise from the pool, a body strikes water with a splash, heavily, music on a radio.

She speaks: "A holy person is arriving. Someone inspired, specially chosen. Go look." Resting my elbows on the low, cramped window sill, I survey our surroundings, and what is there that is unusual? The city is filling with people.

Cars abound on the main street, buses cross the long span of the bridge, to the left (from here they seem to be moving slowly), from Victoria or from inland places, the murky water of the pool that not even the ten o'clock sun can filter or clean, the white skins of guests just arriving, the sparkle of glassware and beer bottles—and in the white lacquered furniture, in the mindless distribution of the chairs, in the round table pushed aside, as if it were drifting away, in the tension among the various square tabletops, in the midst of this disharmony, the still not quite legible announcement of an astonishing event emerging from time.

[*The pale rose dress, fashioned of a supple springy fabric, is piled on top of others, near a wicker basket full of remnants, on the bare table. Translucent tiles filter the wintry daylight, which reflects dimly on the slightly worn wood of the table and intensifies my still immature urge to love. I bury my face in the dress and with eyes closed I breathe in the fading odor of young flesh, of fresh armpits, of popular lotions, Coty or Evening in Granada.*

Who owned that dress? And what was her body like that disturbs and excites me and what name shall I whisper, like a secret, into its folds?]

Even with a full hotel, with waiters and elevators in constant movement, automobiles and buses blocking the entrance, groups playing cards under the white lights of the bar that are multiplied by its mirrored walls, even so he attracts attention—as if he were the hotel's only guest. There we are, reflected in the mirrors of the bar, the small table between us with his beer and my tea, he and I, he with his ivory forehead and I my suntanned leather, he with his long, thin goatee, I my bushy, smoke-gray moustache almost down to my teeth, which are darkened with tartar, he with such placid eyes (although aware, one can see, of the pursuer, the hidden companion), I these delirious spheres about to explode in their sockets, he a scion of some ancient manor house of brocade and dragons, between the Baltic and the Sea of Marmara, I from a place I do not care to know, he and I both marked, bearers of the sign, the black halo.

"I am told the Cretan civilization developed several systems of writing. Somewhat hesitant, a kind of exploration, starting with the ideogram. This was four or five thousand years ago. The lineal expression—straight lines and curves—will come about later."

"You, sir—I interrupt him—are from a country more ancient and respectful of rules than ours, quite obviously. When you meet people in doorways, you bow and let them pass. When you greet them you bend slightly at the waist, your hands a bit closed and retracted. Were your father and grandfather perchance distinguished members of the knighthood? Nobility? High-ranking officers of the military?"

He pours a little more beer in the glass, his hands pallid and his stubby fingers rather shaky. He continues, with a trace of irony:

"It is believed that around 1400 B.C., all the buildings in Crete were destroyed by flames. An invasion or an earthquake? No one knows. After that, the Cretans—strangely enough—stopped writing. As for the writing which they had invented and cultivated (their writing, eh? not the documents), these were also consumed by another kind of fire: oblivion. To this day none has been deciphered."

"What about our Companion, eh? The watcher, almost always on the floor above ours? He's like a death sentence or maybe an executioner, the one who has the ax and the order for execution. We wake up in the night and we know he is lying there, two or three meters above us, in the dark."

"Drink your tea, before it gets cold."

He takes the cigarette holder, a delicate gold-encrusted object, out of his pocket and, with concentration, inserts the cigarette in the holder. Why does he recoil from the burning lighter I extend to him? Can he be so frightened? Through the hallway twenty or thirty young excursionists, burst noisily, some barefooted and with shoes in hand, dragging sacks and suitcases, and accompanying them a male dwarf and two middle-aged women who could easily have posed for a bordello advertisement. He moves his chair and sits with his back to all of them.

I close my left eye, push the teacup away with the back of my hand and observe, with nothing particular in mind:

"When they came in, I could see in your eyes, quite clearly, a sudden golden flash. When you changed places, I noticed the smell of your body and your clothing: bacon, garlic, and dung. I can still smell it. Is it caused by fear?"

Scrutinizing me through the smoke, he answers beneath half-closed lids, his cigarette holder in the air:

"The dependence of people like you and me is terrible. I miss the times when I could sleep outdoors if I wished. Now I need an adjoining room. Above, beside or below mine. Especially above. It's painful, don't you think?"

"Yes, you're right. One can lie in another position, but there is only one in which pain does not interfere. Isn't that so?"

"Yes, the comparison is exact. We can, you and I, go to sleep with *him* next door to us, or on the floor below us. Up there, however, one feels his presence more, he troubles us more, he 'hurts' us more."

The waiter had brought his beer and some minutes afterward my tea. Each has anticipated the sign on the other—and this brings us closer. Some of the young men go through the bar on their way to the swimming pool, drag the lacquered chairs and take their seats, aggravating the disorder fermenting within the pool furniture with its sharp edges and voids. Several youths pick up the dwarf and, for an instant, he is tossed about by thirty hands, a huge, misshapen and frightened crab. The foreigner, tense, closes his eyes. He reopens them and concludes from the other side of the smoke:

"We have no illusions about the meaning of the pursuer's arrival. One never knows death's distance from us. Near or far? People like you and me, however, know: the watcher has arrived and is close by. We have already been set apart and only await the command: 'Take him.' I agree it is disturbing to feel *he* is there watching us. At the same time his vigilance comforts us: as long as he doesn't go away, we are immortal." And all this is so perplexing that I ask myself: "Let's suppose, Velimir Leskovar, that he goes away and by some mistake or chance you are spared. Would you, from then on, be able to stand the uncertainty?"

The last gulp of tea is tepid and smells like a sour pillow. I deliver the words, weighing each one carefully:

"When there is no rain in Egypt, migratory birds come to lay their eggs in Paraíba where grass seeds are plentiful. They lay on the ground and choose not just any, but the most difficult places. Those covered with thorns or under acacias and thistles. They incubate the eggs in silence. Giant toads and turtles eat part of them. The baby birds are fed by their mother's vomit, beak to beak. They flap their wings, the silence is broken, and then the shooting begins. It is mostly the young, clumsy doves that die. Having no experience, they roost in unprotected trees. They are hunted at night, with torches. A depleted, bedraggled, thinner cloud of feathers goes back to Egypt. Sad."

"Today Delos is peopled with sculptures. Immortality has settled on the island and the only ephemeral visitors, shall we call them, are the countless poppies that bloom in May. In the old days, when men still inhabited the island, women who were about to give birth used to be transferred; and likewise the dying. In Delos, nobody was ever born or died. Wouldn't the pursuer be like our Delos?"

[*The wall is not completely white but is painted with green designs, green pea-sized lozenges, vertical scratches and leaves. This made even more attractive, more lively, the shadows somebody was casting with his hands. A frightened Rabbit wiggles its ears. A dog without a tongue opens its mouth over and over and barks, soundlessly. The Bird flies up, up in the air. The Monkey: its rigid profile. The Ostrich's neck rises tall, a questioning beak. I enjoy my small zoo of shadows.*

But who in the world has made me so happy with light, hands, and walls?]

I take Narcelia in my arms and I advance toward the ocean, my knees must not betray me, I must steady myself and keep her from falling, whatever the force of the waves (she pays me to be her agile feet, her youth, and her body's equilibrium), an almost impossible task in the sands at Guarapari, where feet sink as in piled-up rice. The elderly, today less in evidence (do the youths who have been arriving since yesterday frighten them?), rub their stiff joints. Along the beach, burning testicles and hard-tipped breasts pulsate, the young men and women a startling animalesque creature, flexing, bellowing grotesquely with its mouth upon the ground. I start into the ocean with Narcelia and I shudder: Velimir Leskovar hears the black girl, who is pointing with an innocent and lascivious gesture toward the dazzling blue sky. He sees us too and nods respectfully with his broad forehead. When did this man arrive? Yesterday. A gloomy looking man is pushing a wheelchair on the sidewalk:

the invalid, wearing a hat, gloves, and a yellow and red flowered dress, looks thoughtfully out to sea. A larger wave catches us and I almost drop my charge. Narcelia, far from showing fear, sinks her nails into my back and arms, orders me to penetrate deeper and, when the wave envelops us, she rests her face against my shoulder, and I think even licks my salty skin. Velimir Leskovar, very white and hairless, also enters the water, led by the black girl's soft hand. The wheelchair rolls slowly, the woman's right hand waves in the air and her glove exhales a distinct and sharp perfume, a swarm or a buzz that the wind soon dissipates. The man, her attendant, sees only her straw hat, her gloves, her gold bracelets and the flowered silk covering the crippled woman's knees. Velimir Leskovar leaves the black girl and goes into the ocean. He looks happy and nothing suggests in the least that he knows: the sign, the black halo, has disappeared. No longer does he have, despite being condemned, the equivocal protection of the pursuer. The same towering wave that breaks over him envelops us and I whirl with Narcelia, who screams, half-choking, and bites my chest in fear. The foreigner, methodically and with determination, swims out some distance from the beach. The wheelchair travels the uneven sidewalk with its hexagons between the two small inlets, crosses the desolate area and the cutting sound of the saw that comes from the construction work on the left, the woman clenches her fingers inside her gloves and the servant imagines—merely imagines—that she is uttering a shrill agonizing scream like that of the saw. Narcelia, decisive and impassioned, orders me not to be afraid, to penetrate, not to be my usual pusillanimous self, deeper still, more, her inert legs moving back and forth with the flux of the waves and seemingly alive again. Velimir Leskovar perhaps is swimming out to his death or is already drowning. The invalid, facing seaward, near the shallow body of water where parents let their children go alone, extends her hands, speaks of the skies of Capri, the man glances at the gnarled roots of the almond trees in the sand, the curves of girls in the sun or under shade trees, the sound of voices and whistles, the line of the ocean, a sailboat, the perfume: a caustic cloud. The woman faces her attendant, he bends down (the pungent perfume) and he hears her say:

"The only things that happen are those that evolve. Everything else is false. Everything. Now, take me to a shady spot."

"Come on!" Narcelia yells. "Deeper, man, don't weaken." Water at the level of my chest and she almost at the level of my shoulders, the wild waves, back and forth, all our muscles tense, her voice almost choking (that life be damned, she's not concerned about safety or anything else, I should prove I'm a man), now, now! the huge awesome roaring wave, she and I suspended in it, her fingernails in my flesh, the cry, the wave's suction and her mouth riveted to mine, biting. I whirl and feel the sand slipping beneath me, slipping away, but it is sand, bottom. Narcelia, her face the color of lime and looking into the distance, her nostrils quivering, her body heavier. Her feet float to the surface: her toenails are blood-covered. "Now take me in." (I barely hear her voice.) I head for the beach, some elderly couples have approached and are giving me a severe look. I set Narcelia down gently, dry her in my usual impersonal and thorough way, her eyelids remaining closed. Velimir Leskovar, still at a distance, has come back, swimming serenely. The girl leaves the water in her tight-fitting suit, droplets beading her dark skin, the sun catching the movement of her shoulders; her girlish hips swivel when she walks, the disgraceful little bundle of trouble. She turns around and waits for the swimmer, hands on hips, her rounded buttocks two burning spheres. Shameful. Whore.

Narcelia at last opens her eyes. "This afternoon, Canoas, let's"—her voice is neutral—"take a stroll along the beach."

[*A thin ray of moonlight comes through the roof and the cocks crow. No one else is in the room, of which there remain only the spectral walls, the brick floor, the narrow bed where I lie awake. At the other end of the town, they're slaughtering pigs, evidently with dull knives. The sacrificed animals open their throats to the world, cry out for impossible help, their terrifying voices spread deep into the night, the cocks crow and I cry, biting my pillow.*

Am I crying because of the pigs or has someone offended me? Why am I sighing so desperately?]

Percussion instruments reverberate from afar, traffic has been re-routed for the performance by the Apprentice Madmen Carnival Club, dark unpaved streets come alive with the passage of their cars, the bright headlights expose decaying walls, twisted gates, unkept yards, and garbage piles. The city emerges from its lethargy, from its tranquil state of rot, and experiences the intermittent excitement of watering places, familiar to me ever since Narcelia hired me: her wheelchair shuttles between beaches and spas, the stations of this *via profana* coinciding with periods of festivity, in order to disguise the tedium and necessity, to pretend that we have come for pleasure, happiness, fulfillment; the people make way for us as we plow the main street, plow the compact sound of hubbub, cursing, jawbones clacking; the multitude stands back, everyone watching Narcelia, who is indifferent as she moves ahead, her eyes lost in the distance, as if she did not see them, as if the Apprentice Madmen had already performed and dissolved into thin air, as if some of them had not passed us, dressed in satin, as if the souvenir stores, the Apollo Amusement Center, and the restaurants with their filthy tablecloths were not crowded, as if those chairs with which the downtown hotels obstruct the cement walkways were resting indoors, empty, as if it were an ordinary night—the townspeople at home feeding on their own gangrenous hearts, and not this Saturday night before Easter. The energy of the crowd pushes the old people back—scum and detritus of society—to the outer edges, they hug the walls, our passage is blocked by a tighter circle: two Negroes with Mexican hats show off trained dogs and monkeys. I start to go around the circle when a sort of wedge is driven into the group, people totter, scream in fear, bump into each other, some try to turn and cannot, gripped by the confusion which suddenly arises, provoked by no one knows what. Narcelia looks around me and I attempt to back up, but we are also blockaded behind, one of the women who look like prostitutes falls over the wheelchair, the dogs get excited and bark, the two monkeys hide under their hat brims on the shoulders of the Negroes, who try to save their paraphernalia. There is a volley of calls, yells, cries for help. Lifting the chair almost off the ground, I try to reach the sidewalk and at that moment the force overcomes its resistance and spreads out, in tumultuous invasions of stores, something misshapen suddenly grazes Narcelia's knees (the dwarf!), I see that the hem of her dress has been torn, and then I can make out the center, the voluntary mainspring of the commotion, a compact, angry steamroller, ten or twelve young men, none more than twenty years old, the ones from the Hostess Hotel, who arrived the evening before, come at us like a load of falling bricks, snatch up Velimir Leskovar as they pass, the shadowy halo has disappeared and he looks at me—for the briefest second—with his terrified eyes. Narcelia emits a mortal shriek, I am lofted into the air, I let go the wheelchair, see it start to turn over with its invalid passenger, her arms go out to break the fall and it strikes me that in all these days of Holy Week I have not heard in the city a single bell. Not one.

—◦❧ ❦◦—

[*The high walls still exhale the gleaming smell of whitewash and all the door and window frames have been painted green. The wood floor, carefully washed and scrubbed, intoxicates me with its odor of sandalwood, perhaps it is sandalwood, who knows? The door and window of the parlor (or are they two windows?) are wide open as at a wake and the chair backs glisten with their white linen covers. New lamps of a dazzling brilliance are burning in every room in the house. Even the parlor lamp, decorated with a fantastic orange-colored crepe-paper shade, shines through the paper, and the shadows that move on the walls have a kind of clarity.*

Who, meanwhile, has just moved into that strange house, to which I shall perhaps never return and whose lighted lamps, more than lighted, more than dazzling, living, bring me so much joy? Who?]

—◦❧ ❦◦—

The solicitous waiter opens the elevator door and I enter with Narcelia, who turns to contemplate, enigmatically, the empty dining hall, the lengthy table of cold cuts along the windows, the starched tablecloths, the almost homey arrangement still undisturbed by the guests, today in great numbers.

"So, we're free of them," she comments. "That is . . ."

The wheels roll rather stiffly along the corridor. The cloudless sky, the motionless sail of a boat lost in the luminous sea, the rippling cypresses on the isthmus. I open the door.

"That is, what?"

"Nothing. What time is it? Eleven thirty four." Voices in the swimming pool and the splash of falling bodies in the turbid water. I carry her to the bed, take off her shoes, there is a deformity—still slight—of her left foot.

"Bring me my kimono."

"Which one?"

"It doesn't matter. No." (In her voice a note of fatigue.) "I will remain dressed. If you like, you can leave for a while. I don't need anything. Better still: prop me up. I want to smoke."

I cover her feet with a colored silk scarf. Several people swimming at the same time, a sound as of propellers in the water, voices. I go to the window, observe the swimmers, the entire pool area is exposed (no umbrella, no bush, no shade at all). I take the oil can, screwdrivers, and rags from under my bed and start to lubricate the chair. Narcelia's eyes seem to contain both the city and Easter Sunday.

"Anyway, it was good to have lunch early. I don't want to see those people from the excursion."

"Some of them are in the pool."

On the carpet, smaller than her feet, rest the slippers she dreams of wearing.

"The Jew too?"

"Yes."

On the upper floor, my companion watches me; this means I have been found already, that I am marked. I will never see Easter in Seville, but meanwhile *he* protects me, unlike Velimir Leskovar, who is sitting by the pool, his feet immersed in the agitated water, without his special halo and also without any guarantees, mortal, defenseless, abandoned, alone, at the mercy of the unexpected. And how important and seemingly dire for him—a fish back from the abyss, from ephemeral immortality, now exposed to the net—is this madness of chairs and tables by the pool, their tension, the fury taking shape, uncontrollably, among these squares, rectangles, and circles, like storm clouds. Is this why my hands tremble? Is this why I press the oil can so hard I squirt oil on the wooden floor? Narcelia has finished her cigarette and says something I cannot hear over the noise of the clashing voices downstairs. The smell of smoke dissipates and, for a moment, the ruby-red smell of apples is stronger than the scents with which she sprinkles herself, than the wax of the floor boards, than the cedar used in the room and even stronger than the machine oil. The first customers at Angelo's Canteen, threatened by the hungry dogs on the sidewalk and Disney's fraudulent animals hanging from the ceiling, take their ease. In the pool, many are shouting exclamations of rejection and discord. Where did they ever dig up those decalcomanias at Candelabro's, like a forest growing out of the wall and as dark as his green broth? A noise like a mutinous mob, cursing, fighting, splashing water, the sun at its zenith. I stop oiling the chair: my fingernails are purple, purple in a livid, almost luminous tone. Narcelia has her eyes closed, but she is not asleep.

The water in the pool is much filthier so that I cannot see the bottom. The youths have taken it over, more than twenty of them, contesting eagerly for a leather ball, and the chairs and tables around them form a malignant design. Velimir Leskovar reappears perhaps from the bar, and stands hesitantly, following the young men's game with interest. Four or five of them, returning from the beach, scale the wall and dive in, shouting. The girls and the couples leave. The ball spins in the air and falls at random, one of the men grabs it and the rest attack him, yelling obscenities. Hesitantly, the foreigner goes down the steps into the water, but not all at once: step by step. He raises one arm, keeping the other hidden under the agitated water. The ball falls beside him, he steadies it and leans over it, his white back is buried under a mass of muscular arms, legs, torsos, the farthest ones heap on insults as if possessed and suddenly a stain appears in the turbid water. The clamor diminishes. Someone hurries out and escapes over the wall. Bodies disentangle. Why is everybody running? The ball floats red in the sun. Half-submerged—as if between clouds—the light, heavy body of Velimir Leskovar slowly rotates, the blood gushing from his throat darkening the still turbulent water in such a way that I cannot see his face.

I turn and face Narcelia's look: hard and more cross-eyed, a "xaman" priestess, xylographed, double dart strike, an X. I manage to say: "They murdered the Jew."

Am I asleep or am I losing my senses? The day has died, a pink band remains in the changing sky, dissipated by the increasing blue. Did I see Narcelia walking around the room and leaning over me or was it a dream? Did I actually see the feeble, mutilated and abandoned body once more in the impure water?

Narcelia's voice rings clear from the shadows:

"He was not murdered. He died by his own hand."

She still does not move, however. The April stars come out over the city, which falls back into expectation and monotony. A bus slowly crosses the bridge, far off. The pool is empty and the main street is deserted. I go to the window: the sea is the color of steel. A donkey pulling a cart full of empty bottles passes by. At this point I realize that there is *no one* on the floor above us, that my companion—like Leskovar's yesterday—is also gone. Expelled from Delos, I sit in the wheelchair, stunned by the weight of death and uncertainty. The hotel's neon sign starts to pulse. Reflecting off the crumbling building that fronts the beach, it echoes on the wall, unveils the face of Narcelia, who appears to be saying, from the mossy depths of a swamp:

"Now it is your turn."

Dalton Trevisan
—◦❧(b. 1925)❦◦—

A prolific author of dystopian stories aimed at the middle class of Curitiba, Paraná, Dalton Trevisan cultivates very brief, condensed, and refined narratives, based on dialogue and a self-indicting satire. Using understatement, a psychology of cruelty and banality that unmasks the aggressions of the bourgeois middle class, Trevisan's stories present a hidden, expressionistic universe of perversity. His plots may be considered inversions of the exemplary or moral tale. His taste for cultural satire and parody was signaled by his first stories from 1945, "Moonlight Sonata" and "Non-Exemplary Novels." Although the author maintains a reclusive profile, averse to photographs and interviews, Trevisan's works continue to receive prestigious awards, translations in many languages, and film adaptations. Trevisan is almost exclusively a writer of short stories, and in 1996 he received the special prize of the Ministry of Culture for his complete works. His original stories have been pared to their essentials, becoming a kind of haiku of the short story. Author of more than thirty volumes of stories, Trevisan is considered a Brazilian master of the genre. His titles range from parodies of popular and film culture (*Lincha Tarado* [1980]; *Virgen Louca, Loucos Beijos* [1979]) to more abstract, experimental titles, such as the recent *234* (1997), *111 Ais* (2000), *Pico na Veia* (2002) *Capitu Sou Eu* (2003), and *Arara Bêbeda* (2004). In 2003, Trevisan received Brazil's biggest literary prize from Portugal Telecom. The only previously published work of Trevisan's translated into English is *The Vampire of Curitiba* (1972).

The Corpse in the Parlor
—◦❧ ❦◦—

Lying on her back in bed, staring into the darkness, with her hands folded over her breast, she mimicked the corpse in the parlor. The afternoon had passed quickly: it was a novelty to have a dead man in the house. That night Yvette would not have to listen to his eternal argument with her mother: he was convinced that Yvette was not his child. She could hear her mother scratch herself as she sat beside the dead man: the anxious scraping of fingernails over a silk stocking. She recalled the face of the caller who had come to pay his respects to the deceased, how he had afterward slapped at the cuff of his trousers. He had not wanted his clothing to absorb the dead man's cloying mustiness: every corpse is a bloom of a different perfume.

The night breeze rustled the window curtain and gave her arms gooseflesh, but she did not pull up the blanket from the foot of the bed. She could smell the sweetish odor of the wilted flowers and of the tapers at the four corners of the casket. As the wick sputtered, it made the shadows leap against her bedroom door. The man's particular fragrance hovered beneath the mingled odors of the house. There in his casket, his chin caught up with a white handkerchief knotted at the top of his head, he was beginning to stink.

She heard her mother dragging her house slippers over the floor as a different scent, momentarily overpowering the others, reached her dilated nostrils. Her mother was burning incense. At that moment it would have been easier to die than to elude the corpse. The burial had been set for the following morning, and until then the man's odor would furtively spread through the house, seep into the fabric of the curtains, take root under Yvette's fingernails. The caller had slapped uselessly against the cuff of his trousers. He would be obliged to send them to the dry cleaner's.

The dead man had decided to take leave of his home with consummate lack of grace. The burned-out ash of his last cigarette lay undisturbed in his ashtray; his coat hanging on the back of his chair still reeked of his sweat. How could they hide his hat hanging there on the hat rack, his hat whose brim had so often been turned back by hands now lifeless and folded across his chest. If the girl raised her head she would be able to see his pajamas outside the window, hanging on the clothesline. His striped pajamas with stains that no water could wash clean. If she looked in the mirror, it was his ashen face that she would see.

It was not her mother's slippers dragging across the parlor floor, it was his as he leaned against the door to listen to Yvette and her fiancé whispering in the hallway. Suddenly his rocking chair would begin to move again, at the slightest recollection of him. His rocking chair with the cane bottom distended from the weight of him. No matter how frantically she swept the floor, she still found his broken toothpicks in every corner: he had always had a toothpick hanging from his mouth. After digging at his rotten teeth, he would slowly draw a whitish line with his toothpick across his puffy nose. He would roll his bread into little balls and flick them with his fingertips. Yvette had found them in the folds of his napkin, among the lacy fingers of the potted fern, lodged in the frame of the *Last Supper*.

He had taken his own good time in dying. For months on end he had rocked back and forth in his chair with his pajama top open because of the heat, revealing a mass of chest hair so long that it coiled into wiry gray ringlets.

"That girl has no feelings," he railed at his wife. "She looks at me like she wanted me to hurry up and die and be done with it."

He had spent his life as a traveling salesman and had wasted little time with his family, and one fine day he simply came home to die. He sniveled from room to room in his striped pajamas, which he never changed. She could hear his felt slippers as he came near and leaned against the door to listen to the little sounds Yvette and her sweetheart made in the hallway. As he eavesdropped he would chew his toothpick behind the closed door. The girl would cough to let him know that she was aware of his spying, and when she came in again she inevitably found that he had dragged himself back to his rocking chair. She took small vengeance in polishing his shoes, always his shoes. Why polish them if she knew he would never wear them again? She left them resplendent, never waiting for his gratitude, and every week his unused shoes reappeared as smudged as before. There they were now, lined up straight, on top of his wardrobe. If her mother offered them to the milkman or to the baker, the dead man would climb the steps again to reclaim them and the girl would recognize his footfall on the stairs.

It began the afternoon Yvette was dusting the furniture. She was wearing slacks rolled up to her knees, and she noticed that he was looking at her legs. She could imagine his thoughts: "That girl with her birdlegs . . ." From behind his paper he spied on her out of the corner of his eye. The page trembled so violently that it was impossible for him to read. He dropped the page and screamed that she should go change her clothes and not run around the house half naked:

"Cover up your legs. Even if they were pretty, which they're not!"

She was thirteen years old, and since the salesman had returned for good, she never left the house except to go to school, and only then in that dreadful blue uniform. She and her mother were the man's prisoners, he in his woolen socks (even in summer), with the little balls of bread on the tablecloth, and his broken toothpicks in every corner.

"He's just upset because he's sick," her mother implored. "Please be patient with him!"

Yvette did her homework in the parlor. He dozed or read the paper; her mother drudged in the kitchen. Bent over her notebook she suddenly felt the hair on her arm stand erect: he was staring at her. He wasn't asleep; nobody could sleep when his eyelids were moving. He wasn't reading the paper; who could read a paper with his hands shaking like that! The girl went to her bedroom to finish her lessons. From there she could keep an eye on the rocking chair in the parlor. She lifted her eyes from the book and listened hard like a hunted animal . . .

She smoked on the sly in her bedroom. The chair creaked when he rocked and annoyed her so she could not study, but the man who could barely drag himself along by holding onto the furniture knocked at her bedroom. He knocked so hard that it frightened her and she opened the door. He immediately saw the cigarette, still burning where she had thrown it on the floor. With the live ash he burned Yvette's arm, and he made such a hideous face that she did not dare to call out for her mother.

"Don't scream, you tramp. If you do I'll kill you!"

She began to wear only long sleeves so she could hide the red welts on her arms. At mealtime he never took his eyes off her and, if she wanted a second portion, she got up and went around the table for it so she would not have to address him directly. Between them, her mother ate without lifting her eyes from her plate.

When he could not bear it any longer (he rocked in his chair so furiously, why in the name of God didn't he just go flying out the window?), he scratched on her door. He held a cigarette in his hand. It was the only time he ever smoked. He slowly lifted her sleeve, and the girl bit her lip with all her might to keep from crying out. She bore the burn of the cigarette until it crumbled to shreds between the man's fingers.

She always woke up at night when she heard them arguing in the next room. He had been on the road for years and insisted that, in his absence, his wife had enjoyed numberless affairs. Bellowing, he demanded to know what the girl was doing under his roof, since he was not her father. The poor woman sobbed and swore that she had been faithful. In the morning, Yvette looked at herself in the mirror to see whether she could find any family resemblance. It was strange. She was the very image of her father: the same dark hair, just like his before he fell ill, the same large mouth and full lips.

Her mother asked her to take the patient his tea in his room. The doctors had given him up and he could not possibly last much longer, a few days at most. She begged the girl to treat the dying man with kindness. Why not take his tea to him in his room. Yvette's heart softened and she took the tray from her mother. She stopped short at his door: he was only a pitiful old man who was afraid of dying.

Before he died, he begged her to forgive him and kiss him on his forehead as a token of her pardon. He spoke with his eyes closed; his eyelids fluttered. As she leaned down, he suddenly grabbed her and kissed her full on the mouth. It was worse than being burned by his cigarette. She ran to the bathroom and rinsed out her mouth and brushed her teeth with such frenzy that her gums bled.

He could now barely stand the pain of his wracked body and got out of bed only by leaning on his wife's shoulder, in order to reach his chair. He was too weak to rock it. The eyes in his helpless body followed the girl. She never again returned to his room. Her mother never asked why. When he saw that she was beyond his reach, he roared:

"Who's your old man? Which one of your mother's lovers was your old man? Tell me his name. Come in here, you tramp!"

In revenge the girl took to wearing too much make-up. When her fiancé whistled at the front entrance, the chair fell silent. The salesman returned from the transports of his crazed mind. From the dark hallway Yvette could see him in her imagination, craning his neck, trying in vain to sort out the voices. She laughed a little too loudly so the spy could hear through the door. Her boyfriend thought she was crazy. When she came back in, her lips were stripped of the lipstick the boy had kissed away. She deliberately crossed through the parlor so the man could lean from his chair and see for himself the dark circles under her eyes and her disheveled dress.

At dawn Yvette was awakened by their shouting. Clinging to his chair he was in such acute pain that he could not sleep. His wife rocked the chair for him while he demanded to know the names of her lovers. Sleepless with his pain the dying man idly observed the spectacle of his waning life. In her bedroom the girl lit her lamp; lately she could not get back to sleep without a light. Waiting for sleep to come, she fervently prayed that he would die.

Her fiancé had whistled from the hallway and Yvette went to meet him. The man in the striped pajamas had reached his final agony. They kissed so long that her mother had to come to the hallway to get her: she could feel the scratch of his beard with every kiss. Lying in bed with her hands folded over her breast, playing dead, her heart pounded with delight, she fell asleep. Then the man climbed from his casket and came into her bedroom:

"What are you doing, tramp?"

"I'm sleeping."

"Don't you have a mathematics examination in the morning?"

"Yes."

"Why aren't you studying then?"

"You're dead, father. I don't have to take the examination."

When Yvette awoke, she could still hear their voices. She opened her eyes: one corner of the mirror shone in the half-light. She could hear her mother in the parlor, scratching herself. She had caught the dead man's fleas, for sure.

She sat on the edge of the bed and outside the window she caught a glimpse of the pajamas, covered with stains, flapping in the breeze. He was dead. She heard her mother dragging her slippers along the corridor toward the kitchen.

Standing beside the casket, Yvette rubbed her lips against the back of her hand. His kiss burned her tongue. She waited a long moment; it was not an easy matter to escape the dead man. She lit a cigarette and gazed at the old man through the gray smoke. She saw the handkerchief tied about his chin, the handkerchief which kept the drool from oozing from his mouth. Was he staring at her with his half-open eyes through his long lashes? No. This time his eyelids did not flutter. Yvette swallowed the smoke; she was mad with pleasure. He was really dead. In the kitchen, her mother made coffee in preparation for the wake.

The girl leaned over and examined the man: his eyelids, his beard, his mouth. She raised his sleeve and, pushing aside the black beads of the rosary he held between his fingers, she pressed the red glow of the cigarette against her father's flesh. Very slowly she burned a hole in his hand.

The Vampire of Curitiba

Oh, I feel just like dying. Look at her little mouth, the way it's asking to be kissed—a virgin's kiss is the bite of a hairy caterpillar. You shout for twenty-four hours and fall into a happy faint. She's the kind who wet their lips with the tip of their tongue to be more enticing. Why did God make woman a sigh in young men and the whirlpool of the old? It's not fair to a sinner like me. Oh, I'm dying just looking at her, so you can imagine. Stop dreaming, you drunken parrot. It's eleven o'clock in the morning and I won't last till nighttime. If I could only get closer, like someone who doesn't want anything—oh, love, a dry leaf in the wind—and slowly snuggle up to the little bitch. I think I'd die: I close my eyes and I melt away with joy. All I want in the world is two or three just for me. I'm going to put myself in front of her, maybe my moustache will charm her. The devil! She acts as if she didn't see me: there's a butterfly over my crazy little head. She looks right through me and reads the movie poster on the wall. Am I a cloud or a dry leaf in the wind? Damned witch, she ought to be burned alive in a slow fire. She's got no pity in her black plum of a heart. She doesn't know what it's like to moan with love. It would be nice to hang her up head down and let her bleed to death.

If they don't want to, why do they show off what they've got instead of hiding it? I'd like to suck their carotids, one by one. Until then I'll sop up my cognac. All because of a bitch like that one there wiggling all over. I was quiet in my corner, she's the one who started it. No one can say that I'm a degenerate. Under every son of a good family there's a vampire sleeping—don't let him get the taste of blood. Oh, if I only could have been a eunuch! Castrated at the age of five. Bite your tongue, you devil. An angel would say amen! It makes me suffer so much to look at a pretty girl—and there are so many of them. Pardon the indiscretion, love, are you going to drop the stuff of dreams for the ants? Oh, let me, my flower. Just a little, just a little kiss. One more, just one more. One more. It won't hurt, if it hurts may I fall down stiff at your feet. Lord in heaven, I won't hurt you—my *nom de guerre* is Nelsinho the Frail.

Veiled eyes that beg and flee, why can't I face them? A fear that they'll catch the flash of crime in my eyes? I mustn't startle them. Use blandishments and softness. Be very gentle. I lose out because I'm impatient, how many have I chased away with a hasty movement? It's not my fault, they made me what I am—a big chest, a hole in rotten wood where spiders, snakes, and scorpions breed. They're always making up, painting themselves, worshiping themselves in their pocket mirrors. If it's not in order to get some poor soul all aroused, what's it for, then? Look at the daughters of this city, the way they grow up: they neither toil nor spin, and still they're chubby. That one there's one of the lascivious kind who like to scratch themselves. I can hear her nails scratching on the silk stocking from here. I wish she'd scratch me all over and draw blood on my chest. Everything in front of me looks red. Here lies Nelsinho, gone to his reward because of a stroke. Tell me, genie of the mirror, is there anyone in Curitiba more miserable than I?

Don't look, you wretch! Don't look and see that you're lost. She's the kind who ..nuse themselves by seducing adolescents. All in black, with black stockings, whoo-ee. An orphan or a widow? With her husband buried, the wife covers her head with veils so she can hide the pimples that break out on her face overnight—the measles of widowhood in flower. Some go wild, take up with the milkman or the baker. Oh, sad and solitary nights, rolling over in their double beds, fanning themselves, reeking with valerian. Others put on the cook's clothes to go out into the streets hunting for soldiers. She's in black, that nauseating quarantine. But look at her short skirt, she amuses herself by pulling it up above her knees. Ah, the knees . . . Nice and round, with softer curves than a ripe peach. Oh, to be the purple garter that holds up the stocking on that thigh glowing with whiteness. Oh, to be the shoe that pinches her foot. And, being the shoe, to be squeezed by the lady with the small foot and die with a moan. Like a cat!

Look, a car stopped. She's going to get out. Get in position. Oh, don't do that, love, I saw everything. Cover up, her husband's coming, damned cuckold. Some of them attract poor boys to go to bed with their wives. All they want to do is watch beside the bed—I think I'd be inhibited. Underneath it all I'm a hero of good will. That guy at the bar swore to me it happened to him. Is that one there one of that kind? Hell, no, not with that fierce look. Some of them even prefer the boy—would I be capable of that? God save me, it's a sin even to think about it. Kissing another man, all the worse if he's got a moustache—you can tell a man a hundred yards away by the cigarette stink. A woman has her own smell—in her armpits she filters out the honey that intoxicates a hummingbird and drives a vampire into a rage.

Young wives out shopping early. Ah, all painted gold, wearing feathers, plumes, and ermine—tear them with your teeth, leave them with their body hair. Oh, smooth and naked plump little arm—if they don't want to, why do they show them off instead of hiding them?—draw an obscene tattoo on it with the point of a needle. Condemn them to hide under black shrouds, bound in chastity belts—throw away the keys. Lord have mercy, there are so many of them and I'm so all alone.

There goes a schoolgirl. Or could she be that other kind of woman in disguise? If I could only find that famous brothel. All dressed in blue and white uniforms—mother of heaven!—parading by with black stockings and purple garters in a hall of mirrors. Don't do that, love, I arrived in a state of levitation: it's the strength of my twenty years. Look at me, I'm hovering three inches off the ground. I would have taken flight already if it weren't for the ballast of my little turtledove down here. Oh, Lord, let me grow old fast. Close your eyes, count one, two, three, and open them, be an old man with a white beard. Don't delude yourself, you drunken parrot. Not even a patriarch can be trusted, least of all with cold showers, Spanish fly, magic rings—I've known heads of families like that!

What if I got run over by a car crossing the street and the police found this collection of pictures in my pocket? I'd be lynched as a sex maniac, the shame of my city. My godfather would never forgive me. Just like the boy who left a trail of bread crumbs in the forest, I can hide a photograph in a magazine in the dentist's office, send another in an envelope to the little widow for the seventh-day mass. Imagine the surprise, the pretended shame, and finally the hours of delirium in the bedroom—the word bedroom tightens a knot in my throat.

Every family has a virgin burning up in her room. She can't fool me, the devil: first a sitz bath, then she says three prayers and goes to the window, her eyes all set to devour the first male to appear on the corner. And she grows old there, her elbows on the sill, the old maid in her vat of formaldehyde.

Why don't I take my hand out of my pocket, love? It's to hide the hairy hand of a werewolf. Don't look now. You ugly face, you're lost. Too late. I already saw the blonde: a cornfield waving under the weight of ripe tassels. She's bleached, her eyebrows are too dark—how can I stop from chewing my nails? For you I'd be greater than the motorcyclist in the Circle of Death. Let it out, you want a good-looking man with a moustache. Well, I've got a moustache. I'm not handsome, but I'm a nice fellow, isn't that worth anything? It's a shame at my age. There I go following her the way I used to follow the band of the Rio Branco Military Academy when I was a child.

With that face of a little hollow wooden angel and all, I know that she gets fun out of looking up dirty words in the dictionary. Arrogant and disdainful, she moves along with a resolute step that brings sparks out of the cobblestones. She's a regular Attila's mare—the grass no longer grows where she steps. It's impossible for her not to feel my eyes running up her arm like the slime of a snail. If there's some transfer of thought, she must be feeling the seven kisses of passion on the back of her neck.

She's far off now. I didn't give her the rose with the ashes of a swallow's heart to breathe. The blonde gets dizzy, she feels strange and lets herself go at the same time. A select bestiary of bat, swallow, and fly! Mother of heaven, I even used flies as instruments of pleasure—how many did I pull the wings off? A glow lights up in my eyes, I die without getting her. It's not fair. I roar to heaven: how do you get to have a face without pimples?

I despise you, cruel virgins. I could enjoy every one of them—and not a single one has cast her mad eye of lust on me. Oh, if I were only the devil and could bewitch them, be a dark and filthy goat. They'd crawl on their knees to kiss my hairy tail.

Oh, so good that afterwards there's nothing left to do but die. Calm down, boy: admiring the marching pyramids of Cheops, Chephren, and Mycerinus, who cares about the blood of slaves? Help me, oh Lord. Spare me the shame, oh Lord, of an onset of tears in the middle of the street. I'm a poor boy in the damnation of his twentieth year. Should I carry a jar of bloodsuckers and at the moment of danger apply them to the back of the neck?

A blind man doesn't smoke because he can't see the smoke, so, Lord, sink your needles of fire in my eyes. No more being a mangy dog tormented by fleas and turning around to bite his own tail. As a farewell—oh curves, oh delights—grant me the grace of that little woman passing there. In exchange for the lowest female I'd walk on hot coals—and I wouldn't burn my feet. Oh, I feel just like dying. Look at her little mouth, the way it's asking to be kissed—a virgin's kiss is the bite of a hairy caterpillar. You shout for twenty-four hours and fall into a happy faint.

Paulo Emílio Salles Gomes
—◦❧(1916–1977)❦◦—

A specialist in Brazilian cinema, Salles Gomes came late to fiction. In *As Três Mulheres de Três PPPés* (1977; *P's Three Women*, 1984), however, he demonstrated his mastery of narration, stylistic grace, invention, and the satire of psychological and erotic analysis. In the story "Her Times Two," Salles Gomes joined the masters of the urban story through his humor and subtlety, in a satire of male sexual and social dominance, deftly manipulating an ingenuous narrator.

Her Times Two
—◦❧ ❦◦—

First *Carnet*

I open this *carnet* to write of Her. The years I spend with Her are the calmest in a life fraught with hardships that I shall not here recall. If now, as I enter old age, my hour should come to long for repose, and I didn't have Her, the ideal to which my imagination should aspire would be a marriage exactly like ours. I rejoice at not having given ear to the insinuations and even warnings against my choice of Her as a wife. My close relatives and a colleague in my firm never ceased to allude to the numerous inconveniences in marriages where there is a great difference in age between the husband and the wife. I recognize that when I met Her—she must have been about sixteen—an abyss of time was evidenced by the difference in our physical appearances. Spiritually, however, we were always close. As the years passed, the disparity between Her and me lessened and when she became my wife at thirty, I had to make an effort to remember that she could have been my granddaughter. It was as if I had stopped in time and she had hastened to catch up. With her youth smothered beneath austere clothes, her appearance of early maturity was aided by that subtle yellowing of the complexion symptomatic of prolonged virginity. These two points, one subjective and one objective, i.e., my feeling of being young and Her virginity, complicated our wedding night, which was long and laborious. When it ended, its objective had not been achieved. I went so far as to blame this failure on my fallacious sense of youth, which hadn't taken the precaution of conferring with reality repeatedly and at short intervals. Yet the rigidity, not only of my character but of my whole spiritual and physical person, denied the truth of this idea. It was she who interrupted the awkwardness that moved into bed with us as we tried a succession of different positions. Discomfort had infiltrated my consciousness. She took charge and began to speak. First, she explained us, then she explained me, and finally she explained herself, using clarity and tact throughout. Her competence in the area of theory was extensive, as she had studiously followed various premarital courses ranging from those given by the Consolação parish church to the ones offered as an optional credit by the university entrance schools. Her reason for taking so many courses, when young girls generally studied only one, was explained by the length of time she took to marry—more than ten years. Now, during this time the nuptial science and its teaching, like other sciences (notably criticism and linguistics) underwent profound changes. She considered it her duty as a future wife to renew and enlarge annually her sum of knowledge in this field, and she was proven right on this first night which, without her accumulated instruction, could have caused me a long-lasting trauma, perhaps marked me for the rest of my life. I've already mentioned that after our various tries—the anniversary of which we celebrate every year with a bottle of champagne—she gave three short lectures: one about us, another about me, and a third about herself. The first centered on the concept of gauge, not in the offhand sense in which it is employed nowadays, but in the original technical meaning of calculation of proportions, standard measurement to which certain things ought to conform, like the distance between railroad tracks or the width of a tunnel, and the instruments used to verify such measurements. The initial explanation served as an introduction to the other two. In that which concerned me directly, her main theme was gauge, or caliber, which despite her premarital courses she had never imagined so well developed. This part of her dissertation, besides being very enlightening, had the benefit of soothing my self-esteem, which was somewhat battered at the moment. However, the best words she employed that night were used to describe herself. In addition to enriching my knowledge they touched me by revealing that it wasn't only her complexion that had altered during her long wait. To understand her discreet way of broaching this delicate aspect of the feminine condition, an elucidative parenthesis is necessary. Besides the premarital courses, she had taken numerous others, some of a professional order, such as typing, stenography, and English; others of a domestic nature (cooking, sewing, flower arrangement) and still others of miscellaneous types, such as one on binding and gilding books. This partial enumeration demonstrates her superiority over the young girls I knew who while waiting for husbands were wasting precious time on psychology, belles-lettres, or, most useless of all, pedagogy. Speaking of herself on that unforgettable night, she chose terms of comparison in the interesting area of bookbinding. As everyone knows (but I didn't), the celebrated and beautiful French *reliures* in wild boar hide, made during the eighteenth century approximately up to the Revolution (with the decline of the aristocracy pigskin was substituted for wild boar hide) enter into a process of drying and wrinkling which makes impossible not only the reading of the volume but even its simple handling by admirers. It is as if these books enter a profound withdrawal, saving up riches which they can't use due to the impossibility of reading themselves, and at the same time denying curious potential readers the secret joys they could bestow. One must not think, however, that she had any special liking for metaphors. She used them to safeguard her verbal modesty in speaking about the humiliating phenomenon she had suffered. Right afterward she went on to enumerate directly the measures to be taken: make an appointment with a gynecologist for an incision with an electric bistoury, two days to heal and all would be fine. There would be no need for hospitals or stretchers; she would walk into the specialist's office and out again.

She had been speaking continuously for almost half an hour when I intervened to say that the next day we would hunt up a doctor, but her quick mind already had the name of her family physician, a Dr. Bulhões. We went to his office in Marconi Street. *We* is only a form of speech, because when we got to the door of the building I backed out. I explained to Her that doctors' offices made me nervous—which was true—but also I was embarrassed to meet this Dr. Bulhões, or rather, to have him meet me. I would be waiting for Her in a nearby tearoom situated at the rear of a bookshop. I waited for three hours. For the first hour, I remained seated at a table where I partook of hot chocolate and cakes, but I felt uncomfortable occupying a place for so long, in spite of the paucity of customers. Only the bookshop section of the place was animated, where a group of young people was talking and laughing loudly. I ordered more chocolate and cakes and bore up for another hour. The rest of the time I spent pretending to look at books, but really I was extremely restless, first because she was taking so long—I feared some contretemps, one of those unforeseen events that are the rule in medicine once you go beyond routine stomach-thumping and chest-listening. The other, more immediate and disagreeable reason for my restlessness was the behavior of the group of people in the shop. Nobody noticed me during the first five minutes I spent in front of the shelves. They laughed a lot, jeering at one another and especially at certain respectable literary and political names. Upon noticing my presence, they began to talk more softly, as if I were bothering them. Then they whispered, obviously making comments about me. I decided to wait for Her on the sidewalk and look at the window display. But from inside they still watched me through the glass. A big robust boy got up with an air of decision and asked me if I wanted anything. He was not a clerk, and I replied firmly that I had had some hot chocolate and was waiting for my wife. The young man answered sarcastically that if she had delayed this long, she probably wouldn't come at all. I was about to raise my voice at his insolence when she appeared. I pointed to Her with triumph. Thinking the boy was somebody I knew, she extended her hand to him and the fellow, it must be said, behaved correctly, saying politely that the pleasure was his. My good humor restored, I said we must be going and we exchanged cordial farewells. Inside, the others watched the scene with interest, but there was no time for further introductions. I later learned that the bookshop crowd was made up of the new generation of São Paulo intellectuals, which struck me as odd, since they certainly didn't seem to take literature seriously. From what I could observe, they were extremists and perhaps had taken me for a defender of the social and political order, which in truth I am, but only in the area of ideas, not in the active function of a spy. Later

I chanced to meet the owner of the establishment, a very refined gentleman who confided in me his dislike for that gang: they didn't buy books or drink tea and they spent the late afternoon—the best time of day for the serious clientele—raising a rumpus and frightening off customers.

As we walked to the car, our worries dissolved completely. Everything had gone very well. She had been delayed simply because Dr. Bulhões was terribly busy. The check I sent the next day was generous, but he deserved even more, for his competence had made a healing period unnecessary. That very night our marriage was consummated in the greatest comfort and we made up the time lost in the laborious vigil of the night before.

She had a way of facilitating everything. At the firm, where she had worked for so many years, she called me only doctor, the form of address for all men of position. I never explained my vague bachelor's degree to anyone in the circles I frequented, since I consider it unnecessary to justify being called doctor by defending a thesis. I was always called doctor at home by the servants and at work by my employees; doctor because I was the boss, a fact with which everyone agreed, including Her. When we became engaged she didn't change this form of address and in spite of using the familiar *you*, she continued to call me doctor. On our first wedding night she came out with an affectionate "my little doctor," which I didn't appreciate. On our real wedding night, she substituted that with "my big doctor," which was more adequate. The fact of people calling me simply doctor solved a delicate problem: my surname doesn't combine well with that form of address and my first name, though it doesn't combine with anything, is even worse when isolated. A horrible name I've been trying to keep hidden ever since the first humiliations in the kindergarten of the Escola Caetano de Campos; a name I try to forget. On our third night of marriage, she at last gave me an appellation which stuck. It sounded approximately like *pauldior*, pronounced very much à la française. Spoken softly during our caresses, it sounded like one of those erotic verbal compliments she had learned in her courses, the spontaneity of which is well known to specialists. The next morning, however, over coffee and newspapers, she continued to emit the same suggestive nocturnal syllables. I imagined she was making matinal overtures which would cause me to be late for work, but the absence of any provocative tone, as well as Her satiated appearance, gave my thoughts a new direction. She was naturally alluding in a flattering way to the events of the night before and I began to answer the pauldiors with expressions like "my little woman" or "my darling," the only ones my creativity furnishes except when an authoritarian partner dictates what I should call her. Her sense of propriety was distressed at these words so unsuited to the moment, spoken within earshot of the malicious and ill-intentioned domestics who were hanging about, perhaps listening at the door. It was only then that I realized that for more than eight hours she had been calling me by my name. Now, this name had traumatized my spirit to such a degree that I even avoided words that had a similar sound, like *polyglot* or *polyester;* I would actually grow apprehensive when I heard records of the old brand Polydor. My idiosyncrasy reached into distant verbal areas as when, still young, I showed my friends the envy I had of flowers possessing multiple masculine organs; or later, when I reached maturity, I criticized in the same circles women who have more than one man at a time. But I never used the word *polyandrous* (back then written in Portuguese with a *y*), a current expression in the select circles I was part of. Nevertheless, spoken by Her, my name was transformed so much that this time the acceleration of my heart was caused by pleasure, not by the old fear provoked when I was four years old by the cruel children who used to pursue me screaming my name across playgrounds and through corridors until I would hide in the latrine, awaiting the bell that would free me from the fury of the young jackals. In Her mouth, the sounds that had made me suffer so much became a source of joy. In truth, the sounds were others, since she spoke the four syllables in a way unrecognizable to outsiders, especially servants. The first two syllables almost turned into Paul, a handsome name in any language and sufficiently removed from the combination po-ly. Her pronunciation altered still more the other two syllables, do-ro. Between the *d* and the *o* she insinuated a caressing *i* that practically annulled the final *o*, in such a way that one clearly heard *dior*. Moreover, as she also separated the first two syllables from the last two, I received a new name and surname as well: Paul Dior, very flattering to the French side of my personality.

I could mention other examples of Her kindness in the face of my little peculiarities, which outsiders might consider weaknesses but which are part of my being, and without which I would be someone else and not the very reasonable man I am. She, at any rate, accepts me as I am, creating about me a climate of restfulness. She is attentive to all that concerns me and shares my small interests with enthusiasm. A few references to the periods we regularly spend in Águas de São Pedro will serve to illustrate. A tenacious case of arthritis obliges me to take periodic cures at the sulphuric springs. She always accompanies me, doing her best to find a motive in her own physical state so as to leave me completely at ease. She spends days taking doses calculated to the centimeter from the Almeida Salles, Giaconda, or Juventude fountains, and advertises to the maximum their effect on her complexion, sleep, and stomach so I won't think she puts up with such monotony exclusively for my sake. Her consideration for me has no limit. I mentioned the small interests that lend some variation to my present life, which turns completely upon the axles of home and office. As I no longer like to read or attend movies, theaters, or exhibitions, and as television puts me to sleep, I find diversion in the things I see in the street or in the places I go to have coffee. There isn't much variety: façades from the twenties, cement lions, and the scenes painted on blue tiles in the bars of our capital city. I usually am alone when I admire these sights, walking to or from work in spite of having two cars. Walking is good for me. In Águas de São Pedro the two of us walk together a lot, and to pass the time we enter all the places we pass: hotels, bazaars, restaurants, gas stations, branch offices of state and federal savings banks, and cafés. In one of the latter, called Delight's Bakery and Bar, I discovered a picture that aroused my continued interest: medium-sized, it represented a little girl holding a turkey. I wanted to go back to Delight's on the pretext of drinking a cup of the awful coffee they serve, buying a pack of cigarettes I don't smoke, or asking for a useless box of matches, just to contemplate that child with her bird. At first I didn't do so because of Her, fearing to bore Her, but it was she who took the initiative. One afternoon we were vaguely looking into one of the savings banks when she pondered that there wasn't much to see there and suggested we go back to the bar with the girl and the turkey. From then on she acquired the habit of talking to the regular customers of the bar, old people of the region who knew many things. They would explain the difference between the andorinha bird, which had practically disappeared from Águas de São Pedro, and the andorões which to this day crowd the TV antennas as the afternoon wanes. They would recall stories about the early times of the region, when the pioneers were drilling for oil and discovered the waters that cure rheumatism. Not realizing this, they left the gigantic spring gushing for years. Everyone was friendly toward Her, and as they talked I would stare at the girl and her turkey, participating absently in their conversation.

There is still so much I could say. The pleasure I find in writing about Her here in Águas or in the office in São Paulo, during the empty hours of the early afternoon! At times it's hard for me to remember Her real name, I've become so accustomed to calling Her Her, that is, ever since she came to work for the firm so many years ago. Many times I made her repeat the story of this nickname—a little story I never tire of hearing. They had a slightly feebleminded cook who agreed to work for her modest family (father, mother, and a younger brother) in exchange for room and board and some occasional cast-off clothes. This simple soul, a fine person and a good cook, was incapable of remembering names and called the father Mr., the mother Mrs., the younger brother Him, and Her. The family found this amusing and adopted the curious system of names, calling each other Mr., Mrs., Him, and Her. When the old woman went to the poorhouse, everyone in the family reverted to their real names except Her. At school, when they asked her name, she answered spontaneously that it was Her and the director approved, recalling the title of a celebrated English novel and its heroine. Her name became Her permanently. From this story emanated a rather sad poem that I always associate with a small cement lion stationed on the pillar of a gate in Maria Antônia Street. And with the girl holding the turkey. Actually, one of Her charms is her indefinable melancholy. The first time I sensed it was when she broached the subject of her virginity at the beginning of our romance.

She had already been an employee of the company for several years, and our working relationship was excellent. Eventually we came to speak of more personal subjects, though the distance between employer and secretary was not diminished. My private life was not as easy as it is today; I had many worries, and to all effects was married, since I had no reason to go noising abroad the fact that legally my marriage didn't exist. Once I asked Her to type the first draft of a contract where my complete name and civil status had to appear. I myself would normally type this kind of document, the introduction to which the other party never reads, making improbable the embarrassment of their seeing my first name, but on that day I lost track of things and ended up giving Her the rough draft along with some other papers. When she came in holding my original and saying I had made a mistake, my heart sank; I was certain she had seen my name. But no. She only discovered the latter when she insisted on reading our marriage contract, and I've already noted the admirable way she found of circumventing the problem three days after we were married. What she had thought was a mistake was the designation of my civil status as "single." I explained in a summary manner, without going into detail, that under Brazilian law I actually was single. At that very instant I sensed that there stirred in Her a new interest toward me, which was borne out only later. She never spoke to me about it, but it's possible that even then she perceived my domestic difficulties and felt sorry for me, making a special effort to be an efficient worker, with a maternal warmth that did me good. At that time I thought of myself as incredibly older, and I was amused at being cared for like a child. So young, I thought, but like all women she's a potential mother seeking at least a psychic realization in selfless affection. I confess that during all those years I never saw anything in Her beyond the attentive helper who doubled as the vigilant little mother of an almost-old man, capable of serving him with changing dedication, pledged to providing quietly all the dozens of small things indispensable to his well-being. As I think back, I discover that one of Her greatest moments was shown in Her easy delicacy when she came to me in that crucial period mature men pass through: the interval, as difficult as some phases of adolescence, between consummate maturity and senility that fails to arrive. Her historic mission in my biography was to give new dimension and vitality to this chapter, transforming a time which would have been merely transitional into something valuable in its own right, as if instead of old age, what I had been waiting for was Her. The fundamental lever in this miracle was Her virginity. When we first touched on this matter it was the number one mark of my new existence, the zero mark being the luminous morning when she confessed she loved me. This event occurred two or three years after the conclusion of my first marital crisis. Her declaration did me a world of good, although only of a spiritual nature; the distrustful body did not accompany the spirit. When one cold evening I took Her to a nightclub, then rare in São Paulo, the comfort I sought at Her side had no intimation of pleasures more concrete than a good dinner and a high-quality wine. The direction our encounter took was not planned, and I was the first person to be surprised when I kissed Her and delicately proposed we become lovers. The moment she replied in her tiny voice that she was a virgin was the sharpest of my entire life. Mutation, metamorphosis, crystallization, rebirth, horizon, discovery, phoenix, lustrum, resolution, decision, revolution; I would need to use all these words with mastery to describe what I felt. Still, I think I made my basic feeling clear as it came from the depths of the collective masculine memory of the species. I should explain that none of the women who had crossed or accompanied my path up to then had ever been a virgin. In spite of my conservative upbringing, I never gave virginity excessive importance and tended, like the moderns, to consider it an outmoded taboo. All this on the theoretical plane. In practice, I was more severe, and even advised the younger members of my family to exercise prudence when the time came for them to choose wives, inclined as they were to discard with excessive haste a tradition that, like all traditions, has a certain reason for being and needs to be analyzed and understood. On the other hand, more than once I had started a home with experienced women. It's true that things never worked out, but I do not attribute that misfortune exclusively to the circumstance of these ladies' not being beginners. Her virginity brought a new freshness to my aging worldliness, and my imagination broke out of its seemingly permanent lethargy.

—◦֍ ֎◦—

I come to the final pages of this *carnet* and there is still so much I could say. Perhaps I'll start another one, I don't know. But it is necessary to register here that Her love for me is greater and has much more merit than mine. Who would have thought that the autumn of my life would hold for me a woman of such quality and truth?

I write these final lines at home, an exceptional circumstance since I never bring the *carnet* here; I wouldn't forgive myself the absent-mindedness of letting it fall into Her hands to offend her sense of modesty. At this exact moment I've been writing for more than half an hour in the bathroom. I hear Her voice, affectionate and slightly worried: "Paul Dior, you've been in there such a long time! Did something happen, Paul Dior? Answer, Paul Dior!"

My only worry, which I make an effort to keep at a distance, is the fragility of Her health, which obliges Her constantly to visit doctors' offices, clinics, and health centers. Fortunately she doesn't need to be hospitalized, for if that ever happened I don't know what I'd do; my idiosyncrasy toward everything concerning medicine has grown alarmingly pronounced with my age. Before, it was enough for me to stay away from places where medical science was practiced; I even avoided simple contact with doctors. Judging by the number of new hospitals and clinics being built everywhere in the city, the health of our population is deteriorating frightfully, and I don't see the public authorities taking any notice of this grave problem. Sooner or later even the neighborhood where I live will be sacrificed. I already had to bribe a functionary of the Public Health Service who wanted to start a children's clinic right here in Alto dos Pinheiros; from the look of it, children haven't escaped the general decline in health either. I know I won't be able to resist for very long. When my neighborhood is invaded, I'll move to Águas de São Pedro where there are no hospitals and the one doctor limits himself to prescribing the dosage of waters and the temperature of the baths. I can shake his hand without being attacked by the itching that comes over me at the mere sight of the Clinical Hospital when I forget myself and pass along Avenida Rebouças. Her way of protecting me—afflicted as she has always been by poor health, and consulting specialists almost daily—is the ultimate example of Her dedication and must be recorded. The distribution of Her time is organized in such a way that I never know which is the day she doesn't go to the doctor; I always have the impression that it is precisely the present day. Yesterday has already gone by and tomorrow doesn't yet exist, and since (thank God) my happiness is neither retroactive nor anticipatory, memory and imagination do not provoke my itching. What I must avoid are the visual or olfactory evidences, and she manages so that these never come near me. Upon coming home, I find Her bathed and perfumed, without the slightest vestige of injections marring that skin I know so well or the small blue veins whose pulsation I press with such affection. I imagine she must substitute intramuscular or intravenous shots with medications that can be administered in other ways, but the boxes and bottles of medicine that might exist in our house are certainly better concealed than the safe where I keep my stock certificates from Light, Paulista Railways, etc. I also have shares in Melhoramentos and other lesser-known but equally valuable companies. In short, in spite of knowing she is sickly I never perceive it and live in peace. The moments, like this one, when I think about the subject are so rare that I can affirm I am completely happy. Although Her precarious health is at this moment the only cloud in my sky, I don't believe that Destiny would commit the insensitivity of taking Her away from me. Other women besides Her have attributed this constant optimism of mine to egotism, but they were less understanding.

Second *Carnet*

Fresh facts, deserving to be recorded, demand that I open a new *carnet* about Her without which the first, which I wrote a few years ago, would become incomprehensible to me. The tranquility of Águas de São Pedro, where I have come for relief from a particularly sharp attack of arthritis, brings me face to face with the unpleasant duty of filling this second notebook. I have chosen one with a larger number of pages; I have more to write in this one than in the other, and I respect the superstition that pages left blank in a used notebook are a bad omen and presage the cutting off of life. In spite of everything, I don't wish Her any ill, nor myself either, but the fact is, everything has changed. I am not able to say just when the alteration began and I don't know its causes. The reasons she presented in the recent argument that precipitated our separation seem unclear to me. I will not describe in detail the gradual poisoning of our relationship; the process took years, during which the dust of ill feeling kept on accumulating and in the end became unbearably suffocating. If it weren't for the terrible verbal explosion of a week ago—an explosion which had a salutary effect on me—I think I would have pined away and died of the special type of tedium caused by mediocre unhappiness.

I had arrived home lighthearted, prepared for the tiredness that punctually overcame me. I found Her with a new gleam in her eye, herald of decisions. I waited. During dinner she didn't say a single word. She waited for the servants to retire; happily (or unhappily) up to the end of our relationship she was discreet around third parties. Once we were seated in the small lounge where we had our coffee, she began. I heard Her out with polite attention and resolved not to interrupt Her, a system I had adopted during the last two years, with reasonable success. She usually would talk calmly for about an hour, using impeccable language. The content of what she said, always the same, consisted of a list of general complaints about the life she led and criticisms of my fastidious, egotistical, comfort-loving, and false behavior. This behavior was demonstrated particularly, according to Her, in the silence I adopted during these rituals. They only tired me physically, a problem I couldn't get around since, always constrained by good manners, I would never leave a lady to talk to herself, especially in this case, as the insults and laments were couched in polished, civilized words. During those dozens of months she never accused me of anything specific with names and dates, nor did she suggest a solution. She was waiting for me to do so, and I'd had many ideas on how to free myself from that ritual which threatened to go on indefinitely. She and I were like two businessmen who want to make a deal but keep stalling for time, each hoping that the other will make the first proposal. On that night she began as usual, but I was alerted by a new word. The usual expressions answered their roll call: *fastidious, wearisome, vexations, annoying*—and its variant *annoyance*—but when she said outright I was a *bore*, I perceived something different in the air, and my interior attention corresponded, for once, to the attentive face I always maintained. The continuation of Her speech confirmed that the old ritual had undergone a trans- formation as great as those of the mass, or actually even greater, as was verified in the course of the evening. She alluded with new directness to my arthritis, to my cures in Águas where she had suffered the humiliation of being the wife of the most comic figure the porters had ever seen in the constantly changing population of the spa. Example? The entire village commented about my passion for that ridiculous little girl hugging the turkey. At this point she paused as though expecting a reac- tion. There was none. She resumed: actually I knew Her very little, because in spite of being sly I wasn't intelligent; on the contrary I demonstrated a surpassing fool- ishness. She cited the fact of my never having wondered about that brother of hers whom I'd never met. He lived in Rio, but every time we traveled there, he was in the North or the South. In fact, on this point I showed not only foolishness but also lack of family spirit and hardness of heart, since during our life together I had never visited her parents' graves in the Quarta Parada cemetery, nor even those of my own parents, much closer, in Consolação. But the really extraordinary thing was my lack of curiosity to meet this brother. Just as well: this so-called brother didn't exist. No?! No. The Him of Her childhood with the simple cook was an orphaned cousin taken in by her parents. He was the same age as Her. Another, shorter pause creating the impression she had made a mistake. She started talking again, faster, apparently anxious to reach a point at which something was supposed to happen. Her and Him grew up together and until they were ten or eleven, slept in the same narrow bed in the little room which gave onto the plum tree in the back garden. Curious and complacent, they played at the childish game of discov- ering the differences between boys and girls with complete naturalness. The game was interrupted when they grew too big for one bed and slept in separate ones in the same room. Even after she got to be fifteen, when she slept alone in the room and he left to occupy the living room couch, the games continued. She closed this part of her explanation by saying that she and the cousin were the teachers and students in her first course in premarital education: first and only, she concluded. And waited. Her wait was in vain despite the lengthy pause. My silence was not a mere civility; I was prodigiously interested in the plot and anxious for it to continue. She began again, with a reference to a medical exam which I didn't quite under- stand, then drew back and passed quickly to another subject. With a resolute air, she said solemnly that in view of the circumstances, she imagined I would like a divorce. I had been waiting for this proposal for a long time, but the moment was inopportune; just then the only thing that interested me was the continuation of the story. This time there was really a very long silence. I was afraid that if I didn't say something she wouldn't open her mouth again for the rest of the night. She had taken the initiative of making a concrete suggestion and was awaiting my opinion. On any other occasion I would have answered affirmatively, depending on Her intentions, of course. But if we started discussing this now, the conversation would take a practical turn and I would never know anything more about Him and Her, still only fifteen years old. I was obliged to improvise and in my panic I said the wrong word, which turned out to be providential. I meant to ask her if in our situation a separation was reasonable, but instead of "situation" I said "age." She replied vehemently that I shouldn't confuse our ages, she had given me the best years of Her life but she was still a girl compared to an old wreck like me, the cousin was the one who was Her age. The appearance of the word "wreck" for the first time in our conversation, and the return to the cousin, seemed like good omens and induced me once again to be silent. Sure enough, after a few words of sarcasm, she took up Her story at the point where she had left off. When they reached adolescence, the cousin became more imprudent and daring, but she knew how to put Him in his place, thus safeguarding her virginity. The new pause was prolonged, probably because she misinterpreted my impatience, the nature of which was similar to that produced by the television commercials that interrupt a soap opera or film, with the difference that Her story was incomparably more interesting than those on TV.

At this point she went back to the medical examination she had precipitately introduced in a foregoing passage. Its significance only now became clear. She had been slightly hurt, and Her mother, who knew Her recently commenced but very regular menstrual dates by heart, was alarmed by the blood she found on the sheets. She obliged Her to undergo a medical examination. They knew a doctor from the Santa Casa, a worthy young man for whose family Her father had worked as a chauffeur. This same doctor had arranged a place in the poorhouse for the old cook. By this time, she had already mentioned the doctor's name several times, but I only understood this later. It took me a while to recognize the name Bulhões from the way she pronounced it. She didn't include the *Dr.* and practically swallowed the first letter, so that I didn't catch the meaning of the ". . . ulhões" that began to appear with a certain frequency. The doctor examined Her with utmost care, affirmed that she was intact as far as the principal matter was concerned, and as he tinged the secondary problem with iodine, asked why a smart, pretty girl like Her would do a thing like that—because she enjoyed it or because it was a habit? She didn't quite understand the range of the question, and limited herself to answering simply that she didn't much enjoy it, but she didn't want to run the risk of never getting married. That day the doctor didn't say anything more. In the waiting room he reassured the mother as to Her virginity. There was nothing serious wrong with Her, just a small disturbance common in adolescence. In a short time she would be fine and needed only some shots that he himself would give her. He preferred that she be brought to his office in José Bonifácio Street (Marconi Street didn't exist then) because the Santa Casa was for beggars, and he insisted on taking good care of the daughter of an old servant of his family's. The next day, the doctor jokingly asked if she needed more iodine and then went on to explain many things, illustrated with charts and pictures in books. Next he proposed that she relax. He promised on his word of honor as a doctor: whenever she ordered, he would reconstitute her virginity. As she was naturally delicate, two small stitches would be sufficient, maybe only one, even taking into account the growth factor, for she wasn't yet sixteen.

During the next pause, which she threatened to prolong unduly, I discovered a way of making Her continue, which worked well to the end. The rest of the time I talked only when I wanted to. Each time she interrupted her narrative and waited for me to say something, my face would acquire an expression that seemed to ask, "and then?" which had the effect of making Her go on—rather irritably, it's true, which was inconvenient as the increasing pitch of her voice might reach the kitchen. However, soon it became unnecessary to goad her on. She seemed to be confessing her memories to herself while she addressed me. In this abandon the name ?ulhões reacquired a consonant that didn't correspond to the original B. The reason for this intrigued me until the narrative provided an explanation. When she remembered I was listening, she created an ambiguous sound that belonged simultaneously to the first two consonants of the alphabet. Indeed, up to the final seconds of that long evening, Her language remained correct and for the last time I was able to admire the mastery of speech of that girl of such humble origin. It was evident that in place of the mythical premarital courses, and in addition to the one on bookbinding, she had taken many others, both public and private. These must have included one on elocution (pioneered in high society by Dona Noêmia Nascimento Gama) for as I transcribe and condense Her words, I seem to be hearing the sonority of her voice, worked up to the point of artifice.

"... ulhões kept his promise. Of the many he made, it was the only one he kept rigorously, without batting his long eyelashes which have become golden with time. You never met him; you didn't wish to, so you have no way of imagining his eyelashes. In their abundance they resemble those of the writer whose photograph you showed me in the library beside the Leopoldo Fróis Theater, the only difference being that that man was ugly, and Bulhões was very handsome. I recognize that he really couldn't keep some of his promises. He failed to marry me only because his wife's weak lungs were aided by the discoveries of medicine. When she finally died, I had already gotten tired of waiting and married you. The proof of his good faith was his desire to separate from the moribund wife, but I couldn't break the promise I made to my mother on the night she died: to get married properly, with all the papers in order, notarized by the civil authorities and the priest. I often renewed this promise in front of the shallow grave where she was buried beside my father; it remains shallow because you never kept your promise to order the statue with the two angels that I saw in the funeral home on Alagoas Street. In this case, Bulhões showed greater sensibility; he wanted to pay for the statue. I thought it wouldn't be right in spite of our intimacy, as great as that which you and I shared when we were happy. I don't want to be unfair to anyone. You were the two men in my life and when I was still happy, I think I was able to be equitable to both of you. At least I tried. I'll give you an example. Bulhões knew I called you Paul Dior and asked me to give him the same proof of affection, transforming his name as well. I asked him if he disliked his name too and he said he was bothered by the B and added, laughing, that he preferred the neighboring consonant. From then on, as with Paul Dior for you, I always called him by this name, behind closed doors of course, at a safe distance from the nurses and assistants in the places where he worked: his office, the Santa Casa, the Portuguese Beneficiary Home, the Matarazzo Health Center, and the Clinical Hospital, after it was inaugurated by Ademar de Barros. All served for our rendezvous. At first we met almost daily, then less frequently, and nowadays we rarely see each other and then only to talk. But I don't want to think about the present, equally bitter for me with you or with him; I want to remember the golden era with the two of you, when Culhões—better educated than you—said gorgeous things to me using words you never used. On my heart are engraved forever his remarks about how delicate my body was—which didn't impede, he would say, my being a master polyandrist and the happy territory of a diarchy. This isn't the time for insincerity; I loved Culhões much more than Paul Dior, but as long as I was happy I had enough dedication and patience for both. It's true that I would have preferred to marry him, and when you got old and arthritic, ever more set against doctors, I had the hypnothesis that, if we were both widowed, I might finally marry him. He answered that he hadn't thought of this, but if he were to do so, he would choose a younger woman. I am certain you would never offend me so blatantly—one must give credit where it's due—but still we must pardon Culhões, who was going through a difficult phase. Always vain—I would even say pretentious—about himself, Culhões, like all of your sex, would blame his partner for the decline which fatally accompanies age; in men, naturally. And like all of your sex—*you* seem to be an exception—he nurtured an incurable nostalgia for his youth. I thought about Culhões when I read the latest interview with the old soccer star Garrincha, where he recalls with emotion his repeated goals during the great matches here and in foreign countries. Culhões was also very well traveled and, like the champion, had reason to be proud of his past. He was brilliant, not only in São Paulo and Rio, but also in London, Paris, and Berlin, from whence he brought me distinguished diplomas hanging on the waiting room wall. His obsessions didn't bother me as long as life was happy; I've already said that as long as I was content I had patience for you both. Searching my memory I can only remember one occasion when I got irritated with both of you at the same time, but it didn't last long. It was when we had just gotten married. I had asked Culhões to take only one stitch, but he insisted on taking an extra one as a security measure, or so he said. He could have been right; I didn't know you and couldn't have guessed, to inform him, up to what point you are absent-minded about these things. Naturally he imagined, judging for himself, that you belonged to the nosy, investigating type who would want to know, see, and smell everything. You know as well as I do the results of your prudence—no, I'm not disputing how competent you are, I could test this and the results couldn't be more flattering to your skill. After he sewed me up, as a duty to my conscience, I resolved to undergo an examination at the Institute of Legal Medicine; my cousin has a part-time job there and made things easier. The certificate they furnished me could figure beside Culhões's foreign diplomas as additional proof of his knowledge. Even so, our wedding night was a nightmare for me. How I controlled my nerves to avoid the explosion of impatience that would have compromised everything! You have no idea how I strained my imagination to produce the long speech about gauge and caliber, for in reality, next to Culhões you were small fry. Don't think I remained unjustly impatient with you over this point for which the other was exclusively responsible. On our first morning as a married couple (in name at least) I thought about this, and being scrupulous I was remorseful for my feelings of the night before. I changed my mind by the end of the afternoon and if you're honest you will agree with me. While you waited for me in that bookshop you afterward detested for the rest of your life, I poured out to Culhões all the accumulated irritation of the night, blaming him for the impasse. He admitted that perhaps he had been wrong to take excessive precautions. After I described to him your preference for total darkness and the classic embrace, he was convinced that one stitch would have been quite enough, or who knows, none at all. I rejected this last suggestion with vehemence, since it seemed to violate a point implicit in the promise I had made to my deceased mother, but my friend demonstrated my reasoning as absurd and ended up making me agree to the proposal he made. He wasn't convinced that the blame was entirely his, and, after a few theoretical considerations about anatomy, was anxious to put his thesis to a practical test. I still felt that a bistoury incision would be preferable to eliminate the superfluous stitch, but his renewed arguments had a recognizable validity. He reminded me that the night before you had had a psychologically intimidating experience, and that the slightest obstacle might assume for you the guise of an insurmountable barrier. Besides, one mustn't forget that you were no longer young; the best thing for all three of us would be a natural solution. We should at least try, and only resort to medical intervention if his efforts that afternoon should prove as useless as yours of the night before. He repeated that it would benefit you for the reasons he had explained, and me because it would make the incision unnecessary. For himself, the interest in trying would be above all professional: he must find out if he had been wrong or not to take the second stitch. Having no answer to give, I agreed. In truth, Culhões triumphed, but if he had been less pretentious he would have agreed with me that the second stitch had definitely been an error. If you had a lengthy wait in that bookshop it was because things weren't resolved with the ease that Culhões in his boastfulness imagined. He had a hard battle, struggling continuously at first, then resting from time to time to get his strength back. When he won, vain as always, he had the bad taste to compare himself advantageously to you, forgetting his own argument of an hour before concerning your age. I am convinced that you too would have been capable if you weren't so emotional, if you had had more self-confidence. Your age was no problem and your instrument, incomparably narrower than Culhões's, was actually an advantage in the circumstances. But this is past. Everything went well and I'll never forget the years of happiness I owe the two of you. I would hope you in turn might remember all I've done. I've already given up hope of the slightest acknowledgment from Bulhões; he's turning into a poor devil whose mania is staying young, surrounded by a growing group of young girls who fleece him of his money while, in the same proportion, the clients who furnish it diminish. He will come to a sad end. With you it's different; you're a tranquil old man who has known how to age gracefully. Thus we come to my situation. I still have a few years of youth left, and as I wish you a long life, I know that when you die I'll be an old woman, heiress to a useless fortune. The idea of becoming a sad though rich widow horrifies me. I want a separation. For you it makes no difference, but for me there's still time. I will know how to use whatever comes to me of our property. Today my cousin is the best bookbinder in the city; all he needs is some initial capital to enlarge his studio and dedicate himself exclusively to the trade. At present he is obliged to waste time at the Institute of Legal Medicine. Together we will be partners in a great firm, and I will be happy again; you know how I've always liked bookbinding."

—◦❧ ❦◦—

I saw that this pause was final; she had nothing more to add. I had followed Her tale most attentively without letting my mind wander even once, as proven by the fidelity with which I reproduce the story a week later. I was strongly moved by a variety of feelings. It was the first time I had ever heard such a spontaneous confession, formulated moreover with a certain talent. This experience must be commonplace for priests, psychiatrists, and a few foreign police officials; I don't believe the Brazilian ones ever get that kind of confession. When they aren't dealing with potential confessors—by definition distrustful—they hear only lies. If they use other methods, the truths they extract along with the fingernails of the interlocutor are only scraps of truth belonging to a beaten body and spirit. But to hear the confession of a mouth and soul palpitating with ambiguity, although it may be an everyday experience for the professional confidants, was enough to alter the life of an amateur like me. Not that mine was: I'm getting old and my reactions are slow. But there was another motive for my holding back. The one thing that upset me in Her narrative—which I followed almost the whole time as a story unconnected with me—was Her representation of Dr. Bulhões as a person better educated than I, the word "educated" used in the sense of "cultured." Very well, I am fairly modest intellectually but I frequented intelligent circles and knew perfectly well the meaning of the words "polyandrist" and "diarchy" that Dr. Bulhões had taught her. The first I never used for the private reasons described in the first *carnet*; "diarchy" I never used for lack of opportunity. Besides Russia, an alarming country I discuss as little as possible, no other government run by two sovereigns exists. I wanted to make Her see that I wasn't as ignorant as she thought, and I found the opportunity by asking Her about a detail which hadn't been fully clarified. I told Her that the word "polyandrist" that Dr. Bulhões had applied to her seemed correct to me, as well as the derivative adjective "polyandrous." There was no doubt she had had more than one husband at the same time, since the prolonged years of intimacy with Dr. Bulhões permitted her inclusion in this category. Even if there had been other men, the word *polyandrist* was not limiting and would remain valid. About "diarchy" I had doubts, and I asked Her if in truth Her body, in spite of its small-ness, hadn't been the territory of a triarchy. She didn't understand because un-doubtedly she had never heard that word, so thus I got my revenge. Still, I remained curious and I repeated the question in a simpler, more direct form. I wanted to know if, during the time she lived with me, when she visited and was visited by Dr. Bulhões in high hospital beds, she had also been her cousin's lover. A smile crossed Her face before she replied. She began by explaining Her amusement. Decidedly, men were all alike. For example, Dr. Bulhões and I, apparently so different, had reacted in an identical way to a given situation. Dr. Bulhões had never been jealous of me but had harassed Her with questions about the cousin and I, upon learning the whole story, had accepted Culhões but resisted the idea of the other. I replied irritably, accentuating the *B* of Bulhões, that I hadn't accepted or refused the doctor or the cousin, I simply considered myself well informed about one and uninformed about the other. Gently she began speaking again and dissipated the bad humor brought on by the fuss. She confessed that really she never had heard the word "triarchy," but now that she knew what it meant, she didn't consider it accurate to define the relationship linking herself, Dr. Bulhões, her cousin, and me. As the entire argument was based on considering her body a territory, she thought it necessary to make clear that the area in which Dr. Bulhões and I exercised our double sovereignty wasn't the same as that where the first man exercised his: he remained faithful to the memories of adolescence. She asked if the use of the word "triarchy" would be accurate under these conditions. I agreed that it wouldn't, admiring once more Her capacity to learn. There was one more question I wanted to ask but I thought it better to consider Her testimony finished. I wanted to know if the three of us had been the only important men in Her life or if there were still others. I did right to contain my curiosity. The introduction of new characters would make the story at risk of becoming wearisome and, in the final analysis, less admirable. I decided the other things I wanted to say would be better said in a different situation. They were a few practical hints about the viability of a great bookbinding firm. The idea seemed utopian to me; furthermore, I didn't know anything about the cousin's real aptitude. I was afraid she might lose in this adventure the reasonable but after all modest sum I was disposed to give Her—as long as she agreed to a definitive, irreversible contract of discharge to accompany our amicable, discreet, and (insofar as possible) secret separation. My family had snubbed us *en masse* ever since my engagement to Her, and I couldn't bear the idea of the remaining members thinking they had been right to criticize and warn against my marriage. I am a liberal conservative who respects other people's traditions, but I'm subversive when it comes to family; I can't stand mine. I'd be capable of handing over to Her half of what I have just to avoid their learning about the separation and being amused by it. And that half represented a fortune after the skyrocketing of the Petrobrás shares I had bought trembling with fear, since people were saying back then that it was a communist business. Newspaper rumors! But there was no reason to be worried about the separation with regard to my property. She would be content to leave me and take whatever my generosity offered her. She would live in a world of bookshops and libraries where no relative of mine would ever come near Her and no one would know about anything. If by chance she should die before I did, which after the revelation of her stupendously good health seemed very unlikely to me, I was to make some arrangement with the cousin. I would take care of all the expenses, send the notice to the papers with Her married name, bury her in the family plot in Consolação unless she had left instructions to be laid to rest with Her family in the Quarta Parada. But above all, I would be present in the inevitable churches and cemeteries to receive, in the role of inconsolable widower, the condolences of whatever relatives were still alive, since it would be excessive to hope that they would all be dead. I saw nothing inconvenient in having the cousin at my side helping me receive sympathies since he was, after all, Her last carnal relative, that is, granted they really were cousins. The old cook in the poorhouse, if she ever existed, had already died and probably wouldn't be able to say whether or not they were related, since mental disability worsens with time. To get in touch with the old woman's institution, I would need to contact Dr. Bulhões. If he were still alive and practicing, I might avoid the clinic and my attacks of itching by making an appointment to meet him in the bookshop next door, if it were still there. It must have changed a great deal; the young intellectuals wouldn't even recognize me. They would have changed too, grown comfortable. Maybe they wouldn't even be there any more, their time taken up by well-paid positions in the press, government administration, or private enterprise. I would never see them again, but even so the time had come when we would understand each other. I am certain they have asked pardon for their former behavior and we might even become friends, since time would have canceled the difference in age. The bookshop! I never pardoned Her for having made me wait so long on that cursed afternoon. Deep inside, I always blamed Her for the vexation of being harassed and affronted by that band of urchins pretending to be intellectuals and revolutionaries when they were neither, as the future demonstrated: their names were never on book covers nor on the "Most Wanted" list of the police.

My practical reflections and their corollaries concerning Her destiny had begun in a climate of great sympathy but ended up making me feel distrustful and sour. The change must have been reflected on my face. Her expression had altered too. The tranquil silence that had accompanied the beginning of my thoughts about business had given way to an anxious muteness. I prolonged my wordlessness in order to stifle my irritation and think better. I forced myself to take in the whole of Her narrative and the new situation that had arisen; I went over the principal themes, making adjustments and readjustments, trying to weigh everything in an objective manner with maximum honesty toward myself and Her. Once more I managed to face the events as if I had nothing to do with the story. Only this time, what stood out was no longer the pathetic but the comical side of most of the situations. I recognize that the women in my life were all more intelligent than I, and, among them, Her position is prominent. However, they all took such a serious view of life that in the area of humor I come out indisputably ahead. I was a funny fellow as a lad, with success at school and in the German beer halls of old São Paulo. I changed markedly, but behind the severity imposed by business and personal relationships I retained a few traces of my old lightheartedness. Apparently I had bottled up a store of unused laughter, since from the time I was twenty I had been faced with situations that constrained me to austerity both at work and at home. My interior reserve of fun, never finding any chance to escape, had built up past the safety limit without my realizing it. Mentally summarizing the skeletal plot of Her story, I saw a virgin crawling out intact from beneath the superior, inferior, and middle members of a first man to be twice deflowered by a second in order to marry a third. The whole thing had such a similarity to the verbal games in vogue at my *liceu* or the idle conversations in the Rutli, City of Munich, and Franciscan bars, that I was transported back to my youth, and the floodgates of maturity were burst asunder. The result was a deluge of laughter that left me literally stretched out in my chair, shaken by interminable peals of mirth that threatened to choke me, sobbing to the point of convulsion from merriment. The attack must have lasted for some time since I didn't see Her get up. When I managed to compose myself a bit dabbing my wet eyes with my pocket handkerchief, I saw Her standing in front of me, livid, trembling from head to toe. Still coughing, I squelched the desire to start laughing again and gasped a few words of apology for my rudeness. Her lividity changed to redness; her body stopped trembling; she stretched out her hands as if to strangle me and screamed two sentences that pierced through house, garden, and street.

"Paul Dior, you can go straight to hell with your good manners! Shove 'em up your ass, Dr. Polydoro!"

Before she said the last word I had time to observe that Her voice had changed: it had acquired a young tone, vulgar but crystal clear. My reaction was so instantaneous that I only realized what I had done when I saw, covering more than half Her face, the reddish mark left by my hand. A thread of blood was oozing out of Her left nostril and a stronger flow from Her mouth. She shook Her head to dispel the dizziness caused by the dry shock of the blow and fled.

Immediately I grew calm. I could hear Her voice talking on the phone and was worried at what she was saying. Naturally she was speaking with Her cousin and I foresaw the rest: proven evidence of bodily harm from the Institute of Legal Medicine, a litigious divorce, complete victory, my family gloating and me deprived of more than half my fortune. But just then I was more worried about something else. I had just discovered Her and had lost Her in the same moment. I had never really loved Her and now it was too late. At bottom, I had always judged Her to be as artificial and well mannered as I. During our so-called happy period, I had made Her the super-butler of my court of servants and, when this period was over, I had thought of Her as an old domestic whose discharge was complicated by the employment laws. Even after hearing Her long biography I hadn't really come to know Her, because she spoke in the voice she had adopted to please me long ago when she came to work in my office. Whether or not she said agreeable things, she had always remained the same and had only changed in the last seconds of that night when she insulted me. The instant she hurled the swear words at me, that entirely new voice unveiled the existence of a Her different from the three I knew: my three Hers of work, comfort, and tedium—not to mention those of Dr. Bulhões. The new Her was the cousin's, potentially intact inside the others, repressing itself for me and repressed by me, the only one that I could have truly loved. It was Her of the Quarta Parada, a street girl with bad habits, vivid tongue, and shrill voice, Her whom I had met seconds before she pronounced the only intolerable swear word, my name, and left me forever, Her teeth broken from my blow. My only excuse is that I acted in legitimate defense against the rabid jackal that leaped, not out of Her mouth, but out of the depths of my childish hell, to torture me again.

Carlos Drummond de Andrade
—◦❧(1902–1987)❧◦—

The most prolific poet of Brazilian modernism and one of the greatest literary figures of the twentieth century in Latin America, Carlos Drummond de Andrade also wrote extensively in prose, including short stories, journalism, and literary criticism. After moving from his native state of Minas Gerais to Rio de Janeiro in the 1930s, he became the recognized poet of the city, if not the nation, because of his inventive expression of social themes and his technical mastery of poetic form and language. His short stories parallel his imaginative treatment of existential and social cases, problems, and anecdotes. In "Miguel's Theft," Drummond incorporated features of the oral tall tale and mythology into a case of transgression of social and physical boundaries. His stories are collected in *Contos de Aprendiz* (1951) and *Contos Plausíveis* (1981).

Miguel's Theft
—◦❧ ❧◦—

That we are born already adapted to our actions which, once kindled, find their measure in our being, is a well-known fact.

In other words, everything pointed to Miguel's having been born to a destiny of great accomplishment. His carriage was manly, his face radiant, and his whole person acknowledged self-confidence and a calm identification of self with the world at large.

But as for skills, Miguel had developed none, and one day his family ascertained that he had neither learned a trade nor mastered a liberal profession, nor had he found any modern technology whereby he might earn a living. This discovery did nothing to eliminate the dazzled awe awakened at first sight by Miguel's person; it might be that it added to it. Miguel was Miguel: such an assortment of attributes could dispense with exteriorization.

Now, admiration being the extenuating sentiment it is, Miguel's most exalted apologists were, little by little, reducing recognition of his talents to an abstract consideration that certainly required no publicity or, for that matter, much pondering. This was when his talents shone forth most refulgently. Without application, without publicity, gathered unto the bosom of their own pure essence, simultaneously evident and invisible, Miguel's gifts were showered upon family, borough, city and nation in the forms of ostentatious self-importance.

He subsisted on the favoritism of an uncle grown rich in contraband trade, on a gambling brother, and, in a general way, on collective sympathy. Now, it just so happened that certain circumstances cut short the lucrative activities of his relatives, with the result that human sympathy withered somewhat.

It was two o'clock in the afternoon and Miguel, moneyless and without any program for the future, found himself idling alone near a ship docked at the Praça Mauá. He had eaten no lunch and his dinner was in doubt. He had reached that point where nervous people turn their minds to suicide.

Miguel's roving eyes acquainted him with the day's headlines spread out for sale on the sidewalk: Aviation Co. Cashier and Auditor Abscond With Twenty-Five Million Cruzeiros; Bankrupt Bank Director Vanishes; Three Farmer Visitors To Rio Victims Of Lottery, TV, and French Whore Swindles; Sacristan Makes Off With Jeweled Sacramental Articles; Counterfeit Pounds Appear On Market; Falsified Drugs; Armenian Generals Involved In Bribery Scandal; Youth Drugs And Robs Grandmother To Buy North American Bicycle; Statue Of Venus Vanishes From Curitiba Museum; Use Crane To Steal Grand Piano From 20th Floor; Fastest Launch of Maritime Police, Department's Pet, Vanished Year Ago, Theft Just Discovered.

Miguel goggled. Yes, siree! Even a launch, huh? And with the snicker came the idea, an idea destitute of moral value; indeed, one might even call it criminal; but in a flash it revealed all of this exceptionally gifted spirit's originality.

Miguel realized that among all those thefts, in the air, on earth, and on the water, there was one that had not yet been attempted, one that was in itself sufficient to make him rich and powerful. Here it is we find evidenced the adequacy of Miguel to his project and of the latter to Miguel.

What was Miguel's project?

He would appropriate something of considerable value, something vast and overwhelming which would by its very magnitude be unsusceptible of recovery, and this despite the fact that he would be unable to conceal it. Further, it would be an object absolutely indispensable to human life, its possession guaranteeing the holder receipt of just dues and tributes.

To come right out with it, Miguel resolved to filch not a mere launch, not even all launches and seacraft, but that on which they navigated—the sea itself. He deliberated on the theft of the sea with all its coasts, capes, islands, argosies, lighthouses, buoys, algae, gulls, fish, whales, sunken hulls, carcasses, flotsam, jetsam and undersea cables. And, since he thought of doing so, he did so: with the dispatch demanded by the conception, for ideas are fluid, and Miguel might have lost his to the advantage of any receptive citizen.

He drew nearer the sea across the quay, stretched out his gaze, his bearing shrewd and acquisitive, and, mentally establishing the limits of the vast project there unfolding, stole it.

Theft is a mental act, precisely like any other wherein deliberation or intention prevails over the complementary executive measures. The treasurer who steals from a railroad does not take tracks and locomotives home, but only a Socratic subtlety or a crass materialism, which are after all the same thing, and it might be maintained that the objects had not been stolen in essence because they had not in appearance.

To be sure, this distinction was not behindhand in suggesting itself to Miguel, who took great pains to secure a hiding place for his voluminous theft. With concealment in mind, he confided in some of his more intimate friends, but without arriving at the desired solution. Technically, it was still impossible to maintain the sea out of its bed. The country's warehouses were narrow, however much their owners' imaginations had widened them. There are scientists who investigate the means of reducing astronomic quantity to a fingernail's proportions, a plan that is still a mere dream. And Miguel thought of microfilming the sea, so he would be able to carry it with him in a tiny roll. But no; it was not the same thing.

(Those who were aware of the little detail of Miguel at two o'clock not yet having eaten, might consider it strange that he should preoccupy himself with such organizational problems before lining his stomach. Do not permit this to worry you. Miguel knows how to fend for himself, and from the moment he steals the sea, he does not want for profit.)

The sea, however, remained where it had always been, though stolen. There was not the slightest doubt that the theft had been perpetrated. In the newspapers it was recorded as an accomplished fact. Miguel's coup, as headlined in the evening papers, was duly colored by a reporter's excess of imagination; the morning papers were more objective, however, and the *Journal of Commerce* devoted only four lines to him in the police reports. To this veteran organ, which had already given notice to millions of thefts during its centenary existence, Miguel's was no more than one among many. The unheard-of character of the exploit, its modernism, escaped them. Naturally the police discovered what Miguel had achieved; how could they help but discover it?

His first effective provision, after determining that the sea could not be moved, was to boost custom duties twenty-five percent—in behalf, he explained, of the remodeling operations rendered indispensable by the millennial wear and tear on this medium of communication. Miguel promised better fish to the fishermen and better pearls to the prodigious number of women with whom he had acquaintance. Countless laborers were given employment in the remodeling project; but until such a time as the undertaking could be initiated, they would have to continue as stevedores. Joyous and half-naked under the sun and their burdens, they blessed Miguel, who reimbursed them in the coin of his radiant smile.

Miguel's personal fortune soon eclipsed that of his country, that of the continent. There was so much of it that he never found time to count it all. He tried squandering it; but wealth burgeoned from fire, rain, asphalt, fog, and from himself. Miguel was frightfully wealthy in the revenue that issued from (and was larger than) the sea.

Some few piddling annoyances did not succeed in roiling the crystal of his beatitude. For morality's sake, which on the sea must be absolute, Miguel had prohibited excursions by launch and yacht. He would not deign to honor the resulting complaints with replies; in matters of decency he was unyielding. There was only the one little loophole that permitted respectable couples to pay a secret maritime morality tax.

But what really saddened was the interdiction placed on sea bathing. No longer on summer mornings when the surf tempted the mettlesome, when the unruffled baylets with their lifeguard stations seemed to beckon children and young girls in, no longer could one take a little dip, not even in trousered swimsuits, not even in trousers and suitcoats; for, when not immoral, it was dangerous, and Miguel watched over everybody's welfare.

Were someone to allude, no matter how vaguely, to the possibility of a Sunday fishing trip, just for the fun of it, you know—"It'd be a gas to get out on the ocean"—there was always a warning voice nearby: "Shhh! It was stolen."

And to the born voyager in the classic poignancy of exclaiming, "How marvelous it is to travel!" the listener invariably and prudently would retort, "It certainly is, but only by plane or by land."

Farewell, dawns in a yawl amidst rhythmic waves! Farewell, poetry of the wide-open spaces! The tourist trade declined and the tellers of tall tales told fewer of tempests in landlubberly coves.

Disgruntled jurisprudents hammered on the gates of justice. The result was a tiresome succession of litigations marked by conflicts over jurisdictional rights and competencies, all terminating in the decision that the species was totally unknown and escaped every classification of the penal and maritime courts: this was the first time that the sea had ever been stolen.

Out of this situation the grand national movement for constitutional reform originated; to wit, that a clause be inserted to prevent theft of sea, sun, atmosphere or any star, and making such an offense punishable by death. This movement stirred superior spirits and had international repercussions. All to no end. Because the statute, if adopted, could not be made retroactively effective in keeping with the liberal tradition of our legal system. Furthermore, anything so repugnant to our sensibilities as corporal punishment was out of the question. Wreaked on Miguel at that! On such a sympathetic face!

For our Miguel had remained steadfastly attractive, unlike so many heroes of novels who become physically sinister as moral corruption works in them. Miguel's adversaries themselves recognized this and begged him to pardon their attempts at inciting the masses to revolt against his economic power. The masses, on their part, were much too preoccupied with the Chinese struggle and the consolidation of popular democracy in the Balkans to take any note of the situation. "We want bread for Greece!" bellowed the masses through the voice of their representative.

O fortunate Miguel, you who performed so great a feat, and by it gave the measure of your personality, your sovereignty would be eternal if . . .

It just so happens that a six-year-old boy from Ramos, in defiance of all Migueline prohibition and home exhortation, leaping over the head of court litigation and parliamentary inquiry, one morning raced from his house and down to the nearest beach where he stripped and triumphantly plunged into the green, deserted sea. What a commotion! A passing truck jerked to a stop. The driver got out and stood admiring the lad in utter astonishment. Other children gathered. And women. And gaping simpletons. And newspapermen. The boy regaled himself in the immense bath bestowed by the whole ocean. And Miguel, paralyzed somewhere or other in the city, Miguel, inoperative, impotent, could do nothing; he could neither hinder the lad from taking his bath in the sea (with all its thousand foam flowers, pearls, nacres, scintillations, mermaids, and morning tales made out of light, waves and the flitting of birds) nor the sea from bathing the lad.

Then a second boy, emboldened by the other's example, stuck a toe into the water, then another, too, and another, and still another. Young girls in their first bloom, ripe women, and elderly matrons looking for medicinal iodine baths kept the boys company. An athletic youth pushed out his boat and was off to plow the sea's green land. A barge appeared. Everybody managed to get hold of something— a sailboat, a rowboat, a canoe, a raft, a fishing smack, a ketch, anything to hurl against the flood. Ship outfitters then and there decided not to pay Miguel's tribute. They would pay only the hoary, forsaken customhouse. And there was a joy on the littoral and the waters once more. The sea was free. The proper authorities reappeared and drew up a repossession act.

Miguel, learning of this, behaved with decorum and equanimity, and displayed the composure that was one more of the many attributes bestowed on him by riches. Nobody thought of taking him into custody—how? and for what reason? Everybody shook hands in joy and confraternity. Miguel would not admit himself defeated; nor was he. He deposited the better part of his fortune in solid banks and dedicated himself to the collection of chuck shells, the indiscreet and nostalgic souvenir of his oceanic proprietorship:

> *Those shells along the shore that give to view*
> *The colors clouds are when the day is born,*

as Camões has said.

PART IV

Contemporary Visions
—•*(after 1980)*•—

Contemporary Brazil continues to experience rapid modernization and urbanization, and the literary scene since the mid-1980s has been one of eclecticism and diversity. The literary historians speak the endless names of new writers, yet there is no dominant school, movement, or tendency. The mass market, particularly in Rio de Janeiro and São Paulo but also in other major capitals, has greatly increased the rhythm of publication. Instant national communications systems have tended to erase traditional regional distinctions in favor of a wide archive of ideas and techniques practiced in all areas of the country. One of the most import manifestations of the period is the continued presence and dominance of well-established authors, who lend a sense of stability to literary production. In the short story, writers who began publishing in the 1940s (Lygia Fagundes Telles, Dalton Trevisan), 1950s (Autran Dourado), and 1960s (Nélida Piñón, Rubem Fonseca, Moacyr Scliar) continue to pursue their distinguished careers, writing and publishing actively. Even some early modernist figures remained productive to the end of the twentieth century and beyond (Carlos Drummond de Andrade, Jorge Amado, Rachel de Queiroz). At the same time, another important feature of the period has been the acceleration of scholarship on Brazilian literature, encouraged by the high quality of critical essays published in literary supplements in the press, by university studies, and by professional organizations, such as the Associação Brasileira de Literatura Comparada (Brazilian Comparative Literature Association). The presence of literary studies on a much wider scale than before has focused attention on a reexamination of literary modernism and on the most influential authors of mid-century. The overwhelming impact of Guimarães Rosa and Clarice Lispector on the national literature became the subject of a large bibliography dating from the 1970s, and the influence of their works continues to be strong and pervasive. The only major literary movement in the second half of the twentieth century, "*Poesia Concreta*" (concrete poetry) did not produce short stories, yet it set new parameters for experimental writing that pervaded the literary milieu. The open development of literary and artistic ideas was constrained for many years by the military regime, and writers are still struggling to find a common national voice and theme. Yet a lively intellectual culture, particularly active in the major universities post-1985, supports increasingly international perspectives, reflected in the publication of translations, as well as the works of prominent theorists and essayists. The rise of the television *novela* and, more recently, the growth of the Internet, have also contributed to the internationalization of Brazilian culture, which is the main characteristic of the last thirty years. At the same time, one must observe that, within Brazil, this same cultural construct, one of the great products of modernism, has run the risk of becoming stereotyped and commercialized to the point of losing its vitality and the dimension that Mário de Andrade called "research," or continued self-discovery.

Poet and essayist Haroldo de Campos characterized the postmodern period as "post-utopian." The period of the military regime left its mark on subsequent writing, spawning a *littérature noire* concerned with the denial of human rights, torture, exile, and repression. The exile of dozens of writers, artists, and intellectuals during this period had the unexpected positive effect, however, of contributing to the internationalization of Brazilian culture, whether through singers Caetano Veloso and Gilberto Gil, the films of Glauber Rocha, or literary translations. Another dominant theme to come from the regime, also inadvertently, is the country's democratic resurgence, a work in progress often encompassing extreme forms of social interaction, including urban violence and other dynamics of inequality. Perhaps a part of what Haroldo had in mind is that the *cordialidade* (a combination of compromise, grace, and humor) said to characterize Brazilian culture and the Brazilian people by early theorists such as Freyre, who idealized colonial life—and even the spirit of exuberance that animated the modernists (Oswald de Andrade's slogan was *A alegria é a prova dos nove* / Joy is the proof by nines)—were fading if not departed myths of Brazilian life, destroyed by its urban jungles, insecurities, and merciless market economy.

Parallel to stories about the dictatorship, a dystopian strain in the short story captured the anxiety, alienation, and suffering resulting from the failure of the system of *cordialidade*, which had never hidden its partialities. Clarice Lispector is its early radar, with her abstract perceptions of the isolating and even murderous alienation of urban life. Scliar's "The Last Poor Man," an ironically futuristic story of utopia at last discovered in a world controlled by an "Electronic Brain," nonetheless describes society's regression to primitive emotions and acts of jealousy, blame, and crucifixion when a poor man is unexpectedly found in the Amazon by an anthropologist. The turmoil in public opinion, reacting to the presence of this dark atavism in their midst, forms part of Scliar's devastating critique of social idealism. Samuel Rawet's story of the arrival in Brazil of an old Jewish immigrant who has survived the Holocaust contrasts the man's search for understanding and acceptance with a modern material and commercial life so far removed as to be incapable of understanding him. The immigrant uses his last remaining resources to buy a steamship ticket back to the Old World. Other contemporary stories recount and condemn the loss of long-established forms of social cooperation, compromise, and coexistence. J. J. Veiga's "misplaced machine" evokeds the presence of the catastrophic absurd that mysteriously disrupts daily routine, a theme carried to extreme consequences in Victor Giudice's story of a worker who becomes a filing cabinet. Carlos Heitor Cony condemned the arrogance and stupidity of the military mind in his absurdly funny "Order of the Day," and Rubem Fonseca wittily constructed an interview with an iconoclastic writer bent on challenging any traditional opinion or social taste. Lygia Fagundes Telles, Hilda Hilst, and Edla Van Steen portrayed the anxiety of the loss of innocence and youthful sensuality by their heroines, who struggle to remain vital and alive. Caio Fernando Abreu carried alienation into fantasy and myth in his story of an urban youth who evaluates his life in terms of an encounter with a medieval dragon, in a deflation of the expectations of life. Although the panorama of these stories seems bleak, hope and humor remain deeply embedded in them. Milton Hatoum's story about the nymph of the Teatro Amazonas (Amazon Theater), an opera house whose very existence in Manaus is surreal, played on illusion and the recovery of national memory as a means of recontacting a lost yet idealized Brazil, the permanent Brazil underlying mere events.

The presence of myth in the contemporary story attests to the fundamental youthfulness and vitality of Brazilian literature and society. Nélida Piñón's "Big-Bellied Cow" is the story of a ritual relationship between man and animal, in this case, the narrator and his cow, Dapple. The story is an allegory of Dapple's passage through life, her breeding, pregnancy, and faithful belonging to the narrator. Yet Piñón's story is profoundly destabilizing, meant to "unlock life" so as to bring about a profound questioning of the nature of our relationships. The narrator, aided by his precocious son, understands that Dapple is fecundity without end, providing for him unquestioningly, while as a man he has been acting out of the meanness and harshness of possession. Watching the pregnant cow, he becomes aware of the briefness of life and the dignity necessary to understand the daily sharing. The son's feeling that "all of a sudden [the big bellied cow] is going to change into something else" affirms the wisdom of animals, present in the unseen "leap of life" inside the cow, symbolizing the greater strength of the metamorphosis of nature over the imprisonment of possession. The narrator struggles to understand friendship without possession, and when Dapple dies of an illness, he buries her lovingly, having learned the eternal, mythical story of mortality.

Contemporary visions in a period of democratic resurgence follow multiple paths that chronicle, describe, and discover the changing "world world vast world" of the Brazilian short story.

NÉLIDA PIÑÓN
—⋆(b. 1936)⋆—

Coming from a Galician family that immigrated to Brazil in 1920, Nélida Piñón is today one of Brazil's most prominent writers; she entered the Academy of Letters in 1989 and became its first woman president in 1996. During her childhood, Piñón returned to spend two years in Galicia, an experience which would figure prominently in her future writings, especially in her 1984 novel about Spanish immigration to Brazil, *A República dos Sonhos* (*The Republic of Dreams*, 1989). With a degree in journalism from the Catholic University of Rio de Janeiro, she worked as an editor for well-known journals, such as *Cadernos Brasileiros* and *Tempo Brasileiro*, and contributed to international reviews and to Brazilian cultural entities. She inaugurated the chair in creative writing at the Federal University of Rio de Janeiro in 1970 and began a life of literary conferences and teaching in international universities, including those in the United States, France, Spain, and Peru. In 1990, she was awarded the Henry King Stanford Chair in Humanities at the University of Miami, where she lectures each year. Her works create a world of aesthetic and linguistic renovation, full of reflections on humanity's most profound anxieties and the search for personal enlightenment and freedom. She as a writer has the ability to touch these intimate thoughts and consciousnesses, always directed toward the search for a better and more just society. Nélida Piñón's work has been translated into many languages, and she has won prestigious prizes, including the Juan Rulfo International Literature Prize in 1995, the most important prize in Latin America, which was awarded for the first time to a woman and to an author writing in the Portuguese language. Her books of stories include *Tempo das Frutas* (1966), *Sala de Armas* (1973), and *O Calor das Coisas* (1989).

Big-Bellied Cow

It was not really a burial, it was more of a simple ceremony. The family had been reluctant, but when he demanded their appearance he was imposing an authority that had been obeyed ever so many times. There ran through him now that effort that unlocks life as everything drains off in grief.

It had been difficult carrying the animal. And that place had been chosen because it was precisely there that he had come to know the nature of its species.

Even though his wife resisted, you're out of your mind, what will the neighbors say—with the help of his oldest son he opened the great pit, even though the animal had grown thin in its illness. Even so, a great deal of earth was needed to cover those horns. The meanness of a space which his arms could still measure.

"Leave me now." After dismissing the temptations of the world, he looked at the soft earth piled up as a protection. How could he abandon Dapple to animals who would come to eat the remains, and that flesh would soon be divided among beaks and on its way to strange insides after having fallen outside there, and it only brought grief to his heart when he thought of it. Linked to Dapple by so many mysteries, those homey patches that did away with meaning and which only he could understand. It had to be that way, in any other way the transfer would not have taken place, and he would never murder out of love and habit a companion in life, which is the way of eternal possession; it was death by capitulation.

He had not even seen Dapple born. He had bought that foolish appearance when it was still young, for unknown reasons in a marketplace far from home. He had chosen her absent-mindedly, as one who had grown tired of evaluating living things, tying the cord about her neck; the stumps of something soon to be born were piercing her head. When he reached home, a great excitement announced the birth of his grandchild.

"It's a boy, Father," that huge man who considered himself the owner of the father who had conceived him came to announce. Even though the new fatherhood had softened his usual crudeness, the son lamented, but he calmed down with the idea of a grandson. His path was growing shorter, that much the world was making clear. The dialogue died out like an act of accommodation, and he forgot about the animal in need of care, and the grandson who was already upsetting the rhythm of the household. His wisdom excluded pleasant feelings.

There she was in the pasture. As she ate grass, her frailness was not aware of to whom she had come to belong. He smoked his pipe, thinking that things are acquired so that they may start growing. And they were like that for a long time, one close to the other, the man entering into the growth of the animal.

When he needed his neighbor's bull to breed Dapple, he became confused, not knowing how to proceed. Which was not proper. After all, such an innocent request for men of the land who had acquired the habit of yielding to anything that brings on growth. He led her along with the shame of one bringing a daughter to receive the son of some stranger, to lend that beloved flesh to the unknown lust of a procreator. Dapple was innocent, and he masked his embarrassment.

He hid those notions in front of the owner of the bull who was to make a calf in Dapple. But he examined the bull imprisoned in his pen with rage. Still covering up, he asked his neighbor for help. "Get a farmhand, I've got a cramp and I have to go take care of it." He took care of it more than was necessary, calculating the time minutely. When he came back, docilely, like one who had condoned the use, Dapple was through. On the road the man whistled, pretending to ignore the animal. The fear of perceiving something that was visibly changed. What would he have done had he perceived the wound—not what one thinks of as mutilated and requiring care, but something which is done for such a fate and which is resented for precisely that reason. He wanted to say: look, Dapple, you don't know that I'm your owner and that's why this thing bothers me, if you knew it would be easy to explain why I let it be done, but the fact is that we're never aware that someone owns us. And he made an effort, but he never reached that clarity once and for all which would release him and let him live with the earth and its sacred fruit.

Until the calf was born, he ignored her pregnancy, her quivering belly. The whole blame was on him for having allowed the rape. He felt sorry for the animal, something justified only by friendship. The awareness that he used, in its measure and clearness, to judge people of the house, he began to use on Dapple, and more intensely. She had become the release of his secrets. In spite of his affliction, many were the times that he confessed before the animal.

When the cow's body had grown large, bulging out on both sides, he finally responded to the vitality of that growth and came to accept things in their proper places. He became adjusted to the pain that Dapple would suffer. For there was in things a spot of light proportionate to their acceptance. He watched over the brevity of that opulence, and she was silent as she slowly browsed, her eyes so sad, an acute melancholy drawing off whatever blame there was. Like any animal that is relieved, the prosperous belly was being fed.

Interrupting his peace, the oldest grandson asked: "Cows are nice, aren't they, grandfather?"

"Nice, yes."

"So nice you'd like to eat them."

"Eat what, boy?" Annoyed, he looked at his grandson's face, at that avidity which was corrupting his old age.

"Just any old piece. But I feel sorry, that's why I wouldn't. Grandfather, Dapple is a big-bellied cow, isn't she?"

"A what?"

"A big-bellied cow. A cow that's grown so much that all of a sudden she's going to change into something else."

"Oh, you mean that pretty soon she's going to give off something else."

"Something like that. Big-bellied cow, big-bellied woman, big-bellied dog, isn't it all the same thing? They get so big you think they're never going to stop, but I like it. Everything that grows should be respected."

"Who taught you that?"

"I learned it all by myself. I only said it so nice because it came out together."

"Came out together?"

"What I was thinking and what I imagined."

"Oh, I see."

"Like, what would you think if Dapple had baby chicks?"

"Baby chicks?"

"If everything that came out of her came out chicks. How many chicks would Dapple have?"

"That's foolish. Where did you hear of a cow having chicks?"

"Did you ask Dapple if she'd rather have chicks?"

"No."

"Then try to find out before you get mad at me."

The boy's appearance grew calmer as he went away. The man did not lose heart, he tried to forget his grandson with the same harshness of a person who forgets other things which still mattered.

When it was time for the birth of the calf, the patient work was taking place in Dapple. The drivel was flooding out of her mouth just as the blood would flow when the heavy weight had finished deforming her. His wife and son helped him until the gelatinous thing appeared, filthy, raising itself on indecisive legs now in a leap of life, as if inside the big-bellied cow—that grandson could make expressions useless in the same way that he deformed the appearance of branches with his jack-knife—it had been standing for a long time, strolling over the pastures of the world.

With time, Dapple grew used to those uncomfortable maternal duties, the small creature beside her emptying her udder, the exact abundance of that white liquid which would even produce butter, a splendid nature that aimed at fullness and avoided any loss. The strength of the animal had been passed on to the calf, but even so it could benefit man.

One afternoon, in that same pasture, he went over to Dapple. He looked her over with complete audacity, as a person who is shortly going to be lost and stops to find out up to what point he has been saved, how much he understood something that let itself be possessed. More and more tired, he became aware of a briefness in life, so brief that the time of a man was measured according to the action of that same man. Demanding the dignity of analysis in order to understand the world, his life, which rested on a daily sharing of life with an animal. Forced into that mutual contemplation, they would perceive in the end which of them would let himself be more easily exploited.

"Here, Dapple."

The cow approached, her balance softening the nerves that might have cropped out as she walked. And the man and the cow looked at each other. In spite of the meanness of things, any effort at all would clarify what not even the vitality of a friendship had managed to alter. The man owed himself a painful exhaustion in order to understand a friend. A pause invigorated them. He examined that animal who had brought him prosperity, never in revolt against her species, and who belonged to him without such a possession appearing as sores on her body. He did not know whether the animal had given in or whether he had bowed before that animal's necessary habits. "Now, Dapple, we're going to find out what this feeling is like."

The purchase of an animal was a kind of slavery, once its benefit was found, there should be a peaceful clarification of what there is between a cow and a man. But as he accepted the small animal and it grew, the man softened too, as a person stretches out on his bed with fatigue, free of the aberrations that certain kinds of work always instill, free of the life that distinguishes him without the least selection. Could the complete alliance between the man and that cow have been mutual contemplation and time passed? He was feeling more and more isolated under the eyes of the cow, in search of gentle solutions. His mouth wide open and the tight pregnancy of the animal. She was ugly, a cow was, and he tacitly recognized it. The deformation of her loins, the sharp horns that did not even make use of the ferocity of their natural form. The man said: "Is a cow a coward too?" The animal next to her owner, given over to the analysis that was being made of her.

"So cowardly that she accepts my animosity, was that how I understood her?" Then the shortness of the day, and the man was content with what forgiveness had eliminated.

The man spoke, what joins us together is your age. And tranquilly he wanted rest. But even that was not enough for someone who wanted so much. More than age, the living together assured the security of the animal, who accepted all and any land to feed upon. The gentleness that he was analyzing was precisely what had become settled in his flesh, in his time as a man. The resemblance between the man and that cow was the misshapen companionship of those who are equal in the difficult struggle. He patted the animal's head, which she lowered softly in obedience.

"I never want your obedience again."

As one who settles into her comfort, the animal did not move at all. The same sad look lost behind the mountains. Irritated, he rejected that head. Rebelling not against the animal who was enjoying the satisfaction of suffering in her body, but against the life that linked him to things, to that cow, affording him the skill of hesitation. Under the aggrieved eyes of the cow, he had the bitter joy of discovering himself being the only thing looked at. The cow's complete look, along with its intensity, did not leave him, he was the universal cause of an animal. A sob tightened his world, and he knew that he was joined to the sad beast whose solitude embodied his. Having come together in time, identical old age made them obstinate. The cow's wrinkled hide, the forewarning of an illness that would bring her down, and the man's easily irritated skin, not that any wound could be seen, for that was the destruction shown by the cow, but rather a texture without moral uplift, a perplexity in the face of such full powers. The grandchildren were spread over the land, the cow had also spread so many things, even her manure had been a splendid performance, her duty to man.

It bothered him to know that he was the owner of one who, not sensing possession, let herself be dominated by a look, the only virtue of the surrender. Later, things grew calm. The abandonment of old people who can barely resist. Everything in him was tumbling down, his sex too, he would never make another child. She too, the cow, could not give shelter to new flesh.

With time they ceased their examination. They were invaded by the desire of one who does not move. It was understanding. And the cow had to fall ill. The man recognized that servitude and he played the game with death. He pretended not to see the illness that was invading that carcass, the protruding bones were the illness that was establishing itself inside. Severe, the man struggled so that she would die in peace, so that the cow's freedom would not extinguish his.

When his son suggested that the animal be put to death, he sternly hid his face. At dinner, despite his hunger, his eating was different. He abandoned the noise of chunks being chewed and ate elegantly, not letting greed interfere with the operation. His wife looked at their sons, daughters-in-law, grandchildren. A look that communicated the arrogance she had seen in the father. But he did not notice, he had been able to forget the aggressiveness and strength of the meat of the usual meal. After that he returned to the barn, where the cow had discreetly begun to die.

Until she died. Then, energetically, the father notified the family: "Everybody will come to Dapple's burial." Ignoring the reaction provoked, he contented himself with the furtive look of that obedience.

Quite early in the morning they began the work of removal. She was so thin that her bones were showing, but it was not for that reason that Dapple was ugly, ugly, yes, because her appearance was fatal, but the kind of beauty that goes with suffering was there, expressed so well by her horns as they pointed up and cleaned the sky. They dragged the body along the ground over to the wooden cart drawn by other powerful cows who were indifferent to him. The dust cloud filled his heart, and he was made contrite by that scar on the earth that last piece of skillful work done by Dapple, the cow, his friend. Then she was borne to the pasture, where lost in their reflection they could recognize things in that legitimate obscurantism that come with lighting a candle in the darkness: in the beginning the darkness and the shadows are the limiting outline of what is revealed and learned.

Sliding into the pit, the animal remained there. The man went about covering her, and since everything was made of earth, there was not even any need to choose. Veiling forever the softness of those horns that had been reserved for peace.

The family left him as he had requested. He was going to stay there until he was drained dry. From that instant on he would go with other animals, his task would stay the same, except for his heart, for his tranquillity was that of a man who can also die.

BRIEF FLOWER

—◦≫ ≪◦—

Her inconsistency was racial. The sure orientation of her blood. Amidst a glass-like clarity, the softness of her steps as they passed through heaven and earth, such was her framework, her undirected drive. She had lost her direction among the admonitions of her friends, and she would laugh raucously at how funny stones were. She would even decipher them, unlocking secrets, for she had recently acquired the gift of words. She played at hiding, fascinating men, that would be her trick. They would always have to look for her, thinking that she was lost. The offense which they committed on her was funny, it made her vibrate and become aware of herself. In one way or another she would repair the shambles and put on a new dress, with the gamut of its material shining in the light of day.

On certain evenings, right there in front of the mirror, she would get rid of the discovery of her body. She would stare until she enjoyed it, the comfort and the feeling. She did not blush at the thought that she could be dazzled by that minute and exciting examination of her flesh. In that way an area that she had always imagined as dark and dirty was becoming clear and clean. As she mastered the miracle, she would run along the beach, the sand would come at her with the speed of the wind, a tickling that always irritates, even with innocence.

She sat down on a stone to think: now I can decipher any expectation there is. And she got a stomach ache, just as when she had eaten too much chocolate, or when her body went through its modification, altering its flow of blood, the surprise of that initial abundance that upset her, the realization that she was becoming a woman. With that realization, she became shrewd and daring as she faced the exaggeration of the resources she had just received. She would guess at answers until she could learn and breathe.

Men would pass by thinking how nice a woman is when she is young like that, and I am destined to rule that thing that grows in her or in some other one, for I am meant to possess the one who is waiting for me to lead her into the green fields, and if it is not this girl, I will enjoy her in another one for just as long as I live.

She grew tired after eating some ice cream. Despite her courage to go on, for the sun was still shining. The company of small creatures, nervous things protected by a shell and who left a trail, a molecule betrayed by its own brilliance. So funny, and more than company, they offered her astonishment, at any moment she could discover an immediate world, one that had risen up and reached completion through its own precarious science, where guesses were all.

She picked up a periwinkle, with the urge to stick her tongue inside of it, into the restriction of that opening, to taste its savor and its grace. Suddenly taken by the torpor of the small thing and wanting to understand its trick, hiding there inside, so much the prisoner of itself that it became excited and lost, fleeing now into the way of its species and its mystery. And the girl, wanting to stick out her tongue, feared the encounter of her tongue with that soft thing to be undone, until she broke the secret, wresting away the fragility of the little creature, the intimate craving of one who opens her legs, without selection, engulfed in the vital flow of strange resources.

The girl was afraid that with the arrival of the time there would never be any impediments to procreation, better and more serious things, or lost things, which do not cede before the strength of grace and her whim, which is also perfection.

She threw the creature far away, its truth, after the necessary ripening of her inconsistent race. Later, other men, different from the first, tried more daring approaches, preparing for the advances that discipline races. As if they were going about tasks to dominate vague and circumspect women. Who let themselves be sheltered in spring by any domination whatsoever, after which they store up virtues in honey for sweet and strange palates.

My name is Pedro, one of them said to her, and he was boldly waiting for the falling of the fruits. Kicking at the ground, feigning embarrassment, distraction, he sat down beside her. The girl, changing stones, going from the highest one to the lowest, said nothing. Disdainful, the boy smoked a cigarette, and protected by the smoke, he shouted and yours, what's your name? Bewitchingly, she said: a girl is nameless. Like a serene horseman atop the restlessness of his mount, replete with code and shining sword, he answered her: from now on, even if you haven't got a name, you've got a master.

Afterwards she cleaned the house, took care of the wild plants, decorated the table in a dedication to life. Delicate with the cleaning of the objects. Until she was pregnant and pretty, the violence of growth. She had barely noticed it because she was simple, feeling its effects. Such was her modesty. Every day the boy would occupy the house, with a loss of ceremony and respect. He would scratch himself where the chair had abused him, after which he would drag her to bed. The girl, still fascinated, would let herself be led, somewhere between feeling irritated and exalted. As it became a habit, the man drained her of her will and urge. The orientations of her nature were scarcely defined.

And that was how they were becoming, until the child was born. Strong and daring like his father, continuously unfolding with no beauty in him now that would not later change. The boy decided to disappear, never to be seen again. That disturbed the girl profoundly. Even though she had experienced such violent flights, she would still look at the stars, the same intensity. She had a precarious intuition of the freedom of any worthiness that might comfort her, she would make use of the flour that ennobles man after it has received the delicate mixture of some ferment. She dedicated herself to the subtleties that memory suggests, until she attained the vulgarity of such rendering. Only then did she rest a little. To join a new companion in bed and at the table.

At first there was strangeness, the hesitations with a different body, the imposition of other habits. That yellow and dazzling laugh that would always dominate the man, even when they were making love, as if it too were part of the rite. Then his teeth began to fall out from being shown so much, and the girl found herself joined to an old man who, in addition to being ugly, was also imposing the sordidness of his now flabby flesh upon her. Even though it was difficult for her to show her disgust, the sight of those gums, she could barely hold her vomit back, the penury of intense cohabitation. She would run to the bathroom and give herself abundant relief there after the hope, after the abolition of so many things. Even so, the man's presence was strong, and in addition to her body, it filled the whole house, the lust for gold showing on his face. One day she took her son, quite large now, and left the house. Abandoning the city just as she had left shelters so often in the wake of new disturbances. For she had lost the essential notions of living together, and even in a search of kindness, she would release herself in a torment of really wanting to live.

When another man chose her, as one casually chooses something that he is prepared to discard at any moment, she accepted in confusion. She went off to raise chickens, healthy and early-rising, to take care of cows, stubbornly thrusting her hands into the full udders, until her life changed, just as the smell of her skin. Even in that way she was following the path of her star and its false brilliance, as if freedom could be experienced in that way, in its excess. Every morning she would massage the cows, after the man had massaged her body. She would delude herself by thinking that they would rest when they got old. But that was taking time and her son was growing in a rapid and exaggerated way, and the woman hesitated as she faced the innovation of that world that had detached itself from her womb, marginal and operative. The struggle seemed hard and wild.

One day, dragging her son along, she went to the city, where she had not been for a long time. They delicately watched the epic passing-by of men. And they had some ice cream, which she liked so much, giving in to that vital appreciation by closing their eyes and enjoying, the tongue as it slipped across, with no greater demands. As if she were teaching the boy procedures for the future when he would invade the realms of pleasure. And if the boy imitated his mother, it was because the intimacy of that face made him feel good, it had become a powerful presence, and by having to discover his own expression that acknowledged the pleasure he was to feel when, even carelessly, he would be unable to spare his body its necessary exhibitions. Later on there were other things, sordid and colorful, that touched bottom.

After that she could no longer tolerate at all either the man or the cows. It was a disquieting peace and she forgot the attributes of the earth. She admitted again her inborn inconsistency and she laughed in compensation as she met her ancestors. She woke up the boy cautiously, they put a few things into a suitcase and daringly slipped away. The man would never follow them or disturb the earth with his vain pursuit. They rested only when it grew light, and they continued on immediately after, oriented by a simple independence that lays out roads with the illusion of building new cities. Brief stops, the simple necessities of sleep and food. Mother and son were ruling the world with the insouciance of emperors, nothing disturbed them, neither fatigue nor the imperfection of exigent shapes.

At last they came to a house with high walls, surrounded by trees and a lawn. A nun dressed in black came out to greet them, her face protected by a veil. Inviting them to rest and have some hot soup. As one who dares to look so as to observe and appreciate, they entered. The boy looked at his mother as if in reprimand: really, was this what we had fled for? The mother closed her face and, illuminated, she had something that deformed her expression and her patience. In her whole life she had never recorded a deed that had been more heroic. After prayers they ate.

Mother and son were still upset when they looked at each other, imprisoned in a modest cell, a common bed—this before they went to sleep. When bells pealed forth in place of the lowing of the cows, more than the sound, they could perceive the sadness of the prayers, and they arose as if wishing to flee, forgetting the caprice of miracles, changes that, even if they do not come about, dominate the world and make it marginal. But—the high wall and its locked gate—they waited, until the nun asked them: after all, you must be a religious woman, since you've always dreamed of stars. She could not resist the intensity of such wooing.

She went with the nun, her son following. She found herself to be an emotional pioneer, a torch-bearer, and her sudden adolescence was so colorful with its fruits and shrouds. They shared everything, prayers and hates, women made daring by the stimulus of prayer, confusing devotion and martyrdom, for war had honest roots in the world, death and hunger were savage. The boy was dazzled by the freshness of the prayers and the women's work, as they scarcely allowed compliments, a distant trace of friendship, and if, perhaps, they thought of love, they reflected on it as a necessary privation.

The woman had learned to fulfill her human duty as her body inhabited others, and in this multiplicity, the combinations of revolving works, she accepted everything, because here, as before, she found herself convinced that she would rule the stars in their passage, in the briefness of their brilliance. And as she ruled, she would dazzle herself with belief and faith, letting her son grow up among the women's austerity. Until when he was quite large and the mother superior warned her, you must leave, or you may stay and have your son discover the world. Sad and pre-destined, she looked at the son of her flesh, who was imposing successive sacrifices upon her, and in chapel or at the table, she would become upset. She asked her son: what do you think? He did not answer as he lit the candles in the chapel, one of his daily chores.

The mother saw pacification and love in that look, and she put the problem aside. Later on, it rained so much one night that even though she could not bear it, she imagined him leaving, discovering the world and its deep rivers. She knocked at his door, careful not to startle him: even though he was grown now, she called to him in a whisper and told him: whenever you want, we will leave together, I will not be separated from you.

They took leave the next day, stifling a certain faith that can squelch necessary decisions, and even though they could see the beginning of a greater struggle. They walked on, the boy slowing down his pace now so that his mother would not sense her own weakness and become ashamed, and so that the age already showing on her face would not become the only point of interest for the two. Fear that the mother might take a look into some mirror after her dishonor in the life of a recluse. They would only stop when necessary, always talking and looking at the country-side. And they loved one another as never before, now that they were free from things and life had become more difficult. The son was always afraid that he might weep at any moment, and that too was the inconsistency of his race. He would look at his mother, he was learning.

The mother had kept her nun's habit and from time to time, children on the roads would run up and ask for her blessing, offering her bread and trinkets. They found a hut, ugly and in shambles. He took a job at the mill, amidst the thick, white flour. He would return to the house, grave and circumspect, while his mother took care of it, cooking and sweeping the floor. Even though the world around them had forced communication, wounded in their love and glory, they did not pay much attention. Until the woman's body began to pain, it was her spine which hurt. She could no longer walk, and this was followed by a violent trembling, and she was pitiful to see. Age had imposed itself. The boy carried her everywhere on his back, the way one takes a child, so that she could appreciate the changes in nature and would not forget that, in spite of her debilities, she was still alive.

The son liked to look at her white hair, for his eyes did nothing else, and then, of a different race, as they well knew, they found that other joys were strange. Until he became owner of the mill. But the mother could no longer stand the impatience of living in bed, coupled to her son's sight, and he was a compassionate and solitary person. Once she asked him for some gold coins, telling him, if you love me, throw them into the river for me, the time has come for you to begin to suffer and to free yourself. The son did as she asked. Sad, but not over losing the money. His arrogance was something else. He could recognize it in all that hesitation in the face of life of one who is soon to die. They hung in the water for a moment and the mother had given the first sign of her independence.

Later on they ate, and as they filled themselves, she could feel the restlessness of death. She found it strange to die before she had intensely assimilated her old age. Distracted still, she might have let a stranger into her bed and not be offended by any of the actions he might come to practice. Such a disposition seemed like youth to her. Her inconsistency was racial, and she understood, looking up, smiling at the ceiling, that she was approaching the strength of her star. Her son had also inherited from her the illness and gravity of life. They both knew from pungent and audacious attestations.

When her son buried her, he decorated her grave with the brevity of flowers.

LYGIA FAGUNDES TELLES
—◦❧(b. 1923)❧◦—

A professional writer from São Paulo and a specialist in the novel and short story, Lygia Fagundes Telles creates suspenseful stories with economy of means, with urban characters embodying the suggestive problems of their time and social situations. While studying law, she began to publish stories in the 1940s, while in contact with some of the great modernist figures in São Paulo, who influenced her future writings. In works that explore bourgeois family dramas and that are known for their psychological sensitivity, Telles introduces technical innovations, such as the fragmentation of perspectives and voices. Her works pay special attention to the situation of women in Brazilian society, such as separation, inner conflicts, oppression, abuse, and other traumas. Her characters come from all levels of society, high to low, and Telles dramatizes the differences between their dreams and their realities, creating a polarized space in their worlds. Many of her works have been adapted for television, and she was inducted into the Brazilian Academy of Letters in 1985. Her novels *Ciranda de Pedra* (1952) and *As Meninas* (1964; *The Girl in the Photograph*, 1982) received awards and adaptations to television and film. Her prodigious contributions to the short story include fourteen books, the most recent being *A Noite Escura e Mais Eu* (1995), *Invenções e Memória* (2000), and *Durante Aquele Estranho Chá: Perdidos e Achados* (2002).

JUST A SAXOPHONE
—◦❧ ❧◦—

Night has fallen and it's cold. *"Merde! voilà l'hiver"* is the line, which according to Xenophon, is now suitable to the occasion. I learned from him that four-letter words in the mouth of a woman are like a slug in the heart of a rose. I'm a woman; therefore, I can only say four-letter words in a foreign tongue, and if possible, as part of a poem. Then people around me will realize how genuine and at the same time how scholarly I am. A scholarly whore, so scholarly that if I wanted to I could use the foulest slang in ancient Greek; Xenophon knows ancient Greek. And the slug would become unrecognizable as behooves a slug in a forty-four-year old rose. Forty-four years and five months. Jesus, fast, wasn't it? Fast? Another six years and I'll be half a century old, I've thought a lot about it and I feel the cold of a century rising from the floor and penetrating the carpet. My carpet is Persian, all my carpets are Persian but I don't know what's the use of those bastards if they don't prevent the cold from settling in the living room. It used to be less cold in our bedroom, with the walls stuffed with sacking, and the pitiful fiber mat on the floor; he had stuffed the cracks himself and hung portraits of ancestors and engravings of Fra Angelico's Virgin, he was crazy about Fra Angelico.

Where is he now? Where? I could have the fire lit but I've sacked the butler, the housemaid, the cook—I sacked each and every one of them, I was in a fit of despair and ordered the whole gang out, out, out! I was left alone. There's firewood somewhere in the house but it isn't as simple as striking a match and setting it to the firewood the way they do it in the movies; the Japanese used to spend hours messing about and blowing until the fire started. And I barely have enough energy to light my cigarette. I've been sitting here for I don't know how long. I unplugged the telephone, wrapped myself in the shawl, brought the bottle of whiskey and here I am drinking very slowly so that I won't get smashed; not tonight, tonight I want to stay sober, looking at one thing, looking at another. And there are loads of things to look at, inside as well as outside, but mainly outside, hundreds of things I bought all over the world, things I didn't even know I had and I'm only noticing now, now that it's dark. It's because darkness came over both of us, the living room and me. A living room marked by an outrageous, pretentious, affected vacuity. And above all wealthy, excessively wealthy. I poured out money for the interior decorator to go wild. And he did go wild, that fag. His name was René and he used to come quite early in the morning with his fabrics, velvets, muslins, brocades. "Today I've brought a fabric for the sofa that comes from Afghanistan, absolutely divine! Di-vine!" The fabric didn't come from Afghanistan nor was he an out-and-out fag; it was all a put-on, a con job. Once I came upon him unawares when he was alone, smoking by the window, on his face the weary, sad expression of an actor who is sick of acting. He started when he saw me, as if I had caught him in the act of lifting the silverware. Then he resumed his bubbling manner and wiggling all over he took me to see the shrine, a fake antique that shrine of his, everything made three days before but with tiny holes in the wood imitating the dry rot of three centuries. "This angel can only be an Aleijadinho, look at its cheeks! And its eyes with their drooping corners, just a teeny-weeny bit cross-eyed . . ." I assented in the same hysterical tone, although I knew perfectly well that Aleijadinho would have needed more than ten arms to make so many angels like that; Madô's shop also had thousands of them, each one authentic. "A teeny-weeny bit cross-eyed," she repeated imitating René's falsetto voice. High quality colonial fakes. I knew quite well that I was being taken in but I didn't care, quite the opposite, I felt an acute pleasure at being conned. Yesterday I read that people are already eating rats in Saigon and I also read that they don't have any butterflies over there any more, that they'll never have the tiniest butterfly . . . And then I started crying like crazy, I don't know whether it was the butterflies or the rats. I guess I've never drunk so much as lately and when I drink this much I get sentimental and cry at anything.

"You must take care of yourself," René told me that night we got stoned together. I didn't think about it until now. Why should I take care of myself? After that I hired him to decorate my house in the country. "I have the ideal furniture for that house of yours," he announced, and I bought the ideal furniture, I bought everything, I would even have bought Marie Antoinette's wig with all of its moth-made labyrinths plus the dust for which he wouldn't charge me anything, a mere contribution by time, of course. Of course.

Where is he now? Sometimes I would close my eyes and the sounds were like a human voice calling me, enveloping me, Luisiana, Luisiana! What kind of sounds were they? How could they sound like a human voice yet be at the same time so much more powerful, so much purer? And simple, unpretentious, like waves repeated of the sea, apparently identical, but only apparently. "This is my instrument," he said sliding his hand over the saxophone. Cupping his other hand over my breast he added: "And this is my music."

Where, where is he? I look at my portrait over the fireplace. "Your portrait must be by the fireplace," René decided in an authoritarian tone, sometimes he was authoritarian. He introduced me to his boyfriend, a painter; at least he made me believe that he was his boyfriend, because now I can't be sure of anything. And that ephebe with curls on his forehead painted me dressed all in white, a Lady of the Camellias returning from the country, the dress long, the neck long, everything so elongated and lit up as if I had inside me that very candelabra shaped like an angel that stands on the stairway. Everything is now dim in the living room, except the dress in the portrait; there it is, diaphanous like the shroud of an ectoplasm floating delicately in the air. An ectoplasm much younger than I am, no doubt that assLicking ephebe was smart enough to have imagined how I looked at twenty. "You look somewhat different in the portrait," he granted, "but the fact is, I'm not painting only your face," he added diplomatically. He meant to insinuate that he was painting my soul. At the time I agreed; I was even moved when I saw myself with the electric hair and the glassy eyes. "My name is Luisiana," the ectoplasm is now telling me. "Many years ago I sent my beloved away and I've been dead ever since."

Where is he? . . . I have a yacht, I have a silver mink coat, I have a diamond tiara, I have a ruby that was once set in the navel of a very famous shah, not so long ago I knew the name of this shah. I have an old man who gives me money, I have a young man who gives me pleasure, and to top it all, I have a scholar who gives me lessons on philosophic doctrines with such a platonic interest that as early as the second lesson he went to bed with me; he had come so humble, so unhappy in his dusty mourning suit and in his widower's boots that I shut my eyes and lay down; come, Xenophon, come. "I'm not Xenophon, don't call me Xenophon," he said and his breath smelled of a recent Valda lozenge; he was Xenophon, there has never been anyone so Xenophonish as he is. Likewise, there has never been a Luisiana so Luisianaic as me; nobody knows about this name, nobody, not even that pimp my father, who didn't even wait for my birth to see what I looked like, not even that poor thing my mother who didn't live long enough even to register me. I was born that night on the beach and that night I received a name that lasted while love lasted. One dawn when I got stoned and went to see my lawyer about not having any other name engraved on my tomb except this one, he gave that short, loathsome snigger of his. "Luisiana? But why Luisiana? Wherever did you get a name like that?" He restrained himself from shaking me for having woken him at that hour; he got dressed and very politely took me home. "As you like, my darling, you give the orders!" And he sniggered again, after all, a whore drunk but rich has the right to put on her tomb whatever name she chooses, that's probably what he thought. But now I couldn't care less what he thinks, he and all this scum around me: this carpet, this chandelier, that portrait—they're all someone else's opinion. This house with its saints pierced by a thousand torments is someone else's opinion.

But once I did care, and how. Because of those opinions I have a grand piano, I have a Siamese cat with a ring in its ear, I have a country place with a swimming pool, and in the bathrooms toilet paper with golden flowers my sugar daddy brought me from the United States along with a plastic container that plays *"oh! the last Rose of Summer!* . . . while you unroll the paper. When he gave me the rolls of toilet paper he also gave me the pots of caviar. "We must gild the pill," he said laughing with his usual grossness, he's hopelessly gross; if it weren't for the dollars he coughed up I would have told him to go to hell along with his golf clubs and lavender-scented underpants. I have a pair of shoes with diamond buckles and a fishbowl with a forest of coral at the bottom; when the sugar daddy gave me the pearl he thought it very clever of him to hide it in the bottom of the fishbowl and have me search for it: "You're getting hot, hotter. No, now you're cold! . . ." And there I was pretending to be a little girl and laughing while all the time I really felt like telling him to shove that pearl up his ass and leave me in peace, leave me in peace! Him and the fiery young man with all of his fire, and Xenophon with his mint-scented breath—I'd like to get rid of all of them as I did with the servants, those bastards that peed in my milk and doubled up with laughter when I was drunk as an owl.

Where is he now? My God, where? I also have a diamond the size of a pigeon's egg. I'd give the diamond, the shoes with the buckles, the yacht—everything, rings and fingers, if I could only listen, even for a while, to the music of his saxophone. I wouldn't even have to see him, I swear I wouldn't ask for that much, I would be content to know that he's alive, alive somewhere playing his saxophone.

I want to make it very clear that to me the only thing that exists is youth, everything else is poppycock, tinsel, glass beads. I could undergo plastic surgery two thousand times over and that wouldn't provide a solution, deep down it's the same bullshit, only youth is real. He was my youth except that in those days I didn't know it, at the time something's happening you never know, it's impossible to know, everything is so natural like day succeeding night, like the sun, the moon, I was young and didn't think about it as I didn't think about breathing. Who pays any attention to the act of breathing? You do, yes, but only when your breathing goes all to pieces. Then you get the blues: gosh, I never used to get out of breath . . .

He was my youth, he and that saxophone of his that glistened like gold. His shoes were dirty, his shirt hung out, his hair a mess, but the saxophone was always meticulously clean. He also took great pains with his teeth that were whiter than anyone else's; when he laughed I almost stopped laughing just to look at them. He carried the toothbrush in his pocket along with the diaper to wipe the saxophone; he found a box with a dozen Johnson diapers in a cab and after that he used them for everything: as handkerchiefs, face towels, napkins, tablecloths, and to clean the saxophone. And even as a truce flag during one of our more serious fights, when he wanted us to have a baby. He was crazy about so many things. . . .

The first time we made love was on the beach. The sky was throbbing with stars and it was hot. Then we started to laugh and to roll together toward the first waves that foamed on the sand, and there we stayed naked and embraced in the water, tepid like a warm bath. He was worried when I told him that I hadn't been baptized. He gathered water in his cupped hands and poured it over my head: "I baptize you Luisiana, in the name of the Father, the Son, and the Holy Ghost. Amen." I thought he was kidding but I had never seen him so serious. "Now your name is Luisiana," he said, kissing me on the cheek. I asked him if he believed in God. "I'm crazy about God," he whispered, lying on his back, his hands clasped under his neck, his gaze lost in the sky: "What really baffles me is a sky like this one." When we got up he ran as far as the dune where our clothes were, lifted the diaper that covered the saxophone and carried it delicately with his fingertips and dried me with it. Then he took the saxophone, sat down curled up and naked like a boy-faun and very softly he started to improvise, composing with the foaming waves a warm and tender melody. The sounds increased, wavering like soap bubbles, look how big this one is! look at this one now, round, ah, it has burst . . . "If you love me, will you remain naked like that on the dune over there and play, play as loud as you possibly can until the police get here?" I asked. He looked at me without blinking and then started to run toward the dune, with me running after him, shouting and laughing, laughing because he had already started to play at full blast.

A fellow student in my dancing class got married to the drummer of a musical group that played in a nightclub; there was a party. That was where I met him. In the midst of the greatest din you can imagine, the bride's mother shut herself in the bedroom, crying. "Look at the crowd my daughter has got into! Nothing but bums and louts! . . ." I put her to bed and went for a glass of water and sugar but during my absence the guests had found the room and when I came back the couples had already spilled out even there, lying side by side on cushions scattered around. I stepped over people and sat down on the bed. The woman cried and cried until gradually her crying died away and then stopped abruptly. I had also stopped talking and the two of us remained very quiet, listening to the music played by a young man I hadn't met. He was sitting in the dusk, playing the saxophone. The melody was soft but at the same time so eloquent that I became immersed in its spell. I had never heard anything like it, nobody had ever played an instrument like that. Everything I had wanted to say to the woman but didn't have the words to say, he was saying now with the saxophone: that she shouldn't cry any more, that everything was all right, everything was all right when there was love. And there was God, didn't she believe in God? asked the saxophone. And there was childhood, those brilliant sounds were speaking of childhood, think of childhood. . . . The woman had stopped crying, and now I was the one who was crying. All around, the couples were listening in fervent silence and their caresses were becoming deeper, truer, because the melody also spoke of sex, living and chaste like a fruit that ripens in the wind and sun.

Where is he? Where? . . . He took me to his apartment, he lived in a tiny apartment on the tenth floor of a very old building, all his fortune was that room with a minute bathroom. And the saxophone. He told me he had inherited the apartment from an aunt, a fortune teller. Then, another day he said that he had gotten it by winning a bet and when another day he started to tell me a third version, I questioned him, and he started to laugh. "You have to vary your stories, Luisiana, it's fun to improvise, that's what we have imagination for! It's sad to have something stay the same all your life. . . ." And he used to improvise all the time and his music was always agile, rich, so full of discoveries that it distressed me to think that he always composed but lost everything. "You must write it down, you must write down what you compose!" He would smile. "I'm self-taught, Luisiana, I don't know how to read or write music and that's not necessary for a tenor saxophonist, do you know what a tenor saxophonist is? That's what I am." He played with a group that had a contract with a nightclub and his only ambition was to have his own group one day. And also to have a good record player to listen to Ravel and Debussy.

Our life was so wonderfully free! And full of love, how we loved and laughed and cried with love on the tenth floor, surrounded by Fra Angelico engravings and portraits of his ancestors. "They aren't relatives of mine, I found them all in a chest in a basement," he confessed once. I pointed to the most ancient-looking of the portraits, so ancient that only the dark hair of the woman showed. And her eyebrows. "Did you find that one in the chest, too?" I asked. He laughed and to this day I haven't found out whether his story was true or not. "If you really love me," I said, "step on that table and shout at the top of your voice, you're all cuckolds, you're all cuckolds, and then get off the table and walk out, but don't run." He gave me the saxophone to hold while I ran away laughing: "No, no, I was just kidding, don't do it!" At the corner I heard him shouting in the bar, "Cuckolds, you're all cuckolds!" He caught up with me standing among the flabbergasted people. "Don't disown me, Luisiana, don't disown me, Luisiana!" Another night—we were leaving a theater—I couldn't resist asking him if he would dare to sing excerpts from an opera right there in the lobby. "If you really love me, sing now right here on the stairway an excerpt from *Rigoletto!*"

If you really love me, take me to a restaurant right now, buy me those earrings right now, buy me a new dress this minute. He was playing in many more places now because I was getting demanding, if you really love me, if you really really really. . . . He would leave at seven in the evening with the saxophone under his arm and didn't come home until dawn. Then he would clean the mouthpiece of the instrument, polish the metal with the diaper, and begin to finger it absent-mindedly, showing no fatigue and no signs of wear, "Luisiana, you're my only music and I can't live without music," he would say, lips embracing the mouthpiece of the saxophone with the same fervor as he put his lips to my breasts. I began to feel irritable, restless, as if I were afraid to take upon myself the responsibility of so great a love. I wanted him to be more independent, more ambitious. "Aren't you ambitious? It's no longer the thing for an artist not to be ambitious; what kind of a future will you have if you go on this way?" It was always the saxophone that replied and its reasoning was so final that I felt ashamed and miserable for being so demanding. And yet I did demand. I thought of leaving him but I just didn't have the strength; instead, I let our love go rotten, I let it become unbearable in the hope that when he abandoned me, he would do so full of loathing and without regrets.

Where is he now? Where? I have a house in the country, I have a diamond the size of a pigeon's egg . . . I was doing my eyes at the mirror, I had a date, I always had plenty of dates, I was going to a nightclub with a banker. Curled up on the bed, he was playing softly. My eyes began to fill with tears. I dried them on the saxophone's diaper and stood staring at my lips, which seemed to me particularly thin. "If you really love me," I said, "if you really love me, then go out and kill yourself right away."

Murilo Rubião
—◦❧(1916–1981)❦◦—

Making use of fables, biblical allegories and references, and magical settings, Rubião's stories examined reality by transforming daily life through techniques of estrangement, the fantastic, and magic realism. Almost a cult figure in Brazil, Rubião was known for his meticulously slow work and for his very limited number of stories. During four years he spent in Spain, 1956–1960, he wrote only one story, "Teleco, o Coelhinho." His volume *O Ex-Mágico* (1947) was translated into Spanish and English (*The Ex-Magician and Other Stories*, 1979), and he followed that volume with *A Estrela Vermelha* (1953), *Os Dragões e Outros Contos* (1965), and *O Convidado* (1974). His fame in Brazil spread only after the publication of *O Piratécnico Zacarias* in 1975 and *A Casa do Girassol Vermelho* in 1978, when the current of Spanish-American magic realism was in high vogue. There is a lyrical irony and enchantment in his stories, however, that he attributed to his continual rereading of Machado de Assis, perhaps meant as a continuation of the master's dark reading of Brazilian society.

Zacarias, the Pyrotechnist
—◦❧ ❦◦—

> *And thine age shall be*
> *clearer than the noonday;*
> *thou shalt shine forth,*
> *thou shalt be as the*
> *morning star.*
>
> Job, XI:17

Rare is the occasion when, in conversations among friends of mine or people of my acquaintance, this question doesn't arise: Was the pyrotechnist Zacarias actually dead?

Opinions differ in this respect. Some think I am alive—the dead man merely bore some resemblance to me. Others, more superstitious, believe that my death pertains to the roster of accomplished facts, and that the individual whom they persist in calling Zacarias is nothing but a tormented soul, wrapped in some pitiable human garb. There are still others who assert, categorically, the fact of my death, and so refuse to acknowledge the existent citizen to be Zacarias—specialist in fireworks—but rather, someone quite similar to the deceased.

One thing no one discusses: that if Zacarias did in fact die, his body was not interred.

The only person qualified to provide accurate information on the subject is myself. However, I am prevented from doing so because my friends run away from me as soon as they catch a glimpse of me from a distance. If taken by surprise, they stand there appalled, unable to utter even a word.

In point of fact I did die, which corroborates the version espoused by those believing in my death. On the other hand I am also not dead, since I do everything that I did previously and, I have to say, with greater alacrity than ever before.

First it was blue, then green, yellow and black. A heavy black, full of red stripes, of a deep red, resembling dense ribbons of blood. Pasty blood with yellowish pigments, of a greenish yellow, pale, almost without color.

When everything began to go white, a car came by and killed me.

"Simplíco Santana de Alvarenga!"

"Present!"

I felt my head spin, my body roll, as if I were lacking any support from the ground beneath me. I was immediately dragged along by an irresistibly powerful force. I tried to grab onto trees, whose twisted branches, pulled upwards, slipped from my fingers. Further along, I reached out with both hands for a wheel of fire which began to whirl between them, at tremendous speed, without however burning them.

"Friends: in the midst of struggles only the fittest survive, and the moment of supreme sacrifice is at hand. Those who would wish to act in time, take off your hats!"

(Beside me danced fireworks, immediately swallowed up by the rainbow.)

"Simplício Santana de Alvarenga!"

"Not here?"

"Take your hand out of your mouth, Zacarias!"

"How many continents are there?"

"And Oceania?"

Children's playthings were to come no longer from the seas of China.

The schoolmistress, bony, skinny, her eyes glazed-looking, was holding a dozen skyrockets in her right hand. The rods were quite long, long enough to oblige D. Josefina to place her feet apart some two meters above the floor, while her head, covered with strands of twine, almost bumped against the ceiling.

"Simplício Santana de Alvarenga!"
"Children, respect the truth!"

The night was dark. No, black. It didn't take long for white filaments to cover the sky.

I was walking along the road. Acaba-Mundo Road: a few curves, silence, more shadows than silence.

The car did not honk from the distance. And even when it was practically on top of me, I somehow failed to notice the headlights, most likely because it wasn't the right night for whiteness to touch the earth.

The girls in the car shrieked hysterically and proceeded to faint. The fellows talked together in low voices, instantly cured of their drunkenness, and began discussing what might be the best way to deal with the corpse.

First it was blue, then green, yellow and black. A heavy black, full of red stripes, of a deep red, resembling dense ribbons of blood. Pasty blood with yellowish pigments, of a greenish yellow, almost without color. I'd never want to live without color. To live, to get muscles good and tired, walking along streets filled with people, empty of men.

There was silence, more shadows than silence, because the fellows were no longer discussing the matter quietly. They now spoke in natural tones, suitably laced with slang.

The atmosphere, likewise, was relaxed and calm, and the cadaver—my blood-stained corpse—in no way objected to the end these fellows wanted to bestow on it.

The initial idea, rejected almost at once, was to drive me into the city where they might dispose of me, conveniently, at the morgue. After a brief debate, during which every argument was coldly scrutinized, the opinion prevailed that my body might dirty the car. And there was still an additional bother: the probable unwillingness of the girls to ride together with a corpse. (On this point they were roundly mistaken, as I will explain further on.)

One of the fellows, a strapping beardless youth—the only one to have been deeply disturbed by the accident, who remained silently distressed throughout the course of these events—suggested they should leave the girls on the road there and proceed to carry me to the cemetery. His friends, though, paid no attention to his proposal. They limited themselves to sneering at Jorge's bad taste—as they called it—and at the ridiculousness of being more concerned with the fate of a cadaver than with the lovely little ladies who were still in the car.

The boy thereupon acknowledged the stupidity of what he had just said and, without looking directly at the other members of the circle, began to whistle, obviously quite embarrassed.

Impossible not to feel an immediate sympathy for him, in the light of his reasonable suggestion, expressed rather poorly to those who were busy deciding my fate. Anyway, long walks tire indiscriminately the living and the dead. (This argument did not occur to me at the time.)

They went on to consider other possible solutions and finally, decided that throwing me into a ditch—a deep ditch which skirted the roadway—then cleaning up the blood-stained pavement and meticulously washing the car when back home was the solution most adequate to the case, and one that best suited any possible complications with the police, ever eager to find mystery where none abided.

—◦❧ ❧◦—

But that had to be one of the few suggestions that did not interest me. The idea of lying around dumped into a hole, among the stones and weeds, was unendurable to me. And besides, my body might, after being rolled into the gully, remain hidden among all the vegetation, soil and gravel. If that should happen, it would never be discovered in its improvised tomb, and my name would likewise fail to make the headlines in any of the daily papers.

No, I was not to be robbed of that, even if only of a small obituary in the principal morning newspaper. I had to act quickly, decisively:

"That's enough! It's my turn to be heard."

Jorge paled, let out a dull moan and passed out, while his friends, though astonished at seeing a cadaver speak, were somewhat more disposed to hear me out.

—◦❧ ❧◦—

I have always had confidence in my abilities to dominate any adversary when it comes to a discussion. I don't know whether by force of logic or some natural talent, the truth is, while alive, I could always win any debate dependent upon irrefutably solid argumentation.

Death had not impaired this capacity. And my murderers did me justice. After a short debate, in which I explained with great clarity my own views, the fellows felt completely at a loss to find any solution that would apply satisfactorily, as much to my reasoning as to their own program for the evening, still to be continued. But to make things even more confusing, they sensed the futility of giving any direction to a deceased who had yet to lose any of those faculties generally attributed to the living.

Had a suggestion not occurred finally to one of their group, and been adopted immediately, we would have remained at an impasse. The fellow proposed including me in the group, so that, together, we might finish out the evening that had been interrupted by my being run over.

In the meantime, another obstacle intervened: there were only three girls, which is to say, a number equal to the boys. One was still missing for me, and I refused to join them while still unaccompanied myself. The same fellow, however, who had proposed my inclusion in the group, came up with the perfect conciliatory solution by suggesting they abandon the friend who had passed out on the road just before. To improve my appearance, he added, it would be enough merely to switch my clothes with the ones Jorge was wearing, something I declared myself ready to do on the spot.

Beyond a certain reluctance to abandon their colleague like that, everyone (both male and female, the latter now recovered from the early fainting) agreed that he had been weak and had not known how to confront the situation with dignity, therefore it was hardly reasonable for us to waste further time with sentimental reflections upon his person.

—◦❧ ☙◦—

Of what happened afterwards I retain no very clear recollection. The drinking, which before my death had always affected me very little, suddenly produced surprising effects upon my now defunct person. Stars entered through my eyes, and lights whose colors were unknown to me, then absurd triangles, ivory cones and spheres, black roses, carnations shaped like lilies, lilies transformed into hands. And the redhead, who had been allotted me by the group, suddenly squeezed me around the neck with her body which had somehow been transformed into one long metallic arm.

With the coming of daylight, I was roused from my semi-lethargic state. Someone asked me where I wished to be dropped off. I remember I insisted on getting out at the cemetery, which they replied was impossible, since, at that hour, it would certainly be closed. I repeated several times the word cemetery. (Who knows whether I managed actually to repeat it, or only moved my lips, trying to link words to the remote sensations of my polychromatic delirium.)

—◦❧ ☙◦—

For a considerable time afterward, I continued to suffer from the disequilibrium between the exterior world and my eyes, which refused to adjust to the bright color of the landscapes stretching before me, and from the fear that would persist, from that morning on when I first discovered that death had penetrated my body.

If it weren't for the skepticism of men, refusing to accept me alive or dead, I might have taken heart in my ambition to construct a new existence.

I've still had to fight constantly against that madness which, at times, becomes master of my actions and compels me to search, anxiously, in all the daily papers, for any news that might somehow elucidate the mystery still surrounding my decease.

I made various attempts to establish contact with my companions of the fatal night in question, but the results were equally discouraging. And there lay my only hope to prove the real extent of my death.

—◦❧ ☙◦—

As the months passed, my suffering became less acute, and my frustration less extreme, at the difficulty of convincing friends that the Zacarias who walks the city streets is the same pyrotechnical artist of times gone by, with the single difference that the other was alive, while this one is a corpse.

Only one thought really troubles me: What events will fate hold in store for a dead man, if the living breathe such agonizing lives? And my anxiety increases on sensing, in all its fullness, how my capacity to love, to discern things, is far superior to that of the many who pass me by so fearfully.

Still, a clear day might dawn tomorrow, the sun brilliant as never before. And at such an hour, men may come to realize that, even on the margin of life, I am still alive, because my existence has been transmuted into colors, and whiteness is already drawing close to the earth, to the exclusive delight of my eyes.

J. J. Veiga
—◦❧(1915–1999)❦◦—

Known for introducing magic realism into Brazilian literature, J. J. Veiga's stories often carry sinister or menacing overtones in their estrangement and distortion of strangely tranquil everyday realities. His major collections are *Os Cavalinhos de Platiplanto* (1959) and *A Máquina Extraviada* (1968; *The Misplaced Machine and Other Stories*, 1970). Veiga continued to refine his stories of eerie and catastrophic events in *Hora dos Ruminantes* (1966), *Sombras de Reis Barbudos* (1972), *Aquele Mundo de Vasabarros* (1982), and *O Relógio Belisário* (1995).

The Misplaced Machine
—◦❧ ❦◦—

You always ask what is new in this little town of ours and, at last, there is something Big! Let me tell you that we now have a most imposing machine and it makes us all very proud. Ever since it arrived, I can't remember exactly when, I'm not very good at dates, we have hardly talked of anything else; and the way the people here get heated about the most infantile affairs it's a wonder no one yet has started a fight about it (except the politicos, of course).

The machine arrived one afternoon when most families were eating their dinners, and was unloaded in front of the Mayor's office. When we heard the shouts of the drivers and their helpers, a lot of us postponed dessert and coffee and went to see what it was all about. As is usual on such occasions, the men were in bad humor and would not stop to give any explanation; they bumped into the onlookers on purpose, stepped on their feet without excusing themselves, threw the ends of greasy ropes on them—those who wanted to stay clean and unhurt had to get out of the way.

Once the various parts of the machine were unloaded, the men covered them with a tarpaulin and went off to eat and drink in a tavern in the square. A lot of us townspeople gathered in the doorway to stare, but no one dared approach the strangers because one of them, apparently guessing our intentions, kept filling his mouth with beer and squirting it in our direction. We decided their disdain was probably due to tiredness and hunger and thought it best to leave our unanswered questions for the following day. But when we went by their rooming house early next morning we were told they had put the machine together, more or less, during the night and departed at dawn.

And so the machine remained, exposed to the elements, no one knowing who had ordered it or what it was for. Of course, everyone had an opinion (and gave it freely), but no opinion was more valid than another.

The children, no respecters of mysteries as you know, tried to take over the novelty. Without asking anyone's permission (and whose would they ask?) they took off the tarpaulin cover and climbed all over the machine. They still do, playing tag among the cylinders and shafts. They sometimes get caught in the gears and scream their heads off until someone comes along to get them out; it's no use fussing, punishing, or spanking, those kids are plainly enamored of the machine.

Contrary to the opinion of some few who denied any enthusiasm and swore that the novelty would wear off in a few days and rust take over the metal, interest has not flagged in the least. Nobody goes by the square without stopping to look at the machine, and each time there is some new detail to notice. Even the little old church ladies passing by at daybreak and evening, praying and coughing, turn toward the machine and bend a knee discreetly, almost, but not quite, crossing themselves. Brutish types, like that Clodoaldo (you know, the one who shows off in the marketplace, grabbing bulls by the horns and throwing them to the ground) even they treat the machine with respect. If occasionally one or another gives a lever a hard tug or kicks at one of the shafts, you can tell it's just bravado, to keep up his reputation.

Nobody knows who ordered the machine. The Mayor swears it was not he and says he consulted the files and found no document authorizing the transaction. But apparently he does not want to wash his hands of it completely because, in a way, he took it over when he designated an employee to look after the machine.

We have to admit—actually everyone does—that the employee is doing an excellent job. At any time of the day, even occasionally at night, he can be seen clambering over it, disappearing here, reappearing there, whistling or singing, busy and tireless. Twice a week he smears polish on the brass parts, rubs and rubs, sweats, rests, rubs again—and the whole thing sparkles like a jewel.

We are so accustomed to the presence of the machine in the square that if one day it should collapse, or if someone from another town came to fetch it, proving (with documents) that he had a right to, I have no idea what would happen. I don't even want to think of it. It is our pride and glory—and don't think I'm exaggerating. We still don't know what it's for, but that doesn't matter much. Let me tell you that we have had delegations from other towns, in and out of state, wanting to buy the machine. They pretend not to want anything, they visit the Mayor, praise the town, meander around the subject, throw out a little bait, and then show their hand: how much do we want for the machine? Fortunately, the Mayor is honest and smart, and doesn't fall for soft-talk.

The machine is now part of the festivities on all civil occasions. You remember how holidays used to be celebrated at the bandstand or on the football field? Now everything happens near the machine. At election time all the candidates want to stage their rallies in the shade of the machine and as it isn't possible (there are too many), there are always fights. Happily, the machine has not yet been damaged in these brawls, and I hope it won't be.

The priest is the only person who has not paid homage to the machine, but you know how cantankerous he is; he's even worse nowadays, it's his age. In any case, he hasn't yet tried anything, and Heaven help him if he does. As long as he keeps to his veiled censuring we'll put up with it; that's his business. I heard he had been talking about eternal punishment, but it didn't cut any ice.

The only accident of any importance until now was when the delivery boy from old Adudes' store (spiky little old man, smears brilliantine on his moustache, remember?) got his leg caught in one of the gears of the machine, entirely his own fault. The boy had been drinking at a *serenata** and, instead of going home, decided to sleep on the machine. He managed to climb to the top platform, no one knows how, and in the early morning he rolled off; he fell on the gears and his weight started the wheels going around. The whole town awoke with his yelling, people ran to see what was the matter and had to get bars and levers to stop the wheels that were eating into his leg. Nothing happened to the machine, fortunately. The careless chap, without leg or job, now helps with the upkeep of the machine, looking after the lower parts.

There is a movement afoot to declare the machine a municipal monument—but it is only a movement so far. The priest, as always, is against it, wants to know what it would be dedicated to. Have you ever known such sour grapes?

People say the machine has even performed miracles, but that (just between us) I regard as an exaggeration, and I'd rather not dwell on the matter. Personally, I—and probably the greater number of townspeople—don't expect anything in particular of the machine. It is enough for me that it stay where it is, cheering, inspiring, and consoling us.

My one fear is that, when we least expect it, some fellow will arrive from abroad, a resolute know-it-all type, and will examine the machine inside and out, think a bit, and then start to explain the purpose of it. To show how clever he is (they're always very clever), he will ask at the garage for a set of tools and, disregarding all protest, he will get underneath the machine, start tightening, hammering, coupling, and the machine will start to function. If this happens, the spell will be broken and the machine will cease to exist.

---

* A loosely organized party at a chosen house, where all the participants take their musical instruments and play, separately or together, for singing. The participants often bring their own refreshments, but the owner of the house will usually offer something.

Moacyr Scliar
—◦❧(b. 1937)❧◦—

The son of Russian-Jewish immigrants and a prolific writer born in Porto Alegre, Moacyr Scliar is the author of more than fifty books—short stories, novels, chronicles, essays, and children's literature—and has been widely translated into more than twenty languages, with many works finding film, television, theater, and radio adaptations. His works of the mythic imagination have received some of Brazil's major literary prizes, and Scliar has been invited to be a visiting professor and writer by Brown University and the University of Texas at Austin.

His stories "The Last Poor Man" and "The Cow" appeared in his first and most famous book of short stories in 1968, *O Carnival dos Animais* (*Carnival of the Animals*, 1987). Mythology and fantasy figure strongly in Scliar's stories, as do his experiences in medicine and work as a doctor in public health.

The Cow
—◦❧ ❧◦—

During a stormy night there was a shipwreck off the African coast. The ship split in half and sank in less than a minute. Passengers and crew died instantly. There was one survivor, a sailor who had been hurled far away when the disaster occurred. Almost drowning—for he wasn't a good swimmer—the sailor was praying and saying farewell to life, when he saw Carola, the cow, swimming quickly and vigorously next to him.

Carola, the cow, had been loaded in Amsterdam.

A superb breeder, her destination had been a farm in South America.

Holding onto the cow's horn, the sailor let her lead him; and so, at daybreak they reached a sandy islet, where the cow deposited the unfortunate young man, and she kept licking his face until he woke up.

Realizing that he was on a deserted island, the sailor burst into tears. "Woe to me! This island isn't on any sea route! I'll never see another human being again." Throwing himself upon the sand, he cried for a long time, while Carola, the cow, stood gazing at him with her big brown eyes.

Finally, the young man wiped his tears and rose to his feet.

He looked around him: There was nothing on the island except for sharp rocks and a few rickety-looking trees. He felt hungry; he called the cow: "Come here, Carola!" He milked her and drank the good, warm, foamy milk. Then he felt better; he sat down and stood staring at the ocean. "Woe to me!" he would wail at times, but now without much conviction: The milk had done him good.

That night he slept snuggled against the cow. He had a good night's sleep, full of refreshing dreams, and when he woke up, there within his reach was the udder with its abundant milk.

The days went by and the young man grew more and more attached to the cow. "Come here, Carola!" She would obey him.

He would slice off a piece of her tender meat—he was quite partial to tongue—and would eat it raw while still warm, the blood dribbling down his chin. The cow didn't even moo. She merely licked her wounds. The sailor was careful not to injure her vital organs; if he removed a lung, he'd leave the other one in place; he ate the spleen but not the heart, and so on.

With scraps of her skin the sailor made clothes and shoes and a tent to shelter him from the sun and the rain. He cut off Carola's tail and used it to drive the flies away.

When the meat began to get scarce, he hitched the cow to a plow crudely made of tree branches, and then tilled the plot of land lying between the trees, where the soil was more fertile.

He used the animal's excrement for manure. As there wasn't much of it, he ground a few of her bones to powder so that he could use them as fertilizer.

Then he sowed the few grains of corn that had remained stuck in the cavities of Carola's teeth. Soon, seedlings began to sprout and the young man's hopes rekindled.

He celebrated St. John's Day by eating *canjica*, the traditional grated corn pudding.

Spring arrived. At night, from far-off regions, a gentle breeze brought subtle aromas.

Gazing at the stars, the sailor would sigh. One night he plucked out one of Carola's eyes, mixed it with seawater and then swallowed this light concoction. He had voluptuous visions, never before experienced by a human being . . . Overcome by desire, he went up to the cow. And in this matter too, Carola was ready to oblige.

A long time went by, and one day the sailor spotted a ship on the horizon. Wild with joy, he began to yell at the top of his voice, but he got no reply: The vessel was much too far away. The sailor plucked out one of Carola's horns and used it as a makeshift trumpet. The powerful sound roared through the air, but even so he failed to make himself heard.

The young man grew desperate: Night was falling and the ship was sailing farther away from the island. At last, the young man set Carola on the ground and threw a lit match into her ulcerated womb, where a scrap of fat still remained.

The cow caught fire quickly. From amid the black smoke, her one remaining eye looked steadily at the sailor. The young man started; he thought he had detected a tear. But it was just an impression.

The huge flash of light called the attention of the captain of the ship; a motorboat came to pick up the sailor. They were about to leave, taking advantage of the tide, when the young man shouted: "Just a minute!" He went back to the island, and from the smoldering pile he took a handful of ashes and put it in his leather vest. "Farewell, Carola," he murmured. The crew of the motorboat exchanged glances. "Sun-stricken," one of them said.

The sailor arrived in his native country. He resigned from the sea and became a wealthy and respected farmer who owned a dairy farm with hundreds of cows.

But even so he led a lonely, unhappy life, and he had frightening nightmares every night until he was forty years old. When he turned forty, he traveled to Europe by boat.

One night, unable to sleep, he left his luxurious stateroom and went up to the quarterdeck, which was bathed in moonlight. He lit a cigarette, leaned on the ship's rail, and stood gazing at the sea.

Suddenly he stretched his neck eagerly. He had spotted an islet on the horizon.

"Hi, there!" said someone next to him.

He turned. She was a beautiful blonde with brown eyes and a luxuriant bust.

"My name is Carola," she said.

The Last Poor Man
—◦❧ ❦◦—

I—Panorama

1990. The hopes of peace, health and prosperity finally materialized.

The world was at peace. Every citizen had his own car.

The arthropods became extinct. The population explosion had been controlled. Degenerative diseases had been eliminated.

The Chinese, domesticated, worked in an orderly manner, confined to huge corrals.

Bacteria were nonexistent. Happiness was widespread. After a hundred years of useful life, the human being was sent to the freezers of Deimos and Phobos, where he rested in peace, and was awakened every ten years for one hour.

Poverty was abolished for good. A museum in Chicago exhibited a slum in miniature; a great attraction. Thousands of people visited the exhibit and displayed disbelief: "Did people actually live there?" In Rio de Janeiro, a *favela* was preserved just as it had been; ingenious mannequins representing black women walked up and down the hill, carrying cans of water on their heads.

Science fiction disappeared as a literary genre. Reality confirmed the most fantastic predictions. The novel became once more the most popular form of reading.

II—A Fantastic Discovery

In Rio, anthropologist Ellsworth announced a sensational discovery: he had found a strange human being in the still relatively unexplored jungles of the Amazon.

III—João

Old. Maybe a century old. Sparse, yellowish-white hair. Black, rheumy eyes, blinking constantly. Toothless mouth. Veins hard like wires. Ankle bone broken but healed. On his left thigh, a large, suppurating wound, teeming with thousands of tiny white maggots. Between his toes the accumulated filth of years and years. A small loincloth covered his nakedness.

He didn't have a car. He didn't know Mars. He admitted to not having voted in the last World Council elections. He didn't speak Greek. His Portuguese vocabulary consisted of a hundred and seventeen words. He had bitten the thumb of Ellsworth's assistant, an excellent person.

IV—Reactions

Ellsworth expressed his surprise at such a degree of indigence. "I thought that such specimens had become extinct in the Middle Ages," he declared in an interview with *The Times*. He stated his intention of taking the curious creature to London to study him better.

The Brazilian government took issue with him. The era had been witnessing a return to nationalism. "We'll study João right here, with our own resources, which by no means are negligible!" declared Chancellor Alberto.

Public opinion enthusiastically backed up this decision.

A mass rally in Cinelândia. Impassioned speakers. Banners. "Let's protect our poor man!" The Senate nationalized João.

V—Protective Measures

A special budget. A vast tract of land on the banks of the Xingu River: "The National Park of the Pauper." A Special Commission for the Protection of the Pauper. A book by A. P. Lins: *Memories of Poverty*. An Ode to the Pauper, by the Royal College Choral Ensemble. Women's League for the Protection of the Pauper.

VI—Women's League for the Protection of the Pauper

Ladies of diverse ages and social classes. They took turns to stay with João round-the-clock: they fed him, they dressed him, they sang him to sleep, they sprinkled talcum powder on his poor feet.

Frustrated by previous and present disappointments, satirized by the yellow press, suffering from hormone imbalance ill understood by scientists, they went on living and bestowing blessings while waiting to be frozen.

VII—João

Lying all day on a wide bed, wearing pale pink pajamas. Sometimes he'd cry out: "This is the life! This is the life!" He slurped the exquisite broths, and afterwards belched.

His beady black eyes sparkled.

IX—Dona Laura

A woman in her fifties, discreet and virtuous, volunteered to look after João and was immediately admitted to the League. She was the most assiduous, the most diligent, the most well-mannered of them all. "Come on, come on, Senhor João," she'd say, changing his undershirt. "Well, aren't we a nice clean pauper now!"

X—Ingratitude

João looked at her. Beady black eyes, shrewd.

That day, the two of them were alone. He said: "Take off my trousers, Dona Laura."

Dona Laura took off his pajama trousers, devotedly, quickly, gently, skillfully. His thin legs, his left thigh enveloped in gauze appeared. "Remove the dressing." Surprised, Dona Laura obeyed. The wound was exposed, still full of pus despite the dressings. "Kiss it, Dona Laura."

She kissed it. She died the following day, victim of a virulent infection: since diseases had been practically eliminated, human beings had become defenseless to bacteria.

XI—Unmasked

Public opinion had not recovered yet from this violent blow when it was shaken by a new discovery: in the cave where João had slept, Ellsworth found a bag full of very precious coins: dollars, rubles, doubloons, cruzados, sequins, pounds, cruzeiros . . . A great fortune. "João cannot be considered a pauper," Ellsworth decided.

Public opinion in an uproar. The Chancellor resigned. The Special Commission for the Protection of the Pauper was dissolved.

The Women's League for the Protection of the Pauper, in permanent session, demanded the death penalty for João.

XII—The Trial

Data relative to the prosecution and defense were tabulated and sent to the great Electronic Brain in the Capital. The trial was brief: João was sentenced to death. The Electronic Brain specified the mode of execution.

XIII—The Execution

Nailed to a platinum cross to which was attached a cable of two thousand volts. Hawks plucked out his eyes, soldiers fired at his heart, schoolgirls cut off his toes with razor blades. The Choral Ensemble sang the anthem "Hail, hail, Laura."

XIV—A Terrible Mistake

The ceremony was drawing to a close. An urgent message from Ellsworth to the president of the Supreme Court arrived: "Counterfeit coins. João pauper." General uproar among the populars.

Lavish distribution of alcoholic beverages. A race to the drugstores for tranquilizers. Indignation. Marches. Mass rioting, crowds in turmoil.

XX—Indemnity

Early in the XXIst Century João was canonized by the Cybernetic Church. An Electronic Brain quickly reached a decision favorable to João and set the date to be dedicated to his memory, January the thirty-second. This date, which had not existed in the previous century, was added to the calendar in homage to João, the Last Pauper.

AUTRAN DOURADO
—◦❧(b. 1926)❧◦—

Beginning with the novela *Teia* (1947), Autran Dourado has written stories and novels concerned with the decadence of his home state of Minas Gerais, from solitary characters to their tedious and stagnant surroundings. He excels at structuring dialogues and monologues in a continuous narrative stream, in a style reminiscent of Ernest Hemingway and William Faulkner. He is a prolific writer; his production covers five decades, from *Três Histórias na Praia* (1955) to *Cadernos de Narciso* (1996). "Bald Island" is taken from *Solidão, Solitude* (1972). Autran Dourado's novels have been widely translated into English, French, German, and Spanish (*A Hidden Life*, 1969; *The Voices of the Dead*, 1980; *Pattern for a Tapestry*, 1984; *The Bells of Agony*, 1988), yet his volumes of short stories largely remain to be discovered. Dourado resides in Rio de Janeiro.

BALD ISLAND
—◦❧ ❧◦—

Swinging in the hammock on the porch, her legs dangling, her head resting in her clasped hands, she watched the afternoon take possession of the beach. The limpid blue sea stretched out in front of her eyes. Her tired gaze rested in the dust of sundrenched colors. The sparkle of the sun on the sea, the waves executing a long, whitish curve, the bay quiet like everything around it, the hot sand shimmering. Her nostrils, dry from so much light, were filled with wind-carried sea smells.

Tired. A remote desire to cry started to well up from the bottom of her chest, close to the place her sadness was walled in. She detested the darkness she felt in her chest, as much as she hated the weakness of her tears. She wanted to be strong, she relished looking strong, she wanted the sorrowful strength of a man, not the humus of fertile land. That is why, with measured gestures, she dressed simply, and there, in that beach town, where she could wear slacks comfortably, and walk with hard, strong strides, she was happy. But at that moment, Doroteia was not happy.

The afternoon light made her sad eyes burn. Instinctively she moved out of the sun, she tensed up, small and strong, preparing herself for a life in shadow; she feared the virility of the sun, its fertility. She was a shade flower, a lady-of-the-night that opened its pistils to the moonlight. Only the cold, cold moon could understand her—the calm and the dark voices of the night.

Doroteia looked away from the landscape and began to examine the porch around her, the sweet shade which bathed her. She rocked in the hammock, settled in deeper, closed her eyes and waited; she waited long enough for something to happen inside her. Nothing happened, not a thought or a dream, just the drowsiness of the hot afternoon in her body.

There was no point in reading in her present mood. She could try, with a little effort she might get through a few pages. If she were in Rio, she could walk aimlessly through the streets, watch people who wouldn't even notice her. Not on the island. The book gave her another world, but then that world would fade away, and she would be even sadder and more alone. The guitar, since Marcia had become distant, was silent on the shelf. Music, even when it was cheerful, depressed her. She felt moved by the music, but it was the same world as the books, which would vanish into the air. And everything, everything . . .

She stared violently at the ocean, with unfamiliar fury. The imprecise horizon, a gray blue, was the last outpost for her sleepless eyes. That is where Bald Island was, gray as well, but brilliant in the sun. The island was just rocks and cliffs. She saw it as a projection of her soul, with its uninhabitable rocks. She had heard of an ancient god, tied to the rocks, being attacked by a large bird.

A gull glided for a long time in the air, swooped around in a slow curve and dove into the water. Doroteia felt a strong tug in her body, as if the bird had penetrated her.

Everything was calm. Few people were on Castanheiras Beach at that hour of the afternoon. In the mornings, there were the shouts of the children, the colorful canvas cabanas, the suntanned bodies, the wet hair, balls bouncing in the air.

In the afternoon, occasional couples would seek the privacy of the shade of the chestnut trees to lie in the sand, loving.

It was useless, completely useless to try to suppress the questions that filled her soul. Where was Marcia?

The waves broke softly on the beach and the sea was calm. A black man waded into the ocean and started to swim toward the rocks.

Marcia, what had happened to Marcia, whom she had not seen in such a long time? She hated Marcia, she felt like slowly strangling her, sinking her fingers into the slender neck. No, no, she could never kill her, she was sure. She could, yes, lie as if she were dead on the beach, but feeling the soft fingers on her face, running through her hair, the smell of the sea and of her hair. Marcia, however, wasn't worth it, like a bitch that deserves to be kicked out of the house.

She dug her fingers into her thighs, until she felt the nails bruising her skin. She could not go on like that, she could not continue in that state, abandoned, despair blackening her soul. She wanted to be like the other girls, that lightness, those feminine gestures, joking with the men. No, her wish was not sincere, she tried to convince herself, to try to impose a femininity she did not possess on her soul. As a matter of fact, she couldn't stand the gestures, the feminine clothes, the horrible frills, the airy blouses full of lace. It unnerved her, she did not hide her annoyance when Marcia exaggerated her feminine side, when she put on airs. And Marcia did that just to irritate her, she knew, to make her jealous, since then the men paid even more attention to her.

She tried to remember Marcia's face, her gestures, her speech. But the image her spirit reconstrued was not the same Marcia, it did not have the same aggressive reality as the distant model. Marcia really wasn't distant, or was she? Her house was only three hundred meters from Doroteia's. Marcia was slender and firm as a greyhound. She walked to a mysterious music, that only she could hear. The dogs were beautiful when they raised their voices to the moon, howling to its cold and distant clarity. The nights belonged to them, just to them, until that man had jumped from the rocks.

What was the meaning of the death of the man, who one night had found them as they were kissing each other? To her, very little. Why had Marcia become distant, why was she avoiding her?

After that night Marcia became remote, she did not want to have anything more to do with those nightly encounters. Now she had joined the groups of young men and women who gathered on the hotel veranda or at the Praia Bar.

No, it had not been the death of the unknown man that had separated her from Marcia, she thought. Her coldness had begun a while before. She remembered the day after the encounter with the man on the beach, although she searched everywhere for Marcia, at her house, at the places they used to swim, she couldn't find her. She did not know what to do without her. She needed her voice, her eyes, her soft hands *(Marcia was like a little plant, that also needed protection)*, it was impossible to live without her.

Doroteia wandered around the island, alert to any sign of her. When someone laughed happily she would immediately turn around, wanting to know who had reason to laugh. Doroteia's eyes sparkled with oncoming tears. She held her tears back, drowned them in a deep remote corner of her breast, in that walled-in blackness. And the sparkle in her eye became hard and crystalline, sharp, with smooth, cutting edges. She began to search the beaches, the town, other faces. From a distance she watched Marcia's house, her eyes glued to the green shades.

Trying to forget her friend, she started to think about herself again. She experimented with her body, searching for secret sensations that would dissolve her deep sorrow. But the sensations her body gave her were just as sad.

In the hammock, as in a womb, her thoughts gestated.

One Saturday night, tired from wandering on the beach, desperate from her search, Doroteia stopped at the Praia Bar. Inside the blues was playing, the dancing area was decorated with bamboo and things from the sea. A few couples were moving as languidly as the music. Most of them were young girls in colorful blouses. Doroteia sat at a table in the back, where she could hear the music and watch the couples dancing. She greeted a few acquaintances, and when they motioned her over to their table, she pretended she hadn't noticed. The waiter came and she asked for a martini.

—Excuse me, but we don't serve . . .

At her sharp look, the waiter did not try to finish his excuse.

—All right. Dry?

—Yes.

The appropriately melancholy music hardly reached her. Her thoughts, cloudy, desperate, remained absent. She did not look at anyone. Now she felt a strange urge to get drunk. It would be impossible to do that at the bar, they did not like to serve drinks to the young women. She would stay a little longer, until she was mired in melancholy, and then at home, locked in her room, she would try the gin.

The drink made her feel a little better. Her eyes followed a dancing couple. Their bodies were close together, he whispered something into her ear. She laughed happily, letting herself be embraced.

Doroteia felt a strange urge to laugh well up from deep inside her. She would order another dry martini and perhaps that way she could soothe her soul. The men were funny, and would almost seem ridiculous, if it weren't for the strength that sustained them. That fellow dancing looked like a doll. Men never really existed for her. She would have liked to experience the pleasure they felt . . .

The bar was filling up with people. The dim lights, the music pouring from the record player, the couples dancing, the martini, were doing her good. She liked jazz, just as she enjoyed everything that was sad.

The blues that was playing now, she knew well. It was a piece with special meaning for her, it brought back memories of Marcia. One afternoon at her house, her mother was in her room, her father had gone out. She put on the record player and lightly took Marcia's hand. The two girls remained silent for a long time, looking at each other. Marcia was wearing shorts, her pretty legs exposed. Doroteia hugged her and pulled her to the middle of the room. They danced and neither of them had the courage to talk, surrendered to the music and to each other. How long would her suffering last? She was afraid to remember the music, the warmth of Marcia's body. Doroteia felt Marcia's breath on her face, she could hear her rapid heartbeat, the heart she felt like pressing to her own until the bird died, smothered. That was when she had Marcia's face close to her lips, the scent of her skin, her warm hair. She kissed her timidly. Marcia held her tightly, pressed her bare knees against her legs. Then, what happened then? She couldn't remember, there was a big lake in her memory, a lake of slowly moving waves. It seemed like a dream, the mood of a dream, but not really a dream, it was something outside of time, far from reality, as if it had never been experienced. Only the feeling of that moment remained. She could not even remember Marcia's eyes. The record had stopped and the two stood there, with their arms around each other, given to the shadows, to the darkness of their bodies.

—Another martini, Doroteia ordered. The waiter walked away, to talk to the proprietor. Why couldn't she drink, why were these people so backward? But the martini came. The world was different now, it was bathed in a sweet, sad mist. How many martinis would she need to get drunk?

That was when Marcia walked into the bar, accompanied by a young man. When she met Doroteia's eyes, she tried to turn around and leave. Her date pulled her to the dance floor.

What happened then Doroteia could not clearly remember. Everything was shrouded in hate and confusion, the atmosphere of a horrible nightmare, the bitter aftertaste of drink. In her room, she had gotten completely drunk on gin.

In the hammock, as the afternoon deepened and the beach began to be filled with shadows, Doroteia continued to think, to think incessantly, like the waves that broke and returned to sea—but without the peace of those deep waters. Night was falling.

From the garden gate her father shouted:

—Doroteia, look how lucky I was today!

And he lifted up his line full of fish. He came in happy, sunburned, laughing, in a glow. He was truly content.

Doroteia did not say anything, she limited herself to looking disdainfully at the fish that gave her father so much pleasure. At that moment neither the fish nor her father interested her: she wanted peace, she wanted to be alone.

Alone, she thought, looking at Bald Island lost in the grays of the sea.

Her father sat down in the lounge chair, stretched out his legs, tired, his face bathed in sweat.

—I'd give anything to be able to live like this, in the sun, fishing, he started to say.

Doroteia did not pay much attention to him, immersed in her misery. She knew that in a few minutes she would end up arguing with him. Her arguments with her father, although they exasperated her, gave her a great deal of satisfaction, like a wrestling match that required physical effort. When she was younger it was different. She thought her father was the only man who was really alive, who was strong, intelligent. With time, her father began to lose that reality, the powerful shading Doroteia's childish eyes had given him, and what remained was that ordinary man, with the simple smile on his face.

—When I was a boy, I liked to go fishing in the woods, far from the city, hiding out in the backlands. Once I ended up in Araguaia, where I stayed fishing with some friends for three months. That was the life. I came back black from the sun, but with a clean soul, as if the sun had bleached everything inside of me.

Yes, the sun, thought Doroteia, as her father's lively words filled his mouth like pieces of meat. The sun that bathes the earth, that warms humankind, that makes the earth bear fruit.

— . . . and there were some good-for-nothing Indians hanging around waiting for the catfish we'd give them. There was just too much fish. Once . . .

—Isn't that story about Araguaia and the Indians a lie? Doroteia interrupted him brusquely. She wanted to provoke her father, see his hate.

—Lie!? When have you heard me lying? he shouted, his eyes inflamed with rage.

—Maybe it didn't happen that way. Those Indians are too much.

—The hell they are! Why would I want to make it up? Just tell me.

—I don't know, that's what I can't figure out.

She knew her father wasn't lying, but she wanted to see him angry, to have the pleasure of belittling his feats.

—If you want, ask Souza, when we get back to Rio.

—Sure! He's just another fisherman.

Her father did not reply, he fell silent, brooding. What the devil was wrong with that girl? He did not understand her, he thought she was acting strangely, almost in an evil way.

—Come on, Dad, go on with your story. I'm interested, she said.

—No, that's enough, I know it doesn't interest you.

—It interests me very much.

Her father looked at her to see if she were joking. He could not discover any-thing in his daughter's eyes.

—Dad, what's that story about the fish net you had to use in the river one time?

—Don't be silly! I'm not telling you anything.

She could not help but find her father charming, with his fishing, that simplicity, the life she envied.

—Have you been on the porch a long time? he asked.

—A while.

—What's wrong with you?

Could he have noticed something?

—Nothing.

—It couldn't be nothing. No one just sits there doing nothing.

—What do you mean?

—Look, do you think I don't have eyes, that I can't see something is wrong with you?

She could never tell her father what was happening to her. She could never tell anyone.

—Come, daughter, don't you trust me, aren't I your father, haven't we always been friends?

—We were . . .

—We were and we are.

—I don't know.

He loved his only daughter deeply.

—Teia . . .

—Don't call me that, I don't like it.

—Doroteia, don't you want to play the guitar for me?

—I'm tired.

—Do play for me, it's been so long, and you know how much I enjoy it.

—I'm sick of the guitar.

He did not insist, for he sensed the state that the girl was in. Why was she behaving this way?

—Daughter, if you don't want to tell me what the problem is, at least tell me—can I help you with something? Is it money? Do you want to go back to Rio?

—I don't think you can help me. If it were money, I'd ask for it.

—All right, all right, we won't talk about it.

They were silent for some time, he looking at the darkening sea, worried about his daughter; she sunk into the hammock, in anguish.

—Doroteia, why don't you go out, find some friends?

—I don't need anybody!

—You can't just let yourself go like that.

—I'd be better off dead.

—Don't be silly. I don't know anyone who has solved anything by dying.

—Sometimes it helps.

—It doesn't help at all, it just eliminates the problem, it doesn't solve it.

—So eliminating it isn't enough?

—No.

What did her father understand about such lofty problems, about life and death? Nothing, maybe her guitar would be a better companion. But she did not want music, she knew music would only give her sweet melancholia and nothing more, and then everything would be lost in the air. The guitar was the bridge that joined her with her father, she did not want to communicate with him. Her mother was much easier, cold, distant, with lost eyes, another shadow in a wheelchair. At least she did not torment her with questions. She remembered when she was a little girl, her mother was not sick yet, she had tried to love her mother. She spent hours watching her sew, enraptured with her eyes, her tired gestures. Her mother was exasperatingly cold, she did not seem to notice those eyes that followed her so lovingly. Her mother had never caressed her, where were her hands, her heart? They were not made for the gestures Doroteia's soul craved. She left her aside, she started to almost hate her, since in her heart she could find no echo, no answer to her love. It made her feel horribly uncomfortable, physically distraught, to hear in the silence of the house the soft sound of the wheelchair.

—Dad, when are we going back to Rio?

—Whenever your mother wants to go. I'd like to spend the whole summer here.

Suddenly she felt calm, she really did want to talk with her father. Why had she been so rude to him, when he was telling her about the thing he liked most, fishing? A pang of remorse shot through her heart. She saw her father's face, his childlike air, the happiness in his eyes, his simple goodness, the gesture of help she refused. But no, something inside her feared that "weakness," that giving of the heart.

Her father watched her in silence, he saw her silhouette in the shadows of the porch. It was almost dark and he had not even gone inside to give the fish to the maid and to clean up. It was getting late, but he did not want to leave his daughter alone.

—Doroteia, didn't you say the other day that you'd like to go fishing with me? Why don't you come? I'd like very much to have your company.

—Yes, next time I'll come.

—Wonderful, I'll show you a great place I've discovered.

—I'll go, but at night.

—All right, any time.

Again silence separated them. She could hear the creaking of the hammock, the sea in front of her, the little noises of creatures in the garden.

—What happened to Marcia? I haven't seen her in such a long time, he asked to say something, since he did not know how to stay silent for very long, unless he was fishing.

Hearing Marcia's name, a dull thud shook her breast, like something falling down a long way. She had almost forgotten her and once again the sound of her name assaulted her. Her heart beat wildly, her hands shook. It had been a long time since she had heard her friend's name spoken. She herself avoided pronouncing it. She swung more rapidly in the hammock, closed her eyes. She felt the same tug in her chest as when she had seen the gull dive into the sea. Could her father suspect something? She looked at him fearfully. There was nothing in his eyes that indicated a hidden motive.

—You didn't answer me, he continued. Did you have a misunderstanding?

—Yes, I don't want to see her again.

Her father fell silent, he felt miserable in his onslaughts on Doroteia's silence. He liked Marcia because she was his daughter's friend, he was happy when he saw them together.

—Why don't you make up? You'll see it was nothing serious, unintentional . . . it's a shame for friends to separate that way.

—It was nothing.

—Who started it?

—I really don't know . . . Nobody started anything! I don't want to talk about it.

—Fine, fine. I'm going inside. Your mother must be worried. And you want to be alone.

Alone, Doroteia thought again, closing her eyes.

Marcia went over to the record player, whistling a blues tune. She looked for a record, put it on and waited for the music to start. She kept time to the jazz rhythm with her feet.

—Who's playing Armstrong in the living room? asked a voice from the back of the house. It was Marcia's younger sister.

—It's me.

—Wait a minute, I'm coming. I'm crazy about him, you know that.

Julinha came running in, her eyes shining. Her whole body seemed to vibrate to the blues rhythm.

That Julinha is impossible, thought Marcia. She envied her sister a little, since she knew almost all the records, many by heart.

—Marcia, next I'm going to put on a record Orlando lent me. Guess which one it is.

—How am I supposed to know?

—It's *Got No Blues.*

And she continued to keep time to the music.

The two listened to *Got No Blues.*

—Isn't that wonderful? asked Julinha. Did you hear that trombone?

—Yes, but now I'm going to get dressed.

—Hey, don't go yet, let's listen to it again.

—No, I want to go out.

Marcia let herself fall down on the bed. She was tired, after swimming all afternoon at Capelinha Beach. She had agreed to meet Alberto at the Praia Bar, but she did not feel like going. The adventure with Alberto was starting to bore her. She did not have the least interest in him, she had started to date him to get even with Doroteia, since she did not approve of what she had been telling people about the man who had seen them kissing. The man's death had robbed her of several nights' sleep, she was afraid she would dream about him.

She was reluctant to waste another night with Alberto, listening to his vapid chatter. If Doroteia . . . She did not finish the thought. She jumped out of bed and went to the mirror. She straightened her dress, the same lacy dress Doroteia disliked. She pushed the comb through her hair and when she was about to put on her make-up, she stopped for a minute to look in the mirror. Strange, she thought she looked ridiculous. What an indecent dress! It could have been Doroteia's voice. She examined her face, her mouth, her eyes. She saw herself now not with her own eyes but with Doroteia's. She walked away from the mirror and began to change clothes. She would definitely not meet Alberto, he could wait all night for her at the Praia Bar. She put on navy blue slacks, a cambric blouse. She looked at herself in the mirror and she sensed Doroteia's approving glance.

When she went out to the garden, she took a deep breath of the fresh air, the smell of the tide, it was the starry night itself, clear and silent, that filled her breast.

Doroteia had not listened to Armstrong or looked at herself in the mirror. The only music that filled her ears was the savage silence of the night, of the starry sky over the sea, the moon on the water, the cricket in the flowerbed, the small sounds of the night and the sea. The smell of the flowers, the cloyingly sweet jasmine. Her eyes were hard in the darkness, they could no longer see Bald Island, lost in the blackness of the ocean. Her soul . . .

No, she would not examine her soul again, given over to despair. Nevertheless, her eyes did not obey her, the shame she felt at crying was not enough to dull the sparkle in her eyes, and two tears ran down her face.

Suddenly, she heard the noise of wheels near the living room door. It was her mother, certainly, in her wheelchair, coming to see her on the porch. Doroteia squeezed her eyes shut, wiped away her tears and waited, her heart full of fear, for her mother to approach. She waited for several long minutes and the wheels did not move. Why didn't she come? The wheels rolled again and her mother returned to the living room.

Without telling anyone, Doroteia decided to go to the beach, to lie on the sand. There she could surrender to the "weakness" of tears.

And there, she waited for something to happen in the night. The moonlight in her hair, in her body, was like a caress. She opened herself to the night like a flower opening to starlight.

She could not contain a cry of joy when she saw Marcia approach. Yes, she was coming back, she was sure that one night Marcia would return. She knew that for Marcia, love was like words written in the sand, that the sea would carry away by night to its depths.

Orígenes Lessa
—◦❧(1903–1986)❧◦—

A journalist from São Paulo who spent his childhood in the northern city of São Luís do Maranhão, Orígenes Lessa entered the Brazilian Academy of Letters in 1981. While working for the *Diário da Noite* in São Paulo in 1931, Lessa published his first collection of short stories, *O Escritor Proibido* (1929), followed by *Garçon, Garçonnete, Garçonnière* (1930) and *A Cidade que o Diabo Esqueceu* (1931). He was taken captive during the Constitutionalist Revolution of 1932, yet continued to write while imprisoned in Rio de Janeiro, publishing the stories of *Passa-três* (1935) before moving to New York in 1942. During a year in New York, he worked as coordinator of inter-American affairs for NBC. His impressions of the United States were registered in his book *Ok, America* (1943), and his story "Marta: A Souvenir of New York" pays homage to the city. Lessa's novel *O Feijão e o Sonho* (1938) was a major success, and his dedication to the short story continued in *Omlete em Bombaim: Contos* (1946), *A Desintegração da Morte* (1948), *Balbino: Homem do Mar* (1960), *Nove Mulheres* (1968), *Mulher na Calçada* (1984), and the anthology *Dez Contos Escolhidos* (1985). "Marta: A Souvenir of New York" is perhaps his only work ever translated into English.

Marta
—◦❧ ❧◦—
A Souvenir of New York

I do not remember the name of the street. Or rather, the number. It was either Forty-sixth or Forty-eighth. On that street was a Mexican restaurant where I often went to eat, with a longing for highly seasoned foods that the "blue-plate specials" of the U.S. restaurants aroused in me. Food that came with salt and pepper on the side, for the customer to use as he pleased, something that did not tempt a palate that was accustomed to *vatapá* and other spicy dishes. I suffered whenever I sat down at a table in any of those spotless New York restaurants where the food was so photogenic. I took refuge in the Latin American, Spanish, and Italian restaurants, even tried Kosher and Indian cooking. And I feasted on chili and beans, tamales, and *tacos* in that little restaurant whose address I cannot recall.

Only one door, small round tables, exuberant customers. Spanish filled the air, noisily. There was a girl, with slightly protruding ears, fair and not dark, ugly and not pretty, Marta and not Carmen, not Consuelo, not Rosario. Younger, gayer, livelier. She was the best spice in a place that specialized in peppery, imaginative dishes.

"Good morning, Marta."

Marta was everybody's friend. She knew each one's likes and dislikes. Almost from the minute she spotted you, she would be on her way with your favorite dish. Or she would bring what she thought best that day and put it before you with sweetness that defied complaint.

" 'Usted' are going to like it."

We always did.

"Tequila?"

She brought it.

"I kept it for 'usted'."

She spoke English, but systematically substituted "usted" for the banal "you." Her voice had an intimate quality, warm and lifting.

"Marta!"

The restaurant owner called to her all the time. Because whenever she had a free minute Marta would stop at every table and chatter happily. Marta knew that she was all voice. That is why she talked. Her voice made her face beautiful. It lifted her breasts, which—hurrah for *saudade*—were perfectly rounded and made her every movement a melody.

"Chili con carne," someone would order.

"Chili con carne," she would sing, as she set the plate on the table.

All of us—there were not many—more or less knew each other by sight, though we had only one thing in common, Marta. We would often forget the tamales, the *tacos,* and the chili con carne, so intent were we on watching Marta come and go to the sound of her lovely voice. Mostly we forgot the life that passed by outside on its way to the subway, to work, to a cheese sandwich with a lettuce leaf and a slice of tomato, to vitamin pills, or to comic books.

"Have you been out of town?"

For Marta, a trip was the only logical reason any of us could have for staying away for a while. And since I spent my life wandering from restaurant to restaurant, and was not one of the most regular customers there, I always answered yes. Marta began to think of me as a professional traveler.

"Hello, 'viajero'."

And as a "viajero" she knew me.

" 'Usted' who travel so much, have you been in Mexico?"

She had asked in English. I told her in English that I had not. Marta lamented, in Spanish, that I did not know Mexico. And from then on she spoke to me in nothing but Spanish, a privilege that she naturally bestowed only on her fellow countrymen. Thus she included me among those who could bask in the charm of her voice, which was even lovelier in Spanish.

One day, after an absence of weeks, I went to the restaurant.

"What'll you have?"

The voice was hostile. The face was familiar. Dark. Coarse black hair.

"Marta?" I asked.

"I'm talking about food," the man said, holding out a menu.

I made a random selection, the food came, I ate in silence. In silence other men were eating at the gaily decorated tables. The only sound was of silverware and dishes. One fellow was engrossed in a magazine picture story of a steel-muscled hero, rigid of jaw and low of brow.

The tables were crowded, as usual. Before, the owner had sat at the cashier's desk and run the restaurant from there. Now there was a blonde girl with a pretty, vacant face. The owner, Pablo, was waiting on customers. The tables were filled, as I said. But the restaurant seemed empty to me.

Where could Marta be? Was she sick? Or had she gone back to Mexico? Perhaps she was on vacation. I wanted to ask Pablo. But his earlier coldness made me hesitate.

I dawdled over my meal. Maybe she would still show up, maybe she worked afternoons only. A foolish idea, naturally. Marta must have been gone for several days, because the whole atmosphere had changed. Most of the customers were the same. But that silence obviously came from a prolonged lack. Everyone was grieving for the voice that had wreathed all the tables with a smile.

An idiotic notion came to mind. What if Marta had died? It was quite improbable. She was young and healthy. Besides, if she had died, Pablo's reaction would have been different. She must have had an argument with the boss or with a customer. And because of that she had left. But how to find out? I could not ask the other customers. There, it was everyone to his own table. They all had other things to do. Nobody visited from table to table. We plainly were not in a small Mexican village. Finally, I left.

I thought about Marta all day. It was the first time I had thought of her outside the restaurant. And I was quite surprised when I realized that I was thinking about her, that I was vaguely bothered at the idea of never seeing her again. "Al fin y al cabo," as she had said so many times, why was I interested? And what did it matter to me whether I saw her again or not? With this line of reasoning I was able to get her out of my mind that night. I went to a movie, a war story in which the Germans were amazingly stupid and a foreign correspondent fooled all the police, all the undercover agents, and almost all of Hitler's troops.

A week passed. One day I was sitting in torment at my desk. Lunchtime was approaching, and I had an urge to eat chili con carne. Immediately Marta popped back into my mind. I was seized by near-anguish. Had she come back? I left my typewriter as it was, grabbed my overcoat, and hurried out into a snowstorm. When I entered the restaurant, I was upset, searching. There were fewer customers. The expressionless blonde was still at the cashier's desk. The owner was still waiting on table. I studied the menu for a long while, then ordered chili con carne. Yes, Marta must be on vacation. Marta would return. I almost said to myself: Marta must return. I shuddered when I heard a gay "Buenas tardes." It was a young girl, a happy, noisy girl, greeting Pablo, sitting down at a table. No, it was not Marta.

The next day, impelled by some invisible force, I walked by the restaurant. I did not go in. I looked in the door. It was, as it had been the last few times, almost empty. The customers were new, almost all of them. I went on, now really disturbed. Disturbed, in Heaven's name why? I ended up eating tasteless lobster at Dempsey's.

For several days I did not think about Marta. At least, I tried not to. Why should I think about her? There was nothing between us. I hardly knew her. Besides, Mabel was so good-looking and gave me such nice, warm kisses.

But again the memory of Marta had me in its power. Her lovely voice gave charm to her walk. It sent me into a sort of tailspin. I went to Forty-sixth Street, or Forty-eighth, whichever it was. That time I entered, resolutely, very much at ease, like someone going to eat in any restaurant. The place seemed strange, even though the bright tablecloths were the same, the blonde was still ringing up checks on the cash register, and Pablo handed me the usual menu. Even his harsh voice was the same one that had called Marta away from our tables.

I tasted my tamales. I drank a glass of beer dispiritedly. Several times I was tempted to question Pablo. But he was abrupt, his look was dark and unfriendly. He was absorbed in taking the customers' orders.

Since I was now determined to find out, since I now felt I had to find out, to find out why, dear Lord, I went back next day. I went to the restaurant for that one reason. It was surely all in my eyes. It must have been. Because Pablo, as soon as he saw me, came over. Dryly and without preamble, before I uttered a word, he said:

"She's not coming, she's never coming back."

After that I was a more regular customer. Pablo never mentioned Marta again, nor did I. But now he received me as a friend, not just as another customer.

Rubem Fonseca
—◦❧(b. 1925)❧◦—

Originally from the state of Minas Gerais, Fonseca is one of the most prolific writers in and about Rio de Janeiro, mixing elements of detective fiction and the underworld with the social and cultural world of Rio de Janeiro's more exclusive districts. He was once a commissioner of police and later specialized in criminal psychology, before earning degrees in law and public administration. His works document the social transformation of urban, modern Brazil with graphic, dry language in a realistic world of corruption, crime, prostitution, and dramatic situations. His eight blockbuster novels of urban Rio have found a world market in translation, while his twelve books of short stories have remained almost undiscovered in translation, notwithstanding their tremendous popularity and influence in Brazil, to the point that many of his titles are sold at newspaper stands. Five of his first six published titles were short story collections (*Os Prisioneiros*, 1963; *A Coleira do Cão*, 1965; *Lúcia McCartney*, 1967; *Feliz Ano Novo*, 1975; *O Cobrador*, 1979). After receiving a long list of awards for his works in Brazil, Fonseca was awarded the Luís de Camões Prize for literature in 2003 in Portugal, considered a kind of Nobel Prize for literature in the Portuguese language. He is one of Brazil's most distinguished prose writers.

Large Intestine
—◦❧ ❧◦—

I called the author to make an appointment. He said yes, provided he was paid— "by the word." I answered that I could not make that decision, that I would have to talk to the Editor of the magazine first.

"I can even give you seven words free, interested?" said the author.

"Yes."

"Adopt a tree and kill a kid," said the author, hanging up.

The seven words were not worth one cent to me. But the Editor thought differently. They agreed on a rate per word, in a private conversation.

I arranged to meet the author at his home. He received me in the library.

"When did you start to write?" I asked, turning on the tape recorder.

"I think it was when I was twelve. I wrote a small tragedy. I always thought that a good story had to end with somebody dying. I am still killing people."

"Don't you think that denotes a morbid preoccupation with death?"

"It could also be a healthy preoccupation with life, which in the end is the same thing."

"How many books do you have in this room?"

"About five thousand."

"Have you read all of them?"

"Almost."

"Do you read every day? How much? At what speed?"

"I read at least one book a day. My speed today is one hundred pages an hour. But I used to read faster."

"When were you first published? Did it take long?"

"It took a long time. They wanted me to write just like Machado de Assis, but I didn't want to, and I didn't know how to."

"Who were they?"

"The guys who published the books, the literary supplements, the literary journals. They wanted the Guarani Indians, the backlands. I lived in an apartment building in the middle of the city and from my window I saw neon signs and heard car engines."

"Why did you become a writer?"

"People like us either become a saint or go crazy, or turn into a revolutionary or a bandit. Since there was no truth in Ecstasy or in Power, I ended up somewhere between Writer and Bandit."

"People have accused you of being a pornographic writer. Are you?"

"I am, my books are full of miserable people without teeth."

"Your books sell well. Are there that many readers interested in people on the margin of society? A friend of mine said the other day that she was not interested in stories about people without shoes."

"Shoes they have, sometimes. What's missing, always, are teeth. The decay starts, begins to hurt, and the poor guy finally goes to the dentist, one of those who has a plastic sign on the door with an enormous set of dentures on it. The dentist tells him how much it costs to fill the tooth. But to pull it is much cheaper. Then pull it, doc, says the guy. That's how one tooth goes, then another, until the fellow ends up with only one or two, right in front, just to give him a picturesque look and to make the audience laugh, if by chance he has the luck to show up in the movies rooting for Flamengo in a game against Vasco."

The author gets up, goes to the window, and looks out. Then he picks up a book from the shelf.

"But I don't just write about marginals trying to make it into the lumpen bourgeoisie: I also write about fine and noble people. Have you read this book, *Letters of the Duchess of San Severino*? The Duke of San Severino is a very rich man who does not like his wife, the young and beautiful Duchess of San Severino. The mother of the Duke, the Old Duchess of San Severino, does not like her daughter-in-law, because when she married the Duke she was a simple Baroness. The Young Duchess suffers terrible moments in the castle, especially during the solemn dinners, when family trees are being discussed—the family of the Duke goes back to Pepino the Short while that of the ex-Baroness only begins in the seventeenth century. Not being able to stand these humiliations and offenses, the Young Duchess decides to be psychoanalyzed by a mature and wise professor, with whom she finally falls in love. But the analyst refuses to have physical relations with the Young Duchess, alleging that her feelings for him are just a transference and not a spontaneous gesture of love. Desperate, the Young Duchess becomes interested in raising rare orchids, which redeems all her suffering. Of course this is just a summary of a colorful and edifying story, full of interesting characterizations, in a style that permits the reader to penetrate the nucleus of the work without much effort but, despite this, with no less gratification. It is a novel with flowers, beauty, nobility and money. Realize that this is something we all yearn to have."

"And there is also the presence of Science, in the person of the psychoanalyst: a symbol?"

"Deliberately candid. I wrote the book in the manner of Marcel Proust, obviously. In the beginning of the book, the Young Duchess remembers her girlhood, when she was still a little Baroness, in the gardens of the palace, tasting madeleines at dusk, learning how to dance the minuet and play the harpsichord. Then follows the horrible death of her father, in the sinking of the Lusitania; the madness of her mother, the Old Baroness, interned in a Swiss clinic, set among pines and snow-covered peaks. Finally the frustrating marriage, the romance with Professor Klein, and the raising of orchids. The book ends with the orchids, a type of bucolic and pantheistic hymn."

"And the Young Duchess has all her teeth, I presume."

"Well, some are false. But that is not made very explicit. Why disappoint the readers? Just in passing, I refer to the difficulty she has in eating a peach, a poetic citation—do I dare, etc.—for those who know. In addition, her teeth are white, perfect. It has already been said that what counts is not reality, but truth, and truth is that in which you believe."

I got up and held out my hand, asking for the book that the author was holding. On the cover was a Black Dwarf, instead of a Young Duchess. The title of the book was *The Dwarf Who Was Black, a Priest, Hunchback and Nearsighted*.

"This book was interpreted in various ways, including the pornographic. Shall we talk about pornography?"

"Joãozinho and Maria were taken for a walk in the woods by their father who, in collusion with their mother, intended to abandon them so that they would be devoured by wolves. As they were being led into the forest, Joãozinho and Maria, who suspected their father's intentions, surreptitiously dropped bread crumbs along the path. The bread crumbs were to help them find their way back but a little bird ate them all, and, after they were abandoned, the children, lost in the woods, ended up in the claws of an old witch. Thanks, however, to Joãozinho's cleverness, both finally succeeded in throwing the old woman into a cauldron of boiling oil, killing her after a long agony of stabbing screams and pleas. Then the children returned to their parents' house, with the riches they stole from the old woman, and they all lived together again."

"But that is a fairy tale."

"It is an indecent, dishonest, shameful, obscene, immodest, dirty and sordid story. Nevertheless it is printed in all or almost all the major languages of the world and is traditionally transmitted from parents to children as an edifying story. Those children—thieves, assassins—with their criminal parents, should not be allowed to enter anybody's house, not even hidden in a book. That is a really perverted story, in the popular meaning of the word "dirty." And it is, for that reason, pornographic. But when the defenders of decency accuse something of being pornographic it is because it describes or represents sexual or excretory functions, with or without the use of words commonly referred to as 'swear words.' The human being, someone has already said, is still affected by everything which reminds him unequivocally of his animal nature. They also have already said that man is the only animal whose nudity offends those who are in his company, and the only one who in his natural acts hides himself from his fellows."

"And words are influenced by this?"

"Of course. Metaphor is the result of it, so our grandparents would not have to say—fuck. They *slept with, made love* (sometimes in French), *had relations, sexual intercourse, carnal conjunction, coitus, copulation,* they did everything but *fuck.* I had a law professor who was so euphemistic that, when he wanted to describe a case of seduction—which, as you know, is legally confined to copulation—that he spoke Latin: introductio penis intra vas. Philologists and linguists are also bound by taboo. I would like some philologist one day to write a book entitled: *The Fuck.* These restrictions against the so-called dirty word are attributed by some anthropologists to the ancestral taboo against incest. Philosophers say that what perturbs and alarms man are not the things in themselves but his opinions and fantasies about them. Since man lives in a symbolic universe, and language, myth, art, religion are parts of the universe, they are the varied threads which weave the complicated net of human experience. In 1884, a French neurologist, Gilles de la Tourette, described an abnormal behavior in which the patient constantly shouts words considered obscene. Cursing is accompanied by a muscular tic. This combination of symptoms received the name of the La Tourette Syndrome. Even today its causes have not been adequately clarified, and thus there is no definitive cure. Thinking that perhaps the sickness is a reaction against the intolerable rigidity of the taboo structure, an American doctor developed a therapeutic technique that consists of having the patient repeat the obscenities as loudly and as quickly as possible, to the point of exhaustion. Imagine the scene—going on in the consulting room of a psychologist—that is identical to a passage of Burroughs' delirious prose. The patient is tied by electrodes to a machine whose functioning is synchronized with a metronome. This metronome controls the speed with which the swear words must be shouted—up to two hundred a minute. Could you shout two hundred swear words a minute?"

"I don't think so," I answered as I put another cassette into the recorder.

"If you do not shout the obscenities at the necessary speed, electric shocks force you to keep the rhythm. The treatment seems to have for its objective the creation in the patient of a minimum of inhibition; or, rather, because he cannot stand, for lack of temporary relief, the inhibitions he suffers from, the individual explodes, being compelled to a type of antisocial behavior that demands the reimplanting of a new inhibitory casing. The mistake seems to me to be the presumption that inhibitions are necessary to individual balance. The opposite seems truer to me— inhibitions without the possibility of release can cause serious damage to the individual's health. A wise social organization should prevent the repression of these communication channels that provide vicarious relief and the reduction of tension. The alternatives to pornography are mental illness, violence, the Bomb. There should be a National Curse Day. Another danger in the repression of so-called pornography is that such an attitude tends to justify and perpetuate censorship. The allegation that some words are so deleterious that they should not be written is used in all attempts to prevent freedom of expression." "You don't think that spoken pornography is disappearing? In football fields choruses of girls sportively chant songs like this one, which I heard on Sunday:

One, two, three,
four, five, six,
The guys with Flu
Are a bunch of pricks.

"The word prick, like bitch, whore, and others, derives from the key obscenity, which is 'to fuck.' Of course, in this case, the words have a cathartic effect, of relief from tension and pressures. This phenomenon is always more observable when there is a regimentalization of individuals, in time of war or even of peace, in barracks, asylums, prisons, schools, factories, in urban-industrial nuclei with a high demographic concentration. In these cases the use of prohibited words is a form of antirepressive response. But basically the pornography which still exists today is the result of a latent antibiological prejudice in our society. I remember reading the complaints of a writer who feared that pornographic language, because it was so abused, distorted, transformed into clichés, would no longer be the seamy side of the noble language of religion and love, and there would be nothing left to express the opulence of obscenity, which for many people, by the way, is half of the pleasure of the sexual act."

"Your book *The Dwarf*, etc.—can it be considered pornographic?"

"Most books that are considered pornographic are characterized by a successive series of erotic scenes whose objective is to psychologically stimulate the reader—a rhetorical aphrodisiac. All elements are avoided that could possibly distract the reader from the one dimensional involvement to which he is being subjected. These are books of extreme structural simplicity, with a plot circumscribed by the erotic transactions of the characters. The situations tend to be basically identical in all of them; there are only differences in degree of scatology and perversion. As long as they are not excessively exposed to this type of literature, the majority of readers are stimulated by it. There is nothing worse than cheap erotic saturation. The very complexity of the book you mentioned, *The Dwarf*, excludes the book from this category. You know that there is no Dwarf in the book. Even so, some critics affirm that he symbolizes God, others that he represents the ideal of eternal Beauty, still others that he is a Cry of Revolt against the iniquity of the Third World."

"But others have also said that the book does not go beyond a mishmash of gratuitous vulgarities, crude eroticism, and gross actions, unnecessary and futile, tempered by a dirty mind."

"Mash or stew? They said similar things about Joyce."

"Do you think you are like Joyce?"

"I hate Joyce. I hate all my precursors and contemporaries."

"We'll talk about that in a little while. I don't want to leave pornography for the time being, all right? Can the reading of pornographic books lead the individual to morbid or antisocial conduct?"

"On the contrary. For many people it would be advisable to read pornographic books, for the same cathartic reasons that led Aristotle to encourage Athenians to go to the theater."

"Then, for these people, the ideal would be a Pornographic Theater?"

"Exactly. What people call pornography never does any harm and sometimes does some good."

"But many people, including some educators, psychologists, sociologists, don't think that way."

"There are many people who accept pornography everywhere, even, or mainly, in their private life, less in art, believing like Horace, that art should be *dulce et utile*. In attributing to art a moralizing function, or at least, an entertaining one, these people end up justifying the coercive power of censorship, exercised under allegations of security or public well-being."

"Speaking of security, is there a Terrorist Pornography?"

"It exists, and unlike other pornographies, it has an anti-aphrodisiac code, in which sex has no glamor, no logic, no sanity—just force. But Terrorist Pornography is so strange that it has already been called Science Fiction Pornography. Distinguished examples of this genre are the books by the Marquis de Sade and William Burroughs, which cause surprise, revulsion and horror in simple souls, books where there are no trees, flowers, birds, mountains, rivers, animals—only human nature."

"What is human nature?"

"In my book *Large Intestine* I say that in order to understand human nature, it is necessary that all artists excommunicate the body and investigate—in the way that only we know how to do, contrary to the method of scientists—the still secret and obscure relations between body and mind, minutely observe the functioning of the animal in all his interactions."

"Does pornography, like space voyages and measles, have a future?"

"Pornography is linked to the organs of excretion and reproduction, to life, to the functions that characterize resistance to death—feeding and love, and its exercises and results: excrement, copulation, sperm, pregnancy, labor, growth. That is our old friend, the Pornography of Life."

"Is there a Pornography of Death, as Gorer wanted it? Excuse me for citing someone by name, I know you don't like it, but you were the one who established the precedent, quoting Aristotle, Joyce and Horace."

"Yes, it is creating itself. In the measure that copulation becomes more mentionable and its chorus of little girls in football stadiums chants songs with dirty words of the Old Pornography, something else is being hidden which is increasingly less mentionable, which is death as a natural process, resulting from physical decay, which is Pornographic Death, death in bed, by sickness—and which is becoming continually more secret, abject, objectionable, obscene. The other death—by crime, catastrophe, conflict, violent death—is part of the Fantasy Offered to the Masses by Television Today, like the stories of Joãozinho and Maria used to be. A New Pornography is growing up that we could call the Pornography of Gorer."

"On the telephone you gave me a motto: adopt a tree and kill a kid. Does this mean you hate humanity?"

"My slogan could also be, adopt a savage animal and kill a man. This is not because I hate, but on the contrary, because I love all my fellow beings. I am just afraid that human beings will change, first into devourers of insects and then into devouring insects. In short, there are too many people, or there will soon be too many people in the world, creating an excessive dependence on technology and a necessity for regimentalization similar to that of the ant hill. The day will come when the greatest inheritance that parents can leave their children will be their own body, for their children to eat. As a matter of fact, the moment has come for us, the artists and writers, to start a big universal cultural and religious movement; in the sense of creating the habit of feeding ourselves on the flesh of our dead, with Jesus, Allah, Mohammed, Moses, all involved in the campaign. A terrible waste of protein is going on. Swift and others already said something similar, but they were making satire. What I propose is a New Religion, Superanthropocentric, Mystic Cannibalism."

"Would you eat your father?"

"Not in a *churrasco* or a stew. But in a biscuit, like in that movie, I would not have the least repugnance to devouring my father. It is still possible that someone would want to devour his mother roasted, whole, like a chicken, to afterwards lick his fingers and lips, saying: 'Mom was always very good.' It's a matter of taste."

"Do you write books for an imaginary reader?"

"Among my readers are also those who are as idiotic as the human vegetables who spend all their leisure hours watching television. I would like to be able to say that literature is useless, but it is not, in a world in which ever more technicians pullulate. For every Nuclear Plant a group of artists and poets are needed, otherwise we're screwed even before the Bomb explodes."

"Is there a Latin American Literature?"

"Don't make me laugh. There is not even a Brazilian literature, with a semblance of structure, style, characterization, or whatever. There are people writing in the same language, in Portuguese, which is already a lot and everything. I have nothing in common with Guimarães Rosa; I am writing about people heaped together in the city while the technocrats sharpen the barbed wire. We spent years and years worried about what some cretin English and German scientists (Humboldt) said about the impossibility of creating a civilization South of the Equator and we decided to roll up our sleeves, cut out our lazy café conversations and, starting with our plastic luncheonettes, make a civilization like they wanted it, and we constructed São Paulo, Santo André, São Caetano, our tropical Manchesters with their mortipherous seeds. Until yesterday the symbol of the Federation of Industries of the State of São Paulo was three chimneys belching thick funnels of black smoke into the air. We are killing all the animals, not even an armadillo can stand it, several species are already extinct, a million trees are cut down each day, in a little while all the leopards will become bathroom mats, the alligators from the swamps have turned into purses and tapirs are eaten in native restaurants, the kind a guy goes to, asks for *Capybara Thermidor,* tires a little bit, just to tell his friends, and throws the rest out. There is nothing left for Diadorim."

"But is there or is there not a Latin American Literature?"

"Only if it's in Knopf's head."

"What do you mean with this about writing your book? Is that the advice you give young people?"

"I am not giving advice. Just because someone can try to write the *Comédie Humaine* applying to his fiction the laws of nature or write the *Metamorphosis* breaking those same laws, sooner or later he will end up writing his book—his own. Sooner or later he will also end up dirtying his hands, if he persists."

"Last question: do you like to write?"

"No. No writer really likes to write. I like to make love and drink wine. At my age I shouldn't lose time with anything else, but I can't stop writing. It's a disease."

"I think we have enough," I said, turning off the tape recorder.

After the interview was transcribed, I went to the Editor.

"This interview looks like the *Dialogue des Morts* of French classicism, bottoms up."

"We'll publish it like it is," said the Editor.

I called the author.

"You said two thousand six hundred and twenty-seven words and we will send you a check for the right amount."

The author did not even thank me. Once again he hung up on me.

"These writers think they know it all," I said, irritated.

"That's why they're dangerous," said the Editor.

CARLOS HEITOR CONY
—❧(b. 1926)❧—

Author of twelve books of short stories and fourteen novels, elected to the Brazilian
Academy of Letters in 2000, Carlos Heitor Cony has mixed journalism with an
impressive literary career, notable for the attention and awards given to his work.
His first novel (*O Ventre*) was influenced by Sartre and considered too strong to be
published in 1956. With a publisher's contract, however, Cony continued to write,
and in 1996 the academy awarded him the Machado de Assis Medal for his complete works.

While a journalist in Rio de Janeiro in 1964, Cony was imprisoned six times
during the dictatorship and lived in exile in Cuba in 1967–1968. Even while imprisoned, he continued to publish, and his novel *Antes, o Verão* (1964) was made
into a film. Cony's story "Order of the Day" satirizes the mentality and brutish
stupidity of military rule in Brazil. Cony received the Ordre des Arts et des Lettres
from the French government, while his prose works continue to receive the highest
awards in Brazil.

ORDER OF THE DAY
—❧ ❧—

"Men!"

He passed his hand across his forehead, which he thought was sweaty. Sweaty
it was, but cold. Before his eyes was the formation of men, standing at attention.
The bugler had sounded the call, a dry clamor of boots against boots came from
the courtyard, and there in front of his men was the colonel, wiping his hand across
his forehead which produced sweat and cold but not a single thought.

To gain time he raised his voice one tone higher. When he was a captain his
authoritative voice had acquired fame; he had been sought for all important ceremonies. Few men in the entire First Military District knew, as did he, how to
command a drill.

Again he shouted: "Men!"

He did not have time now to curse the confidence he had felt that "When I'm up there I'll think of something." After all, for more than five years, on the same date, for the same reasons and in the same words he had been extolling the heroism of that Regiment which in times past, at the battle of Lomas Valentinas, had written a page of glory in the annals of war. In addition, it was the birthday of the Military District Commander, which should have made his speech easier. Impossible that out of his head, soaked with sweat and cold, should not emerge the speech in praise of these two events.

In past years he had gone armed, like a good soldier: he had taken a speech solidly set down on solid sheets of paper, and when the bugler used to sound the call to attention, his only concern was to achieve the right tone of voice, so that his words, soaring and consecrated by love for the Fatherland, should acquire beauty, virility and emotion.

He was going to repeat for the third time "Men," but he ventured on to a sentence that more or less committed him:

"We are here, once again united at the feet of our sublime Fatherland, to worship . . ."

Problems were already arising, sooner than he had expected. Worship which event first of all? The victory of the battle of Lomas Valentinas or the birthday of the Military District Commander? If he had had the time, occasion and forethought to write down his speech, he would have duly weighed the pros and cons of a choice. But there, thrown suddenly before the troops, he could not inventory the advantages or disadvantages of choosing one or the other.

He felt his lips trembling, not out of uncertainty but out of hatred: they'd pay for it! He would be cruel, cunning, implacable. That affront would not go unavenged; he would nurse his wounds and still leave himself a margin wide enough not only for defending himself, but for attacking as well. Since he had become *sindico*, in charge of the condominium where he lived, he had never gone through such a crisis. A crisis, above all, of authority. And authority for him, colonel and *sindico*, was a sacred thing, untouchable, God given. That scoundrel on the third floor would see whom he had to deal with. And the Argentinian? That bastard—and he had a fright: he had almost pronounced the word bastard out loud.

He concentrated on the ceremony. He remembered vaguely that the sentence had ended with "to worship," but now he did not know what or how they should worship. It wasn't a time for worship, but rather for horse whips, for spurs. A libertine who brought loose women home, who besieged the honest women in the building, for whose honor and defense he had vouchsafed and was responsible! It was too much! Were we to worship knavery and shamelessness? No! A horse whip! Spurs!

". . . to worship, my friends, the beloved Fatherland which gave us life, this Fatherland of the blue sky, the perennial blue sky, on which are engraved the five immortal stars, the Southern Cross, which guide us and lead us to a glorious destiny . . ."

The sky was not blue, neither on the outside, nor within himself. Clouds hovered over the entire courtyard, from one end to the other, but he was speaking in the poetic, the figurative sense. He had overcome the most difficult part of the talk, the beginning, the first few words. The image of the blue sky had been in his mind for a long time, since his high school days when he used to like to speak of the perennial blue.

Actually, he felt as if he were overcast. There were clouds everywhere, in the sky and in his heart, and even in his eyes: all of a sudden he no longer saw the troops in front of him as a single man in a single correct stance, befitting a military review. What he saw before him was the debacle of the previous night.

It all started after dinner, just as he was preparing to write his order of the day for the following morning. He knew that he had to present an important speech and, although he had already selected some ideas, he did not think much of impromptu talks; he liked to have everything written down.

He had sat down at his writing table, used practically only on these occasions, to compose the address for this historic date. He selected a piece of satiny paper, the best pen in his possession, and with vigorous capital letters put on the top of the first sheet, "MEN!"

He had not completed writing the word *men* when he heard the noise. Glass was breaking with a racket down below. With some effort of concentration he finished putting the exclamation point after the word *men* and went to the window to have a look at what was happening.

He was a *sindico* and a colonel. When he had sat down at his writing table he was the colonel, but by the time he got to the window and looked down he was the *sindico*.

He did not need to think very long to understand what was happening: someone had flung a chair out of the window, and the chair had fallen squarely on the glass roof of the greenhouse that he had built to protect his wife's plants. That roof, that greenhouse, had been a victory he had sweated out, the greatest victory of his life, more important, in a certain sense, than the victory of Lomas Valentinas, of which he had only vague and distant notions.

It so happened that his wife loved plants, but she had always restricted herself to third-rate cultivated types and to vases which were balanced on top of the narrow window sills in the small apartments in which she had always lived. His wife's dream was to have a greenhouse made to order, with a special glass roof to retain the light but keep out the wind. Some time before, at a meeting of the condominium, he had proposed that a greenhouse be built at the end of the parking lot, sacrificing a few of the parking spaces. His idea had been opposed by everyone, especially by the man who was then *sindico*, a lawyer for the weavers' union, a meddlesome communist and savior of the poor. The idea of the greenhouse was ridiculous, said the *sindico* right to his face, "and if the colonel's wife wants greenhouses, let her put them up elsewhere."

The colonel had swallowed the insult, but not for long. One night at the end of March, he was already in bed, wrapped in fine hand-finished sheets, when a phone call came. It was Quincas, a friend of his who was a general. He was agitated:

"We're going to put troops in the streets! This time we'll bring down the government!"

The colonel felt weary; he had already gone into the streets so many times, and it never did any good. The next day a new government stepped in and he was left holding the bag. He was going to argue against the idea of putting troops inthe streets, but Quincas was very enthusiastic and yelled from the other end of the line:

"We're going to take this country in hand! It's the end of this madness of civilians telling us what to do. We're going to be in charge now!"

He shuddered. The first thought which occurred to him was about the greenhouse. He was going to explain the problem of the greenhouse, but Quincas was raving:

"Get down here, man! If not, you won't be in on it and when we split up the goodies there won't be anything left for you!"

He did not really want anything. Like everyone else, he thought that general disorder reigned in the country, a real mess. He measured the national confusion by the internal confusion of the building in which, after twenty-some years of a hard barracks life, he had managed to buy a two-bedroom apartment with a small balcony overlooking the back, whose ledge served as the pasture and domain of his wife and her potted plants.

The confusion had increased considerably of late, especially when that lawyer was elected *sindico* and immediately undertook to improve the situation of the doorman and the two janitors, ordering that they be paid their thirteenth month's salary, which had been held up. This upset everyone in a general way and the colonel very much in particular: to him the doorman was a communist who read the leftist paper *Última Hora* every day. There was even a special antipathy between them. It was enough for the colonel to appear in uniform and the doorman would immediately open the *Última Hora*, as a silent, deadly affront.

When meetings of the condominium took place, it was always the colonel who was humiliated and offended. One night, after a bitter argument in which he had once again defended the idea of the greenhouse, he heard an unidentified voice from the back call him "gorilla." He was going to retaliate, but the *sindico* cut him off and cited some statutes. The colonel resolved to appeal to brute force. He threatened to go up to his apartment and arm himself with his SW.45, but the peace-lovers cooled him off and the affront—which was not to him alone but to the Armed Forces—remained unavenged. The following day, when he went out, the doorman, although he had the *Última Hora* spread out in front of his face, had a smile even wider than the newspaper page. On that sneering mouth, in a gigantic grin, the colonel could make out the word "gorilla"

That was water over the dam. Quincas—Brigadier General Joaquim Osório de Lima, descendant of the military hero Caxias and a hero of 1937 when, in a very successful surprise maneuver, he had managed to take over the snack bar of the law school where two students had hidden after a demonstration—Quincas was now on the phone telling him that everything was working out smoothly.

He put on his uniform and went to headquarters, not knowing exactly what to do and with only two ideas fixed in his head: get the troops into the streets and set up a greenhouse for his wife.

The troops went into the streets. There were doubts among the general staff whether the brass band should go along, but several pieces were missing, so they ended up going without it. The soldiers left the barracks, went once around Camp

São Cristóvão, halted while the colonel consulted the maps to know which direction to take, and finally managed to reach the intersection of Avenida Presidente Vargas where they stood, not knowing whether to go down to Tijuca, or up toward the center of the city. The decision was important, audacious. It was indeed a serious moment, happily resolved by the boldness and insight of the colonel. He recalled the great military decisions of Alexander, of Caesar, of Napoleon and Hannibal— and decided to set up camp in Ponte dos Marinheiros, near the Perola Sugar Refinery.

He took a Petrobras gas station, closed down the cash register and had the national flag raised on the mast from which fluttered a pennant for Traffic Accident Prevention Week. And since the drivers of cars and buses were stopping, astonished, to see what was going on, he ordered a tank to be placed across the middle of the road—which made a traffic detour necessary and provoked irritation and obscenities.

He set up his headquarters over the gas station and ordered the communications team to locate Quincas. But no one knew where anyone was and the solution seemed to be to wait by the radio, listening to a program of tangos, the weather forecast, the cotton quotations from Melbourne, advice to the lovelorn in which a lady with a velvety voice counseled how to catch a husband, the Tea at Five program—on which he heard an old samba by Orlando Silva (Lips That I Have Kissed!)—until the radio announced that the Revolution had ended with the victory of God and Democracy.

He ordered his men back to the barracks, but when he was approaching São Cristóvão he saw, returning from the opposite direction, a neighboring regiment, of cavalry, also marching gallantly.

And now what? After all, who had won the Revolution? While he searched for an inspiration to cope with this situation, his men passed by the adjoining troops and not a shot was fired. Each man looked straight ahead, without seeming to notice the troops to the side. The colonel then took the initiative of doing nothing. When he passed the other commander—a fat colonel, of whom he knew only that his name was Aristarco—they exchanged a cold, regulation salute, but he had time to notice that the other colonel too did not know for sure who had beaten whom.

Only on the following day, with the information published in the newspapers, did the colonel learn that he was a hero, a victorious soldier who had risked his life for Brazilian unity and for the integrity of the national territory. He was decorated with many medals, and he distributed many others among the men under his command. However, since he was not a political colonel, but rather a man of the barracks, up from the ranks, he did not get a larger slice of the cake.

Quincas was named minister of something of which the colonel had never heard: Coordination of Economic Planning. And he himself, returning home a decorated hero, had the greatest personal triumph. He learned that the *sindico* had saved his skin and ditched his responsibility, running off to take refuge at the Honduran Embassy.

Despite his exhaustion from the toil of that day, the colonel could not refuse to make still another sacrifice for the Fatherland, for the tranquility of Christian society, so sorely tried. A meeting of the condominium was called to settle the internal problems of the building and, as the absence of the *sindico* was noted and con-firmed, an absence clothed in ignominy since with his flight the records were lost, the colonel sensed that his moment had arrived and that it was a time for bold action.

"I am the new *sindico*!"

No one objected to this. A slight murmur was heard in the back of the room, but it was not a resident of the building who was protesting. It was the doorman who, in view of the latest events, had also decided to flee for good.

That very night the colonel had taken his tape measure to the back of the parking lot and noted down the measurements. Soon the workers came; pilasters were erected, walls went up, and later the glass arrived, the best for use in green-houses, specially ordered from Belgium. A resident from the fifth floor who had been in Holland affirmed that not even in Europe were there such perfect and functional greenhouses. The colonel took to the description and adopted it:

"Yes, yes, unassuming but very functional."

His wife enthroned her pots, and other residents also wanted to make use of the new and important internal improvement—since the construction had been fi-nanced by them all—but this right never got to the point of being claimed because the colonel, who now also had a car at his disposal, started going to Friburgo every Saturday and bringing back carnations and other flowers and plants, with the result that the greenhouse was soon stuffed and monopolized by his wife.

His chest too was feeling stuffed, and it was then that he remembered he was in front of his troops, his soldiers standing at attention, the sun beginning to filter through the cloudy sky, tiring everyone. Where was he?

At headquarters, giving a speech, that he didn't doubt. But where? A kind of auditory memory brought back to him the word "glory." He had been speaking about glory, and since he was no longer able to recall to what glory he was referring, he decided to speak of the only incontrovertible that he knew: that of the National Flag.

". . . the glory of our beloved Flag, which has fluttered and will always flutter over our battle camps, from which we will drive out the betrayers of our Nationality and the enemies of our dominion . . ."

He was ablaze. At last he had picked up the thread of the speech, the correct and appropriate tone both for the ceremony and for his reputation as a competent and inflammatory orator.

"We will never permit, never, that ruthless demagogues threaten the peace of the Brazilian family . . ."

The Brazilian family. There it was; that's what he got for being tolerant. He should have evicted the libertine on the third floor a long time ago. It was he who was a threat to the Brazilian family. Always bringing loose women to defile the chastity of that building, chastity of which he, the colonel, was the guardian and caretaker. At first he had pretended not to notice, but anonymous letters began to appear every day underneath his door. His neighbor on the seventh floor left him an anonymous letter in which she denounced the profligate on the third floor, the lecher who brought home go-go girls for orgies into the wee hours.

He had looked the other way; after all, the boy had been very understanding about the greenhouse. He had even cooperated, suggesting some details, and brought along a guy who knew about interior decoration and gave him hints on ornamental plants. Basically a good boy, although influenced by bad companions.

It would have remained like that—the orgies on the third floor and the knowing complaisance of the *sindico,* had it not been for the precipitous events which took the form and figure of an Argentinian fellow whom the boy brought home one night as a guest, and who ended up staying for good. The boy had rounded up the Argentinian in a bar, drunk, with nowhere to go. In the solidarity of drunkards, he invited the Argentinian to sleep in his apartment that night, and the Argentinian stayed on and slowly became involved in the life of the building.

He was a middle-aged man, thin, wore glasses, was striking, the nose somewhat large and aggressive, hair almost graying. He spoke a complicated jabber; had it not been for the accent, he could have been taken for a Brazilian from Bras de Pina or Rua Miguel Lemos—for the Argentinian went around putting the squeeze on the women in the building. He liked mature women, in their forties, and began to inflame hearts weakened by menopause or by the inevitability of the end.

On a certain morning, picking up the anonymous letter lying under his door, the colonel was about to tear it up, as he always did, but a sixth sense alerted him to the size of the envelope, bigger and thicker than usual. He opened it and read.

The old woman on the seventh floor was making abominable insinuations concerning the recent conduct of the colonel's wife, who had also fallen within the purview of the satyr from Buenos Aires. The old woman had come upon the Argentinian strutting by the colonel's wife. Tongues were beginning to wag and, as was inevitable, at least once the colonel's wife had been seen at the door of the lascivious third-floor apartment: she had gone with the Argentinian to pick up some instructions on how to cultivate a particular species of begonia. The Argentinian, in addition to other and innumerable specialties and skills, was a connoisseur of begonias as well.

That day the colonel had gone around crestfallen, gloomy, every now and then sighing deeply, not knowing what to do. He analyzed his wife's behavior and realized that she had been acting strangely recently, had given herself over to silences and sighs. He shuddered: he remembered that some days earlier his wife had dug up some old long-forgotten records, covered with dust and oblivion, and now the phonograph played only tangos, "Dusk," "Nostalgia," the standard repertoire of Francisco Canaro, "The Day You'll Love Me . . ."

He did not have the knack or the style to approach his wife to speak about such an unexpected and brutal subject. This did not mean that he was henpecked, a man dominated by his wife; he was the rooster in their yard, and when he was in a bad mood his wife suffered his insults and, if there were cause, he ended up slapping her.

But these were routine mishaps in the life of any couple: his coat missing a button, carelessness in preparing his dress uniform, an imprudence with the household budget which caught him off-guard and irritated—and his wife would get it. Apart from this, she had always deserved his trust; she was an honest woman, that she was, not like the others, and he felt he knew the world.

Then, all of a sudden, those tangos, those silences and sighs, the satyr from

Buenos Aires in the building all day long, not working, not doing anything, forever sponging off the fortuitous friend of that continuing drunken bout.

Well, time would provide some solution, and the colonel resigned himself to waiting for the Argentinian to move out from one moment to the next. But time passed and the Argentinian stayed on, until just two weeks before, the scandal had erupted: the satyr was caught with his fly open inside the service elevator. A maid from the fourth floor unexpectedly took the elevator and saw the Argentinian hurriedly trying to button up his fly. She gave a cry and ran out in time to see Dona Alaíde, the wife of a storeowner from Praça Serzedelo Correia, scuttling down the service stairs.

The scandal shook the building from top to bottom. The colonel still tried to minimize the thing, asking for more concrete proofs; the testimony of the maid could be fanciful: many times a man alone in the elevator, discovering that he had not done up his fly completely, might take advantage of his solitude to complete the job. And the fact that Dona Alaíde was going down the service stairs could be a coincidence. She was an honest sort of woman, almost a grandmother, heavy with her forty-nine years, treasurer of the Apostolate of Devotion of Our Lady of Peace Parish. No, it was too great a perfidy to suspect such an honorable lady, whose virtue had been proven and confirmed.

It was then that the colonel's wife, for the first time in her life, took the initiative in picking a domestic quarrel: either her husband do something about Dona Alaíde, she demanded, or she too would give herself to lewdness, to shamelessness, and be like the others. The incident was an affront to the morality of them all, especially to her morality, a colonel's wife's morality. What was the good of years and years of honesty if her husband, at the end of his life, turned out to be an accomplice to vileness, to orgies?

"But there's nothing I can do about Dona Alaíde! That foreigner on the third floor is the culprit. I'll report him to the police!"

The colonel's wife became more infuriated.

"That's a good one! She's shameless, yes she is! She's the one who should be reported to the police. She doesn't even consider her children and goes around offering herself to the Argentinian! She's the guilty one, she went around tempting him, offering herself, a hussy!"

"But look, woman, Dona Alaíde has a husband and children. Let them do something. I can't do a thing! And I don't have proof . . ."

His wife looked at him with contempt, more contempt than hatred.

"Chicken! That's what you are—chicken! Colonel Chicken!"

Chicken! Out of pride, and to prevent the crisis from getting worse, he decided to write a letter to the boy on the third floor, calling attention to the strange situation regarding his perpetual guest. The colonel had the law on his side: on his resident's form, the boy had stated that he lived alone, he had filled out one form only, for bachelors. Either the "guest" fill out a form too, or he would take the case to the police.

The boy filled out a new form, and everyone found out that the Argentinian, besides being a foreigner because he was from Argentina, was doubly foreign, being a Jew: Jayme Jacob Goldschak Novallis. When he signed his name, just Jayme

Novallis. Fifty-one years old, born in Mendoza at the foot of the Andes, an artist by profession (what kind of artist? the colonel wondered), without a fixed income, previous residence in Calle Tucuman in Buenos Aires. He was separated from his wife, worked in an export-import firm, and held passport number 53,697. Everything legal. The colonel apologized for the inconvenience and then related to his wife: "Nothing can be done."

But she remained obstinate in her battle with Dona Alaíde. She undertook some research and grew suspicious that one of Dona Alaíde's children was not by her husband: she had always devoted herself to her lovers and had ended up having a child by one of them. Her husband had accepted his horns and the child—shameless! In another building, she had fallen in love with a Guatemalan who sold powdered milk from America. And with a customs dispatcher, who embezzled funds from an electric appliance firm.

Things were on this footing when an event facilitated a solution. There was a huge orgy one Saturday night, the two inhabitants of the third-floor apartment brought in minors, there were drinks and drugs, a radio singer appeared with a dog who was addicted to shameless behavior with women, one of the minors hit the bottle and wanted to kill herself. In the middle of all this was a lady married to an assistant police chief. All hell broke loose. The building was awakened by the curses, the cries, the obscenities. A drunken woman went to the window and shouted to the remainder of the building: "Wake up, you cuckolds! Come on over for a fuck!"

Without consulting the *sindico*, someone notified a squad car and, by the time he decided to go downstairs, the colonel was confronted with a fait accompli. He had to fight a free-for-all, on exposed terrain. The police took everyone to the station, and the colonel made a pledge to the commissioner: "I will not tolerate any more equivocation!"

Equivocation. The troops in front of him, immobile in their position of attention, were waiting for the speech. He had paused for a long time, the speech was crawling out, advancing little by little, dragged out of him. At his side, other officers stood immobile, assuming that emotion was impeding his voice. But now he had a direction to head for. He screamed out, with all possible force:

"We will not equivocate with the enemies of our dominion, with the traitors and false patriots who conspire against the life of our institutions and against the national security! We will not equivocate! Never!"

He had achieved the exact note, the precise voice, the true passion.

The men were tired; he noticed that some of them were stirring, in an impatience which little by little arose from all sides. Even near him, the most important officers were surprised by such a disconnected speech. At first they had thought of the emotion experienced by the colonel, a sensitive man, his soul open to the great and glowing historical events of the Fatherland. But now, in the face of so many pauses, so many silences, they feared that the colonel would suddenly make some revelation of great importance.

He noticed this and lowered his tone of voice, as if making a confidence that could be heard throughout the courtyard:

"I will never keep silent in the face of the catastrophes of our times, and we will all remain on the alert to maintain our dignity before those factions which are conspiring against our happiness and well-being."

It was almost a password. Some officers moved; a major from the Heavy Artillery Company thought: the colonel's going to start a revolution! He's going to put the men in the streets!

But the colonel had not yet found the precise tone for his proclamation. His mouth felt dry; a little fleck of saliva was burning the corners of his lips. And hatred.

Hatred was a sheet, white and thick, covering his eyes. He saw that he was making a fool of himself in front of his men, in front of his troops. After this speech, he would never again be cited as the vibrant and impassioned orator he had always been. And it was all the fault of that boy, and his Argentinian "guest." After the trip to the police station, open war was declared by the two third-floor residents against the entire building.

One morning the boy went downstairs naked to take a bath in the tank that was there for washing the cars. And one night the Argentinian brought home two queers to create a scandal inside the building.

Dona Alaíde was finally unmasked when the boy called everyone to his apartment and they all went and saw Dona Alaíde hurry out of the Argentinian's bed and lock herself in the bathroom. The colonel's wife, on that inauspicious day, went through a crisis of rage and mortification, threw plates at him, the colonel, and declared that from then on she was going to be a prostitute, because "they're the ones who win in the end."

Said and done.

The next day the scandal was repeated, only this time it was not Dona Alaíde who was in the lascivious third-floor apartment. It was the colonel's own wife who was seen half naked in bed, embracing the Argentinian. The colonel did not happen to witness the great outrage, but the incident circulated so widely and extravagantly that at night when he came home for dinner he learned that his wife had been in bed with the Argentinian and the boy together—an indignity!

The colonel then re-inflated his pride and resolved to settle matters by force. He armed himself with his SW.45 and left for the third floor. He scattered shots in the air, on the ground—and the Argentinian almost hurled himself out the window at the thought of the impending disaster. The boy tried to placate the colonel, but was punched in the nose.

After so many shots, much talk and many guesses, it was muttered that the two satyrs were going to move. They were seen at Leblon, apartment-hunting. And on the previous day, the great moment finally arrived: an enormous truck was edged up to the curb and the move began.

But it was just at the end, when night had fallen and he was preparing to write his proclamation, that the colonel heard the noise of glass shattering. He ran to the window and saw that the greenhouse had been demolished.

At first he thought a rock had been thrown, but soon he saw another chair descending from the window of the third floor, falling ridiculously and awry on another part of the greenhouse roof. Now he had no doubts and he made a decision and reached for his revolver: the same SW.45 which during twenty-some years of professional life he had brandished before all his most serious adversaries, fortuitous and recurring.

When his wife saw him armed, she tore her hair, howled, promised to repent of her one sin in so many years of faithful and nearly monastic life, threw herself at his feet and wet his trousers at knee-level with tears of remorse.

He was unyielding. Too impatient to wait for the elevator, he stormed fiercely down the stairs. When he reached the fifth floor, the staircase was already jammed with neighbors who had come to find out what was happening—although they all knew very well.

They saw the colonel and his mighty .45. And since they knew that these two things—the colonel and the weapon—were the elements missing for the consummation of the scandal, they grew more excited still.

An old man from the eleventh floor tried to mediate informally: the colonel should go alone, without the weapon. But he soon gave up; everyone agreed that this time colonel and weapon were necessary to clear up the situation.

The convoy that was going downstairs met up with the convoy going upstairs, and both merged in a small crowd around the door of the lethal apartment. It fell to the colonel to open the door, and everyone expected him to break it down or shoot it open. There was surprise when the colonel delicately rang the doorbell, like any visitor. They all waited for a while, and then the colonel pressed the doorbell insistently, excusing himself to the neighbors:

"Maybe they didn't hear."

At about the third ring, the door opened. Face to face, the colonel and the Argentinian looked at one another, ready for battle. The apartment was almost empty, devoid of furniture; there still remained a few chairs which had not gone down via the window because the Argentinian was drunk and, after the third chair, lost interest in destroying the greenhouse which, in any case, was already destroyed more than enough.

Everyone awaited the inevitable, the shot or the blow, but after making sure that the Argentinian was alone, the colonel, revolver in view, said in a forceful voice, "I demand an explanation."

The Argentinian staggered with drink, and what he said was heard by everyone: "Go to your whore of a mother!"

Behind the colonel the crowd roared an "Oh!" like the chorus of a Greek tragedy, and continued to wait for the bloodbath. But the colonel, as far as that was concerned, merely maintained his sangfroid.

"Where's the boy?"

"He's gone. I stayed, alone."

Through the colonel's head passed the phrase "Prepare to die!" but what his mouth said was something else:

"You can't stay in this apartment. You are not the tenant; you are an intruder."

He liked the exalted tone with which he had ended the phrase, and repeated the word, still more exalted:

"An intruder!"

The Argentinian did not move from the door, and exclaimed:

"Your mother's the intruder. I'm here, and I'm not moving."

The colonel heard an inciting din coming from behind: "Shoot him." "Put a slug in the foreigner's face." But the colonel did not want to spill blood in vain.

"You are evicted. I am evicting you from this building."

The Argentinian countered with another curse which was not precisely understood, given the mixture of languages, but which certainly was a curse and had the noun "mother" and the verb "gave birth."

Soon after the bilingual curse, the colonel was pushed back and the door closed violently. The crowd was demanding blood, clamoring for blood. The colonel made a sweeping gesture, asking for silence.

"My friends, I came downstairs to reach an agreement with the resident of this apartment, the boy who has already moved. The gentleman who is now occupying the apartment is a foreigner, he has no legal right to the apartment. As *sindico*, I can do nothing about him. But I will take measures. I will evict him, not only from this apartment, but from the country. This very night!"

He went upstairs, accompanied by the neighbors, and when he arrived at his door he asked that they all withdraw: he was going to take measures. But the neighbors entered anyway, and witnessed the undertaking to the very end.

The first step was to locate Quincas, General Joaquim Osório de Lima, minister of he didn't know quite what, but a minister.

He was not easy to locate, and the colonel ran up against the ill will of various people who were awakened to find out where Quincas was. Toward dawn, he managed to get the phone number of a certain Ângela Luisa, former entertainer from Tiradentes Square, at whose house Quincas encamped once a week to relax from his ministerial hardships.

It took Quincas some time to understand the story, and when he had heard it all, he said decisively that the case had nothing to do with him, but rather with the Minister of Justice, under whose jurisdiction fell the expulsion of foreign nationals who became undesirable for the security of the country.

The colonel persisted, expressing the gravity of the situation, the prestige of the Armed Forces at stake in the episode. He had been slighted by a foreigner, a libertine, a drunkard who showed no regard for the high rank he, a colonel, held, decorated, cited in the bulletins as a revolutionary hero of April 1, one of the moral reserves of the Army and of the Nation, an exemplary soldier.

Quincas finally gave him the number of another general who was serving on the cabinet of the Minister of Justice. This one showed himself more understanding and patriotic.

"Count on me. The foreigner will be expelled tomorrow."

He wanted to have some details, and the colonel embroidered the facts: in addition to being a libertine and a drunkard, the Argentinian was a communist, had ties with Fidel Castro's regime, was an international agent of Peking.

The general took notes and promised to complete a report against the Argentinian that same night; it would just need the Minister's signature. He asked the colonel to wait; he would call him back in half an hour.

Dawn approached, and the negotiations moved even faster than the dawn. Half an hour later the general called the colonel. The report was ready, the minister was on his way—a civilian minister, when called upon by a general, really has to come running to sign any paper—and the colonel should write a memorandum expounding the case and accusing the Argentinian in detail of being a professional terrorist.

"But I said communist."

"It comes down to the same thing! What interests us is the expulsion."

The colonel took the sheet on which he had begun his speech, crossed out the word "Men" and outlined five paragraphs of direct accusations against the third-floor resident. But soon the general rang up again and said:

"Requisition an escort to take the Argentinian. The papers are signed. Manduca's already here."

"But who's Manduca?"

"He's the Minister of Justice!"

The colonel telephoned his headquarters and requested an escort, but it took a while to find the Officer of the Day. He spoke with the acting sergeant, the escort set out, and the colonel went down to the street to wait for it. The neighbors had disbanded; one or another lingered, waiting for something to happen.

With the arrival of the escort, the colonel tried to command some type of unified order on the sidewalk, but the soldiers were soon going up the stairs to the third floor. They found the door closed, and a note affixed to it saying in English "DO NOT DISTURB." This they could not understand, and they had to call the colonel to translate the cryptic phrase. The colonel, seeing the paper from afar, thought it was some obscenity, or another offense stated against his person, his dignity. He shouted:

"Break down the door!"

The soldiers broke down the door and found the apartment empty.

Day came. After a search through the rooms, the escort went away. The colonel looked at his watch; he had an hour and a half to get to the barracks, the anniversary of the battle of Lomas Valentinas, the birthday of the Military District Commander, and he had not drafted the Order of the Day!

There was time barely to shave and get dressed. He shaved and dressed; and dressed and shaved, there he was before the troops, mumbling his patriotic speech in praise of Lomas Valentinas.

"The Armed Forces are cohesive, my friends, and will know how to repel attacks which come from within and without . . ."

In one of the corners of the courtyard, a tired soldier let go of his rifle and fainted. But the rest of the troops continued immobile, vigilant, cohesive.

SAMUEL RAWET
—◦❧(1929–1984)❦◦—

Born in Poland, Samuel Rawet arrived with his family in Brazil at age seven. He worked as an engineer in the construction of Brasília alongside another poet/engineer, Joaquim Cardozo, while producing short stories, novels, plays, and essays. Considered shy and even strange, Rawet wrote about existential and anguished characters, often treating the problems of Jewish immigrants in Brazil. His best-known book of stories is *Contos do Imigrante* (1956), and the posthumously published 1998 anthology *The Prophet and Other Stories* was his first appearance in English.

THE PROPHET
—◦❧ ❦◦—

All illusions lost, the only thing really left for him to do was to take that step. The gangplank already hauled off, and the last whistle blown, the steamship would weigh anchor, He again looked at the cranes wielding bales, the piles of ore and other minerals. Down below, people hustling and bustling and foreign tongues. Necks stretched out in cries toward those who surrounded him on the rampart of the upper deck. Handkerchiefs. In the distance, the honking of automobiles revealing the life that continued on in the city he was now abandoning. The sneering looks of some mattered little to him. At another time he would have felt hurt. He understood that the white beard and the long overcoat well below his knees made him a strange figure to them. He had become accustomed to that reaction. Right now they would be laughing at the thin figure, all in black except for the face, the beard, and the even whiter hands. However, no one dared challenge those eyes that commanded respect and instilled a certain majestic air to his demeanor. With fists folded against his temples, he resisted interior escape into the serenity that had brought him to this point. Hearing the ship's muffled toot, he became fully aware of his plunging into solitude. The return, the only way out he had discovered, seemed to him empty and illogical. He thought, at the moment of hesitation, that he had acted as a child. Lately, the idea had been building into gigantic proportions and had culminated in his presence on board the ship. Now he was afraid of seeing that decision effaced by the glimmer of doubt. The fear of solitude terrified him more so because of the experience obtained in his daily contact with death. There was still time . . .

"Step down the gangplank, please, step down!"

The fat figure of the woman to his side turned upon hearing, or upon thinking that she heard, the words of the old man.

"Sir, did you say something to me?"

Useless. He knew the language barrier would not allow him to say anything. The woman's face changed with the old man's negative nod and supplicating eyes. With exceptions, the true recourse would be mimicry but that would accentuate the childishness that tyrannized him. Only then did he realize he had murmured the sentence, and ashamed, he closed his eyes.

"My wife, my children, my son-in-law."

Confused, he gazed at the group that kept on hugging and kissing, a strange group (even his brother and cousins, if not for the photographs mailed ahead, would also seem strange to him), and the tears then rolling down his cheeks were not of tenderness but of gratitude. He had known the older ones as children. Thirty years ago his own brother was little more than an adolescent. Here he had married, had sons and daughters, and had also seen his daughter marry. Not even after settling into the cushioned springs of the car the son-in-law was driving did his tears stop flowing. To the onslaught of questions, he responded with gestures, evasions, or else silence. Despite its age, his thin but hard body had enabled him to work and, moreover, had saved his life. Now it swayed with the traffic's hesitations and never once did his eyes gaze upon the landscape. He seemed to be concentrating more on responding to the avalanche of tenderness. What was going on inside would be impossible for him to convey through the superficial contact now being initiated. He figured his silences were embarrassing. The silences following the series of questions about himself, about the most terrifying thing he had experienced. To forget what had happened, never. But how to belittle it, to eliminate the essence of the horror as one sat down to a beautifully set table, or as one sipped tea ensconced in elegant cushions and comfortable armchairs? The avid and inquiring eyes around him, hadn't they heard or seen enough to be horrified as well and to share his silences? One world alone. He expected to find on this side of the ocean the comfort of those like him who had suffered, but whom chance had marginally saved from the worst. And being conscious of that, they shared this meeting with humility. However, he had an inkling of a slight mistake on his part.

The apartment occupied by his brother was on the top floor of the building. Open to the sea, the veranda absorbed the nightly crash of the waves with more furor than during the day. There he liked to sit (having returned from the synagogue after evening prayers) with his grandnephew on his lap, both babbling nonsense. The child's fingers would get tangled in his beard and sometimes forcibly grope for a tuft of hair or two. Pincus would then rub his hard nose with his roundish and cartilaginous finger and both of them would let loose a carefree laugh. They would amuse themselves until the time the brother got home and they went in to dinner.

During the first weeks there was much commotion and many houses to visit, many tables to eat at, and in all the homes he felt indignant for being taken for granted as a *curiosity*. With time, once the enthusiasm and the curiosity had cooled down, he ended up spending time only with his brother. Actually talking only to him or to his wife. The others hardly understood him, nor did his nephews, and even less so the son-in-law, toward whom he began to nurture a real aversion.

"Here comes the 'Prophet'!"

He had barely opened the door when the son-in-law's derisive words and laugh surprised him. He pretended as if he hadn't noticed the others' uneasiness. He had taken his time on the way home from the synagogue and they were already waiting for him at the dinner table. He glimpsed his brother's disapproval and one of the children's shortened laugh. Only Paulo (that's how they called the grandson, whose real name was Pincus) moved his hands babbling as though to complain about the lost playtime. Mute, he placed his hat on the rack, keeping only the black silk cap on his head. He still hadn't learned a thing about the language. But, being a good observer, even though he didn't dare say anything, by association he managed to memorize a few things. And the word "prophet," delivered with mischievous laughter as he came into the house, was becoming familiar. He didn't get its meaning. Little did it matter, however. The word was never uttered without an ironic look, a smirk. In the bathroom (while he was washing his hands) he was reminded of the innumerable times the same sounds were said in front of him. He made the connection with other scenes. From down deep surfaced the memory of something similar having occurred in the temple.

The mistake he sensed on the first day became more pronounced. The sensation that their world was really something other than his—that they had not participated in anything that (for him) had been the horrible night—was being slowly transformed into concrete reality. The dinner gatherings where he would remain in the background were to him quite tiresome. When the children were sleeping and the other couples came over to chat, he felt foolish listening to the tone of the conversation, the bawdy jokes, the numbers always being bandied about in reference to everything and, at times, to nothing. The war had stripped him of all his prior illusions and had confirmed the precariousness of what once had been solid. The only thing remaining intact had been his faith in God and in religion, so deep-rooted that even during the most bitter ordeals he hadn't been able to expel his belief. (He had already tried, he knew, but in vain.) A year had scarcely gone by and he found himself still repeating monotonously what he imagined to be over and done with. The son-in-law's parasitic situation awakened in him feelings of hatred, and at great expense, he controlled himself. He had seen other hands making other gestures. But the manicured nails and the rings, the roly-poly body, the stupid laugh, and his uselessness intensified his overall disgust. How many times (long past midnight), on the veranda with his cigarette lit, he would let himself forget while listening to the vulgar (to him) guffaws uttered bilingually from one card game to another.

"So this is what it's all about?"

The others thought it was senility. He knew very well it wasn't. Monologues had been useful to him when he thought he was going crazy. Today they were a habit. When alone, he would release tension by saying one sentence or another with no meaningful connection, except for him. He remembered one day (right in the beginning), in the middle of some conversation, he had halfheartedly attempted some flimsy complaint by making some weak sign of protest, and perhaps his index finger did cut the air with gestures of ominous intentions. The same thing in the synagogue when the congregation's rudeness had disturbed a prayer.

"Those fat, bossy men of plenty don't belong here," he had murmured to himself one day.

Perhaps for that reason, the *prophet*. (Afterwards he had discovered its meaning.)

He thought about changing a little his topics of conversation and began to narrate stories about what he had once denied. But now it didn't seem to interest them. Condescendingly (they didn't understand what degree of sacrifice that meant to him) they listened to him at first and no tears were missing from the women's eyes. Afterwards, noticing their annoyance, indignation, he thought he discovered reproof in some looks and second-guessed sentences like these: "What do you expect from all this talk? Why do you torment us with stuff that has nothing to do with us?" There were wrinkles of remorse when they remembered someone who was connected to them, yes. But these moments were brief. They disappeared as a crease does in a rubber doll. It didn't take long for such behavior to become obvious, albeit masked.

"You are suffering from all this talk. Why do you insist so?"

He shut up. And more than that, he became silent. Very seldom did they hear a word from him, and they didn't notice that he was putting himself into a marginal situation. Only Pincus (that's what he called him) continued to braid his beard, rub his nose, and tell endless stories with his round eyes. Uselessness.

The sea brought back sad memories and launched enigmatic ones. Solitude upon solitude. At times, he asked himself about his capacity to last in an environment that was no longer his. The whoosh of the waves. A small finger plunged into his mouth and then a laugh at the jolt. An unrestrained laugh. Did he have the right to condemn? Not really, if this was pleasurable reward after the torment. No, he couldn't even condemn himself if for some reason he gave in, despite his age. But the others? Blind and deaf in their insensitivity and self-sufficiency! He'd then get up. He'd walk through the rooms, examining the household comfort for signs of contrast he knew beforehand did not exist. He lured himself into useless arguments. And from down deep came a bitter and disappointing taste. The days piled up in a routine manner but the time in the synagogue on Saturdays was painful for him. With his prayer book open (unnecessary since he uttered all the prayers by heart), he would close his eyes to the intrigues and would remain to the side, always to the side. On his way home, he would admire the showy colors of the shop windows, the skyscrapers disappearing in the distance with the turn of his neck, and the incessant crawl of the automobiles. And in the midst of all that, solitude weighed him down, the spiritual state that had not found any affinity whatsoever.

He knew his brother's good fortune to be recent. In one of his rare moments of rest, he had told him about the years of struggle in the suburbs, and triumphant, with sweeping gestures, he capped his story with the success of his present security. More than any other sensations, that one affected him profoundly, echoing deep inside. He realized that any kind of affinity was impossible since their experiences were totally opposite. His, bitter. The other's, victorious. And in the same interim of time!? God, my God! Nights of insomnia followed. He tried to reach the conclusion that a feeling of envy had burdened him with hatred. Impossible. Being really honest with himself, he easily saw right through that conclusion. And stood by the opposite one, the more difficult one. The forms in the dimness of the room (he slept with the grandson) composed scenes he didn't expect to see again. Horrible and skeletal daybreaks. Anguished faces and prayers flying away from human ashes. His wife's figure wrapping her shawl at the last minute. Where are the eyes, where are the muted eyes that disclosed the animal cry? Roguish laughter. Card games. Numbers. Look at the "prophet" over there! And faces of laughter, giggling at the overcoat draped on the chair. Impossible.

—⋅❧ ☙⋅—

The increasing cries made him notice the time of departure. He looked at the docks. Slowly the strip of water expanded with the final gestures of good-bye. He tightened all the muscles in his body. When the family returned from the resort, they would find his letter on the table. And the protests would be useless because they were too late. He had taken advantage of their two-week absence. The passport with his tourist visa (after, they were thinking about changing it for a permanent one) made his plan easy. The money he owned was all spent on the ticket. Return. The maid found it a bit strange to see him leave with his suitcase. But she attributed the fact to the eccentric figure who in the beginning had instilled in her a little fear. Plans? He didn't have any. He was simply going in search of the company of people who were the same, the same, yes. Perhaps in search of the end. The energies this step demanded had wiped him out, and his debilitated state had brought some doubts. And facing the irremediable, his frustrated eyes swelled in the anxious attempt to quell his tears. Already tiny by now, the figures waving good-bye. The mountainous background, bluish in the midday sky. Green blocks of little islands and spray on the bows of the barges. (There are always seagulls. But he couldn't see them.) Again, his fists closing and moving crosswise, his head resting in his arms, and the black figure, in the form of a hook, trembling in tears.

HILDA HILST

—◦❧(1930–2004)❧◦—

Hilst was an experimental writer whose works were once considered to be pornographic for their frank sexuality; her stories are now gaining attention in Brazil and
in Europe. After *Contes sarcastiques* (*Fragments Érotiques*, 1994), there followed
French translations of *Com os Meus Olhos de Cão* (1986) and *Contos d'Escárnio,
Textos Grotescos* (1990). Hilst's versatility and experimentation covered the major
stylistic tendencies of literary modernism: the interior monologue, fragmentation of
syntax, and open forms that collapse time and theme into the narrative moment.
In 1982, Hilst became a resident artist at the State University of Campinas in São
Paulo. Her extensive creative works included plays, poetry, and fiction, and she was
awarded prestigious literary prizes.

AGDA
—◦❧ ❧◦—

Take care of yourself, Agda, it's time to hold the fruit in your hand, just look at it,
how can your yellowed hand touch the one who says he loves you, that fragile
young man, Agda, go back to your chores, take care of the pigs, clean off the porch,
water the cactus, examine the ferns, the anthurium, walk slowly, slowly, how you've
aged, and so much more this morning. Remember your mother telling you just
before she died you won't be able to stand it, daughter, the way you take care of
yourself, orange cream on your face, another for your hands, the light green one
for your body and ashes from the stove to whiten your teeth, you won't be able to
stand it daughter, you'd be better off dying Now Now life is all around you, clean,
clean, look at me, and above all don't love, NEVER AGAIN, should you be so shameless, if anyone touches you you'll know how sad your flesh has become, all of it
darkened, darkened, and your hands, look at your hands, that's called keratosis,
daughter, that's from old age, first the stain, then a thin scab, you think it will go
away, the doctor smiles, says it starts with middle age madam, it's the time, you
understand, madam? You smile. The time? Yes, what nobody sees, mucus stretched
thin almost to transparency. And how your Ana smiled when she realized he loved
you, she smiled even wider when you started to pretty yourself, could you do the

hem on this skirt for me? And if you have time, put some gold trim here, look I've already bought it, looks nice, doesn't it? Gold and brown go so well together. Never again, never again they said to you. Ah yes I'll clean off the porch, water the cactus, ah yes my God you have to forget the touch, the trim, the gold earrings, you have to forget, knife your memory, you never felt anything and much less now, you don't feel anything, no, no I don't feel anything, I dreamed about the new girls at school, they were in green and were going to chapel, I was in black, going in the opposite direction, towards a door-window opening to nothing. From now on it will always be the abyss, I look down into the depths, what's down there? Dryness, everything consumed. Never again. Never again, mend a collar, look at the row of flowerpots on the bench, true, the cactus didn't need fertilizer, the bulbous white one is drooping in tangles, I'll have to put up some small stakes, I'll become like that myself if I get satiated, Agda, satiated, drooping, closer and closer to the abyss, closer to the earth, after all the shame, yes, shame, he'll tell his friends the old woman quivered in my hands, the yellow old woman rattled even to the tips of my fingers, fingers your hand my love you shouldn't place your whole hand on my tarnished one, your sunny hand on my shadowy body, I root pushing under the earth, root-body-flesh, something that spoils, no no you shouldn't touch it, don't mistreat that light that comes out of your fingers, NEVER AGAIN should I be touched, after all, it exists, and can I say I am my body? If I were my body would it hurt me like this? If I were my body would it be this old? What is the language of my body? What is my language? A language for my body: a funeral for myself, irrigated, fat, a funeral of daisies and lilies, someone repeating a useless cadence: sunflowers for the woman-girl. For my body a funeral and for the GREAT INNER LIFE, THE ALL ALIVE, what? Agda is like that: THE ALL ALIVE does not follow the body, it is intact, nothing corrupts it, THE ALL ALIVE has many hungers, it searches, it never tires, never grows old, it filters through everything that sprouts, in the static as well, into what seems tacit and adjusted, into apples, water holes, into the rich swamp that your body doesn't see. THE ALL ALIVE is what lives this love, not the body, Agda. Is that true? I examine myself. A small nodule in my vein, a knotty vein, a varicose nodule, knot, I probe it, one thing, doctor, this won't burst, will it? It might, madam. And another thing, doctor, this flabbiness here, under my arms, this, this, will exercise take care of it, do you think? He smiles: wear long sleeves. I know, but to the touch, you understand? Does someone touch you, madam? A thousand pardons, madam, I didn't mean to say, well I mean that to get rid of that kind of flab, at your age, fifty? fifty-five? Well, there's nothing you can do about that kind of flab, madam, classical music, who knows . . . might take your mind off it . . . are you indifferent to classical music? No, on the contrary, doctor, I like it very much. Stockhausen and. Really? Stockhausen is fine, but perhaps Scarlatti would be better? Fugues concertos fifteen cantatas? Does someone touch you, madam? he said that. Yes, they touched me, my father you touched me, your fingertips running along the lines in my palm, your middle finger on the life line, you said Agda, just three nights of love, three nights you'll give me and then you squeezed my wrist and looked at the wall and next to us the old women whispered yes its's his daughter, the head is the same and so are the eyes, lovely daughter, so white . . . My father, the cement bench, the mosaics, the rubber plants, the nurses at a distance. They smiled. I say: it's me,

Agda, Daddy, Mommy didn't come but she sends her love, she hasn't been too well the last few days, but she'll come, it's me, Agda, Agda, Daddy, it's me, your daughter. You will have a long life, Agda, as long as from here to China, everyone will go by, you'll say wait, my friend, it's me, Agda, can it be true you don't remember? Will they go by silently? Or like this looking from side to side, trying to guess where she will come from, she she THE GREAT TURBID THING. He touched your wrist, keep going, don't dwell on the landscape, the wall, the mosaics, the rubber plants, and when he touched you, admit it Agda, tell me that you want to lie down right here, yes, but it was beautiful, it wasn't just lying down, it was something flowing, a passion thing, he stretched out, fragile on top of me. As fragile as this other one who now says he loves me. So three nights Agda, and the discovery of the islands, our disinterred dead, you will remember your lovely mother, mommymommy-mommy, here he is now, come with us to the beach, hedgehogs under the rocks, we three motherfatherdaughter, we three intertwined twisted fiber, and these flowers here, we put the flowers in the bottom of these graves, nothing else is left inside them, all resurrected, our flesh clean, naked, we are naked and in bliss, here we will build the stone house so that time will pass without a trace, we'll say go away time, there's no place for you here, here there are just the three of us, those, the same three, not the usual holy trinity, the others of flesh and astringency, of blood and astringency. I have to take care of the pigs, water the cactus, examine the ferns . . . if I take you away from this corner who knows if you'll come back to life, did you wilt suddenly, could it have been a draft? If I put you here, in the middle of the patio, near the well, no, too much sun, those delicate things want shade, shade this instant in the squareness of the patio, yes he will come, even if it's Ash Wednesday, he'll come because I exist, I am my body, Agda's body, a body that will wake up next to another fragile body, the small rosy circles, no, I never had children and that's why they're pretty, he will touch them, he'll say they're very pretty Agda, and when I lie down my face becomes smoother, I'll loosen my hair, and when I lie down it seems that my mouth is always smiling, I will keep smiling and I must be careful when I reach my pleasure, no grimaces, no shouts, just a tremor, and for the love of God, Agda, don't let your nostrils flare open, no, that's no good at all, your nose is tapered, a little of your father, a little of your mother, they both had a nice nose, at least that part of you is decent, your nose, ah yes, your breasts are decent too, you have to take care of your mouth, and no watery glances, look straight into his eyes, don't close your eyes, you can show your feet too, they are very nicely shaped, the curve is pronounced that's nice too, now your legs, never, remember the small nodules in your veins, the small nodule on the vein, a knotty vein, a varicose nodule, knot. Ana can clean off the porch today, Ana can take care of the pigs today, that's what she's for, Ana, today you'll clean off the porch, today you'll take care of the pigs. She smiled, she smiled because she knows that I can't tire myself out today, I've got to put my legs up, a compress on my eyes, change the bed linen, white embroidered sheets, eucalyptus leaves under the pillow. One thing, daughter: everything's just fine, I've been feeling very well, the body, you know, but you have to tell your mother to tell the doctor that my memory . . . that they have to pull out my memory, understand? That the boats are too heavy, they put a thousand things in them, I asked them to empty the boats but they put stones in them, ropes, enormous anchors, I can't do it that way, daughter, I can't get to the island, and another thing, Agda, my dreams, they have to pull out my dreams, at night another life, a life of others starts to happen, they call me from all sides in those dreams, your mother always refuses in those dreams, I take walks in the dark, I don't see the rivers and I fall, people wave at me, people I never saw before, daughter, others I know but I don't want to see them again, Agda, tell your mother to tell the doctor that the dreams and memories have to be devoured, I will stay here on the cement bench and someone will devour them, that way I'll expel dream memory and someone next to me will eat them. Did you understand, Agda? Body-limit, a contour in repose or tense, how far until I am most myself? Palm of my hand, that I know is mine, palm of your hand, father, that inner now intimate absorption of us two, perplexity of perspiration, body-limit-poor thing, suddenly you move, you go into the pig sty, you ask yourself what is this, a pig? Suddenly you remember that someone already asked, that many will ask, what is this, a pig. What is this-me? A young pig, pink piglet, I tenderly pick it up I say pretty piglet, it would be nice to have one like that in the house, then a big stuffed pig, then I wouldn't pick it up any more, I say good to eat at tomorrow's party, in commem-oration of one hundred years from the day after tomorrow, at the fireworks ex-ploding in an immense bonfire and to feed the blaze three days from now, big stuffed pig I devour you. Thus, this-me: pink baby I caress you, you give me spittle, piss, I love you then delicate girl pubis, I give you candy, boots, contraband, I give you smiles, you're all soft, hard, buckram, then a woman I give you contraband again so you'll give me just that, I give it to you, you give it to me, then old whore, foulmouth shut up you stink yellowed, I don't give it to you, you don't give it to me, nobody touches you, I ask you: is the pig-body still yours? Agda limit of your-self, you agonize: so nothing more from here on? Was that your father on the cement bench yes yes I know, mosaic walls rubber plants, don't hide it, forget the landscape, that was your father damaged neuron, prefrontal without antennas, sum-mer summer, useless crossing from the bench to the bed, vice versa, your father without a quiver, splendid head in immense disorder, yes quiver yes, he took my hands, asked me for love, father how I wanted everything yours to live again a hundred thousand times in me, that love OH NEVER NEVER WOULD DIE, now loving this fragile one is like seeing you grow, it's like seeing you a seed, everything inside you waiting to explode, explosion in me, you will give all of yourself to me, Agda, you are delirious, you said once that you weren't that you weren't like that full of love and perplexed, you said. Or were you? Were you always like that? Old and quivering like that? Another thing, daughter, another thing, my love: don't let them sing slow boat to China any more since . . . I don't want to hear slow boat to China, we won't get anywhere, the flesh rots, there's no time to get there. Another thing: don't let them repeat this too too solid flesh, solid nothing, it's a lie, every day I feel it soften, inside and out, every day it gets yellower touch me here and there, you yes are still alive, touch me if it doesn't sicken you, I'll open my mouth wide so you can see, here daughter, there's nothing left, they gnawed away my teeth, the big kiss of pleasure that I would give you, that I would never give your mother again, Agda-mother-daughter, my body is nothing any more, I'm nothing more, I never was anything because if I had been, I wouldn't be this nothing-body today.

Evening is falling. Even though it's Ash Wednesday he will come, a green shadow empties ashes over the squareness of the patio. Or is it still morning? Yes, it's still morning, the sun is just on this side, Ana, you have to put the birds in the sun, a chicory leaf for each one, you always forget, and look how the anthurium leaf is stained, Ana Ana, the anthurium was so pretty. Whose fault, Agda? Your demagnetized yellow hand, it is your hand that touches the former brilliance of that leaf, it is your hand that makes it die now, you walked a long way, yes I walked but I never saw what they said I would see, THAT SERENE WHITE FLAME AT THE END. Flame. The desire to see everything again, see, touch for the first time. Not the first caresses, nor the second, the first. What great wonder. Afterwards my mouth on the shoulder of this fragile one, this father-lover-son for the first time, this my resurrected one, this joy stretched over me, what THE GREAT TURBID THING will not touch because I'll be there in front of it, immense, and I'll say as I say: get lost filthy thing, death, black-winged broom, this nothing, this no, this indelible fragility, truth keeps watch inside me, this whole life on my-body-his. Yes it is, the love of the whole world washing itself in my song, then they'll try to dry up the well, they'll say: Agda ask everything the others asked, pretend to be wearing a crown and it's just the same ghost, let's repeat then. *who are you that usurp'st this time of night?* When night falls I will not be discoursing saxophoniously like this, no, body-aroma on embroidered linen, lily mouth, lovely, lovely, lily mouth satyr butterfly and plant, Agda horsey with her rider, as if time . . . as if the great body time were just one immobile whole, irremediably tangled and immobile.

Wait a minute, they are already coming to get me, listen: above all, before they tear out of me what I just told you, above all, Agda, your mother should thank them for me for the absence of the object. Have her tell it this way to the doctor, write it down, take a pencil, like this: he thanks the doctor for the absence of the object-demon steel and silver, that abominable whole, like this, daughter: he thanks you for all of us. And that this-unique-I never again doubled is happy to exist in nothingness, that this-unique-I is, uses well-conceived expressions, daughter, is . . . is stupefied, that's it, in capital letters now: STUPEFIED BY HIS LUCID CRITERIA, doctor . . . because this life, Agda, of the object-demon-abominable, this multiplied existence added weight to this-unique-I, it was even in your mother's silver, in the window panes, even in the metal trays, I always asked her to cover them, to wrap the knives in flannels, everything in that house was a thousand times the I-other, at the end of the corridors, in the vestibule, even next to the bed your mother put the object-demon-abominable, even in the bathroom, daughter, I woke up wet because I was coming out of the river, I would get up, to defecate, and there there the other stranger spying on me. How many times I spit on that other one, I rubbed the shit in his face, or then, listen, I brought myself to say pretty words, I brought myself to that, yes I said: cloven, extremis, algae, fleeting, I said dissolve yourself, I'll give you a little time, smoky I said, dilute yourself, I'll give you some time, defiant image I brought myself to say softly, pantomime of nausea I'm going to tear you to pieces. I socked him ten fifteen times and he would open his bloodied mouth but wouldn't give up. Then I would breathe, daughter, my forehead on the tiles, I would look slowly, and would you believe the other one was still there? Crushed but there. Just thinking about him, look at my hand, it's wet, just thinking that he was around, perhaps on the other side of the wall, trying to break through the thickness, he and his useless calendar, because that was it, daughter, every morning the other was not the same, understand? Yes, because if he didn't change his face until he were well received, it's good to have a shadow friend, waving, I'm here, it's good, one ought to have it. I don't have much time, recess is over, they're coming to get me, now a snack bread and cheese, so listen: far from the main house, near the pig sty, there is some golden dirt, at the second stake, in the right pen, freshly dug earth, I discovered it very late there wasn't time, your mother called the men, I had to come here, but you can take advantage of it, swallow that golden earth, swallow it, that's what I heard, swallow it later daughter, when you're old, put a fistful in your hand and the object-demon-abominable will show his other face, regression, sad earth. What, father? Regression, daughter, youth again, adolescence, childhood, then nothing, but it's worth it. One single time and it's worth it. You'll walk a girl to nothingness, but the mechanism is easier, little by little you'll identify with the inanimate, girl-plant, girl-stone, girl-earth. Don't forget, write it down: my father told me that many years from now when I'm old I should swallow the golden earth, the dirt near the pig sty, at the second stake, in the right pen. I dig. It's still morning. How long should I dig? The earth is blacker and blacker, if I planted roses, imagine, black roses, in the center a clearing, bison, golden bulls, I Agda-pretty-daughter all white under the rose bushes. Agda rosemary dallying in the rose garden. Every morning, every afternoon, full moon, Agda old woman-quivering digs digs under the rosebushes. Of course, gentlemen, I'll show you the place, yes yes I've worked for her for a long time, yes my name is Ana, let's go, you know the young man didn't want to see her any more, he was right poor thing, here from my room I heard what went on in there, what he said in Agda's room, he said: just like you are, I want you like you are, your body has nothing to do with it, what does your body matter? It's your luminosity, your magic, your energy, nothing in you is shadow, may the light in you live, I exist because you dreamed me palm to palm, I exist because at each instant you remake what isn't sad in me. The vertigo of your existence, beloved, I swear, gentlemen, it was like that, that's what the young man said. You know, in the beginning, it was hard to believe, he was slender, almost a boy, his twenty years didn't show, I'd laugh because . . . well, after all he was inadequate, Agda wasn't a small person, you'll see, she was a lot of woman poor thing, I would laugh because . . . you know, gentlemen, it's just not usual for an old woman and a young calf like that, but I didn't mean it badly, no sirs, it was just amusing, very amusing, the young man was strange, a beautiful mouth, enormous eyes, a sight for sore eyes, big, a treasure, and his hair, so smooth, it was a shame, you know, Agda heavy slow, but what fire gentlemen, before everything happened, dying in the hole she shouted: flame at the end, I never saw that white serene flame at the end. Who knows what she was thinking when she was shouting.

I DIG. Constancy. Ten arm-lengths deep. How much farther? Snails. Mud in my face. Not even a reflex. It would be good to have a yellow light gilding the snails, the larvae, my hand. It would be good to invent words, cross them, say of the light filter sparkling faceted, to say of the dark simply strange, to say of the search what it is, searcher and searched for, reveal the two sides, here you are, here I am looking at you, the pleasured orbit shattering fear, here when you were a child

on the wall, hiding your face, the light splintering your eye, the violet eyelid shrink-
ing, arm, forearm vertex of the elbow pointing at the woman taking your picture.
Who is taking your picture? Mommymommymommy beauty, your beret at an angle, snails in your hair covering your rosy ears, mommymommymommy beauty, let
me touch your tender skin, or . . . fly fly Medea, go away, cross spaces, cross all
the bridges or go live under the sea, so that father's reflection will be just for me,
vere dignum et justus est, aéquum et salutáre so he'll be just for me . . . because . . .
because . . . I would have to spend many nights to explain it to you or just shout
it like that one: woe, woe, Ah me, Ah me! Now I am really getting to know myself
with this mud on my face, chewing myself, burning wax consuming my body,
consuming myself and knowing myself without disgust, wide-open gullet, livid al-
chemist, go Agda, but down deeper, without knowing your body is a sieve, a thousand and one minuscule orifices separating out what is worthwhile, tasting and
letting the rest slide down into the well. Go, Agda, go down deeper. OH, I'm going,
never again will I have that fragile body on top of me, oh, never again, life death
expelled, oh I was lucid, clean, my flesh was smooth, ah those mysterious pleasures,
the pleasureful in me, the great pleasure it is to burrow my yellow and aged flesh
into this mud and never again will anyone TOUCH ME, NEVER AGAIN NEVER AGAIN

VICTOR GIUDICE
—∘❧(1934–1997)❦∘—

Born of Italian immigrant parents, young Victor Giudice showed an early fascination with performance after attending a concert conducted by Arturo Toscanini. A voice student, he attended recitals and operas before writing his first story. The theater and cinema fostered his interest in suspense and the unforeseen. Along with his interest in the stage, Giudice practiced photography and published his photos in major magazines, later working as a graphic artist. It was possibly as an employee of the Bank of Brazil that Giudice picked up his taste for absurd situations, and "The File Cabinet" ("O Arquivo"), his third story, became a classic and was translated into eight languages. While he was an artist and performer, Giudice also enjoyed the simple life of his neighborhood and ethnic background. His imagination was always at work, and one of his last interests was divination with tarot cards. The 1990s was the most productive period of his career as a writer of short stories. His books of stories include *Necrológio* (1972), *Os Banheiros* (1979), *Salvador Janta no Lamas: Contos* (1989), and *O Museu Darbot e Outros Mistérios* (1994).

THE FILE CABINET
—∘❧ ❦∘—

After only one year on the job, João was given a fifteen percent salary cut.

João was a young man. It was his first job. He did not show his pride, even though he was one of the few considered. After all, he had made an effort. He had never once missed work or come in late. He limited himself to smiling, to thanking the boss.

The next day, he moved to a room farther away from the center of the city. With his reduced salary, he must pay a lower rent.

He started to take two buses to work. Nevertheless, he was satisfied. He got up earlier, and this seemed to brighten his disposition.

Two years later, another reward came.

The boss called him in and informed him of his second salary cut.

This time, the firm was in excellent shape. The cut was a little larger: seventeen percent.

More smiles, more thanks, another move.

Now, João got up at five in the morning. He waited for three buses. In compensation, he ate less. He lost weight. His skin became less rosy. His contentment grew.

The fight went on.

However, in the next four years, nothing extraordinary happened.

João was worried. He lost sleep, poisoned by the intrigues of jealous colleagues. He hated them. He tortured himself with the lack of understanding of the boss. But he did not give up. He started to work two more hours a day.

One afternoon, almost at the end of the day, he was called into the head office. His breath quickened.

"Mr. João. Our firm is greatly indebted to you."

João lowered his head in a sign of modesty.

"We are aware of all your efforts. It is our desire to give you substantial proof of our recognition."

His heart stopped.

"In addition to a salary reduction of sixteen percent, we decided, in yesterday's meeting, to demote you."

The revelation dazzled him. Everybody smiled.

"From today on, you will be assistant bookkeeper, with five days less vacation. Happy?"

Radiant, João stuttered something unintelligible, paid his respects to the board of directors, and returned to work.

That evening, João did not think about anything. He slept peacefully in the silence of the suburbs.

One more time, he moved. Finally, he stopped eating dinner. Lunch was reduced to a sandwich. He became thinner, felt lighter, more fragile. He did not need many clothes. He eliminated certain superfluous expenses, laundry, meals. He arrived home at eleven at night, got up at three in the morning. He drained his energy on a train and two buses to be sure to arrive at work half an hour early.

Life went by, with new rewards.

At sixty, his salary was the equivalent of two percent of his starting pay. His organism had accommodated itself to hunger. Once in a while, he tasted a roadside weed. He only slept fifteen minutes. He did not have any more worries about lodging or clothing. He slept in the fields, among refreshing trees, he covered himself with the rags of a sheet acquired a long time ago.

His body was a mass of smiling wrinkles.

Every day, an anonymous truck transported him to work.

When he had completed forty years of service, he was summoned by the directors.

"Mr. João. We have just eliminated your salary. There will be no more vacation. And your job, starting tomorrow, will be to clean our bathrooms."

The dry skull shrank. From his yellowish eyes, ran a tenuous liquid. His mouth trembled, but he said nothing. Finally, he had achieved all his objectives. He tried to smile:

"I am grateful for everything you have done on my behalf. But I would like to hand in my resignation."

The boss did not understand.

"But, Mr. João, now that your salary has been eliminated? Why? In a few months you will have to pay the initial tax to remain in our organization. Throw all that away? After forty years? You are still strong. What do you say?"

Emotion ruled out any reply.

João walked away. His wilted lips extended. His skin hardened, turned smooth. His stature diminished. His head fused to his body. His forms became dehumanized, plane, compact. His sides formed angles. He turned gray.

João turned into a metal file cabinet.

EDLA VAN STEEN
—◦❧(b. 1936)❧◦—

Originally from Florianópolis, Santa Catarina, and bilingual in German and Portuguese, Edla Van Steen is a journalist, scriptwriter, and author of short stories, novels, and theatrical works who lives in São Paulo. She has won national prizes and been widely translated (*A Bag of Stories* [1991]; *Early Mourning* [1997]; *Scent of Love* [2001], *Village of the Ghost Bells* [1991] are all books of stories translated by David S. George). Her stories incorporate many innovative approaches, influenced by her work in theater and film, as well as outspoken cultural criticism. She especially addresses issues of Brazilian women in society, including love, eroticism, and problems of secondary social status. Her contribution to the short story extends to the organization of anthologies (*Love Stories: A Brazilian Collection*, 1978; *O Conto da Mulher Brasileira*, 1978; *O Papel do Amor: Antologia e Contos*, 1979). The 1978 anthology of Brazilian women's stories shocked the public with its explicit content and promoted the awareness and greater reception of women's writing.

CAROL head LINA heart
—◦❧ ❧◦—

For Joyce Carol Oates

The man leaves his suitcases on the table, opens the window, and looks at the apartment that from now on will be his.

The fern in the earthen pot and the vase of flowers are vivid reminders of the owner's presence. This Tomás Ferro must be a considerate fellow, the man thinks

The woman paces back and forth, feeling a hollow pain in her stomach. She eats a slice of cheese. Can pain before he touches the clay statues and examines the furniture—could he have left these flowers intentionally?

be hollow? Hers is. A sensation of irretrievable loss. Or is it just hunger? She cuts another slice. He said: Carolina, you have to improve your diet, drink less coffee, and don't smoke so much. Yessir—she lies on the bed, picks up a magazine, and tries to relax. It doesn't work. She decides to take a walk in the garden.

The tall wet grass feels unpleasant, but the plants, washed clean, glisten in their beds.

The man perches uncomfortable on the edge of an armchair as if he were a visitor waiting for someone to show up. He lights a cigarette.

He remembers the owner's reticence, the shyness in his voice. The fellow practically shoved the keys into his hand, a gesture of confidence in the accuracy of his ad. No reason not to rent the cozy, discreet apartment—a stroke of luck. He gets up and closes the window, shutting out the traffic noise.

She slowly breathes in the posthumous smell of the rain— posthumous smell? Her head sure is muddled today—or is it just the opposite? It will be dark soon; she can make out the city in the distance: the first streetlights go on—the electric company's fireflies?

He opens one of the suitcases and takes out a bottle, winds the alarm clock, and turns on the transistor radio: a report on a new crisis in the Portuguese government. So what else is new? He turns it off.

She has a sudden desire to climb a tree and rub off the mud spattered on her legs—why doesn't she go go back in the house? Painted blue, from that angle, at that hour, it looks black. A mausoleum? No, a coffin.

The hem of her skirt catches on the absurd rose bush that no one planted. She hates roses—she gives her skirt a firm tug: the harsh sound of cloth tearing. She pricks her finger on a thorn—and sucks the warm liquid.

He goes into the bedroom: the bare, double mattress makes him slightly queasy. He finds some sheets in the closet and smooths them out on the bed; there's a raincoat on one of the hangers. Left behind? He tries it on. Too small—he finds a lottery ticket in the pocket. Expired.

After he's unpacked his belongings, left his typewriter in the living room, lined up his books on the shelf, and put away his suitcases, he feels settled in.

A drink of scotch at the right time hits the spot—he leans comfortably back into the sofa. He thinks about Penélope; too bad the condominium association won't allow dogs. Then, against his will, he remembers his ex-wife, a frame accidentally spliced into the wrong film. He tries to change the subject by admitting he's not keen on the job he's starting Monday, editor of a medical journal. Who knows what's in store for him! In the first place, he knows little about the field. Second, he hates medicine. Third, he's sick and tired of working in those crummy editorial offices.

Ice in the pit of his stomach: he downs his drink in a single gulp.

The flame reveals the wrinkles on his hand: hundreds of lines make up the honeycomb of old age—he throws the match in an ashtray.

No, he's not resigned to getting old. If the likelihood of an aneurysm fails him, the magic bubble that will enable him to burst on the beach, in the office, at the movies, he'll have to rely on the accident—should he close

Heavy drops of rain begin falling again. (As if drops of blood poured from the sky?)

She heads back toward the house feeling unexpected anguish, as if the house were about to disappear.

She's panting by the time she arrives. She takes a few deep breaths—the pain is gone. For how long?

In the shadows, someone is breathing. Standing still, her senses alert, she tries to locate the sound: it's coming from the right. Did she see a glow just now? She waits to find out. He's finally come back, unannounced. Her heart thumps desperately. He wanted to surprise her, didn't he? That's it. Another heart beats wildly in the silence, one here, another over there. The glow fades in and out, flying through the darkness.

Tomás will get tired of the game. He's well aware of her affliction, the anxiety taking hold of her. She'll kneel down and lick his feet—a bitch grateful for the return of her master.

Then their bodies will slowly envelop each other, pulsing with love. Forever.

One day she said: near you I'm as submissive as a puddle of water.

The click of the light switch in the empty room seems more like a scream.

Carolina scalds her body in the hot shower. Pity she can't warm up her soul. She hears the distant sound of the neighbor lady's contralto voice. She tries a little warbling herself. It sounds more like a moan.

his eyes when he crosses the street?
Or will he jump out the window? It's
ten floors. Guaranteed success.

Is there a sound of silence? No. Is
silence soundless? Perhaps. He pours
another scotch and turns on the
radio. A Portuguese lesson. He gives
up. Loneliness, the best refuge.

Strong bolt of lightning. It keeps
raining.

When he was a child he was
afraid of the dark. Now . . . Now, too—
he turns on the gold-colored lamp.
There was a time . . . Stop it, no there
wasn't. Memory lies. Makes up
situations he never experienced. All a
dream. Pointless fantasy. This is the
only truth: a man drinking his scotch,
in a city somewhere, the night before
starting some job. A man listening to
himself sipping and looking
indifferently at his shoes.

The telephone rings, startling him.

Her breasts are all that's left of
her firmness. They'll eventually be
flopping against her navel. Damn! She
works out. If it's up to her—instead
of thirty repetitions she'll do a
hundred a day and she'll stretch those
lousy muscles—they won't sag, oh
no. One, two, three, four, five . . .
She'll try a new hair style, she'll cut it
very short, and she'll gain a few
pounds. Their bodies, more in
balance, will flow enchantingly
together . . . Heavens, thinking's not a
good idea . . . Tomás surrendering
totally, exposing himself to her
adventurous impulses. Oh, how she
loved exploring that rugged terrain,
its valleys, its rivers. He was her
country. She wanted to live and die
there, amen.

She lies down, wrapped in a
towel. What if he's changed his mind
about the separation? "I'm moving to
a new address. Don't try and find
me." That damn hollow pain again.

Carolina picks up the telephone.

"Hi, Tomás. Decide against moving? I can't take this loneliness. I'm sorry, I promised I wouldn't call, it's not easy, not a bit . . . Are you listening to me? (*The man grunts*) I know your tricks. You hem and haw so you won't get caught saying something dumb. Well, it doesn't bother me. I say whatever nonsense comes into my head. For example, I want you here, by my side. It's been so long since anyone's asked, 'how are you, little bird?' A day, six months, a year? No matter. (*The woman's body doubles up in pain, and she covers herself with a quilt.*) This afternoon a bird was pecking at a begonia in the bedroom window. I felt such agony . . . (*The man stretches out his leg on the sofa.*) Oh, my god, say something, Tomás, please. Do you know what it means to feel physical longing for someone? Every pore on my skin misses you. And my Lina does too. Don't laugh. It was your idea to make up nicknames. If you were with me, now, I'd ask you to stroke Lina's hair,

the silky down that's all yours . . . (*The man is startled. Did he hear that right?*)
The thing I found most touching was our poetic game of creating images and names
for everything. Believe me, Carol head and Lina heart wouldn't exist if not for you.
Hey, that sounds like samba lyrics . . . (*She laughs*) Patience. Darling, do you think
that a person who's shared so many delights can forget about love, just like that?
Chocolate covered cherries, chocolate mousse—remembered?—strawberry jam.
You think all you have to do is say: it's over, I'm leaving? No, sir. A man and a
woman truly coming together, like two identical seashells, that doesn't happen very
often in people's lives, do you understand? It doesn't happen. Didn't you tell me
that you had affairs with all kinds of women? It's true, I also had my share of
lovers. And yet . . . I'll repeat everything I've already said: I spent my whole life
getting ready for you, learning to give and take pleasure, which after all is what
love is all about. (*Pause.*) Don't just shut me out of your life, Tomás, at least give
me some time . . . A few more days and . . . (*The man wonders if he should hang
up. After all, he's robbing a priceless treasure—he rolls his eyes, relaxes his facial
muscles, there's a flicker of a smile: if he had a woman like that . . . He imagines
his ideal type: dark, Indian face.*) Call me your little bon-bon, come on. (*Silence.*)
This is your Lina asking. Your Lina. Don't be so quiet, I don't deserve that. (*She
crawls out from under the quilt.*) It's funny, I can't stand the idea of sudden break-
ups, even though I realize they're more efficient. And at the same time I can't bear
the idea of love dying a slow death, the daily grind destroying us bit by bit . . . (*The
man's glass is empty. He needs another drink bad. He tries to reach the bottle but
the cord is too short. So he puts the phone on the sofa and grabs the scotch. He's
missing something important.*) . . . don't you think we could find a better way to
say goodbye? Get together one last time, affectionately, as friends . . . a final picture
for us to remember, how about it? A tribute to the fond memories we have of each
other. A proper goodbye is a refined touch, a civilized touch. How about it? Listen,
my love, you know what, I'm coming over. (*The man sits down in a panic.*) I
promise this'll be the last time. Please. I love you."

The man sits for a few moments
with the phone to his ear, indecisive.
Oh no. What should he do? He gets
up. An uncontrollable urge to throw
up. His stomach churning, convulsing, until the vomit spews out.

Feeling better, he puts on some
music and fills the glass with ice. He
downs another scotch.

Then he decides to change his
clothes—he checks the closet—but
only picks out a cardigan—he's in a
cold sweat—and mirror reflects a
worn out, doleful, unshaven face.

The woman quickly gets dressed,
puts on a bit of makeup, and slams
the door without looking back. The
yellow beams of the headlights seem
to violate the night. Threads of rain
look like falling stars disintegrating
on the pavement.

What bad luck—she has to park a
long way from the building, she'll be
soaked by the time she gets there—
she runs. The rain wets her face—a
baptism of love?

She runs like someone trying to reach the horizon. Like someone trying to embrace infinity.

Terrified, he hears the sound of the elevator coming up.

Is it time to jump out the window?

The woman rings the doorbell once, twice, ten times as she feels the water running down her body, down her legs, to her feet.

The puddle of water, entering the apartment, licks the floor.

CAIO FERNANDO ABREU
—◦❧(1948–1996)❦◦—

Born in Santiago, Rio Grande do Sul, Caio Fernando Abreu studied dramatic arts at the Federal University of Rio Grande do Sul before working as an editor, journalist, writer, and playwright in São Paulo, Rio de Janeiro, and Porto Alegre. His first literary success after *Inventário do Irremediável* (1970) came with *O Ovo Apunhalado* (1975), which received honorable mention in a national fiction contest and was named by *Veja* magazine as one of the best books of the year. Other books of stories followed in this period: *Pedras de Calcutá* (1977), *Morangos Mofados* (1982), *Triângulo das Águas* (1983), and *Os Dragões Não Conhecem o Paraíso* (1987). English and French translations soon followed (*Dragons . . .* , 1990), and Abreu began an intensive period of travel and participation in international literary conferences. His novel *Onde Andará Dulce Veiga* (*Whatever Happened to Dulce Veiga? A B-novel*, 2000) won the prize of the São Paulo Association of Art Critics as the best novel of the year. Abreu published an anthology of stories, *Ovelhas Negras, de 1962 a 1995* (1995) before his premature death in 1996 at age forty-seven. Along with the theater, the abiding influence of journalism in his style can be seen in his collected newspaper columns, *Pequenas Epifanias: Crônicas, 1986/1995* (1996).

DRAGONS . . .
—◦❧ ❦◦—

Because he sees with great clarity causes and effects, he completes the six steps at the right time and mounts toward heaven on them at the right time, as though on six dragons.

Ch'ien, The Creative: *I Ching:*
The Book of Changes

I've got a dragon living with me.
No, it's not true.
I haven't really got a dragon. And even if I did have, he wouldn't live with me

or with anyone else. There's nothing harder for dragons to imagine than sharing their space, whether with another dragon or with some ordinary person like me. Or an unusual person, as I imagine others must be. They're solitary creatures, dragons. Almost as solitary as I felt when I was left alone in this flat after he went. I say *almost* because during all that time he was with me I nurtured the illusion that my isolation was over forever. And I say *illusion* because the other day, on one of those mornings barren with his absence, though fortunately it's getting less and less frequent (the barrenness, not his absence), I had this thought: *Men need the illusion of love in the same way that they need the illusion of God; the illusion of love so that they won't fall into that awful well of utter solitude; the illusion of God, so that they won't lose themselves in the chaos of disorder and anomie.*

It sounded grandiloquent and wise like an idea that wasn't mine, that's how stupid my thoughts tend to be. And I made a quick note of it on the napkin in the bar where I was sitting. I wrote down something else too but I spilled coffee over it. To this day I haven't been able to work out what it says. Or else I've avoided trying, afraid of my—fortunately undecipherable—lucidity on that day.

I'm getting confused, I'm drifting off all over the place.

The napkin, the sentence, the coffee stain, my fear—that'll have to come later. All these things I'm talking about now; the specialness of dragons, the ordinariness of people like me, I only discovered later. Slowly, as I tried to understand him in his absence. Understanding him less and less, attempting to make my understanding seductive enough to convince him to come back, and deeper and deeper so that this understanding might help me *to*. I can't say. When I'm thinking like this I make a list of propositions such as: *to* be a less ordinary person; *to* be stronger, more sure of myself, calmer, happier; *to* get by with the minimum of pain. All those things we decide to do or become when something we assumed to be great comes to an end, and there's nothing to be done but go on living.

So, let it be sweet. Every morning, when I open the windows to let in the sunshine or the grayness of a day, that's just what I repeat, let it be sweet. When it's sunny and the sun strikes my face creased with sleep or insomnia, as I watch the particles of dust floating in the air like a little universe, I repeat seven times for luck: let it be sweet let it be sweet let it be sweet and so on. But if someone asked me what had to be sweet maybe I wouldn't have an answer. *Everything* is so vague it might as well be nothing.

No one will ask anything, I think to myself. Then I carry on telling myself about it, as if I were both the old man telling the story and the child listening, sitting on my lap. That was the image which occurred to me this morning when, opening the window, I decided I couldn't bear to let another day go by without telling this story about dragons. I managed to avoid it until the middle of the afternoon. It hurts a little. Not a fresh wound any more, just a little rose thorn, or something of the sort that you try to dig out of the palm of your hand with the point of a needle. But if you don't manage to pluck it out, that little thorn might stop being a little pain and turn into a big sore.

That's how things are at the moment as I sit here. The sharp point of a needle balanced between the fingers of my right hand hovering over the open palm of my left hand. A few notes around me, made a long time ago, the paper napkin from the bar with those wise words that don't sound like mine and those other coffee-stained ones which I can't or don't want to or pretend I can't decipher.

I still haven't begun.

I really wish I could say *Once upon a time*. I still can't.

But I have to begin somehow. And I reckon that, after all, this way, not beginning properly, confused, drifting about, repetitively like this, is as good or bad as any other way of beginning a story. Above all if it's a story about dragons.

I enjoy saying *I've got a dragon living with me*, even though it's not true. As I was saying, a dragon never belongs to or lives with anyone. Whether it's an ordinary person like me or whether it's a unicorn, a salamander, a harpy, an elf, a wood nymph, a mermaid or an ogre. I doubt whether a dragon gets on better with those mythological beings that are more akin to his nature than he does with a human being. Not that they're unsociable. On the contrary, sometimes a dragon can be as kind and submissive as a geisha. It's just that their customs are different.

No one can really understand a dragon. They never show what they're feeling. Who could comprehend, for example, that as soon as they wake up (and this can happen at any time, at three in the afternoon or eleven at night, since their day and night take place inside them, although it's more likely between seven and nine in the morning because that's the time for dragons) they always thrash their tails three times, as if they were in a rage, breathing fire through their nostrils and incinerating anything within a radius of over five meters? Today I wonder; perhaps that's their clumsy way of saying, as I tend to say these days, when they wake up—let it be sweet.

But at the time he was living with me, I tried to—let's say—adapt him to circumstances. I'd say please try to understand, darling, those common people on the next floor down have complained about your tail thrashing on the floor last night at four in the morning. The baby woke up, they said, he wouldn't let anyone sleep after that. Besides, when you wake up in the lounge, the plants get burnt up in the searing heat of your breath. And when you wake up in the bedroom, that pile of books on the bedside table turns to ashes.

He wouldn't promise to mend his ways. And I know very well how ridiculous this all sounds. A dragon never thinks he's wrong. In fact he never is. Everything he does that might seem dangerous, eccentric or in the slightest bit rude to a human being like me is just part of the strange nature of dragons. The following mornings, afternoons and nights, when he woke up again the neighbors would complain again and day by day the yellow primulas and the purple and green begonias and Kafka, Salinger, Pessoa, Lispector and Borges would get more and more scorched. Until just the two of us were left in that flat amongst the ashes. Ashes are like silk to a dragon, but never to a human because they remind us of destruction and death, not pleasure. They cross with impunity, with relish, over the threshold between two zones; one hidden, the other more worldly. Something we find hard to understand, or at least to accept.

Aside from anything else, I couldn't see him. Dragons are invisible you know. Did you know that? I didn't. It's so slow and difficult telling this story—has your patience run out yet? Of course, obviously you want to know how, after all, I was so sure of his existence if I claim I couldn't see him. If you were to say that he'd laugh. If, like men and hyenas, dragons possessed the dubious gift of laughter. You would think him perhaps ironic, but he would be quite unconcerned as he asked, but do you only believe in what you can see, then. If you said yes, he'd talk about unicorns, salamanders, harpies, wood nymphs, mermaids and ogres. Perhaps about fairies too or voodoo *orixás*. Or atoms, black holes, white dwarves, quasars and protozoa. And he'd say in that slightly pedantic tone, *"Anyone who only believes in what is visible has a very small world. There isn't room for dragons in those small worlds with walls that are inaccessible to what is not visible."*

He really liked those words beginning with *in—invisible, inaccessible, incomprehensible*—which mean the opposite of what they should. He himself was quite the opposite of what he should be. So much so that when I thought he was being intractable, to use a word he'd like, I actually suspected him of being the opposite— oozing with affection. I sometimes thought of dealing with him like that, the wrong way round, so that we'd be happier together. I never dared. And now he's gone it's too late to attempt any refined harmonies.

He smelled of mint and rosemary. I believed in his existence because of that green smell of herbs crushed in the palms of both one's hands. There were other signs, other auguries. But I want to dwell on the smells for a moment before going on. Don't believe it if someone, even someone who doesn't have a small world, says that dragons smell of horses after a race, or of dogs from the streets after it's been raining. Of closed rooms, mold, rotten fruit, dead fish or the beach at low tide— that's never been the smell of dragons.

They smell of mint and rosemary. When he got in, the whole flat would be impregnated with that aroma. Even the neighbors, the ones from the next floor down, asked whether I was using incense or burning herbs to exorcise the flat. Everything all right, the wife asked. She had innocent blue eyes. Her husband didn't say anything, didn't even say hello. I reckon he thought it was one of those Indian herbs that people tend to smoke when they live in flats, listening to very loud music. The wife said the baby slept better when that smell started to drift down the stairs, more strongly in the evening, and that the baby smiled as if he were dreaming. Without saying a word, I knew that the baby must be dreaming of dragons, unicorns or salamanders, that was one way that his world could gradually become bigger. But babies usually forget those things when they stop being babies although they possess the strange faculty of seeing dragons—something of which only more ample worlds are capable.

I learned the trick of noticing when the dragon was next to me. Once, we went down in the lift together with that woman with the innocent-blue-eyes and her baby, who also had innocent-blue-eyes. The baby stared at me the whole time. Then it stretched out its hands to the left of me where the dragon was. Dragons always stand on your left, so they can talk straight to your heart. The air next to me became light and vaguely purplish. A sign that he was happy. Him, the dragon, and the baby too and me and the woman and the Japanese woman who got in on the sixth floor and a young man with a beard on the third. We smiled sweetly, a bit stupidly, going down together in the lift on what I remember was an April afternoon—that's the month of dragons—in that atmosphere of fluid eternity that only dragons, but only sometimes, know how to convey.

I loved him for things like that. And I still love him, maybe even now, maybe even without quite knowing the exact meaning of that arid word—love. If not the whole time, then at least when I'm remembering moments like that. Which, unfortunately, is not often. Severity and contrariness seem to be more constant in the nature of dragons than levity and straightforwardness. But I wanted to talk about the time before the smell. There were other signs, I said earlier. Vague, all of them.

On the days leading up to his arrival I'd wake up in the middle of the night, my heart beating wildly. There'd be a cold sweat on the palms of my hands. Without knowing why, on the mornings afterwards I'd start to buy flowers, clean the house, go to the supermarket and the market to fill the flat with roses and palms and those nice plump strawberries and gleaming bunches of grapes and shiny aubergines (dragons, I found out later, love looking at aubergines) which I couldn't eat myself. I'd lay them out on dishes, in the corners, with flowers and candles and ribbons, so that the place would look nicer.

I felt a kind of hunger. But a hunger for seeing, not eating. I'd sit in the neat and tidy lounge, with the carpet brushed, the curtains washed, baskets of fruit, vases of flowers, I'd light a cigarette and sit there chewing over with my eyes the beauty of these clean ordered things, unable to eat anything with my mouth, just hungry for seeing. As the house became more lovely I became uglier and uglier, thinner and thinner, with heavy bags under my eyes and hollow cheeks. For I couldn't sleep or eat as I waited for him. Now, now I'm going to be happy I thought the whole time with a hysterical certainty. Until that smell of rosemary and mint began to get stronger and then, one day, slipped just like a breeze under the door and ever so slowly settled in the hallway, on the living-room sofa, in the bathroom, in my bed. He had arrived.

I only discovered those rhythms little by little. Even the smell of mint and rosemary, I only found out that was what it was when I came across some herbs on a market stall. My heart leapt, I imagined he was close by. I followed the smell until I was leaning over the stall and saw two green bunches, the mint with its tiny little leaves, the rosemary with its long stalks and leaves like thorns, but they didn't hurt. I asked what they were called, the man told me, and I didn't forget. With the sheer intoxication of it, on the following days I'd say again and again when the longing came over me, rosemary mint rosemary mint rosemary.

Before that, still earlier, my premonitions about his visit brought only anxiety, palpitations, nail-biting distress. It wasn't good. I couldn't work, go to the cinema or sink into any other of those mundane occupations which people like me occupy their lives with. All I could think about was pretty things for the house and getting myself nice to meet him. My anxiety was such that I became uglier as the days went by. And when he eventually did arrive, I'd never looked so ugly. Dragons don't forgive ugliness. Let alone ugliness in those whom they honor with their rare visits.

After he came, with the prettiness of the house contrasting with the ugliness of my body, everything gradually began to fall apart. Like pain, not happiness. Now now now I'm going to be happy, I kept on saying—now now now. And I strained to look in all the corners to see if I could find at least the reflections of his greenish-silver scales, a fleeting light, the arrow-shaped tip of his tail through the crack of an open door or the smoke from his nostrils which changed color depending on his mood. Which was nearly always a bad one, and the smoke black. On those days I'd get crazier and crazier, wanting so urgently to be happy right now. Noticing my distress, he became more and more distant. He'd stay away, withdraw and pretend to leave. His smell of herbs became fainter and fainter until it was no more than a green hint in the air. I breathed deeper, getting breathless in my effort to see him, day after day, while the flowers and fruits rotted in the vases, baskets and corners, and those tiny little black flies buzzed ominously around them.

Everything was rotting away more and more without my noticing, so grief-stricken was I with the impossibility of having him. Concerned only with my pain; which was rotting too and smelling bad. Then one of the neighbors would knock at the door to find out whether I'd died and yes, I wanted to say, I'm slowly rotting, smelling bad or not smelling at all like ordinary people do when they die, waiting for a happiness that never comes. They wouldn't understand, no one would understand. I didn't understand in those days, do you?

Dragons, as I said, can't stand ugliness. He'd leave when that smell of rotten fruit, flowers and, worst of all, feelings became unbearable, matching the smell of the happiness he had once again failed to bring me. Asleep or awake, I took his departure like a sudden punch in the chest. Then I'd look up and around, in search of God or something like that: wood nymphs, archangels, radioactive clouds, demons or whatever. I never saw them. I never saw anything apart from the walls that were suddenly so empty without him.

Only someone who's had a dragon in their home can know how deserted this house seems after he's gone. Dunes, glaciers, steppes. No more greenish reflections in the corners ever again, no aroma of herbs in the air, no more colored smoke or shapes like serpents peeping through the cracks in half-opened doors. Sadder still; no more desire inside you to be happy ever again, even if that happiness leaves you with your heart beating wildly, your hands clammy, your eyes shining and that hunger when you can't swallow anything. Except for that loveliness which is seeing, not chewing, and for that very reason is a form of discomfort too. In the barren dimness of a house emptied of the presence of a dragon, even as you start to eat and sleep normally again, as ordinary people do, you no longer know whether that old swamp that was full of unrealized possibilities might not be preferable to this barrenness now. When everything, without him, is nothing.

Today I think I know. Does a dragon come and go away again so that your world will grow? I ask this because I'm not sure, perhaps things are rather elementary, for example, does a dragon come and go away again so that you will learn about the pain of not having him, after cherishing the illusion of possessing him? So that human beings will learn how to hold onto him, if he comes back one day?

No, that's not how it is. That's not right.

Dragons don't stay. Dragons are just the announcement of themselves. They are forever rehearsing, and never make their debut. The curtains never actually open so that they can go on stage. They give a glimpse of themselves and then go up in smoke without ever revealing their shape. Applause would be unbearable for them; the confirmation that their nonconformity is understood and accepted and admired, and therefore—the wrong way round, the same as the right way round—misunderstood, rejected, despised. Dragons don't want to be accepted. They flee from paradise, the paradise that we ordinary people invent; the way I invented a wondrous world of tricks to await him and trap him here with me forever. Dragons have no knowledge of a paradise where everything goes perfectly and nothing hurts or sparkles or gasps in an eternal monotony of peaceable falseness. Their paradise is conflict, never harmony.

When I think about him again, on those nights when I've taken to leaning out of the window looking for moving lights in the sky, I like to imagine him flying along with his big golden wings, free in space, heading for everywhere which is nowhere. That is his more subtle nature, averse to the paradisiacal prisons that I was stupidly preparing for him with snares of flowers, fruits and ribbons when he came. Artificial paradises that gradually rotted, my own paradise—so ordinary and thirsty—tolerating all of his extravagances, which must sound ridiculous, pathetic and wretched to you. Now I just glide about, not too desperate about being happy.

The mornings are nice to wake up in, drink coffee, watch the time go by. Objects are nice to look at, they don't give you too many frights because they are what they are and they look at us too, with eyes that are thinking nothing. Since I sent him away, so that I could at last learn about the great disillusionment of paradise, that's how I've been feeling—hardly feeling at all.

All that's left is this story I'm telling, are you still listening? The odd note on the table, full ashtrays, empty glasses and this paper napkin where I noted down some apparently wise phrases about love and God, together with a sentence I'm afraid to decipher and which maybe, after all, just says something simple such as, none of this exists. And that nothing would include love and God, and dragons too and all the rest, visible or invisible.

None of this, none of it exists.

Then I'm almost sick and weep and bleed when I think these things. But I breathe deeply, rub my hands together and generate an energy from within. To keep myself alive, I go out in search of illusions like the smell of herbs or greenish reflections of scales around the flat and when I find them, even if it's just in my mind's eye, then again I become able to claim, as if it were harmless vice—I've got a dragon living with me. And in this way I begin a new story which this time *will* be absolutely true even if it's a total lie. I get tired of the love I feel and with a huge effort which gradually turns into a kind of modest joy, late in the evening, alone in the flat in the middle of a town where dragons are scarce, over and over I repeat this confused apprenticeship of mine for the child-who-is-me sitting anguished and cold on the knees of the calm old-man-who-is-me:

"Go to sleep, only dreams exist. Go to sleep, my child. Let it be sweet."

No, that's not true either.

Milton Hatoum
—◦❧(b. 1952)❧◦—

Part of the Lebanese community in Manaus, the capital city of Amazonas, son of an immigrant father and a Brazilian daughter of immigrants, Milton Hatoum grew up listening to the Arabic spoken in his community. His childhood memories were formed in the still belle-époque surroundings left in Manaus from the elegance of the rubber boom, where his family became more Brazilian over the years. Hatoum's first novel, *Relato de um Certo Oriente* (1989; *Tree of the Seventh Heaven*, 1994), won the Jabuti Prize in 1990 and catapulted him to prominence as one of Brazil's most promising young writers. It was almost immediately translated under different titles into French, German, and English. Based on the author's life and identity in Manaus, the novel is a mixture of confession, memoir, travelogue, and novel of education. Hatoum's second novel, *Dois Irmãos* (2000; *The Brothers*, 2002), was an even greater success, continuing in his third, *Cinzas do Norte* (2005). Delving in more detail into the psychological and cultural side of his family story, Hatoum's novel contrasts the lives of two twins, Yaqub and Omar, one scientific and studious while the other is completely licentious. The novel is narrated by Domingas, a maid of indigenous origins who has always lived with the family, although her role is more complex. The presence of the Lebanese is part of an epic story of the development of the city, caught up both in the sweep of family passions and the currents of national culture and history. Hatoum's short story "The Truth Is a Seven-Headed Animal" ("A Ninfa do Teatro Amazonas," in *O Estado de S. Paulo*, 4 February 1996) is set in the famous opera theater that now seems anachronistic and surreal, part of a world gone by, just as Hatoum's family was absorbed into greater Brazil. Hatoum was professor of French at the University of Manaus and is now professor of Brazilian literature at the Universidade de São Paulo. He has been a visiting writer at Yale University and a visiting professor at the University of California, Berkeley.

The Truth Is a Seven-Headed Animal
— ◦❯ ❮◦ —

She was a shadow lost in a flooded world. We still don't know her name or where she lives. Some say the poor woman's from a hole in the wall in the ragged Colinas district; others have seen her roaming the alleys of the Céu neighborhood, and God only knows whether she's a daughter of the city or the jungle. They say she tried to check into Santa Casa Hospital, but the security guard shooed her away and she was caught in a fierce downpour in the middle of Praça São Sebastião. The church was closed, the square deserted, house fronts silent. Somehow it all seemed linked to the dread that comes with the December rainy season here in Manaus. She must have felt the first contractions as she wandered the square outside our majestic Opera House. We can imagine her eyes searching for someone to help her, but there was not a living soul in sight. Rather than struggling with the stairs, she dragged herself up the nearest ramp to the entrance, somehow managed to pull open the massive wooden doors, and crawled inside.

The Opera House was empty. Now and again a sudden flash of light would scratch the window and a rumble boom down from the sky like a warning. Hauling herself along, the woman plunged into a shadowy place where nothing—except her damp body and wet hair—recalled the wet tumult outside. She found herself in the Opera House auditorium, where a sloping aisle led her down near the stage. She lay down on the velvety red between the rows, waiting for the propitious moment to give birth.

Maybe it was the thunder's crack that broke the silence reigning over the refuge—no one knows for certain what set the chandeliers that dangled from the high dome to swaying. We do know, however, that the disturbance registered in a small attic room where, stretched in a hammock, the self-proclaimed watchman of the Opera House lay drifting far from the world. Álvaro Celestino de Matos—a taciturn eighty-seven-year-old with the accent of an immigrant from the Minho region of Portugal—woke with a start. There it was again—the strange noise he'd imagined he'd been dreaming: the voice of a singer from a distant night in childhood. He floated for a while in that shifting place where sleep and dream mysteriously merge, unsure whether what he heard was a product of the storm or of a certain Thursday in 1910: the famous day—still crystal in memory—when as a boy he had waxed and waxed the stage, lovingly preparing it to receive the precious feet of Angiolina Zanuchi, Soprano.

Nothing, or almost nothing, had changed about his modest room since that day: conspicuous on the wall beside the window was a photograph of the singer descending the gangplank of the Queen Elizabeth. But it was impossible to look at the photograph without also taking in the view out the window: a single church spire with a belfry and a bell as regular as the rain—until nightfall, when the silhouette of the church faded and a lunar disk appeared in the center of the window. These two images—the picture of the soprano and the profile of the Church of São Sebastião—were unalterably linked in both vision and memory. For how many years had he been gazing at them before sleep—sixty, seventy? He would drift off with those two images in his head, and on waking the first thing he'd do was to light the kerosene lamp, so that a flame lit up Angiolina's face beside the moon-flooded landscape.

Yesterday, when Seu Álvaro opened his eyes, the view from his window looked like an aquarium full of brownish water, and the contours of the singer's face had disappeared; only the broad side of the ship emerged from the murk of his attic room. The watchman wasn't sure in this lingering night whether the sound he heard was a human voice or the chords of a piano, but it no longer belonged to sleep or dream. It seemed to come from a long way off, probably from inside the Opera House, down below.

For a man approaching his nineties, the distance from the attic to the ground floor was practically an abyss. This did not discourage him. He decided to brave the journey armed with his Winchester, which had intimidated countless men and brought down countless animals in times past. Now, almost the same height as his stooped frame, the rifle served as a cane.

The descent was slow and arduous, but it wasn't fatigue that set him to shaking the moment he stepped onto the carpeted ground floor. Seu Álvaro realized that this sudden trembling had nothing to do with age; instinct told him that something ominous was about to happen this rainy morning. Was the half-open entryway door a sign of an intruder? He glanced out at the monument. Of the four bronze boats, only one was visible, seemingly adrift in the center of the square, and the wings of a submerged angel looked like an anchor floating free in space. Pushing the door fully open with the butt of the gun, the watchman noticed a red stain that trailed along the floor and disappeared into the auditorium. Choosing another route, he turned down one of the side corridors: a winding wall of doors that gave onto the main floor boxes. He had decided to slip into the seventh box and was already turning the doorknob when he heard the sound again—odder now, more threatening. And so he stood and waited a few seconds, and this moment of hesitation—the anxiety of an old man?—caused him to change his mind. Turning away from the door, a strange sensation led him to the backstage area. There he found a safe haven on the stage, with the painted canvas curtain separating him from the concert hall itself.

Wary but not unsteady—his past, his profession, and perhaps his rifle all helping to keep him calm—the watchman felt his way along the closest wall and found, among the spider webs, a wooden handle. He yanked it upwards. A thread of light shot toward him through a hole in the curtain, which glowed with sudden brightness from the other side. The watchman could well envision the shapes and colors of the immense paintings now visible in the hall: herons and storks surrounded by white lilies and other aquatic flowers, and a water nymph reclining on a shell that floated atop the "Meeting of the Waters" of the Rio Negro and the Rio Amazonas. Seu Álvaro moved up to the curtain, bringing his right eye directly to the hole, and shivered when he realized that the ring of light coincided with the water nymph's outlined navel. Steadying himself on his rifle, he scanned the hall, searching for the source of the noise that had awoken him. It was disheartening, somehow, to find the hall deserted, chandeliers and upholstery dusty, plaster busts of Bach and Shubert—in past times honored by famous pianists—lusterless.

Today the hall looked utterly abandoned, the boxes empty . . . until that one wide-open eye detected a shadow—perhaps a body?—down front near the stage. For the first time the watchman was a little afraid. He put on his glasses, bringing the hall into a clearer focus: more of his old friends, busts of Carlos Gomes, Racine, and Molière. And, there in a front row seat, the glistening body of a dark-haired woman.

The watchman lurched back from the curtain and stood there, imagining the painting on the other side: the water nymph lying on her shell, almost naked, a white and luxuriant body accented by the light. Then he touched his right hand to the curtain and gently caressed the nymph's belly; the roughness of the canvas on his skin jolted him into remembering that it really was a painting. He lined his eye up with the hole in the curtain again: the woman had crossed her legs. Her hair hung down over her breasts. From this distance he couldn't make out the expression on her face, but the eyes seemed large, almond-shaped maybe. Her posture, demeanor? That body was simply a body. Not more than twenty years old, he thought to himself, as the woman leaned back in her chair, cradling a baby in her arms. She enfolded the infant tenderly, and, when she opened her mouth, he expected a voice or a song; but it was merely a yawn. Then the woman began licking the baby's face, her lips and tongue gleaming in the light from the chandelier. As if in a dream, the hall suddenly went black, just like that. The watchman closed his eyes and struck the floor several times impatiently with his rifle. As the noise echoed through the theater, he guffawed once, then smiled at himself. Giving in fully to laughter, he didn't notice the loss of his gun until he staggered and fell to his knees. Two men dressed in white dragged him downstage through the gloom and deposited him in the middle of some old scenery: a small room with wooden walls and a single window that framed a church spire and belfry in a sky bright with tin foil stars, with a cardboard moon hung in the air like a mobile. One of the nurses flicked a light on and lunged at Seu Álvaro when he tried to climb into the hammock that was part of the old set. He was breathing heavily, his eyes never wavering from a certain spot on the curtain, as if to drill through to the front row seat just on the other side.

Night had fallen by the time they arrived at the Estrada de Flores Mental Hospital. We found him lying on a straw mattress. His hands were shaking badly, but on his wrinkled face he wore an enigmatic smile. Raspy-voiced and somber, he related what had happened yesterday morning in the Opera House. Dr. S. L., the psychiatrist on duty, stated that Senhor de Matos' declaration was consistent with that of a man who had for some time been suffering the swamp of senility. Before hospitalization, his nomad's life had followed the course of the seasons: in summer, dawn would find him in one of the bronze boats of the monument in the Praça São Sebastião, where he spent hours contemplating the statue of a woman. During the rainy season, he took refuge in the abandoned scenery of the Opera House, where he'd been found on several occasions, either singing or staring at one of the seats in the front of the hall.

One particular element in the former watchman's story caught our attention. In one of his pockets, the doctor found a very old photograph of a woman and a boy holding hands. The woman's fleshy body under her tight skirt, two plumpish arms, a fan clasped in her left hand—all of this is clearly visible in the picture. But the upper section of the photograph is blotchy, worn, making the woman's face unrecognizable. Could she be Angiolina, the alleged heartthrob of the watchman in his adolescence? Our archives confirm that "the divine Milanese soprano," as she was proclaimed by the citizenry, did in fact make a visit to Manaus on a December night in the year 1910.

Another hypothesis, suggested by Dr. S. L., proposes that the woman in the photograph is a local Amazonian pianist known to have given several recitals during the time Seu Álvaro worked as a watchman at the Opera House. Who could forget the story of how she later drowned not far from the "Meeting of the Waters"? Her last concert, *Sunrise Sonata in F Minor*, also looms large in the memory of the whole city, though no doubt recalled with greatest intensity by that boy, now so ancient.

Senhor de Matos's psychological condition remains undiagnosed. Will he turn out to be merely a mythomaniac? Simply suffering from somniloquy? A victim of a crisis of delirium tremens? What he saw, or said he saw—will it prove to have been lunatic delusions? A resident of the Praça São Sebastião swears that she saw a pregnant woman dragging herself into the Opera House. Yesterday's thunderous downpour didn't cause her to veer from her course for a minute, said our informant, who, we should point out, is a regular reader of this weekly column, *The Truth Is a Seven-Headed Animal.*

Selected Bibliography

This bibliography contains references to sources in English about Brazilian literature and selected studies of the short story and of some of the authors in the anthology.

An Anthology of Twentieth-Century Brazilian Poetry. Elizabeth Bishop, Emanuel Brasil, eds. Middletown, CT, Wesleyan UP, 1972.

Azevedo, Fernando de. *Brazilian Culture.* William Rex Crawford, trans. New York, Macmillan, 1950.

Bandeira, Manuel. *A Brief History of Brazilian Literature.* Washington, DC, Pan American, 1958.

Barbosa, Maria José Somerlate. *Clarice Lispector: Spinning the Webs of Passion.* New Orleans, LA, UP of the South, 1997.

Borzoi Anthology of Latin American Literature. Emir Rodríguez Monegal, ed. New York, Knopf, 1977.

Boxer, Charles R. *A Great Luso-Brazilian Figure: Padre Antônio Vieira.* London, Hispanic and Luso-Brazilian Councils, 1957.

Brant, Alice Dayrell Caldeira. *The Diary of Helena Morley.* Elizabeth Bishop, trans. New York, Ecco, 1977.

Brazilian Literature: A Research Bibliography. David William Foster, William Rela, comps. New York, Garland, 1990.

Brazilian Poetry, 1950–1980. Emanuel Brasil, William J. Smith, eds. Middletown, CT, Wesleyan UP, 1983.

Brazilian Short Stories. Isaac Goldberg, ed. Girard, KS, Haldeman-Julius, 1925.

Brazilian Tales. Isaac Goldberg, ed. Boston, Four Seas, 1921.

Brazil Reader: History, Culture, Politics. Robert M. Levine, John J. Crocitti, eds. Durham, NC, Duke UP, 1999.

Brookshaw, David. *Paradise Betrayed: Brazilian Literature of the Indian.* Amsterdam, CEDLA, 1988.

Brookshaw, David. *Race and Color in Brazilian Literature.* Metuchen, NJ, Scarecrow, 1986.

Caldwell, Helen. *Brazilian Othello of Machado de Assis.* Berkeley, California UP, 1960.

Caldwell, Helen. *Machado de Assis: The Brazilian Master and His Novels.* Berkeley: California UP, 1970.

Cambridge History of Latin American Literature. Vol. 3, *Brazilian Literature.* Roberto González Echevarría, Enrique Pupo-Walker, eds. Cambridge, Cambridge UP, 1996.

Caminha, Pero Vaz de. "The Discovery of Brazil," in *Portuguese Voyages, 1498–1663.* C. D. Ley, trans. and ed. London, Dent, 1947, 40–59.

Cândido, Antônio. *On Literature and Society.* Howard S. Becker, trans. Princeton, NJ, Princeton UP, 1995.

Catalog of Brazilian Acquisitions in the Library of Congress, 1964–74. William V. Jackson, comp. Boston, Hall, 1977.

Chamberlain, Bobby J. *Jorge Amado.* Boston, Twayne, 1990.

Chamberlain, Bobby J. *Portuguese Language and Luso-Brazilian Literature: An Annotated Guide to Selected Reference Works.* New York, MLA, 1993.

Clarice Lispector: A Bio-bibliography. Diane Marting, ed. Westport, CT, Greenwood, 1993.

Closer to the Wild Heart: Essays on Clarice Lispector. Cláudia Pazos Alonso, Claire Williams, eds. Oxford, Oxford UP, 2002.

Concrete Poetry. Emmett Williams, org. New York, Something Else Press, 1968.

Concrete Poetry: A World View. Mary Ellen Solt, org. Bloomington, Indiana UP, 1968.

Coutinho, Afrânio. *An Introduction to Literature in Brazil.* Gregory Rabassa, trans. New York, Columbia UP, 1969.

da Costa, Emília Viotti. *The Brazilian Empire: Myths & Histories.* Chapel Hill, U of North Carolina P, 2000.

De Jong, Gerrit. *Four Hundred Years of Brazilian Literature: Outline and Anthology.* Provo, UT, Brigham Young UP, 1969.

De Oliveira, Celso L. *Understanding Graciliano Ramos.* Columbia, U of South Carolina P, 1988.

Dictionary of Brazilian Literature. Irwin Stern, ed. Westport, CT, Greenwood, 1988.

Dixon, Paul B. *Retired Dreams: Dom Casmurro, Myth and Modernity.* West Lafayette, IN, Purdue UP, 1989.

Dos Passos, John. *Brazil on the Move.* Garden City, NY, Doubleday, 1963.

Downes, Leonard. *An Introduction to Brazilian Poetry.* São Paulo, Clube de Poesia, 1944.

Driver, David. *The Indian in Brazilian Literature.* New York, Hispanic Institute in the United States, 1942.

Ellison, Fred. *Brazil's New Novel: Four Modern Masters.* Berkeley, U of California P, 1954.

Empire in Transition: The Portuguese World in the Time of Camões. Alfred Hower, Richard A. Preto-Rodas, eds. Gainesville, U of Florida P, 1985.

Experimental, Visual, Concrete: Avant-Garde Poetry since 1960. K. David Jackson, Eric Vos, Johanna Drucker, eds. Amsterdam and Atlanta, Rodopi, 1996.

Fitz, Earl. *Clarice Lispector.* Boston, Twayne, 1985.

Fitz, Earl. *Machado de Assis.* Boston, Twayne, 1989.

Fitz, Earl. *Sexuality and Being in the Poststructuralist Universe of Clarice Lispector: The Différance of Desire.* Austin, U of Texas P, 2001.

Freyre, Gilberto. *The Masters & the Slaves.* Samuel Putnam, trans. New York, Knopf, 1946.

Gledson, John. *The Deceptive Realism of Machado de Assis: A Dissenting Interpretation of Dom Casmurro,* Liverpool, Cairns, 1984.

Goldberg, Isaac. *Brazilian Literature.* New York, Knopf, 1922.

Haberley, David. *Three Sad Races: Racial Identity and National Consciousness in Brazilian Literature.* Cambridge, Cambridge UP, 1983.

Hallewell, Lawrence. *Books in Brazil: A History of the Publishing Trade.* Metuchen, NJ, Scarecrow, 1982.

Hartness, Ann. *Brazil in Reference Books, 1965–89: An Annotated Bibliography.* Metuchen, NJ, Scarecrow, 1991.

Hers Ancient and Modern: Women's Writing in Spain and Brazil. Catherine Davies, Jane Whetnall, eds. Manchester, U of Manchester P, 1997.

Hulet, Claude. *Brazilian Literature.* 3 vols. Washington, DC, Georgetown UP, 1974–1975.

Jackson, K. David. "The Brazilian Short Story," in *The Cambridge History of Latin American Literature*, vol. 3, Roberto González Echevarría, Enrique Pupo-Walker, eds. Cambridge, Cambridge UP, 1996, 207–232.

Johnson, Randal. *Literature, Culture and Authoritarianism in Brazil, 1930–1945.* Commentary by Nelson Vieira. Washington, DC, Latin American Program, Wilson Center, 1989.

Jorge Amado: New Critical Essays. Keith H. Brower, Earl Fitz, Martínez-Vidal, eds. New York, Routledge, 2001.

Latin America and the Caribbean: A Critical Guide to Research Sources. Paula Covington, ed. Westport, CT, Greenwood, 1996.

Levine, Robert M. *Historical Dictionary of Brazil.* Metuchen, NJ, Scarecrow, 1979.

Library Guide for Brazilian Studies. William V. Jackson, comp. Pittsburgh, PA, U of Pittsburgh Book Centers, 1964.

Lima, Luiz Costa. *Control of the Imaginary.* Ronald W. Sousa, trans. Minneapolis, U of Minnesota P, 1988.

Lima, Luiz Costa. *The Dark Side of Reason: Fictionality and Power.* Paulo Henriques Britto, trans. Stanford, CA, Stanford UP, 1992.

Lisboa, Maria Manuel. *Machado de Assis and Feminism: Re-reading the Heart of the Companion.* Lewiston, ME, Mellen, 1996.

Loos, Dorothy. *The Naturalist Novel of Brazil.* New York, Hispanic Institute, 1963.

Marting, Diane. *Clarice Lispector: A Bio-Bibliography.* Westport, CT, Greenwood, 1985.

Machado, José Bettencourt. *Machado of Brazil.* New York, Bramerica, 1953.

Martins, Wilson. *The Modernist Idea.* Jack E. Tomlins, trans. and ed. New York, New York UP, 1970.

Modern Brazilian Poetry: An Anthology. John Nist, ed. Bloomington, Indiana UP, 1962.

Moog, Viana. *An Interpretation of Brazilian Literature.* John Knox, trans. Rio de Janeiro, 1951.

Morse, Richard. *New World Sounding: Culture and Ideology in the Americas.* Baltimore, MD, Johns Hopkins UP, 1989.

Needell, Jeffry. *A Tropical Belle Epoque.* Cambridge, Cambridge UP, 1987.

Nist, John. *The Modernist Movement in Brazil.* Austin, U of Texas P, 1967.

One Hundred Years of Invention: Centenary of Oswald de Andrade. K. David Jackson, ed. Austin, TX, Abaporu, 1992.

Oxford Book of Latin American Short Stories. Roberto González Echevarría, ed. Oxford, Oxford UP, 1997.

Peixoto, Marta. *Passionate Fictions: Gender, Narrative, and Violence in Clarice Lispector.* Minneapolis, U of Minnesota P, 1994.

Poesia Brasileira Moderna: A Bilingual Anthology. Neistein, José, ed. Washington, DC, Brazilian-American Cultural Center, 1972.

Putnam, Samuel. *Marvelous Journey.* New York, Knopf, 1948.

Rodrígues, José Honório. *Brazilians: Their Character and Aspiration.* tr. Ralph Edward Dimmick, trans. Austin, U of Texas P, 1967.

Santiago, Silviano. *The Space in Between.* Durham, NC, Duke UP, 2001.

Sayers, Raymond. *The Negro in Brazilian Literature.* New York, Hispanic Institute in the United States, 1956.

Schwarz, Roberto. *A Master on the Periphery of Capitalism: Machado de Assis.* John Gledson, trans. Durham, NC, Duke UP, 2001.

Schwarz, Roberto. *Misplaced Ideas: Essays on Brazilian Culture.* John Gledson, ed. London, Verso, 1992.

Staden, Hans. *The True History of His Captivity.* Malcolm Letts, trans. and ed. London, Routledge, 1928.

Sternberg, Ricardo da Silveira Lobo. *The Unquiet Self: Self and Society in the Poetry of Carlos Drummond de Andrade.* Valencia, Albatros, 1986.

Suárez, José I., and Tomlins, Jack E. *Mário de Andrade: The Creative Works.* Lewisburg, PA, Bucknell UP; London, Associated UP, 2000.

Sussekind, Flora. *Cinematograph of Words.* Paulo Henriques Brito, trans. Stanford, CA, Stanford UP, 1997.

A Tentative Bibliography of Brazilian Belles-lettres. J. D. M. Ford, Arthur F. Whittem, Maxwell I. Raphaes, comps. Cambridge, MA, Harvard UP, 1931.

Transformations of Literary Language in Latin American Literature: From Machado to the Vanguards. K. David Jackson, ed. Austin, TX, Abaporu, 1987.

Tropical Paths. Randal Johnson, ed. New York, Garland, 1992.

Veríssimo, Érico. *Brazilian Literature: An Outline.* New York, Macmillan, 1945.

Vincent, Jon S. *João Guimarães Rosa.* Boston, Twayne, 1978.

Wasserman, Renata. *Exotic Nations: Literature and Cultural Identity in the United States and Brazil, 1830–1930.* Ithaca, NY, Cornell, 1994.

Williams, Edwin B. *From Latin to Portuguese.* Philadelphia: U of Pennsylvania P; Oxford, Milford, 1938.

ACKNOWLEDGMENTS

Abreu, Caio Fernando. "Dragons . . ." David Treece, trans. In *Dragons . . .* (London: Boulevard, 1990), 139–149. Originally published as "Os Dragões não conhecem o paraíso," in *Os Dragões não conhecem o paraíso* (São Paulo: Companhia das Letras, 1988), 147–157.

Accioly, Breno. "João Urso." R. P. Joscelyne, trans. In J. M. Cohen, ed., *Latin American Writing Today* (Harmondsworth, England: Penguin, 1967), 235–246. Originally published as *João Urso* (Rio de Janeiro: Epasa, 1944).

Alphonsus, João. "Sardanapalo." Darlene Sadlier, trans. *Latin American Literary Review* 17.34 (1989): 101–106. Originally published as "Sardanapalo," in *Contos e Novelas* (Rio de Janeiro: Edição do Autor, 1965).

Amado, Jorge. "How Porciúncula the Mulatto Got the Corpse off His Back." Edwin Honig and Margot Honig, trans. In Barbara Howes, ed., *The Eye of the Heart: Short Stories from Latin America* (Indianapolis, IN: Bobbs-Merrill, 1973), 253–261. Originally published as "De Como o Mulato Porciúncula Descarregou seu Defunto," in *Histórias da Bahia*, ed. Adonias Filho (Rio de Janeiro: Edições GRD, 1963).

Andrade, Carlos Drummond de. "Miguel's Theft." Robert Stock, trans. *Delos* 5 (1970): 170–175. Originally published as "Miguel e o seu Furto," in *Contos de Aprendiz*, 2d ed. (Rio de Janeiro: José Olympio, 1958), 167–178.

Andrade, Mário de. "It Can Hurt Plenty." In William Grossman, ed. and trans., *Modern Brazilian Short Stories* (Berkeley: U of California P, 1967), 12–25. Originally published as "Piá não sofre? Sofre," in *Belazarte, Contos* (São Paulo: Piratininga, 1934). "The Christmas Turkey." Richard Brenneman, trans. *Latin American Literary Review* 7.14 (Spring–Summer 1979): 96–102. Translation revised by K. D. Jackson. Originally published as "O Peru de Natal," in *Contos Novos* (São Paulo: Martins, 1947).

Assis, Joaquim Maria Machado de. "Wedding Song." Neil Miller and Karen McLean, trans. Originally published as "Cantiga de Esponsais," in *Histórias Sem Data* (Rio de Janeiro: Garnier, 1884). Reprinted and revised from *Américas*, a bimonthly magazine published by the General Secretariat of the Organization of American States in English and Spanish (30.1 [1978]: 7–9). "The Siamese Academies." Lorie Ishimatsu, trans. *Latin American Literary Review* 14.27 (January–June 1986): 35–41. Originally published as "As Academias de Sião," in *Histórias Sem Data*. "The Fortune-Teller." In Isaac Goldberg, ed. and trans., *Brazilian Tales* (Boston: International Pocket Library, 1965), 47–60. Copyright 1921 The Four Seas Company. Originally published as "A Cartomante," in *Várias Histórias* (Rio de Janeiro: Laemmert, 1896). "Life." In Isaac Goldberg, ed. and trans., *Brazilian Tales* (Boston: International Pocket Library, 1965), 61–70. Originally published as "Viver!" in *Várias*

Histórias. "The Nurse." Neil Miller, trans. Originally published as "O Enfermeiro," in *Várias Histórias.* Reprinted and revised from *Américas,* a bimonthly magazine published by the General Secretariat of the Organization of American States in English and Spanish (24.4 [1972]: 37–41). "The Secret Cause." Helen Caldwell, trans. In *The Psychiatrist, and Other Stories* (Berkeley: U of California P, 1963), 66–75. Originally published as "A Causa Secreta," in *Várias Histórias.* "A Woman's Arms." Helen Caldwell, trans. In *The Psychiatrist, and Other Stories* (Berkeley: U of California P, 1963), 46–55. Originally published as "Uns Braços," in *Várias Histórias.* "Dona Paula." Jack Schmitt and Lorie Ishimatsu, trans. In *The Devil's Church & Other Stories* (Austin: U of Texas P, 1977), 59–67. Originally published as "Dona Paula," in *Várias Histórias.* "Father versus Mother." Helen Caldwell, trans. In *The Psychiatrist, and Other Stories* (Berkeley: U of California P, 1963), 101–112. Originally published as "Pai versus Mãe," in *Relíquias de Casa Velha* (Rio de Janeiro: Garnier, 1906). "Wallow, Swine!" Jack Schmitt and Lorie Ishimatsu, trans. In *The Devil's Church & Other Stories* (Austin: U of Texas P, 1977), 146–150. Originally published as "Suje-se, Gordo!" in *Relíquias de Casa Velha.*

Barreto, Paulo (João Paulo Emílio Cristóvão dos Santos Coelho Barreto, pseud. João do Rio). "The Baby in Rose Tarlatan." K. David Jackson, trans. Originally published as "O Bebê de Tarlatana Rosa," in *Dentro da Noite* (Rio de Janeiro and Paris: Garnier, 1910), 155–164. "An Episode in a Hotel." *Inter-American Monthly* 1.6 (1918): 350–354. Originally published as "Aventura de Hotel," in *Dentro da Noite,* 129–140.

Cony, Carlos Heitor. "Order of the Day." Daphne Patai, trans. *Latin American Literary Review* 4.9 (1976): 27–42. Originally published as "A Ordem do Dia" in *Sobre todas as coisas: Contos* (Rio de Janeiro, Civilização Brasileira, 1968).

Dourado, Autran. "Bald Island." Elizabeth Lowe, trans. In Edla Van Steen, ed., *Love Stories: A Brazilian Collection* (São Paulo: Indústrias de Papel Simão, 1978), 113–127. Originally published as "A Ilha Escalvada," in *Solidão, Solitude* (Rio de Janeiro: Civilização Brasileira, 1972), 21–33.

Fonseca, Rubem. "Large Intestine." Elizabeth Lowe, trans. *Review 76* 18 (Fall 1976): 70–75. Originally published as "Intestino Grosso," in *Feliz Ano Novo* (Rio de Janeiro: Artenova, 1975).

Giudice, Victor. "The File Cabinet." Elizabeth Lowe, trans. *Translation* 5 (Spring 1978): 84–86. Originally published as "O Arquivo," in *O Necrológio* (Rio de Janeiro: Edições O Cruzeiro, 1972).

Gomes, Paulo Emílio Salles. "Her Times Two." Margaret A. Neves, trans. In *P's Three Women* (New York: Avon, 1984), 101–136. Originally published as "Duas Vezes Ela," in *As Três Mulheres dos Três PPPs* (São Paulo: Perspectiva, 1977), 77–101.

Hatoum, Milton. "The Truth Is a Seven-Headed Animal." Ellen Doré Watson, trans. *Grand Street* 64.4 (Spring 1998): 103–107. Originally published as "A Ninfa do Teatro Amazonas," in *Caderno Especial, O Estado de S. Paulo* (4 February 1996). Commemorating 100 years of the Teatro Amazonas.

Hilst, Hilda. "Agda." Elizabeth Lowe, trans. In Edla Van Steen, ed., *Love Stories: A Brazilian Collection* (São Paulo: Indústrias de Papel Simão, 1978), 157–168. Originally published as "Agda," in *Qadós* (São Paulo: Edart, 1973); rpt. in *Ficções* (São Paulo: Quíron, 1977), 47–60.

Lessa, Orígenes. "Marta: A Souvenir of New York." *Americas* 12.3 (1960): 22–23.

Lima Barreto, Affonso Henriques de. "The Man Who Knew Javanese." Clifford E. Landers, trans. *Brasil/Brazil* 5 (1991): 94–103. Originally published as "O Homem que Sabia Javanês" in *Histórias e Sonhos* (Rio de Janeiro, 1920).

Lins, Osman. "Baroque Tale or Tripartite Unity." Adria Frizzi, trans. In *Nine, Novena* (Los Angeles: Sun & Moon, 1995), 169–192. Originally published as "Conto Barroco," in *Nove, Novena: Narrativas* (São Paulo: Martins, 1966). "Easter Sunday." Fred P. Ellison and Ana Luiza Andrade, trans. In *South American Trilogy* (Austin, TX: Studia Hispanica, 1982), 17–31.

Lispector, Clarice. "The Buffalo." Giovanni Pontiero, trans. In *Family Ties* (Austin: U of Texas P, 1972). Originally published in *Laços de Famíla* (Rio de Janeiro: Editora do Autor, 1965). "The Chicken." In *Family Ties*. Originally published as "Uma Galinha," in *Alguns Contos* (Rio de Janeiro: MEC, 1952), 42–45. "The Smallest Woman in the World." Elizabeth Bishop, trans. *Kenyon Review* 26.3 (Summer 1964): 501–506. Also published in Barbara Howes, ed., *The Eye of the Heart: Short Stories from Latin America* (Indianapolis, IN: Bobbs-Merrill, 1973), 320–325. Also published in *Laços de Famíla*. "The Breaking of the Bread." Eloah Giacomelli, trans. *Antigonish Review* 18 (1974): 69–72. Originally published in *A Legião Estrangeira* (Rio de Janeiro: Editora do Autor, 1964). "The Fifth Story." Eloah F. Giacomelli, trans. *Antigonish Review* 16 (1974): 77–79. Originally published in *A Legião Estrangeira*. "Miss Algrave." Alexis Levitin, trans. In *Soulstorm* (New York: New Directions, 1989), 7–14. Originally published in *Via Crucis do Corpo* (Rio de Janeiro: Nova Fronteira, 1974). "The Body." Alexis Levitin, trans. *Literary Review* 21.4 (Summer 1978): 465–471. Originally published in *Via Crucis do Corpo*. "Plaza Mauá." Alexis Levitin, trans. In *Soulstorm* (New York: New Directions, 1989), 54–58. Originally published in *Via Crucis do Corpo*. "Beauty and the Beast, or The Wound Too Great." Earl Fitz, trans. *Latin American Literary Review* 19.37 (January–June 1991): 112–120. Originally published as "A Bela e a Fera, ou a Ferida Grande Demais," in *A Bela e a Fera* (Rio de Janeiro: Nova Fronteira, 1979).

Lobato, Monteiro. "The Funnyman Who Repented." *Atlantic Monthly* (February 1956): 161–165. Originally published as "O Engraçado Arrependido," in *Urupês* (São Paulo: Ed. Revista do Brasil, 1918).

Machado, Aníbal. "The Death of the Standard Bearer." K. David Jackson, trans. Originally published as "A Morte da Porta-Estandarte," in *A Morte da Porta-Estandarte, e Outras Histórias* (Rio de Janeiro: José Olympio, 1965). "The First Corpse." *Americas* 9.2 (1957): 22–26. Originally published as "O Defunto Inaugural," in *Vila Feliz: Novelas* (Rio de Janeiro: José Olympio, 1944).

Machado, Antônio de Alcântara. "The Beauty Contest." Elisabeth Sprague Smith, trans. *Atlantic Monthly* 197.2 (February 1956): 122–124. Originally published as "Miss Corisco," in *Contos Avulsos, Novelas Paulistanas* (Rio de Janeiro: José Olympio, 1959). "Gaetaninho." In William L. Grossman, ed. and trans., *Modern Brazilian Short Stories* (Berkeley: U of California P, 1967), 71–73. Originally published as "Gaetaninho," in *Brás, Bexiga e Barra Funda* (São Paulo: Edição do Autor, 1927).

Mello, Emília Moncorva Bandeira de (pseud. Carmen Dolores). "Aunt Zézé's Tears." In Isaac Goldberg, trans., *Brazilian Tales* (Boston: International Pocket Library, 1965), 89–96. Originally published as "As Lágrimas da Tia Zezé" in *Um Drama na Roça* (1907).

Piñón, Nélida. "Big-Bellied Cow." Gregory Rabassa, trans. *Mundus Artium* 3.3 (1970): 89–96. Originally published as "A Vaca Bojuda," in *Tempo das Frutas* (Rio de Janeiro: José Álvaro, 1966), 147–156. "Brief Flower." Gregory Rabassa, trans. In *The TriQuarterly Anthology of Contemporary Latin American Literature*, ed. Jose Donoso and William A. Henkin (New York: Dutton, 1969), 309–316. Originally published as "Breve Flor," in *Tempo das Frutas* (Rio de Janeiro: José Álvaro, 1966), 47–60.

Queiroz, Rachel de. "Metonymy, or The Husband's Revenge." William L. Grossman, trans. In Alberto Manguel, ed., *Other Fires: Short Fiction by Latin American Women* (New York: Potter, 1986), 24–31. Originally published as "Metonímia, ou a Vingança do Enganado" in *100 Crônicas Escolhidas* (Rio de Janeiro: José Olympio, 1958), 263–270.

Ramos, Graciliano. "The Thief." In William L. Grossman, *Modern Brazilian Short Stories* (Berkeley: U of California P, 1967), 41–52. Originally published as "Um Ladrão," in *Insônia* (São Paulo: Martins, 1961). "Whale." Elizabeth A. Jackson, trans. Originally published in *Vidas Secas* (Rio de Janeiro: José Olympio, 1938).

Rawet, Samuel. "The Prophet." Nelson H. Vieira, trans. In *The Prophet and Other Stories* (Albuquerque: U of New Mexico P, 1998), 1–8. Originally published as "O Profeta," in *Contos do Imigrante* (Rio de Janeiro: José Olympio, 1956), 7–17.

Rebelo, Marques. "Down Our Street." *Life & Letters Today* 38.71 (July 1943): 5–13. Originally published as "A Rua Dona Emerenciana," in *Oscarina* (Rio de Janeiro: Schmidt, 1931).

Rosa, João Guimarães. "The Girl from Beyond." In Barbara Shelby, ed and trans., *The Third Bank of the River and Other Stories* (New York: Knopf, 1968), 205–211. Originally published as "A Menina de Lá," in *Primeiras Estórias* (Rio de Janeiro: José Olympio, 1962). "Much Ado." In *TriQuarterly Anthology of Contemporary Latin American Literature*, ed. Jose Donoso and William A. Henkin (New York: Dutton, 1969), 418–433. Also published in Barbara Shelby, ed. and trans., *The Third Bank of the River and Other Stories* (New York: Knopf, 1968), 35–55. Originally published as "Darandina," in *Primeiras Estórias*. "Sorôco, His Mother, His Daughter." In Barbara Shelby, ed. and trans., *The Third Bank of the River and Other Stories* (New York: Knopf, 1968), 213–218. Originally published as "Sorôco, sua mãe, sua filha," in *Primeiras Estórias*. "The Third Bank of the River." In William L. Grossman, ed. and trans., *Modern Brazilian Short Stories* (Berkeley: U of California P, 1967), 125–130. Originally published as "A Terceira Margem do Rio," in *Primeiras Estórias*. "Treetops." In Barbara Shelby, ed. and trans., *The Third Bank of the River and Other Stories* (New York: Knopf, 1968), 227–238. Originally published as "Os Cimos," in *Primeiras Estórias*. "Those Lopes." Richard Zenith, trans. *Grand Street* 61, no. 1 (1997): 177–180. Originally published as "Esses Lopes," in *Essas Estórias* (Rio de Janeiro: José Olympio, 1969); "The Jaguar." David Treece, trans. In *The Jaguar and Other Stories* (Oxford: Boulevard, 2001). Originally published as "O Meu Tio, o Iauaretê," in *Tutameia: Terceiras Estórias* (Rio de Janeiro: José Olympio, 1967).

Rubião, Murilo. "Zacarias, the Pyrotechnist." Thomas Colchie, trans. *Translation 6* (1978–1979): 129–135. Originally published as *O Pirotécnico Zacarias* (São Paulo: Atica, 1974).

Scliar, Moacyr. "The Cow." Eloah F. Giacomelli, trans. In *The Carnival of the Animals* (New York: Ballantine, 1985), 11–14. Originally published as "A Vaca," in *Os Melhores Contos* (São Paulo: Global, 1984), 171–174. "The Last Poor Man." Eloah F. Giacomelli, trans. *Antigonish Review* 18 (1974): 73–77. Originally published as "O Último Pobre," in *O Carnaval dos Animais* (Porto Alegre: Editora Movimento, 1968), 23–27.

Steen, Edla Van. "CAROL head LINA heart." David George, trans., in *A Bag of Stories* (Pittsburgh: Latin American Literary Review Press, 1991), 117–127. Originally published as "CAROL cabeça LINA coração" in *Até Sempre* (São Paulo: Global, 1985), 171–182.

Telles, Lygia Fagundes. "Just a Saxophone." Eloah F. Giacomelli, trans. *Literary Review* 21.2 (Winter 1978): 225–233. Originally published as "Apenas um Saxofone" in "Trilogia da Confissão" in *Os 18 Melhores Contos do Brasil* (Rio de Janeiro: Editora Bloch, 1968), 52–61.

Trevisan, Dalton. "The Corpse in the Parlor." Jack E. Tomlins, trans. *Mundus Artium* 3.3 (1970): 61–66. Originally published as "O Morto na Sala," in *Novelas Nada Exemplares*, 3d ed. (Rio de Janeiro: Civilização Brasileira, 1970), 17–22. "The Vampire of Curitiba." Gregory Rabassa, trans. In *The Vampire of Curitiba and Other Stories* (New York: Knopf, 1972), 107–112. Originally published as "O Vampiro de Curitiba," in *O Vampiro de Curitiba* (Rio de Janeiro: Civilização Brasileira, 1965).

Veiga, J. J. "The Misplaced Machine." Pamela G. Bird, trans. In *The Misplaced Machine and Other Stories* (New York: Knopf, 1970), 89–93. Originally published as "A Máquina Extraviada," in *A Máquina Extraviada* (Rio de Janeiro: Civilização Brasileira, 1974).

Veríssimo, Érico. "Fandango." *Atlantic Monthly* 197.2 (February 1956): 112–116. "The Guerrilla." *Mexican Life: Mexico's Monthly Review* 36.4 (April 1960): 10. "The House of the Melancholy Angel." *Americas* 6.2 (1954): 42–45. Originally published as "Sonata" in *As Mãos do meu Filho* (Porto Alegre: Meridiano, 1942).

Veríssimo, José. "Going after Rubber" and "Returning from Rubber Gathering." Bob White Linker and Francis Simkins, trans. *Poet Lore* 39 (1928): 467–472, 154–158. Originally published as "Indo à Seringa" and "Voltando da Seringa," in *Cenas da Vida Amazônica*, 3d ed. (Rio de Janeiro: Organização Simões, 1957).